Heroes of
Gold Country

By Kirsten Miles

In memory of Eric Grodberg, an amazing writer and friend.

Contents

Chapter 1- The Strange Girl

Anna Claire lived in daydreams. She enjoyed escaping reality, as reality usually disinterested her as much as watching weeds grow. On this particular day, the little girl was thinking how wonderful Montana Territory was and how she wished she could fly as high as the birds that mocked her from the trees beyond the little log cabin. If she could fly, she'd travel the whole world- to the rolling hills of Italy, the warm sand beaches of California, the ice-cold huts in Greenland- and be back to the cabin in Montana Territory before supper.

Anna Claire, looking to her side, noticed a boy watching her play on the grass with Berthie and Peter, her siblings. The look on the boy's face was quite despondent and contained one of lonely wistfulness and a bit of jealousy. His bright blue eyes squinted across the yard, sunburned cheeks aglow, as he watched the little girl twirling in the field like a little prairie flower.

Tommy Cooper was not a boy who had many playmates. He hadn't gone to school a day in his life and did not know how to interact with children his age. He was a ten-year-old mess of a child and had landed on the Freiler's doorstep the moment he had found out that new settlers had arrived nearby.

Caroline, the oldest Freiler child, had been sewing on the porch when she saw the boy walk up bashfully to Anna Claire, Pete, and Berthie. She had closely observed him, noting his unwashed, tattered clothes and his uncombed, wild brown hair, and immediately disapproved of him.

"Who are you and what are you doing on our land?" Caroline asked the boy as she made her way across the field in front of the house.

Suddenly overcome with delight, the boy's eyes went wide in his cheekbones as he squinted at the girl, much older than himself, trying to get a better look.

There was no doubt that Tommy Cooper knew a pretty girl when he saw one, and Caroline Freiler was the most beautiful girl he'd seen yet. However, Miss Caroline had no such inkling of what was going on in the little boy's head.

"This ain't *your* land," the boy explained, not harshly, but simply explanatorily. "This is Old Man Hatfield's."

Caroline was not agreeable and did not have much patience with pesky little boys. She was certainly not one to be lied to.

"It *is* our land, you dirty, ungrateful boy, and if you were smart, you'd get out of here!" Her hands were on her hips, and she lifted her chin as a gesture for the lonely soul to leave.

"Caroline, dry up!" cried Anna Claire, hoping her sister hadn't scared the boy off. This boy had been the first child she had seen since the mining camp days besides her siblings. To Tommy, she said, "We just traveled here from Minnesota!"

"Oh," was all Tommy said as he turned his attention back to Caroline, who looked angrier than before, with her eyes smaller and cheeks flushed. "Pretty soon you'll wish you hadn't."

"What do you mean?" Anna Claire asked, her green eyes growing wide-not with fear but with the fluttering in her heart that told her something adventurous was on its way.

"Don't listen to him," Caroline called as she walked forward. She had already been in a sour temper due to Helen, the second oldest Freiler child, spilling milk on her dress, and she wasn't in the mood for playing around. "Anna Claire, get away from him right now."

"Shut your mouth," replied Anna Claire vigorously. She then turned to Tommy with a look of frustration. "That's my sister Caroline, and she's always sour. I'm Anna Claire."

Tommy spit in his hand, wiped it on his pants, and stuck it out for her to shake. She did so without a flinch. When he looked up at her, he stopped for a moment.

"I'm Tommy," he said. "I'm a Cooper. I don't think your sister likes me."

"She doesn't like me either," Anna Claire assured him, turning around to give her older sister a nasty glare.

None of this was audible to the oldest girl, who was rolling her eyes at the uselessness it was to asking Anna Claire to do anything.

Tommy gazed for a moment at Anna Claire before turning to Caroline.

"You like marbles?" he asked with such a funny grin that Caroline thought he was mocking her, even though in truth, he was simply asking a question.

"Get out of here, you dirty little boy," she spat, her blood flowing swiftly to her face.

"Come on, you can play with me," Anna Claire instructed, dragging his arm as they ran into the cluster of trees so quickly that Caroline almost admired the speed at which the children bolted away.

She watched them run and then decided that she was too tired to make her sister come back, and that it was far too hot to do such a thing, so she sat down with a sulky sigh and picked up her sewing again.

In the forest, the two little ones played away, Tommy talking about his life and Anna Claire rattling on about hers.

As Anna Claire found out, Tommy wasn't an orphan, but he might as well have been. His parents had met ten years ago and "kinda liked each other at first," as Tommy put it. They had lived near Bannack, only about a mile the opposite way, even though Bannack wasn't even there yet. Although both of his parents were alive and kicking, they were not married, and he lived with his mother while his father came in and out of town when he pleased, which was not often. Anna Claire had never met anybody with parents who did that. Every couple she had met who had children was married! It didn't make any sense, but when she said so, Tommy looked very sad, and so she stopped talking any more about it.

"Pa didn't want me, and neither did Ma," he said sadly. "And they fought over who was to have me. Finally, in court, they decided Ma should have me 'cause she's a woman and she gave birth to me, and my pa was busy travelin'. So, I lived with her, and when I was five, Pa wanted me back, but Ma wouldn't let him because she kinda started to like me. I used to see Pa a lot when he wasn't traveling, but he doesn't stop here no more. Me and Ma , you can spot us anywhere! We're right in the center of town. Sometimes I stay there. But I usually don't wanna. I usually play with Rocks and Ebb. They're in a gang, but they won't let me join it 'cause I'm only ten and they're twelve. Oh well, someday I'll start my own gang and they'll be awful sorry!"

Anna Claire had never met anyone she liked so much as Tommy Cooper. She told him about how rotten her older sisters were and how much she missed Minnesota.

"I had a lot of friends there," Anna Claire told him. "We had the best of times! We used to play this game where we would throw rocks at each other until someone would back out. One time, I was the first one to back out. Erwin hit me in the eye and I cried so loud! But that was only once. Usually, I won. I can really throw rocks!"

The children talked for nearly an hour, which felt like much longer to them, and when Tommy had left, Anna Claire found herself anticipating in earnest the next time he would visit her.

Caroline told her mother all about it, and that is when Charlotta, their mother, called him a "sacrilegious infidel." Although Charlotta and Caroline were not thrilled with the little boy, Anna Claire was happy she had finally found a friend.

"Anna Claire!" called Caroline from across the field a week later, interrupting her daydreams.

Anna Claire was not in this particular field, at least not in spirit- instead, she was Cleopatra the Seventh, daughter of the Nile, staring up at the pyramids and swimming in a pool of golden water-

"Anna Claire!" She was suddenly yanked out of Egypt by the hard tug of her sister pulling her up with a strong grip right onto her legs. "That was very rude of you to ignore me, Anna Claire," Caroline said in her best *"Mama"* tone, for Caroline was always trying to be like their mother.

"I wasn't *ignorin'* you," Anna Claire replied. "I just wasn't *listenin'*." Her small, slightly freckled nose turned up at her sister, and her lips pursed.

"Well, maybe if you'd pay attention as much as you daydream, you wouldn't be in scrapes all the time!" But Caroline was calming down now, and her breathing slowed. "Mama wants you to pick as many raspberries as you can find down by the creek."

She said this much more softly than before, but Anna Claire still felt aggravated for being "taken out of the Nile," and as she stalked down the field, she turned back at her big sister and stuck out her tongue. Most appalled, Caroline scowled back, but Anna Claire missed it because she was already halfway toward the trees, running as fast as a wild jackrabbit.

She stopped short with a sudden realization that she had forgotten her basket. She ran again across the field, passing Caroline along the way, and to the front of the door of the wooden cabin, where there was the little basket. The child grabbed the basket swiftly and darted from the porch, knocking her older sister to her side.

"And Mama told me to tell you to be quick about it!" added Caroline angrily, flattening her blue cotton dress.

Anna Claire, once again, ran through the sagebrush-covered field and did not stop to breathe until she had reached the clump of trees known as the "forest," although there were not enough trees to be an entirely *real* forest, at least not there. She could still see the log cabin when she looked behind her and the mountains rising far behind it, but the trees hid most of it, and Anna Claire felt thoroughly safe. But then she remembered what Tommy Cooper said of the woods being haunted, and she wasn't so sure of her shelter. Anna Claire shuddered and tried to forget what Tommy had told her for, as Mama said, Tommy was just a "downright sacrilegious infidel," whatever *that* meant. But the trees crowded around her and whispered in her ear as if haunting her, making Anna Claire frightened of all the ghosts that were bound to be lurking around.

Tommy's just a downright sacrilegious infidel, thought Anna Claire in triumph, although she had not a single idea what the phrase meant, but, if Mama said it, it must be true.

As she headed further down toward the water, she sighed with delight, looking at the creek that wound around and down away from her. It ran around that part of the territory like a piece of ribbon, and Anna Claire, in her mere couple of months in Gold

Country, had already grown so familiar with it. Grasshopper Creek, or "Gold Creek" as many called it, was like a person to her. This was what many of the people called it, as the men at the mining camp explained that they had found a good amount of gold there. Anna Claire had spent many moments reading by the creek when she was supposed to be doing chores.

Their mother and father sometimes sent the little ones to stay outdoors to play or read while they kept the two older girls inside to help them with all of the many chores. Most of the time, though, Anna Claire and all of her siblings were stuck working. Anna Claire helped with the chores, although she hated to do it. There were many inside chores to do and so much food to cook and store for the winter. Anna Claire tried to help and do everything right, but her mother usually told her that she was in the way.

This was all fine with Anna Claire. She was never bored when she was outside, for she could not get enough of how magical the outside world was. There were so many paths to explore, so many animals, birds, and plants to discover here, and there was also that sacrilegious infidel, Tommy Cooper, to run around with. But it was a shadow over the infinite mass of golden prairie that Anna Claire was "little." Anna Claire had been little for so long that it seemed like she'd be a little girl forever with no special privileges and the punishment of being talked to like a baby.

"That girl is always doing some strange thing," her mother, Charlotta, would say. Her father, Joseph, who seemed to understand his spirited daughter and her queer habits, would only shake his head and grin. There was no doubt that Anna Claire was the misfit of the family, although Peter was a close second. Because he was a boy, he could do those sorts of things without grown people paying much attention.

When Caroline was little, she never would have gone "toad-catching" or pretend to be somewhere she wasn't, or hunt for mythological creatures. Caroline was presumed to be too good and proper for such behavior. When she was nine, she would have been seen indoors crocheting or playing with dolls quietly in their old Minnesota parlor. Anna Claire would never, *ever* be caught in her coffin with a doll, which she called a "silly fake person."

Caroline Freiler, on the other hand, was a prim and proper fourteen-year-old girl. She was very pretty with curly hair as black as a crow's wing and dark lashes surrounding pools of vivid cerulean in her eyes. Her skin was ashen, but her cheeks flushed with a vibrant pink. She was well-mannered, critical, and extremely disapproving of any idea that was not within the scope of what she had been taught by the adults she had grown up around. She was a natural-born conformer and despised Anna Claire's more unruly behavior.

Caroline, however, was not Anna Claire's only older sister. Helen Freiler was *hardly* mature, though. At twelve years old, Helen believed herself to be a very important person. She had almond-shaped brown eyes, a pleasant smile, skin browned from the sun, and chestnut hair. Helen was mindful of her looks but not at all mindful of her temper, which flickered on and off very often, especially when people complained too much or annoyed her. Although sometimes charming and good-natured, Helen had her faults and was so lazy that she would rather cry than do her chores. Helen always took the easiest way out of anything that she could.

Anna Claire was the middle child, as she had two younger siblings as well. Younger than Anna Claire was Peter Freiler, whom everyone just called "Pete". Pete had just turned seven, and Anna Claire sympathized with him because he was full of mischief and always vexing people. Pete enjoyed bothering others and often meant to cause mischief. Pete took pleasure in irritating his family whenever possible, whether it was sneaking rocks into the soup bowls or tricking a sister to bite a cookie full of dirt. Whatever that mysterious mischief was, it was in his telling blue eyes and his gap-toothed smile. By now, the family was very good at catching Pete in his pranks, but not good enough to outwit him. One morning years before, Caroline woke up with honey stuck throughout her hair, and on another, Anna Claire found herself locked in the outhouse. There was one person Pete never played pranks on, however, and that was Bertha.

Bertha Freiler was a very small slip of a five-year-old girl who was as timid as a mouse but gentle as a flower. Berthie, as they called her, had hair almost as white as clouds that hung straight down to her shoulders. Her skin was very pale, and there were always dark rims around her big brown eyes. Her cheeks were as rosy as her little, heart-shaped lips, and there was a connection in her eyes to the outer world, or universe, or space- so rich and deep were those soulful brown eyes. It was almost as if she could detect things that others could not.

Anna Claire did not like this position of being in the middle, squeezed together by overbearing superiors and little tattletales. She wished she were the oldest so she could boss around Caroline and Helen, who were always telling her how to behave. Or maybe an only child- that sounded even better. She once had a friend back in Minnesota who was an only child, but she said she would give up her best China doll for a brother or sister.

As for Anna Claire, she despised dolls with as much ardor as one would dislike a papercut. She had equal distaste for dresses with silly, uncomfortable ribbons and tight, itchy hems. Caroline talked often of owning a dress made with bustles and hoops, as was the style now among the older girls and women. Their mother had said she was far too young to own such attire, and Anna Claire pronounced passionately that she would rather "hang my neck on a rope than wear one of those stupid, ugly balloons!" even when she got old enough. She made a solemn promise to herself that when she grew up, she would never, *ever* dress like that.

What Anna Claire wanted most of all was to travel the world. She never wanted to be an old sourpuss, like Grandma Lund, and she had made up her mind long ago that she never wanted to get married like all the other women did. She would hate to have to stand by and watch as a husband went off doing the things *she* longed to do! Then she would end up like her mother, of all the miseries! Besides, she thought that boys were all alike- prideful and boastful- and it wasn't fair that men could go off and fight bravely in wars and earn medals of honor while Anna Claire would have to stay inside and knit. She was only nine years old but was already beginning to feel the sting of being different from boys. She often wished she, herself, were born a boy so that she could fight, explore, and travel all around the world to all the places she had only read about.

So far, moving to Montana Territory was the most exciting thing that had happened in Anna Claire's life by far. She and her family had settled on "Grasshopper Diggings," which was called so because of Grasshopper Creek, and was close to where the mining operations were. The boomtown of Bannack near Grasshopper Diggings was filled with danger, which Anna Claire loved, and included masses of outlaws, cowboys, saloons, wild horses, and gamblers. Their mother said it was the land of the devil, but for Anna Claire, it was the touch of heaven. Although she had only been to town once with her father to get some supplies, she had loved what she saw. In town, there was so much noise and commotion that Anna Claire had felt compelled to cover her ears at times. However, the talk of the wild, raggedy-bearded men stirred a feeling of belonging deep within the small girl! She silently wished that she could live in town, where all the excitement was, instead of an isolated wood cabin built in the middle of No Man's Land.

Their father did not want the family living in town, and while they were staying in the mining camps, he went off to build the house. He worked day and night to build their home while providing food with the small rations he was earning in the camp and getting accustomed to the hard work of gold panning. The town could be dangerous, and their father saw to it that they were close enough to call for help when in trouble, but far enough to be distant from the sources of most of the peril.

But their mother did not like to go to town. Whenever the occasion befell, she would bury her head in her husband's chest and shut her eyes tight, fearing a conflict or something even worse.

Charlotta, her mother, and Caroline were all reserved, proper, and elegant. Grasshopper Diggings and the wild town of Bannack were not a place fit for them, but Anna Claire loved it. She was like her father, who, because of his eagerness to travel, crossed the many, many miles from Minnesota all the way to "Gold Country."

Joseph Freiler had heard about the streak of luck miners had when entering Montana Territory three years earlier, and he immediately jumped at the excuse to travel. But then, the war was growing bloodier, and Joseph served for a very short time in the Union before falling from an injury to his leg. Since then, he had a very slight limp that was nearly undetectable except when he tried to run. That is when he was determined to move the family, which made their mother furious at first. Charlotta loved her family and friends back in Minnesota, but her husband coaxed her and promised that if they moved to Montana Territory, riches awaited them undoubtedly. At first, she put up such a fight that he almost gave in. Soon, however, she reminded herself that whatever Joseph thought was the right thing to do was best because he was the husband, father of her children, and provider for the family. She believed he was appointed by God to make the big decisions for the family, since he was the man.

Joseph Freiler himself was a firm but loving husband and gentle father. He wanted to make his wife and children happy, but he also had a desire for wealth, and his dreams of riches convinced him that he needed to explore the west to the territories that were new and brimming with discoveries. Joseph Freiler was dedicated to his country and always longed to see more of it, and was thrilled with the Union's victory. He had many family members of old colonial blood, and he had a deep love and affection for the United States. When he was discharged for his leg injury, he was horribly upset as he dreamed of serving his country and wanted to be a war hero. Even as a couple of years went by, it was a sore spot for him to be reminded of when he could not fight in the war. However, his mind was now set on gold and proving to his family that he could provide whatever they wanted and needed.

Although his wife eventually surrendered, she would not pretend that she was happy about it. For the last couple of months before the move, she did nothing but clean and sew, never smiling. She wouldn't even look at Joseph. But as time went by and prayers were numerous, she began to accept the idea of a new life in Montana Territory.

Charlotta Freiler was a bold, brave, but soft woman. She was a creature of habit and enjoyed her way of life. She could never bear too many changes at once, and the thought of moving *anywhere* was petrifying to her. She was tall and pale with strong blue eyes and voluminous dark hair. Charlotta was strict with her young ones but loved them very much, making sure she spent time with everyone. She was hardworking and diligent, a true perfectionist, as everything had to be in its proper place. Luckily for the Freiler children, Mrs. Freiler was a strong believer in playtime and would often order one of the children to "go outside" or "play hoop" after a chore or such. She knew exercise to be good for the mind and spirit, as she used to do much of it herself, taking walks in the woods as a child.

Joseph Freiler, on the other hand, didn't mind change, as he was ambitious, friendly, and had a desire for wealth. He had dreamed of becoming wealthy all of his life, but despite his love of coins, Mr. Freiler was not greedy. He mostly wished for riches to support his family and help out friends. He wanted wealth somewhat for his ego, also, as he wanted to prove that he could claim gold with hard work and a sparkle in his eye.

Anna Claire loved her father and admired him in all ways, and she was happy to move, for the most part. She did miss her family. She especially missed Katie, her cousin, with whom she had a very strong bond. Their homes were not too far, and every week-end, Grandma Lund and the whole family would have a Saturday Night Gathering at Aunt Louisa's, Uncle Karl's, and Cousin Katie's large home. Then, they would all go to church together the next morning. Anna Claire would never forget the feeling of closeness- the nights of tenderness and laughter- which made her so happy. She loved Saturday Night Gatherings- this was the one true thing that Anna Claire missed with all of her heart.

It took her father a good month and a half to build the house while the rest of the family stayed at the mining camps. The mining camp was so interesting that Anna Claire didn't want to leave it. Joseph Freiler was very lucky to have met some generous men during his short time camped out on the southern part of Grasshopper Diggings, where most of the mining took place, and he, along with about twenty or so men, built his house.

The men were kind, and Joseph had helped them with some of their construction needs for their own homes. That was the great thing about the camps- so many people were willing to help, even though they did not know anyone. Both the men and women were sympathetic to the Freiler's cause as they, too, had once been new and struggling on Grasshopper Diggings. Some of the men couldn't understand why the family did not just stay in the mining camps and thought building an entire house was a bit "high up," but most were still willing to help, especially when Joseph explained that Charlotta was severely anxious and homesick.

Those few weeks at the camp from April to the end of May were the most exciting in Anna Claire's life. Most of the family was rather frightened, as this was a new experience for everyone, but not Anna Claire. At the mining camp, she helped her father with setting up the tent and watched with wide eyes as he and the other men laughed, joked, and worked, talking about places, people, and things that she had never before heard of. While the others stayed close to their mother, Anna Claire was getting to know the men at the camp, and they had made somewhat of a pet out of the girl, calling her "the mining queen" out of affection.

"The mining queen" took much pleasure in staying awake all night listening to the men cheer and play the banjo, complaining about this and that. She relished in watching the men take the goods out of the freight train and trying to find the coffee for her mother so that her father could buy some for her. She loved snuggling up next to Berthie and watching the firelight from outside hit the tents, moving around like wind. She loved playing with the mining children who, unlike her sisters, were much wilder and more fun, and did not wear neat clothes or have to bathe so much like her family did. Some of the children were even allowed to run amok alone, wandering around the camps and getting themselves dirty in the creek.

Anna Claire loved to swim, make mud pies, and play Rattlesnake with the children of the mining camps. She wholeheartedly enjoyed spending time with all of the new and interesting families that were

camping on Grasshopper Diggings for the same reason as the Freilers, making a better life for themselves
and their families.

She missed the camp very much and, even
though she was now nice and settled in a suitable
house, she no longer had the luxury of being thrown
on top of the big men's shoulders while they called
her "the mining queen," or playing in the mud with
the other children without being yelled at for it. Her
parents had been so distracted with all the work that
needed to be done that they didn't have time to constantly yell or scold her. It was sometimes a relief to
let her run around with the other children, even if she
was getting into a bit of benign trouble. At least then
she would not dirty the laundry, spill the boiled water,
or knock over her mother's prized plate from back
home.

She remembered with fondness the Chinese
family who were camped just down the road, and
how she loved to play with the couple's twin babies.
The mother and father were always making interesting food and letting Anna Claire help make it. Anna
Claire had the opportunity to meet quite a few people
of Chinese descent, as many Chinese immigrants had
come to find the gold and build businesses. She had
loved meeting all the new people in the mining
camps.

Now, in the present moment, as Anna Claire
ran her tiny fingers through Gold Creek, she felt a
pang of sadness that sprang upon her very suddenly.
It would be many years until Anna Claire would see
Cousin Katie and the rest of her family again. What if

Anna Claire had grown taller than Katie? What if Anna Claire *never* saw them again?

She pondered this thought as she unlaced her stiff black boots. Her basket lay beside her, still empty of raspberries. She slowly dipped her swollen feet into the cool, clear waters and at once felt released from the pain her old boots had brought her. Her father didn't have the money to buy her a new pair of boots before their trip, and Anna Claire's feet had grown considerably.

She stopped thinking about Minnesota for a moment as she gazed around with her big eyes in childish wonderment. Whenever Anna Claire was outdoors, she felt that the earth was speaking through her and comforting all of her sorrows and cares away. Her mother and Caroline said it was God. Maybe it was God, maybe it was something else, but it was everywhere at that moment. It was in the long ash trees whose green leaves swayed in the wind, and in the dirt that was beginning to cover her dress. When Anna Claire was outside the house, she felt that she could breathe. The air and the wind kept her from feeling closed in. The little scurrying voles and the whispers of the uncultivated land around the creek kept her from being lonely. The outdoors was always enjoyable and fresh. There was never a dull moment outside, and usually never the voice of an annoying older sister calling for her to hurry up.

"Anna *Claire*!" cried Helen dramatically as if her life depended on it. Anna Claire could see her through the trees when she turned around. "Hurry up! Mama's almost got supper ready!"

"I'm *hurryin'*!" yelled Anna Claire in her loudest voice. She watched Helen turn around and head back to the house before she began her hunt for berries.

The raspberries around Gold Creek were safe and good to eat. During the days at the mining camps, she and the other children would often pick the berries surrounding the creek and smash them in each other's faces. Their parents would use the other ones to make jam together, and all of the families would sit around the fire late at night and eat jam and bread. Anna Claire relished in those delicious pies, and she knew they would always remind her of those days when she got to stay up too late and eat dessert far past her bedtime.

She found a few of the raspberries under some willow bushes and even on the ground. It was not many, but it was at least something to put on the table. It also didn't help that she ate quite a few of them herself, grabbing some and licking the juice clean off her red-stained hands. As she completed this task, a song began to fill her mind, and she hummed the tune out loud. She plopped a few more berries into her woven basket and sang away in that loud, indistinct way young children often do when they aren't paying attention.

She left the creek and emerged from the large cluster of trees, swinging her basket this way and that. It wasn't long before she was full-fledged singing, forgetting completely about the berries, dropping herself onto the field, and staring into the sky.

The sky was so much bigger in Montana Territory than it was in Minnesota. It was deep and so very blue, sometimes seeming endless. Anna Claire loved looking at the big lumps of mountains in the distance- huge, towering over the people of Bannack and the surrounding areas of Gold Country. Anna Claire had never seen such big, towering mountains before moving to Montana Territory. They were *so* big and *so* towering that they seemed to be angrily hovering over her in a menacing and sometimes eerie stance. However, she loved these enormous palaces of hope, and the mountains instantly became friends of Anna Claire's. She stopped singing to take a big breath, gazing at them. She *never* wanted to leave this beautiful scenery and the plush hills of green, but soon she was once again interrupted by the snub voice of Helen, calling her for dinner.

"Oh, just leave me alone!" Anna Claire muttered.

She slowly and regretfully arose from the field, gasping when she saw that her blue plaid dress was brown with dirt and her sleeves had berry stains all over them. She quickly ran to the creek to try and scrub some of the stains off, rubbing a rock against them and covering it with water, but it would take hours for even her mother to wash out the stains- if that was possible.

"Anna Claire!" Helen's impatient voice called again through the trees. "*Anna Claire!*"

"Comin'!" she called, quite annoyed.

She ran through the trees, unhappy to leave her little paradise. When she entered the field once again, there stood Helen with her hands on her hips and her lips pursed.

"*That* took you long enough, didn't it?" she said with a haughty frown. "Mama wouldn't start dinner before you got back, and so now the food is cold and I've been calling you for *hours*."

"I wasn't no more than twenty minutes!" retorted Anna Claire with a defiant glare, squinting up at her big sister.

"It's been over an hour! And, oh, where are your shoes?" Helen's light brown eyes glared back with even more fervor.

Anna Claire realized that she had left her boots by the waters of Grasshopper Creek as, in her delighted state of mind, she had completely forgotten about them.

"I forgot them!" she cried in a high-pitched squeal. "I'll be right back!"

"Well, don't be down there fooling around. We're all starving!"

But Anna Claire was already among the trees.

Supper at the Freiler's was never very thrilling for Anna Claire, as she was often full from sneaking food out of the kitchen or eating berries while collecting them, but she always got her helping anyway.

The wood cabin was well-built, but not quite big enough for a family of seven to live in, which is why their father had built another room so that they would have more storage. For now, there were only a few raggedy buckskin hides protecting that part of the cabin from the great outdoors, although it was almost finished. Joseph Freiler had carved out another small cellar in the ground for storing and canning food. The house was set with a table big enough to squeeze everyone in, a table that was, in fact, made by Joseph and one of the men at the mining camps. The table just barely fit in the space, but it was something.

The children had two sides of the loft, with Caroline and Helen sharing one side and the three little ones sharing the other. There were some small ladder stairs leading upward to the two separate sides of the loft.

Anna Claire thought it bitterly unfair that her older sisters only had to share a side of the loft between the two of them, but she didn't mind sleeping with her other siblings much. Sometimes they would even stay up late when everyone was sleeping to talk and laugh. Berthie slept soundly, even if she did kick every once in a while, and Anna Claire was grateful that she wasn't Caroline, who had to put up with much flapping of the arms and snoring from Helen.

Because the cabin was made of logs and their father used buffalo hides to protect the foundation and clay, the whole upstairs acquired a funny smell, like stinking leather, especially now that June had come and the weather was hotter. It did not help that the rainwater would sometimes leak right onto their beds, and they would wake up with a small puddle around them when a big storm came through. Anna Claire tried to like the loft, but the hides were scary at night, and the smell woke her up countless times.

Downstairs smelled much better because of the meals their mother would cook during the day. Whatever they would eat that night, the house smelled like it throughout. Anna Claire only wished it would pervade into hers, Pete's, and Berthie's side of the loft!

Back in Minnesota, their mother had a notable talent for housewifery, cooking, and cleaning so well that any true wife would envy her talents. Charlotta Freiler worked tirelessly to excel at all wifely and motherly duties, and she was, above all, a true perfectionist when it came to domestic affairs.

"We've got corn!" exclaimed their father that night, holding up the wooden bowl. Everyone grew silent, for corn was their main source of food for the past couple of months.

"Papa, again?" cried Berthie, a profound look of disappointment on her little face.

"*Yes,* dear," Charlotta said, her eyes sharpening, "and we are all going to enjoy it, aren't we, children?"

The children looked into their laps. Caroline nodded, but even *she* looked unhappy, her long black locks hiding her flushed cheeks.

Joseph's eyes were kind and merry as he said, "I know you all must be tired of corn." He began laughing and stretched his arm out to touch Charlotta's hand. "I'm even startin' to get tired of it myself! But listen to how I got it."

Anna Claire was too full of the berries to be thinking about corn. Groaning with her stomach aching, she turned her face from the table.

Hero, the Freiler's watchdog, whom they found wandering around the creek alone the week prior, came over to the table to sniff around. With his long teeth and big snout for a nose, Hero could and *would* eat anything.

Anna Claire patted her leg softly to summon the mutt to her side. Hero came wagging his tail over, his tongue protruding out of his mouth. Anna Claire looked about the table to make sure no one was watching her before she broke off a piece from the corn husk, causing Hero to put his paws on Anna Claire's lap.

"Get down!" pleaded Anna Claire in a harsh whisper, throwing the piece of corn on the floor where Hero scrambled to eat it.

"Well, today I was ridin' into town for some seeds," began Joseph, a kind twinkle in his dark eyes. "Of course, I took the mules with me on the wagon or, at least, *tried* to. They were as stubborn as two old pianos, and I couldn't even get them to look at me! Now I wasn't goin' *anywhere* with those two, so I took my whip out and-"

"Oh, Papa! You didn't huwt them!" cried Berthie with her funny way of speaking.

"Now, now, now," Joseph had that teasing look in his eyes. "I didn't whip 'em. I just took the whip out to scare 'em into budgin' an inch."

"Did they budge, Papa?" Pete asked. Anna Claire took this time to spoon off another few pieces of corn and throw it at Hero.

"No, sir," Joseph laughed merrily. "Not even an inch. Those two dang on mules didn't even glance at me. You would have thought they were blind! They found a small patch of short grass and nibbled on it.

They stayed like two ol' barnacles, they did. They didn't even know I was there!"

Everyone chuckled except for Anna Claire, who was now throwing her berries at the dog unsuccessfully.

"Well, I knew I had to do somethin' if I wanted to go to town today. So, I walked."

Just then, Charlotta noticed Anna Claire throw a handful of berries onto the floor.

"Anna Claire Freiler!" she cried.

Everyone else turned towards the child with equal curiosity. "What did I tell you about feeding the dog at the table? It is not good for you *or* suitable for Hero."

"Yes, Mama," Anna Claire frowned and put her head in her hands. She looked down at the table and began to sulk.

"Well, as I was sayin'," said Joseph, trying to take the attention away from his shame-faced daughter, "I had to follow the hills close to town to get there. By now, I had walked nearly a mile, and it was gettin' real toasty outside." Joseph's eyes flickered on and off from the candlelight. "As I was beginning to get real tired, I happened to look behind me and those two ol' mules were trudgin' along. Now, I thought to myself, hadn't I tied the reins good and well? Turns out that, in my frustration, I had completely forgotten, and so here they come down the dust path bawlin' at me."

"*Why*, Papa?" questioned Berthie, tilting her head as she usually did when asking questions.

"Oh, I don't know, those animals are as unpredictable as the weather," Joseph went on. "I walked over to them and tried to walk them into town, but they had stopped movin' again. Well, now I've had about enough of these two. I nudged their legs and their backs, but they weren't phased a trifle. Then I saw they were sniffin' and kickin' in the dirt. I grabbed at them and hollered, but they stayed put just as they were. I thought of givin' up goin' into town, but then I saw why they stopped." He paused again for a drink.

"What, tell us, Papa!" cried Pete.

"There, right under my nose, stuck in old dirt, were a couple of dozen corn husks growin' right out of the dust, too!"

With this recount presumably ended, the children laughed while Charlotta rolled her eyes at her husband's silly story.

"Now wait just a minute here," Joseph raised his hand for them to be quiet. "I'm not quite finished. After I saw the corn growin' out of the ground just in the middle of all that dust, I inspected them good to make sure it wasn't a trick."

"Why?" asked Helen with curiosity. "Who would trick you?"

"Mother nature," Joseph answered, amused. "I sniffed their husks, and part of it still clung tight to the soil. Then I took a bite to make sure it hadn't spoiled. I still don't know what all that corn was doin' there. When I pat the mules on the back, they rode me to town and back without so much as a sniff. Those animals are dang smart."

"Don't say that word, Joseph," admonished Charlotta.

"But Papa," spoke up Helen, a look of confusion on her face, "why were you so excited? We've had corn every day for weeks!"

Joseph laughed. "Well, Helen, sometimes you have to find happiness in small victories. Isn't that right, Char?"

Charlotta hid her smile and nodded her head.

Anna Claire suddenly became hungry. She wasn't sure if it was because of her father's story or just because her stomach had cleared some room, but she ate the rest of her dinner quickly.

"Now we have enough corn to last us a couple of days!" cried Charlotta in jubilation. "It's providential, I suppose, that you forgot to tie the reins on those two mules."

"Oh, not another week of *corn*!" cried Helen, her hair falling into her plate.

"What did your father just say?" snapped Charlotta, raising her eyebrows.

Helen sulked quietly as the table began to be cleared.

Anna Claire hated helping her mother wash the food off the dishes. She thought of that "sacrilegious infidel" Tommy Cooper and remembered he had told her that he *never* did a single chore at his house.

I wish I lived with an infidel, thought Anna Claire miserably. Then she tried to guess what an infidel was as she wiped down the bare plates.

Once dinner was cleared and cleaned, Anna Claire was allowed to go sit outside the cabin. She loved to be outside at night under the stars.

She thought of her cousins back at home. She thought of all the fun she had at the mining camps and all the nice families she got to meet there. She thought of her parents, sisters, and brother, and the adventure they had experienced together of traveling all this way to this new territory. She also thought of how lucky she was not to have to go to school these past months.

Deep in thought, she began counting the stars and squinting to be able to see some of the more distant ones.

"Hey, Anny-Claire!" she heard a voice call out to her.

Startled, she looked around her but didn't see anyone- only the dark fields and some of the outlines of the trees to the side.

"Anny-Claire, over here!" the voice said again, a bit deeper and more aggressive than before.

When Anna Claire turned her head around, Tommy Cooper was hiding around the side of the cabin and beckoning her to come forward with his hands, his eyes wide and begging. Looking both ways around her first, she approached Tommy.

"What are you doin' here?"

"I was bored, and I knew you were probably bored too, so I thought, how 'bout I come down and see how Anny-Claire's doin'?"

Anna Claire thought Tommy Cooper to be the most interesting and adventurous boy and couldn't wait to see him again. But he hadn't come in a week, and Anna Claire was insulted with misery for his failure to return.

Now, though, after all of this time, he had interrupted her star-gazing and was about to get her into trouble. Tommy was not very good at being prompt or coming at convenient times.

"It's too late, Tommy," whispered Anna Claire. "If Mama or Papa sees you, they'll make sure you never come back again!"

It was Tommy's turn to sigh. "I hate bein' alone. I wanted to have fun. Don't you want to play in the woods or somethin'?"

Yes, actually, she would, but Anna Claire knew the cost of this was too high.

"Sure, Tommy, I'd like to a lot. But I can't." She waved her hand at him. "I still have to go inside and do my night chores and wash my face, and go to bed. Mama and Papa and everyone else are awake, and they'll know I'm missin'. I can't do nothin' tonight. I'll get in loads of trouble! And why haven't you come around here in weeks? Last time you said you wanted to be friends!" Just then, Anna Claire heard the sound of Caroline calling for her to come inside and help.

Tommy frowned. "No fun. But hey, we *are* friends. Maybe tomorrow?"

"Go away!" returned Anna Claire as she ran around the cabin. Looking behind her, she added, "Fine then. Maybe tomorrow! And you better be back here!"

Satisfied with that answer, the boy went skipping away through the dark field to where he lived in town, glad to have a friend. Anna Claire went inside to do her night chores and was giddier than usual, knowing she wouldn't have to wait long for her friend to return.

Chapter 2- The Sacrilegious Infidel

Summer had just begun. The family had lived in Gold Country, Montana Territory, for some time now and was getting used to the feeling of no longer being in Minnesota. The family was very busy making the small log cabin a home. Joseph Freiler spent most of his time panning for gold outside, harvesting the fields, and digging ditches for the water supply. Charlotta sometimes helped him in the fields, too, and gathered together plants, such as gooseberries and wild turnips, which she put into the little oven to make for suppers.

Caroline sewed new dresses for the girls and a new pair of summer trousers for her brother while Helen helped with the canning and sweeping. Peter had learned how to fish and obtained the underwater wildlife that ended up on the plates of the family. He was learning from his father the chores of their little farm, such as caring for the cows, mules, and horses. Berthie stayed by Charlotta's side and learned sewing, cooking, and planting from her mother. Anna Claire was the one to pick the berries and bring water from the creek to the house, which sounds easy enough, but for a girl as tiny as Anna Claire was, the bucket was half her size. The water was so heavy that it dragged her down so that she had to take frequent stops on the way from the creek to the house. She often dropped the water bucket and would have to turn around to go back.

The summer began with beautiful weather but turned scorching hot very quickly. It was so hot that the Freilers had to keep the door open at times while Joseph kept watch with his shotgun to make sure there was no danger, such as a traveling wolf or another unwelcome guest. The family spent their days sweating inside, taking turns doing their chores, going to the creek for relief, and catching every gust of breeze that they could. Life in Montana Territory was hard. The chores were endless, and sometimes it felt like they were living just to merely survive. Back in Minnesota, they knew everyone in their little part of the woods, but here they were still getting to know the other miners and their families.

Joseph had the dangerous job of digging out the well, which was a laborious task, while everyone else went out to find wood and sticks for the little fireplace. Their father made a patch next to the wagon in which to begin growing more corn and wheat while their mother stayed busy husking the corn and constantly sweeping the wooden floor. During the rain, it got so muddy that Charlotta and the girls had to go to the creek to wash and scrub their boots with the lye and grease from the game-whichever game their father could catch that week.

Charlotta and Joseph built a little crooked fence that they put up around the garden. Joseph was able to buy food with the small rations and the little meager dusts of gold he found here and there, but it was never enough to fill the whole family. They had nights where they went to bed hungry, although this was thankfully rare due to Joseph's good aim for hunting and his very hard work panning by the creek.

However, it was still awful to go to bed without supper on those more unfortunate nights.

Charlotta always worried about disease and, as she often said, "Cleanliness is next to Godliness." She encouraged her children to bathe at the creek very often and use the lye soap that they had, but to be very careful not to drink it in case the water was polluted. The water that they drank was boiled in a big tin pot on the fireplace before consumption.

The typical diet was the game their father caught, which varied from elk to moose, and slices of bread obtained from the town. Many times, there were salmon, especially in the summer months, as it was easy for Pete to catch them then. Sometimes, for a rare treat, Joseph would buy coffee in town for his wife, as Charlotta loved coffee. Occasionally, Joseph was able to buy canned fruit, which Helen and Anna Claire loved. But the town prices could be expensive sometimes for poor frontier families, so they often did without the little luxuries.

Charlotta and Caroline did most of the hemming and made some new trousers for Joseph and Peter, as well as began knitting hats and gloves for the upcoming fall. Charlotta, Caroline, Helen, and Anna Claire always seemed to be washing clothes in the big keg before placing them on the line outside to dry. This was a tedious chore for Anna Claire, as she hated scrubbing all the filth and dirt off, particularly on her own dresses as they were always the dirtiest. They would also wash their braided rag rugs and the little muslin curtains in the keg every once and a while when they could.

The animals took up a lot of work, but this part Anna Claire didn't mind, as she loved being near them. They had to be fed, washed, their hooves cleaned, and their nails trimmed. Anna Claire loved watching the chickens lay eggs and peck at the ground. The horses and the mules had to eat very often, and it seemed that most of the food was grown for them, such as the grains Joseph had been harvesting. In any case, Anna Claire loved going up to them and giving them big hugs, nuzzling her face into their necks.

Joseph had his work cut out for him, too, as he often sharpened and oiled his tools for the next day, trying to expand their little farm. He worked very late nights by the creek with the many other miners, panning and trying to find that sparkly yellow that was so treasured. He found some gold dust, which was exciting at first, but less so when he realized how little the gold dust went in Bannack. He could only focus on making the best out of the gold he was able to obtain.

Caroline was always so preoccupied with her beautiful hair and insisted on washing it first before any of the others could wash in the big keg. Charlotta let this little vanity slide because Caroline was a "good" girl and an obedient daughter who nearly did no wrong in her eyes. Most of the time, they all used the same water to bathe. Most families bathed once a week, but due to Charlotta's near obsession with cleanliness, the Freilers bathed twice a week. Charlotta insisted, after their bath in the keg, that they each take a rag dipped in clean boiled water to wash themselves after to be even more mindful. It was always oldest to youngest in the water keg. The parents would bathe first, and then Caroline, before Helen, Anna Claire, Pete, and finally Berthie.

Caroline liked to weave and sew, so she took on these tasks happily. Helen was the laziest of everyone and always did her chores so slowly. It took her more than twenty minutes to run to the creek and gather a pan full of water, and even longer to collect eggs from the chicken coop. Peter liked to fish and be by the water, and he liked spending time with his father, so he spent many a day outside on the farm or by the creek. Little Bertha couldn't do very much, but she liked to stick by Charlotta's side at all times, so she learned how to do her chores by watching her mother and her sisters. Anna Claire wished she could be like Pete and fish and farm with her father, but instead she had to learn the chores of girls, which were mainly inside. She relished those times when she could finally go outside and collect raspberries from the creek or tend to the animals when she had the chance.

Anna Claire had been in a poor mood for a while because the boy who lived in town had not come to meet her the next day as he said he would, or the day after that, or even the day after that. Anna Claire was growing bored and glum, and even Grasshopper Creek couldn't console her much.

That all changed one day, about a week after he had sneaked to the Freiler's house in the evening.

"Anny-Claire!" cried Tommy Cooper from outside Anna Claire's window. "Anny-Claire!"

"That sacrilegious infidel!" exclaimed Anna Claire furiously to herself, annoyed at being woken up so early. She hit the ground with her feet and rubbed her eyes. "What is he doin' standin' below my window?"

"Anny-Claire!" called the insistent voice. "Where- oh," his voice softened into a tone barely audible behind stuffy glass windows. Caroline had promptly appeared at the door in her jam-covered apron, looking annoyed.

Anna Claire ran down the ladder of the loft, through the room, and over to greet him, still wearing her nightgown.

"Where are you going, and who is that boy outside?" Charlotta asked, peeking her head out of the door.

"I'm going outside, and he's Tommy, the sacrilegious infidel," answered Anna Claire as she sprang out the door, using her mother's own insult to describe him.

"Wait right here," her mother admonished, "and go back up that ladder. Change into your dress before running outdoors. It's still very early- why, the sun is hardly up!"

Anna Claire groaned, ran up the ladder, and threw her dress on inside out before leaping back down anxiously. She was so happy that Tommy was back that she could hardly contain her excitement. She wasn't sure if she would ever see him again.

"You!" she cried as she ran into the squelching hot air, her lips pursed and her eyes narrow.

"Anna Claire, you're awake! It is time you learned how to sew properly," said Caroline, thrusting the spool and thread into her arms. "I'll teach you now."

"Get your needles and cloth away from me," Anna Claire commanded, dropping them onto the ground and running towards the boy. "Tommy Cooper, why haven't you visited?"

Tommy looked confused. "Sorry. I just didn't. I guess I didn't know you wanted me to."

"Well, now you do," she said as she pushed him straight into the ground, "and don't you ever not come visitin' for a whole week again!"

Tommy got up and brushed the dirt off his pants. They were already so muddy that it really didn't matter how many times he fell.

"Anna Claire, come into this house at once!" cried Caroline next to the door with tangible irritation.

"I already told Mama I was going to play with the infidel!" and with that, Anna Claire stuck out her tongue. Then she turned to Tommy and added, "My mama says you're a sacrilegious infidel."

Tommy, having no concept whatsoever of the phrase, took it as a nice compliment and nodded. "Really?"

"And she's right." Caroline's lips shut taut after that comment, and Tommy stared with amazement at this beautiful fire-head who so clearly disliked his presence.

"We're goin' into the forest," Anna Claire told her sister.

Caroline ignored the excited girl and her tattered bumpkin of a friend and went into the house, slamming the door as hard as it would slam.

"Your sister's awful pretty," Tommy said in admiration, "but she don't like me one bit!"

"Caroline's awfully nasty, but don't you ever say that she's pretty again!" Anna Claire, being the little tomboy that she was, took great offense to the word "pretty" and thought it a very silly, undesirable thing.

"Well, she is!" Tommy spat in the dirt and wiped his mouth. "You're a fire-head too, like she is. I was gonna see if you wanted to go to town, but I guess you're too high and mighty for that."

This idea was very appealing to Anna Claire. *Town!* To just say the word brought chills to her body. The thrill of adventure entered her danger-seeking soul and filled her with energy.

"I'm not high and mighty!" she declared indignantly. She then brushed her hair, which was shoulder-length and darkened gold like honey, with her hand. "I'll come to town with you!"

Tommy was pleased that he had found this strange but bold comrade, even if she was a girl.

"I like you," he said frankly. "You're a girl but you ain't a sissy. I hate sissies. But you're a real fire-head!"

"I'm not a fire-head!" she protested with great offense. "But I do like town much better than this stupid ol' house."

And so, with that, instead of going to the creek as Caroline and her mother thought they were, the children headed off into town.

They walked through the willowy bitterroot milkvetch and the white, lilac-filled sego lilies, skipping and talking like old friends. They crossed over into the itchy blue grama and the arching stems of heath asters before walking into seemingly endless grass, Anna Claire talking a mile a minute and Tommy listening in awe.

"Why did you and your family come to Montana Territory? Is it 'cause of the gold?"

Anna Claire liked Tommy's way of speaking. He had that Western drawl she found so interesting, and he pronounced his words differently than the people back in Minnesota- in fact, most of the people she came into contact with were much different than those in Minnesota.

"Yeah, the gold," she answered. "Mama didn't want to come. Papa had to beg her, and she was angry. So angry! Sometimes, me and Berthie could hear her yellin' at Papa late at night when we were supposed to be sleepin'."

"Well, why didn't she want gold?"

"I think she does want gold," Anna Claire stopped to think, "but she didn't want to leave Minnesota. She said she misses her own mama and her sisters, and my cousins. She has friends there, too, and she misses them and all the people from church. She didn't want to come all the way out here so far away."

"Well, I sure hope she's not angry at your pa anymore," said Tommy.

"No, she told him that he's the provider and will listen to him. She always says that about him bein' a provider."

"What's that mean?"

Anna Claire shrugged. "I don't know, but she says it a lot."

"Are you happy you came?" Tommy asked sincerely as they skipped along.

"Yes!" Anna Claire answered. "I miss my cousin Katie sometimes, but I love it here. Montana Territory is the most exciting place I've ever been in my whole life! I hope we live here forever!"

"How old are ya? You look younger than me," observed Tommy.

"I'm nine-years-old," Anna Claire said, straightening herself up as if to look taller. Tommy was only a year her senior, but tall for his age.

"You're younger than me," said Tommy, "'cause I'm already ten and turnin' eleven in October."

"Well, my birthday is at the end of the summer!" bragged Anna Claire with great pride. "I'll be ten-years-old like you!"

"I'm still older and you're just a little girl," said Tommy with a grin.

"I am *not*!" Anna Claire cried indignantly, imitating her newly found friend by spitting on the ground. She couldn't come up with an argument for her statement, so she walked a bit ahead of Tommy with her arms folded about her chest and a pout on her face.

They walked on in a tense silence for some time until Anna Claire began to see the outline of the town on the horizon.

"Look, Tommy, look, it's the town!" she cried with delight, clasping her hands together. "We're almost there!" She spun in circles, her dress like a flower as it flowed around her legs.

"It's just town," answered Tommy nonchalantly. He couldn't understand why this little, frantic girl got so worked up about everything.

"Are there cowboy races every day?" she asked excitedly. "How 'bout rodeos and music and lots of candy?"

Tommy laughed. "There's cowboys, but I reckon they don't have much races," he answered with some confusion, "and there's music and all, but it gets loud at night when I'm tryin' to sleep."

Tommy had always hated that music and never got the proper amount of sleep he needed.

"Boy, that sounds wonderful!" Anna Claire tugged at his arm to make him go faster. "Come on and hurry up, you slowpoke, we have to get to town!"

"I don't see why you gotta get all excited about everything," Tommy said, but yielded to her ecstatic behavior.

The two walked some more through the field until they reached town. The little girl watched with huge eyes, taking in the stout buildings painted all sorts of bright colors- pink, green, blue, yellow; anything! She went open-mouthed at the saloon in which two older men were throwing drinks at each other over an unfair game of poker. She nearly jumped in the air with excitement when she noticed the young men carrying whips in their rough-skinned hands as they sat on wild black and brown horses. They yelled cusswords at each other as they rode out of town. She marveled at the grand red entrance of the City Drug Store and the strong smell of the butcher shop. There were young women in flouncy bustles and children with dirty faces spitting tobacco in the road. She listened intently to the hammering of nails into wood and the sound of springs and bolts at the blacksmith's shop, getting out of the way of the rickety carriage axles riding by her methodically.

To the child of nine, the town of Bannack was a huge citadel among a vast heavenly land, and stood big and proud against the prairie sky. Anna Claire felt that she *must* live here in this wild and dangerous place where nothing could ever get boring.

"This is my house," said Tommy as they entered a building with an awning and a large porch, the words "Swiner's Saloon" written at the top. It was one of the town's few saloons, where most of the miners and people of Bannack went to see their friends and businesses, and to find amusement during the difficult times of living on the frontier.

"You live in a *saloon*?" cried Anna Claire in shock.

"Yeah. It's terrible," Tommy answered, tugging on her small hand and pulling her inside. Had he not made this gesture, the girl would have stood outside the building for a very long time with her mouth hanging open and her feet stuck to the floorboards.

Anna Claire walked into the saloon tentatively. She looked around at the people sitting down at the tables and at the countertop. A man was getting a haircut from the barber in the corner, and some of the men in the middle of the room were yelling about a game of Texas Hold 'Em. There were windows on the other side of the building and a long brass chandelier hanging precariously on the ceiling, swinging back and forth as if it was about to fall any minute. The walls were covered with nails for the men to hang their hats on, and a big set of antlers was placed right above the bar. The counter was elaborately carved like a sculpture, and bottles were displayed temptingly on the ledge. There was a tall man with a long beard behind the counter pouring drinks into steel cups from bottles, and a flouncy woman standing next to him and smiling at her.

Tommy had let go of her hand, and immediately after he did, he wished he hadn't, for Anna Claire was not a bit intimidated by all of the grown-ups sitting on the stools and the tables.

"Tommy, is this your friend you were tellin' me about?" said the flouncy lady with too much makeup. She had big red lips and wore a skimpy red and white not-quite-a-dress, staring down at Anna Claire with a teasing smile. "You're a little one, ain't ya?"

The men at the counter laughed, not because of Anna Claire's size, but simply because of the expression on the child's face. Never before had she been so insulted!

"Well, bein' young is better than bein' *old*!" she retorted, hands on her hips.

"Come on, Anny-Claire," begged Tommy, pulling her sleeve.

"And you wear too much red on your lips!" cried the winded, offended little creature in a final attempt to hurt the lady's feelings. She hadn't succeeded much, for the woman was laughing along with the men.

"She's a little sprite, isn't she?" cried one of the men, laughing into his whiskey and hitting his friend on the arm.

"What a kid!"

Now Anna Claire was even more insulted than she already had been. She didn't know what a sprite was, but she sensed it wasn't a good thing. Her golden-tanned face red from anger, she wiggled out of Tommy's grasp and stalked over to the man.

"I'll show *you* what a sprite is!" she cried, her hands clasped in a fist. And she would have let him have it had it not been for Tommy, who pulled her to the other side of the room.

"Ma, we're gonna play upstairs," Tommy said to the lady in the short dress wearing "too much red" on her lips.

The woman smiled again as the men continued to laugh and laugh, some of them teasing the man she had wanted to hit, shouting, "You met your match, Jasey! She got ya, Jasey!"

Anna Claire was furious. She did not try to run back to the howling crowd of men but instead yelled nasty insults at them as Tommy dragged her up the stairs.

"Gee, be quiet!" Tommy yelled at her. "You're gonna get yourself jabbed!"

"Your mama isn't very nice to call me little," said Anna Claire, a calm hurt taking the place of her previous anger.

"My ma was only tellin' the truth!" Tommy started but, seeing Anna Claire's face becoming red again, added, "I think she was tryin' to make you laugh."

"I'm not laughin' at all," said the injured little girl.

They entered a very small space with a wooden door, which Tommy declared his "room." It was very tiny, nearly small enough to be a closet, and was a dirty, unsanitary place that held the small bed, a little wooden barrel which Tommy called his "dresser," and various posters of women dressed in shorter attire than his mother was wearing and with the red lipstick Anna Claire most dreaded. The pictures had the women pulling up their skirts past their knees, winking, and even exposing parts of their bosom. Anna Claire had never seen anything like this before and was puzzled. Next to the pictures of the women were cowboys riding wild horses with whips in their hands, looking much like the ones Anna Claire had seen with her own eyes that very day.

"I like your cowboy pictures," Anna Claire began, "but I don't like those ones with those ladies in them. Why do they dress like that?"

"I don't know, but Rocks and Ebb collects lots of 'em," bragged Tommy, referring to the two boys in town he admired. "They have even more than I do and put them up on every inch of their walls. See this lady here?"

Anna Claire did see her, and she felt more confused than ever. Not only was the woman wearing very little, but she was also standing on a table in a dancing-like motion. She didn't know why, but the odd woman gave Anna Claire a feeling of dread.

"Ebb said he knew her," Tommy bragged. "He said she danced on him."

"Why?" asked the innocent girl slowly, gazing in bewilderment at the lady above her head.

"I don't know, but it sounds alright to me." Tommy sat on his bed and turned his attention back to Anna Claire, who had her head down and a frown on her full lips. "What's wrong?"

"Mama wouldn't like me seein' these ladies. She would say they're sinnin' by wearin' clothes like that."

Tommy laughed. "Maybe they are, I don't know, but aren't they pretty?"

Anna Claire nodded. "But why do they wear their dresses like that?"

Tommy shrugged, honestly unsure of the answer.

"Do you wanna have a bottle of whiskey?" he asked suddenly, reaching over onto his "dresser" for two bottles containing a putrid-looking, yellow-brown substance.

Anna Claire put her one hand to her mouth. "Papa always said whiskey is real bad and that only men drink it! Whiskey ain't for children."

Tommy just looked at her. "I'm no child, I'm a *man*." The look on his face was so serious that any real grown-up would have a hard time stifling a chuckle at this declaration. "You're not scared of it, are ya?"

"Of course not!" she cried indignantly.

"Well, alright then," and Tommy opened the bottle, promptly giving it to her.

She hesitated. "It looks dreadful! And it smells awful! Will I die?"

Tommy laughed at his friend's ignorance. "You ain't gonna die from a bottle of whiskey. It might make you tired, though."

"You sure?"

"' Course I'm sure," Tommy told her firmly. "Taste it. It's bad at first, but you get used to it."

Anna Claire did as she was told, and as soon as the bottle reached her lips, she took a big sip and grimaced. "The smell! What's in this?" she gave the bottle back to Tommy, who was taking his in big gulps.

"I told ya, it's whiskey. Tarantula Juice," he answered, taking another swig. "Come on, drink some more. After the first bottle, it's like magic."

Now she was intrigued. "It's *magic*?"

"Sure, it is," Tommy said, now finishing the bottle and throwing it to the ground so that it made a clinking sound against the wooden floorboards.

"Well, kind of. It makes your mind see things. Like right now, I could swear you had three heads!"

"Three heads!" she touched her face self-consciously. "I don't have three heads!"

"Exactly!" Tommy exclaimed, lying back down on his bed. 'Cause whiskey is magic. It makes everything come to life."

Anna Claire wanted to see magic, too. So, heeding her irresponsible friend, she took another large sip of the drink. And then another. Already, her head began to play tricks on her.

"I bet you want me to tell you a story," Tommy slurred, taking the bottle out of her hands. "But you can't be drunk. You have to listen."

But Anna Claire didn't want any more of her drink. She yielded without a fight, clenching her stomach and feeling a bit nauseous, her throat burning from the alcohol. She belched loudly and groaned.

"This drink made me sick," she said, closing her eyes.

"No, don't fall asleep!" beckoned Tommy. "Listen to this story."

Wearily, Anna Claire opened her eyes.

"Go on then," she instructed with a queenly wave of her hand.

"Remember when I told you that you live where Old Man Hatfield used to live? Well," he continued, "I was right. But if I tell you the story, you gotta promise not to tell a livin' soul."

"I won't tell!" Anna Claire promised, spitting in her hand and shaking his.

"Alright, then, I'll tell ya. But you'd better not tell or I'll smash your face in your skull!" The threat didn't frighten Anna Claire at all, but she nodded, wanting to hear the tale.

"About a hundred years ago," began Tommy, his blue eyes growing by the second, "there was a nice young man named Davie Hatfield. Always nice and friendly to everyone who happened to drop by. He was so nice that he got good jobs buildin' buildin's. He wanted to find gold, just like your pa. Well, Davie Hatfield became rich with piles of gold when he mined it. He decided to marry Minnie Waters. Minnie was pretty and real nice and liked Davie a lot. Well, we all know that happiness never came to Davie Hatfield."

"I don't!" Anna Claire cried, her interest exceeding her stomachache.

"Will ya be quiet and let me tell the story?" cried Tommy with exasperation. "Gee. Anyway, Minnie and Old Man Ha- Davie Hatfield moved to a real small cabin which used to be where your house is before they teared it down. One day, Minnie was thrown off her horse in your very field and she died. Davie ran out and guess what he saw?"

"What!?" asked Anna Claire in rapture, sitting up.

"Flies," he stopped to watch her face, "*eating* her flesh."

Instead of making a face, Anna Claire relished the grotesque tale. "What else did the flies do?"

"They bit her." Tommy pretended to bite her nose off, and Anna Claire giggled. "And then, Davie

Hatfield became so sad. Minnie left him with a daughter. She was three. Her name was Daisy."

"That's sad," reflected Anna Claire.

"Shh," Tommy rolled his eyes, annoyed at Anna Claire's constant interruptions. "*Anyway*, Daisy and Davie lived together, and he raised Daisy all by himself. He did good by her, but missed his wife 'cause she could cook the greatest meals, and Davie wasn't very handy with a pot and spoon."

"That's the only reason he liked his wife?" Anna Claire interrupted with a baffled look.

"*No*, stupid," Tommy made a face. "He liked her because she was pretty!"

"That's *it!?*"

"He was in love with her!" Tommy threw his hands up in the air in exasperation.

Anna Claire made a face. Although the flies did not bother her in this tale, being "in love" really gave her a sick feeling in the pit of her stomach.

"Love is awful!" cried Anna Claire passionately as she wrinkled her nose and sank deeper into the old, yellowed mattress of Tommy's cot.

"Can I continue?" asked the little boy with much exaggeration. Anna Claire nodded sulkily and put her hand over her mouth to keep from any more outbursts.

"Davie used some of the gold to buy her food and clothes, but saved most of it for Daisy to use when she grew up. Daisy finally grew up. When she was eighteen, her father let her make a choice. To live with him or go on her own. Now Davie thought she would choose to live with him."

"But she didn't!" guessed Anna Claire.

"Daisy Hatfield wanted to see the world, and so she decided to leave. Davie was angry because he really loved Daisy and thought she would choose to live with him. So, as she was packin' to leave, he ran her out of the house and chased her up the mountains or somethin'."

Anna Claire laughed. She laughed so hard her face turned a bright red and her eyes began to water.

"What's the matter with you?" asked Tommy, very offended that his little companion took his tale so lightly.

"It's funny to think of a man chasin' a girl up a hill!" Anna Claire laughed again, but sobered up when she noticed the ambitious tale-teller's frown.

"You won't think it's so jolly in a minute," he snapped. "Daisy became real scared and didn't ever come back. But Davie Hatfield gave up because of his sadness and didn't care about life anymore."

Anna Claire was perplexed. Life here seemed so interesting that she could never imagine someone not caring about mere *existence*.

"How can you stop carin' about life?" she asked naively, her heart feeling heavy in her chest.

Tommy looked down as if he knew but wouldn't say.

"Davie Hatfield sure didn't care no more. He buried all his riches and gold that he found in the mines and dug them deep in the mountains- *those* mountains up there-" he looked at the wall over his shoulder, "and he died from a heart attack. Now, everyone calls him Old Man Hatfield." Tommy took a sip from Anna Claire's bottle. "They say Daisy felt home-sick and she missed her father."

"But he's dead!" Anna Claire jumped up from the bed. "You said he buried all his treasures."

"Yeah, he did," Tommy said mournfully. "She came back to Idaho Territory, that's what it used to be, and to the house she grew up in. *Your* house, Anny-Claire."

"That wasn't their house! I saw my papa build it!" she reproved with tenacity.

"Well, his house was on the same land!" Tommy rebuked. "How was *I* supposed to know they took it down? Well, now, Daisy was surprised when she found out her father was dead. They say that she couldn't handle the grief and went and killed herself. Some say she jumped off the mountain, but I heard some other men sayin' she poisoned herself. They say Daisy had a child. They say she's still alive. Her name's Darlin'."

"That's a funny name!" Anna Claire shouted, bursting into laughter again.

"I don't know, I didn't make it up, that's what they called her," said Tommy resolutely. "All I know is that she's real old. Maybe forty."

"That's older than Mama and Papa!" Anna Claire cried with shock.

"I know," Tommy shook his head as if he couldn't believe people as old as forty were still walk-ing the earth. "I heard that she's somewhere with a hidden identity."

"What's a hidden identity?" asked Anna Claire.

"Are you dumb or somethin'? It means you're keepin' your name a secret and callin' yourself someone else."

"Sometimes I have a hidden identity," she whispered. "When I play Uncle John, I sometimes pretend I'm him and make a long beard out of Caroline's gloves. Does that mean I'm bad?"

By now, Tommy Cooper thought that this "Anny-Claire" was the strangest girl he'd ever met in his life, and this sealed his doubts.

"No, it doesn't mean you're bad, but it *does* mean your nuts," he told her with a serious expression, as was custom in him when expressing opinions.

"I am *not* nuts!" cried Anna Claire indignantly. "But whatever happened to the treasure?"

"It's buried in the mountains, 'course," explained Tommy, a glow in his eyes. "And men have tried to dig it up, but no one has ever found it. *I* think they're lookin' in all the wrong places, if you ask me. I have a feeling I know *just* where it's at. Mr. Dobbins thinks so, too. Someday I'm gonna go back to those mountains and get that treasure. You just watch me, Anny-Claire; I'm gonna be rich someday! Someday, real soon. I swear!"

Anna Claire gasped. "My sister Helen told me that you go to hell if you swear!"

"She's about as nuts as you are," Tommy answered, lying back onto his pillow. "There ain't no such thing as a heaven or a hell or God. I don't know where people got that bosh from anyhow."

"Oh, Tommy," Anna Claire frowned. "You're a very bad boy. Mama said I mustn't play or speak to anyone who doesn't believe in God."

"Well then, go home!" cried Tommy, much offended. The boy was very sensitive about his feelings and beliefs, and his feathers ruffled every time someone criticized him. "I don't need a sissy girl stickin' around here anyway. 'Specially if she's gonna say things like *that*."

Now Anna Claire's own sensitive soul was pricked painfully. "Tommy Cooper, you said it yourself that you like me because I'm *not* a sissy! And I ain't. I was only tellin' you what Mama told me. But I like you even if you are a bad boy. Caroline always says I'm a bad girl, but she says she loves me. I guess she has to 'cause I'm her sister, but I like you anyway. I don't wanna leave."

"Well, then don't go preachin' to me unless you're the pastor and I'm in the church!" Anna Claire frowned so pathetically that even red-tempered Tommy softened.

"Listen, it's all well and good if you believe in Jesus and all that stuff," he told her, his voice lighter, "but that don't mean I got to, ya understand?"

Anna Claire nodded, still feeling a bit hurt at her new friend's degrading tone.

Tommy noticed this and awkwardly put his small hand on her bony shoulder. "Aw, come on, don't be mad. I didn't mean to yell. I like talkin' to you, even if you're nuts."

"I am *not* nuts!" repeated Anna Claire, her fire returning like a lit match.

"Alright, a *little* nuts," resolved the boy with a defined cross of his arms.

"No, not even a little nuts," Anna Claire replied.

Tommy frowned and gave in. "Fine, whatever you say, but I still think you're a little nuts."

Anna Claire didn't hear this comment because her eyes moved around his room and stopped on one of his most beloved posters. This one contained a well-drawn picture of a cowboy holding ropes of gold in his hand as he rode away into an orange sunset towards the mountains.

"Don't that picture remind you of the story you told me?" she asked, pointing to it.

Tommy looked up with hopeful eyes. "Yeah. That's gonna be me someday when I find that treasure in the mountains. Old Man Hatfield's long forgotten treasure. I'll be smilin' just like that man is and I'll be holdin' that gold just the same."

"If I got lots of gold, I'd do what Daisy did and travel everywhere. I'd go to Egypt first and then probably Greece. Did you know the Egyptians had secret chambers in their pyramids?"

"No," said Tommy honestly. "I don't know nothin' about the Egyptians."

"I love learnin' about Egypt," Anna Claire went on. "All the pharaohs and queens...I think some of those people had to have magic to be able to build all of those pyramids. I wasn't allowed to talk about it in school 'cause the teacher said it ain't proper, but I still kept readin' about it, though. My aunt had lots and lots of books, and so does Mama. Mama loves to read, even though she tells me I can't read her books 'cause they ain't proper for me. Well, if they're not proper, then why does *she* read them?"

Anna Claire thought of Minnesota and Grandma Lund's home. She thought of all of the books- dozens of books- that were kept on the shelf in her Grandma Lund's spare room. Some of the books had been Anna Claire's grandmother's, and many of them had been her mother's growing up. Mrs. Freiler loved books, possibly more than anything in the world besides her family. Many of the books in her Grandma Lund's home held stories and truths of ancient civilizations, old miracles, and myths from Sweden.

"I ain't read nothin'," said Tommy, taking a bite out of a stale piece of bread from his box of dresser and tossing it at the ceiling of the room. "Readin' sounds boring."

"Oh, you're wrong, Tommy," said the avid adventurer who, being unable to fly away like a little bird to all the places she most desired, could at least read about them. "Can't you read?"

Tommy frowned and shook his head. "Nah. I could if I wanted to, but I don't, so there."

There was a look of shame on his face, which was not unnoticed by Anna Claire.

"Well, didn't you ever go to school?"

"Nah, and I never will," he spat on the floorboards underneath him. "School is for sissies."

Anna Claire was amazed. She wished she had

never had to go to school. She loathed school and always had, and had been happy not to go when she moved.

"I hate school," she said aloud. "You're lucky your mama doesn't make you go."

Tommy sighed. "I *am* lucky. School…" he shuddered as if saying a bad word. "I never went to school, even when I lived in the shanty."

"The shanty?" Anna Claire asked with interest.

"Yeah, the shanty. I used to live there when I was little. We moved into town when Pa told Ma about all the businesses that were comin' out here 'cause of the gold. Before that, though, we lived in the little shanty."

"Where was the little shanty?" Anna Claire asked with interest.

"How am I supposed to know? I was only seven."

The children went quiet for a moment as they heard a loud bang from down the long stairway and the sound of glass shattering.

"Don't pay no mind, that's how it always is here," sighed Tommy, his piercing blue eyes gazing up at the ceiling.

Anna Claire looked at him, at the door, and then back at him. "I think livin' here must be wonderful!"

Tommy shrugged. *He* certainly didn't think it was wonderful.

"I like it sometimes," he said slowly, "but most of the time it gets too loud here. And my ma works all night. Sometimes I hear her up talkin' to men from the town. They come in here and drink, and then they stay with my ma durin' the night. I don't know why. Ma says they're her customers, but she won't tell me what they're buyin' from her so late."

Anna Claire thought her friend's life must be absolutely thrilling- to be in town, living on top of a saloon with a mother who didn't care if Tommy learned how to read or not.

"Do you think my papa will find gold?" asked Anna Claire, thinking once again of the pyramids of Egypt she so badly wanted to see.

Tommy shrugged, leaning against the wall. His small, oval face looked pensive before he said, "He might. I reckon I don't know. He might."

Anna Claire was reminded of something her father had told her when she was very small.

"Papa told me that havin' a family is the best kind of gold in the world," she said. "Don't you think it is?"

Tommy looked at her blankly. "I wouldn't know," he replied, the bottle cracking as it hit the ground.

It had been several hours since Anna Claire had left her house, gone to town, and reached the Freiler homestead again. She was exhausted and tired, but full of energy in spirit. She had made Tommy retell the tragic story of Old Man Hatfield once again before she left, finding that the story charmed her unlike any other that she had heard be- fore. She felt pity for Mr. Hatfield and sadness that his daughter had taken her own life. She was also very curious about the granddaughter with the funny name "Darling" that still might be alive at that ancient age of forty. But even her imagination could not keep her from intense tiredness, and the walk home had been long and boring, as Tommy had fallen asleep after drinking more whiskey and couldn't even walk her down the stairs.

As she walked nearer to the homestead, she could hear shouts and calls from the forest. They seemed to be screaming her name. Swiftly, she made a beeline for home, her heart quickening in pace. She knew she was late and, even worse, in big trouble.

"I'm here!" she cried as loudly as she could, panting as she ran. "Mama! Papa! I'm here!"

She saw a small figure turn her way. It was Helen, and she had a smile on her face.

"Papa! Mr. Clemmons! She's here!" cried her sister, running to the men. "I found her!"

Joseph and Mr. Clemmons, a man from the mining camp who had settled not far from the Freilers, both came out from the trees to inspect the dirt-faced little thing that emerged in the yard, eyes weary and dress torn.

"They've been looking for you," Helen warned her with brevity in her voice.

The men reached Anna Claire, Papa shaking her shoulders.

"Where in heaven's name were you for six hours?" he demanded hoarsely. "Your mama said you left at six in the morning! It's past noon! I came home to eat with Mr. Clemmons. We've been lookin' all through the woods and fields for you until we finally decided to follow the creek."

"I must admit, I was worried that you might've drowned," said Mr. Clemmons, shaking his head, his mustache beaded with sweat.

Mr. Clemmons looked sour, but not nearly as wild with rage as her father was. Anna Claire struggled not to flinch under his harsh gaze.

"You do the most foolish things!" he cried in a torrent of anger, his eyes darkening. "How many times have your mama and I told you not to go runnin' off anywhere you please? One of these days you're gonna get yourself killed."

Anna Claire glanced at Helen, who was pretending to feel great sorrow for their father and Mr. Clemmons, even though Anna Claire could plainly see the smirk in her eyes.

"You can't keep runnin' off," Mr. Clemmons added. "Ever since I met your good family, your mama and papa have been worried sick about your wanderin' different places whereas you don't belong and ain't got no right to be."

Mr. Clemmons was a good-humored man whom Anna Claire liked greatly, but at this moment, Anna Claire wished he would leave her alone.

"Why don't you climb a tree?" she cried angrily, beginning to storm off as she shot him a look.

As soon as those terrible words escaped from Anna Claire's lips, she regretted them. She knew she was in for a good spanking- very soon.

"Anna Claire!" Joseph shouted, furious. "Don't you speak to good Mr. Clemmons like that. He's been lookin' for you just as long as I have, wantin' to make sure you're safe. Now get out of my sight!"

She wanted to apologize, but she couldn't open her mouth.

"Git!" repeated her father, a wild look in his eyes.

As Anna Claire ran across the yard as fast as her skinny little legs could carry her, she heard her father's voice in the distance.

"And you can be sure of a spankin'!"

Chapter 3- Grasshopper Diggings

The next day was not a day Anna Claire would look back on with fondness. She washed the clothes in the keg and put them on the line to dry, churned butter with the dasher, cleaned the dreadful out-house, fried eggs above the fire, and felt the painful bruise of last night's spanking on her bottom. It was something Anna Claire thought she would never get over.

She also felt sorely guilty about telling poor, kind Mr. Clemmons- the same man who had given her a lemon drop just last week- to "go climb a tree." She never thought she could look at that man again with-out cringing in embarrassment.

"You know, you're a very ungrateful little girl," Caroline said reprovingly as Anna Claire scrubbed the windows that next day. She was sitting in a chair watching her, a book open in her hands.

Anna Claire didn't reply. Instead, she scrubbed harder than ever, dipping the rag into the castile-filled water bucket.

"Papa and Mama have so much to do, what with settling in Montana Territory and taking care of us children," Caroline continued. "They are very busy. You talk to them so scornfully, even though they feed you and give you pretty little dresses to wear, at which you throw mud all over anyway. When I was a little girl, I never did such terrible things. I was thank-ful for Mama and Papa, and I was always respectful."

Still, Anna Claire said nothing. Caroline always thought she could mother Anna Claire just because she was older, and Anna Claire sometimes thought she hated her older sister with as much passion as she hated dresses or dolls.

"Anna Claire, are you even listening to a word I'm saying?" the elder sister asked, dropping the book on her lap, eyes concentrated on the girl's frustrated face.

"Yes," the younger sister answered without turning around.

"You really are a terribly bad girl," Caroline continued with her usual superior air, "and I was shocked when you told us you were at that dreadful boy's house. What a heathen if I ever saw one!"

Now Anna Claire dropped her rag into the bucket and threw her hands on her hips. Turning to face her sister, anger pinching her nose, she said in her cruelest tone, "Tommy *ain't* a heathen!" She had no clue what a "heathen" really was, but she knew it could be nothing good. "*You're* a heathen, Caroline Freiler! You think you're somethin' important just because you're the oldest! Well, just because you're the oldest don't mean you're the smartest!" and with that, the younger one fled the room in a whirlwind of fury, leaving behind an amused sister who simply rolled her eyes.

"You are so entertaining!" Caroline cried, shrugging her slender shoulders and picking up the book she was reading, the corners of her lips tugging up slightly.

Caroline Freiler was a tough sister and an obedient daughter. Most of the time, her bossiness was meant to guide her siblings. She yelled at Anna Claire because she wanted to see her sister grow up into a morally refined, proper young woman, and because she cared. But to Anna Claire, it always seemed that Caroline was seeking ways to make her miserable.

The despairing soldier in her family's marching order dropped the rag into the water again and sat on a box, sighing. She was tired and she didn't feel well at all.

"Did you scrub the windows from the outside as well?" asked her mother, turning over the flapjacks.

"Yes," she lied.

"Did you hang the clothes outside on the clothesline?"

"Yes."

"Did you feed Patty and Leo? Those mules were powerfully hungry this afternoon."

"*Yes,* Mama." Anna Claire could not hide her frustration in her voice.

Mrs. Freiler considered and nodded, satisfied. Anna Claire's spirits lifted at the thought of a break from her punishment of cleaning.

"Alright, you have been working very hard today," Charlotta said. Anna Claire smiled. "Now you can help set the table and pour the milk."

Anna Claire frowned and sighed. She'd never run off again without letting her parents know where she was. For a moment, she wished she could just be spanked again instead.

Hastily, she set the table, placing the spoons, knives, and forks in any spot she chose.

"You're doing it all wrong," Helen reprimanded, coming into the room that was now hot from the oven. "You put the spoon and knife on the right side of the plate, and the fork on the left." She fixed it for her, pursing her lips and rolling her eyes.

Anna Claire shrugged and began to pour the milk. As she was pouring, she noticed Pete running down the ladder with red berries all over his face.

"Look, I'm a wolf!" he cried, running over to her. "Ah, I'm going to get you, you ugly girl!"

Anna Claire laughed. Unfortunately, she laughed so hard that she quite forgot about the milk she was pouring.

"Oh, Anna Claire!" Charlotta cried as she ran over to the mess. "You spilled it all over the table!"

"Can't you do anything?" Helen snapped with a hand on her hip. "You are as stupid as a rock!"

Anna Claire surveyed the mess and frowned at Pete. "He distracted me, Mama! He was pretendin' to be a wolf!"

"Was not," lied Pete, running out of the kitchen and chasing little Berthie up the wooden ladder.

"Anna Claire, you've done enough damage in one day than I can possibly count," her mother said. "Please just call everyone to supper."

Anna Claire did so, but not without tears in her eyes.

Helen's right, she thought miserably. *I can't do anything right.*

That night, Anna Claire ate all of her supper without even feeding it to Hero the dog. She was so hungry from cleaning that she doubted an elephant would satisfy her cravings.

"Mr. Clemmons is thinkin' of startin' a barn-raisin'," Joseph said, sipping the milk from his cup. "He thinks it's a good way to be a part of the community; meet people and all."

"Oh, Joseph, that sounds like a good idea," Charlotta said, daintily patting her mouth with her napkin. "Imagine all the families that are settling here, not far from us. The children should really have some friends. I wouldn't mind someone to talk to either. The West can be so lonesome without company."

And it was true. During the long weeks when the Freilers were camping out and traveling from Minnesota, the miles of cold night air and endless yellow fields often made Anna Claire feel caged and closed in, even though there was nothing around her.

"Mr. Clemmons is a good man," Joseph commented with a fervent glance at his middle child. Anna Claire shrank a little smaller in her seat, remembering the unkind words she had said the night before.

"Mr. Clemmons seems like an honorable gentleman, even though his mustache frightens me," Caroline said practically, touching her soft black locks with her small hand.

"That he is," Charlotta agreed, taking a bite of deer. "His wife is a very nice woman also. So kind and generous in spirit. It was so nice of Mrs. Clemmons to make me that cherry pie when we first moved here."

"She's nice," agreed Helen, "but Mr. Clemmons sure didn't choose her to be his wife on account of her looks!"

"Helen!" cried both parents in horror.

"What an evil, malicious thing to say!" Charlotta said, her sharp eyes narrowing. "Helen, how could you say such unkind words about such a lovely person, who has been nothing but kind to us?"

"Oh, Helen, how horrible!" cried Caroline, glancing at her mother for approval.

The criminal bent her head with remorse. "I'm sorry," she peeped.

Anna Claire smiled. Finally, it was *Helen* who was in trouble.

"You must not say such things about fellow Christian people, or *any* people for that matter," their father admonished. "Mrs. Clemmons has a pretty heart, and a pretty heart is much better than a pretty face. Pretty faces won't get you into heaven. Only pretty hearts will."

"Yes, Papa," Helen answered quickly, glaring at Anna Claire.

"I like both of them!" said Pete, his mouth full of food. "Mr. Clemmons said he's gonna give me a rabbit's foot for good luck. He says if I wish for somethin', it has a good chance of comin' true if I just hold the rabbit's foot. Aint that somethin'?"

"It's *'isn't it'* something, not 'ain't'," corrected Charlotta gently, "and there is no such thing as luck, only providence. Mr. Clemmons can be very strange when it comes to those funny things, but he is a good Christian man nevertheless."

"Mama, what's pwov-dence?" asked Berthie with her mouth full.

"It means the gifts that God gives us, sweetheart," Charlotta replied, smiling at her littlest child affectionately.

"Like my new hat?" asked Berthie, referring to the straw hat Caroline had made for her the week prior.

Charlotta laughed. "Not quite, Berthie dear. It is more like an answered prayer, if you would like to think of it that way."

"Mama, how do I know if it's been ans-ewed?" asked the child, her large brown eyes growing even larger.

"If it is something that's meant to happen, then it will happen and it will be God's plan," Joseph interjected, now staring at his wife with an affectionate smile.

"Yes, something that is supposed to happen," Charlotta said softly, smiling back at her husband.

"Like us?" Berthie asked.

"Yes, all of you," their father laughed heartily and reached over to squeeze Berthie's little nose. "You're all our providential children!"

"Oh, yes, I'm *sure*," Helen said sarcastically.

"Maybe some of us," Pete said, his lips still stained with berries, "but Anna Claire's always messin' things up!"

Anna Claire, who had been quiet the whole supper-something very unusual for her, now piped up. "Pete Freiler, you're an awful little pest! You just shut your pie hole!"

"Anna Claire," her mother begged, wanting to get through a peaceful supper for once. "Please. Just eat."

Begrudgingly, Anna Claire obeyed, finishing the last of her deer and flapjacks. But when her parents weren't looking, she stuck her tongue out at her little brother.

"Hey!" shouted Pete.

"I saw that!" Helen cried anxiously, pointing at Anna Claire.

Joseph and Charlotta, who were grinning at each other and looking very much like they had fifteen years earlier when they were first married, now looked over at Anna Claire and frowned.

"Don't you stick your ugly tongue out at me!" Pete said, his blonde hair wildly stuck up in a comical manner. "You don't do nothin' right!"

"You make more messes than me!" cried Anna Claire with fire, standing up from the table.

"You both oughta be horse-whipped," Helen commented, banging her fists on the table and looking at her father as if expecting him to run and grab the whip at that instant. "Papa, shouldn't they?"

"Shut up!" yelled Anna Claire to Helen. "You ain't got no say in this! You ain't no mother of mine!"

"Well, *I* am," interjected Charlotta, putting her hands to her face, "and this quarrelling business at the table has been happening more frequently since we moved, and I will not allow it!"

The table quickly silenced with only the occasional dirty look from the children.

Things were much calmer after that. Charlotta and Joseph began talking about plans for the barn-raising, and Caroline and Helen began giggling about old memories at their school back in Minnesota.

Anna Claire, who was sitting next to Berthie, poked her and whispered, "Tonight I'll tell you a story. Would you like that?"

"Yes, I would!" Berthie answered, staring up at her big sister with full admiration.

Berthie Freiler was a spunky, intelligent child who looked up to Anna Claire with all the love a little sister could have. She wanted to grow up to be just like her, although her personality was essentially nothing like hers. Even so, she admired her big sister and often followed her around the house when she was not with their mother. Anna Claire, being older, sometimes didn't like her little sister tagging along, but usually the two got on splendidly, and Anna Claire loved having a sister to read and tell stories to.

"Anyone wanna hear a story?" asked Anna Claire, cheering up at the thought of the delicious rumor of a real live treasure buried in the mountains she could see from the back window.

No one was listening to her, and so she stood on her chair for attention. "I *said*, does anyone wanna hear a story?"

"Get off that chair!" her mother pleaded, pulling on her dress. "Anna Claire, why are you being so naughty tonight?"

Charlotta Freiler was a woman who was very proper and usually in complete, calm control, but this night was particularly agitating, and she was ashamed

that she was losing her maternal power at this particular supper.

Anna Claire jumped off the chair with a sneaky grin and threw her elbows on the table. "Do ya wanna hear a story Tommy told me?"

Her parents frowned.

"I really don't think you should be bringin' up that boy after all that happened last night," reprimanded Joseph with a quick glance at his wife.

"No, but it's a good story," Anna Claire said with a smile. "It's awful exciting."

"I wanna hear!" Pete agreed, pretending to be a dog by panting with his tongue out of his mouth, a piece of flapjack falling out unflatteringly.

"Can I?" she begged, looking at her parents for approval.

"Oh, go on," Charlotta consented. "How awful can it be?"

"I don't *think* it's awful! Wait 'til you hear what Tommy told me yesterday."

"I'm sure I can't wait," muttered Charlotta.

And Anna Claire told the story, retelling it just as Tommy had, only with more passion and earnestness. She even used voices to make the characters come alive.

"Look at her," Helen whispered to Caroline. "You would think nothing could make her stranger than she usually is!"

Berthie was silent through the story, her brown eyes big and wide. Pete *oohed* over nearly every part, especially the part about the flies biting Davie Hatfield's dead wife, as Anna Claire made sure to point out this detail especially. Helen rolled her eyes and yawned during intervals, pretending to be bored but secretly wondering if the whole gold story was true. Caroline twirled her black hair that was in perfect curls around her face and watched Anna Claire as she would watch a clown at the circus, with a perplexed expression.

When Anna Claire finished her tale, she grinned with pure delight. She stared over at the audience with satisfaction, but the only ones who seemed to share this satisfaction were Pete and Berthie, who were amazed by the whole thing and began asking many questions.

"I hope you don't believe in such a tall tale," their father said, clearing his throat.

"Sure, it's true!" cried Anna Claire with hope. "Tommy told me so, and Tommy knows everything!"

Charlotta frowned and pressed her hand against her cheek.

"There's gold near these parts," said Joseph reluctantly, "but I doubt there really was an Old Mr. Hatfield."

"And I don't approve of such false storytelling," Charlotta added with a grim expression. "It's a bunch of nonsense, is what it is. Please, try to have more sense, darling."

"Darlin'!" Anna Claire cried in rapture, thinking of Daisy's daughter. "She might be listening to us by the window right now!"

"Be quiet," Helen snapped, glancing at the window with fear.

"It really isn't true, dear," her mother said, firmly but lightly. She knew what it felt like to have childhood dreams, but she did not fancy one of her daughters running up to the mountains or some such nonsense to treasure-hunt for gold that didn't exist.

"Well, Papa's sure there's gold and no one laughs at him when *he* goes treasure huntin'," Anna Claire said with a taut nod of her head.

Joseph surprisingly laughed. He looked over at Charlotta, who looked horrified, and added, "She is right, my dear! You never know what could be found out there." He winked at her. "There's lots of silver and gold strikin' here now. You really can never tell. Remember the big strike back in '62? That's the whole reason we're sittin' here at this table right now!"

"I told you!" cried Anna Claire with a decisive grin. "Listen to Papa! He understands!"

Joseph winked at his spirited little girl, and she beamed with pride. Unlike his wife, he appreciated his daughter's tenacity and love for the unknown.

"You're a silly goose," Helen added to her sister.

"Someday, you'll see, Helen Freiler," Anna Claire huffed. "Someday, I'll be richer than a queen and have ropes of gold wrapped all around me like the cowboy in Tommy's poster, and you won't get a *cent* of it!"

"Anna Claire!" cried Mrs. Freiler reprovingly. "I can't believe you went to that strange boy's house."

"It was fun!" Anna Claire retorted. "Tommy lives in a saloon. Can't you think of the excitement it would be to live in a *saloon?*"

"A saloon! Do you hear this, Joseph?" said Charlotta. "No, I cannot think what it would be like, and I do not see the reason you should neglect the good, solid home you have here, away from all that noise and rowdiness."

"Oh, but I like town so much better," Anna Claire went on, not realizing her words were making her parents frustrated. "Don't you wish we at least lived in town?"

"Not even a little bit," Caroline hissed.

"From the Ten Commandments," Charlotta reminded her, "You shall not be greedy nor jealous of another's possessions."

"I know, Mama," Anna Claire took another bite. "But it's *thrillin'*. Me and Tommy-"

"Tommy and I," Mama corrected.

"Tommy and *I* were drinkin' whiskey when he told me the story and-"

"Whiskey!" cried Joseph, panic in his voice.

"Don't worry, it ain't bad to drink whiskey, Tommy said."

"I doubt you were drinking *real whiskey*," Charlotta told herself more than her daughter, chuckling at the notion. "I'm sure he told you that you were just to have a fun time."

"But I was," insisted Anna Claire, tilting the glass of milk to her lips. "Tommy lives in the saloon and his mama isn't very nice at all, and Tommy gave me a bottle of whiskey, but I didn't like the taste of it and-"

"I hope you're teasin', Anna Claire," Joseph said severely with that look of wild fury in his eyes again. "I don't like this kind of joke. Jokin' about whiskey is very bad, Anna Claire."

"Whiskey!" Charlotta had risen from the table after nearly falling out of her chair. "You really did have it, didn't you? How much did you have?"

"Only a gulp of it," Anna Claire lied, seeing how angry her parents were. "But it ain't good. And it looks like somethin' that comes from the outhouse."

"Anna Claire!" cried Charlotta suddenly, throwing down her handkerchief. "Do you know how wicked drinking is? Do you know what whiskey can do?"

"I know it can make me magical," Anna Claire told them earnestly.

"Magical!" her papa scoffed. "You mean *drunk*! In *my* household!"

"But it wasn't in *your* household," reasoned the little girl. "It was in Tommy Cooper's saloon."

"Anna Claire, who gave you alcohol?" her mother demanded, a look of profound sickness on her face.

"Tommy did," Anna Claire answered nonchalantly. "He had a bottle under a box."

Charlotta's eyes widened as she clutched the table to steady her balance. She could not believe what she was hearing. Tears began to well up in her eyes and, for a moment, she almost left the room. "You must not ever do a thing like that again!"

"Alcohol changes your mind," Joseph explained. "It makes you do things you wouldn't normally do, don't you understand? You should never drink it. It will harm you."

"But I know *you* drink sometimes!" Anna Claire fired back.

"That's because I'm a grown man," answered Joseph, "and not a little girl. I know how to drink and what to avoid. And I don't drink often!" he added, glancing at his wife.

"I didn't know all that," peeped Anna Claire, now frightened. "What'll happen to me?"

"Well, you should be fine," Joseph replied, as Charlotta could not speak. "The amount of whiskey you had surely wasn't enough to harm you. You probably just felt dizzy."

"I sure did," agreed the little girl.

"I have a good mind to go right over there and inform this boy's mother," said Charlotta, and, when their mother said something, she usually meant it. "Anna Claire, you are never to play with this wretched heathen again! Joseph, please come with me to this saloon. Anna Claire, do you know which it was?"

Anna Claire trembled. "It said 'Swiner's Saloon' at the top."

"I will come," Joseph agreed, burying his head in his hands as the children stared at him, anticipating what would happen next. "This boy should be whipped properly. I must talk with his father."

"No, please don't," begged Anna Claire, tears flowing freely. "Please stop!"

"Anna Claire-" began Charlotta.

"Tommy hasn't nobody in the whole world except me, and he'll be betrayed if he found out I told you. Please, Papa! Tommy is my only friend! He doesn't have a papa to look after him, and he didn't know whiskey was bad. He even said that he thought it was a magical drink 'cause he sees all the men drinkin' it at the saloon. He didn't know no better. Please don't hurt my only friend! His mama works at that saloon, and she called me 'little.' She's not nice at all. And Tommy wants so much for her to like him, but she's sad because his papa's gone, and she never pays him any mind. Tommy told me himself that he was lonely for her sometimes. And he never had nobody to play with 'til I came along, and he said he likes me fine even if I am a girl because I ain't no sissy. Please, don't tattle on him, he'll be awful sore!" and with that, the small girl burst into a fit of tears, sobbing loudly into her plate.

The other children watched the scene with interest while their father's face began to soften, and their mother looked down at the table quietly.

"Anna Claire, drinkin' is an evil, terrible thing for a child to do, and you must know how bad it is," Joseph told her, but no longer harshly. "Promise me you'll never do that again."

"I promise," she said solemnly. Although Anna Claire wasn't usually obedient, she rarely broke her promises.

"This boy does seem neglected," Charlotta contemplated, tapping her finger to her chin. "He came running down here in clothes with holes in them and bare feet. This is not a child who is being properly tended to. He is a dreadful boy. He is not a suitable playmate for our children."

Joseph nodded slowly. "Yes, my dear, you're right."

Before Anna Claire had a chance to protest, Pete began asking questions about the saloon.

"He hasn't been taught what's right," said Charlotta with finality, ignoring Pete and thinking of Tommy. "Anna Claire, you are not to play with this boy again. Do you understand me?"

Anna Claire's eyes widened, and a look of pure grief spread onto her small face. "He's my only friend! I gotta! I gotta!"

"That's enough!" shouted Joseph.

Anna Claire continued to sob but stopped talking lest she receive another spanking. Everyone dropped the subject of Tommy Cooper and continued to eat, Anna Claire licking the tears that were falling onto her lips.

Charlotta was very tired when she went to bed that night. Brushing her long, dark hair in her small mirror, she stood up from the little stool and walked methodically into bed, her head aching and her chest tense with anxiety.

"My dear, I know this was upsetting," said Joseph, coming over and putting his strong hands on her shoulders. "Our little girl...goin' off to a saloon and drinkin' whiskey...I still can't believe it myself. But we have to trust that she learned a big lesson tonight."

"And what would that be?" snapped Charlotta.

"How whiskey is *magical*?" This last word sent fresh tears to her sparkling blue eyes.

Joseph sighed and sat on the bed, unbuttoning his shirt and taking off his boots. "No. Didn't you see that little girl's face? She was scared half to death when we told her what whiskey could do!"

"That's true," Charlotta was beginning to calm down, if only slightly.

"The child is terrified!" continued Joseph, coming over to put his arm around his wife's waist. "I will never let her forget it, and she knows how much trouble she'll be in if she ever decides to try any more of that." His handsome face, glowing from the hot air, broke into a grin as he pulled his wife toward him. "Now, my dear, let's forget about this for now. Forget goin' to the saloon just yet. I don't want any trouble over somethin' as silly as a little boy. Anna Claire will not be playin' with him anymore, so she won't have any chance to step foot in that saloon again."

Charlotta sighed, feeling like there was a knot in her chest.

"She is so disobedient, Joseph. What if she decides to go into town like she did yesterday?"

"After the spankin' I gave her last night, I don't see how that's possible," said Joseph with a chuckle. "You know I didn't want to do it, Char, but she has to remember that night. She can't go traipsin' off and gettin' everyone worried about her. She's far too young to be disappearin'. Keep her close by your side, and if the boy comes around again, well, we'll tell him to go back home. Simple as that."

"I do hope so," whispered the exasperated mother, her eyes closing in spite of herself.

"Come here," Joseph said with a big smile as he opened his arms. "Let's rest and put this night behind us."

Still feeling sick with fear, Charlotta lay her head in the nook of his arm and wrapped her arm around his chest.

"Alright, Joseph," she sighed. "I just want our children to be safe, is all."

"And they will be," her husband promised her, kissing her forehead. "You are doing a wonderful job with all of the children. Anna Claire just has a mind of her own."

"Just like her father," laughed Charlotta.

The pair huddled closer together and thought about the recent events of the week.

"Everything will be fine," said Joseph gently. "She's learnin' her lessons and makin' mistakes. She just happens to make more than any child I know."

Charlotta began to genuinely laugh at this. "You have just the right words to make everything better. I do hope you're right. Coming to Gold Country has been so difficult- there have been so many changes, Joseph. I only wish we could make it easier for the children."

"It *will* get easier," replied her husband, grazing his hand through her hair and blowing out the candle. "We must have faith in the Lord. He will not forsake us. Now, let us put that to the side." And he took her in his arms.

Charlotta tried to put the incident of the week behind her, but it was quite difficult. She was worried about all of her children, but for Anna Claire, the most. She had more reason than she even realized to be worried for Anna Claire.

Chapter 4- An Accidental Adventure

Life in Montana Territory was not easy for anyone. The frontier was a challenge and became the home of determination and willpower. The land that was auctioned off to Joseph somehow seemed to never want to cooperate and produce the plants Charlotta so wanted in the little garden, which was unpoetically surrounded by a mere wobbly, wooden fence. She and the girls began to plant flax, corn, and wheat with little success, but they were resolved that it would succeed despite the disappointment of seeing only dirt when looking into the garden.

Joseph had bought cattle from one of the men across town and quickly began building a barn, lest the cattle rustlers steal them and sell them far away. Joseph became quickly accustomed to the gulches and made fast friends with many of the men, as he was sociable and had a good sense of humor. He was known to occasionally walk into a saloon and "bend an elbow" from time to time with some of the men. Many of the men that he worked with had come from the gold rush in California at Sutter's Mill, and prospectors were eager to get their hands on some of the purest gold in the country in the Montana Territory.

The history of Bannack and the surrounding region was a unique one, no doubt. A few years before the Freiler's move, John White and William Eads found gold along the Beaverhead River, and people began claiming the whole length of Grasshopper Creek, which got its name from the numerous insects that persistently hopped around all over the area.

Word about the gold rush traveled through newspapers and pamphlets throughout the country. Once the prospectors got settled into the new territory, merchants and businessmen bee-lined swiftly to the region to ensure that they were there for all of the miners' needs, such as supplies, equipment, and tools, making quite a good amount of money from the families that were there. That very next year, a group on their way from the Yellowstone River region arrived. They camped by a stream surrounded by alders called Ruby River Valley and happened to find $200 worth of gold. That became a fourteen-mile-long town called Virginia City, miles away from Bannack, but another popular spot for the hunt for gold.

There were men of all ages, but many were very young, not even thirty, and they were hard-headed, believing with all of their hearts and souls that they would make it rich. Many pioneers came from the steamboat on the Missouri River to Fort Benton, which then took them on a stagecoach or a wagon to the area of Bannack. The steamboat was crucial, as it brought supplies, food, equipment, and household necessities before heading back down to St. Louis. Some of these items consisted of sheet iron cookstoves, candles, supper utensils, and other necessities like panes of glass and nails. Joseph loved to buy the three-dollar frozen onions to give to Charlotta so that she could cook them in with the next meal, as onions had always been a favorite delicacy of his. The steamboat also brought sardines, oats, ranch, and herb butter, No.1 California liquors (which Joseph had purchased subtly once), and tobacco pipes. The steamboat would then bring back from the Gold Country a wide array of bison hides and furs to supply the people in the East.

Many of the new prospectors had traveled the 624 miles on Mullen Road from Walla Walla and through Deer Lodge Valley to the brain of it all, Fort Benton. Freight trains provided much relief to the pioneers, as much food was supplied from this method. Many people, such as Joseph, cut valleys into farms. There were farmers and prospectors of all kinds hoping to improve the lives of themselves and their families. Among them were Chinese, French, Canadian, German, Mexican, Black, Jewish, and Irish people, all wanting a taste of a better life. Everyone there was striving for betterment and wealth, aiming with confidence at the abundance of gold that may be hidden under the dirt, like pearls in an oyster. Every day, the men would head to their claims and throw their picks into the ground, scarves around their necks, and sweat upon their foreheads.

The miners had their claims going approximately 100 feet next to Grasshopper Creek. A man would put the notice in and report it to the recorder, which instilled the rule that a miner needed to work on it every single day when water was readily accessible, lest after three days it was forfeited or jumped. Sometimes the rules were bent if someone was gravely ill or if one of their wives was giving birth, but, for the most part, the miners did their work every day, even on Sundays.

Of course, one had their fair share of conflicts in a place such as this. A miner's court was put into place to ensure that men's claims were protected, and judges warranted that these claims would stay in the hands of the rightful owners. There was always the possible threat of attacks from other settlers in the area, as well as threatening weather, and life in Montana Territory was as unpredictable as they came. Yet this didn't stop people from creating a big, boisterous town in which there were hotels, black-smiths, butcher shops, meat markets, hotels, drug stores, and hurdy gurdy houses. The saloons were used for a lot more than drinking, too. Many important people of the town, such as the governor, gave speeches at the saloon, as that is where many men congregated, and sometimes a reverend would conduct his services there. There was even a doctor and a barber who were found on occasion setting up shop in the corners of the building. People were anxious to be a part of this amazing piece of American history, and they created a life full of optimism and courage.

It was a hot and humid day in mid-June when Charlotta decided to write a letter to her "Mor" back in Minnesota. "Mor," which means "mother" in Swedish, was what she had always called her mother since childhood. Charlotta loved the art of letter-writing and could write for hours on end if she was not constantly interrupted by small feet and little voices.

She sat down at the kitchen table and gathered all of her thoughts in her mind before putting quill to paper.

Dear Mor,

I miss you so much more every day. I pray every night for you and the family that God will protect you all. It has been lovely air here in Montana Territory, although it has been so hot and I work until I am sore in the bones. I suppose a woman's work is never quite finished, is it? I miss Minnesota indescribably, especially you, my dear mother.

Summer seems not to be a season but rather a custom here. Joseph and another man who settled close by want to have a barn-raising party. They wish to work on Mr. Clemmons's barn and then continue on with the other men's barns. I think it is a splendid idea, although I fear for Joseph's health. He works to the marrow every day, and I know he is very tired, especially with his bad leg, and I can't do much to make him stop. He is such a blessing to me, and I do not know what I would do without him.

Joseph found some corn while he was walking to town. It's a rather funny story, actually. He was trying to get one of the mules to take him to town, but they were in a stubborn fit. Because of this, Joseph decided to walk and, about halfway there, he turned around and noticed both of the mules following him! That is when he realized that he had forgotten to tie up the mules. They seemed to be sniffing something in the ground, and that's how it came to be that we ate corn that night and for the rest of the week. It is only my Joseph who could gather food in such a way.

I've been noticing more frequently how God can change everything around so quickly. If we let God work His miracles, we may reap the benefits. Not in an indolent sense, of course, but more in trust. I am quite fond of the house Joseph built for us, and I like that the children have such wide, open spaces to run in. I even find myself almost liking this odd way of life at times, but there are many things that need to be improved upon. For one thing, I do not know what will happen in the fall. I am far too busy to teach the little ones at home. I suppose Caroline is getting to be old enough to look upon her own studies, but as for the other ones, I know not what I shall do. Caroline is not old enough to be their teacher, but if there is no one else, she will have to help me construct lessons for them. I have thought about letting them go to the town's school, but the town is so wretched, I'm afraid for them to walk there. Yet, I shall not have them growing up to be ignorant. Montana Territory is a much uncivilized place, I'm afraid.

I was able to put some money aside to buy a new sun bonnet. It is a bit elaborate for my taste, but Joseph liked it on me so much that I gave in. I usually wear the old straw one, but I have decided to use the sun bonnet when I am in town.

There are some things here that are beautiful that cannot be bought. I took a walk the other day, closer to the mountains, and saw some very nice plants. The bitter root is so lovely, and it is beginning to bloom with golden flowers. There are so many kinds of willows here, and I even saw some balsamroot. That is nothing compared to the lilies. They are perfectly white flowers with yellow in the middle and just a touch of violet peaking around the pollen.

Other than a lack of playmates, the children are well. They have each other to frolic with, which I can honestly say they do. I am becoming increasingly frightened of Anna Claire. You know what a wild little thing she is! It seems all she does is get into scrapes. As soon as she has made one mess of things, she goes right off and gets into more trouble than she was in before. She runs off and pays no mind to me without thinking twice. Yesterday, she went off to town with the strangest little boy imaginable. Not a word did she tell me before doing such an impulsive thing!

She seems to be very fond of this Tommy child. She says he lives on top of the saloon where his mother works- can you imagine? His father is almost always away. I confess I feel some sympathy for the creature. When I saw him from the window, I could hardly believe how tattered and dirty he was. He was not even wearing shoes! I am vexed to find how much Anna Claire fancies him. She likes anyone who curses and spits, I'm afraid. I have forbidden her to ever see this boy again unless by happenstance. Anna Claire does not need more encouragement for her wild ways.

Caroline wants me to send her deepest love. She is just as much of a proper girl as she always was, although something is troubling me about her. I should be quite satisfied that she is not roaming all the odds and ends of the world like Anna Claire is, but I fear for her girlhood. Since the move, she hardly seems like a child anymore. She is so well-behaved that it frightens me a bit. I almost wish she would laugh and shout like the little ones at times, because then I would know she was a child. I try to encourage her to go outside, for I believe it mends the soul and spirit. I know coming to the territory was difficult for her, and perhaps that is why she has been confining herself to her sewing and books all of the time.

As for Helen, she certainly has a temper of her own. It flashes at the worst of times, and it does not bother her a bit. I am very disappointed to say that she has become sharp and sarcastic, especially with the younger ones, and I daresay I am not sure what to do about it. I have tried keeping her indoors to tend to her chores and scold her when she does not mind her manners. She always seems so sorry about her temper and promises to control it, but the very next day, she is angrier than a hen.

Pete is also well in body, although quite a troublemaker himself. He can be quite a lot to manage. He has Joseph's adventurous soul and never stops running around doing something shocking, like Anna Claire, although he is still young, and I can keep him by my side most of the time. The other day, Pete pretended to be a bird and jumped from the table. He jumped so high! He laughed and he laughed. It vexes me. I am grateful that Pete is in good health and will soon be helpful to Joseph as he gets older, but he is much too wild now.

I do not fear for Berthie very much. She seems to have a mind of her own, and she never strays far from me, although she is getting to be far too fond of Anna Claire's bedtime stories. When I tell the two to go to bed, they tell me they will, but then when I come up to the loft, I can hear the girls talking, for they all share the loft.

Mor, how did you do it with us? I know I could be a trial when I was a child. How did you ever handle it? I praise your kind patience and loving attitude. I only wish it would work with my five young ones! I have such disobedient children that it makes me ashamed sometimes, as if I do not try hard enough to discipline them. But I do not believe in that notion about hitting a child. I cannot bring myself to do it, although Joseph has on a number of occasions. My children are dreadfully ill-behaved, all but Caroline and Berthie, and I must confess that my wits are greatly being tested.

Oh my, there goes Anna Claire out the door again. I just know she is up to some mischief! Give the whole family our love and tell them we miss them all dearly. Please write soon with any advice you have for me. I will continue to pray to our Lord for my strength and courage.
Loving you with all my heart,
Charlotta

Anna Claire tiptoed out of the door, throwing her dust cap and pinafore onto the table, while Charlotta was writing the letter. She tried to sneak out quietly, but she fell and tripped over her own clumsy feet.

"Anna Claire!" called her mother, but Anna Claire was already out the door and running through the fields to the clump of trees. "Be careful down there!"

Anna Claire nodded and ran to the creek. She sat down by the water and smiled.

"I'm glad I got away," she said aloud, "and I'm even gladder Caroline didn't hear. That old goose would tattle-tale, and then I would've smacked her hard."

Anna Claire liked to talk aloud at times. It was a habit that she relished because it was the only habit that allowed her to express her opinions openly without being worried about receiving a lecture. She sat by the yellow sweet clover, thinking about Minnesota and wondering what her cousin Katie was doing. Then, very suddenly, a feeling of sadness clenched her heart. She didn't know why, but she was suddenly struck with a deep pain.

She missed Helen.

Of course, she could have skipped right to the house if she really wanted to see Helen at that moment. She could've run up the loft and seen her lying on her bed, reading a book or admiring her hair. But this wasn't the same Helen that Anna Claire missed.

Once upon a time, a time that seemed very far and distant to Anna Claire, her big sister wasn't quite so terrible. In fact, she and Helen were as inseparable as the closest of friends at one period of time, and Anna Claire reflected with grimness all of the fun the two little girls used to have together. They used to laugh at everything and share all of their secrets. They used to do all of the things kindred spirits do, and Anna Claire always tried to make her sister laugh, with much success. They were friends a long time ago.

Dipping her toes in Gold Creek, Anna Claire reflected on how they used to catch fireflies in the midnight summer air or when they used to go swimming in the big lake back in Minnesota. She thought of the times when Berthie was a baby and how the two little girls loved to help their mother tend to her. They had hiked and chased deer together in the forest. They had laughed at the old, grumpy reverend and at the boring teacher at the little log schoolhouse. They had held hands as they picked berries and cuddled together by the fireplace as their father told Bible stories.

About a year ago, things changed. Anna Claire tried not to think about it as she moved her feet back and forth in the cold waters of the creek, but she thought of it anyway. She remembered when Helen began to change and develop new interests. This meant that she had stopped having an interest in her troublesome little sister. Helen would rather play with girls her own age and have tea parties and talk about fancy dresses. Anna Claire was like that doll one outgrows- the kind one used to love and carry with them everywhere until they wake up one day and realize that they've moved on. Anna Claire didn't like being left behind on Helen's dusty shelf.

"I hate that mean ol' Helen anyway," she decided with a nod of her small, upturned nose, dipping her feet and then her body into the water. She wouldn't waste another second thinking of her "mean ol'" sister.

Anna Claire floated on top of the surface of the high creek and smiled at the sun peeking through the trees. She giggled as a brown frog jumped and narrowly missed her arm. Anna Claire was a good swimmer and learned long ago in Minnesota how to swim. Her father always thought it was important that children learned to swim, since water was everywhere and drowning could happen easily, and Anna Claire seemed to just have a natural knack for it.

"I can never catch these dang'on frogs," she sighed as she dived in.

A cold rush spread throughout her skin, and she yelled out loud under water, a gurgling sound muffling anything else. When she returned to the surface, she shivered.

Trout and minnows swam in circles around her as her toes lightly brushed coons tail on the bottom of the creek. The sun hit her already golden skin and made her feel warm again. Her hair flowed in the water, the pressure bringing it close to her face and back out again. The sound of birds whispered in her ears, free from scolding and disapproval, and, upon looking up as she floated, she spotted a golden eagle soaring above her proudly and smoothly. The leaves hit the water from the trees above, and the reflections from clouds and the sun made the water look like heaven. It was all so delightful that Anna Claire never wanted to go back to her boring house. She wanted to stay in Grasshopper Creek forever and drift down its beautiful waters.

Soon, little logs began to float downriver. Anna Claire attempted to stand on top of one but fell just as she was crowning herself the queen of Grasshopper Creek. Little tugs beckoned her to swim more as little creek waves ruffled up against her skin like silk. She propped her back in a floating position and let the water take her where it may. To her, it seemed as though the water stood still and that her "boring house" was still right behind her through the trees and up the fields. But she was wrong.

Little did she realize that the creek was actually *moving* and that she was floating down it like a leaf. The small currents were making her fly down fast like a bird in the water, and soon she realized that she could no longer feel the grainy stones on the balls of her feet. In fact, as she flew up in a panic, she couldn't feel *anything* on her feet.

She quickly grabbed onto a large log and let herself pass through the creek, which was becoming as wide as a lake. Frightened, she held onto the log with her wet and shivering hands until she realized that the water was calm enough to swim to the other side. Although she was no longer nervous and could easily reach the shore, she did not do so immediately. Instead, she thought it would be a deliciously exciting plot to fall downstream and be helpless, even if it wasn't true.

So, she decided to play a game with herself. Pretending she was wildly afraid, she clung to the log and said out loud, "Oh no! I'm fallin' downstream! No one can help me! Help! Help! Oh, no one can hear me now. I guess it ain't good for my throat to keep on shoutin' if no one ain't gonna come; it'll just waste my air up. Oh no, here I go! I wonder what'll happen to me. I could get eaten alive by a bear!"

Anna Claire, of course, was not the least bit scared, but she told herself that she was helpless until she quite believed it.

In truth, she *wanted* to get lost. She wanted her father and Mr. Clemmons to hunt for her. She wanted Caroline and Helen to be sorry for all of the terrible things they had ever said to her. She could almost picture the scene- Caroline and Helen, holding onto each other and sobbing, while Anna Claire was lost and "afraid." She could picture her mother weeping and saying with deep regret, "Oh, if only I hadn't yelled at the little darling!" and her father shaking his head with the tears streaming down, saying, "My Anna Claire! I wish I hadn't spanked her for bein' bad. Now she's probably dead and it's all my fault!"

Anna Claire couldn't help smiling to herself when she thought of this. How sorry everyone would be that they treated her like a baby! Anna Claire would avenge her hurt spirit.

"Dang, I'm goin' real fast now," said Anna Claire in pretense worry. "I guess I can't do nothin' but let myself go. I don't wanna waste the little bit of energy I got."

In only a few minutes' time, things began to grow very unfamiliar as the soaked creature floated down the lake on the log. The trees became more and more numerous, and even the sounds that Anna Claire had grown accustomed to were not the same. Soon, she didn't recognize a thing.

"That'll teach Helen not to make fun of me anymore," thought Anna Claire dourly.

"Where is Anna Claire?" Charlotta asked the family when the food was ready.

It was past one o'clock, and Anna Claire had not been seen since early that morning. She did not come when she was called for chores, and Charlotta simply did not have the energy that day to run around and try to find her. Also, if she was being honest with herself, Anna Claire would not be able to do the chores correctly, which would have taken Charlotta even longer to complete. The family figured she must have been at Grasshopper Creek or in the trees exploring, as she usually was.

"I bet she went to town," Helen suggested haughtily. "Probably went to visit that Tommy-nobody."

"Ridiculous," Charlotta answered, but feeling nervous at the thought. "Anna Claire and I had a long talk about that, and she promised not to do it again."

Helen looked up at her mother with a smirk in her brown eyes. "Yes, Mama, but when does Anna Claire keep promises?"

Charlotta sighed. "She has her faults, but one thing she never breaks is her promises," she answered with certainty, although she was beginning to look out of the window nervously, that previous knot coming back into her chest.

The other children looked at each other and shrugged. Caroline was sitting at the table with a book in her hand and could not be bothered with the whereabouts of the little girl.

"Caroline, go call on your father and tell him dinner is ready," Charlotta said finally. "I believe he is at Mr. Clemmons's farm."

"Yes, Mama," Caroline answered sincerely, rising from the table and walking to the door, the whole time reading her book.

"Helen, please go and call Anna Claire in," Charlotta instructed, her chest becoming heavy with anxiety. "She must be at the creek."

"Yes, Mama," answered Helen with sulky obedience. She rose from her chair and ran out the door.

Helen did not exactly *despise* her sister all the time, but Helen was the kind of little girl who wished to grow up, and associating with the likeness of someone who was practically a *baby* did not suit her interests.

As she ran through the forest, calling Anna Claire's name, it suddenly occurred to her that she wasn't answering back. Usually, although Anna Claire did grumble, she would at least make the effort to express her annoyance. But, as Helen ran up and down the creek calling out her name, no Anna Claire Freiler answered back.

"That stupid girl has run off again," said Helen aloud in irritation. "Unless she could be hiding from me. Oh, Anna Claire! Anna Claire! You're stupid and ugly and smelly! Anna Claire! Didn't you hear me? I said you're stupid and ugly, and you smell like manure!"

No reply. Now, Helen began to feel a bit worried. Anna Claire sometimes played hide and seek, but whenever insulted, she would spoil the game by coming out of her hiding place to tell her opponent off. But now, Helen began to get those strange chills up and down her spine that signify when one is suddenly and unexpectedly isolated.

Helen ran up and down the creek for a long while, and still no Anna Claire.

"That wretch went to town," she said aloud with her characteristic roll of the eyes. "Anna Claire, if you're in here somewhere listening to me, I'm gonna maim you!"

Helen, being of the lazy sort, hated to waste her time running around trying to collect her little siblings. Instead, she ran out of the little cluster of trees and back through the field to explain to her family that their middle wild-child had mystically disappeared again.

"She's gone," Helen cried out as soon as she reached the house.

Although Helen was irritated at being asked to look for her, she was extremely pleased that Anna Claire had run off. This would mean great excitement and worrying, which would mean that once Anna Claire was found, there would be an interesting punishment, especially if she went to town, which their parents had made her promise never to do again without permission.

"Oh, Helen, she must be at that creek somewhere!" sighed a poor and very tired Charlotta, feeling angry that Helen was not trying her best. "She must be there! You must not have said her name loud enough."

Helen shrugged and plopped down into the chair, her fingers tracing the patterns of the wood on the table. "I shouted her name, Mama. I looked *for-ever*," she exaggerated, rolling her eyes. "She's not nowhere."

Charlotta was too worried to correct her daughter's grammar. Suddenly, the sound of the door creaked open.

"Joseph," she cried when he entered, "Helen went by Grasshopper Creek to call Anna Claire, and she is nowhere to be found. Please tell me that she is with you."

Joseph frowned and took off his hat. "No, no, I'm afraid she isn't."

He seemed very tired at that moment, and Helen grinned with delight. Her sister was going to be in so much trouble!

"I bet she went off to town, just like you told her not to!" she offered, her hands on her hips.

Charlotta looked at her husband, who looked back at her with a hint of fear in his eyes.

"I'll go into town," Joseph sighed as he put his hat back on, only seconds after taking it off. "Pete! Come with me."

Pete glowed and ran over to his father's side.

"Can I come, Papa?" cried Helen wistfully, wanting to see her sister get spanked.

"No, you can't, this is a man's work!" Pete said, flopping his tongue at her.

"Helen, you may stay inside with me," Char-lotta told her. "Anna Claire is most likely on her way home now."

"What should we do, Mama?" asked Caroline softly, genuinely wanting to help in any way that she could.

"You and Helen go outside and run by Mr. Clemmons's. Tell him we've lost her again and just ask him to keep a lookout for her." Charlotta sat in the chair and buried her head in her hands. "I simply cannot go running all over God's green Earth for her today. I just cannot."

Caroline and Helen glanced at each other, and Caroline patted her mother's arm affectionately.

"Alright, we'll look in town," Joseph said as he opened the door. "Don't worry, Char. I doubt she's very far off." And with that, he left, taking the proud little boy with him.

"Mama, Anna Claire will be all right," Helen said with a suppressed grin.

"Yes, please don't fret," said Caroline with a curious glance at the window. "Papa will surely find her."

"You girls just mind what I say and go tell Mr. Clemmons." Sharp was the tone of Charlotta's voice, and the two girls heeded without another admonishment.

"Oh, I do not know, Lord," Charlotta said aloud, Berthie reaching out to hold her hand. "She just keeps on running away. Never lets us know where she is going- no, that would be too sensible for her. Berthie, are you sure you haven't seen Anna Claire today?"

"No-o-o," Berthie said with her tiny, lilting voice. "Just this mowning."

"Did she tell you where she was going?" asked Charlotta.

"No-o-o," replied the five-year-old. "I'm hungwy."

"I know you're hungry, Berthie, but we have to find Anna Claire before we can eat." Charlotta was now at her wits' end with that whole crazy week, and she was not sure how long her temper could stay intact.

"Maybe she wan away," suggested the little girl, sneaking a piece of veal from the plate on the table and cramming it into her mouth.

"Well, your sister's going to be in a good deal of trouble once she gets home," Charlotta said, not noticing as Berthie stole another helping of veal.

"Mama, why?"

"Because she is very naughty to run away," Charlotta answered with furtive glances out the window.

"Why?"

"Because I am her mother, and I told her to never run away."

"But why, Mama?"

"Because running away is a dangerous game. There are wild animals, and God knows what else is out there in the wild. Your sister can get hurt. I do hope I'll never have to chase *you* around someday."

"Why?"

"Oh, hush, dear, you ask far too many questions," but Charlotta smiled and wrapped her youngest in a little embrace. "My baby," she cooed, "My

Berthie. Please always listen to your mama. Please never run off."

Charlotta's chest held that anxious feeling again, and her breath felt sharp. It had been so many difficult months since leaving Minnesota. The journey was tiresome and long, and the mining camps had been frightening and ridden with mosquitoes, pests, and dirt. She had hoped that, if she worked hard in the new place, life would be a bit easier again. Instead, she was caring for five children, four of them too young to do all of the housework correctly, and home all day without her husband, while she took care of the house. She loved her children, but she longed for adult company, as she was lonely, aggrieved, and worried about where the next meal might come from or if her husband was chasing a silly dream that would never come true, making her leave her dear family as well as all of her friends.

She held Berthie tighter to her, stifling the sound of her tears as they fell haphazardly from her eyes, the same eyes that were so determined to hold them back.

Nearly an hour had passed when Anna Claire finally banked to the pebbled shore after nearly falling down a small waterfall. She had passed through little hills and was a distance away from the mountains now. She had seen lodgepole pines and red cedars as well as little lupins and dryads growing not far away. The basin wildrye had called out to her, and the violet fairy slippers beckoned her so gently. How could she possibly go home? However, now she had no idea how far she had gone or which way to walk home. There had been forks in the water, and she had taken a couple of different turns.

"I only wanted to scare everyone a bit," said Anna Claire to the fox squirrel that was climbing the tree next to her. "Don't you understand? I just wanted Helen and Caroline to be sorry for yellin' at me, and for Papa to feel guilty about spankin' me. I didn't mean to go this far away."

But far she had gone, and it seemed to her that she had traveled many more miles than she actually did.

"Maybe I'm back in Minnesota again," thought Anna Claire.

Although she felt sorry for doing it, it must be stated that she had a swell time floating on that log. She had made-believed she was a desperate child, clinging on by a thread. She had another adventure. She had seen a bear on the shore, throwing fish in the air, as well as chipmunks, minnows, and even a moose from far away. But now she could hear the grumbling of her stomach, and it suddenly occurred to her that floating away was not a very good idea. Her eyes began to feel strangely heavy as her whole body lay numb on the ground.

"I suppose I'll starve out here and die," she thought grimly. There was a good amount of dirt on her cheeks, and anyone who may have passed by would have suspected her to be homeless.

Anna Claire hated to cry, but now she felt she needed to. She sat under the same tree on which the fox squirrel had climbed up and broke into loud, pitiful sobs.

"Little bird, you sure are pretty," said Anna Claire dramatically at the magpie that was sitting above her. "I wish I could borrow your wings and fly back home. I wonder why people can't make their own wings. I guess when they find my body, they'll be awfully sorry. Caroline will cry and cry and say that she never meant to scold me. Helen will throw flowers at my grave and tell me she loves me and that she wished she had been a kinder sister. Mama and Papa will be so sad, and they'll both be sorry that they ever shouted at me. Pete'll cry, too, and he'll say how he wishes he had not put that mouse in the bed. But what will Berthie say? Who will tell her a bedtime story?" With that thought, Anna Claire dug her hands into the soil and sobbed much louder than before. "I'll miss Berthie most of all!"

The little bird that had stopped and watched Anna Claire peculiarly had fled and flown into the trees. Now it was just Anna Claire and the bellows of the frogs around her.

"They'll be sorry," she muttered as she fell fast asleep, dreaming of her mother's hot broth and of her father's heart-warming stories.

Joseph ran to Paul Clemmons, who lived not far across the creek and over the field a bit, and told him about his daughter's disappearance once again. Mr. Clemmons felt awful for his new friend, for one of his children had run away once, and it was some of the most frightening moments of his entire life.

"Did you check the creek?" offered Mr. Clemmons, his wife Nettie coming along beside him, handkerchief in her hand and sweat from the oven on her forehead.

"I did, twice, and so did my daughter."

"Let's go into town," suggested Mr. Clemmons. "I know that little one loves to go to town!"

The two men, Mr. Clemmons bringing his rifle, rode their horses into town. As there was still a good bit of daylight out, they started looking around the outskirts first, going around the little cabins and huts and in the bushes and shrubs. Then they started looking in the saloons, including Swiner's Saloon, the bakery, the three hotels scattered throughout town, the blacksmith's shop, the meat market, and stables all over. They even checked the restaurant. There wasn't a sign of Anna Claire.

"Please, have you seen my daughter?" Joseph said, knocking on one of the many homes that outlined the town. "She's about this high" (he demonstrated by putting his hand toward the ground and crouching down) "and's got light hair. She's wearin' a pink dress and black boots. She's nine years old."

The man inside looked at him suspiciously as Mr. Clemmons began knocking on the other house next door.

"I don't reckon I have," said the man gruffly. "If I do see her, I'll bring her to the Bannack Hotel."

"Thank you, sir," Joseph answered, pausing to look around him.

Where could she have gone? She loved the town. Why was she nowhere to be found in all of Bannack?

"If you see her, bring her to the hotel," Mr. Clemmons was saying as he left one of the little houses.

The two men knocked on the houses, and before long, Joseph had gathered more than two dozen new and older settlers to join him in his search. Many of the townsmen wanted to help the family find the child, who was far too young to be wandering around alone, and generously offered their time.

One of these men was Mr. Henry Dobbins, a man in his fifties who knew Tommy very well, as he frequented the saloon and was friends with his mother. Mr. Dobbins, a portly man with a small gray beard, balding head, and a wide, round face, had overheard the commotion in the saloon and grabbed his rifle along with two of his close friends, Mr. Chesham and Mr. O'Reilly. He found some of the other men in the town, who explained the situation of Joseph Freiler's little girl "Annie" (as some thought her name was) and that she had been lost all day.

The men searched the area consistently without any luck, up and down the creek, throughout the fields, in the buildings of town, and in the surrounding areas. Charlotta, with the help of Nettie Clemmons, had gathered a small group of women, some of whom she knew from the mining camps, and they all decided to act by searching for the missing girl.

"Oh, Mrs. Clemmons, I cannot thank you enough," Charlotta said when Nettie Clemmons ran to the house, bringing a bag of tea and putting it above the fireplace. "You are so kind."

Mrs. Clemmons grinned. "No. I'm a mother."

Charlotta smiled despite feeling like her heart would come out of her chest. She could not speak anymore, for the tears were choking her throat, and her mind was scattered all over the place.

Caroline had joined the women who had made it their mission to also go to town and spread the word, while the younger children had fallen asleep after hours of looking around the fields with their mother. Charlotta, her feet sore from walking so much in her boots and her dark hair halfway out of its bun, was beginning to panic. The other women told her that she must rest so that she could help them again the next day, but Charlotta just wanted to keep looking. She knew, however, that if she walked any further in those boots, her already blistered feet would start to bleed.

"I cannot believe she did this again," Charlotta managed to say as she took a very short sip of tea. "Your husband was kind enough to help Joseph look for her a couple weeks ago when she ran off to town. I have talked to her so many times about her wandering off. I'm simply out of ideas, Mrs. Clemmons."

"Please, call me Nettie," said the woman warmly. "I know how you feel. Two years ago, my Rebecca went missing for a day, and I was in a fit! We will find your Anna Claire. She couldn't have gone that far."

Mrs. Clemmons had a soft, high-pitched voice that was soothing and sincere. It made Charlotta feel relaxed and even hopeful.

"Thank you for the tea, Nettie," she smiled. "I hate to sit here and do nothing, but Mrs. Skelley was right. If I keep walking, my feet will only blister more, and I will be in awful pain." She looked up at her new friend and pressed her hand to hers. "You are a good friend. I am glad to know you."

Mrs. Clemmons smiled, fixing her curly auburn hair back in her knot, and poured Charlotta another cup of tea. The women fell fast in silence for some time, both of them trying to come up with new ideas of where the child could have gone and where she might be then.

Meanwhile, Tommy Cooper had found out she was missing when Mr. Elmer Grimm broke into the saloon and told the men that a little girl named Annie had run from home and her parents could not find her. Tommy had promptly decided to go on his own little search party and find his friend.

A few hours after the Freilers and the Clemmons's grouped their search party, Tommy ran as fast as he could to the Freiler cabin where he burst through the door, red and panting.

"Is she back!?" he cried, his nose running and his eyes wide.

Charlotta was stunned to see the little boy, but not appalled at his lack of manners. Mrs. Clemmons looked surprised and stared in wonder at this little boy who had the tenacity to run through their home like that.

"No, she is not," Charlotta answered, tears welling up in her eyes. "Have you seen her at all? Did she come to the saloon? Did you see her in town? You must be truthful!"

"No, ma'am," said Tommy honestly. "She didn't come to town today. She hasn't come to see me in a while, ma'am."

Charlotta buried her face in her hands. "What if-what if she drowned?"

"Oh, she hasn't!" cried Mrs. Clemmons, rushing over to comfort her friend.

Tommy came over and pressed his hand to Charlotta's. "Nah, Anny-Claire can swim really well. I saw her. She likes to get lost. I'm gonna go find her. I'll bring her back, you'll see!"

Although Charlotta knew the ten-year-old boy would not be able to find her daughter, she felt a burst of appreciation that he wanted to try.

Forgetting that he was the reason she had ever been to town and had a taste of whiskey, Charlotta reached up to touch his cheek. "Be careful, dear."

The first place Tommy went was Grasshopper Creek, where everyone had gone. The creek was searched around the home so thoroughly that everyone but Tommy had given up looking there.

When he had searched under every rock and stump, he had run back to town and told his mother to look out for his friend. He then ran throughout the town, telling everyone to look for the pretty little girl with a small nose and golden hair. Although only knowing Anna Claire for a short time, he considered her to be his best friend and would sorely miss her should she be eaten by a grizzly bear or clawed by a wolf. He knew he needed to find his friend, no matter how long it might have taken.

By the next morning, the whole town of Bannack was on the lookout for Anna Claire, and some men were even posting missing signs around, offering a prize, even though she had not been gone terribly long.

Joseph insisted on a $100 prize, although it was almost too much to spare and was all the Freiler's had saved up. In a wilderness like Montana Territory, no one was quite sure how long it would take for her to turn up- if she ever did.

Yes, Anna Claire was still alive and, in fact, well. She had followed the stream back a bit, and she was waiting for the perfect opportunity to get a ride.

She had docked right in the heart of a lush field with all types of wild plants from camas to watershield. Afraid of running into bears or worse, she hid under a peach-leaf willow where it was too wide to see much of her tattered figure. Hopefully, a kind human being would spot her looking hungry and offer her a piece of bread or even pie, which Anna Claire relished. She was beginning to long for her mother's good cooking and even the bickering of her siblings. And she missed that sacrilegious infidel, Tommy Cooper, who had so far been her only friend in Montana Territory.

She forgot why she so dramatically floated down the creek. Even if she told them that it was an accident, she would still be in trouble for swimming in the creek and not getting to shore before she was swept away. She was going to be in trouble either way, and Helen would have the last laugh.

She sighed and moved a bit further away from the tree toward a narrow dirt path. Perhaps someone would take pity on her and bring her home. She watched forlornly as the squirrels and pocket mice scurried along through the rattlesnake fern, the sweet smell of showy milkweed flowing around her. She was afraid to touch any of the plants, as her mother had always warned her about strange and poisonous ones, and, despite her hunger, she refrained from taking a piece of blue grama or a colorful anemone. She silently prayed that she would be found because she realized she did not want to die and would rather have a chance to explore the town.

"Why did I do this?" she thought to herself, her hair damp and matted, and her dress soaking and cold against her skin.

Joseph and the men searched from that next morning well into the next night, but they did not find Anna Claire. Joseph and Paul Clemmons had begun to look further than the town and the house, and were now beginning to search the hills. Mr. Henry Dobbins had come along with them and was telling them all about the area, as he had lived there all of his life.

"You see now," he said, "don't fret too much. The little girl ain't gone far. Don't fret. I know these lands like the back of my ol' hand and I'm tellin' ya, she's just fine. The animals 'round here are used to people from town, so they ain't gonna touch her. The creek don't get that rough 'round these parts. We just gotta look in these here hills, ya see. She's prob'ly in the hills. It's damn hard to see with all the sagebrush and the trees and the mountainside. I've no doubt she's out there somewhere close. You see now, Gold Country ain't all that scary. It used to be worse 'round here when Sheriff Plummer was killin' people, but it ain't so bad now. No one would dare harm a little girl. There be some hard folks out here, folks you would never wanna meet, but they would never do no harm to a little girl. You gotta believe me there."

Joseph was appreciative that he had made some new friends who were so invested in helping him find his daughter, but he was worried sick to his stomach. Prairie life was dangerous. There were oxen that could get loose and trample her, bears in the forests by the mountains that could maim her, and so many sloping hills that it would be easy to get lost. He knew Anna Claire was strong and resilient, and he was sure she did not drown, but there was a possibility she might be out somewhere severely injured, which was why she had not come home. Perhaps an animal had gotten her, and she was bleeding somewhere, unable to move, or someone had stopped and kidnapped her.

Joseph had so far been able to put these feelings to the side, knowing that fear and panic would not help him find his daughter. He reminded himself of her swimming ability, her knack for adventure, her outright disobedience of rules, and her tendency to run very fast when she wanted to. She had to be alright out there.

"We need to cut dirt if we're gonna find her tonight," said Mr. Clemmons, putting his hat on tighter. "Don't worry about this mess, Joseph. Anna Claire's got smarts. She'll be alright."

"Let's lope, men," said Mr. Dobbins with a serious expression on his face. "We gotta get doin'. The quicker the better. Don't I know it!"

In the early morning hours, as the sun was just beginning to peak out behind the golden hills, Joseph regretfully walked into the home, now two days after Anna Claire went missing. Half of the men would keep searching while the other half would go home to rest and eat with their families. Then, in the late afternoon, they would switch again.

Upon seeing his wife's face, Joseph sighed and said, "Now, Char, do not panic. The men are out there searchin' for her, and no one is stoppin'. I need to rest before I go out there again. Paul Clemmons is restin' now, too. Now Char! Don't look at me like that! We will find her and bring her home. We will bring her home. I'm too tired to continue searchin' now, and I gotta get some sleep before I go back out there. But the others are lookin' and then I'm goin' back out again."

"It's been nearly two days," sobbed Charlotta, her blue eyes appearing red from the constant wiping with her handkerchief. "She has never been gone for this long. She is out in the wild all by herself out there."

"We don't know that for sure," reminded Joseph, putting down his hat and sitting in the chair, his face cut from the brush and his eyes also red with exhaustion. "Maybe someone found her and is lettin' her stay the night before bringin' her back. Yeah- I reckon that's what happened. They found her and are gonna bring her back today."

Charlotta buried her face in her hands and sobbed, not caring if she woke the other children. She could not speak. She was so angry. Angry at her husband for not finding her, angry with Anna Claire for running off again, and angry with herself for not paying more mind to her young child.

She got up from the table and feebly walked across the room, her hands holding the wall as she leaned over her stomach. Joseph, too exhausted to fight it anymore, followed her and closed his eyes, falling asleep for some time. When he woke up a couple of hours later, he went out to try to find Anna Claire again.

It was mid-afternoon, and Anna Claire was ravenous.

"I must go back now," she thought a little sadly, as though the entirety of Bannack and the surrounding camps weren't out looking for her.

Her adventure was over, and home, Anna Claire realized, was much better when one was tired and hungry. She was ready to leave the little patch of grass under the larch tree that she had slept on that night and continue walking home.

Despite being far from home, Anna Claire was fully aware of how beautiful Montana Territory was. She admired the red clay peaks rising next to her and the hemlocks that were growing so tall. She relished in the asters and bitterroots that grew in surprising places around the creek and venerated the crevasses and supple river valleys that poured from the big hills around her. She was mesmerized by the dips of the earth and the pines sticking out from the slopes. She could stay here forever- that is, if she had some food.

As she was walking, she saw a man fishing by the creek. She wanted to ask him if he could spare her a fish to eat when she heard a familiar voice.

"Excuse me, sir," said a little boy, tall for his age, with sun-streaked brown hair and tanned-brown skin. "Have you seen a little girl? She's got gold hair and green eyes. Kinda small and real skinny?"

"Tommy!" cried Anna Claire gratefully, tripping over her bare feet.

Tommy looked at her incredulously. "Anny-Claire!" he responded, looking quite the picture himself, his face sweaty and dirt covering his hands. "Never mind, sir, I found her."

The man looked at Tommy, then at Anna Claire, and shrugged.

The two children ran to each other, and Anna Claire excitedly flung her arms around him. "Tommy, I'm sure glad to see *you*! I have to tell you all about my big adventure!"

"Your big adventure!" huffed Tommy, brushing his hair out of his eyes. "Hmph! Is that what you call it when you got the whole town runnin' around and your pa offerin' to pay $100 for you?"

Anna Claire was puzzled.

"Are you youngins all right?" asked the red-bearded man as he heard them.

"Yes, sir," Anna Claire and Tommy answered at once.

"Well, be careful, kids," the man admonished as he continued to fish.

"Do you know the way home?" asked Anna Claire as the two children walked away up the creek.

"Sure, I do," Tommy replied. "It'll take us some time to walk all the way back, but we might be back tonight."

"Let's go then," she said, feeling the sudden effects of her adventure in her weary bones.

The two worn-out children turned a corner and walked through the trees surrounding the creek, which sparkled under the sun, and began to walk the very long walk back home.

They spotted antelopes, gophers, and wild turkeys wandering around the land as they journeyed forward, and Anna Claire chattered on about her fun adventure while Tommy shook his head sensibly.

"You really are an odd stick, ain't ya?" he asked her with a hopeless sigh.

"I am *not* an odd stick, you sacrilegious infidel!" objected the girl, stomping her foot. "My mama says that I'm *puzzlin'*."

"What does *that* mean?" Tommy asked, scrunching up his face. "And why do you always use such strange words?"

"I don't know, but I think it means I like adventures," replied Anna Claire, snapping a skinny branch off a tree and swinging it around her.

"Put that cussed thing down!" Tommy cried, ducking as the branch nearly missed his face.

Anna Claire did as she was told, wanting to make Tommy happy because he had gone through all of that trouble to look for her.

"Gee," he muttered, grabbing a clump of berries and stuffing it in his face.

Hungrily, Anna Claire reached for the leaves and carefully picked a berry off. She then finished it and reached for more.

The two walked on in some silence. Anna Claire was quite impressed that Tommy had found her, and Tommy was irritated that Anna Claire didn't seem the slightest bit put off by the event.

"Tommy, how come you knew I was here?" asked Anna Claire.

"Lucky guess," answered the little boy. "You're always talkin' about driftin' downstream and goin' somewhere. And you don't know how much gird it took. At least *you* could sleep! I had to watch out for everything. Poison Ivy, bears, foxes, and wolves. And vultures who think you're dead."

Anna Claire shivered with delight. She truly loved a good adventure!

"How come you didn't float downstream?" she asked innocently.

"No thanks," Tommy answered with a wave of his hand. "I would never do that."

"Well, why not? You woulda gotten here a lot faster!"

"It's easier to walk," Tommy said practically. And walk they did for over an hour.

"Tommy?" asked Anna Claire during the walk. "Do ya think they'll recognize us?"

"' Course they will," Tommy rolled his eyes. "It's only been two days. Hey, you sure are thick sometimes, ain't ya?"

"But look at us!" persisted Anna Claire. "I look like I've been rollin' around in the mud!"

"Oh well," said Tommy with a slump in his shoulders. "You could look worse."

But Anna Claire had a point. After the long night, both of them were dirty, tired, and very, very hungry. Anna Claire had floated miles away on that log, and, for the children, it was a very long way to walk back.

"I wanted my sisters to be sorry," Anna Claire said softly.

Tommy looked at her with his curious, deep eyes. "Why? Sorry for what?"

"For always yellin' at me!" said Anna Claire defensively.

"At least you ain't lonely all the time," Tommy whispered, a sadness in his eyes that Anna Claire had never noticed before. But now, seeing it, she realized that it had always been there ever so slightly.

"Well, at least you ain't got nasty older sisters tellin' *you* what to do all the time," reasoned the little girl. "Or little pesky brothers puttin' honey in your bonnet."

"Oh, gee," answered Tommy with a scowl. "At least you don't gotta put up with music in your ears at three o'clock in the mornin' or people who don't care 'bout nothin' 'cept their drinks and guns!"

Anna Claire listened in rapture.

"I want to live in town!" she declared, her eyes sparkling. "It's better than livin' in the middle of nowhere with nothin' but fields. I like fields sometimes, but it gets awfully boring after a while."

"I wish I lived where there's nothin' but fields and trees and the wild animals everywhere," Tommy responded with a faraway look in his eyes. "I don't like it when it's crowded."

"*I* do," said Anna Claire. "I don't like bein' alone."

Tommy sighed and squinted up at the little puzzle of blue sky in between tree leaves.

"Sometimes you can be completely alone in the most crowded places," he answered with a small and unhappy sigh.

Anna Claire scrunched her face. "If it's crowded, you ain't alone," she reasoned, confused by her friend's comment.

"You can be," answered Tommy, just before they heard a loud sound.

Monstrous and echoing, it was a sound so startling that both children put their hands to their heads.

"Duck!" cried Tommy.

"Why?"

"'Cause that was a gunshot!"

Chapter 5- A Wanderer and his Dog

The gunshot came out of nowhere, and both Anna Claire and Tommy flew onto the ground, Tommy's arm protectively around his little friend's shoulders.

"Dang missed 'em!" shouted a deep male voice.

"He means us!" Anna Claire cried, watching Tommy with huge eyes.

Tommy was too frightened to say anything, but he covered Anna Claire's mouth to keep the man from hearing them.

"Shh," he beckoned as Anna Claire struggled to break free of his grip.

"Hey, anyone there?" called the man.

Both Tommy and Anna Claire sat stock still. Neither of them dared to breathe. The ground crackled in front of them, and they could now see the man coming into view.

He had a shaggy but short gray beard and a balding head. His trousers looked even worse than Anna Claire's gingham, and he carried a long, silvery rifle.

"Hey!" called the man again. "Anyone there?"

When he heard nothing, he shrugged his shoulders and continued moving throughout the forest, leaves crackling under his worn moccasins.

Anna Claire tried not to move around in the leaves, but it was difficult, and the leaves rustled loudly.

The man turned wildly around, not seeing the children.

"I'm gonna get ye!" he said as he drew nearer. "Hell yeah. I'm gonna eat ye up for supper tonight and cut ye into tiny, little pieces. Tinier than my pinkie nail, that's what ye'll be!"

Anna Claire made a little gasp as Tommy shut her mouth tighter. Her heart was beating loudly, and her palms were sweating. She could never remember being so frightened.

Tommy himself did not look or feel any better. Beads of perspiration wet his forehead as cold shivers ran up and down his spine. Not only did this man *look* like he would kill two very frightened children, but his voice was determined and angry. Tommy had a feeling that this was a man who would not give up or relent once he had made up his mind to do something.

"Here, come on," the man was saying, spinning wildly in Tommy and Anna Claire's direction. "I'm gonna catch ye!"

Suddenly, Anna Claire made a loud squeal of helplessness and jolted up right out of Tommy's grasp, making a run for it. She fled across the crunching leaves but tripped and fell face-first on a rock, causing a cut on her forehead.

The man was at her side, and he grabbed her elbow, lifting her off the ground.

"Let me go!" she squealed, squirming out of his reach. "Let me go! You bad man, get your hands off of me!"

"Anny-Claire!" yelled Tommy as he ran to her side. He grabbed the largest stick he could find in two seconds and swung it at the extremely tall man, hitting him hard in the back.

"Children!" yelled the man, bending over with pain. But Tommy kept at him as Anna Claire took the big rock and threw it at his face. The rock landed squarely on his nose, and he moved his hands from his back to it, crying out in pain.

"Stop! Stop!" he cried, grabbing Tommy and stilling him.

"Get away!" Anna Claire shouted, throwing another rock at the man. "You leave us alone! And if you shoot one of us, we'll come up from our graves and haunt you!"

"Yeah!" Tommy bellowed. "We'll murder you, and there'll be a trail of blood all the way to Mississippi!"

"What?" cried the man in confusion.

"You leave us alone or we'll kill ya!" screamed Anna Claire, kicking his leg and then whacking him in the chest with her palm. "Mean rotten son-of-a-gun!"

"Stop!" begged the man, suddenly grabbing both the children by the arms and twisting them a bit, for it was the only way to save himself from the angry little beasts. "Stop now!"

"Get off!" cried Anna Claire in her high-pitched voice, kicking him where it hurts men most.

The man winced but did not let go. "Why ye tryna kill me? All I was tryna do was get my dinner!"

"Dinner is what you call us?" Tommy shouted, his face red and sweat dripping down his shirt. "Well, you're gonna have to catch another boy and girl because *we* aren't *anybody's* meat!"

Suddenly, the man laughed heartily, his eyes curving into his cheeks in a big, wide gap-toothed smile, his breath foul, frightening Anna Claire and Tommy to the brink of their nerves.

"Ye youngins are crazy," he laughed. "What, ye think I was tryna shoot you? Stop it! Stop kickin' me, li'l girl!"

"You *were* tryin' to shoot us!" cried Anna Claire. "We saw you!"

"Not ye, not ye!" said the man, still laughing mightily.

Anna Claire's face went from furious to upset and then to worried all in one swift motion. She fell limp in the man's grip and finally let her legs dangle in the air as the large man held her up.

"Listen here," began the man with a smile. "I wasn't aimin' at *ye*, I was aimin' at the deer that I almost shot a li'l while 'go."

"What deer?" Tommy asked suspiciously.

"It ran away," the man nodded regretfully. "Little scared-cat ran away faster than a jack rabbit."

"You weren't shootin' at us?" asked Tommy, beginning to feel the prick of his conscience.

"Hell naw," the man shouted, looking surprised. Anna Claire shook with terror at the scars on his cheeks and the overgrown white bushes above his eyes. "Ye believe I'd shoot a couple-a youngins?"

Tommy shivered with relief. "Well, all we heard was a gunshot!"

The man smiled and released the two horrified children, laughing with enjoyment and wiping a bit of the blood off his nose.

" 'Course I wouldn't do such a thing- I'm an honorable man, ye know," he laughed again, that same high and crackly "hee hee" that reminded Anna Claire of a blood-hungry animal. "Ye youngins really hurt me, ye know. My back aches now, and look, I'm bleedin' all over the place!"

Anna Claire let herself fall to the ground, rubbing where the pain was and letting herself breathe. Tommy sat on a rock beside her and struggled to catch his breath.

"Ye youngins see whatcha did to me?" he asked with annoyance. "And all I was tryna do was get me some dinner."

"So, when you told us you were gonna cut us up into tiny little pieces smaller than your nail, you weren't talkin' to us?" gasped Tommy with a new flood of relief.

The man laughed more powerfully than ever, "hee-heeing" so much that his ruddy face turned a bright red.

"Yer nuts!" he cried, chuckling as he bent his back. "Naw, I wasn't talkin' to ye, I was talkin' to that deer that got away from me. If ye dang'on youngins hadn't been so loud, maybe ye wouldn't have scared 'em off!"

Anna Claire felt a wave of guilt as she and Tommy exchanged a happy glance.

"Did we hurt you somethin' awful?" she asked with concern.

The man laughed again. "Well, ye made me bleed all right, but I think I'll be fine."

"Gee, sir," said Tommy, shaking his head with sorrow. "I'm- *we're*- awful sorry. We didn't mean to hurt you like that. We thought you was after us!"

"Naw, but I'll be all right," the man assured them, that amused look still in his eyes.

Anna Claire wished he would stop smiling- his yellow teeth, the few that he had, were starting to scare her.

"Say," he said, taking one good look at each of them, "why ye youngins out playin' in this here forest? Forests ain't such a great place for ye to be playin', what with hunters and all."

"We weren't playin'," Tommy told him. "I was out lookin' for Anny-Claire after she ran away, and now we gotta go home."

"Who's Anny-Claire?"

"I am!" called out the little girl with an eager voice. "I'm Anna Claire! He says my name wrong."

"Well," he bent down to her level and stared her in the eyes. "What's a li'l girl like ye doin' runnin' away from yer home?"

"I...don't know," faltered Anna Claire, feeling annoyed that he had called her "little." She was still wary of the stranger and did not yet know if she could trust him. "I...I floated down the stream by accident."

"You did *not*, stop lyin' Anny-Claire," said Tommy with force. "You ran away."

Anna Claire lapsed into silence as the man watched Tommy very seriously. "Are you brother and sister?"

Both children gasped.

"How could *I* be related to such a numbskull?" cried Tommy, as if the idea was most absurd.

Anna Claire jumped from her rock and stood in front of him, hands on her hips. "No one's a numbskull 'round here except *you*!" she fired, nodding curtly before huffing back onto her rock.

"I guess ye ain't related then," the man said slowly with an amused grin. "Well, how do ye know each other?"

"I live on Grasshopper Diggin's," Anna Claire said. "Tommy lives in town, but I have to live far away in the field."

"Anna Claire likes town better," Tommy explained, "but I don't see why."

The giant man sighed and sat down next to the children. "Town is nice for a while, but I couldn't stand too many people all at one time. I'm Jim Turner, by the way. And yer Anna Claire and Tommy?"

They nodded.

"Well, I'm sorry I gave ye such a scare," Jim said kindly. "I didn't mean no harm. Really was after that deer."

"Sorry I hit you in the face...and threw a rock at you...and kicked you," said Anna Claire, her stomach making a loud growling sound.

"No harm done," Jim Turner answered kindly. "Hey, don't ye youngins need a ride or somethin'?"

Anna Claire and Tommy looked at each other.

"Well, we really should be gettin' back to Grasshopper Diggin's," Tommy responded, looking up at the sun.

"I'll give ye a lift," Jim smiled at them. "My wagon's right 'round here."

Together, the three weary travelers made their way out of the trees to Jim's wagon.

It did not feel so very long when the little rickety wagon had traveled an hour. They rode through the soft, clear air and around the winding, glittering creek as the saskatoon berries and dryads spread along in flushing colors of creams and purples. Anna Claire came to find that they were extremely fond of this man who called himself "an ol' keener." He listened to the children's summaries of their lives with much interest and amusing comments, making them laugh throughout their time with him.

Tommy told him all about Rocks and Ebb, his "friends" who excluded him from their gang, and went on to talk about how his father once took him to a rodeo and how they had a great time, but his father hadn't shown up since, and that was over a year ago. Anna Claire talked about her old life in Minnesota and about how, if she had one wish, she would wish to be the oldest of her siblings.

Throughout the children's pouring of hearts, Jim's spirit slowly lifted. He had been awful lonely lately, and the children were just what he needed to perk up.

"It's still early. I'm sure we'll get ye back before nightfall. I ain't so good at ridin' in the dark. No, not in the dark I ain't."

Jim shared with them some pieces of bread he was keeping in his wagon, along with some jam he had kept in an old wooden box.

"I know yer families must be worried," Jim said. "I hate to think of them lookin' for ye."

"My ma won't care," Tommy answered. "She probably doesn't even know I've been gone."

And so that's how a close friendship began with the giant man who claimed to "cut them up" into tiny little pieces just that very day.

"Mama and Papa won't be happy to hear that I floated downstream, but I couldn't stay in that boring old house anymore," Anna Claire explained as the wheels jolted up and down. "I needed an adventure."

"So ye *did* run away?" asked Jim, who up to that point had been skeptical.

Anna Claire realized what she had confessed. "Maybe I did, and I ain't sorry either! If you had a bunch of nasty brothers and sisters, you would too!"

"I've had my full share of pesky sisters," Jim stated. "I was the middle'n. Ye both got restless spirits," he told them. The children looked confused, and Jim added hastily, "It's a good thing to have. I have one myself, in fact."

"Tell us what it was like when you were our age!" begged Anna Claire, not feeling tired or hungry anymore.

"Yeah, we wanna know about you, since we've told you about us," Tommy reasoned.

Jim laughed. He hadn't felt this glad in a very long time. "Well, I s'pose a li'l story for the ride ain't gonna hurt nothin'. As long as ye youngins promise not to keep runnin' away."

"We won't!" the children cried at once.

And so, Jim Turner began his tale.

A Jim Turner Day in 1814

Ten-year-old Jim Turner lived at the edge of a small town in Kentucky with his five-year-old sister Betsy, seven-year-old sister Alma, and thirteen-year-old sister Sally. They lived with their ma and pa in a big wooden cottage that lay just beyond a sea of grassy fields and poppy flowers.

Today was supposed to be just a normal day for little Jim, not unlike any other. Wake up early- too early in Jim's mind- after the rooster crowed. Get dressed in his old pair of overalls. Run downstairs and give a kiss to Ma while she handed him a baked flapjack to eat on his way to school. Walk slowly up the riverbank to the little log schoolhouse that awaited him in its wooden agony, knowing he'd have a tough day ahead of him. Work hard at his lessons and be careful not to let Sam Hinger and his friends get him in trouble. Play with Borner, the dog, at break. Go back and endure school, being careful not to show his fear when the boys mercilessly teased him. Walk after school over to the riverbank and hang around Rock Pond and throw stones in the water until evening. Come home and have a hot supper with his family. Help Pa outside with the farm chores; milking the cows, brushing the horses, loading and unloading the hay, as is expected of every farmer boy. Go inside and change into his nightgown. Betsy would beg him to tell her a bedtime story if she wasn't already asleep when he came inside.

But this day wasn't like most days.

Jim started out on a fresh Tuesday morning in his regular routine. He quickly jolted up out of bed, the darkness persisting through the house, making him wish he could climb right back into that soft, warm bed.

He changed into his ragged overalls and stomped loudly down the stairs, full of the energy most common in little boys of ten. Ma handed him his usual flapjack and smiled kindly at her son, her plump face spreading into a warm smile.

"Have a good day at school, Jim, and try to be as good as you can."

Ma always said that phrase, and Jim often grew tired of hearing it. But he nodded and grinned, running out of the door and into the fresh Kentucky air. He ran across the field but then slowed down his pace when he heard Alma's high-pitched voice behind him.

This year was Alma's first year in school, being only seven. Jim decided to be kind and wait for her, for Pa told him to keep an eye on his sister, especially since she was so little.

Alma was clutching her brown lunch basket, skipping as she sang a tune. Jim hummed along with her as the two went singing and whistling down the forest and alongside the riverbank.

"Jim, why do I have to go to school?" Alma asked, her wide eyes looking up at him.

"We all have to," Jim answered. "It's because we're children. All children go to school until they're grown up."

"Why don't men and women go to school?" Alma inquired.

"Because then they have to work," Jim replied. "Unless they're girls. Then they have to keep house."

"Keep what house?"

"What Ma does."

"But why do they make children go to school?"

"'Cause they know just how to torture us," answered Jim as Alma, satisfied with the answer, ran along the brook, throwing rocks into the water.

Once they reached the schoolhouse, Jim already had a feeling of dread. Sam Hinger and the boys would surely pick on him as usual. Jim wasn't in the mood, especially not today when he was so tired. He took his seat and prayed silently that Sam wouldn't taunt him.

So far, the school day was going smoothly. The children sat up straight with their hands folded on their laps, doing their arithmetic sums in complete and total silence. It was so quiet that Jim could hear his heartbeat. His legs began to ache from dangling, for he was still too small to reach the floor.

The teacher, who was very kind and pitied Jim, gave him a sum to do on the board. He solved it quickly and without much of a problem. He was very good at arithmetic and always got the highest marks in that subject. But reading and history were a different story.

The teacher praised Jim, and he flushed with pride. This day was going so well. No one talked to him so far, which was a good thing, for when they did talk to him, it was usually to say something nasty or mean.

Jim ate all alone at dinnertime, watching as his sisters had fun with their friends. He watched as Alma ran races, a bit envious of her popularity. Sally laughed and flirted with some of the boys. Jim saw the other Fourth Reader boys playing four-square and wished he weren't so shy so he could join them. But he was only chubby, sensitive Jim Turner. He wasn't like Sam Hinger, who was cheerful, rude, and wild. Although his teacher much preferred Jim over Sam any day of the week, Jim wished he could be loud and talkative like Sam, who always seemed to be so loved and admired among all of the little boys and girls.

That's when he remembered Borner.

Excitedly, Jim ran along the side of the schoolhouse where Borner, the little brown-haired white-spotted mutt, stood waiting for him. He was not quite sure where the lively dog got his peculiar name, or exactly what breeds he was mixed with, only that he was Mr. Smith's two-year-old pup whose house stood right next to the school yard and was blocked off by a low-wooded fence. Borner was an amiable, friendly dog who would cleverly catch and bring back whatever Jim threw at him. He would stay inside the fence, waiting for Jim until break came.

Because the fence was low, Jim could climb over and out during the break hour. This day, he did just that, letting the dog escape from his captivity. Jim subconsciously knew that he could get in big trouble if ever his teacher or Mr. Smith found out, but decided that the risk was well worth it. Borner was essentially Jim's only good friend and loving companion, and Jim adored the little dog with all of his heart.

"Hey, Born-boy," he greeted the dog with a smile on his chubby cheeks.

"Roof!" cried the dog, excitedly jumping to and fro inside the fence.

Jim climbed over it, careful to guard the windows in case Mr. Smith was there.

It was a known fact that Mr. Smith was not kind to his dog. In fact, the students had heard on a number of occasions the yelling and hitting of Borner from the windows of the school. Whenever Jim heard this, he'd close his eyes and cover his ears, not being able to withstand the thought of his dearest friend being abused.

Gently removing the poor dog from the yard, Jim gave him a pat on the back and the two went running wildly down by the forest, where the students couldn't see.

"I wish I could take ye home with me, Borner boy," said Jim. Borner looked up at him as if to nod, his ears flapping.

"If only Mr. Smith would let me," thought the sensitive boy. "I already asked him twice. It ain't fair, no, it ain't fair one bit. That ol' man don't treat ye right, does he, Born boy?"

The dog barked in response, wagging his tail around in little circles.

"He never cares right for ye," said Jim. "He licks you bad and yells at ye all the time. It ain't right.

If *I* could take care of ye, I would take the best care of ye that ye could ever want."

"Roof!" Borner agreed, jumping up and laying his paws on Jim's thighs.

Jim grimaced when he saw the red marks on Borner's back and around his ears. He gently reached to stroke them, but the dog moved carefully back with a little whimper.

"Oh, my Born-boy, ye know I'd never hurt ye," said Jim, his voice soothing. Instead of reaching for the sores, he patted the dog on the back, and Borner wagged his hungry tongue at him.

"Ye look awful skinny," Jim remarked. "I bet that ol' mean Mr. Smith don't even feed ye."

The dog barked again, and his chest flexed in, his ribcage very visible. Jim looked down at his hand and realized a piece of ham was still in his pocket from lunch. Usually, Jim would try to save the dog a piece of lunch every day. As Sam Hinger said, "That fatty Jim Turner doesn't need any lunch, just look at him!"

He threw the piece of ham on the ground and- wildly and savagely- the dog bent down and ate it in one breath, looking up with pleading black eyes for more.

"Oh, Borner-boy, I'm sorry, I don't got no more ham," Jim said with sadness. "' Morro I'll bring ye some more. I promise. Yer a good boy."

The dog barked and stood on his hind legs. Jim could see traces of scars along his flat, pink stomach.

They played fetch and catch with a pinecone until the twenty-minute break was concluded. Hearing the bell, Jim regretfully walked back up the little hill, the dog following him with pleading barks.

Jim gently and kindly put Borner back into his fence, careful to watch out for Mr. Smith. Then, knowing he was already three minutes late, he scurried back into the schoolhouse, not without a sharp reprimand from his teacher.

"Be a good boy!" he called as he ran to the schoolhouse.

"Roof!" promised Borner, trying to jump the fence without success, watching the little boy run away with sad eyes.

"Jim's queer," said Sam Hinger rudely. "He's always playin' by himself in the forest."

"Lord knows he needs his exercise!" whispered John Perks.

Jim frowned and stared down at his desk, his face flushed.

"Don't say that 'bout my brother!" shouted Alma. Although small, the little girl was as tough and stubborn as a mother hen. "He ain't so fat and he ain't so queer, either!"

"Aw, we're upsetting the little baby," teased Sam. "Poor little baby. Why don't you go cry to your mama about it?"

"Jim's a queer stick, that's what he is, and so are you, Alma!" shouted John Perks, sticking out his tongue.

Alma made a face and shouted, "You just stop teasin' my brother now, John!"

"Is something the matter?" the teacher had heard the conversation and now turned around from the board with her hands on her hips.

The children shook their heads, but Alma turned her head towards Jim and smiled.

Jim was always being made fun of because of his looks. His sisters, Sally and Alma, were both so pretty and skinny. No one ever made fun of them. But Jim was big, stubby, and ruddy. His eyes were set very far apart, making him look wild. His nose was large, and his teeth were crooked. Although Jim was not considered so beautiful on the outside, he had a heart worth of envy.

When the tough school day ended, Jim dashed out in a flash and ran along the pond, throwing rocks in the water.

"Whatcha doin'?" asked a devilish voice behind him. Only in this case, even the devil himself would have been more welcome than the true speaker.

"Nothin'," Jim answered, feeling his cheeks flush again.

Sam Hinger smiled an evil grin, his two best friends snickering with cruel eyes.

"You're the fattest boy I've ever seen," pronounced John Perks, glancing at his ringleader for approval. "And you're the dumbest boy in school."

"That's why he has no friends," said Arnold Johnson.

"I think he's pretty skinny, myself," Sam mocked. "At least for a grizzly bear, he is."

"Yeah," spat John. "You look like a grizzly bear—all fat and ugly!"

"And dumb!" added Arnold with a howl.

The cruel boys chuckled and patted Jim on the back.

"Hey, let's be friends," Sam said. "Here, come on, play with us. You wanna?"

Jim wanted to disappear.

"Let's shake on it," but when Sam stuck out his hand and Jim tried to take it, Sam jerked it away in one swift motion and stuck it in his pocket instead. "Hey, Jim's a sore loser!" he cried, and his loyal followers yelped with laughter.

"Well, hey, why are you backin' away like that?" hissed Sam with a smirk. "We ain't gonna hurt you now. We've gotta help our pa's with the chores. But we'll be back later, don't you worry," and with that, they were off, running and shouting through the forest.

"Jimmy the sissy!" they called back, all the while glancing at him and throwing rocks at each other.

Jim shook his head and sat by the creek, watching the water flow by. He was so used to the bullies' teasing that it almost didn't hurt so much after a while.

Suddenly, while trying to drown out his faults in that stream, he heard a shouting voice. He jerked his head up and stretched his neck. The sound stopped. Jim turned back to the water, willing himself not to cry.

"You dumb ol' piece of shit," cried the voice again. It was coming from behind the forest. Jim jumped up with a start.

"Bad dog. You're a no-good little shit," said the voice. "Next time you jump on me like that, you're kicked!" He heard two loud thumps and then Borner's gentle voice, whimpering in pain.

Frantically, Jim ran through and out of the forest.

He could hear the straps hitting his friend with a cruel, merciless force. "Snap- Snap- Whip- Snap," said the wooden stick, beating the dog with a passion unknown to any human with a heart.

"No!" cried Jim in panic, not knowing what to do. "No, no, please stop!" He ran to the fence where he found Mr. Smith with the stick in his hand, Borner lying on the ground with blood marks on his back and stomach. "Don't hurt him! He's a good dog!"

Before he even realized what he was doing, Jim was already climbing the fence, wrapping his arms protectively around the helpless animal.

"What you doin', boy?" shouted Mr. Smith, waving the stick dangerously in front of the little boy's face. "Get out of my yard."

"No," Jim said sternly, but with a quivering voice. He couldn't stop the tears from flowing down his face. "Let me have Borner, please. Ye don't want him, and I'll take care of him. Please, Mr. Smith, please. I'll do whatever ye want, just please let me have Borner."

Mr. Smith frowned, his wrinkles growing even larger.

"What good will that do for me?" he asked, narrowing his black eyes at Jim.

Jim considered. It was now or never. Borner alive or Borner dead. Something had to be done- he just had to save his friend.

"Well, I'll rake the leaves for ye in yer yard," said Jim. "And I'll work for ye. I can do almost anything a grown man can do. I can cut those weeds out and fix that roof, and patch up those walls! I'll do anything, Mr. Smith."

Borner's head turned, and his helpless eyes watched Jim with hope.

"Please, Mr. Smith," tears flowed freely now. "Please let me take care of him. I'll do anything ye want."

Mr. Smith's hardened face did not soften, but he was silent for a few moments, pondering all the work that needed to be done for his house.

"Alright, alright, you can have him," he said in a tone not to be tampered with. "Lord knows I don't need him. Damn dog, more useful dead than alive. Just rake these leaves when they get plentiful and fix this fence. Then you can worry about the roof and the wall. I don't need this no-good goddamn dog messin' up my yard no more."

"Yes, sir," said Jim obediently. He was a clever young lad and knew the best way to get what you wanted with a man like Mr. Smith was to make it seem as if everything was his suggestion.

Borner pricked up his ears at the sound of Mr. Smith's front door slamming.

"Yes!" cried Jim in a torrent of joy, unable to believe how easy his success had come to him. He bolted up on his feet and jumped up into the sky. "Yes! We've got each other now, Born-boy! I can have ye! I can take care of ye! We've got each other, boy! We'll never be lonely, not ever again. Oh, Borner-boy! Yer a good dog!"

The starving creature found the strength to get up on all fours and stand on his hind legs, hands on Jim's thigh.

"Roof!" barked Borner.

"Good boy!" cried Jim, rubbing the back of his ear softly and kissing the top of his head, tears hitting the soft brown fur. "I love ye, Borner boy. We're going to have the best times."

Borner barked as if he understood. His tail began wagging as he paced back and forth, tongue hanging out and dripping hungry saliva onto the ground.

"Oh, Borner, I've got ye and ye got me," cried Jim. "Pa already told me I could have ye if Mr. Smith let me. Oh, Borner, I'll take care of ye! Ye'll never get beaten or be hungry again! Not ever."

Borner barked happily and licked his new master's face. Borner didn't care if Jim was chubby or if those cheeks were ruddy. All Borner could understand was his love for Jim, and all Jim could understand in his young years was how much he cared for the dog. He would have a good home now filled with children, good food, warm firesides, and loving pets, and Jim and Borner would always have each other.

"Come on, boy," murmured Jim with overjoyed disbelief, "it's time to go home."

And home they went, with Borner wagging his tail and jumping up and down onto Jim's weightless legs, which seemed to soar across the forest.

"You have tears in your eyes," Anna Claire said, waking the older Jim Turner out of his daydream.

Jim woke up suddenly and smiled over at the two little ones.

"I miss that dog," he said with sad, gray eyes that were far apart from each other. "He was the best friend a man could have."

"That was a sad story," Anna Claire stated. "But I liked it so much. Especially Borner. He reminds me of Hero. Hero is a good boy, too, just like Borner. I miss Hero lots. I'm gonna give him a big kiss when I get home! What happened to Borner, and why do you miss him? And did you really sit all by yourself at dinnertime?"

Jim nodded. "I sure did. Them kids didn't like me much, I can tell ye that." He chuckled with the memory twinkling in his eyes.

"But what happened to Borner?" asked Tommy, looking out of the wagon as if the dog would simply pop up out of thin air.

"Borner's long gone," Jim reflected sadly. "Died about forty years ago. But let me tell ye he was the best dog a man could ever have, and the happiest one at that."

"Did your sisters like him?" asked Anna Claire curiously.

"They sure did," Jim answered. "Not as much as I did, but no one could've loved him like me. Little Betsy took to the dog almost just as well, and Borner and her became good friends. That dog was at every picnic, hike, or walk we ever went on." His face glowed from the memory of it. "Pa and Ma loved him too."

"Did you really work for that mean old man?" asked Tommy.

"Yessir, but not for long," replied Jim. "Mr. Smith died not long after that, and that's when I stopped. Me and Borner did have some great times. I stopped goin' to school the next year to become a farmer. Farmin' life never quite agreed with me. I always wanted to do somethin' with arithmetic, but I never did."

"Where do you live now?" asked Tommy.

"Wherever I feel like," replied Jim.

"Are you married? Where's your house?" asked Anna Claire.

"No, I am not married, never found a woman I liked as much as she liked me," Jim teased with a smile. "And I don't have a house. I kinda like to go with the flow, see what happens down the road."

The children looked up at Jim with expressions of rapture.

"How did Borner die?" Anna Claire's green eyes were now like huge saucers, soaking up Jim's bittersweet tale.

"Got old." Jim was happy to answer the children's questions. He had a need for companionship and always enjoyed when people listened to his stories. It felt as though he had made a name for himself in his own strange way. "But I can tell ye that while he was livin', he had the best life a pup could ever have. And he loved us just as much as we loved him."

Jim sighed. He could still see Borner clearly in his mind, as if he was standing on his hind legs, wagging his tail with his tongue out right in front of him.

"Me and Borner were like brothers, although we didn't look much alike," laughed Jim with recollection. "He even went with me to school sometimes. When I was workin' at the town mill, he even followed me there, all the way until he got old and sick. But I'll tell ye this, we were the best of friends."

"Did that mean Sam boy still tease you?" asked Anna Claire.

"He sure did, all the way until I stopped goin' to school," said Jim, although no emotion was in his voice. "Good ol' Sam Hinger." He chuckled lightly and smiled, showing his crooked yellow teeth.

"What happened to your sisters? And your ma and pa? Don't you ever see them no more?" asked Tommy, blue eyes ablaze.

Jim's face fell into a look of sadness. "Well, Ma died a while back now. In fact, she passed away from fever not long after Borner died. Pa passed on ten years ago, although I ain't seen him for twenty. Pa and I had our differences. Sally, my older sister, married o' course and had four children. Never really kept in touch with Sally. I had already left home to move to the east by the time the second one was born. Alma, sweet li'l Alma, is long dead now, too."

Anna Claire and Tommy looked at each other. They hadn't expected that. For some reason, they both thought Jim's tale would have a happier ending.

"She died almost twenty-five years ago," Jim reflected sadly. "Dang, I can't believe it's been that long. Sweet li'l Alma. Always so kind to me. When she was seventeen, she married John Perks."

"But John- wasn't he that mean boy who made fun of you, too?" asked Anna Claire in surprise.

"He used to," admitted Jim. "But when he grew up, he wasn't so bad. Kind, even. Loved my sister with all of his heart, he did."

"And why did Alma die?" asked Tommy.

"She had a child. There was some problem when she was givin' birth. By that time, I was in the east, workin' at a paper factory." His eyes beheld that sad, far-away look again. "I wasn't even there to help 'er. I couldn't even do nothin'. Alma didn't deserve to die so young. Such a sweet li'l thing she was. Once I heard of her death, I came back home right away. John was sittin' in her old chair, sobbin' and carryin' on. He loved his wife. Poor John."

"What happened to John?" whispered Anna Claire.

"John moved away with his only daughter, the one Alma died givin' birth to," Jim said sadly. "I loved that child like she was my own from the day I first saw 'er. Her and John were the only ones I ever kept in touch with. Her daughter is still alive. I see her often; in fact, she doesn't live far from this very town. Looks just like my sweet li'l sister. As for the littlest, Betsy, she left home without tellin' anyone at sixteen. Didn't like the country and moved to the city, so I heard. I've never seen or heard from her again."

Anna Claire felt a pang of sadness for the kind man who was helping her get back home. He seemed like he had lost almost everyone he loved.

"Thank ye for listenin' to me. Hope I didn't bore ye too much. Ye both are real good youngins."

"Oh, you didn't bore us at all!" cried Anna Claire.

"No, I want to hear more!" agreed Tommy.

Jim laughed. "Seems to me we don't got much time left."

As the fields seemed to stretch on and on, Jim following the creek religiously, Anna Claire was beginning to recognize where she was. Very soon, she could see her home in the distance. It was still partially light out, and Anna Claire easily recognized her mother with a small group of women walking down the creek towards her. When one of them saw the wagon, the women began walking more briskly until Charlotta spotted her daughter, putting her hand over her eyes and squinting to make sure the sun wasn't playing any cruel tricks on her.

Jim smiled and stopped the wagon, letting both of the children run through the field. Charlotta came closer and closer until Anna Claire ran into her head-first and embraced her.

Jim rode the wagon up a bit until he was next to the group of women, Charlotta sobbing into her daughter's hair, and the other women comforting them. Tommy had his hands on his hips and a fierce look on his face. He stood proudly and boldly, knowing he was a part of her rescue.

"Anna Claire," Charlotta's voice was breaking, the tenseness in her chest dissipating. "You're safe. You're home. Oh, sweet girl. Where on God's green Earth were you? You know the whole town has been looking for you? Are you alright? Are you hurt? There's a cut on your head!"

"Oh, I'm fine, Mama!" she said cheerfully. "I hit my head on a rock."

The women turned towards Anna Claire and enveloped her, all taking a glance at her head and telling Charlotta it would be healed.

Charlotta looked up at Jim, who was in his wagon. "Hello, Sir! Sir, where did you find her?"

Jim jumped down and shook her hand. "I'm Jim Turner. I found yer here youngin' with this boy down the creek, miles from here. I knew they was lost and hungry, so I brought them back and gave them some of my bread and jam. I reckon they're gonna want a lot more than that though."

Charlotta turned to Tommy and gently put her hand to his face before turning to Anna Claire. "What on Earth happened?"

Anna Claire knew it was going to be the most difficult moment of the reunion. She closed her eyes and sighed, her legs trembling underneath her.

"I went swimmin' in the creek and I went too far," she said. "Way too far. I didn't realize I had gone so far 'cause I was floatin' for a while, but then I started movin' real quick and was scared to swim off the log I was on, and then I almost fell over the waterfall but that was after I saw the bear and then I got to shore." She was panting now and out-of-breath. She looked over at Tommy and added, "Tommy came to find me."

Charlotta was in shock. Mrs. Clemmons held her by her waist to steady her as the other women began inspecting Anna Claire and checking to make sure she was all in one piece. Then they did the same to Tommy. The other children had run out of the house and were now surrounding Anna Claire with embraces and kisses, for even Helen was beginning to get frightened that perhaps something had happened to her little sister. Even Hero came wagging his tail out of the house, licking Anna Claire's face roughly as she bent down and giggled, hugging and kissing him with all of her might.

"Oh, Anna Claire," cried Caroline, tears flowing down her face. "I was so worried- we- we were all so worried," and then she stopped in a bundle of sobs.

Anna Claire couldn't speak, for the pressure of their bodies was nearly making her choke.

"How did you know where she was?" asked one of the women to Tommy.

"I didn't," the boy said shortly. "I know she loves the creek, so I figured she probably just swam or walked down it."

Charlotta burst into another flood of tears. "Tommy, thank you! And thank all of you for helping me. I am always at your service. You have all been so kind to us."

The group of women helped Charlotta walk back into the house while Anna Claire and Tommy skipped happily next to Jim.

Mrs. Clemmons and the other women went to find Mr. Clemmons, who would then find Joseph to tell him that his daughter had been found alive and safe. Charlotta put on some tea, and Jim had some tea with the family as they talked about Anna Claire's journey and Tommy's willingness to sojourn after her.

"You must stay for supper," Charlotta pleaded to Jim. "My husband should be here any minute. Please, Mr. Turner. You have done so much for us all. That is the least we can do."

"I fancy I just might," agreed Jim. "Thank ye."

When their father returned, more tears emerged, and Joseph briskly wiped them away. He was so relieved that his daughter had been brought back safe and sound. Charlotta recalled the tale to him, and his face went from overjoyed to angry, then to relieved and curious.

Charlotta's face was brighter than the sun. She turned to Tommy, who was picking apart a piece of wood on the chair awkwardly.

"You went all the way downstream, just to find my Anna Claire?" she asked, her voice softer than a dove.

"He sure did!" exclaimed the little troublemaker. "He saved me, Mama! You should've seen him. He was so brave! If he hadn't come along, I wouldn't have heard Mr. Turner!"

"You traveled all that way to save my sister?" Caroline asked him, blue eyes glowing.

Tommy didn't reply. Instead, he half-nodded, staring down at the chair with an embarrassed frown.

"My dear boy," cooed the grateful mother, arising from the chair to give Tommy an embrace. "You are a hero for doing that. Had you not found her, she would've been all alone, and who knows who could've picked her up."

"Thank you, son," Joseph said, a smile forming on his lips. "My family will not soon forget your bravery."

Tommy blushed and turned his face in the corner of the chair. All of this attention was too much for him.

"You are a hero," repeated Charlotta, tears rolling silently down her pale cheeks. "I was so worried- so, so worried." Then she turned her attention back to Jim, where she arose again to give Mr. Turner a big, grateful embrace.

"And you," she told him, "are just as much of one. I do not know how I can repay your kindness. Here is the $100 we promised to whoever found our Anna Claire."

"No," said Jim. "I ain't takin' any of yer money. I do appreciate it, but I'd rather ye spend the money for the children. Ye let me stay for supper. Yer cookin's so good, I feel like the luckiest man in Montana Territory right now!"

Charlotta flushed with delight. "You can do more than just stay for supper. You can be a guest at our house for as long as you'd like!"

Jim politely turned down the offer. "Thank ye, ma'am, ye don't know how much that means to a man like me. But I'm a travelin' kinda man. I'm going to see my niece and her new baby real soon, so I gotta get prepared. I'm gonna have to get back on my wagon and journey on. But that was mighty good of ye."

"You are always welcome here," said Joseph. "What you have done for us cannot be repaid."

Jim smiled. "Thank ye, sir."

"And Tommy," said Joseph, "you are welcome here anytime as well. You helped get my Anna Claire back safe and sound."

Caroline, the girl who had despised little Tommy Cooper from the moment she laid eyes on him, now stared coyly but sweetly at Tommy with admiration. This made Tommy feel as though he could drown in happiness.

Soon, the table was set very nicely, and johnny-cakes, rye mush, and roasting corn ears were placed on the one good China set that had made it all the way from Minnesota.

"Anna Claire, where did you go to the outhouse?" questioned little Pete with a boyish grin.

"Pete, not at the table," begged Charlotta.

"Weh you scawed?" asked Berthie, her huge brown eyes wide.

Anna Claire grinned. "I was scared sometimes," she answered. "But I wasn't *too* scared! I'm a very brave person, you know."

"I just find it odd that you could've floated down the creek for so long," said Joseph doubtfully. "That's the strangest thing I ever heard."

"Well, I did!" said Anna Claire. "And I couldn't get out of the water."

Tommy rolled his eyes and said with his mouth full, "Anna Claire did it on purpose."

"I did *not*!" lied the little girl. "You just shut up, Tommy Cooper!"

"Now, please, Anna Claire," Charlotta pleaded, "be kind to the hero who helped save your life."

Tommy brightened up at that comment.

"I thought you died, or you were hidin' from us or somethin'," Pete confessed, biting off a piece of his johnny-cake.

"Peter Freiler!" reprimanded Charlotta.

"Sorry, Mama," said Pete. "But I'm glad you're not dead, Anna Claire."

Joseph turned to Jim. "Where do you live, sir?" he asked.

Jim shrugged and swallowed a spoonful of rye mush. "Wherever the land takes me. I don't got a house, but I manage. I like to just follow my own path and see where it takes me."

The family gazed on with interest.

"Don't you ever get lonely by yourself?" asked Helen.

Jim shook his head. "Sometimes I do, but I like wanderin' 'round with nothin' but the trees and the animals to keep me company."

"Oh," said sociable Helen, who couldn't imagine a life with nothing but trees and animals.

"Why don't you settle down here?" asked Joseph, who did not quite understand Jim.

"I couldn't do that," said Jim. "I don't like stayin' in one place for too long. I like to be on my feet."

"Well, know that you are welcome here at Grasshopper Diggings anytime."

"That's mighty nice of you, sir," Jim answered.

"Oh, Berthie," Charlotta said with a worried frown, looking down at the youngest, for the child had not touched a piece of food once during the entire meal. "Eat your supper. You haven't eaten a single thing practically all day."

"I'm not hungwy," whined Berthie, putting her hand in her chin with frustration.

"Eat your supper now," ordered their father strictly.

Berthie relented, but Anna Claire saw her give a piece of her roasted corn ear to Hero, a trick she had taught her little sister.

After the supper, which had ended happily with lots of laughter, the girls helped Charlotta clear the table. Jim, Joseph, and Mr. Clemmons (who had come back to see that everything was alright) talked about farming and of the barn raise they would be having.

"You should join us," offered Mr. Clemmons to Jim. "We're holding one at my house first, then we'll have many more for all the other settlers. It'll be a swell time."

Jim considered. "When is it?"

"The first one's next week," replied Mr. Clemmons. "Please join us."

"Yes, we'd all love have you," agreed Joseph. "We can't describe our gratitude to you for takin' care of those wild ones."

Jim laughed and nodded decidedly. "It sounds awful nice, but I need to get back on the road."

"Please come," Charlotta said kindly. "You have been a blessing to all of us."

"Yes, please do come," agreed Caroline properly.

"I would love to, and I thank ye all for your kindness, but I can't," he said, standing up. "But maybe I'll return and visit someday. Would that be alright by ye?"

"It would be wonderful." Charlotta looked particularly beautiful that night, her blue eyes sparkling and her skin glowing. She was so happy and relieved to have her girl back at home. "Please come back soon."

Jim offered to take Tommy back to his house as they all walked to Jim's wagon, the night air warm and soothing to the tired bodies.

"Anna Claire must have a bath immediately," said Charlotta. "This child is simply covered with filth."

"I ain't so bad!" retorted the little fire-head.

Charlotta frowned but smiled as Joseph grabbed her hand and quickly twirled her around.

"Tommy," said Caroline, turning to face the boy with gratitude. "I want to thank you again for saving my sister's life. Anna Claire gets into a lot of trouble, and it's hard to discipline her. I do hope you will come to the barn raising."

At that moment, Tommy would've done any-thing to appease that beautiful, dark-haired girl.

He nodded sheepishly as he stepped into the wagon.

"Tommy, boy, here," said Joseph, handing him $100. "Make sure you spend it well. Give some to your mother."

"You don't gotta give me money," Tommy said sheepishly.

"Please take it," said Joseph, taking the money and placing it into the boy's hand. "It's the least we could do to show our appreciation for findin' Anna Claire."

"I don't need that much," said Tommy, embar-rassed. "I ain't takin' it."

"At least take this," said Joseph, handing him $20. "Just for the trouble and all."

Tommy looked over at the man who had placed his arm on his shoulder and taken the money, his eyes going wide at how much it was. Tommy Cooper had never seen so much money in his entire life all at once!

"I was gonna go tell some of the men in town that we found them," said Joseph to Jim. "I'll take Tommy home."

"Alright, I best be off," said Jim, looking at the family a bit sadly as Tommy jumped out of his wagon.

Anna Claire rushed to embrace him. "Mr. Turner, don't go. Please!"

Jim smiled as he shook hands with Joseph and Charlotta. "I promised I'd try to come visit ye some-day, didn't I? But for now, I gotta get ready to see that niece I was tellin' ye about. And before I do that, I gotta take a bath!" He pretended to smell both of his armpits, which made all of the children laugh.

He gave Tommy and Anna Claire one last embrace and patted them on the back.

"Now go and do somethin' important!" he said. "Be the best ye can be! Maybe I'll be seein' ye all again. Thank you, sir, ma'am," he nodded to Joseph and Charlotta, who had their arms around each other.

"Please know that you are welcome here anytime," Charlotta reiterated, lacing her hand through her husband's.

Suddenly, without thinking, Anna Claire ran to the wagon where Jim stopped abruptly.

"What's the matter, li'l miss?" he asked, leaning over to look into her eyes.

"I just wanted to say thank you," she answered.

Jim smiled. "Well, yer quite welcome, Anna Claire. I hope we'll be good friends, even if I don't see ye for a long, long time."

"' Course we are," she smiled. "Bye, Mr. Turner!"

Anna Claire walked back to her family, where they all waited for her with smiles. They didn't even seem angry! She turned to Tommy and gave him a wide grin.

"Thanks for comin' all that way to find me. I'll pay you back someday."

"Aw, shut up!" cried the very embarrassed Tommy, blushing from ear to ear.

"Does that mean I can play with Tommy again?" shouted Anna Claire to her parents, afraid of the answer. She instantly breathed a sigh of relief when Charlotta laughed.

"Yes, of course you can. You must just tell us where you two are going! And no more whiskey!"

Tommy looked over at Anna Claire with a horrified expression, humiliated that she had spilled this news to her family.

"We can play again soon. Come back the day after tomorrow," demanded Anna Claire.

Everyone embraced Tommy, even Caroline and Charlotta, who had previously forbidden Anna Claire to ever see him again. Anna Claire gave him the biggest embrace, wishing he didn't have to leave.

"Anna Claire!" Helen cried. "You're *crying*!"

This was an extreme situation, for the Freiler family rarely saw the middle child shed a tear. Anna Claire caught it in her hand and stared at it as if an insect just exited her eye.

"What's the matter?" cried Charlotta, full of concern.

"I- I don't know," she answered slowly. "I didn't know I was cryin'."

"She's just relieved, I reckon," Joseph said, smiling at the little girl whose tears were now numerous.

"Let's get you a warm bath and some hot tea," suggested Charlotta.

Anna Claire nodded, rubbing the tears off her cheeks. She didn't know why she was crying. She didn't think it was from relief. Just something stirred in her heart that night; something like gratefulness and friendship all at once. They weren't necessarily tears of sadness, but more like tears of hope. So many people cared about her. Sometimes she forgot.

Tommy and Joseph began heading into town, and with that, the family walked inside, their arms around the little girl they had not known if they'd ever see again.

The night surrounded Anna Claire and pushed down her eyelids. She was so tired from hardly sleeping, and she was anxious to get to dreamland. She had stopped crying a while ago when she realized that she was embarrassed by it, and had decided never to cry again, even when she got hurt.

"Why weh you cwying?" said a voice which startled Anna Claire enough to open her eyes.

She looked beside her to see the outline of Berthie's face, her eyes shining of the moon's bright glow.

Anna Claire sat up and looked at her. "Don't you say anything more about that, Berthie Freiler! I didn't cry *that* much."

"You cwied when you weh taking a bath and when you weh dwinking yeh tea," Berthie observed, holding her head in her hands. "How come yeh sad?"

Anna Claire sighed. "I don't know. I don't why I was cryin'- I couldn't stop cryin'." She shook her head shamefully and held back the new tears that surprisingly sprang into her eyes.

"Tell me what happened," Berthie begged, her high-pitched voice pleading. "What happened when you went all the way down the cweek?"

Anna Claire shuddered at the thought. "Well, the current took me down and I was so scared. I tried to yell and yell, but nobody came. I saw a bear in the water, too! Soon everything was dark and fearsome, and I knew I was far away from home."

"What did you do?" gasped Berthie, her voice sweet and innocent, full of admiration for her big, brave sister.

"Then I swam to the shore," Anna Claire said. "I stayed in the forest that night and slept. I was so scared because I heard lots and lots of funny noises. But then Tommy found me." Anna Claire was now fully awake and telling the story with bravado. She told all about her adventure and about poor old Jim Turner, who had captured her heart with his bitter-sweet tale.

"Anna Claiwe," peeped Berthie from under the covers. "Is the dog still alive?"

"Nah," answered Anna Claire. "Jim told me he died a long time ago. But he also said that he had the best life a dog could have. I wish I was a dog like Hero. Then everyone in this family would have to be nice to me and play with me when I wanna." She sighed and glanced over at her youngest sibling, who was gazing up at her in wonder.

"I'm nice to you and I always play with you," Berthie said.

Anna Claire put her arm around her. "I know you do. Hey, Berthie?"

"What?"

"Do you ever feel like you shouldn't be stuck indoors all day?" Anna Claire said in a whisper. "Don't you ever feel like you were meant for somethin' else? Oh, forget it. I can't explain it."

Berthie turned to her. "I don't know."

"You're such a good little girl. I wish I could be a good girl 'cause maybe Mama and Caroline and Helen would like me a little better. They always say I'm a tomboy, and they always say I'm a heathenish. I don't know what a heathenish is, but I don't think I like it."

"Anna Claiwe?" asked Berthie.

"Yeah?"

"Can you tell me the stowy about Old Man Hatfield again?"

"Oh, I told you that ten times already!" sighed Anna Claire. "But I'll tell it again, only for you."

And she did tell it again, adding little bits and pieces here and there to make it more interesting. Although Anna Claire had told the story to Berthie numerous times, she felt an unbreakable connection between her and her sister that bonded with this strange and sad tale. She never tired of telling it.

"I like that stowy," sighed Berthie when it was over.

Anna Claire then had a wonderful idea. Berthie, already being tiny and fragile, had been looking so thin and frail lately that it was beginning to worry her. Their mother and father had been trying to push Berthie to eat more, but that rarely ever worked.

"Do you wanna make a deal?" asked Anna Claire.

Berthie glanced up suspiciously from under her covers. "What kinda deal?"

Anna Claire paused and thought. "How about I tell you a story every night that you eat your supper?"

Berthie groaned and kicked Anna Claire's legs with her own. "Aw, I can't do that! I'm not hungwy at suppeh time."

"I know. I'm not very hungry either," Anna Claire confessed, brushing her wild hair out of her eyes. "But I heard Mama say a while back that she was worried about you 'cause you're not eatin'. She's scared that you'll get sick. You're too skinny and pale! I'm worried, too. I don't want you to get sick."

"But I can't make myself eat!" shouted Berthie in a voice so loud that Anna Claire had to shush her with her hand.

"Now, you listen to me," Anna Claire said impatiently. "I don't care whether you eat breakfast or dinner or not. Only supper. Think how happy you'd make Mama! She's been awful unhappy. And think of all the trouble she goes through just to make our meals, and how sad she gets when you leave everything on your plate! Now, you listen here, Berthie Freiler. I like stayin' up late and tellin' you stories, but I ain't gonna do it no more if you don't promise me that you'll eat your supper. And don't try to feed it to Hero! I see you givin' away your food to the dog! I'm sorry I taught you how to do that. Now I love you lots, Berthie, and I don't want you to get sick. You're either gonna eat your supper-everything on the plate- or I ain't gonna tell you no more stories."

Berthie responded by putting her arm around her. "I'll eat if you tell me the stowies."

Anna Claire sighed with relief, although she had to admit that she was a little fond of being bossy, since she was so often being bossed around herself.

"That's smart of you, Berthie," she said, trying to sound years older. "I'm mighty proud of you. You're a good girl, but you need to eat your supper from now on. The days that you don't eat your supper or I see you givin' it to Hero, no stories!"

"Aw, alwight," consented Berthie with a sigh. "But you have to eat suppew, too!"

Anna Claire sighed. "Fine, fine, I'll eat the dang supper, if it'll make you eat it."

"Good night, Anna Claiwe!" said Berthie, kissing her on the cheek and turning over in the bed.

"I love you, Berthie," whispered Anna Claire. The two slept soundly, arms across each other's backs as they both fell into dreamland.

Chapter 6- Barn Raisin' and Spit Cheerin'

July came quickly to Gold Creek, and the ground became hot to the touch. The sun hung large and menacingly in the sky, and the Freiler family found themselves working hard to keep themselves cool. There was much work to be done on their little homestead, and everyone had to do something outdoors, as the little garden on the side was refusing to grow properly, and the animals seemed to never be full enough. The children worked long hours, tending to the chickens and the cows, which Joseph had purchased for a steep price from Mr. Miller beyond the other side of town. It was proving to be a hard summer for them.

Little Berthie was responsible for gathering the eggs and helping her mother cook and sew while Pete helped his father in the fields on their growing little farm. Helen brought water out from the creek, scrubbed and washed the clothing, set the clothing outside on the lines to dry, swept the floors and furniture, and helped her mother clean the little kitchen and the dishes. Caroline fixed shoes, made dresses, sewed Pete new trousers, made little handkerchiefs decorated with colorful flowers for if guests were to come to eat, and worked tirelessly in the little garden to which she was beginning to feel very offended by. As for Anna Claire, she helped with various projects where her parents believed she might not make such a big mess. She helped her father clean the shed and care for the animals, which was her favorite chore because it required her to be outside of the house and in the barn. She aided her sisters in scrubbing the floors and polishing the windows, as well as picking raspberries and bringing them back home to sweeten their meals. Anna Claire didn't mind the chores so much in the summer.

In the middle of the month, Anna Claire was grateful that she was allowed to go into town with her father to pick ingredients for a fresh apple pie and was even able to stop at the saloon to see Tommy, albeit briefly. Joseph had allowed her to say a quick greeting, and had the chance to meet Ms. Cooper, who he was a bit judgmental of. He later questioned her character, stating that "any woman dressed like that has no morals."

Joseph was also hard at work, continuing to mine day in and day out. When he wasn't mining in the creek, he was digging shafts into the side of hills and digging out the ore to send to the stamp mill for extra money. When getting lucky and finding a bit of gold dust at the creek with his pick and pan, he was sometimes able to purchase rare goods the family desired. He did this by carrying the gold in his buckskin poke and going into town to the drug store or the meat market, whichever store he wanted to obtain goods from. He then had the gold placed on a pocket scale in the shops as he found things to buy.

Joseph was a skilled miner. He had physical strength, but also a good sense of the earth around him. He found gold in places where erosion had interfered with the soil and, sometimes, he found flakes within the quartz. When it was time to go home, Joseph always cleaned his sluice box with his tin scraper, hoping to find a bit of gold in the cracks. He had gotten lucky on a number of occasions when he shook a sagebrush plant and saw little pieces of gold dust hitting the pan that could be a dollar's worth. If Joseph was very lucky and could gather a teaspoon of gold, this was enough for a whole month's provisions. Much of the time, however, he dug into the shallow soil until leaning over to inspect particles of sand and soil without luck.

Joseph dressed the part of a miner, too, now that he was working. Charlotta had carefully constructed him a cabbage tree hat along with an undershirt and a smock. She later made him a bright red overshirt and bought him a pair of gaiters to hold up the boots. He had obtained a neck-kerchief and cotton trousers from the general store, and made sure to have two pairs of leather boots, usually attached with bowyangs. He never left the house without his bowie knife, as he knew he could easily fall into danger, and always wore his face gauze to keep him from the dust and all of the many flies that were gathered around the creek. Mining was grueling work, but Joseph loved anticipation and adventure, and relished in the golden opportunity to live in the West.

He was a good farmer, too, and was able to juggle this along with all of the other tasks he had to do. He was attempting to grow mangels, corn, and oats, which had made their way above the dirt. Meanwhile, Charlotta and the girls were busy planting seeds of beans, peas, cabbages, and parsnips.

A little over a week after her wild journey down the creek, the Saturday began with a fresh burst of sun in Anna Claire's window, reminding her that it was the day of the Clemmons's barn raise!

The entire family was already gathered in the kitchen, eating rye mush and sipping tea.

"I was just about to wake you," Charlotta said. "I let you sleep in this morning. I'm quite pleased with how hard you've been working."

"I'm still tired from last week," Anna Claire said, referring to the moment in which she had stayed outside too long and nearly fainted from lack of water and too much heat.

"Nonsense. It's been over a week now. And you, Anna Claire, must eat a very quick breakfast if you're planning to come to the barn raising."

The words once again lifted her heart. "Oh, Mama, I ain't hungry! Can't I eat somethin' when I get there?"

Joseph, coming in from the outdoors, took Anna Claire's plate and served strawberries on bread. "Eat, my girl. Pete, come with me to hitch the horses!"

"Alright, Papa!" Pete said happily, spilling some of the strawberries all over his smock.

Anna Claire sighed and took a bite out of her bread. She was too excited to eat.

"Will there be other children there?" asked Helen eagerly. "I do hope so!"

"There should be," Joseph answered. "We've got a lot of men from around Grasshopper Diggin's and Bannack to come to Mr. Clemmons's."

"And I know Tommy said he's going!" shouted Anna Claire, dropping her bread and berries on her plate. "I like Tommy an awful lot. Not just for rescuin' me, you know. He's strange and funny."

Charlotta smiled softly, feeling no worries about Anna Claire's young friend now that he had helped to save her life.

"What dress should I wear? My yellow one or my blue church one?" Caroline asked, thoughtfully playing with her berries with her fork.

"It's a barn raise, dear," Charlotta said. "You don't need to dress fancy."

"I want to go *now*!" cried little Berthie, rubbing her eyes. "Let us go *now*!"

"Soon, dear," Charlotta promised, bending down to kiss her on her pale cheek.

"Tommy said he's walkin' over," Anna Claire reminded the family.

"That boy is a lot braver than I thought," Caroline conceded, taking another bite of her bread. "He surprised me. I suppose he isn't so bad after all."

"Well, he certainly proved *me* wrong," said Charlotta, glancing at Anna Claire suspiciously. "Anna Claire Freiler, eat that breakfast! You must have something in your stomach, or you will not be going to the barn raising."

"Oh, Mama," she sighed as she threw a fistful of berries in her mouth and took a big bite out of the bread. "See? I'm eatin'!"

Charlotta shook her head, fixing Helen's hair into two long brown braids.

"Caroline, wear the yellow dress; it isn't as fancy as the church one. Helen, your hair is getting far too long; I shall have to cut it soon. Pete! Why aren't you dressed? Go upstairs and change immediately! Berthie, you need to finish your breakfast, too. And Anna Claire, please stop talking so loudly!"

Anna Claire, who was shouting out exclamations of excitement to her siblings and Hero, fell silent. She had not been to a party in such a long time, and a barn raising was as much of a party as anything could be right now. She would get to see the Clemmons's, who had become the family's dear companions, their children Rebecca and Matthew, Tommy Cooper, and some of the other men, women, and children she knew from the mining camps. She hadn't seen some of them in months. This was going to be a great day.

After a long hour of preparing to go to the barn raise, the Freiler family finally walked to the Clemmons's cabin, which lay not far over Gold Creek. Joseph had set up big rocks to walk across the brief water gap between the two sides.

Anna Claire could not wait to see what a real barn raise would be like. She just couldn't wait to taste the home-cooked corn bread and the hot chicken soup they would be having. She was even more excited for the late-night campfire where she would persuade her father to tell one of his frightening tales and would catch fireflies in the summer air.

When the family arrived at the Clemmons's homestead, many people were already there, shaking hands and greeting each other with friendly faces. Anna Claire immediately spotted Tommy walking just beyond the field.

"Look, Tommy's here!" she cried excitedly, running out to greet him.

"Anna Claire, don't get your dress dirty!" Charlotta called after her, but Anna Claire wasn't listening.

"Tommy, you came!" she yelled, embracing her friend, nearly knocking him over with her force.

Tommy stood straight, patting his friend on the back, embarrassed to be seen hugging a *girl*. But nonetheless, he was pleased to see his friend. He was wearing a torn button-down smock over yellowish trousers that were far too short for him and came to his calves, wettened from the creek. His brown hair was wispy over his very handsome, oval-shaped face, and his blue eyes sparkled in the sun. He was very tan and a bit dirty on his hands and legs.

"Hello, Anny-Claire," Tommy said. "You look like a girl!"

Anna Claire looked down in horror. This was the first time Tommy had ever seen her in a dress this nice before. She was wearing her bright yellow dress with a bit of lace on the sleeves, and her hair, fixed by her mother, had been slightly pressed and curled. A little yellow bow was placed congenially at the side where her ear met her hair.

Embarrassed, she instinctively placed her hands across her chest. "That's not a nice thing to say, Tommy Cooper. At least I don't look like Caroline!" she motioned to her older sister, who was beside Charlotta, looking prim and proper in her own yellow dress and white hair ribbon.

Tommy's mouth dropped at the sight of Caroline. "Oh, Gee. Oh, Gee. She's so pretty."

Anna Claire rolled her eyes and took his hands, pulling them towards the house. "I've never been to a barn raise before. I wonder what it'll be like. Come say hello to everyone."

"Everyone" was talking outside in the fresh July air, drinking lemonade and laughing with their new friends.

"Hi, everyone!" cried Anna Claire loudly, tugging Tommy by the arm.

The adults smiled at her, giving her the dreaded "She's simply adorable!" face, as the other children stared.

"This is Tommy," she said, motioning to the boy. "He's from the town. He's my best friend."

The men and women came over, and one by one they greeted the children. Anna Claire had not seen some of them for what felt like so long. She felt the embraces of the men who once crowned her "the mining queen," and all of the mothers who used to make her little pies. She greeted some of their children and introduced them to Tommy. Then, she took Tommy by the hand and led him over to Mrs. Clemmons.

"This is Tommy," she said. "Remember him? He went lookin' for me when I got lost."

Mrs. Clemmons smiled, showing her crooked teeth. Although she was not considered pretty by most, her face had a special quality about it that made children fall in love with the benevolent woman.

"How do you do, Tommy?" asked Mrs. Clemmons, extending her hand. "It's wonderful to see you again, dear."

Tommy took it awkwardly, frowning as he did so.

"Are your children here?" Anna Claire asked anxiously. "Me and Tommy want to play."

Mrs. Clemmons nodded. "Go get your brother and sisters. I will introduce the lot of them to some of the other children who have settled near here."

Tommy pulled on Anna Claire's sleeve. "I don't wanna meet nobody," he whispered.

"Are ya *scared*?"

Tommy ground his foot in the dirt and wrinkled his nose. "I ain't neither. But I don't like settlin' children."

"Why not?" Anna Claire asked with a roll of her eyes. "What's the difference between settlin' children and town children? Aren't I a settlin' child?"

Tommy looked down at the ground and shrugged.

"Come on, you poke, it'll be fun," and Anna Claire pulled on his hand, dragging him to where the four siblings stood next to the little log cabin.

"Mrs. Clemmons wants you all to meet some of the other children," Charlotta said.

"Aw, Mama, do I have to?" moaned Pete.

"I think it would be good to go meet some of the other children who are new here," said Joseph. "All of you, go have a swell time!"

No one moved. Then Anna Claire said in an impatient voice, "Mrs. Clemmons is waitin'!"

Slowly, the suddenly shy Freiler children walked over to the porch where Mrs. Clemmons had gathered five children of all sorts of ages.

"Now, here are the Freiler children," Mrs. Clemmons announced.

The boy standing beside her was taller than most boys, around fifteen or so, and very nonchalant in his mannerisms.

"This here is Jacob Mast." Mrs. Clemmons was beaming from head to toe. She enjoyed introducing people. "Jacob, this is Caroline. You are both about the same age."

Jacob glanced up for the first time and, unsurprisingly, could not stop staring at Caroline.

"Helen, this is Nikola Sikorski. Nikola, this is Helen Freiler," the enthusiastic Mrs. Clemmons beamed at the little ones. "Both of you are twelve-years-old and I think you two will get a long swimmingly together."

Nikola was a pretty girl with very white skin and big, blue eyes. Nikola smiled shyly at Helen, but Helen only wrinkled her nose and looked at the ground.

Mrs. Clemmons then pushed forward a timid, small girl and presented her to Anna Claire and Tommy.

"This is Lisa Howler. She moved here just two weeks ago, all the way from Washington, D.C! Her parents live not too far away through that patch of woods yonder. I think the three of you will be very good friends."

Anna Claire looked at the girl skeptically and quickly noticed that everything about her was brown. She had mousy but shiny brown hair and a very bony, tan body. Her face was much too long for her small frame, and she had big, almost scared brown eyes. Her nose was like a mouse's- small with a rounded tip. Her lips were full and plump, and the overall effect was very pleasant. Anna Claire didn't much like girls, though, and she was very ambivalent about Lisa Howler.

"And this, little Berthie, is Samuel Howler. He's Lisa's little brother. Look how nice they both look together!" And they did.

Both children were standing side-by-side as Berthie grinned and took his little hand in her own.

"And we can't forget you boys!" Mrs. Clemmons said to Pete and another little boy. "Peter, this is Tim Johnson. Tim, this is Peter Freiler."

Pete and Tim stared, not knowing what to make of each other.

"Oh, this is all very splendid. Our little settlement will soon be a nice, big township!" and Mrs. Clemmons smiled and bid all of the children to go off and play.

Caroline and Jacob decided to sit down on the porch and talk. Helen and Nikola, although eyeing each other suspiciously at first, had become fast friends and were now playing jump rope with Rebecca Clemmons and another girl. Pete and his new friend Tim were making fun of Berthie and Samuel as they chased them around and around the log cabin. Meanwhile, Anna Claire, Tommy, and Lisa hadn't moved a single inch since Mrs. Clemmons's departure.

"My name's Tommy," Tommy said.

Lisa said nothing.

"I'm Anna Claire," said Anna Claire.

"I know," replied Lisa, looking at the grass underneath her.

"Do you like it here?" asked Tommy, tilting his head to the side.

Lisa shrugged.

"How old are you?" asked Anna Claire.

"Nine," answered Lisa.

"Me, too," said Anna Claire, growing more suspicious.

"I'm ten," said Tommy proudly.

"What's your favorite game?" asked Anna Claire.

"I don't know."

And that summed up the first five minutes of their conversation. Anna Claire had quickly decided that she didn't like this Lisa Howler, and she wished that she and Tommy could go by the creek somewhere and catch grasshoppers until it was time to eat.

"What do you both wanna do?" sighed Anna Claire. "I'm awful bored."

Lisa shrugged, and Tommy crossed his arms.

"I wish I lived in town so we wouldn't have to walk all that way just to go to the store," sulked Anna Claire as the three children sat down in the grass.

Anna Claire glanced at Lisa and made a face. Lisa was dressed in a very pretty flower-print calico dress with a frilly lace collar and a big straw hat. On her feet, she wore small, white, buckled shoes and, on her hands, rested tiny white gloves with a little pearl in the middle of them. Lisa seemed like the neatest, stingiest little girl Anna Claire had ever seen.

"I don't like frills," said Anna Claire saucily, looking at her up and down.

"Aren't you hot in those gloves?" Tommy asked.

Lisa shrugged and stared at a piece of grass that she twisted in her hand.

"Well, I'm glad I'm not a girl so I don't have to wear those hot gloves and hats and dresses," said Tommy.

"I'm a girl and *I* don't wear those silly things," Anna Claire snapped, wrinkling her little freckled nose at the girl to her side. "Only today, just today, because it's a special day, Mama said."

The children watched in silence at the people in the front yard of the house. The men had begun to gather big, heavy wooden boards and were now setting up the groundwork for the new barn. The women all looked nice in their colored dresses and their hats. The other children were running around the yard, and Caroline and Jacob were both laughing over something one of them had said. Everyone looked completely happy. Everyone except the three miserable children on the grass.

"This is boring," whined Tommy. "I knew I shouldn't have come."

"Well then, you can just leave!" cried Anna Claire, her face turning pink. "I don't wanna talk to you anymore today anyway!"

"Gee, calm down, I was only *sayin'*," and Tommy lapsed into a sulky silence.

"It's hot out here," said Lisa, itching at her gloves.

"Why don't you take those stupid gloves off if they're botherin' you so much?" hissed the moody tomboy, crossing her arms and pursing her lips.

"I can't," peeped Lisa, a bit afraid of this wild child. "Mama wouldn't like it."

"Of course your *Mama* wouldn't like it," mimicked Anna Claire, "and you're too much of a sissy to take them off anyway."

Lisa glanced at Anna Claire and pulled off her gloves one by one, tossing them into the grass. Anna Claire pretended not to notice.

"Hey, Lisa, do you have any other brothers and sisters besides Samuel?" Tommy asked kindly, feeling sorry that Anna Claire was in one of her snits.

Lisa shook her head and concentrated on the tiny piece of grass that she was twining in her hand.

"Oh, I'm the only child," Tommy said.

"Really?" Lisa looked up for the first time. "That must be nice."

"Not really. Actually, it's kinda lonely. At least when you've got-"

Anna Claire made a noise of impatience and stood up. "Tommy, do you wanna play in the creek? I don't think *miss fancy* would wanna play with us."

"You're bein' mean, Anny-Claire," and Tommy ignored her question and continued talking to Lisa.

Furious and not without envy, Anna Claire stalked off and ran up the porch steps, coming over and sitting on Caroline's lap.

"What's the matter, dear?" asked Caroline with uncharacteristic patience, as she wanted her new friend to think of her as very nice.

"Caroline, go tell Tommy to stop playin' with that other girl," mourned Anna Claire, watching as Tommy and Lisa enjoyed themselves, talking and giggling in the grass.

"Why, whatever is the problem?" said Caroline, her hand up to her mouth and her back straightening. Anna Claire noticed with annoyance how her sister's voice was even more Mama-like than usual.

"I wanna play with Tommy, but he keeps on talkin' to that Lisa girl, and she's no fun at all!" She crossed her arms indignantly.

"Don't be silly," Caroline said, giggling sheepishly. "Why don't you go on and talk to both of them?"

"I don't wanna talk to her. She thinks she's a princess. Look at what she's wearin'! I don't like her a bit."

Suddenly, Jacob spoke up, looking at Caroline the entire time. "Maybe if you join in with both of them, Lisa won't seem so dull to you."

Who did he think he was, to be telling Anna Claire what to do?

"I wasn't talkin' to *you*!" snapped Anna Claire, sticking out her tongue.

"Oh, Anna Claire!" cried Caroline in embarrassment. "Don't be spiteful! I'm sorry for my sister, Jacob. She's awful."

Angry and feeling lonely, Anna Claire walked over to Helen and Nikola.

"Can I play with you?" she asked.

"Where's Tommy and your other little friend?" asked Helen.

"She is *not* my friend!"

"Well, no, you can't play with us; we don't like babies," laughed Helen, unsympathetic to her sister's plight. Nikola laughed along, and Anna Claire felt lonelier than ever.

She looked over to where Tommy and Lisa were talking and decided that she was going to be very bad-mannered to Lisa Howler. Anna Claire was jealous because she was used to having Tommy's full attention all to herself and did not like someone else taking over Anna Claire's role as Tommy's best and only good friend.

As Anna Claire stomped over, Tommy and Lisa glanced up only for a moment and then continued giggling.

"What are ya'll laughin' about?" yelled Anna Claire.

"I was tellin' Lisa how Rocks and Ebb threw stones at the windows of the saloon all night and no one ever found out who cracked 'em," said Tommy without looking at Anna Claire. He couldn't understand what had possessed his friend to behave in such a way.

"That ain't what you was talkin' about, Tommy Cooper!" cried the indignant girl. In a fume, she fell down next to them and glared at Lisa with intense eyes.

"Anyway," continued Tommy, "I live on top of a saloon. It ain't nice like a house, but I get all the free drinks I want!"

Lisa giggled at him shyly. Anna Claire wanted to throw a rock at her head.

"Someday, I'm going to be in Rocks and Ebb's gang," said Tommy. "They won't let me in 'cause they think I'm too young but I'm gonna ask again when I turn eleven 'cause that ain't so little anymore."

Lisa laughed, dimples showing. Anna Claire pretended to throw up.

"Hey, anybody wanna have a spit contest?" But no one was paying Anna Claire any mind. She stomped her foot for emphasis. "I *say*, does anybody wanna have a spit contest!?"

Tommy looked up, and Lisa looked down at her hands.

"'Course the princess wouldn't wanna play a *real* game," snarled Anna Claire. "You'd rather go play dolls or somethin', wouldn't ya, Lisa?"

Hurt, Lisa looked up and said, "I'll play."

Tommy beamed.

"Ok, come on, Tommy, we'll stay far away as not to spit too close to her and her princess gloves," Anna Claire took his hand with a satisfied grin and narrowed her eyes at the poor little girl who had tears brimming.

Tommy pushed Anna Claire away and shouted, "You hurt her feelings, Anna Claire! Lisa, wait!"

But Lisa was running away, tears coming down her brown cheeks.

Anna Claire didn't pause. "Let her run off. Let's have a spit contest. Bet I can spit further!"

But Tommy had run away and caught up to the baffled Lisa, who quickly dried her tears.

"You're cryin'! She made you cry!"

"I'm not," Lisa insisted, wiping away another tear. "My eyes hurt. And I don't wanna play with that nasty girl. She's dreadful!"

"Anna Claire's nice most of the time," Tommy said. "I don't reckon why she's so dang nasty today. Oh well, can ya spit?"

Lisa was hesitant. "I never tried."

"Come on, give it a gird! I'll teach ya. We'll show Anna Claire real good! That'll punish her!" and without waiting for a reply, Tommy grabbed Lisa by the hand and the two ran back to where Anna Claire stood with her hands on her hips.

"The queen is going to play?" she asked, furious at the sight of Tommy holding hands with the enemy.

"Yes, she is," said Tommy decidedly, "and she's going to beat you, too!"

"I bet she's never even done a spit contest before, have you?" She narrowed her eyes down at the small figure who looked as if a breeze might blow her over.

Lisa shook her head and looked at Tommy for support.

"Well, I doubt you'll be very good at it," said Anna Claire saucily.

Tommy shook his head as if embarrassed by his friend. "You're a real croaker today, ain't ya?"

"Hey, what're you guys doin'?" asked a small male voice who had crept up behind them.

"Pete, go away," sighed Anna Claire, who was already annoyed and did not want to deal with her bothersome brother.

"No, we won't until you tell us what you're doin'!" said the little boy, poking his new friend in the ribs.

"We're having a spit contest," answered Lisa.

"Shh!" cried Anna Claire. "You weren't supposed to tell them what we're doin'!"

"We wanna play," Tim demanded, glancing at Pete mischievously.

"We wanna play, too," cried Berthie and Samuel Howler, coming up behind them.

"Fine, you can play, but don't be all pesky!" Tommy answered, despite angry looks from Anna Claire. Smiling, he looked over at Lisa.

"Look, here's how you spit. You just have to hack up everything you got in your throat and try to see how far you can send it. Watch me." He made a very unattractive sound in the back of his throat and spat a few yards away. "You try."

Lisa glanced around at everyone and tried to ignore the harsh stare of the very jealous Anna Claire, who was growing more indignant by the second.

"She's a *girl*," said Pete. "No girls can spit."

Lisa tried her best to make something rise from her throat like Tommy did, but she only made a short little sound.

"Everyone, watch me!" cried Anna Claire. "I'll show you how a real girl can spit!"

She backed up a few steps, hacked up real good, and spat, letting it fly past Tommy's head. Her saliva ended up further than anybody would have guessed from such a small girl.

Simultaneously, everyone ran to see where it landed.

Anna Claire beamed with pride. "Wait'll I tell Papa how far I spitted today!" she cried anxiously.

"Dang, Anna Claire," said Tommy, running a hand through his chocolate-brown hair. "Dang."

"Look at me!" cried Berthie, trying to spit and failing miserably.

"Alright, alright, let's do this the right way!" said Tommy. "I'll go where Anna Claire was standin' and let's see if I can beat her. Now you'll see a *real* spitter." He grinned at Lisa as he took his place beside Anna Claire. Pete grabbed a rock and placed it at the spot where they stood to mark the starting line.

"Berthie, when someone spits, put a stone there so we remember," said Anna Claire. Happily, Berthie skipped over and began to gather a few stones. Samuel ran after her to help.

Tommy pushed Anna Claire out of the way and took a deep breath. Gathering all the air he could in his mouth, he jerked his head back. The children's eyes followed as it soared like a bird in front of their heads. No one said a single word as they watched; they only stared at it with their mouths gaping.

When it finally landed, Samuel and Berthie put down a red stone at exactly the spot, and the others came running.

"My *stars*!" cried Lisa in an awed voice.

"You beat Anna Claire!" shouted Tim Johnson.

No one said anything for a few seconds. They only looked from Tommy back to each other.

"It's my turn!" shouted Pete. "Quiet, every-one!"

He took his place by the large rock and hacked. Unfortunately for Pete, it landed only about a foot away.

"Oh, well, that was my bad try, lemme try again," said Pete.

"No one can try again, that isn't fair!" declared Anna Claire. "Who wants to go next?"

"Aw, I wanted to go," moaned Pete.

"I won the spit contest!" said Tommy, sounding like an auctioneer. "Bada-bing bada-boom! Let's go! Next person, step up!"

"I wanna go!" cried Samuel.

"Me, first!" protested Berthie.

"Let Samuel go, then it's your turn, Berthie."

Tommy smiled. "How about we let Lisa have a turn. She hasn't gone yet."

"I don't think I wanna," said Lisa timidly.

Tommy took her arm and whispered, "Come on. Anna Claire thinks she's so great because she can beat everybody. Let's see you beat her. I showed you how, now it's up to you to do it."

Lisa shrugged and walked up to the rock. Her eyes were shut as if a million feet up in the air, and her hands were clamped tightly by her side. In a moment, everyone was looking at her with their mouths wide open.

"You- you beat me," said Tommy a moment later.

Running to it, the children witnessed a true miracle. Although only just about a centimeter ahead of Tommy's, it was still ahead.

"Wow!" cried Pete.

"Holy cow!" shouted Tim.

"Mother of spit!" said Tommy.

"My *stars*," said Lisa.

Before she knew it, the others were crowding around her and lifting her up. "She's the new champion!" they cried, cheering and clapping. "Hip hip hooray!"

Anna Claire stood off to the side and felt greener than ever.

"She did it!" they all shouted. "Hooray for Lisa Howler, the new spit queen!"

Lisa herself looked very flustered as she smiled with building pride. She glanced at Anna Claire and couldn't help but tilt her nose up.

Laughing and screaming, the children ran around to the front of the cabin to where the women were standing with lemonade in their hands.

"She did it!" they cried.

"Did what?" asked the women, looking very dignified and proper.

"She won the spit contest!" Pete answered.

Charlotta wanted to shrink into the ground and turn into one of the little earth worms so that she could crawl away.

"And what in heaven's name is a *spit* contest?" asked Mrs. Johnson.

"It's where you hack up spit and see how far it goes," answered Pete.

Mrs. Johnson looked reprovingly at Charlotta, and Charlotta looked reprovingly at Pete.

"How disgusting," a few of the ladies muttered, grimacing as they sipped their lemonade.

Charlotta narrowed her eyes at her son before changing the subject, commenting on the beautiful weather.

"I reckon we're all gonna be rich by the end of all this," said Mr. Elliot Reynolds, one of the men Joseph had gotten to know from the mining camps, while they all took a break. "There's lots of gold simmerin' all throughout this territory. Just a matter of time before we find it."

Joseph smiled and nodded, sweat already beading on his forehead.

"You ever regret comin' out here?" asked Mr. Matthew Sully, hitting Joseph lightly in the shoulder. "You ever wish you stayed in Minnesota?"

"No," Joseph answered sincerely. "Yeah, it's been pretty dang hard out here and things sure ain't easy, but the journey's been worth it. I think you're right, Reynolds. I think it's just a matter of time before we're all rich men. Anyhow, land is cheap and big here, and men can make their own way."

Joseph was an unfaltering optimist. He saw opportunities when other people saw nothing, and created plans where other people saw downfalls. Joseph knew how to take risks and how to convince others to take risks, too, like his wife.

"I wanna thank y'all for comin' out here and helpin' me with this barn," said Mr. Clemmons, wiping the sweat from his forehead. "I know everyone's busy and this ain't no easy feat."

"That's what friends are for!" said Mr. Chesham. "We wouldn't have you doin' all this alone."

"You helped me with my house," said Joseph. "We didn't even ask you to do it, but you did it anyway. Like hell we're not gonna be out here workin' with you!"

Mr. Clemmons smiled, his gray eyes shining and his mustache catching drops of sweat. "Well, I'm grateful to all of ya."

"How did y'all hear about the big rush?" asked Mr. Chesham, hand on his hip and eyes out towards the clouds.

"Novels," answered Mr. Clemmons honestly.

"I kept hearin' all these tales of people gettin' rich and gettin' everything that their family needed," said Joseph with a long sigh. "I kept hearin' about heroes who sacrificed everything to find gold for their families. I wanted to be one of 'em. It wasn't easy, though. Damn, I thought we'd nearly drown crossin' those lakes and streams!"

"I'm surprised there weren't more attacks," jolly and Irish James O'Reilly sighed, drinking out of his canteen, speaking of the nearby Native Americans. "They aren't happy we're here, but here we are! The big gold was found in '62, but there had been some found ten years before that when White and his prospectors found gold. They were lookin' in Pike's

Peak when they made a wrong turn and found Grass-hopper Diggin's. The White Bar. What a blessin' that mistake turned out to be! They found them deposits along Gold Creek, and then they all started filin' claims here. Some of 'em came from hard luck in California. That was back when it was Idaho Territory. They named the town Bannack, but they spelled it wrong 'cause 'Bannock' was spelled with an 'o' and not an 'a'. I reckon who messed that one up? Probably some miser over in Washington."

"You should have seen this place a couple years ago," said Mr. Sully with a snort, stopping to sip water out of his canteen. "So many people floodin' in, you couldn't believe. Always a blizzard around here. Even more than now. A lot from California and even more from the Bozeman Trail. Now we got gamblin' houses and a billiard hall. Thank Jesus for the Manheim Brewery! That place takes everyone with a dollar. Hey, I could really use a Kentucky Bourbon."

Everyone laughed and took a swig of blackstrap.

"There's more than just the people comin' here," said Mr. Sully. "There were so many murders those first couple of years, you woulda thought we were cursed. Remember Birdie Nellie? Poor girl. Her man caught her dancin' with another man and shot her dead right in the saloon."

"Remember when those three dimwits from town attacked and killed those three people two years ago?" said Mr. Tucker, referring to a few Native Americans whom were killed. "Fergus felt that this was an injustice, he did. I reckon he was right, in this case. They hadn't done no harm to no one yet. You beef a man, you beef a man. But to kill a baby! Now damn, that ain't right no matter what the circumstances."

"The Yankee Flats trials," said Mr. Sully knowingly with a snort. "They killed one of 'em, and the other one was chased off. The last one was overturned, lucky son of a gun."

"It was wild out here," agreed Mr. Tucker. "The Road Agents started their foolery, and ain't no one was safe. Sheriff Plummer was out and about tryin' to catch 'em, so we thought- turns out the keener was the leader of the Road Agents all along. All those men killed, and our own Sheriff was havin' a good laugh. His hangin' was a splurge, I'll tell ya!"

Joseph shook his head and sighed. "Sounds crazy."

"It was foolery," repeated Mr. Tucker. "Downright foolery."

"How did everyone figure out it was him?" asked Joseph, sitting down on one of the logs next to Mr. Clemmons.

"Yager," said Mr. Sully with a shake of his head. "He admitted it was Plummer. That man had it comin' to him; he was a troublesome man long before that! He ended up hangin' off the very noose he built himself."

A couple of the men chuckled darkly.

"It was wild around here," reiterated Mr. Sully. "There was more murders, robbin's, and gun fight's you ever could see."

Joseph took another sip of water. "It seems like it can still get dangerous in these parts."

A couple of the men nodded and laughed.

"Hell, the road goin' this way to Virginia City is real dangerous to travel," said Mr. Tucker, looking ahead of him. "So many goddamn kids in their twenties wantin' to find the gold, but they ain't ready to deal with what comes before the scad. Damn kids. Workin' their tails off, but they too young. Get themselves killed tryin' to travel to Virginia City."

"News from Bozeman City said that some men were murdered by some Sioux up at Fort Benton the other week," went on Mr. Sully. "Remember Reeves? In '63, some odd fellow named Reeves bought a Sioux girl, but she refused to live with him and went back to the tribe where she came from. Reeves went on over there and tried to force her to come back with him, but that ol' chief put his foot down. Reeves shot at him. The very next day, him and some fella named Moore got real slewed from Old Red-Eye and went back to that tribe with some other fella named Mitchell. They shot at a couple Sioux and poured a volley with an ounce ball and a charge of buckshot. They killed a White man along with the chief. They lamed a boy and killed a papoose. That's just one of many stories 'round here."

"It gets even worse," said Paul Clemmons. "Joseph, you remember what they said over in Yankee Flats?"

Joseph nodded, shuddering.

"They told us they found a man named Phil walkin' right into town eatin'," went on Mr. Clemmons. "Now that don't sound so strange, does it? Until you find out that Phil was eatin' a man's leg! No one knows where he got that leg. He told everyone a robber killed his friend, and he had to fend for himself to eat. Now, who knows if that's what happened or not."

The men chuckled at the morbid thought.

"My wife is so ornery," said Mr. Tucker with a grin. "She went crazy on me for forkin' out money for this. But I say it's worth it!"

"We ain't leavin' without gold!" agreed Mr. O'Reilly with a flushed face. "Then we'll take the silver. They say there's silver lodes runnin' from here all the way to Prickly Pear. I wouldn't mind some silver either, but gold's comin' first!"

Joseph nodded his head again and looked behind him over at the cabin, where he could see Caroline sitting properly with Jacob Mast, and then over at Anna Claire, who had her hands on her hips and a smirk on her face.

"I just wanna keep my family safe," said Joseph. "I don't want nothin' bad to happen to them."

"We all wanna keep our families safe," nodded Mr. Sully. "That's why we gotta watch each other and take care of each other. These are our lives, boys."

The children soon ran into the cabin to eat refreshments. Anna Claire was in a poor mood and feeling left out. She hated that Tommy was talking to another little girl besides her and wanted nothing more than to scare that girl away.

"I hate that Lisa Howler," she said aloud to herself. "She thinks she's somethin' else now, just because she won a little spit contest. Her and her fancy dress and her silly gloves! Well, I'll show her!"

And feeling particularly naughty, even for sneaky Anna Claire, she tiptoed up the porch steps, ignoring the questioning looks from Caroline and Jacob, and walked carefully into the house.

Sliding her small body easily through the crack in the door, she crept into the back of the room. She could hear the children's voices from the small kitchen, and she carefully did her best not to laugh out loud. Grabbing a handful of bright red and dark black berries, she ran outside and threw them at the side of the house to save for later.

Within the next hour, the men came back for their dinner break, and the women gathered in the house with them, everyone making new friends and getting to know each other. Anna Claire could smell the cornbread cooking on the stove and the intoxicating smell of the chicken soup. She thought of how nice the campfire would be, and she was trying to think of the most frightening tale she could tell when she saw Tommy and Lisa walk out of the house.

Anna Claire cringed and sulked. It was a terrible feeling to be left out. Anna Claire was reminded of horrible times at school, where the girls used to tease her for not being like them. She was ruthlessly mocked for her tree-climbing, doll-killing, insect-collecting ways and never felt much like anybody else. Being forgotten without even a second thought was not a feeling Anna Claire liked very much.

Slowly, she got up and followed the two new friends outside to where they were playing hide and go seek.

"I'll seek, you hide," said Tommy as he began to count.

Snickering, Anna Claire ran to where she had thrown the berries by the side of the house and turned them over in her hands, squeezing them until the juice dripped in between her fingers. She watched as Lisa hid under some shrubs. Giggling evilly, Anna Claire ran to her arch enemy and pulled her from the shrubs.

Lisa gasped, mouth open and eyes wide with surprise. Before she could say or do anything, Anna Claire squeezed the berries and threw them all over her nice dress, rubbing the juice all over the clean, snow-white petticoat.

"How's your nice new dress now, miss spit queen?" laughed Anna Claire viciously. "I think red goes *perfectly* with your dress!"

With a piercing scream, Lisa untangled herself from Anna Claire's berry-stained hands and ran away, crying and yelling across the yard.

Tommy ran to see what had happened as he watched Lisa run into the house. "What's wrong with her?"

"Shh, I did it," Anna Claire whispered proudly. "I threw the berries on her. But don't you tell anybody!"

Tommy looked at her and then at Lisa, who had run inside the house. "Gee, Anny-Claire," frowned the boy. "What're you gonna tell everyone?"

"I'll say I didn't know what happened," shrugged the little girl maliciously. "They'll think she fell. You don't think they'll find out?"

Tommy shook his head in disbelief. "Probably."

A feeling of fear began to crawl inside the pit of Anna Claire's stomach. Perhaps she should have thought this out more before delving into trouble.

"Don't tell, Tommy!" she cried, beginning to panic. "Please, don't tell! I'll do anything you want!"

"Fine, I ain't gonna say nothin'," for although Tommy was angry and felt sympathy for Lisa, he was still once and for all loyal to Anna Claire. "You better run!"

Anna Claire took off. She was going to run into the house and make it look like she had been inside the whole time, but she was able to do no such thing. She was grabbed by her mother, who caught her just on the porch.

"Oh, h-hello, Mama," stuttered the terrified girl, trying to smile innocently.

"Don't 'hello' me!" shouted Charlotta, grabbing her by the collar of her dress. "And don't you act innocent! I saw what you did to poor Lisa Howler! How could you?"

By now, most of the adults were standing by the door watching with sympathetic faces, both for Lisa and for poor Mrs. Freiler, who had to face the embarrassment of being the mother of an untamed child.

"I didn't-" tried Anna Claire, now sobbing loudly. "Mama! Stop! You're hurtin' me!"

"As well you should be!" said Charlotta, although taking her hand off of her collar as she hadn't realized how tightly she was holding on to it. "Look at those red hands! You have disgraced me again, Anna Claire! And you have ruined Lisa Howler's dress! You go right into that house and apologize!"

Anna Claire was a brave little thing, but she knew better than to go against her mother. Feeling her boastful pride squeeze out of her, she treaded slowly into the house where Lisa was crying into her mother's arms.

"I'm sorry about your dress," piped Anna Claire softly.

Lisa's mother scowled at her, and Anna Claire wanted to fly away.

Charlotta was a few steps behind, and she said to Mrs. Howler, "I cannot tell you how sorry I am. Please, accept this." She held out some of her money from her small purse that she was going to use to buy new White Pine Compound. "If you need more, I will bring it to you."

"Don't be ridiculous," barked Mrs. Howler sharply. "I won't take your money."

"But her dress is ruined!" cried Charlotta in humiliated agony.

"It cannot be helped," Mrs. Howler pat her daughter's hair as she sobbed into her arms. "Lisa has other dresses."

Everyone was staring at this disastrous scene. Anna Claire had never felt more humiliated in her entire life.

"Please, take some of it," begged the horrified Charlotta, her cheeks crimson.

"Please, Mrs. Freiler, take my word. Lisa has plenty of dresses. I am sure I can salvage this one if necessary," and Mrs. Howler smiled. Not a nice, friendly, "I understand" smile, but a prim, tight, "get out of my sight" grimace. Anna Claire felt more embarrassed for her mother than for her own self.

"Tell my husband that I'm taking Anna Claire home," said Charlotta, not able to look anyone in the face. "She is going to be severely punished."

And with that, Anna Claire was forced to leave. Lisa looked back at her as the other children whispered words of comfort to the berry-stained little girl. No one said anything to Anna Claire.

She looked back once at Tommy, who waved goodbye, looking forlorn and very sympathetic.

The walk back home was not a cheerful one. Anna Claire was nearly dragged all the way over Grasshopper Creek and then pushed inside the house, Charlotta grabbing her by the back of her dress. She was in more trouble than she had ever been, even after returning from her journey down the creek.

"Never have I been more ashamed in my entire life," said Charlotta, tears brimming in her eyes. "What possessed you to do such a thing? What on

God's earth made you throw berries on that poor little girl?"

Anna Claire just sobbed, not able to answer. Thinking back, she was no longer quite sure why she was so mean to Lisa.

"Her dress is ruined, and I am going to have to pay for it," shouted her mother. "You are to stay inside every day for a very long time, Anna Claire! You are lucky you did not get spanked in front of those people, which is what I should have done!"

Anna Claire was crying so hard that she could barely breathe. She felt humiliated and angry with herself. Most of all, she felt disappointed. She wanted so badly to taste the cornbread and the chicken soup and to catch fireflies while listening to one of her father's tales. Now her friends and family would be having a jolly time at the barn raise while Anna Claire would be stuck up in the loft, crying and feeling bored.

"I'm sorry, Mama," peeped Anna Claire when inside and a safe distance away. "I won't ever do it again."

"I can't look at you at this very moment," and Charlotta's voice broke. "Get out of my sight and do *not* leave this house! You are a *very* naughty child, Anna Claire."

Anna Claire ran up the ladder and flung herself onto her bed, weeping and hollering, feeling terrible. She went to her window and stuck her head out. She could see a campfire on the horizon, already sprouting amid the growing darkness of the hot summer night. She longed to be there with everyone having fun and running around with the children.

Why did I do that? she asked herself. *What's wrong with me? Now Lisa's dress is ruined, and everyone is angry with Mama. I want to go back and say I'm sorry! I want to eat chicken soup and tell scary stories!*

But no soup or stories came to Anna Claire that night. Instead, a sharp feeling of remorse flooded her heart and made her eyes sting with pain. It was a night that she would never forget.

Chapter 7- The Little Heroes

Unbeknownst to the children, Montana Territory was not a very safe place to live, especially in and surrounding the town of Bannack. The town had already made history the previous year when their sheriff was hung for being part of the Road Agents, the gang he claimed to want to stop, and there had already been murders of men who were robbed of their gold. Bannack had exploded with a population of people who wanted to get rich off of striking gold, and others who established businesses where they could attract consumers. This sudden influx made the once nearly barren area full of people, and not everyone got along. There was much blood around the town of Bannack, and it was becoming known in Montana Territory as a boomtown of greed, violence, and crime.

Anna Claire and her siblings did not know the level of danger there was around Gold Country, but Joseph understood. Joseph heard the rumors of the Sheriff and the Road Agents, who were responsible for the murders that happened on the roads leading to and from Bannack. He knew the darker history of the place, which was ridden with drinking, fighting, and killings if at the wrong place at the wrong time. What was even worse was that Joseph did not know whom to trust besides a few of the men he had met at the camps and befriended.

He was grateful to have met Mr. Clemmons and Mr. O'Reilly and some of the other men who had become a part of his and his family's life, and the men promised each other that they would look out for one another's families and livelihoods. Joseph, however, still heard tales of evil from men who wanted gold and would kill anyone to obtain it. He knew if he did find a good amount of gold in the creek, he would have to be very quiet about whom he told. He could not risk the safety of his wife and children, and he would do absolutely anything to protect them. Now that they had made the long journey to Montana Territory and had settled down, he knew that they would have to spend a long time there, and he also knew that this meant he must protect his family at all costs.

Joseph warned his wife of some of the dangers of being robbed, but did not tell her about all of the killings. He did not want to frighten her or make her regret coming to Gold Country more than she already had. He and Paul Clemmons made a promise to watch out for each other's houses when the other was gone as an extra precaution, and Joseph had bought multiple bolt locks for the door of the house and the barn. He saved up with the little wages he earned for the gold hunt to buy himself a rifle, which he kept above the dresser at all times. He warned all of the children about the rifle and never to go near it for any reason. He scared Anna Claire and Pete by telling them that the rifle was poisonous and could burn them to the touch. He didn't have to worry about the other three children, but Anna Claire and Pete were the adventurous children in the family, and he could not take a chance of them playing with his rifle. He also felt safer knowing the rifle could not be reached by the children without a chair and that his wife was most often with them, should they be curious to go near the weapon. He felt as though this rifle would keep his family safe and frequently mentioned it in town casually, as if to warn others that he was armed and not to come around the Freiler's house looking for trouble.

Someone who knew even more about the dangers of the town and surrounding areas was little Tommy Cooper, who had lived close by his whole entire life and had known men who had been murdered; in fact, more than just a few. Growing up, Tommy's mother had many suitors, and some of those men ended up being stabbed, shot, or robbed for their possessions. Tommy witnessed some of the robberies, but none of the actual killings, as they usually happened on the road heading from town in the direction of Virginia City. In his short ten years of life, Tommy had seen many a drunken brawl, heard the late-night sounds of his mother and other women in the upstairs rooms with men, saw gambling gone wrong and violence strike, and had even witnessed a man grabbing his mother and beating her to the ground for what he called "bein' a miserable hussy." Tommy didn't know what a "hussy" was, but he knew he must never say that word. It must have meant something very bad, and his mother had cried about it later as he helped her apply ointment to her bruised face.

Most of Tommy's young life consisted of loud noises when he was trying to sleep, being woken up by saloon fights and his mother's suitors, and sneaking whiskey from the bar when he could. His mother knew he drank sometimes because he did it in front of her before, but she must have been too tired to stop him- or maybe she just didn't care.

A few weeks passed since Anna Claire's naughty moments at the Clemmons's cabin, and Anna Claire had spent the rest of that month alone in her room- sad, tired, and helping Charlotta with all of the chores. Tommy was allowed to stop by and say hello to the family; however, Anna Claire was not permitted to spend time with him. She had done a very bad thing to cover the girl in berries at the barn raising, and she had to be punished in a way that she would remember.

Anna Claire never did forget, for that month was exhausting, long, and lonely for her. She was forced to weave with Caroline, read the Bible on Sunday nights, and help her father sharpen his mining tools. She had to scrub the floors, wash the windows, and keep up with the little garden, which desperately held on to corn, beans, carrots, and cabbages. She helped her mother with the pickling and canning, and did her usual chore of obtaining the water for drinking and bathing. Eventually, her mother began feeling sorry for her, as she was sullen and appeared anxious, and decided the punishment would come to an end. Much to Anna Claire's delight, she was once again allowed to go running in the fields and down to the creek, where she could play with her brother and sisters, and make up games.

Charlotta, becoming very fond of Tommy Cooper, had, on a beautiful and cool summer's day, allowed Tommy to take his friend to town. This was to the shock of everyone since Charlotta never let any of the children into Bannack. However, she was acquainted with more of the men who lived in the town, including Mr. Dobbins whom she had befriended while everyone was on the hunt for Anna Claire and who had helped in the search for her daughter. She felt that, so long as Anna Claire followed a strict timeline and stayed with Mr. Dobbins and Tommy, she would be alright. She did not like the idea of Anna Claire going to the saloon, but because Mr. Dobbins was often there, she knew he would take care of her.

Tommy promised to take Anna Claire to the saloon to meet Mr. Dobbins, and the two would take a walk. So, with that, Tommy walked to his friend's house and took her to town, excited that she was finally allowed to go somewhere with him.

Tommy and Anna Claire were quiet for a while. Tommy wanted to ask her about her punishment, but knew that Anna Claire would be in no mood to talk about that dark day at the barn raising. They chit-chatted about what they wanted to be someday (Anna Claire an "adventuress" and Tommy a cowboy) and walked through the fields to the dirt road where they finally approached town.

Tommy, forgetting to mention the little detail of meeting Mr. Dobbins in the saloon, walked in and introduced the two.

Mr. Dobbins was the kind, plump fellow with the short, untamed, gray beard, ruddy cheeks, bushy eyebrows, and gray hair sticking out from all directions. He was wearing a pair of overalls over a red flannel shirt that looked older than himself, and had a huge hole in the front of one of his shoes. He may have looked like a bit of a mess, but his smile was bright, wide, and very welcoming. Anna Claire liked him immediately.

"We don't need no introducin', do we, Anne-Claire?" said Mr. Dobbins with a laugh, embracing the girl.

"Oh, me and him know each other!" she said to Tommy. "We met at the mining camps once! Mr. Dobbins played in the creek with me there!"

Mr. Dobbins gave a big hearty laugh again, his voice echoing throughout the saloon. "That's right! I go to those camps sometimes to greet the newcomers. We played all day sometimes, didn't we?"

Anna Claire smiled and nodded as they walked in and sat at one of the little round tables.   Swiner's Saloon looked exactly like a place Anna Claire wanted to be. Nails were attached to the walls for the men to put their hats on, and above them were antlers covering the borders. All of the alcohol was displayed behind the ornately designed wooden counter and was being poured generously into the men's glasses. Although quieter than it was the last time she had visited, there were people in every corner, toasting drinks, laughing, and talking about their day. Everyone looked happy and cheerful in the saloon. Anna Claire only wished she were old enough to play the card games they were playing.

Tommy, on the other hand, wished that they could be somewhere else. He looked up and saw his mother wave at him from across the counter, her bright red hair hanging in long curls around her hair combs. She was wearing a revealing bright pink and white dress that showed off her voluptuous figure and very high-heeled boots. Tommy waved back, but ducked a bit further down in his seat.

"So, I take it you like it here in the back country, Anne-Claire?" asked Mr. Dobbins, grinning widely at the girl.

Anna Claire nodded as Tommy's mother put out a fresh plate of bread.

"Thank you, Tommy's ma!" she said. The woman smiled.

"We never run out of bread around here!" said his mother. "You just ask and I'll get some more, ya hear?"

Anna Claire nodded giddily and began stuffing the bread in her mouth, the heat from it hitting her tongue.

"I love Gold Country," she said. "My papa says it can be dangerous outside of town, where the roads are. I think it sounds exciting."

Mr. Dobbins waved and greeted another man who walked into the bar before saying, "You ain't heard nothin' yet, little missy. If you knew half the dangers that are out here, you'd wanna stay right close to your ma and pa!"

"What dangers?" asked Anna Claire curiously.

Mr. Dobbins sighed. "I don't want to scare ya or nothin', but it's wise that you children be aware of what can happen 'round here. Now Tommy knows."

Tommy nodded and sat up straighter in his chair as he watched his mother go into the little kitchen in the back.

"It gets scary here sometimes," the boy said, lowering his voice. "I've seen people get robbed right here in the saloon! And I've seen people hit other people in the eye and beat people until they were bloody. I've seen men come in here with rifles, and one time a man even shot at another man, but he didn't hit him, so the men had a fight right over there." He pointed to a table a couple of seats over. "That's what always happens. Some of the men were caught and taken away, but we all know that there are more murderers. One time, Mr. Grimm found a man's body right down a road across from the town. The man was dead, but no one knew who did it to him."

Anna Claire shivered and looked around.

"That's only some of it," said Mr. Dobbins, lowering his head. "Ya see, there's a band 'round these parts called the Road Agents. Now they're the ones goin' and stealin' people's money and gold. When men find gold and try to leave, they find 'em and kill 'em if they so much as protest. If a man goes about his own business, makes an honest wage, and gets lucky and finds some gold, you can be sure some other man'll try to get that gold from him when he's leavin' town or even before that, if the man can get him alone. That's why I tell your pa to try not to come into town at night. In the darkness is usually when the worst of it happens. That's when people end up dead. That's right, they're on the war path again. When I was a boy, it was quiet 'round here. There was no Bannack town, just a few cabins in the hills. Now that there's people everywhere, it's gotten dangerous.

Now look at what it's become! Look at all these people! Can't get a moment's rest in this town!" He shook his head and threw his arm down on the table. "Ever since those Road Agents started doin' their sly work, we all got to watch our backs. Even our own Sherriff Plummer was hanged up on those gallows for pretendin' to be against the Road Agents when he was one of 'em himself! Huh! Maybe even the leader. Sherriff Plummer and his deputies got themselves tied at the neck. It'd be a damn shame if they were innocent, but Plummer was a shady one either way."

Anna Claire looked at Tommy with wide eyes and then back at Mr. Dobbins. "Tell us more!" she demanded, jumping in her seat a bit.

"Oh, there's plenty to tell," went on Mr. Dobbins. "Before your family got here, they started the group of vigilantes. Now the Montana Vigilantes are tryin' to stop the killin's and robberies in these parts. At least most of them are. That's why you see all those posters 'round here tellin' everyone to watch out and be aware. It's a reminder of that night those men got roostered and grabbed the Sheriff and the deputies. The worst part is, like I said, the Agents usually come out at night and hide out on the roads, waitin' for people. Word gets out real fast here in Bannack when somebody strikes gold, and we haven't been able to catch all 'em. Some of 'em may even be in here now."

Tommy and Anna Claire looked around the room and back at each other.

"I know your ma and pa prob'ly wouldn't like me tellin' all this to you, but I think you oughta know where you live and what you need to do," Mr. Dobbins continued. "Now, Anne-Claire, I know your pa got that rifle now. That'll protect all you in that house in case there's ever any trouble all the way up there. Usually, the trouble happens here or on the other side of town, where the roads are, but it's good he has the rifle all the same. The Road Agents don't care who you are. If you got the gold they want, they're gonna do what they can to get it. They've lost before, though. People have left in the dead of night and went a different route or even bloodied up a Road Agent and got away. It happens. Just depends on the night. Oh, hey now, don't look so fearful! It *is* dangerous, but they don't come after no children. They worry 'bout the men who have the gold. And as for your father, he's got the rifle now. Still, you gotta know what's goin' on to be safe. Don't be goin' outside at night. Tommy will tell ya. And don't be wanderin' 'round town, 'specially at night. Stay with your family, come here in the daylight, and if your pa gets lucky, don't tell anyone he got gold! Or someone might overhear and start plottin' somethin'."

Anna Claire shook her head rigorously, looking at the men around the saloon and wondering which of them could be Road Agents.

"Are you a part of the Montana Vigilantes?" she asked.

Mr. Dobbins laughed. "With these old bones? I don't think so, although I do keep watch on this place when I can. Ask Tommy. Tommy, don't I keep a good eye on you?"

Tommy nodded. "You sure do, Mr. Dobbins. You come here most every day to see how I'm doin'!"

At that moment, a man dropped his glass of whiskey on the floor, the drink splashing across the floorboards, and the man stood up angrily, his face hot and red. He began to yell about winning Faro before he threw his chair across the other side of the room and stormed out of the saloon.

"Now that temper is good compared to many of what I've seen," said Mr. Dobbins.

Tommy leaned in to whisper in Anna Claire's ear. "Sometimes the men don't leave here. Sometimes they stay during the night."

"Why would they want to do that?" asked Anna Claire innocently. "Do they want to play games all night?"

Tommy frowned, his wide eyes narrowing. "They stay upstairs with my ma. I think they might play games up there because there's always so much noise. Sometimes they fight up there, though. My ma says she has to have men come upstairs because they give her money for her company."

"She must be good company," said Anna Claire, surprised.

Mr. Dobbins attempted to distract the children with a new subject, discussing the summer heat and the problems some people were having with their crops. Anna Claire could not take her eyes off of the various men coming in and out of the saloon. Some wore broad hats and big buckled boots, while others only wore their pants and no shirt at all. Some of the men looked happy and cheerful while others looked miserable and angry. There was a barber in the corner taking orders for haircuts, and there was another man selling cigars in another corner. Men were drinking, talking loudly, and flirting with Tommy's mother, who carried drinks in her hands with a wide smile on her face, her red lipstick bright amidst the crowd. Another woman came in later wearing nearly the same dress as Tommy's mother, only green, and the two conversed like old friends. The other woman took a man's hand and led him upstairs, winking at him while the man's friends cheered. Anna Claire wondered why they were all so happy.

"I told her about Old Man Hatfield," said Tommy in a hush whisper, looking around him.

Mr. Dobbins's eyes went wide for a moment, and he leaned back into his chair ever so slightly, yet Anna Claire noticed.

"Tell her, tell her!" encouraged Tommy excitedly. "Come on, Mr. Dobbins! Tell her the story! I told her already, but you told it more interesting!"

Mr. Dobbins sighed as if Tommy had asked him to disclose secret governmental information.

"Well," he said, "I'm sure you did a fine job tellin' it yourself- but I'll go through it one more time."

Anna Claire sat up in her seat, feeling much older in the company of Mr. Dobbins in the saloon with all the others.

"Like Tommy prob'ly said, there used to be a man in these parts," continued Mr. Dobbins. "A real nice man. Before the word of gold had ever reached anyone, rumor has it that he found gold in these parts. Now he couldn't have been all that rich 'cause he stayed here- that was when it was still Idaho Territory. This was many years ago, you see. His name was Mr. David Hatfield, but everyone called him Davie."

"Did you know him?" asked Anna Claire excitedly.

Mr. Dobbins nodded. "That I did. But I never heard much about him strikin' gold. You see, sometimes he'd help my pa, but I was just a boy when he married that Minnie Waters girl. Now, everyone liked Davie. He was real kind and a real good fella. That's what I heard anyway. I was too young to remember, but I know my ma and pa liked him, too. He was always helpin' everyone and makin' sure things was goin' smooth. That was long before Bannack."

"And didn't he live where Anna Claire lives now?" asked Tommy, his voice getting higher.

Mr. Dobbins laughed. "Well, not exactly. Yes, he lived somewhere up there in those parts, but I don't reckon it was in the same place. They tore it down long ago, so maybe it was for all I know. Anyway, let me get there. So, he met this sweet girl when her family rode in with their wagon here and married her. That's Minnie Waters. Two of the nicest people anyone could ever meet in these parts.

"Now they was real happy and had their own little house and their own little animals. Minnie was a good cook, so I heard. They had a little girl named Daisy. Poor little Daisy wasn't even two years old when her mother was thrown off her horse on her way to town and hit her head on a rock. Killed her right on the spot.

"You can imagine that Davie wasn't the same no more. He was a changed man. Became broodin'. Didn't wanna talk to nobody. Stayed away from everyone in that cabin of his. When he did come around, he didn't look anyone in the eye, and if anyone talked to him, he would stare right into their eyes and give the most terrifyin' look. It scared 'em right off!

"Davie raised Daisy, but he missed his wife somethin' awful. His wife meant the world to Davie. He loved his daughter, but was too protective of her, too set on keepin' her right next to him all the time that he made her downright miserable! Daisy grew up to be a lonely girl. Yeah, I have met her before. She was real nice and real pretty, but real sad. She was never allowed to leave her father's sight! When she was grown, she stayed with her father, who wouldn't let her breathe without him! He was scared, you see, that what happened to Minnie would happen to Daisy. I never talked much to Davie myself and hardly knew Daisy growin' up. She was younger than I was, anyway.

"I hate gettin' into all the details, but it's important you children know what's goin' on, just like I said. In any case, eventually Daisy fell in love. That's right! She fell in love with a man from the south and left her father to be with him.

"You can imagine how angry Davie was. That's when people started callin' him Old Man Hatfield. He was a mean, nasty old hardcase who scared off everyone who went near him! Well, the daft man Daisy ran away with left her. Never married her and left her with a baby and all. Daisy went back to make amends with her father, but Davie had died of a bad heart years before. My ma new Davie well and she told us what happened before he died. Daisy even came lookin' for him at our house with the baby. Some people say he died of a broken heart after losin' his wife and watchin' his daughter run away with that man. Either end, he was dead, and Daisy was heartbroken."

"Tell the rest!" cried Tommy after a moment of silence. "It's not over! Tell her what the men were talkin' about that day when I was listenin' by the stairs!"

Mr. Dobbins sighed and looked up at the ceiling. Quickly, he said, "I hate tellin' this part, but granted Tommy told you anyway." He looked at the children, his mouth open, and said, "Daisy was so upset she ended herself. Yes, but you must not tell this story to everyone you meet! It's a sensitive spot here in these parts. Or maybe just with me now. People liked Daisy. She was like a flower, they said- kind and beautiful. She climbed part of that mountain and jumped to her death, she did. At least that's what we think. I hate tellin' it, but it needs tellin'. Their memories can't be forgotten."

"And Darlin' is still out there," continued Tommy, his eyes wide. "She's Daisy's daughter, right, Mr. Dobbins? Tell her!"

Mr. Dobbins sighed, his thick, gray eyebrows bunched in concern. "She called the baby Darlin', but no one knows where the baby is now. No one's so much as heard that name in a long while."

By this point, Anna Claire's elbows were on the table, and her hands were holding her head.

"Tommy said Old Man Hatfield buried gold in the mountains," she said.

Mr. Dobbins nodded. "That's what they say, anyway."

"Who says?" asked Anna Claire.

Mr. Dobbins paused. "Well, it used to be my ma and our friends down the hill, but they're all dead now. You see, my pa died when I was real young, too. I guess no one but me remembers Davie, Minnie, and Daisy anymore."

Suddenly, they heard the sound of the doors being pushed and loud boots on the floor. "Hey, it's Tommy!" proclaimed a man who had just walked into the saloon, his friends joining him.

Tommy smiled wide as the men ruffled up his hair and pat him on the back.

"How's our favorite hero?" asked one of them.

Tommy had become somewhat of a town luminary since he had rescued Anna Claire and helped to bring her back home, as many men had been a part of that search party.

"Fine!" said Tommy sheepishly, although very much enjoying the attention.

"And is this the little girl you helped to rescue?"

Anna Claire winced at being called "little" and wrinkled her nose.

"This is Anny-Claire!" cried Tommy.

The men pat her on the back, too, and said very nice things to her, like how much her father loved her and how worried everyone was. Anna Claire's face of disgust softened.

"Oh, I didn't know so many people liked me!" she pronounced.

The men laughed and said goodbye, going over to the counter to get their drinks.

"Welcome to Montana Territory!" and Mr. Dobbins laughed heartily again, his hand hitting the table. "There ain't no dull day here anymore. Not with all these hotels and stores. There's nothin' like Swiner's Saloon, though, where our Tommy lives. Everyone likes to come here. Right in the center of town, and his ma is kind to everyone. Good bread, good drinks, and some real good brawls. Nothin' like Swiner's!"

Anna Claire agreed. Never had she seen a place so full of excitement and enthusiasm. There was cheering, yelling, playing, drinking, and even dancing. She could have stayed there forever, except that she was on a strict time limit from her mother and could not risk getting punished again. She wasn't sure if she could bear another day all by herself in the loft.

"Tommy, I have to go home," she said to her friend. "I'm gonna miss it here, Mr. Dobbins. I promise I'll come back!"

Mr. Dobbins stood up and shook hands with the girl. "I look forward to it. But don't come here when the sun goes down! Promise me you won't come here when the sun goes down!"

Anna Claire nodded, her sea-green eyes looking up at him.

"We'll see you later, Mr. Dobbins!" called Tommy as they left the saloon.

Anna Claire's mouth hung open as she spun around in the middle of the dirt street. "I love this town! Tommy, we gotta come back again as soon as we can!"

Some of the men and women stopped to stare at the excited little girl. She could not have been happier in that moment.

"Yeah, fine, let's go," huffed Tommy, wanting to go back to the quiet calmness of the fields.

Anna Claire took in the stores, the hotels, the blacksmith shop, the bakeries, the meat market, the stables, the grocery store, the drug store, and the billiard hall. The men looked fearless and tough, spitting tobacco in the ground and holding their pistols in their hands. There were some women, too. Some looked bright and revealing, like Tommy's mother, while others wore drab clothing and stood next to their husbands in silence. Children ran down the roads, men came out of stores holding bottles of medicine, women passed by in carriages, and everything was alive. In fact, Bannack was the liveliest place Anna Claire had ever seen. It was just booming and brimming with people, food, wagons, and music. Anna Claire could hear the sound of the fiddle playing outside another saloon, and she could smell the mixture of sweat from different people around her in the hot sun. She did not want to leave. However, they eventually crossed through town and were walking back to Anna Claire's cabin again.

"I love town," said Anna Claire again. "I've never seen so much rowdiness! Mama doesn't like when things are rowdy, but me and Pete do. I think Papa does, too, but he won't say it."

"Yeah," Tommy shrugged and walked in front of her. "I guess it's alright sometimes. It's just so dang loud. I can't never get good sleep. And there's always someone rufflin' with someone else. Everyone's always fightin' all the time. They're always shoutin' and yellin' about cards and women and money and God. I'd like to get one good night of sleep! Just one!" He kicked a rock that was in his way and crossed his arms.

Anna Claire skipped ahead, catching up with him. "But you get to be with all those men! You can hear all the stories you want and stay out as late as you want, and no one cares where you are or where you're goin'!"

"That's right," sighed Tommy. "No one cares."

He fell silent, becoming irritated with Anna Claire. She didn't realize how lucky she was to have a mother and father who loved her, who punished her, who made her go to bed and come home, and looked for her when she was lost. There was a time when Tommy had been gone two whole nights, and no one ever came looking for him except for Mr. Dobbins, who found him near Buffalo Creek far away.

Anna Claire sensed that she had said something wrong.

"I'm sorry, Tommy. I know people care about you. Your mama is real nice. I'm sure she cares about you!"

"My ma don't know when I'm here and when I'm not," Tommy shook his head sadly. "She's nice, I guess, but she don't care. I ran away two years ago, and she didn't care. When Mr. Dobbins found me by the creek and brought me home, she told him she thought I was upstairs. That was for two whole days. She don't care a lick about me, and that's the truth. One time she came into my room and started kissin' this old man and forgot I was even right there!"

Now Anna Claire was starting to understand Tommy a bit better.

"My pa didn't want me, and neither did she. I already told you. They had a fight about who was to keep me and ma lost and kept me. She liked me after a while, but that don't mean she cares about me. She don't care a lick. I don't care either," he lied, trying not to let hot tears of anger sting his eyes.

Anna Claire fell silent, watching Tommy. He had turned to the side and was facing the other direction.

"I care," she whispered, running slightly to catch up with him.

Tommy looked back at her and gave her a toothy grin. "You promise?"

"I promise, Tommy Cooper."

"And you mean you care about *me*? Not just about comin' to town and seein' the saloon?"

Anna Claire rolled her eyes. "I like town, but I would never go again if it meant I couldn't see you anymore."

Tommy brightened, his face glowing. He reached out his hand to Anna Claire's. "You really mean it?"

"I mean it, of course, or I wouldn't have said it!" Anna Claire instinctively pulled her hand back from his, as she did not like anyone touching her or getting too emotional around her.

Tommy brightened, his eyes lighting up and his big smile widening.

"Guess we'll always be friends, that means," he said.

"Well, you can't stop bein' friends with me now. We already said we'd be friends, so that means we always will."

The two skipped and chatted along, the sun hitting their skin. Tommy felt good inside, for he knew that he had a friend who cared about him. He very seldom felt cared about except by Mr. Dobbins, who was a trusted friend. He looked over at Anna Claire, her eyes sparkling, her gold hair brighter under the sun, little freckles on her nose, and her skin the color of honey. Her lips were formed into a pout without her being conscious of it, and her small, thin body had to walk a bit faster to keep up with Tommy.

"You know what I like about you?" Tommy asked.

"What?"

"You don't give up. You wanted to go down the creek, so you did. You wanted your ma and pa to let you go into town, and they did. You wanted to know about Bannack and Gold Country, so you did. You wanted me to come back to your cabin, so I did. You don't give up easily."

Anna Claire nodded. She knew one of her strengths was her fierce determination.

They eventually arrived back at the house, and Charlotta allowed Anna Claire to take Tommy to the creek.

The two young ones each sat on a rock and talked, gently feeling the coldness of the water on their already dirty toes.

"Did you get in awful big trouble after the barn raisin'?" asked Tommy, his eyes squinting in the daylight.

Anna Claire nodded. "I had to stay in the house for weeks!" She crossed her arms angrily at the terrible memory and stuck her whole foot in the water.

"I feel bad, Anny-Claire," said Tommy. "I mean, it was awful rotten what you did to that girl, but I didn't have nobody to play with all week! Every time I got even a little close to your house, your ma or your sisters would tell me that you couldn't play because you were in punishment."

The little girl sat up with a furious start as she stared at Tommy with her large eyes. "No one told me that you came! Dang, I was awful bored and lonely. Why didn't you just go play with that cry-baby Lisa? You seemed to like *her* an awful lot." She grimaced at the name and jerked her head away from her friend, frowning at the trees ahead.

Tommy watched her in stunned silence. "I liked Lisa fine."

"Well, you should've gone to her house instead! Why bother comin' around if you like Lisa better than me?"

The confused boy rattled his brain for a minute, trying to come up with a reason why his friend would think such a thing.

"What makes you say *that*?" asked Tommy, feeling a bit of anger surge within him. "I liked Lisa fine. I never said I liked her more than you. What's the matter with ya? Puttin' thoughts that don't mean nothin' into my brain."

Anna Claire sighed, looking at the leaf that she was twisting in her hands until the leaf had crumpled up completely.

"You ignored me."

"I never ignored you. I was tryin' to be nice 'cause she seemed shy and all... you're my best friend, Anna Claire."

"Anna Claire?" she looked up and narrowed her eyes. "You said my name right this time! You really think I'm your best friend?"

Now Tommy was feeling shy. "I guess so, but don't go pushin' it or rubbin' it in. If you want me to be your best friend, I will."

"You gotta promise that you'll always be my best friend."

"Alright, alright, I promise," he said begrudgingly.

"No, no, that ain't good enough! That's what Helen said a long time ago, and Helen hates me! No, we have to make a sake-er-id vow." Getting an idea, she took a sharp twig from the ground and held it to his finger. "We have to make somethin' bleed and then mix our blood on a rock. That way, our blood will always be on that rock, and rocks never die, you know. That way, neither of us can ever not be best friends."

Tommy looked doubtfully at the twig on his finger and then at her. "Stick looks awful sharp."

"' Course it does, it has to be to make your finger bleed." Anna Claire rolled her eyes.

"Here's a rock," offered Tommy, picking up a gray, bumpy one that was by his side. "This is kinda stupid. I promised I'd always be your best friend, and I don't break promises."

"Helen said the same thing, and she broke it. If we have a rock, it'll forever be stained with our blood. It'll never go away, and I read once that if you are bound in blood, you'll always be bound in spirit. Stick out your hand!"

Tommy sighed and did as he was told, flinching as she cut it. Taking the drip of ruby red, she rubbed it on the rock and instructed her friend to do the same to her.

"Hurry, before your blood dries," she commanded as he pricked her finger. She didn't flinch as she took the rock and mixed her blood with his, watching as the vitality of each other's friendship mixed together in the ruby concoction. Neither of them could tell the two drips of blood apart. It made a big smear on the charcoal gray, where it would forever be clung together.

Tommy laughed at Anna Claire and picked up the rock.

"What's so funny?" she demanded, hands on her hips.

"Nothin'; just that you have awful funny ideas. But I'm glad that you're my best friend," he said. "You're strange, though."

The little girl picked up the rock, which held the stain of their friendship, now dried and permanent. She lightly felt it with her small fingers and smiled. "Look, Tommy, it's dried. We're forever friends!"

The two then commenced swimming in the creek, leaving their rock to rest in the sagebrush. They splashed each other until they nearly drowned from laughing too hard, and then they dramatically threw each other into the air.

"Let's go underwater and I'll wave to you," suggested Tommy.

"But I won't be able to see you."

"Just open your eyes!"

"Underwater?"

"Come on," he said in amazement. "Tell me you at least can open your eyes under water!"

Anna Claire shook her head. "I never tried. I'm scared."

"There's nothin' to it," said Tommy. "Just go down real quick and open your eyes. It don't hurt at all."

Reluctantly, she sprung down and then sprang up again. "I can't!"

Tommy splashed her face. "I promise it doesn't hurt at all. It feels nice on the eyes."

"What does it feel like?"

"I don't know. Watery," answered the boy with a shrug of the shoulders. "Come on, do it, then we can talk to each other under water!"

"I... I don't think I can," said Anna Claire.

Tommy disappeared from her sight. Anna Claire watched in the water but couldn't see anything, especially not a human form.

"Tommy?" she called. "Where are you? Dang it, you better come up now!"

And she screamed in terror as her feet were pulled underneath the water, her head going under. Tommy swam up beside her and laughed at her fright.

"¡Ha ha, I scared ya!"

"Only for a minute," and she broke into a squeal and continued throwing water in Tommy's face.

"I saw your feet under water," he told her, still chuckling. "Now you try. Think of how fun it would be if we could wave and talk underwater!"

"That'd be a lot of fun," admitted Anna Claire hesitantly. She ducked into the water and rose back up in a heartbeat.

"I can't do it," she said, angry with herself. "I'm too scared."

"Aw, come on, don't be a baby," teased Tommy. "Do it! I dare you to. Or are you just a scared little baby?"

"Shut up!" Anna Claire looked at the water. It looked dark and murky, waiting for her to sink underneath of it. She looked at Tommy, who was waiting for her to go under with a smirk on his face.

"Come on, you can do it, Anna Claire! I know you can."

Anna Claire looked straight into his eyes and nodded. "Of course, I can! Go under water and I'll wave to you."

She took a deep breath, closed her eyes, and went under. In less than a second, she opened her eyes and pushed back into the air again.

"Did you see me, Tommy? I did it!" she splashed him, arms out-stretched.

"That's nothin'- you gotta wave to me, and then maybe I'll call it somethin'!"

Anna Claire, feeling more confident, engulfed herself back into the dark waters of Gold Creek and forced her eyelids apart, seeing Tommy as he waved back to her. The water was much clearer than she expected, and she could see Tommy grin and stick out his tongue from the depths of the translucent clearness.

She stuck out her tongue back and gave him a big wave, feeling prouder of herself than ever before. Together, the two swam quickly upstream, pointing at the lady ferns and marigolds and making funny faces at each other, lost in their own enchanting world that was all their own.

When the night finally blew out the sun's luminance and a dark hush filled the small forest, Anna Claire and Tommy swam ashore and dried off, neither of them wishing to return home. Sitting down, Anna Claire took the bloody rock and turned it over and over in her hands.

"Why doesn't Helen like you no more?" asked Tommy gently.

Anna Claire frowned as she traced the blood smear up and down with her finger. "Helen's not nice. When we were littler, we used to be friends. We always did everything together, like me and you do now."

"Why don't you anymore?" asked Tommy innocently.

"I don't know. We always played together and told each other all of our deepest secrets. But then she stopped talkin' to me. It was when school started-she was in the Fifth Reader, and I was only in Second. Then she started makin' new friends and she didn't like me anymore. She ignored me and made fun of me with her new friends. She forgot all about her promise," she sighed and glanced at Tommy.

He felt sad for his friend, who looked like she was on the brink of tears.

"Well, I don't care about that old sourpuss," she continued. "She can fall off a cliff or drown for all I care!" But she did care, even if it was only a little bit. "I'm sick of bein' little. She treats me like I'm just a baby, and so does Mama, and even Papa sometimes. Caroline's the worst. I just wanna grow up."

"I'm gonna be eleven this year," reminded Tommy with a grin. "Growin' up ain't that great sometimes." A silence hung in the air for a moment as Tommy stared into the water thoughtfully. "Don't you ever just wanna get away? Go somewhere and be far away from everybody?"

Anna Claire nodded and stared at the moon's glow that made it appear as if it was swimming in the water, its pale illumination the only light around them.

"I want an adventure," Anna Claire said, her eyes going wide again, "and I don't care nothin' 'bout gettin' in trouble. I'm tired of that boring cabin. I want to do somethin' *thrillin'*."

Tommy smiled excitedly, his eyes widening in anticipation. "Anna Claire, I have a great idea!"

She glanced at him, beginning to feel the familiar tingle of naughtiness gather quickly in her stomach. "What?"

"Well, you know how I told you that I'm aimin' to find that treasure?" His eyes held a mysterious longing that Anna Claire had not yet seen in them. "I think we gotta do it. I think we should go find Davie Hatfield's treasure."

Anna Claire looked at him as if he had asked her to stand on her head and sing Yankee-Doodle.

"It could be anywhere," she told him. "Besides, won't his ghost get mad?"

Tommy laughed, eagerly working a plan in his head. "Nah, Old Man Hatfield likes us, I know it. Everyone this side of Gold Country knows that he buried his treasure up in them mountains. It'll be easy to find it. I heard he buried the treasure on that big one over there." He pointed behind him, although all they could see were the trees. "All we have to do is look for cracks in the ground."

"Do you really think we'll find it?"

"I *know* we'll find it," answered the confident boy, feeling the anticipation run through his veins. "Especially if you come with me. We'd double our chances of finding it. And you know me, I'm as strong as a bison! I can do anything!"

"Do you know where it is, really?" asked Anna Claire, already grinning at this unexpected turn of events.

"I know it's the biggest one they say, and on the very top! That big one behind your house!"

"That's a lot of walkin'."

"Yeah, but just think of what will happen if we find the treasure." His eyes began to sparkle and glow. "What do you want more than anything?"

Anna Claire tilted her face in thought. "I wanna be like Tom Sawyer and run around wild."

Tommy considered. "Ah, that's a stupid wish. Name somethin' else."

"How 'bout a big boat so I could travel all over the world and not have to worry about anyone takin' care of me?"

"That's better," said Tommy. "Now think about this- each piece of gold is worth hundreds and hundreds of dollars! You'd have a boat in every country if you wanted to!"

"I'd like that," agreed Anna Claire, already imagining herself gazing up at the Egyptian pyramids.

"And you can have anything else that you want in the whole world. *Anything*," said Tommy intensely. "Think about it. You can have the biggest house in all the world and have your own carriages and servants and just about everything! Your ma and pa'd be so proud of you, and your sister will be sorry that she was mean to you, but you don't got to give her a single piece of gold!" He paused and added dreamily, "I'll have so much gold that Caroline will become sweet on me."

Anna Claire was beginning to like the sound of this exploration. "Helen would be sorry that she was mean to me. She'd see that I'm not a baby. Maybe everyone will like me a lot better if I make everybody rich. We gotta find that treasure!"

"Alright, but we got some serious plannin' to do."

They lapsed into a silence. Anna Claire was imagining her family on their hands and knees, crying out how much they adored and loved her. She thought of all the boats she would buy and of a big mansion by an azure blue sea, eating lemon drops and swinging on ropes of pearls. Tommy thought about running away to the desert and building up a store of his own where he made nothing but candy and chocolate. He'd make a house full of rubies and live all by himself with just his own musician to keep him company. He'd buy every type of rifle he saw in the mercantile, and he'd never have to worry about whether or not his ma could buy him a new pair of shoes. Soon she'd be the one begging *him* for pity money.

"I've got a plan," said Tommy, a mysterious grin spreading across his face.

The trees whispered softly to each other as the leaves rustled in peaceful agreement. The summer night air blew against the children's backs as they devised their plan.

Both of them wanted so badly to prove something. Both wanted to prove that they, as young as they were, could make a difference and help their families. Anna Claire wanted to show her family what she could really do. Tommy wanted to make his own way in the world, and he hated to depend on his inconsistent mother for anything. But, most of all, the children longed for an adventure that would alter their lives forever in Gold Country.

Chapter 8- The Plan

"Can I please let Jacob take me to town?" begged Caroline, her usual obedience simmering away.

Charlotta, who was making bread and firmly pressing on the dough, looked up and pursed her lips in thought. Caroline was consistently respectful to her parents and always followed the rules.

Charlotta sighed begrudgingly. "Alright, you can go."

Caroline practically jumped for joy. She and the Mast boy she had met at the barn raising had made quick plans to see each other, and Caroline could not wait to go into town with her new friend.

"Thank you, oh, thank you, Mama!"

Helen, who was sitting at the table with her needle and thread, rolled her eyes.

"How come Caroline gets to go into town just 'cause she's got a beau?" asked Helen. "Even Anna Claire goes, and she's just a baby!"

"I am not a baby!" cried Anna Claire indignantly, reaching up in the little cabinet for the baking pan.

It was Charlotta's turn to roll her eyes. "Helen, if someone comes to take you into town that I know, you are welcome to go. I know and trust Tommy, although he is just a boy, and I trust Mr. Dobbins to watch out for him and Anna Claire when she goes into town. Why do you not go with them? I daresay it is only in the daylight. Caroline is older than you and is going with a boy who is also older than you. We can go into town together sometime, dear."

Helen crossed her arms and kicked the leg of the chair in frustration, her face squinting with anger

"Thank you, Mama!" Caroline cried again, her big ringlets flying around her face and her cheeks red with excitement. "I'm going to go get ready!"

Charlotta, happy to have pleased her daughter, smiled to herself as she continued kneading the bread. In about an hour, young Jacob Mast showed up at the door and took Caroline away to town, the two chittering away on the wagon. Helen began asking Charlotta when the two of them would go to town together, when two knocks were heard on the door. Anna Claire knew instantly who it was.

"Hey, Tommy!" she said, letting the wooden door swing open.

"Hello, Tommy," said Charlotta cheerfully.

Tommy bowed his head shyly and nodded.

Anna Claire, her face red from raspberries she had so thoughtfully picked and eaten for herself, held a finger to his face.

"Wait, I'll be right back!"

She sped off up the ladder into the loft and grabbed some rocks from next to her bed. When she came down, she held them out to Tommy.

"Oh, these are nice!" he said, feeling the different colored rocks with his hand. "This red one is bully!"

Anna Claire smiled, and Charlotta and Helen shook their heads. She knew he would like the odd rocks she had been collecting from the creek, even if nobody else did.

The two, with her mother's permission, went back into town. Anna Claire simply could not get enough of Bannack- the crowds, the people, all the men talking about striking gold and getting rich, the pretty ladies with their short dresses and red lipstick, the children who ran through the streets chasing each other. It was a sort of heaven for a nine-year-old girl who loved nothing more than fun and adventure.

This day was no exception. The sun glared down on the children as they reached the town, and Anna Claire could feel the sweat dripping from her scalp. Both she and Tommy were thirsty, and their throats were dry. With the few dusts of gold that was given to her, she bought herself and Tommy a soda from the drug store, and the two sat on the stairs.

They were too hot to speak for several minutes. Instead, they watched.

There was a family who dressed far nicer than anyone Anna Claire had seen yet in Montana Territory- even nicer than the Howler's- walking around the porch of the hotel across the road. She watched with wide eyes as a little girl about her age turned to face her, her big yellow hat shading a small, pretty face, and her gloved hands reaching the pole to lean her yellow dress against the railing.

Anna Claire and the girl stared at each other for a moment before the little girl turned up her nose and grabbed the hand of a man presumed by the children to be her father. The woman, very tall and yellow-haired, took the girl's gloved hand and the hand of another older girl with an even bigger yellow hat. An older boy with a yellow mustache, maybe eighteen, came to stand next to them as the owner of the hotel bowed and let them inside. Then, the "yellow" family disappeared through the big mahogany doors.

Anna Claire looked over to her left and saw some young men grabbing canisters from wagons and bringing them into the drug store, their heads beaded with sweat. One man lifted the canister over to another man, who then gave it to another man, who then brought it into the store. Their wagon had big blue letters painted on a wooden sign on the bottom that said, "Harvey's Milk" and a huge painted drawing of a canister. The young men were shouting to each other when the other one reached for a new canister, and one by one, they got them inside the store.

There were some small children on a corner playing a game with some stones and stepping on and off of them, their laughter loud. There was one small girl with a plaid red dress and two small boys, both wearing overalls and neither wearing shoes. Their faces were dirty, as was their hair, hands, and clothing. Anna Claire wondered if the children lived in town or in the fields, like she did.

Next to the children was another saloon- a different one than where Tommy lived- and a few men were chewing tobacco and spitting in the dirt. They were men with long looks on their faces and eyes as sharp as knives. Two of the men wore overalls, and the other two had plaid shirts tucked into their trousers. They watched the people pass by, their hands on their hips and their arms crossed. Their mouths were moving, and Anna Claire yearned to know what they were talking about. It had to have been so interesting!

Stores and stores went down the road further than Anna Claire could see. The drug store, the blacksmith's shop, the butcher, the tonic shop, the bakery, and the meat market went on and on down the road. Wagons and people moved on by, some stopping at the stores and engaging in conversation with each other. There were the hotels, the stables, the billiard hall, and even more saloons.

Anna Claire took one last sip of soda from her bottle and looked over at Tommy.

"Let's walk," she said with a mysterious grin.

Forgetting to take the bottles, the children left them on the stairs of the saloon and walked on, struggling to hear their own thoughts amidst the noise and chaotic clamoring in the town. They passed the men with the tobacco, Anna Claire staring at them wide-eyed as they watched her with expressionless faces and hard eyes. They felt the dryness of the road underneath their feet, and Anna Claire kicked a small stone out of her way with her boot.

Passing by the blacksmith, she heard the high-pitched sound of metal on metal and watched the young man wipe sweat from his brows, stopping to take a gulp of water. Walking on, the smell of meat was so strong that Anna Claire wrinkled her nose and Tommy held his, watching as the men sold packages while other men were in the back, clearly ripping away hide and cutting off meat from the bones with knives. The butcher was laughing with a man and a woman, and they all looked happy as a package was handed from the butcher to them.

They walked by the tonics and saw little rows of medication bottles in the windows, an older woman with gray hair sticking out of her bun watching them silently by the door. Anna Claire's stomach grumbled with hunger at the sight of the little Johnny cakes and oatmeal cookies in the windows of the bakery, as well as the smell of cinnamon and molasses permeating through the air. Men and women making purchases, painted ladies holding on to drunken men, men with tobacco riding atop horses, boys and girls holding hands and laughing... these were the sights that Anna Claire loved. Everything felt so alive, so enthralling, so filled with promise. Anna Claire never wanted to leave.

"Hey, you two!" cried Mr. Dobbins, finding them sitting down on the steps of Swiner's Saloon. "Well, look at you, you both look like you've been cookin' in an oven! I must say it ain't no better in there than out here."

Anna Claire smiled, happy to see a friendly face.

"I'm freezin' for water!" begged Tommy, looking up longingly at Mr. Dobbins.

Mr. Dobbins sat down next to Tommy, offering them water from his canteen, to which they both took gratefully.

"It's so loud all the time," grumbled Tommy, wiping his wet brown hair from his forehead.

Mr. Dobbins nodded. "It does get mighty loud. It wouldn't be Bannack if it wasn't pourin' in with people!"

"I saw rich people," chimed in Anna Claire. "They were wearin' fancy dresses and hats. What are rich people doin' here in Bannack?"

Mr. Dobbins put down the water and leaned against the foundation of the saloon.
"Lots of people come here for lots of reasons. Maybe the man is investin' in somethin' here, or maybe he's tryin' to get ahold of gold, although don't sound like he needs it!"

Anna Claire thought again of the little girl in the yellow dress who had so coldly turned her nose up at her, as if she was just as common as a mouse.

"I don't want to be rich anyway," said Anna Claire, turning up her nose like the little girl had. "I would hate to wear those awful dresses and hats and gloves- it would be terrible!"

Mr. Dobbins laughed heartily. "Oh, you amuse me, little flutter-bug! You really do!"

Anna Claire looked around at the crowds of people and then back at Mr. Dobbins, her face falling. "Why do those people look so sad? And why are they wearin' that?"

Tommy and Mr. Dobbins followed where she was pointing. People were coming out of their shops and windows, and were gathering in the road. Many had gone outside to see what the commotion was all about.

Struggling, Anna Claire stood up and moved around Tommy and Mr. Dobbins, squirming her way through the little crowd, standing on her tip-toes. She tried to see above the adults, but finally she and Tommy, who had come up beside her, crouched down beside a young man and looked through a peephole between him and a girl.

"Mister, mister," cried Tommy, pulling on the sleeve of the man standing next to them.

The young man looked down and kindly smiled.

"Why's everyone out here starin' at the road?" he asked, bright eyes naïve and youthful.

The man smiled again. He explained that they were watching the Native Americans.

Mr. Dobbins had come up behind them and was watching the scene with a sad look on his face. "You see, children, the government is pushin' them off of their homeland and makin' them go into reservations. Reservations are patches of land arranged for them by the government, but they don't choose it. And they gotta stay there. It's not legal for them to move off of 'em. Not since they were murdered in the thousands all those years ago. It's a terrible thing."

Anna Claire looked on wide-eyed.

"Well, what's the difference between where they lived before and their reservations?" asked Tommy practically.

"Reservations split families up and make it illegal for them to practice any of their beliefs," said Mr. Dobbins, frowning deeply. "I don't doubt that their beliefs are strange, but to me, a person's belief is their own belief, and no one should force 'em otherwise. I think sometimes people forget that they're people, too. I tell you, it's downright terrible what this country is doin' to these poor people. Just awful."

Anna Claire watched as the small group of Native Americans began to walk down the dusty road of the town, stopping to point at stores and the man counting shells from a belt on his waist. It was as if they had no idea people were staring at them. The two women were dressed in long suede robes while the men and children barely wore anything, their almost bare bodies sweating in the heat.

"Where are they goin'?" asked Anna Claire, confused.

Mr. Dobbins shook his head shamefully. "I don't know, but I can tell you that these here folks don't deserve what they get. They should be allowed to practice any way of life that they want instead of havin' to be just like us."

"Us?" asked Anna Claire, confused.

"Us. You know, White folks."

Tommy and Anna Claire looked at each other with worried eyes and then frowned, lapsing into a silence of confusion as the family of Native Americans made their way towards them. They all looked tired but also peaceful for some reason that Anna Claire could not understand.

Anna Claire had only seen Native Americans in her picture books. Never before had she seen one in her real life. The family had skin the color brown and eyes that were soft and dark. Their hair was dark as well, and their clothes were made of animal hides. The two women and the little girl wore beads draped over their attire, while the men wore necklaces made of teeth from animals. Their ornaments were so grand!

As they walked on, heads high and proud, Anna Claire caught the eye of a little girl about her own age. The little girl wore the same brown buckskin hide and was holding the hand of a little boy, presumably her brother. Her eyes were so dark that they were almost black, and her skin reminded Anna Claire of an autumn leaf; brown but with a hint of auburn gold. Her hair was black and very long, almost touching the ground, and fell in one big silky waterfall down her back. The little girl was the most beautiful girl Anna Claire had ever seen.

Thinking she was being friendly, Anna Claire waved cheerfully to the girl. Instead of returning her amiable gesture, the girl deeply frowned and held her proud head higher in the air, making Anna Claire scrunch her eyebrows with confusion.

"You shouldn't wave at 'em," said Mr. Dobbins, his voice sharpening. "They think that you're mockin' 'em."

"I was only tryin' to be friends," said Anna Claire, feeling ashamed.

The crowd of surprised people, who were now looking about as if they had not been trying to stare at the family, split apart, and the Native Americans were able to walk on with only subtle stares and open mouths.

They seemed like citadels to Anna Claire. Although they were alone, they were also confident and brave. Although they were being forced into a new way of life filled with confinement and a culture that was not their own, they knew who they were and were proud of it. Some of the men stared at them with hard eyes and a cross look on their faces as they spat their tobacco on the ground. The other people walked around them in an embarrassed fear, a look of shame crossing their faces.

"It's dang'on merciless what this country's doin' to these here folks- people like you and me." Mr. Dobbins shook his head again as he talked about the Native Americans and hit his hand on his leg. "These folks have been in this country longer than any of our folk. They've been here a thousand years! Then us White folks come and pillage 'em, slaughter 'em, beat 'em, and make 'em leave their families and their homes. For no good reason, really. Yeah, I reckon some of them done bad things to people, but they're no different than us. Some are bad, some are good, just like us. The good ones don't deserve their own land to be stolen from them. I even heard that the government is gonna try and make them poor folks dig the silver and gold instead of doin' it themselves. These lazy White folk want these folks to help them find all the gold while the people doin' the work get nothin'."

Mr. Dobbins looked disgusted. Anna Claire suddenly felt sick and went to sit on the stairs of the saloon, watching carefully as the Native American family continued walking, finally stopping at a drug store.

"But all she wanted was to stay home," Anna Claire said aloud, thinking of the girl with the beautiful hair and feeling a sharp pain in her gut. She, of all people, knew what it was like to be forced to move from the only home one ever knew. She might see all of them again, working on the hills and the mountains, searching for riches that they could never keep. "She just wants to be home."

"It's a shame that these people ain't accepted anywhere they go by Whites," Mr. Dobbins sighed. "It's another form of slavery is what it is. Even the Chinese don't get it as bad, and they're tortured, too! It's wrong. All of it."

They fell silent for a moment, all of them feeling quite awful, when they heard a loud, squeaky voice behind them.

"Tommy, my dear!" It was his mother, coming out in her flouncy dress and her bright red hair very high upon her head, little pieces hanging down around her neck. She leaned over to kiss her son.

Tommy instinctively pulled back, recoiling from his mother's kiss, the residue of her red lips staining his cheek.

"Ma," he merely said, looking down at the scuffed wooden panels of the stairs.

"Oh, and little Anna Claire again!" she said, coming over to the child and giving her a quick kiss on the cheek.

Anna Claire, trying but failing to move her head away from the kiss, sighed and tried not to protest at being called "little," although she truly hated that word directed towards her.

"Nice to see you," she said, remembering what her mother had taught her to say when greeting someone.

Tommy's mother's pale face brightened, and her wide lips widened even more.

"It's far too hot for the kids to be out here dawdlin', Kathleen," laughed Mr. Dobbins. "Don't worry, I had them drink some water. I don't reckon it'd be good for them to go inside. It's worse in there than it is out here. So dang hot!"

"So dang hot!" Anna Claire repeated in agreement, spitting in the dirt.

Kathleen Cooper and Mr. Dobbins laughed.

"You are just simply adorable," said the woman to her, coming closer so that Anna Claire could see a bit down the top of her dress. "Do you like it?" she said, pointing to the collar of the dress. "Tell you what, honey, I'll make one for you someday when you get a little older."

Anna Claire hated the dress, but was able to keep her mouth shut.

"Ma, I was showin' Anna Claire around town," Tommy said, standing up and pulling her hand. "We gotta go because she gotta go back soon."

"Oh," said Ms. Cooper. "When will you be back, Tommy dear?"

Tommy gripped his friend's hand harder. "Tonight."

Mrs. Cooper frowned for a moment and then smiled, showing a few missing teeth. "Alright, then. It was nice seein' you, Anna Claire! Mr. Dobbins, you'll be comin' in with me now. The fellas are settin' up a new game of cards in there. Care for some Faro?"

Mr. Dobbins stood up, giving a quick nod to the children, and said, "I guess that means I better be in there!"

"Bye, Mr. Dobbins!" yelled both Tommy and Anna Claire.

They waved as Tommy pulled her hand quickly onto the road.

"Why are you pullin' on me like that?" asked Anna Claire, annoyed and confused.

"I don't want Ma askin' a bunch of questions," Tommy answered curtly as they walked back down the road the other way in which they came.

Leaving the hustle and bustle of the town, Tommy and Anna Claire walked on through the fields, a pensive look on Tommy's face.

"You look crazed!" cried Anna Claire. "Have you gone crazy, Tommy?"

Tommy rolled his eyes at his friend's silliness. "Shut it! No, I'm not crazy! I was meanin' to tell you somethin', but I don't know if you can handle it."

Anna Claire stopped in her tracks and threw her foot down, the dusty dirt making a cloud. "I can handle it! I can handle anything, Tommy Cooper, so you tell me what it is right now!"

Tommy broke out into a smile, his wide blue eyes softening. "Fine. I'll tell ya. But you gotta swear not to tell a soul, dead or alive!"

The two began walking slowly again.

"I won't tell no one!" promised Anna Claire. "I swear I won't tell no one, not dead or alive!"

Tommy brightened.

"I've been thinkin' a lot about the treasure in the mountains that Old Man Hatfield hid there."

"What about it?"

Tommy walked ahead of Anna Claire. "I was thinkin', if there really is buried treasure up there, I want to be the first to find it. I think it's time."

"You mean," started Anna Claire, "you think we can go lookin' up there right *now*?"

"Well, I was thinkin' sooner rather than later." Tommy turned his head towards her, pieces of unruly brown hair falling in his face.

Anna Claire frowned. "I've been thinking, too. I wanna come, but how do you reckon I'll be able to do that? Mama and Papa will know if I sneak out of the house. They know everything." She sighed and shrugged her shoulders, wiping the sweat from her forehead.

"That's why we gotta be smart about it," said Tommy. "I know we can think of some way to do it. I think we could find the treasure and be back by suppertime! No one would even know!"

Anna Claire looked ahead at the mountains doubtfully as they shrouded the sky in the distance.

"I do wanna find the treasure," she said seriously, her green eyes almost golden in the sun.

"Alright, but we got some serious plannin' to do."

"Those mountains are so tall. We couldn't climb to the top in one day!"

"Alright, maybe it'll take two," admitted Tommy, squinting from the sun's sharp rays. "We just have to be smart about it, like I said. I bet Mr. Dobbins would help us. Do you think your pa and ma will let you stay over town one night at the saloon?"

"The saloon!" cried the girl doubtfully. "Mama won't even let me go into town alone! She'll never let me stay over."

"Well, we gotta think of one way she'd let you. We gotta come up with somethin'. I need you to come with me. Findin' and diggin' up that treasure ain't gonna be easy, and I can't do it by myself. Don't you see?"

Anna Claire nodded, her soul filling with wonder. "Imagine if we got that treasure, Tommy. Just imagine it. Imagine what Mama would say! Mama hates bein' poor. Think what Papa would say! They wouldn't ever have to worry about a thing again. And that'll show Caroline and Helen! They'll be sorry they ever hurt my feelings and teased! They'll know that I'm the daughter who found the gold and saved us all from bein' poor!"

"Exactly." Tommy nodded. "Now you're thinkin' like a real treasure-hunter! Now, we just have to think of a good reason your ma and pa would let you stay in town. Just one night. We'll be able to climb the mountain and sleep there, and then be back by the next day! But what can we say to make them let you?"

Anna Claire considered it as they turned the little bend, walking more slowly.

"Maybe we can say that my mama needs your help 'cause she ain't been feelin' too well," thought Tommy.

"My mama doesn't think your mama is a *lady*. I heard her say so. And I also heard that she doesn't think your mama-" Anna Claire stopped herself, for she was about to make a comment about his mother not taking care of him, and she knew that would injure her friend. "She doesn't think your mama would have a lot of time to watch children."

Tommy thought and paused. It made sense.

"How about we tell them that I feel sick and you have to take care of me?"

"Then Mama will just come over herself and nurse you. She won't let me go, especially if someone is sick."

"Maybe we can say that I'm sad about somethin' and you need to stay over to make me feel better." Tommy's face lit up at the idea, but Anna Claire shook her head.

"Mama is too smart," she said. "She won't let me stay overnight for that. She'll just let me go in the day."

Stumped, the two children walked until they reached the field surrounding the Freiler's small log cabin. Turning to the creek, they ran, chasing each other and screaming with laughter until finally plopping down on the rocks by the stream of clear water.

"I wanna look for the treasure," said Anna Claire determinedly. "We gotta think of somethin'! I'm sick of bein' treated like a baby. This'll show 'em!"

"Well, I'm at sea." Tommy thought for a moment. "What if- what if you come into town in the mornin' and we go then? When they don't find you, they'll look for you for a while. When they find us, we'll tell them a couple of robbers dragged us up the mountain and left us there. And we'll have the gold by then, so your ma and pa won't get wrathy with us. We'll be too rich! They'll be so surprised about the gold that they won't punish you, Anna Claire."

"Then when I show them the gold, they'll be plum shocked, that's what they'll be! Plum shocked!"

Tommy smiled, and the two spat in their hands, giving each other a long handshake, as the creek flowed on.

"Let's go tomorrow," Tommy said enthusiastically. "Meet me at my saloon as early as you can, and we'll go. Maybe it won't take us as long as we think it will. Maybe we'll even get back at night! Either way, you won't get into trouble, I promise. We got a good story. The robbers grabbed us on the road when we was playin' and took us into the mountains, but left us when a bear came to chase them. So, then we tried to leave, but saw a little nugget of gold in a corner of a rock. That's when we knew we struck it big!"

Anna Claire's eyes shone like the gold she wanted to find. The plan sounded brilliant, too good to even be true. They would go in the day when no one would suspect anything, perhaps even find the gold early, and be back home. Or they would stay the night on the mountain and find the gold the next morning and be back to share all the gold they found. Anna Claire would be able to buy as many books as she wanted, and her mama and papa could get fancy clothes and fancy furniture and even afford electricity! Caroline would humble herself and realize that she need not boss Anna Claire around anymore, while

Helen would be jealous of her for making them all so rich. Peter could have as many cowboy hats as he wanted, and Berthie could pick out any doll from any store in town! It was the perfect plan.

When the night slowly began to blow out the sun's brightness and an evening hush filled the small clump of trees and sage bushes, Anna Claire and Tommy still sat in place, neither of them wishing to return home although it was past supper. Anna Claire took the bloody rock that they had made their friend-ship pact on and turned it over and over in her hands.

The children watched the sun, slightly fading in the blushing Montana Territory sky, hit the water, making Grasshopper Creek brighter and more golden than ever.

The two looked at each other mischievously. Their stomachs flopping with excitement, they thought how wonderful it would be in a couple of days when they finally uncovered the mysterious treasure buried by Old Man Hatfield on the hills of Gold Country.

Chapter 9- Two Weary Travelers

"Anna Claiwe!" cried Berthie very late that night when it was time to go to sleep.

The girls and Pete were up in the loft, neither of the girls asleep, and Berthie was surprised to see her sister gazing wide-eyed outside of their window next to the bed.

"Shh," hushed Anna Claire, "don't wake up Mama and Papa!"

"What aw you *doing*?" asked the littlest.

Anna Claire turned to her and sat back down on the bed.

"I'm watchin' the stars," she answered. "Berthie, look how bright they are tonight! I'll tell ya a secret if you promise not to tell."

"What?"

"You have to promise not to tell!"

"I won't tell!" cried the little girl anxiously, her eyes growing bigger. "Tell me!"

"That's what you said that time when I told you that Pete smells like a dead pig and you went and told Mama and I got in trouble."

"No, I pwomise, I won't tell," said Berthie, giggling as she moved closer to Anna Claire's side.

"Berthie, I'm leavin'. Maybe forever if I get eaten by a bear."

Berthie jumped up and gasped. "Yeh leavin'?"

"Me and Tommy are goin' to the mountains and we're gonna be diggin' for treasure. I'm gonna meet him early tomorrow, so that's why I can't go to sleep." Her eyes were big and wide, and her mouth spoke quickly. "I just have to find that treasure so we can all be rich. When me and Tommy find it, I'm gonna share it with you. Just think of it, Berthie, we'll be rich!"

"I wanna come, I wanna come!"

"Shh, you *can't* come."

"Why not?"

"'Cause it's dangerous for little girls," whispered Anna Claire as if she herself was not one, glancing furtively over at the buckskin separation in front of them. "But I do know a way you can help."

"How?"

"I need you to pretend like I'm here. In the middle of the day tomorrow, tell them you saw Tommy and I at the creek or in town, so they don't worry about me and come lookin' for me."

"But what if they find out?" said Berthie in a frightened squeal, causing Pete to stir from the other side of the bed.

Anna Claire put her finger to her lips to silence her sister. "They won't if you're a good enough secret-keeper," insisted Anna Claire. "And I *know* you are, Berthie."

That was a bold-faced lie, of course, for little Berthie had the tendency to say whatever was on her mind regardless if it was a secret or not. But Anna Claire had to convince the youngest Freiler to go along with her plan. It was the only way she and Tommy might ever reach the mountains.

"And if you keep Mama and Papa believing for even just a day, I'll tell you three stories in one night when I get back! That is, *if* I get back."

"You've got to come back!" and with a small shriek the child leapt from the bed and encircled her arms around Anna Claire's waist, burying her pale face into her sister's nightgown.

"I'll do my best," she answered slowly. "That is if I don't get kidnapped or stolen by gypsies. Anything can happen. Now let me go!"

Berthie untangled herself and crossed her arms over her chest defiantly. "I wanna come."

"You can't come on this trip, Berthie, but I promise next time."

"But I wanna come *now!*" and with a tragic frown, Berthie fell face-flat on the bed and began to cry.

"Shh, please don't cry," said Anna Claire. "You'll wake Pete up, and Pete doesn't keep secrets! Listen, I'll tell you four stories a night for a week!"

If there was anything the little child loved more than listening to her sister's stories, she didn't know what it was.

Berthie poked her head up from the covers and dried her tears with her sleeve. "Alwight," she answered slowly, still not quite satisfied. "As long as you tell me stowies evewy single night!"

"For a week," reminded Anna Claire. "Just think, Berthie, you get to be part of Old Man Hatfield's secret plan! Mama will be able to afford those China sets she's been wantin' and Papa can get himself a pair of brand-new boots! His boots are so worn now, they have holes all over them, and he works hard for all of us. And you, Berthie- you can have all the porcelain dolls and necklaces you could ever want!" Her eyes were dancing, and her lips turned up in a sincere grin of excitement. "This will be wonderful, Berthie! Let's just see what this family thinks about me when I come home with a barrel full of gold in my hands!"

"Will thew be lots and lots of tweasuwe?" asked Berthie innocently, trying hard but failing to say "treasure" correctly.

"Lots and lots."

"What kind?"

"Gold and silver, maybe even rubies and jewels! Remember what I told you to do. In the afternoon, tell them you saw me and Tommy and that we're fine. Then, when they ask again, tell them Mr. Dobbins took us to town. It should only last a day and a night. The next time you see me, we'll all be millionaires!"

"Yeah!" chimed in Berthie, eyes big and wide. "I'll have all the dolls I want!"

With a kiss on the cheek, Anna Claire laid down, heart fluttering so that it would be impossible to sleep that night.

As planned, Anna Claire bid her mother and siblings farewell that next morning, claiming she was going into town with Tommy and Mr. Dobbins. Charlotta, being in the middle of a food battle with Berthie, let her go without much of a thought.

Anna Claire could hardly wait to meet with Tommy. Excitement burned in her stomach as if a torch had been lit, and her heart thumped in her chest like a big rock. She had gathered her brown carpet bag- the same one she had taken with her months earlier when she moved from Minnesota- and packed a couple of johnny cakes that she was able to clear off from supper the night before. She hadn't brushed her hair, so it was tangled and wild, and she didn't even think to pack an extra pair of clothes.

"Look at all this good food!" Tommy bragged the moment Anna Claire sat beside him. "I took some beer from the saloon, and then I stole some candy from the drug store since we were out."

"Dang, Tommy," gasped Anna Claire in delighted shock. "Dang. That's a lot of candy!" For his entire knap sack was filled with all sorts of little sweets in all the brightest versions of colors. "You've got the perfect life. You can just take anything, and your mama don't even notice!"

A look of sadness crossed Tommy's face, but it was fleeting. "Ma had another party and she left the beer all over the tables."

"I'm thirsty, let me have some," said Anna Claire. Tommy handed her the bottle and watched with amusement as she struggled to get it open.

"Here, give it to me," and he opened the tight cap with his teeth and spit it out.

Taking a big gulp and swallowing all too quickly, Anna Claire spit the rest out with a gag. "That is still the most disgusting thing I have ever tasted! I'd rather drink castor oil."

Tommy rolled his eyes and grabbed the bottle out of her hand, only to drink it himself in less than a minute.

"What did you tell your mama?" asked Anna Claire.

Tommy shrugged. "Nothin'. She don't care, never has."

"Oh."

The two sat in a brief but uncomfortable silence. Anna Claire ended the quietness by grabbing his hand and pulling him towards the trees.

"We'll be livin' like kings! But we've got gold diggin' to do if we're gonna find Old Man Hatfield's buried treasure."

"Dang right we do," Tommy answered. Tommy carried his little shovel and pick in a worn-out burlap sack, chattering constantly until they reached beyond the town and into the field. The hills rose beyond it as they ran through the grass sprinkled with morning dew, spreading their arms and hands as far as they could.

Neither of the children had slept hardly a wink the night before, as they were both too excited thinking of the treasure hunt. They walked on and on, tirelessly and full of inspiration and the determination to keep moving forward. They ate candy, sipped beer, and both told stories of times past, embracing the strong branch of friendship which sometimes is thicker than those of the family tree.

The grass was as green as Tommy's candy-stained tongue, and the sun shone brightly on the two chums as they walked on and on for what seemed like days, although it was only a few hours. Anna Claire's mouth moved quickly and without pause, telling Tommy about her home back in Minnesota, the family she had there, and all of the fun she had at the mining camp. She talked of the children running in the mud, the parents anxiously tending to sick members of their families, and excitedly marking their stakes for their own missions. She told of long nights riding into the dark aimlessly in the wagon until arriving at the camp, and the dangers of the prairie, including the dust storm that nearly destroyed their wagon and blinded their horses. She gave Tommy a colorful and descriptive picture of the journey and the hardships of camp, such as when she cut her knee on a rock or when one of the elder members of a mining family passed away at the camp. She also spoke of the best moments of her experiences, such as making up games with the other children and hearing ghost stories from one of the other fathers.

Tommy listened, enraptured. The adventures sounded thrilling and dangerous, and he was a bit jealous that he had not been there for some of Anna Claire's dramatic moments. More so than jealousy, however, was awe. He admired the way Anna Claire talked about her life with bravery and excitement of even the most frightening moments, such as when her mother began screaming and crying halfway through the journey from homesickness and regret. Anna Claire never seemed to mind much about the emotions of others, and this was surprising in a little girl. Although she cared about other people, Anna Claire was strong, and it was obvious to her friend that she did not yield to fear or panic easily.

"You must have had to be awful brave, Anna Claire," he said to her after she talked some more about the mining camps. "You had to leave all your family and your grandma, and all your aunts and uncles and cousins to come here. Ya'll came so far to be here. We'll find that gold and no one will be disappointed, not even a little bit!"

Suddenly, Tommy crouched down as they finally came upon the entrance of the forest and pointed in the distance.

"A deer!" he cried too loudly. The deer jerked up its head and darted away through the trees, the white of its tail bouncing to and fro.

"And look, a baby eagle!" cried Anna Claire wildly.

"It's not a baby eagle," guffawed Tommy with a roll of the eyes, "It's called a sparrow."

Anna Claire stuck up her nose defiantly. "It looks like a baby eagle!"

Sparrows and deer were not the only specimens of interest to the children. There were elk, mocking birds, large sunset-colored leaves bigger than their hands, small creeks filled with geese and ducks, and some of the loveliest flowers either of them had ever seen. There were beautiful wildflowers of yellows and blues, and green goosefoot near the creeks. The sky was blue and wide, and the air was so clear and fresh. The Rocky Hills Peaks hovered in the distance of rolling valleys and sloping gulches, and the earth felt firm under their feet. Everything was so quiet when the children were not talking- almost eerily so- except for the sound of a bird or their ankles through the green grass.

The two eventually plopped down, exhausted, into clusters of chokecherries and cordgrass, each grabbing another piece of candy.

"This is your twentieth piece!" protested Tommy selfishly.

"It's less than how many *you've* had!" snapped Anna Claire. "I'm so hungry and sick of walkin'." To prove her point, she leaned back on her palms and yawned up at the cumulous clouds that covered the vast sky.

Anna Claire dipped her head back down, taking in the scent of the warm sweet grass, and whispered, "I'm tired, Tommy. Don't you think we oughta rest? And what's a better place than here where the flowers are just like pillows?"

So, the two travelers took a break from their walking to take a nap, reveling in their own dreams and desires, praying that they would get to the mountains by the next day and find that treasure the lonely old man had hidden so long ago.

"Where's Anna Claire gone to?" asked Charlotta, cracking a couple of eggs above the fire as the afternoon sun shone high in the sky.

"She went to the cweek," lied Berthie, nodding her head with innocence, "with Tommy."

"The creek?" Charlotta put both her hands on her hips and looked at Berthie curiously. "For heaven's sake, it's after noon! She has her chores to do! They will not do themselves. Can you tell her to come inside to eat?"

"She told me to tell you she wasn't hungwy," lied Berthie again, feeling the presence of guilt and also the desire to tell her sister's secret rise within her.

"The girl has to eat!" exclaimed Charlotta with annoyance.

"She's gonna eat the bewies in the fowest," Berthie smiled triumphantly, feeling clever.

"Berthie dear, please go to the creek and make sure that she's there. If she isn't, I suppose she went traipsing off to town again. I can't trust that little bug anymore."

"Yes, Mama," said Berthie with a giggle. She flew through the door and out into the trees, not even reaching the water, coming back with a proud grin on her face.

"She's not theh!" she cried.

"Oh my, what shall I do with her?" frowned Charlotta as she set food on the table.

"You should punish her when she gets back, Mama," said Helen, mixing the rye mush on the table with a mischievous smile. "She didn't ask if she could go to town."

"She did ask me, I believe," sighed Charlotta. "I told her she could go. She should know that she must be back for chores, and it is very naughty of her to stay in town. I must tell everything to that girl!"

Berthie began giggling mysteriously, catching the attention of her brother.

"What's so rich?" asked Pete.

"Nothin'" replied the five-year-old, covering her mouth with her hands, putting a bony chin in an even bonier hand.

"It is time to eat," said Charlotta suddenly, hurriedly putting the plates down on the table and helping Caroline set it.

She thought of her middle child and sighed. Why didn't Anna Claire come back for her chores when she knew she had to do them? It was the summertime, and the cows were not going to milk themselves, and the flowers were not going to wait nicely to drink while she went off into town, doing whatever she pleased. "I just cannot understand that girl sometimes."

When Anna Claire and Tommy woke up from their nap, the sunlight was already dimming. The world looked like a giant peach- the orange-yellowness of the sky, the grass lightly touching it like a stem- and it brought a lonely kind of ache to Anna Claire's heart.

"I wonder how Berthie's lyin' is comin' along," thought Anna Claire out loud. "Berthie's not very good at keepin' secrets."

"I don't know, but if it's anything like the last time, your pa'll have a search party out lookin' for you soon," Tommy replied, stretching his arms behind his back. "We better get goin' so we can get to that gold. We shouldn't have slept so long. We won't be back by tonight, that's for sure. Keep your eyes skinned for wolves or bears or snakes."

"What if everyone's already lookin' for me? I'll be in so much trouble!"

"Well, that's why we need to go."

They gathered their strength, which wasn't very much considering they had eaten nearly nothing but candy and drank nothing but beer for a whole day, and continued to walk up and over the many small hills that wrapped around the center of the bigger mountains.

The beautiful bluffs that surrounded them seemed to be bigger than ever before as the large Montana Territory sky colored beyond them everywhere they could see. The long red cedar trees standing firm and upright for miles, the bright greenness of the grass below, the towering gray rocks around them, the sounds of creaking branches and birds of the forests- they all gave the children feelings of gladness and even melancholy, for everything was almost too beautiful to soak in.

Spruces and alders lined the hills in such orderly fashion that they almost appeared like tall, green soldiers. There were columbine and daisies, poppies and primroses, and heart-stopping willow bushes. The lovely hyssops stood erected in the groves as the mahogany trees curled like snakes on the sides of the uneven cliffs.

As they began the upward journey, they briefly passed through a small meadow before the ground started to become rocky and jagged. They walked along through the wildrye, their eyes widening at the colors around them and their souls feeling invigorated. As they ascended further, their noses inhaled the smells of pine and artemisia, while their ears listened to the muskrats running through the ponderosas and the voles wiggling their way through the grass. For the children, it was very magical.

To most adults, it would seem to be a very silly idea to walk across mountains in search of a clue that could lead them to a "buried treasure" which they knew nothing about. But for the children, instead of thinking about how or why on Earth there would be a treasure buried deep in the mountains, they only knew that there *could* be a treasure. For the children, just that mere idea was enough to keep them inspired. While adults need clarification, children only need hope- hope that something better lie just beyond their very noses.

Although both Tommy and Anna Claire were tired, very hungry, and feeling sick from the beer and candy, they were undauntedly excited by the mystery of what could happen to the both of them, and they enjoyed the company of their best friend by their side. Tommy and Anna Claire were very different in some ways, and they argued half the time they walked together. However, they were not so very different altogether, and it was their spirit that kept them forging through unknown forests, huge rocks, and finally to the sight of an enormous mountainous peak rising above them that seemed to touch the heavens with its superior height.

"It looks awful big," said Anna Claire with wide eyes as she gazed up at the fortress, which rose far above her head.

"I bet you're scared," Tommy teased with that familiar twinkle in his eye. "You're scared to walk up that little hill, ain't ya?"

"I ain't!" spat Anna Claire with disgust. "I'll show you just how scared I am, you silly, stupid boy! I ain't scared of nothin'!" and throwing her legs wildly out beneath her, she began to hike up the little wooded hills of the mountain with very large, hard steps.

The mountain was becoming much steeper now, and they no longer felt like they were simply walking up through a forest. Some branches must be held on to, and the chances of falling on the stones beneath them grew.

Tommy sighed, shook his head, and followed suit, eager to keep up with the fast pace of his comrade.

"Can't you slow down?" he asked a few minutes later, panting for breath. "You're goin' too fast."

Anna Claire looked behind her and grinned. "Too fast for little Tommy to keep up?"

"No, no, not me," said Tommy, wiping the sweat off his forehead. "I'm just worried about you, of course."

"Of course," Anna Claire smirked silently as she reached up to grab onto a rock with her hand and took it back with a scream.

"What?" asked a baffled Tommy. "What's wrong?"

"Something sharp is there!" She stopped walking and nursed her hand, a trickle of blood forming a small bubble on her finger.

Tommy grabbed her arm instinctively and pulled her over towards him, taking her hand and looking at the cut.

"It'll be alright," he said. "It's just a little cut. Besides, I thought nothin' scared you."

Anna Claire had no answer except to stick out her tongue, which was a bright blue from the candy that had long been eaten now.

The children continued their ascent up the mountain with many laughs, for Anna Claire seemed to think everything was funny suddenly. Whenever she or Tommy nearly slipped off of a rock, Anna Claire would burst into giggles that couldn't be quieted by Tommy's repeated smack on her shoulder. Whenever she or Tommy fell onto the bare granite and looked behind them at the bottom of the mountain, which was growing smaller and smaller, Anna Claire laughed, much to the annoyance of Tommy, who couldn't understand what was so funny.

"Gee, why do you keep on laughin'?"

"You look silly when you trip!"

"You're a real big bug, ain't ya?" Tommy shook his head. "I saw you trip too, and you don't look so graceful either!"

What sent Anna Claire into soberness was the next part of their climb when they reached a landing. The sky was already darkening, and she could even see the moon watching from behind her. Even though she and Tommy had climbed a good portion of the mountain during the day, they had the sun to guide them along. Now, there was nothing that could help them except the occasional firebug that darted in and out of the little coal-black caves.

"Is there another way?" peeped Anna Claire, trying to remain brave.

"No," answered the boy. "This is it. We've got to do it, Anna Claire. The rest of the mountain's right up there. We ain't too far. Come on, we've come this far, we can't turn around now. What would Old Man Hatfield's ghost say if he knew we turned around in the middle of our great adventure?"

Anna Claire looked behind her and shuddered. She could barely see the bottom of the mountain where they had started their climb. Everything was dark and uncertain now and getting steeper. Instead of solid ground surrounding them, the mountain was becoming sharper, and there were more peaks to climb, increasing the risk of falling a further distance on the widening granite surface.

"What if everyone's out lookin' for me?" she asked in a whisper. "Mama's never gonna let me out of the house again. And I know I won't be allowed to play with you anymore if they found out what we did."

"They won't." Tommy was unsure and growing wearier, but he wanted to appear brave. After all, he was the oldest. "If they don't have a whole team out lookin' for you now, that means your sister must've done alright with her lyin'. Remember, when they do figure it out and find us, we got kidnapped by the robbers who made us climb the mountain and ran away because of a bear."

"I'll be brave," said Anna Claire, but her voice was trembling. "Hey, Tommy?"

"What now?"

"I think I'm afraid."

Giving each other ominous looks, the two began to climb up a bit higher, reaching out to grab the little ledges, their hearts beating rapidly in their chests. Everything was dark, and neither one of them could hardly see. After a minute, they reached a wider ledge and placed their hands in front of their bodies so they wouldn't hit a tree. Tommy was feeling stronger as he walked. He felt more like a man than a little boy now because he had a little girl to protect. A little girl who was wild, self-assured, but so naïve. He had to find this treasure; if not for his sake, for hers. She looked up to him, even though she wouldn't admit it. He had to prove to her that he was as brave as she thought he was. And this treasure was the only way to do it.

"Tommy, where are you!?" cried Anna Claire, her knees locking and unlocking. "Tommy, help, I can't see you!"

"I'm right here!" His voice was beginning to sound distant.

"I can't see anything," she repeated. "It's dark. I'm afraid!"

Tommy bit his lip after almost saying a sarcastic comment about her false confidence. Instead, he listened carefully to her footsteps and followed them until he accidentally walked right into her.

"I thought you were a tree," he said apologetically.

"What tree in this forest is *this* short?"

"Sorry," he mumbled.

The two walked on side by side, hands outstretched and eyes squinting to make out any little light they could scrape. They walked and they walked, and they walked. They walked until their arms and legs were bleeding from the thorns that they couldn't see. They walked until they had to constantly reach up and brush the bugs out of each other's hair. They walked until Anna Claire tripped and fell flat on her face in a thorn bush.

Wiping tears from her eyes, she sat up in frustration and pulled Tommy's hand until he was sitting down next to her.

"Who knows if we're even goin' the right way," she said into the darkness. "We could be goin' around and around in circles. We gotta wait until mornin' comes. It's too dark. I can't see nothin' out here!"

"You're right, I reckon," conceded Tommy with a sigh. "But I don't wanna sleep where all these bugs are."

"Me neither," said Anna Claire.

It was silent for a few moments. They listened to the sound of the beetles scraping against the leaves and the *hoot-hoot* of the owls high up in the trees. They tried to ignore the sounds of the wind rustling through the leaves and the distant cry of a presumed wolf, hungry on the prowl.

"Are you cryin'?" whispered Tommy softly.

"No," sobbed Anna Claire in a muffled voice. "I don't cry!"

"It's gonna be alright," he promised. "I swear. Nothin's gonna happen to you while I'm sittin' here. No, Sir!" and to make his point, he crossed his arms and set his eyebrows down in anger. "Tomorrow we'll find the gold. I know we will."

"But Mama and Papa will be so angry!" She had her hands in her face now. "And I can already hear Caroline and Helen laughin' at me and pointin' their fingers and sayin', *'Look who tried to run away from home again? You should punish her!'* What am I gonna do, Tommy?"

He sighed and put his arm protectively around his panicked friend. "When we find the gold, your ma and pa will be so happy they'll forget all about how you ran away, and they'll be worried about how to spend their gold. It'll be a ton; it'll make up for everything. I promise."

He sounded so sure of himself, and he was older and wiser than Anna Claire. Wiping the tears off of her cheeks and lifting her head out of her lap, in that order, she smiled up at the darkness and rested her head against a tree, feeling protected. No matter what happened that night, they would be all right. And by this time next night, they would both be millionaires.

Charlotta was growing nervous now. The sun had set, and Anna Claire was still presumed to be in town. Joseph had come back from his day panning gold, and Charlotta admitted to him that she had let her go into town without giving her a time to get back.

"Char, you know she will take advantage of anything you give her, including time," he said, brushing his wife's hair back from her face. "That little girl has gone off to town with no time to come back home. Now she'll be back when it pleases her. I'm sorry, my dear, but she has a reason to be in town."

Charlotta frowned, shaking her head, her blue eyes narrowing. "But Joseph, she has chores to do, and she knows that. Now the sun is setting, and she's not even home! She knows she cannot miss a day of chores."

"This is true," nodded her husband. "That is what we will say when she comes home. Oh, don't be afraid; you know our daughter well! She will be in town until the absolute second she has to leave. She'll be here for supper."

But Anna Claire was not there for supper, nor was she there for cleaning up or for bedtime.

"That's it," said Joseph finally, putting his newspaper down and standing up from his chair in the room as Caroline and Helen came to stand beside him.

"She is going to be in so much trouble," said Helen with a small grin.

"Don't smile, Helen," Caroline admonished. "That is unkind. Papa, what will you do?   Joseph walked to the door, scuffing the hair on Pete's head. "Well, I'm going into that town and bringin' her back. I would have hoped she'd have the good common sense to come back of her own accord at least by supper, seein' that she's always runnin' off and gettin' in trouble, but it seems she made other choices. Oh, Char, don't be worried." He turned to his wife, whose face was beginning to pale.

"Be careful, Papa," said Caroline, her eyes concerned. "It's getting dark!"

"Yes, be careful of the robbers," nodded Charlotta.

"They don't come 'round this side," said Joseph, although a bit doubtfully. "We're too close to town and not near enough to the roads. Anyway, nothin' to fret about. She's at Swiner's Saloon with Tommy. The two of them are probably sayin' goodbye now, and I'll meet Anna Claire on my way there."

But Joseph was wrong. When he entered the saloon, he was greeted by the men, some of them his friends, who asked him to play cards. He stated that he could not be obliged, as he had to take his little girl back home from town. That is when they, including Kathleen Cooper and Mr. Dobbins, explained that there was no little girl in the saloon- in fact, there was no little boy either. When Kathleen went to check on her son in his room, his bed was empty, and there were pieces of candy all over the floor.

Mr. Freiler, becoming much alarmed with the realization that Anna Claire had, once again, ran away, gathered several of the men from the saloon and began another search for the girl, the third one since moving to Montana Territory.

Joseph was more than concerned this time. He was afraid, yes, especially since it was dark and Anna Claire was nowhere in sight, but this time he was also angry. The anger bubbled up in his chest and spread throughout his limbs. She had no right to go off again! How dare she, after all the family had been through and all of the talks they had with her? How could she run away after all of those times getting into trouble and finally earning some trust? She had spoiled it now, and for good.

Joseph hastily and rightfully decided that this would be the last time this would happen. He would see to it that Anna Claire would never be able to go anywhere as long as her childhood would last. She would never be allowed to go off to town, even with a friend, or be allowed to play alone in the fields. She would never be allowed to go with anyone anywhere again unless Joseph and Charlotta themselves were with her. No more freedom in Gold Country, not anymore. It was far too dangerous.

After he went home with the men to tell his poor wife, who fell apart in his arms immediately at the news, a pang of sadness and fear combined hit him in his gut. He could not believe he had allowed Anna Claire, after she had run away more than once and was but nine years old, to continuously leave home and go play in the town.

What had he been thinking?

Tears stung his eyes as the search party hit the creek first, thinking to himself that if anything happened to his dear little daughter, it would be his fault.

Berthie was rarely sneaky, and her little lie was becoming more difficult to bear upon her small shoulders. Her father was out looking for Anna Claire, and her mother was wiping tears away with her fingers, talking aloud places her daughter might be. The night had yielded to the sun again, and another day had dawned. No one had slept, not even Pete who was kept awake by Caroline's crying and his mother's laments of prayers. Berthie needed to tell. She *had* to tell. This had all gone too far.

"Mama, Mama!" cried Berthie that morning, running to her mother's side in the kitchen. Her eyes filled with tears, and her mouth trembled as she spoke. "I-I-don't feel well."

"Berthie, what on earth is the matter?" cried Charlotta, kneeling down with the small girl. When Berthie only shook her head, her face turning bright red, the frightened mother shook the girl's shoulders.

"I- I can't bweathe!" cried Berthie, changing her mind about telling, showing a very fine demonstration by putting both of her small hands to her throat and whispering hoarsely.

More terrified than she could ever remember being, Mrs. Freiler dropped the berries and bread she was trying to prepare for the children and grabbed Berthie by the waist, slinging her over her shoulder. Running as quickly as she could, she threw Berthie down upon her and Joseph's bed behind the buckskin curtains.

"Caroline!" she called in a voice so unlike her that Caroline hardly recognized it.

Caroline came barreling down the ladder, her hair in a fluffy dark puff around her pale face, looking startled and anxious.

"Mama, what is it?" she cried, looking from Berthie to Charlotta and back to Berthie again. The little child was lying down and breathing too hard.

"Helen!" cried Mrs. Freiler, her face ashen. "Helen!"

Helen, who was reading a dime novel in the loft, rushed downstairs to see what all the commotion was about. Looking rumpled and tired, her long brown hair everywhere but where it was supposed to be, she rushed to her mother's side.

"Mama, what- what's happened to Berthie?"

"Berthie, are you alright? Tell us what the matter is!" said Charlotta.

Berthie looked up and stifled a laugh.

"Helen, go get my bottle of eucalyptus and some pillows." Her eyes never left Berthie's calm face. "It's alright darling, everything will be fine."

Berthie shook her head suddenly. She couldn't do it anymore. Little Berthie knew she had made a big promise to her sister to keep her secret, but she couldn't do it any longer.

Charlotta breathed deeply and burst into tears, sobs tightening her throat. "This is all too much," she muttered, pulling on her nightgown. "Too much."

"I know whey Anna Claiwe is," said Berthie in an almost whisper.

"Where's Anna Claire?" asked Pete, appearing suddenly from the ladder and yawning.

"Mama, Anna Claiwe went to Tommy's house in town." Berthie felt herself tremble as her voice shook. "But then she said she was going to go find the gold."

"Wha-what?" her mother was stunned, turning around to look at the other children who were equally as surprised. "Gold? What gold? When did she tell you this? Where did she go?"

Berthie shrugged. "When we went to sleep. Not last night, the other night. She said that she was going with Tommy up in the mountain to find Old Man Hatfield's gold! She said I could have all the dolls that I wanted once we get which one!"

Charlotta nearly fainted. She leaned against her heels and stood up shakily. "The mountain- the hills. She went to go find treasure in the hills. She and Tommy are climbing the mountains." She turned to Caroline. "Oh, but which hill? I must find your father. Tend to the children while I'm gone. And Berthie- that was naughty of you to lie!" Caroline nodded dutifully, beckoning Pete and Berthie to follow her into their little kitchen alcove. Charlotta, without getting changed, ran through the fields in her nightgown, her long dark hair flying uncharacteristically and wildly about her head. She didn't have time to get dressed or do her hair up or hardly think. She had to find her husband so that they could search the mountains for their missing child.

"I think we're gonna find it today," Anna Claire said as she woke up, happy to see the daylight. "I just have this feeling. I just know we're gonna be millionaires today!"

"I have the same feeling," admitted Tommy, trying to ignore his thirst. Looking up, he paused, then sighed. "Do you think..." he paused and blushed.

"Well, ask me already!" cried out the impatient and hungry Anna Claire.

"Do you think Caroline will take notice of me once she knows I'm rich?"

Anna Claire laughed and shook her hair, which was filthy and resembled hay.

"Caroline's fourteen. You're ten. She's never gonna notice you," replied Anna Claire casually.

"That ain't true," Tommy said indignantly. "That's a bunch of bull. I'm almost a man!"

"You're still a little boy," Anna Claire remarked, laughing until her stomach hurt. "Tommy, a *man*! Sure. And I must be the Queen of the Nile! Caroline's almost a lady."

"So what? Someday I'll be a man and then it won't matter much."

"Sorry, Tommy, but you have as much of a chance catchin' the moon than courtin' my sister." She laughed and stood up, brushing the dirt from the night off of her tattered dress.

Tommy said nothing. Instead, he picked a piece of white yarrow from the ground and twisted it in his fingers, thinking of Caroline's lovely black curls and her wide blue eyes.

"Ever think about Helen? She's not so ugly and she's only two years older than you!"

"Helen's real pretty, too, but I like Caroline," he said firmly. "I like her an awful lot. I wish I didn't."

"Caroline's a mean old witch!" declared the little girl with a prideful raise of her head. "You're a lot nicer than she is, even if you're a boy."

"Thanks, I guess," muttered Tommy, feeling glum. If only Caroline could feel the same way about him that he did about her! Maybe once they found that gold, she would realize her true love for Tommy.

The two children, admitting their hunger and thirst, ate the remainder of the Johnny Cakes Anna Claire had snuck and walked around looking for any source of water. Most of the mountain was now rocky cliffs, and water was hard to find. Eventually, they found a little stream across one of the bigger landings, and they each took long, thirsty gulps with their hands.

"Tell me, where do we go now?" asked Anna Claire, looking up at the peak of the mountain that still seemed to be so far away.

Tommy sighed. "We gotta keep climbin'. I think we're gettin' closer. I'm sure the gold is close. I know it's near the top, but it can't be at the very top because there's no dirt, it's all cliffs. That means we're gettin' real close. We're almost there."

Excited, the two children talked more about Old Man Hatfield, the legend of the gold in the hills, and all of the fancy things they would buy once they found the gold. Anna Claire was worried she might get into some trouble, but she knew once her parents saw the amount of gold she'd be carrying, they would relent and fall into her arms and say how sorry they were that they ever doubted her!

The daylight shone between the long aspen trees, and the rocks grew greater and greater. Bright, soft, and dark hues colored the area around them. The musty smell of hemlock that was positioned dangerously in little corners thickened in their nostrils as the feeling of touching the cliffs and trees were beginning to wear on their hands. Their breaths quickened as they hastily skipped around the bends, their chests holding the excitement of childhood, and their eyes sparkling in the sunlight. They knew they were getting very close now.

As they walked around a small bend, they both heard the sound of some leaves rustling, no doubt some kind of animal. Curiously, Anna Claire bent her head before being pulled and shoved over the other side of Tommy. He had grabbed her arms when he noticed the slithering body of a snake, knowing that the animal was most likely poisonous, for every story he ever heard with a snake in it, it was a poisonous one.

Anna Claire gasped and squealed, excited.

"A snake!" she cried happily. "What did you push me for?"

"Because snakes are poisonous!" exclaimed Tommy. "I know they are! Mr. Dobbins and his friends say they are. They can kill you! All they have to do is bite!"

Heeding her friend's warning, Anna Claire backed away from the snake and the two ran in the other direction, both taking a bit of pleasure in the thrill of danger.

Soon they reached a landing in which they were not able to climb any longer, lest chancing falling to their deaths. The peaks above were granite and rock, and this was the only and last logical place to bury a treasure that high up.

"We don't have much land anymore," said Tommy happily. "It's gotta be in this area. There's not even a lot of trees here. This must be where the treasure is buried. They said it was this mountain near this peak. We can't climb anymore. That can only mean we're standin' above the gold."

Anna Claire did a little jump in the air and grabbed Tommy by his elbow. "Let's get diggin'!"

Getting the pick and shovel out of his burlap sack, Tommy began digging, and Anna Claire helped get the rocks and sticks out of the way. They dug and they dug and they dug. They dug a couple of feet before moving to a close area and digging again. They soon had big holes all around the landing, the dark soil tossed haphazardly through the bushes and the rocks. They dug until their fingernails began to break and until their knuckles bled, cracking with the dry dust. The sun beat down on them, causing them to sweat profusely, and their faces were soon burned and wet. Anna Claire's golden hair was nearly completely brown from the sweat and the dirt, and Tommy's piercing blue eyes could hardly be seen behind all of the dust in his face.

Hours went by. Their throats ached with dryness and thirst, and their stomachs were empty and hollow. They were tired, worn out, and ultimately disappointed. Impressively big holes were nearly everywhere, and they still hadn't found any gold. They even went a bit above and below where they had initially begun digging, and still no luck.

Hoping that the gold was buried deeper, they turned to the holes they had already dug and kept digging deeper. It was arduous and tedious. Time went by slowly, and it felt like days since they had slept, drank, or eaten. The worst was the heat. Both were drowning in their own sweat, and their skin was hot to the touch. Their eyelids hurt from rubbing them, and every time they took a breath, it was only hot air that entered their lungs.

Tommy's face quickly went from excited to hopeful to worried to doubtful, and then to clearly giving up. He looked over at Anna Claire, who was still taking the shovel and digging, her little face scrunched with determination, and her small hands tossing the stones and dirt aside as she got deeper.

"What if they were wrong?" Tommy dared to speak. "What if the treasure is buried another place or another mountain? We would've found it by now. Oh dang, we would've found it by now!"

Anna Claire was surprised. "You're givin' up too easily! We gotta keep goin'! The treasure is here, it must be here! They all said so, even Mr. Dobbins!"

Tommy, feeling quite silly and sad, gave her a look of doubt but kept digging with her, moving back around to another side of the landing.

It felt like time stopped when their shovel hit something hard. It was as if the world stopped spinning and the skies had opened all around them, bringing their dreams to life.

"Gold!" cried Tommy, slapping the ground with a hand. "We did it, Anna Claire! We did it!"

Anna Claire collapsed in relieved happiness, getting the pick and digging a little around the area where the shovel had hit the hard surface. However, with a few little pricks, it was obvious that they had not found any gold. The surface was a crusted, pearl-white, and what looked like a small, thin tree branch.

"That ain't gold!" cried Tommy, his face growing even redder.

"That ain't gold!"

"What is it?" asked Anna Claire. "Maybe it's somethin' better than gold!"

The two continued digging until Tommy gasped, his legs hitting the ground.

"What's the matter with you?" asked Anna Claire in an annoyed tone, continuing to dig around the structure that was looking larger and longer.

"Anna Claire," he choked out, steadying his hand on her shoulder. "Get away from there. You heard me, get away!" His voice was loud and shrill, his eyes wide, and his body trembling.

Anna Claire, feeling startled and frightened, jumped up from the dirt to look at what she had been digging up. Looking closer, she only saw a long white stick in the ground.

"What are you fussin' for?" she asked with a roll of her eyes and a stomp of her foot.

"Look closer," said Tommy.

Anna Claire looked again at the stick. It was quite a long stick and it looked like it was connected to another hard surface, almost like a tree trunk- but much too thin to be the trunk of any tree.

"Oh!" she cried, walking back and tripping over a rock.

For in the ground, covered up with the dust and the dirt of time gone past, were the bones of a human being. The skeleton of someone who, like them, was once alive and breathing.

"Anna Claire..." his voice shook. "We're *really* up a tree, now."

Almost as if he had spoken the words himself, Tommy heard the search crew from a way down the mountains calling their names.

Tommy! Anna Claire! Tommy Cooper! Anna Claire Freiler!

"We're here!" yelled Anna Claire instinctively.

Even Tommy, being slightly injured, empty with hunger, and mad with thirst, waved his hands in the air and called out to the crew. They yelled and yelled until they could see Mr. Clemmons, Mr. Dobbins, Mr. Freiler, and some of the other men coming towards them, canteens of water in their hands, and food and candles in sacks over their shoulders.

When Mr. Freiler reached his daughter, he gave her a hard smack on her cheek and then drew her close to hug her.

"You foolish child!" he said with tears in his eyes. "How many times must you learn? How many times will I have to come find you? How much longer will the Lord bless me by keepin' you safe?"

Mr. Dobbins gave Tommy a big embrace and the other men immediately began feeding the children bread and water.

"What have you youngins been doin'?" asked Mr. Dobbins, shaking his head as the search crew and the children sat down upon the dirt. "Y'all look plain terrible!"

"Why did you two run off again?" asked Mr. Grimm, looking irritated and tired.

"We've been lookin' for you all night long!" added Mr. O'Reilly.

Tommy and Anna Claire sighed and looked at each other. They knew that nothing they could possibly say would make this situation any better for them. Suddenly, their plan of telling them they were kidnapped by robbers and dragged up the mountain, left alone with a bear, sounded ridiculous to say aloud.

"Sir, we went to find the lost treasure," admitted Tommy sheepishly. "I'm awful sorry. I was the one that asked Anna Claire to go with me. It was all my idea."

"But I wanted to go," said Anna Claire, jumping in defense of her friend. "I ran away on my own. They all said that Old Man Hatfield buried all his gold here and I just wanted to make you all rich and proud of me!"

Joseph Freiler shook his head and apologized again to his friends who had been so patient helping him find his daughter over and over again.

"I suppose I had somethin' to do with all of this," said Joseph, giving Anna Claire a sympathetic look.

"Don't say that, Joseph," said Mr. Sully.

"Talkin' on and on about findin' treasure and diggin' up gold and gettin' rich," sighed Joseph, looking at his daughter. "Of course, it made you curious. Of course, you wanted to find gold yourself. But you know that runnin' off like this is dangerous, and you have made your mama very ill. If you had eaten the wrong plant or had run into the wrong animal, you both would be dead. You will never go traipsin' off again without us."

Anna Claire wanted to protest, but instead she nodded.

"This little one is always on the shoot!" said Mr. Chesham with a shake of his head.

"It's my fault," said Mr. Dobbins. "I was the one tellin' the children that story about the gold bein' in the mountain. I'm awful sorry."

Joseph sighed. "It's not your doin'. Anna Claire knows better than to run away from home."

No one said a word for a minute. Everyone was drinking water, eating the bread, and thinking of the long trek back down the mountain.

"I have to ask," said Mr. Chesham, breaking the silence, "did you kids find anything while you were out here? I know there's no gold, but did you children see anything interesting?"

Anna Claire and Tommy looked at each other and pointed silently in the space yards away from where they were sitting.

The men paused to look at where they were pointing but shrugged, as they couldn't see anything noteworthy. However, Mr. Dobbins walked closer to one of the big holes that they dug, squinting to see and bending down slowly.

"My God," he said, stepping away from the grisly sight. "My God."

The others came to where he stood to see what he was pointing at. Some of them removed their hats to pay respect to the skeleton that lay in the dirt, while others knelt down or were too shocked to speak. They examined the bones all dried up in the dirt, barely visible but just visible enough to be seen and identified as the remains of a human being.

Joseph pulled Anna Claire close to him and kissed the top of her head, a piece of pine falling out of her hair. Tommy moved to where Mr. Dobbins was standing and stared down at the sight with wide and curious eyes. No one could believe what the children had raked up and, after a bit more digging with Tommy's shovel, they saw the tattered remains of a shell-pink shirt and old worn-out brown boots.

Chapter 10- Danger in Gold Country

The bones had been taken to the courthouse to be examined by the doctor and the diplomat. They had gone under intense scrutiny and were soon deemed to be the bones of a Mr. Gus Winkler, who had died very young- still in his twenties- after he had been trekking the mountain. There were no signs of trauma or struggle. It had been too cold and treacherous to take a trip up the mountain, so they planned to look for Gus Winkler and excavate his bones in the spring, but could not successfully find his skeleton the year prior.

The children were praised for finding the body, even amid the trouble they were both in. Tommy and Anna Claire did not like finding the skeleton, as it only reminded them of their utter failure looking for gold that was probably never even there in the first place.

Anna Claire couldn't believe it. What about Old Man Hatfield and Daisy? Did he ever really bury the gold?

Mr. Dobbins assured the children that rumors stated there was gold buried in the hills, but admitted that he might have been wrong about the exact mountain and placement of the gold. Tommy was angry that he had wasted his time and didn't talk to Mr. Dobbins for three whole days.

Tommy and Anna Claire were, once again, famous in Bannack for the discovery of the Winkler body in the mountains and for "bringing Gus back home." Obviously beloved, Mr. Winkler finally had his proper burial and was laid to rest in the cemetery just outside of town.

Life kept moving forward and Joseph kept the fight to find gold. Joseph Freiler was nothing if not a hard worker. Ever since he was just a young boy growing up in Wisconsin with six brothers, he always had the drive to do big things with his life. This didn't stop when he married Charlotta. If anything, the marriage and the children made him strive even harder to be the man his family needed and then some. This was a big part of the reason he had enlisted in the war. He was already married and had his children by then, but his love for the United States of America and fighting for freedom caused his desire to enlist and fight for the freedoms he believed his great nation deserved-his family deserved.

Joseph, although bravely doing everything he could to fight, was not able to stay in the army. After only a mere month of camping and battle, Joseph was dismissed and sent home due to the bad injury to his leg from being crushed by a wagon wheel during the travels. His leg had nearly broken, and Joseph, despite forcing himself through willpower, could hardly move it. His general sent him home against all of his wishes, and, since then, the Civil War had been a very sore subject for Joseph. Even these days, when the weather was gloomy and rainy, his leg would hurt and cause him to have a slight limp when running. It was hardly noticeable except to Charlotta, whose heart stung every time she saw that limp. She was reminded of how hard her husband had tried to fight for his country and how devastated he had been when he was forced to come home with that leg nearly crushed underneath him.

Since then, Joseph did not want to talk much about the Civil War, although he was happy the Union won. He also did not want to discuss his difficult month with hardly any food and trekking miles on the land to fight before that horrible accident. He wanted to be with his men- he wanted to stand by their side and fight, to conquer Dixie, to display his honor and courage upon President Lincoln himself- but, alas, he was unable to.

Joseph understood his middle child well. Anna Claire was a lot like he had been as a child- determined, stubborn, and brave. She had that same sense of careless adventure and risk-taking that he had, as well as his gold hair and sun-kissed skin. He saw himself the most in Anna Claire and who-if he was being honest- he never wanted to change. Although Charlotta saw her bad manners and excessive energy as unladylike and improper, Joseph loved his middle child's courageous ways and her need to discover everything about the world around her.

Moving to Gold Country had not been easy, and he knew it wouldn't be. The most difficult part was, of course, leaving the family and convincing his wife to be open to accepting a possible new reality in Montana Territory, so far away from Minnesota and their family. Charlotta had protested gravely and refused to go until she had a change of heart and told him that she trusted in his vision of a new life. He wasn't sure what he had done to deserve such a loving, beautiful, and gold-hearted wife, but he was grateful to God for her and promised Him that he would make sure she would be safe in this new place, wherever it took them.

He had certainly managed to do so, at least so far, and now it was the hard work- the toiling in the stones and wet ground, the farming, the panning in hopes to see even just a glimpse of bright yellow peeking out from his pans. He was never certain he would find any of the metal, but he was hopeful enough to find such brilliance in any amount that might have truly mattered economically. It seemed far too good to be true, like something from the horizons of his boyhood dreams, yet it compelled him and pulled him to go to Montana Territory in search of the substance in the small chance that he would get lucky. Even the meager gold dust he obtained was a miracle for him. That little tiny chance was the reason for leaving family, for Charlotta leaving her mother and sisters, their children leaving their grandmother, aunts, uncles, cousins, and friends, and for him to leave behind all he had built.

Joseph knew deep down that this was important. He knew the family needed this fresh start, and prayed nightly that he would be able to deliver his promise to them. Even if the Freiler's never did become rich and only found a sufficient amount, it would be worth it. It would mean that, not only was he right, but that God did have a plan for his family. He would be able to give them a bit of a better life than he ever could being a deliveryman in Minnesota.

But the days were long and very trying. Nearly every day, Joseph sat at the far end of the creek, down where the camps were, and panned for gold. He would work side by side the other men, all of them chasing a dream and hoping to strike lucky. Tirelessly, his eyes searched for large sparks of brilliant metal which meant that he had succeeded in his journey, that he had reached a wildest dream. He understood that this was a dream most would laugh at, a dream that he might have been foolish to pursue. Yet it was a wish he felt in his bones, almost as if this move to Montana Territory would give his restlessness closure and his family peace.

He and the men spent their days and even some evenings separating quartz from the earth of the creek. He already had his claim, although this was quite far from his home, and posted a notice to the others. Sometimes on his own and other times with help, he shoveled out huge piles of dirt and gravel while sweating through his clothes before using his pick to break down the hardened sand. He would then use his pan to gather the dirt and move it around with the creek water before checking the bottom, as real gold would sink. Other times, he would simply use his sluice to gather those rare little pieces of gold dust he found often but not nearly often enough. When he did get lucky to find little pieces of dust, he would gather them in his poke to take to the Assay office in town, where they would measure the gold on the scale.

Early mornings and late nights, Joseph searched for the gold. Each day he had high hopes that he would find it, just like they did back in 1862. He woke up with the sun, worked in the fields, and then went to the creek. He had his friends, also gold miners who had lofty hopes like himself, and he was grateful for their company, which made the hours go by much quicker as they all toiled away, day in and day out. They prayed for wind and erosion to bring down the gold from the streams and uncover their bright loveliness in the soil or quartz.

After spending months doing so, he was starting to become a bit worn out. Charlotta missed him terribly when he was gone, as did his children. Little Caroline, his firstborn child and the girl that he and Charlotta first adored, was not so little and was now courting a boy in town. Helen was becoming secretive and angry, while Anna Claire could not help but run away over and over again from the life that she had. Peter was lonely and dreamy, while Berthie could hardly eat and was constantly ill. Joseph dedicated his life to his family and did what he could to spend as much time with them as he could when he was not working.

Joseph was especially grateful to the Clemmons's, who were always by their side when they needed a friend. Paul would be with him mining, while Nettie would sometimes invite Charlotta over for tea or to discuss problems they were both having in Gold Country. Both women depended on each other for comfort and companionship while their husbands were away working for their families. Paul was the first to help Joseph organize a search party whenever Anna Claire went missing, and always the one making Joseph laugh during the roughest of moments. Nettie held Charlotta's hand when she cried over the possible fate of her children and the impossibly lonely moments when she realized with terror everything she had left behind and everything that was at stake for the family.

The family had grown very close to the Clemmons's. Rebecca Clemmons had become a point of sanity for Helen, who was beginning to become frustrated with Montana Territory in general and needed someone to complain to. Matthew Clemmons was nice enough to take Pete by his side and hunt, fish, and cook with him. Matthew and Anna Claire were friendly, but Anna Claire was always on her own or with Tommy, whether that was fishing alone, playing by the creek, or reading about ancient Egypt. Matthew did not stand a chance in friendship when it came to Tommy Cooper, who nearly worshipped Anna Claire as the only girl he would ever consider his equal and the only one who actually understood him.

Joseph did not want to punish the little girl he saw so much of himself in, yet he did it. She had blatantly disobeyed all rules and went against her parents yet again. She had put herself in danger and climbed a mountain in search of her own treasure. Although he could relate to this very well, Joseph also knew that he must keep Anna Claire safe at all costs, even if it meant that she was very bored and very sad for a long time.

And that she was. Anna Claire was permitted to play with Tommy Cooper when Tommy came to the Freiler's cabin; however, that was the extent of

Anna Claire's boundary. She was not allowed to go anywhere else without her parents. Because of this rule, she was not able to go to town or wander the creek any longer, which was what she lived for, and this was a bitter point in her life.

Anna Claire turned ten years old in August, and she was still not permitted to go into town, although Charlotta had baked her a nice cake and Joseph had bought her a children's dime novel about a parrot.

The night of Anna Claire's tenth birthday was a beautiful night that she would never forget. Anna Claire was always fond of her birthday because she usually got to eat sweets and was treated like she was special. She was allowed to choose which game to play, what she wanted to do that day, and could take a break from most of the chores.

"Anna Claire," said her father very late at night. Everyone else was asleep at this point, and he woke her up by whispering in her ear.

"Papa?" she asked, disoriented and wiping her sleepy eyes.

"Come with me," he said, allowing her to follow him quietly down the ladder and then outside of the house.

"I didn't want to wake everyone," said Joseph, smiling and sitting on top of the keg. "I thought that, since it's your birthday, you'd want to see this."

He pointed up in the sky just then, grinning and looking up as if seeing a new world.

Anna Claire's mouth dropped open and her eyes went wide.

"Papa! What is that?" she asked as her father brought her closer to him, his arm around her.

"That is a lunar rainbow, darlin'," he answered in awe. "Look at that moon!"

"It's beautiful!" said Anna Claire, looking up at the sky, which beheld a half-circle of a ring of light that was extraordinarily white. The ring, white with just a tinge of colors, seemed to cover a vast majority of the hills and was shining down on Gold Country as if to bless it.

"It *is* beautiful, isn't it?" sighed Joseph, still smiling in admiration of the natural beauty. "I never seen one like this before."

"Me neither!" said Anna Claire. "I never saw a white rainbow before! Do you think that's what heaven looks like? Mama said heaven is real bright."

"I reckon I don't know," said Joseph, his arm squeezing his daughter's waist as she leaned her head on his shoulder.

"I'm glad you woke me up," she said with a nod of her head.

They watched the mystical manifestation in silence for a while, both in awe of the majestic beauty of what they were witnessing. The night air was warm, and they could hear the light sound of crickets chirping in the distance. All seemed right with the world. It was certainly an unforgettable birthday.

"Now, time for bed," Joseph said as he stood up, ruffling her hair.

Anna Claire didn't want to leave the lunar spectacle, but she knew it was far past her bedtime.

She felt lucky that she was the only one who her father had woken up to see this spectacular sight.

"I love you, Papa," she said from the ladder as he kissed her cheek.

"I love you, my ten-year-old girl," he beamed, walking over to the buckskin curtain.

***

Summer set quickly during this time, as Joseph worked tirelessly panning gold while Charlotta worked in the home and the fields, and the children learned to do more chores that were new to them. Anna Claire herself had learned to properly scrub the floors, clean the chicken coop, cook meats and pies, and sew gloves for the upcoming winter months. Anna Claire frequently splashed dirty water all over the walls on accident, broke eggs while putting them into the basket, undercooked the meats and burned the pies, and pricked herself with the needle while sewing the wrong stitch. The rest of September was dreadfully long for her, as sometimes Tommy was even turned away when approaching her house, due to Anna Claire being "busy" with chores.

Charlotta dutifully wrote to her loved ones in Minnesota as she often did, explaining Grasshopper Diggings and Gold Country in extraordinary detail, even in small conversations. She was still a bit lonely, but the company of Mrs. Nettie Clemmons had done wonders for her soul, as the two spent long hours helping each other wash clothes, bake, sew dresses and pants, and enjoy several cups of lemon tea. Sometimes, Matthew and Rebecca would come along and play with the children, which gave Charlotta time to discuss adult matters with her friend, such as her fear of Anna Claire going missing someday, her husband's nonchalant manner about finding gold, and the difficulty living on their small farm. They lived close by, so Nettie knew this life well and the two related to each other in a way that brought sanity and companionship to poor Charlotta, who was in over her head with her children and the recent move.

The fall brought some big changes to the children. A couple of years prior, a young woman had traveled with a very important man named Mr. Sidney Edgerton, who had been appointed by President Abraham Lincoln himself to govern Montana Territory. Mr. Edgerton had come along with his wife, children, a couple of friends, and his niece- a Miss Lucia Darling- all the way from Ohio, where he was a colonel and US Congressman.

Lucia, much beloved to her uncle, was an attractive young woman in her twenties with raven-black hair, skin like porcelain, and dark, sad eyes. She had come to Bannack and immediately was drawn to the town, confirming to herself that Bannack needed a school for the children.

Miss Darling had begun a school in the family home where she oversaw twelve children and taught them reading, writing, and arithmetic. The next year, a few townsmen had come together and built a small schoolhouse for Miss Darling to teach, which was successful. Miss Darling, along with the families of Bannack, obtained whatever chairs, desks, slates, and books that they could to aid in the help of student education. Miss Darling was a compassionate, kind, and skilled young teacher who the children adored and who was determined to see the children succeed.

Charlotta Freiler was thrilled to send her five children off to school in October, despite it being close to town. Berthie was old enough and well enough to go, and Peter was the appointed chaperone for his little sister. Caroline, who had loved school in Minnesota and was a very diligent student, was delighted to be able to go to school once again, although this school was smaller than the schoolhouse she had previously attended. Helen was to see that Anna Claire was safe while walking to and from school, and Anna Claire would keep an eye on Pete and Berthie. Caroline was to watch them all. It was all a very good plan, as they all looked out for each other.

The first day of school was tough for Anna Claire. She never cared for school and believed that it would be terrible. But then she met Miss Lucia Darling- the kind-hearted, young teacher of the little schoolhouse- and decided that she liked school. Anna Claire rushed home from school that first day and proclaimed how much she loved the school and how much she adored her teacher.

Miss Darling herself had taken to Anna Claire almost immediately. She appreciated Anna Claire's boldness, her frankness about what she disliked, and her genuine honesty towards everyone around her. Although Anna Claire did not possess the best manners, she was a smart and passionate student, much to the surprise of the Freilers, who still could not believe that she woke up actually *wanting* to go to school.

Anna Claire felt very at home in school now. Her siblings were with her, Tommy had started attending school too (despite his initial refusal), and she knew some of the other children, including Jacob Mast, Rebecca and Matthew Clemmons, Nikola Sikorski, Tim Johnson, and even the Howler children. This time, though, Anna Claire and Lisa Howler had ended their hatred for each other and, being young with short attention spans, had nearly forgotten their earlier quarrel at the barn raising.

"Why do children always have to go to school?" whined Tommy in his room, only a week after school had begun.

He and Anna Claire were doing their usual routine of eating candy, playing cards (which Tommy had taught her), and talking about nothing and everything. Anna Claire had finally been allowed to stay with Tommy after school for a short while.

Anna Claire shrugged. "So we're not stupid, I guess."

Tommy sighed, throwing a broken piece of wood from the floor against the wall. "It's kinda hard to be in school when you don't read."

Anna Claire looked over at him, her eyes wide. "I forgot you couldn't read!"

"Bosh! I could read if I wanted to!" spat Tommy angrily. "That is, if I wanted to learn how. But I don't. I see no use for it, so long as I know where I'm goin' and what the signs mean. That's easy as pie."

Anna Claire rolled her eyes. "This is dull. Let's go look at the clouds."

The two ran outside, out of town, and up a little hill where they fell down in the field, sighing as they leaned back into the grass.

"That looks like a cat," mused Anna Claire as she and Tommy lay in the field, staring up at the bright sky.

It was already beginning to get cold, and the children were shivering in their long coats. Yet, they were having too much fun making clouds into shapes with their imagination and did not have any intention of leaving just because it was a bit chilly outside.

"Eh, I think that looks more like a horse," answered Tommy, his hands behind his head. Anna Claire sighed, breathing in the pure air of Montana Territory. "I think I'd like to live in the clouds. Imagine that!"

"No one will ever be able to go inside a cloud," said Tommy. "It's too high!"

"I read that there are mountains in the clouds all the way in Asia!" declared Anna Claire dreamily, imagining herself being able to reach out and touch a cloud.

"You know a lot," Tommy said, sounding impressed. "I don't even know where Asia is!"

"I do know a lot," agreed Anna Claire, "but that's only because I read. If you read more, you would be able to know a lot, too."

Tommy sat up, his fingers running through the tall, yellowing grass. "I don't like readin'. It's for girls."

"No, it ain't. Everyone reads. Even cowboys read."

"They do not."

"They do, too!"

"Well, it ain't no matter 'cause I don't like readin'. What's so important about it anyway?" said Tommy.

"You can be anyone and go anywhere!" declared Anna Claire passionately. "I'm only allowed to read some books, but my aunt had so many books!" She put her hands above her head to demonstrate the number of books the collection contained. "She had books from all over. I got to read all about Egypt and Israel, and even Turkey. Someday, I'm gonna be a traveler."

Tommy laughed. "You can't travel. You're just a girl!"

Insulted, Anna Claire sat up in the grass, wiping it from her hair. "Take it back, Tommy Cooper! I ain't just a girl!"

"Fine," grumbled Tommy. "You ain't just a girl. You're Anna Claire."

Anna Claire crossed her arms and nodded. "I'll show you someday! I'll go everywhere!"

Tommy shook his head. "I'm stayin' right here. I ain't ever leavin'. Not ever."

Anna Claire stood up and patted her blue plaid dress. "You know what I just thought?"

Tommy lay back down in the field, looking bored. "What?"

Anna Claire, delighted, shook him by his shoulders.

"What is it?"

"I can teach you!" she exclaimed with all the zest she had, her eyes sparkling. "Why didn't I think of that? I can teach you how to read anything! You'll be the best reader in the whole school when I'm done teachin' you! Next to me, of course."

Tommy shook his head. "No way! I don't wanna read."

Anna Claire rolled her eyes. "Oh, Tommy, you gotta learn to read! Otherwise, you'll look stupid at school! Everyone will think you're dumb as a rock."

Tommy looked over at his slate, which was still empty even though he was supposed to be writing on it.

"I don't think I can," he said sadly.

"Of course, you can. I'll help you. That'll give Mama an excuse to let you come to our cabin! And me to town!"

Tommy nodded, finding that idea wonderful, thinking of seeing Caroline.

"Tomorrow, come over and I'll show you some of my books and I'll teach you to read."

Tommy smiled bashfully. "I guess it'd be good to know for school. I never been schooled before. Ma doesn't care if I don't go, but I wanna go 'cause you all go to school. I don't wanna be the only one not goin' to school."

Anna Claire showed her gap-toothed smile and stood up. "You're gonna be smart, Tommy Cooper. Real smart!"

Tommy smiled too. He supposed being smart wasn't the worst thing in the world. Maybe he could even get used to reading.

"Daisy Hatfield's daughter is out there some-where," said Anna Claire suddenly and randomly. "And her name is Darlin'."

"Yeah, so?"

"So! Miss *Darlin'*! How could we not have seen this before?"

Tommy sat up with a start, a surprised look crossing his face. "Gee! How could we not see this? Anna Claire, you're a genius!" He stood up and grabbed his friend's little hand. "Miss Lucia Darlin'! She must be! She's the only one that came here from so far away with the name Darlin'!"

"It's her family name, though," said Anna Claire. "I thought Daisy named her daughter Darlin' as her first name."

"Me too," Tommy said, pacing back and forth. "I thought so, too! But maybe we were wrong! Maybe they were wrong! Maybe Darlin' was the family name of the man Daisy ran away with! Darlin' would be an odd first name, wouldn't it?"

Anna Claire nodded. "I always thought so!"

Tommy jumped in the air and howled. "Whoo! I think we did it!"

Anna Claire jumped up and down excitedly. "We have to tell Miss Darlin'!"

"No, no, she can't know our secret yet," said Tommy, his eyebrows narrowing. "If she knows, she might get real wrathy at us. We don't wanna tell her we know yet. We should wait until the summer when school is out, so she has time to stop bein' embar-rassed and all. When she knows that we know her ma killed herself and that her pa ran away, she'll feel awful. We gotta wait. In the summer we'll tell her, and then she might be angry, but she'll be right cheered up by the time school comes again! She might even help us find the gold. Once she hears that we're lookin' for the gold and that the gold is still out there somewhere, she'll be happy we knew 'cause then we'll all be rich! Maybe she even knows where the gold is!Anna Claire nodded and spat on the ground. There were so many mysteries about Miss Darling and how much she knew. "We gotta wait, Tommy. Just like you said. We gotta wait 'til school is over. Maybe she doesn't even know! Maybe no one told her about her real mama and papa!"

Tommy smiled and the two made a pact that only they would know the dark secret- that Miss Lucia Darling, their sweet school teacher, was actually the granddaughter of the legendary Old Man Hatfield, and had lost both of her parents as a baby, and may not even realize her own identity. Coming from Illinois, maybe she had been handed off to other people who raised her as their own. Maybe she had no clue who she was or where she really came from. Maybe Governor Edgerton knew this and brought her home.

Tommy and Anna Claire swore that they would be the ones to tell her if no one else was able to figure out the secret. How could they not have thought about this before? Darling. Darling, of course! Of *course*, she would come back to her land, especially if she did know her history and wanted to see the place her mother grew up. She would want to see the place where her family's roots began and where her mother so tragically ended her own life. It was all being put together now.

And, under the big, beautiful blue skies of Montana Territory, Anna Claire Freiler and Tommy Cooper had begun to put together an old secret, dozens of years in the making.

When Anna Claire threw the door of her home open, Caroline was standing there with her hands on her hips.

"You're late," she hissed, her eyes narrowing.

"Dry up," answered Anna Claire, scowling and walking past her.

"I need you to help me slice the beef!" called Charlotta, her body bent forward towards the fireplace. Anna Claire took one of the little store boxes by the table. She then helped carry the pan to the table, where Charlotta handed her the knife. Anna Claire cut happily and threw in some linseed for flavor, wondering what book she would help Tommy to read the next day. It had to be a book that wasn't so complicated- perhaps *A Pirate's Tale.* It was interesting, but short and simple.

"Please, may Tommy come over tomorrow?" she asked sweetly. "I'm teaching him how to read!"

"He can't *read*?" interjected Helen. "No wonder he never answers when it's his turn to read the board!"

Charlotta looked at her excited little daughter and smiled. "Of course. You are teaching him how to read, which is one of the greatest blessings of all."

Caroline walked over to where Anna Claire was cutting the beef in clunky, shapeless forms and said, "You aren't cutting it right. Give it to me."

"Take it!" yelled Anna Claire, happy to be relieved of the chore. "I think Tommy might learn how to be smart."

"Dear," said Charlotta gently, "I think Tommy is already very smart. Just because he cannot read does not mean he is not smart. He just has not learned *how*."

"I suppose so," said Anna Claire, grabbing the store box and putting it back by the table. "I think he'll be able to read real well."

"The poor boy can't even read!" exclaimed Caroline, a look of sadness on her concerned face.

"That is truly terrible," Charlotta agreed, coming over and placing the little tin plates on the table. "Anna Claire, if you need help, we will all help him."

Anna Claire brought the little tin spoons and forks over to the table and put them upside down before walking away and petting Hero.

"I guess I'll start with the pirate book," she said, letting Hero lick her face. "It's simple but it ain't boring."

"*Is not*," corrected Charlotta.

"He is welcome to read my poetry book," offered Caroline, standing up from the chair and walking over to the fireplace where she took the corn off of the stick.

"He can read my Reader!" said Pete in his earnest, high voice. "I hate readin' that thing!"

"Peter," Charlotta said firmly.

Anna Claire and Pete looked at each other and began to chuckle.

"In any matter, that is very kind of you that you want to help Tommy," said Charlotta, her face glowing in the light of the fire. "He is a good boy. Everyone should know how to read!"

At that moment, Joseph burst through the door, carrying a goose over his head and with a huge grin on his face.

"Papa!" yelled Helen, coming to his side and wrapping her arms around him.

"My girl," he said, playfully pulling on one of her brown braids.

"Well, you look happy tonight," Charlotta helped him take the goose and place it on the plate on the box by the fireplace.

Joseph kissed Charlotta before grabbing his buckskin sac.

"I found enough gold to buy us some extra food this week!" he said happily, throwing the poke down on the table.

The children gathered around and watched the little flakes of gold dust in awe. It wasn't much, but it was more than they had ever seen.

Charlotta smiled and kissed Joseph. "This will do quite well!"

"Does that mean I can get the dolly I saw in the stowe?" asked Berthie sweetly.

"No, you cannot get the doll you saw in the store," answered Charlotta, still smiling. "I promise you will get a new doll, but we need this money for food. Lord knows we have no flour or butter, and we are getting low on canned peaches and honey."

Joseph took his wife's hand and spun her around, extending his arm as she bent back.

"Joseph!" she scolded, standing up straight and wiping her apron. Yet, she was still smiling.

"Does this mean we can have the peaches?" asked Helen. She loved the canned peaches more than anything in Gold Country.

"I don't see why not," said Joseph, holding out his arms so that Helen and Pete could hug him. "Maybe I'll even buy some coffee!"

Caroline perked up at this idea. She and Charlotta loved coffee and had it in the mornings when it was available to them.

"I want the gingew snaps!" said Berthie, licking her lips.

"For you, I might be able to find some," Joseph bent over to kiss his youngest. "I can get that Western Reserve cheese and that Japanese green tea, too. I know you've been wantin' that, Char."

"We can use a couple of new candles, too," said Charlotta happily. "Perhaps Werk's Star?"

"I don't see why not!" agreed Joseph, his eyes sparkling.

The happiness vibrated throughout the entire cabin, and the smiles could be felt from every corner.

"I'm going to teach Tommy how to read!" exclaimed Anna Claire proudly.

"I think that's a fine endeavor," Joseph agreed cheerfully as they all sat down to supper. "I didn't know the poor boy couldn't read!"

"I know how to wead, too!" stated Berthie excitedly.

"Yes, you certainly do," Charlotta smiled, a look of serenity finally on her face.

The table was full of joy that night. The children were glad to see their parents smiling and happy, and the husband and wife were glad that they could help each other with the little bit of gold Joseph had found. Charlotta's usually anxious face was calm, and her blue eyes were softened. Joseph's typically wrinkled forehead was smooth and flat, as he was not scrunching his face up in pain or worry. They laughed, they talked, they even sang. Caroline grabbed the hymnal book from the other room, and they all sang one of Charlotta's favorite hymnals, "For the Beauty of the Earth."

Anna Claire was a dreadful singer and hated it, so instead she pretended Hero was singing and knelt down to sit behind his narrow head.

"Oh, Papa, may I go to the town dance with Jacob?" Caroline asked suddenly. She knew this was her chance.

"The autumn dance at the billiard hall?" asked Joseph, eyeing Charlotta.

"Yes, Papa," Caroline held her breath in anxious anticipation.

Joseph looked over at Charlotta, who gave him a worried glance.

"Do you think it is safe, Joseph?" she asked, taking a sip of water from her cup.

Joseph paused. "Jacob will be taking you?"

Caroline nodded, her eyes sparkling with hope. "Yes, and I promise not to stay too long, and I promise to be back as soon as you would like me to!"

Charlotta smiled and nodded at Joseph.

"She's only fourteen," said Joseph with a sigh. He looked over at Caroline.

"Jacob is fifteen!" she exclaimed with a nod, as if fifteen was drastically older.

Joseph sighed again. "Well, if you think it is safe, Char, she can go."

Before he even said the last word, Caroline rushed up out of her chair to hug him and kiss him on the cheek.

"Now wait a minute," he went on, looking at her sternly. "You may go, but only for a couple of hours. And only if I take you and Jacob in the wagon myself."

Caroline was a bit disappointed at this thought, but knew not to say anything.

"And," Joseph continued, "I will also be takin' you home. Two hours."

Caroline nodded happily, her face lighting up.

Joseph and Charlotta smiled.

"You *are* growin' up," said Joseph, affectionately rubbing her head. "Caroline at a dance with a boy! I never thought I'd see the day!"

"I can help you with your hair, dear," Charlotta offered, standing up to clear the plates.

"Why do you want to go with Jacob Mast?" Helen said with food in her mouth. "He is the strangest-looking boy I've ever seen!"

"Helen!" exclaimed Charlotta as she turned around to look at her reproachfully.

"*You're* strange looking!" Caroline snapped back. Seeing the look on her father's face, she calmed down and hastily helped clear the table.

"I think dances are silly," said Anna Claire, still sitting on the ground and playing with Hero. "I ain't never goin' to a dance."

"Stop saying 'ain't'," Charlotta admonished, beginning to wash the little forks in the bucket of water with the cloth rag. "It is terribly rude and ignorant." Anna Claire said nothing.

"The only way I'd go to a dance is if there was apple pie!" said Pete.

"Me too!" agreed Anna Claire, now wishing earnestly that she could have pie, her favorite treat.

Helen, Caroline, Anna Claire, and Berthie helped Charlotta clean the silverware while Joseph took Pete outside to help him with the horses. Then, Charlotta and the girls began to skin the duck to cook it and prepare it for food the next day. Berthie always hated this part- she loved animals- and Charlotta always explained to her that "God gives us animals to eat and they know this is their purpose on Earth." This vague explanation did not help Berthie much, so Berthie was always permitted to play with her dolls up in the loft at this time.

Anna Claire skinned the duck, helped put it on the stick, and placed it above the fire.

"Tommy's birthday's soon!" said Anna Claire. "Maybe we can get him a book!"

"If we can afford it," reminded Charlotta. "We need all the money we can to store food for the winter."

Anna Claire sighed. She wished they had enough gold to buy Tommy a thousand books!

"Can I go outside and help Papa and Peter with the animals?" asked Anna Claire eagerly.

"Because you cleaned up and helped cook so well, you may," answered Charlotta, bending down and wiping a piece of beef off of Berthie's lips with the rag.

With that, Anna Claire darted out of the house and into the night sky. The summer air had long faded, and she could feel the coldness of fall.

"I reckon we have enough hay," Joseph was saying, patting one of the horses on her side. "I could pick up some more in town for the winter. Now watch, Peter." He went around the horse and picked up her foot, showing his son the hoof. "Now, like I told you, you never stand directly in back of the horse. They can kick ya. Stand a little off to the side, like this." He positioned Pete next to him before giving him the little pick. "Now gently start diggin' in. Make sure you get all the dirt out of there, but don't pick too much in the middle, else it'll hurt him. There ya go. Good."

Anna Claire was silent as she watched her father teach her little brother.

"I wanna do it myself!" said Pete, going around the front of the horse and standing to the side of the other hoof. He picked the hoof gently but firmly, getting rid of the dirt and grime of the day.

"Very good, Peter!" Joseph's face lit up with pride.

Anna Claire stayed silent for a while as she watched Pete finish the hooves. She wished deeply that Joseph could teach her how to take care of the animals, and not just the little stuff like brushing them, feeding them, and trimming their nails.

Joseph noticed Anna Claire standing off to the side, looking sad. He went over and gave her the pick.

Anna Claire looked up at him and smiled in disbelief.

"Well, you saw Pete, you know what to do," Joseph smiled at her kindly, his bright brown eyes twinkling.

Anna Claire eagerly stood to the side and picked the dirt from the front hooves with pride. She then gently kissed the side of the horse, feeling its coarse brown hair, before handing the pick back to her father.

"Good girl," he said, his face beaming. He put his arm around her and Pete's shoulders. "Let us go back inside."

The three walked slowly back to the house, Anna Claire watching the moon with big, wide eyes. There was something about the moon that had always excited Anna Claire. She wondered if there would ever be a time when someone would be able to go to the moon and touch it. It was a ridiculous thought, but one she sometimes entertained.

Soon, it was time to get ready for bed. They first gathered around Charlotta while she read a passage from the family Bible, and then they each kissed their parents on the cheek. The children went up to the loft- Helen and Caroline on one side and Anna Claire, Pete, and Berthie on the other- the sides separated only by some buckskins that were nailed to the top of the roof.

"Do you think anyone will ever go to the moon?" mused Anna Claire as she dressed into her little nightgown.

"I can hear you!" shouted Helen from the other side of the loft. "Be quiet! And also, no one can go to the moon. People can't fly. You're a half-wit, Anna Claire!"

"Not as much as *you* are!" yelled Anna Claire back, turning around and getting into bed. "Please, let us just go to sleep now!" Caroline yelled back, annoyed.

Anna Claire huddled in the bed with Berthie and Pete. Pete was a good sleeper and practically dozed off as soon as his head hit the pillow. This was not the case for Anna Claire and Berthie.

"Tell me the story about Old Man Hatfield," begged Berthie, snuggling into the covers. Anna Claire rolled her eyes and sighed.

"I've told you that story a thousand times."

"Please?" Berthie asked so sweetly, her big brown eyes like a puppy dog's.

Anna Claire smiled. "Fine. Alright. So, there was once a man named Davie Hatfield. He was kind and nice to all he met..."

When the story was over, Berthie had fallen asleep, and Anna Claire went over to the little window to look up at the moon again. It was so full and bright and glowing. Anna Claire thought that there may not be anything prettier than the moon. Soon, she climbed back into the bed, snuggled under the blanket, and fell asleep.

It was a beautiful fall day and finally the day of the big autumn dance.

Caroline had been so excited all week. Jacob had come to visit and bring the family apples. Caroline went to the Mast's and brought some ginger snaps over, the same ginger snaps that Berthie so loved. The day of the dance, she had awoken early, ate one of the apples for breakfast before anyone else was even awake, and then immediately started her chores as quietly as she could, cutting the rest of the apples for the others and setting up the table.

"You're up early, dear," yawned Charlotta from behind her and Joseph's space, which was set up in the same fashion as the loft, with the buckskin partly separating it from the rest of the house.

"It's the day of the dance," laughed Joseph. "Of course she's up early!"

Joseph went outside to tend to the animals while Charlotta began cooking the eggs on the fireplace. It was so early that it was still somewhat dark outside.

A bit later, Berthie woke up and was asking for eggs, and then Pete came down the ladder. Anna Claire was next, and Helen, as usual, was last and had to be woken up by Caroline.

"I daresay, I have never seen you so thrilled," Charlotta observed, watching Caroline eat her eggs as quickly as she could.

"I must admit," Caroline said, "I am happy to go to the dance. Oh, thank you for letting me go!"

"Remember what we discussed," said Joseph sternly.

"I will, Papa."

"No dancin' with anyone other than Jacob."

"Yes, Papa."

"No leavin' the billiard hall at any time."

"Yes, Papa."

"When I come in, it is time to go home."

"Yes, Papa."

Caroline's eyes sparkled with excitement, her heavy, dark lashes beautifully framed in the way.

"Caroline is always so obedient and good," said Charlotta, smiling at her oldest child and reaching out to touch her hand. "I know she will be just fine at the dance."

"I will, I will!"

"I'd never go with Jacob Mast," said Helen, her nose in the air.

"You're just angry because you're too young to go to a dance!" hissed Caroline, her eyes sharpening.

"I'd rather not go than to go with him!"

"Children!" boomed Joseph, the windows shaking a bit.

Everyone was quiet then, and Caroline and Helen ate their breakfast silently, not without giving each other nasty looks.

When breakfast was over, Caroline hastily helped her mother wash the silverware and plates, scrub the table, and churn the butter. She did this quickly, wanting nothing more than to begin preparing for the special night.

Charlotta took pity on her, watching her as she began to crouch down to scrub the floor.

"Never you mind that," she said softly. "I think you have done enough for today. Go choose which dress you want to wear."

Caroline's face brightened as she hugged her mother tightly. "Thank you, Mama!"

She ran up to the loft and opened the little chest. Caroline loved to sew, and she had three beautiful dresses. One was her church dress she had brought from Minnesota, one she had made herself during the summer, and another one in which her father had just bought for her with the extra gold dust.

Caroline looked over the options, ignoring the loud sounds of Anna Claire and Pete playing horses downstairs, and imagined swirling around in each dress. She loved the one from Minnesota, but it was plaid and yellow, and more for little girls with the hemline just reaching the knees. The one she made herself was pretty and blue like the sky, but would be a bit hard to dance in. She took the light white dress with the little bow on the collar, the one made of muslin. It was free-flowing enough that she should be able to dance in it, and it was also the longest dress she had, which meant it would hit her ankles. That meant that she had grown up.

She hastily began to brush her hair, as it was curled in her clothes the night before for the dance. Her hair was silky and more curly than usual. She tried on the dress, and it was perfect. She swayed back and forth, looking in her small mirror, admiring her trim figure and her very pale skin. She liked the dress, and the dress certainly liked her.

She could hear the sound of her father leaving, and she called goodbye from the loft. She sat on her bed and looked at her lovely curls in the mirror again. She hoped that Jacob would think she looked pretty, too. At fourteen, she could not have been more excited to go to her very first dance alone with a boy! She wondered what it would be like. Would Jacob take her by her hand and waltz her around the billiard? Would other boys try to take over and dance with her, too?

Wanting to show her family her hair and her dress, she crept down the loft very slowly. When she arrived, Charlotta praised her, clapping her hands as her eyes filled up with tears.

"Dear, you look beautiful," she said. "Radiant."

Caroline smiled and curtsied playfully.

"You look nice," admitted Helen, her nose still in the air.

"That dress is *pretty*," said Anna Claire, not meaning it as a compliment.

Caroline smiled and turned around to show everyone how she looked. When she turned back around, no one was smiling anymore.

"What's on the back of your dress?" asked Helen, scrunching her face.

"What? Did I get something on my dress?" Caroline was frantic, taking the back of her dress and trying to see it from the side.

Charlotta quickly came to her side.

"It looks like you're bleedin'!" cried Anna Claire when Caroline turned around. "Mama, she's bleedin'!"

Charlotta's face flushed.

"I am going to take care of Caroline. Helen, go to the creek and get some water. Anna Claire, go with your sister and help. Berthie, go with them. You watch your little sister now!"

And with that, Charlotta helped Caroline crawl back up the ladder.

"My dress! My dress!" Caroline cried. If she were injured, she could bear that, but she could not bear to ruin her beautiful new town dress.

"Stay here and take that dress off," instructed Charlotta, a slight look of panic on her face. She left the loft and went down the ladder to her side of the room.

Caroline, practically wailing, quickly took the dress off, wanting to see if she had sat on anything in particular. Her eyes went wide when she saw the blood stain. She patted down her body from head to toe but could not find the source of the injury.

When Charlotta came back up the loft, she held out a rag and what water was left in the little bucket.

"I knew this was bound to happen soon," she muttered, "but of all days!"

"Mama, where am I bleeding? I cannot feel anything!" Caroline's face was red hot, and her nose was running as tears spilled down her cheeks.

"I will explain," said Charlotta, "but first, wash yourself underneath. Yes, like that. You are going to wear this-" she held out a buckled contraption with a rag in the middle of a belt. "You see, remember when I told you that someday you will bleed when you get older?"

Caroline nodded, sniffling and rubbing her eyes.

"This is supposed to happen," Charlotta helped her daughter put the Hoosier belt on. "Don't be afraid."

"This means I'm getting older?" asked Caroline, remembering her mother telling her a long time ago that women and girls bled for several days when they were growing up.

Charlotta sighed, helping Caroline change back into her nightgown. "Yes, dear. It does. It has happened, and it cannot be helped. But do not fret. It will be alright. This means you can have children now, once you are married."

"My dress," she sobbed into her mother's arms, her curls in disarray from all of the crying.

"I am sorry to say that this dress may be ruined, but I will try to clean out the stain. There, there, no more crying."

"Now I can't go to the dance," said Caroline with great despair. "All I wanted was to go to the dance!"

"I suppose you can still go," said Charlotta slowly. "You have the belt on. It will take care of the bleeding."

"I never had this happen before," Caroline sobbed. "I do not feel very well. My stomach hurts an awful lot. How will I dance like this? I do not want Jacob to see me in this state! If something were to happen at the dance, oh, I could never bear it!" She sent herself through another rain of tears.

"Oh, darling," her mother cooed, sitting down on the bed and wrapping her arm around her. "What a terrible day for this to happen. But it is well that this happened now instead of while you were at the billiard hall."

Caroline nodded sadly. This was true.

"If you are not feeling well," Charlotta continued, "do not go to the dance. Give yourself some time to learn what to do. Go to the next one. Oh dear, do not cry! I promise that you can go to the next one."

But Caroline could not stop crying. She crawled into bed, her hand over her stomach, and put her arm over her face. She looked so small and pitiful that Charlotta nearly started crying herself.

"I am going to bring you some soup and we are going to talk about what you shall do when this happens," said Charlotta, going towards the ladder.

"It will happen *again*?" Caroline was sent into another wave of despair when Charlotta nodded, leaving her on her bed. This was absolutely dreadful, and Caroline was horrified.

In a few moments, her mother came up with bread and chicken soup.

"What shall we tell the others? And Papa?" Caroline could hardly stand to think of it.

Charlotta smiled. "Well, I don't see why your Papa has to know unless he asks. I am sure he will not ask. As for Pete, he has been in the barn the whole time and will not know. I will tell the girls not to say anything. As for your sisters, we will tell them that you sat on something sharp and pricked yourself. Lies are truly terrible sins, but in this case, God may forgive it. There, there. It will be alright, dear."

Caroline cried and cried, feeling vulnerable and so disappointed that she would not be able to attend the dance at the billiard hall, something she had been excited about now for weeks.

"What will we tell Jacob?" sniffed the unfortunate girl.

Charlotta looked to the ceiling for answers. "You shall not worry about that. When the girls return, I will ride to the Mast's and tell them that you are ill. That is not a lie."

"Thank you, Mama," said Caroline softly, burying her head full of dismembered curls into her mother's chest.

The girls believed the story about the injury, and they felt sorry that Caroline had gotten hurt. Charlotta went over to talk to the Mast's and to apologize to Jacob. All seemed to be well for now. Yet,

Caroline could be heard crying softly to herself up alone in the loft for the rest of the day.

Chapter 11- Iá daxpitchée

As the Freilers became closer to the people in town and developed more friends, the nights grew longer and longer. Bannack itself had already been known as a party town, the town where the cowboys could escape for a night and where the miners could throw down a drink or two while playing some cards with friends and foes. However, it was becoming evident that Gold Country was growing a bit less friendly and a bit more dangerous. Joseph and Charlotta had heard stories of the robbers and how they hunted down families who had struck gold, injuring or killing them to obtain the treasure.

It was no secret that men were being killed on the roads to and from the town because of the Road Agents. The Road Agents, being greedy and obsessed with gold, would kill anyone who tried to resist and bring the gold or other currency from the treasure with them. Families moving to Virginia City were particularly vulnerable, as they traveled on some of the most dangerous roads alone. The roads became tainted with blood as more and more men fell to the insatiability of the Road Agents.

While the Road Agents were terrorizing the people of Montana Territory, there was another group that was attempting to counteract the violence and deaths from the wild group. They called themselves the Vigilantes, started by the governor's nephew. Some of the men only pretended to be vigilantes to disguise the fact that they were actually

Road Agents, but many were valiant, brave, and determined to create a safer life for themselves and the families of Gold Country. The Vigilantes worked tirelessly to promote peace, even if it meant coming down hard on the criminals.

The Vigilantes often wore bandanas to look intimidating, which succeeded, and would target those suspected of being part of the Road Agents gang. When catching a member of this group, they would threaten to murder or maim them if they continued frightening the families of Bannack and the surrounding areas. These men protected the people and frightened the Road Agents into compliance while also catching more than two dozen of them and hanging them for their slaughters and robberies.

The Freilers began to see the posters of the Vigilantes with the mystic numbers "3-7-77." Mr. Dobbins had said this meant that the Vigilantes were prepared to put anyone who would terrorize the community into the ground- three feet wide, seven feet long, and seventy-seven inches deep. Some of these posters were more obviously sinister, with crossbones and skulls drawn on the front to scare off the Road Agents. The Vigilantes brought a great amount of justice to Gold Country, especially to the victims of the dreadful murders. Joseph became one of the Vigilantes and helped where he could. He was mindful of his work and his family, but did on occasion go to a house or two disguised with a bandana around his face and threaten harm if ever there was word of robbery or murder.

Joseph Freiler was always mindful when he was panning for his gold. Taking his pick and his pan, he was careful not to talk too much of the precious substance and tried to stay friendly with all of the men, even the surliest ones, to prevent them from finding his home and hurting his family. Although he had not found gold, he vowed that he would never tell anyone if he did, except a few trusted friends and the workers at the Assay.

There was a reason why everyone wanted the gold of Montana Territory. This gold was nearly completely pure, and many had luck finding some. The pamphlets advertising the gold rush were all over the big cities of the East and drew even more people to the West in search of this wonderful and bountiful life. This new "El Dorado," as the people called it, had drawn in thousands to search for gold in hopes of becoming one of the lucky ones. Many new miners built huts and tents to camp in, while some made due in caves and dug-outs. Others simply stayed in their wagons, where they slept and ate the hunted game. Bannack was popular among men who had fought in the Civil War, as well as businessmen who gained profit from the new people who flooded into the town. These families and individuals traveled in wagons, stagecoaches, and steamboats from the popular Fort Benton, and some men even came to Bannack by walking.

Joseph was beginning to grow a bit disappointed and doubtful, although he still had high hopes that providence would shine down upon him and his family. He only made a meager couple of dollars a day, which was just enough to go into town and buy some necessities such as cough syrup and dry goods- and, on occasion, little food treats for the family. He made less of a living than he had in Minnesota, but he was determined that it would pay off. He was steadfast in his decision to stay in Gold Country until they became at least somewhat stable with money.

Anna Claire loved Gold Country. She did not always love when her father was gone late at night or all of the many chores she had to do indoors, but she loved living by Grasshopper Creek. Life, despite being much more placid up in the prairie where the cabin was, was still exciting and new. Anna Claire had seen more in less than a year than she had before in her whole life. She could be herself here, as free as the Montana Territory winds, as tall as the Gold Country mountains, as unpredictable as the weather, and as wild as the sagebrush growing along the banks. She loved nothing more than the feeling of her hair, which had started to grow longer, trailing behind her as she ran through the grass, the star-like asters hitting her knees as the sun peered slowly from the hills on her way to school. She relished in the excitement of town, showing her all kinds of people from all over the country who had come to Gold Country to pave their own way, just like her family did. She felt sometimes as if she was as much a part of Montana Territory as the soil in the ground or the caves in the rocks. It fit her, and she fit it.

Autumn in Gold Country was unbelievably beautiful with its rogue hills and brown leaves, and the golden crops ready for their harvest. Chores were becoming rough as Joseph allowed Peter to begin shooting the game himself before Charlotta and the girls cooked the meat and skinned the animals for their fur, which could be very tedious. Some weeks it rained too much while others rained too little, and the weather was volatile, which made Joseph anxious about that year's crops. Anna Claire helped her father and Pete sow the grass seed for the hay and care for the animals on their little farm. There was even a small fire at the Clemmons's barn, which, thankfully, was quickly put out when Charlotta noticed the beginning of a flame on her way to Nettie Clemmons for tea. The two women had been able to take blankets and put out the fire after Charlotta began screaming for Nettie until her tonsils ached, and Nettie noticed the flame, screaming herself and running into the house for the blankets. The autumn did not fail to create interesting situations for the Freiler's as well, who were at the whims of the prairie and the throes of the western climate.

At the end of October, Tommy turned eleven-years old and the Freiler's had a small cake for him at their home, as his mother had forgotten his birthday. Tommy had expected his mother would forget, as she often did most years, but was surprised when Mr. Freiler showed up at the saloon to take him out of town to the house to see the family. When they arrived, there was a little cake in the center of the table that which Charlotta and Caroline had baked for him. Tommy had been stunned and touched, and nearly cried on the spot until he remembered that he was

Tommy Cooper and Tommy Cooper didn't cry. Charlotta and Joseph found themselves very fond of the little boy, even though they worried about his influence over Anna Claire at times.

"I'm giving you this book," said Anna Claire as the two talked up in the loft.

The others were still eating cake downstairs with each other. It was only Tommy and Anna Claire now.

Anna Claire extended *A Pirate's Tale* to her friend.

"I like this one," said Tommy, taking the book and looking at the dark blue cover. "And I can read it now! Thanks."

"You're gettin' much better," said Anna Claire, taking the book from him and opening the first page. "Let's read."

Tommy sounded out the letters slowly and remembered what all of the letters symbolized and the sounds they made. He read very slowly, but Anna Claire was a patient little teacher. She helped him sound out the more difficult words and taught him the words with the silent letters in them. Tommy was making remarkable progress in just a couple of weeks.

Tommy was quite aware of how much his life had changed since meeting the Freilers. Before then, he spent his days looking at posters in his room and wandering about all over Bannack and the surrounding lands, not caring about anything or anyone. Then he met Anna Claire, and everything became bright and vivid. It was almost like she had lifted a gray veil from his eyes so that he could finally see clearly. He found himself thinking about holidays, visiting the Freiler's cabin, and how wonderful it was to see Caroline's beautiful face when he came over. He thought about sassy Helen, playful Peter, and adorable Berthie, about Joseph's stories and Charlotta's kindness, and most of all Anna Claire's friendship. For the first time ever, he felt he had a real family.

He liked his mother well enough, but sometimes he wondered if she liked him back. Sometimes he felt that he would be fine without her and would possibly be better off. No more loud noises in the middle of the night, no more drunken brawls on the stairwell, no more strange men knocking on the bedroom doors, and no more agitating requests from his mother to fetch her something to drink or help her with her stockings. No more of her complaining about how his father ran away, no more whining about how she had little money because of him, no more casual dismissals to do whatever he pleased, and- most importantly- no reminders of how he felt unloved by her.

Kathleen Cooper was not the type of woman who ever wanted to have children. She was high-strung, rapidly fluctuating in mood and taste, and had an intense dislike of caretaking. She had raised Tommy the only way she knew how, which was not to raise him at all. She had to remain focused on obtaining the money and getting support from lovers whom she took on various nights to sustain her standing, her pride, and her finances. She did, however, care for the child, but he was too young to be much of a big help in her life, and, therefore, she did not know what to do about him.

Tommy was becoming cherished by the Freilers, including Caroline, who had grown used to the boy's adoration of her and took it all in stride. She thought Tommy was brave for everything he had done to save her sister when she had gone down the creek, and so he had won her over as part of the family. Helen loved having him around because he was silly and made her laugh, and Helen loved anyone who could make her laugh. Pete thought Tommy was absolutely remarkable, as he knew so much about cowboys and rodeos, and talked of excitement and gore, which was everything Pete so desperately loved. Berthie was pleased with Tommy because he often told her stories and called her "Little Ber" as if she was his own little sister. And, of course, Anna Claire thought of Tommy as closer than a brother to her, her very best friend.

Life was hard, but gentle at the same time. The work was difficult and could be very futile and frustrating, but the closeness the family felt and the people around them made it all worth it. After so many months in Gold Country, Charlotta did not feel alone any longer. She felt like she was finally a part of a community, albeit a small one, and she adored the Clemmons's as if they were her own family members. The two families depended on each other to watch their children if one of the mothers was sick, to provide food when there was too much to go around, and to provide support for each other, especially now that the days were growing short and the nights would soon be long and cold. They became very close, and the children grew to like the Clemmons children.

However, not everyone who was settled around the banks of Grasshopper Creek could be trusted. The lawlessness, the rough and drunken men, and the consistently growing murders around the roads of Bannack were a serious concern for many of the people of Gold Country. Everyone had to tread lightly and watch their step, for there were people out there who were keeping track of who was finding resources and hunting down those who did. Death was ever-present in Gold Country, although it was often easy to forget in the quiet of the fields or in the cheerful tone of the town.

The two young children who had found the bones of Gus Winkler were also gold-hungry, and neither of them had given up on the hope of finding the treasure. Although they had not been able to find the gold on that spot of the mountain, they knew it was up there, and someday, maybe when they got a little older, they would journey back up that mountain, more ready and prepared than ever before to find what had been hidden for years. Together they planned it, hoping for the opportunity to show up at any moment. They decided they would wait no matter how long it would take. They themselves would rescue the gold and save their families. They were going to be the ones.

"I don't think we should be goin' all the way over there," said Tommy one day, watching as Anna Claire waded through the water, throwing her bonnet onto the shore.

It was an unusually warm day in Gold Country at the beginning of November, and it almost felt like Spring again.

"But we never been across there before," she said, referring to the other side of the creek where she was swimming to.

Tommy followed her, the water creeping up to his neck.

"Ain't your ma and pa gonna be downright angry?"

Anna Claire shrugged as she reached the other side of the bank, squeezing her hair so that some of the water came out. "They don't gotta know."

Tommy thought for a moment before nodding.

"I just wanted to see what was over here," said Anna Claire, gazing ahead, the sky an exceptionally light blue and the grass various shades of green and yellow.

"Maybe there ain't nothin'. Maybe there's somethin'."

The children looked behind them at the shrubs, the creek, and the trees on the other side before beginning to walk. They walked and walked, and walked some more. There was nothing but blue sky and bristly grass, the hills rising and falling in the distance, much too far away for two young children to walk to.

"I guess there ain't much here," Tommy looked around him, making sure he did not miss anything.

"I suppose," sighed Anna Claire, disappointed.

They were about to turn around when Anna Claire put her finger to her lips.

"What?"

"Don't you hear that?"

"Hear what? I don't hear nothin'," said Tommy.

Anna Claire could hear something, although she did not know what. Voices faintly calling, laughing, chattering.

"Come on!" She took Tommy's hand and began running.

The two stopped short when they saw something unidentifiable in the distance and began walking briskly instead. As they got closer, they could see the faint outline of the top of a tower- only it wasn't the top of a tower because there was no tower.

Tommy was shocked to see the camps of the Native Americans. "Everyone always talks about them, and sometimes they've come to town, but not often." He started backing away slowly, as if he had seen a fox and was trying to creep away from it.

Anna Claire looked at him and then over at the little triangular shapes ahead.

"We should say hello!" She motioned for him to come closer, but he stayed still.

"They're bad," said Tommy, his face frightened. "They scalp and kill anybody who's White! They cook and eat them for supper!"

Anna Claire rolled her eyes. "Oh, stop it. I'm goin'. Are you comin' or not?"

In truth, Tommy really, *really* did not want to go anywhere near there. But he also couldn't let little

Anna Claire go over there by herself, so he began to walk next to her, the two silently heading towards the tee-pees.

As they got closer, they drew the attention of the Native Americans. They, in the middle of their activities, stopped to look at them, their faces curious but guarded.

Anna Claire swallowed, feeling nervous. She wasn't sure any longer if this was a good idea.

"You saw it," Tommy said, "now let's go!"

Ignoring him, Anna Claire walked on, her head high.

"Anna *Claire*!" cried Tommy uselessly.

As she approached, one of the men wearing bright colors around his neck and long feathers in his hair began walking toward them. He put up his hand to stop them.

Anna Claire stopped short and looked up. He had some light wrinkles crossing his forehead and his cheeks. His eyes were sharp and fierce, and he held Anna Claire's gaze without blinking an eye.

Neither Anna Claire nor Tommy could speak. Instead, they could just look up into the man's eyes, trembling and daring not to breathe.

"Why are you here?" he asked in a deep, confident voice.

Anna Claire gulped. "We- we were just walkin', sir. We just wanted to see- to see what was on the other side of the creek!"

Before the conversation could go any further, a beautiful woman with two black braids and earrings brighter than the sun came to stand next to the man.

That is when Anna Claire noticed the outline of a bird on the man's arm. After exchanging some words in a language Tommy and Anna Claire didn't understand, the man sighed.

"Come." He was very direct- so direct that the children dared not disobey him.

Getting closer to the Native American camps, Anna Claire's heart began to beat loudly in her chest. She looked around her as the people stopped what they were doing to stare at her and Tommy.

There were Native Americans of all different ages, some of them with white hair and innumerable wrinkles while others were merely toddlers sucking on their mothers' breasts. Some of the younger children stared with big eyes and curious faces, while others buried their faces in their parents' chests. Their tee-pees rose tall above them, covered with buffalo hides. The people of the camp wore the finest jewelry Anna Claire had ever seen in her life- amethysts, rubies, and colored beads draping around the necks and heads of the men and women. Anna Claire had rarely seen people with such dark skin, and she never saw anyone with such elaborate clothing on their bodies. It both frightened and excited her beyond measure.

"Gee, let us go home!" begged Tommy, his eyes wide and his hands tense by his side. "Please! We didn't mean to cause no trouble!"

The woman who had been standing next to the man turned around. She slowly took Tommy's hand in hers and covered it with the other hand. She bent her head forward and smiled kindly, causing

Tommy's hand to stop shaking. She then smiled warmly at Anna Claire.

Anna Claire smiled and bowed her head, admiring the woman's sparkling brown eyes.

Tommy looked over at Anna Claire. Anna Claire made a quick face at him to be quiet.

The teepees were large and tall, and covered with brown and red pictures- drawings of spears, of men running, of bears standing straight and fierce.

Children were running around, laughing, and smiling at the newcomers. Some of the women sat in front of the teepees, making beautiful necklaces and earrings from colorful beads. Most of the men had hair so long it dragged on the ground, while the women had hair much shorter. Some of the younger girls had long braids, and some of the boys did, too. Anna Claire had never seen such clothing before- clothing of buckskin, shoes of leather, and head-dresses of the most beautiful long feathers. One man, an older man watching them carefully from the side of a teepee, had a headdress so expressive that it made Tommy stop and point. Horses were seen throughout the camps, too. There was brightly colored pottery in front of one of the teepees, some with what appeared to be dried vegetables in them. Many women were outside sitting down on wooden chairs, sewing, tending to children, and washing clothing. They wore long, thick dresses made of hide, decorated with bones and elk teeth. They stopped what they were doing to watch the two excited and somewhat frightened children, some looking solemn while others smiled warmly.

"Hungry?" said the stern man, looking at them straight into their eyes without blinking.

Anna Claire and Tommy both shook their heads no. However, a young woman came out of one of the teepees with a basket of bread.

"Eat," said the man, motioning to the bread.

Anna Claire and Tommy glanced at each other and slowly took a piece of bread from the basket, chewing hesitantly, before realizing it was actually quite soft and delicious, and then eating the rest quickly.

Anna Claire noticed the same girl she had seen during the summer- the strikingly beautiful one with the long black hair and face like a doll. The girl turned to look at her, giving her that same cold look.

"Thank you for the bread," said Anna Claire to the woman who still held out the basket with a warm smile. "This is the best bread I've ever had!"

The woman continued to smile, but her eyes looked confused.

"She does not speak much English," said the man. "I learned some. I had to learn."

Tommy and Anna Claire nodded, sharing curious glances at each other.

Speaking in a language neither of them understood, one of the boys ran up to the man and asked him a question. The man replied gruffly.

"Hello," said the young boy, looking from Anna Claire to Tommy and back to Anna Claire, a curious but confused look on his face.

"Hello," said Anna Claire and Tommy at the same time.

The boy must have been about ten years old. He was lean and wiry, his black hair disheveled around his face. His teeth were spread apart a bit, and his face had a wild but softened look to it.

"You speak English?" asked Anna Claire, feeling delighted and surprised.

"Very small," answered the boy. He then looked at the man, who appeared to be his father, and spoke more in the interesting language that they couldn't understand.

"My son speak only a bit of English," explained the man. "He only know a few words. He is learning. He must learn."

Tommy put out his hand to shake it, but the other boy only looked at him blankly.

"What's your name?" asked Anna Claire.

The father said something to the boy, who responded with "lá daxpitchée," the words sounding to Tommy and Anna Claire like *iak doc-peet-che.*

"Anna Claire," she said, putting her hands to her chest.

"Tommy," and he put his hands to his chest as well.

"His name means 'Little Bear,'" explained his father, smiling with pride and putting the top of his hand on his son's head, "in your language."

The boy said a few words to his father, who paused before nodding and answering.

"My son wants to show you," the man extended his arm. "This is where we live."

And where they lived was quite fascinating, and even more so, *how* they lived. There were children running around freely, laughing so easily. Some of the children played games, such as one using a hoop, while others did chores like bringing water into buckets and helping their mothers make buffalo-meat stew.

Men with bearded hair pipes sat together and talked in deep, low voices. Young women with elk teeth on their dresses and men carrying knives and stone ball clubs were adorned with colorful beads. These beads were mostly of pinks and blues and hung around their necks, wrists, and even waists. Women ground saskatoon berries and prairie turnips on stones. Some were making pottery and carving out utensils from mountain sheep horns, while others were making bags out of salmon skin and tanning hides. Anna Claire and Tommy noticed a very tall man standing off to the side, smoking tobacco and watching them with narrowed eyes and a sharp frown. He had long stripes of black over his face.

Iá daxpitchée motioned for Tommy and Anna Claire to come with him, and the three of them ran around a few of the teepees, the structures alive with paintings of animals and depictions of humans. The boy then let them gingerly step into a long, large teepee and pointed at the people, saying their names one by one. There was an old woman with gray hair sitting by the fireplace and smiling. The woman who they had met before was there, and by the way Iá daxpitchée stood at her side and held her hand, it was clear she was his mother. There was an older man with a very young child in his lap. Mattresses of buffalo hides were placed around the edges, and there was a big fireplace at the center, the smoke escaping from a flap at the top.

Anna Claire and Tommy admired the beadwork on the women's necks and the long buckskin shirt of the old man. The little baby was plump and happy, cooing gleefully to see the two odd children.

Soon, lá daxpitchée motioned for them to leave his teepee. He walked them a short way beyond it, through a few more teepees and people, all who were looking at them- some in fear, some in shock, others in curiosity- and then sat down in the grass. When Tommy and Anna Claire did the same, he held out a necklace with a tooth hanging from it. They had never seen such a thing.

"Ooh," said Anna Claire as he allowed her to touch it, her small hands taking the tooth while her eyes moved around it.

"That's ace high!" said Tommy, impressed. "Maybe I can get one like that?"

Anna Claire rolled her eyes. "He doesn't understand you!"

"I understand," said the boy slowly but confidently. "I understand you want it." With a shrug and a sigh, the boy handed over the tooth necklace to Tommy.

"For me?" Tommy couldn't believe his eyes.

The boy nodded.

"Gee, thanks!" Tommy said, taking the tooth in his hands and smoothing it over and over.

The boy nodded and then looked over at Anna Claire.

"I do not have," he said sadly. "Come back in few days. I will have something for you."

Anna Claire smiled. "You don't have to give me nothin'!"

Iá daxpitchée smiled brightly. "I give."

The children sat underneath the sun for a while. There was so much that Anna Claire wanted to say to Tommy, but it would have to wait.

"See," said the boy, pointing to the ground. "Bikkée."

"Bee-ka?" asked Tommy.

The boy took a blade of grass into his hand and repeated the word.

"Grass!" said Anna Claire excitedly. "He's telling us his language!" She then took the blade of grass from his hand and said, "Grass."

Iá daxpitchée smiled. "G-rass. Grass."

"That's good!" said Anna Claire. She nodded to him, repeating the word "good."

"Good," Iá daxpitchée said slowly. He then took a small rock and put it in his hand. "Biiá. Biiá."

"Bee-ya... biiá," said Anna Claire happily, taking the rock from his hand.

Tommy then piped in, snatching the rock from his friend's hand and pointing to it. "Rock."

"Rock," said the boy. "Rock."

They were all smiling now, huddling into their own little circle and pointing to various objects, such as their shirts, their shoes, the teepees, and the horses.

"Iichíile. Iichíile," said Iá daxpitchée, pointing over to where a horse grazed next to a teepee.

"Horse!" the two others said, excited to be learning and also to be teaching a language. "Horse!"

Anna Claire thought for a moment before looking away and pointing at two horses. She then put up two fingers and said, "Horses."

"Horses?" Iá daxpitchée sounded confused.

Tommy put one finger up and said "Horse." Then, he put two fingers up and pointed at the other horses one by one. "Horses."

Iá daxpitchée smiled confidently. "I understand! Horses!"

He then pointed his finger at himself, Tommy, and then Anna Claire. He did this again, and they wondered what he meant. And then he said, "iilápaache." He repeated the motion and then put his hands on his heart. "Iilápaache."

"Oh!" cried Anna Claire, also pointing to him and then to herself and Tommy. "Friends! Friends."

The children laughed and talked, teaching each other new words and forming a bond that was, albeit different, sacred. They were good friends by the time they parted.

"I'm sorry, but my mama's gonna be so sore at me!" explained Anna Claire. "I was supposed to be home long ago!"

Iá daxpitchée tilted his head slightly.

"We have to go," said Tommy to him. "Anna Claire has to go home. I could stay all day, but she can't."

"You must go," said Iá daxpitchée, nodding. "Come back. I have something for Anna Claire."

The three children smiled, having developed a friendship that only a few words helped to grow.

Iá daxpitchée followed them down a bit, answering the Native American people's questions with answers in his own language.

He stopped in front of his father and said something. The man smiled ever-so-slightly before extending his hand.

"Táachiiate ihké," he said firmly but gently, the words sounding like "tah-gee-da ee-ka" to Tommy and Anna Claire. "My name. It means 'Bright Star.'"

"Pleased to meet you, sir," said Tommy.

"Thank you for lettin' us come," said Anna Claire.

The man nodded. "You may come again. If you wish."

The children smiled and shook their heads "Yes."

Then, they ran across the field, away from the camps, and back to Grasshopper Creek.

"You're awfully quiet tonight, Anna Claire," said Joseph at the table as the family ate supper.

Anna Claire was enthralled. She had never formally met any Native Americans, and meeting Iá daxpitchée had been one of the most thrilling and exciting moments of her entire life. Even better- they were friends, now. She was friends with a Native American. Her elders had been wrong. The Native Americans weren't dangerous and bad people like her parents and the other miners always told her.

"I got nothin' to say," she answered, slowly and methodically breaking off a piece of bread.

"That is the first I've heard of that!" said Charlotta with a smile.

Anna Claire smiled back happily. They had no idea what had just happened to her- the amazing, rare, beautiful moments at the Native American camps with Iá daxpitchée and his family and friends. She was not going to tell them, either. They could not know what happened. They would forbid her to go anywhere near the creek again, let alone the camps.

"Why don't you just finally run away and don't come back this time?" sneered Helen at Anna Claire, her mouth full of jam.

"Helen Freiler!" shouted Charlotta.

"It's alright, Mama," said Anna Claire gently. "Jesus teaches us to forgive. Doesn't he, Mama?"

Charlotta nearly fell out of her chair. "W-why yes, yes he does."

"I forgive you, Helen!" said Anna Claire, a hint of sauciness in her voice that went undetected by her parents but was not missed on Helen.

"You little.." Helen huffed and pursed her lips, turning to look at her plate. Anna Claire smiled to herself sneakily.

"Did you hear up near Bozeman's another man was attacked and killed by a Crow?" Joseph took a drink from his glass.

Charlotta shook her head. "Joseph, not now, not with the children."

Joseph sighed. "They have to know how dangerous those people are!"

"Why?" sighed Charlotta. "Why do they have to know?"

"Because they must know never to go near them if they ever meet them. And they must be prepared when they do. They are everywhere; they'll no doubt see them. O'Reilly told me there's a tribe of Crows not too far from here." Joseph put down his glass, a feeling of anger stirring inside of him.

Anna Claire looked up at this and resisted speaking.

Joseph muttered an unkind name for the Native Americans, leaning against the table to look into the children's eyes. "There are many men from many areas of Montana Territory. Many of our men and even women and children have been mercilessly killed."

"Why?" asked Pete, shivering.

"No good reason," said Joseph. "They're angry with us because we dare make a life for ourselves out West. They want the land all to themselves. You see, they are a selfish people. A murderous, simple, primitive people."

"What's pwimtive mean?" asked Berthie innocently.

"Unintelligent," replied Joseph, sitting back in his chair. "You must tell me if you ever see one and you must always stay away from them!"

"They're not all bad," spoke up Anna Claire. She paused, hoping they wouldn't ask her more questions.

"Well, I reckon that must be so," said Joseph after a long pause. "But most of 'em are. Now, mind me and tell me if you ever see one."

"I will, Papa," said Helen obediently.

"I will, too," said Caroline, her face ashen.

Anna Claire so wanted to tell her father that he was wrong, that she knew the Native Americans nearby, that she had made a friend in one and had grown to like those at the camps. They were nice, they treated her and Tommy well, and they offered them bread. They could not be bad people. But Anna Claire knew that if she were to say anything else, her parents would grow suspicious, so instead she kept her mouth shut.

After the plates had been washed and the bread folded back into the napkins, Anna Claire went quietly up to the loft where she looked out of the window. She tried to imagine what Iá daxpitchée and his family were doing now. Were they singing songs in their teepees by the fire? Were they dancing outside in the quiet wind? Had Iá daxpitchée finished eating, too? She wondered what he had for supper.

Papa is wrong, thought Anna Claire. *They aren't all bad.*

Anna Claire's heart sank at the thought of her father being wrong. He was always right, always fair, always true. Why did he despise the Native Americans so much?

She felt sick to her stomach that night. Her father was actually wrong about something- and not something small, either. He was wrong, like so many other people were, about the Native Americans.

Why didn't they try to understand?

Chapter 12- Miss Darling and Her School

Miss Lucia Darling was an educated young woman who had traveled with family members from Ohio to the little town in Idaho Territory a couple of years before. She had come with her uncle, the very astute governor Sidney Edgerton- appointed by Abraham Lincoln himself, who had traveled all the way to Washington, D.C, to talk to Congress, fighting for the land to be a territory. He had brought with him $2,500 worth of gold, sewn into his coat lining to impress the congressmen. They certainly were impressed, and so the land had thus become Montana Territory.

Governor Sidney Edgerton even had the Legislature of Montana come into his home while Bannack was being pronounced the capital of the territory. For financial purposes, the governor left Montana Territory in September of that year with most of his family members; however, the schoolteacher, Miss Lucia Darling, stayed behind in the cabin. This same cabin had been used the previous year to teach the students before the proper school was built closer to town. She had been appointed by the superintendent of public instruction and had charmed the administrator with her wit and smarts.

Only in her mid-twenties, Lucia Darling was mature for her age and very resilient. Not only had she made the arduous journey from Ohio, but she was determined to succeed and ensure that the children of the mining camps and of the rough-and-tumble town received proper schooling. She was a hardworker, serious and bright, and deeply cared about the children of Bannack and Gold Country. She had makeshift school supplies, including desks and books received from various families around town, and she was resolute that her school would create a sense of order in the community.

She succeeded somewhat, at least among the children. Some of the children from the mining camps had never learned to read, and others had not been to school in years. Miss Darling wanted to ensure success for all of her students, no matter whom they were, and she was not a woman who gave up easily.

It was only a few weeks that the little school by the bank was in session as Anna Claire raced off to school one foggy morning, forgetting to tie her boot laces and brush her hair. She was excited because this was the day of the big exam. This was the day that Anna Claire could prove that she was a good reader and had excellent skills in literary metaphors.

Miss Darling had instructed the children in her Fourth Reader group to read the book, *Eva Green,* which was about a girl growing up in the South. Anna Claire did not love reading the book, but she could not help but want to impress Miss Darling. Miss Darling was so fond of her, and she wanted to prove that she could do what was asked of her and then some.

"Anna Claire, you forgot your lunch!" said Caroline, running to hand her the little burlap sack with the bread and apples.

"I'm sure my presentation is going to be the best," said Helen saucily, her ribbons slowly unraveling from her hair.

Anna Claire smiled to herself. She wasn't even going to try to impress her sisters. They would find out soon how much she had taken from the book and how great she was going to be in her presentation.

Reaching the school, Anna Claire met Tommy outside of the door.

"Hey, you gonna tell me how that book ended?" he asked, his eyes widening.

Anna Claire nodded and whispered in his ear. She knew Tommy was never going to get around to finishing the book, despite the children's ability to share copies, so she was his entrusted confidant.

"That book sounds so stupid," said Tommy, frowning.

"It was," agreed Anna Claire. "But there were some really good parts in it, too. You just wait and hear. I'm going to talk about all of the best parts of the book. Miss Darlin'll be real happy with me and then she'll know I'm a good reader, just like she is."

The children, including Anna Claire and Tommy, gathered into the schoolhouse, Anna Claire tripping on the plank wood, and took their seats. Caroline, sitting in the back upright and proper, gave Jacob Mast a warm look from across the room. Helen sat down on the seat so hard she hurt herself and was rubbing the back of her behind. Pete, holding Berthie's hand, separated from her so that they could both take their places on opposite sides of the room-boys on one side and girls on the other. Anna Claire glanced over at Lisa Howler and gave her a smile.

"I can't wait to present!" she declared.

"I'm sure you'll be the best," said Lisa, giving her a look of confidence.

"Thanks, Lisa," smiled Anna Claire.

"Now class," said sweet Miss Darling, pausing to write the name of the book, *Eva Green*, on the board. "Today is the day we will have presentations from our Fourth Reader students and our older students. I will call you by name, and you will come to the front of the classroom and tell us about the book, a lesson you learned from the book, and how this lesson has affected you."

Anna Claire nodded happily, squirming in her seat. She couldn't wait to go. She began to raise her hand, but Miss Darling called on Rebecca Clemmons first. There were a few more children that Miss Darling called on, and Anna Claire listened to each one, trying to keep herself from smiling at the fact that she had a much better perspective of the book than any of her classmates.

That is when things began to get sour.

"Alright, Anna Claire," said Miss Darling, looking down at her with a smile. "Let us hear your presentation."

Anna Claire, nearly giddy with anticipation, headed up to the front of the classroom. As she was walking, she suddenly felt the world spin around her and everything go upside down. She landed on her side with a loud thud, right as she was about to reach the end of the room.

Some of her classmates erupted in laughter, mainly the boys. She sat up shakily, rubbing her forehead and trying not to cry. Someone on the boy's side of the room had deliberately tripped her by putting their foot out.

"Little baby is gonna cry!" said the culprit, whose foot had quickly disappeared behind the other desk.

"I-I'm not," faltered Anna Claire, still shocked by her fall. She stood up slowly with Miss Darling helping her.

"I saw that, Ebb Drummond," said Miss Darling to the boy who had tripped Anna Claire. "I will have to send you home today."

Ebenezer Drummond, known as the most trying and callous boy in the school, laughed and stood up tall. At fifteen, he was taller than Miss Darling herself and was not intimidated by her in the slightest.

"Oh yeah?" he sneered, walking towards her. "Maybe I won't go home. Maybe I'll just stay around the schoolhouse for a little while. You know, hear everyone's presentations."

"Go home, Ebenezer," said Miss Darling softly. Miss Darling rarely got angry, but this time she was definitely having trouble keeping calm.

"Yeah? What're ya gon' do about it now?"

"If you don't leave immediately-"

"Yeah?" Ebenezer tested, walking up to her face and looking down at her.

"What? Nothin'?"

"Leave at once!" Miss Darling yelled, her voice shaking, the whole classroom in raptured silence wondering what was going to happen next.

"I ain't goin' nowhere," said Ebenezer, sitting back in his chair and yawning. "Go on teachin'. Ann-Claire, go on with your presentation."

The children were shocked. No one had ever spoken to kind-hearted but firm Miss Darling that way.

Miss Darling's face went from angry to shocked and then to slightly embarrassed. She wasn't able to necessarily force Ebenezer Drummond to leave her classroom, and he was far too big for a whipping. For a moment, it was very clear that she had no idea what to do next.

"Please, I do not want to have to expel you," said Miss Darling as calmly as she could manage.

"*Expel*- that's a big word," laughed the boy, looking at the other boys next to him who were not laughing any longer. He stood up from his seat again, this time with his eyebrows narrowing and his eyes ominously shrinking.

"No one is gettin' expelled. *No one.*"

With this move, he grabbed Miss Darling by the elbow and squeezed it just enough that she could not move out of his grasp. She made a little cry before gathering up her senses and remaining calm.

Anna Claire, never having actually gone back to her seat, stood there with her mouth open and her eyes wide. She felt her face flush and her fists clench. No one dared to touch her, Miss Darling!

Without thinking, she grabbed the ink quill on Miss Darling's desk, turned to face them, and stabbed Ebenezer Drummond with the quill, right behind him where his shoulder met his backbone.

Ebenezer let out a loud cry that nearly rever-berated throughout the schoolhouse. He let go of Miss Darling, who was too surprised to move, and took the quill out of his skin from the back of his shirt. He then grabbed Anna Claire by the arm, held the quill menacingly to her face, and suddenly dropped it, making another loud cry. This time it was Tommy.

Tommy had stood up on one of the desks in his row and jumped on his back, pounding his head with small fists.

"Get off her, get off her!" he cried, blinding Ebenezer with his hand.

Miss Darling, gathering her wits, rushed over and pried Tommy off while he was still kicking and screaming. She then yelled for everyone in the class-room to safely leave the building and go home, except for Tommy whom she told to run into town and get someone to help. Anna Claire huddled under a desk for a moment before jumping up as Ebenezer's big arm came towards her.

"That stupid little girl!" Ebenezer yelled, his voice thundering. "Come back, you baby! Baby Ann-Claire! Stupid little baby!"

Miss Darling yelled for Ebenezer to calm down and stop, but he was up and chasing Anna Claire around the classroom. Anna Claire, much smaller and nimbler than him, ran around and under the desks, climbing up and then down quickly, until she reached the door of the schoolhouse, where she ran into Mr. Kenneth Hoffman, one of the blacksmiths, who had come to help with Tommy.

"What's goin' on in here?" he asked as he ran to block Ebenezer from getting to Anna Claire. "Son, slow down!"

With his strength, Mr. Hoffman pinned Ebenezer to the wall as the boy tried to kick and hit. Screaming, his face as red as a cherry, he yelled more insults toward Anna Claire, who was staring with big eyes at the scene before her.

"Thank you, Mr. Hoffman," said Miss Darling once Ebenezer began to grow weary. "Thank you ever so much."

"Don't mention it," he answered. "But what happened in here?"

"He touched Miss Darlin'!" cried Anna Claire, rousing Ebenezer's anger again.

"Let me handle this from here," said Miss Darling, explaining what had happened after he had tripped Anna Claire and grabbed her elbow.

"My, my," frowned Mr. Hoffman. "You did a bad thing, Anna Claire, but I know you were just tryin' to help your teacher. Ebenezer, you never touch a teacher! I'm going to have a long conversation with your father about this one. You're really ridin' the rail now, boy."

"Ahh!" yelled Ebenezer, the anger returning to his face. However, Mr. Hoffman was much bigger and stronger, and took him out of the building by the ear, dragging him all the way.

"Anna Claire, are you alright?" asked Miss Darling once it was safe, giving her pupil a small embrace.

"He didn't get me, Miss Darlin'," she answered, looking up at her teacher with a smile.

"Thank you for defending me," Miss Darling said, "but you can never stab anyone with a quill! He may be seriously injured! I will have to tell your mama and papa, you see?"

Anna Claire sighed. "I know."

Miss Darling noticed the forlorn look on her face and added, "But of course I'll also have to tell them that you saved me today and I am forever thankful to have had you by my side this afternoon."

Anna Claire smiled again.

"And thank you, Tommy," continued Miss Darling, "for all of your help. If not for you, Anna Claire would have gotten very hurt, and I'm not sure what would have happened to me!"

Tommy nodded, attempting to look tough, but was hiding a slightly noticeable grin.

"Go home and please rest," said Miss Darling. "I will stay behind in case any of the parents want to talk with me. Anna Claire, I trust you to tell your parents. Please tell them to come see me this week when they can after school."

"I will," promised Anna Claire disappointedly. "I didn't even get to present."

"Don't worry, dear," said Miss Darling kindly. "You can present tomorrow. I know it will be wonderful."

Anna Claire and Tommy skipped happily out of the door, feeling like little heroes.

"You know what?" said Tommy as they walked quickly through the town, the sounds of the wagons and voices filling the air.

"What?"

"I think you're braver than that stupid Ebb Drummond. I think you might be as brave as a boy!"

"Of course, I am!" declared Anna Claire, spitting in the dirt to prove her point. "That boy didn't scare me none!"

Tommy laughed as the two of them went into Swiner's Saloon.

"My sisters have to be home now," said Anna Claire as they opened the flimsy doors. "They don't know how long we had to stay. I knew stupid Caroline and Helen wouldn't wait for me. They were too scared to hang around the school. I'm glad though 'cause now we can go upstairs. But I can't be too long else they'll come lookin' for me, and Mama will be awful mad when she hears what I did."

The two, giving a quick wave to Kathleen Cooper, who was serving drinks at the counter, ran up the stairs heavily, their boots hitting the steps with loud thuds.

When they arrived in Tommy's little room, messy with his clothes on the floor haphazardly and his posters of cowboys and women thrown around in various places on the ground, they both sighed.

"I feel like you haven't been here in forever," said Tommy, sitting down on the floor. "I wish you were allowed to come to town more instead of just to school."

Anna Claire fell down next to him and put her arms around her knees. "Not after that time we went to the mountain. My papa was so scared he cried! I saw him! He said it was all his fault for lettin' me do what I want and that I'm too young to say where I go and where I don't go, and that you're too young for me to go alone with, and that I could've been killed on the mountain. Ain't that kinda silly? We wasn't killed and we even helped find that man's body! If it wasn't for us, his bones would still be up there. But I still can't go to town unless it's for school with my sisters and Pete. Maybe when I'm older or at least when you're old enough to take me to town by yourself."

"I'm eleven," said Tommy, sitting up a little taller. "I'm mighty old enough."

"No, you're not," said Anna Claire matter-of-factly.

Tommy sighed as Anna Claire looked at the posters that were strewn across the wooden floor which was stained with licorice and old candy.

"I don't like the way those ladies dress," Anna Claire shook her head. "Their dresses are too short and they have too much paint on their face!"

Tommy smiled. "They sure are pretty though, ain't they?"

Anna Claire didn't answer but instead scrunched her slightly freckled nose.

"Someday, I'm gonna get me a girl like that," he looked down at his poster, his blue eyes wide with admiration.

Anna Claire laughed. "I thought you wanted Caroline!"

Tommy paused and nodded. "Yeah, well I wanna marry Caroline the most, but if she can't marry me, then I want a girl like this."

"Caroline would never wear dresses so short," said Anna Claire. "Never in a hundred years!"

"I said only if she didn't marry me!" declared Tommy unhappily, standing up and sitting on his bed. "Gee, I'm awful hungry. Do you want to sneak some candy?"

"Sure!"

The two ran down the creaky stairs, careful not to get splinters from the railing in their hands. Giggling, they ran behind the counter and took handfuls of colorful hard candies, Tommy stashing some in his pockets, before running back outside.

"I have to go home," said Anna Claire as she popped a gumdrop in her mouth, "before Mama and Caroline and Helen and Pete and Berthie come back to the schoolhouse."

"Oh, alright," said Tommy sadly. "But maybe soon your pa can come to town with you!"

"He don't like saloons," Anna Claire pronounced, "but maybe he'll come anyway."

She then left the saloon. She stopped to run through a little alleyway before skirting off into the surrounding fields of the town. When she arrived home, her mother and Caroline came up to hug her closely.

"Oh, Anna Claire," said her mother, a worried expression on her face, "I heard what happened. I heard that you saved your teacher by hitting a bigger boy and getting him away from Miss Darling!"

"She *stabbed* him, Mama," said Helen, rolling her eyes next to the fireplace.

"What you did was not very smart, for that matter," admitted Charlotta with a twinkle in her eyes, "and you really should not have done it. He could have hurt you, and you should never hurt others. I cannot imagine what his mother and father will say about this. But, Anna Claire, I must say that I believe you thought you were doing right by Miss Darling. It seems as though he would have truly injured her."

"Oh, Mama, he was!" Caroline said much to Anna Claire's surprise, putting her arm around her. "He grabbed her arm! Anna Claire yelled at him and took that quill and put it right in his back!"

"Yeah, Mama, Anna Claire got him good!" cried Pete, extending his arm and pretending to stab an invisible quill in someone's back.

Charlotta made a small face but could not hide her amusement. "I do hope he's alright. I also hope you never do such a thing again. But I am proud that you had courage and conviction. That is what I want for you. I hope you will not give us a scare such as that again!"Anna Claire, confused but relieved, added, "Miss Darlin' wants to see you sometime after school. She also wants me to tell you that I was a hero!"

Helen threw her rag down on the ground. "That is ridiculous!" she said before stomping up the stairs.

Anna Claire, glad to see her sister jealous, was wrapped up in another embrace with Caroline. She kissed the top of Anna Claire's head affectionately as she helped her get seated at the table. "Oh, Anna

Claire, you were so brave! Naughty perhaps, but brave!"

Anna Claire pursed her lips to keep from smiling too wide. She didn't want to spoil this rare moment. Hero came up to her then and started licking her leg while she bent down to pat his head.

Anna Claire didn't get to present that day, but she had a wonderful day regardless. She had helped Miss Darling from danger, ate candy with Tommy, and made her family proud. She couldn't wait until her father got home to hear the news!

It was another chilly fall day when Anna Claire and the Freiler children experienced something else that was foreign to them.

They were walking to school when they finally reached town. Caroline, now that she was in the sight of human eyes, walked ahead of them, lifting her head up in the air and pretending like she didn't know her own siblings. She quickly met up with Mary Sully, the two girls arm in arm and clearly gossiping about their pests of sisters and brothers.

"She's so silly," said Helen as they entered Main Street. However, only a mere moment later, she met Lucy Grimm in the middle of the street and began looking over her shoulder and laughing.

"I hate them both," grumbled Anna Claire as she took Berthie's hand.

"I don't like girls," said Pete, crossing his arms and shuffling his feet.

Anna Claire, Pete, and Berthie walked along Main Street and turned on Clover Street, reaching the other side of town. Anna Claire noticed some of the people pointing and staring. When she looked over, her mouth dropped.

Three Black pioneers were coming out of the general store. The man, who was tall and stern-looking, was shouting something at one of the men who worked at the store. The man was yelling back and putting a fist in the air. This continued for some time, all the while people were watching and shaking their heads. The woman and little boy behind him stayed off to the side, looking helpless.

Anna Claire had never seen a Black person before, but only read about them in stories or heard about them from family members. She rubbed her eyes to make sure she was seeing correctly. Pete did the same. Berthie stared with her mouth wide open.

"You oughta be ashamed of yourself," said the Black man, coming to stand next to the woman and child. "Not lettin' a customer in on the account of bein' Black. My family shouldn't have to go without because of racist Whites like you!"

"You saw the sign," said the portly man from the general store.

"'No Blacks Allowed.' Go home." Then, the store owner proceeded to call the man a very ignorant and cruel word.

"Come on," said the man to his family. "We're leavin'."

He gave a long look and scowl toward the man at the store, who had now crossed his arms and was spitting into the dirt. He took the woman and the boy lightly by their arms and led them away from the scene.

Anna Claire, Pete, and Berthie watched them turn around and pass them on Clover Street as they made their way to Main Street. Many people stopped and stared. It was not often that a Black person came into town and Anna Claire herself had never seen one before.

"Ooh!" said Pete in awe. "Real Black people!"

Anna Claire shared his sentiments and glanced over at Berthie, who still had her mouth open and watched them as they continued to walk through town.

"Wait 'til I tell Papa!" Pete remarked, jumping up excitedly.

"Why is they skin so dawk?" asked Berthie, putting her fingers in her mouth like she usually did when she was feeling uneasy.

"It just is," answered Anna Claire. "Come on, let's go."

The three children walked a bit further before heading up to the school. They walked in and hung their coats in the cloakroom. When they sat down in their seats, taking out their copybooks, they realized that they were not the only ones shocked by the Black pioneers. The class was still standing up, talking excitedly among themselves.

"I can't believe I missed it," Helen said, frowning.

"They were so *dark*, too!" shouted Rebecca Clemmons, dropping her slate on her desk.

"I don't know why they're comin' to town," said Jonathan Brick. "They should know they ain't welcome here."

"I just can't believe they came here," said Suzanna Sloan. "Why would they ever come here? It must be dangerous for them!"

"Oh, who cares?" said Theodore Grimm. "Y'all are gettin' all worked up over nothin'. They're just people."

"They ain't people," said Ebenezer Drummond, spitting right there in the middle of the classroom. "They ain't even human." He then called them the ignorant word that the store owner had used earlier. "They don't deserve to be here."

Anna Claire shuddered as the door to the classroom shut. Miss Darling came in, her hair perfectly placed in its usual curly brown bun and her sweet face full of expression. She had Anna Claire and Lisa Howler get the cordwood to make the firewood in the pot-bellied stove while a few of the boys washed the inside of the windows, as everything had become frosty.

"Good morning, class!" she said happily, opening up her teaching book. "Now I know it has been cold. Thank you all for coming. Let us now say the Pledge of Allegiance."

"Can't we talk about the Blacks?" asked Samuel Thorn, coming from the group to sit down at his seat. Except that Samuel did not use the word "Black," but instead, used the far more ignorant and cruel word.

Miss Darling frowned and looked around the room. Anna Claire watched as Tommy entered the school building, late as usual, and plopped down in his seat. His eyes were puffy, and his hair was disheveled.

He was wearing the same dirty outfit he had on the day before. He looked like he hadn't slept in days.

"I will not permit that word in my classroom," said Miss Darling, obviously uncomfortable.

The class fell silent for a moment. No one could hear a sound. Then, Ebenezer Drummond stood up. Anna Claire felt her heart drop. She knew that whenever Ebb Drummond stood up, things were going to get bad.

"What word?" he said, his hands on his waist. And then he repeated it.

Miss Darling inhaled sharply. "Yes, Ebenezer. It is not a kind or appropriate word for this classroom."

Ebb Drummond laughed, looking over at his friends. "Well, I for one thing like the word. And whoever has a problem with it is probably a Black-lover themselves."

Anna Claire looked up at Miss Darling, wondering what she would do. No one said a single word, not even Ebb's friends. All was quiet.

Miss Darling shook her head and opened the book, knowing that sometimes the best way to deal with a problematic child was to ignore them.

"Now, the fireplace," she said awkwardly, purposefully looking away from Ebb. "I think we may take a vote to-"

"I wanna talk 'bout them Blacks that was in town this mornin,'" Ebb hissed, still standing with his hands on his waist. "Did you see 'em, Miss Darlin'?"

Miss Darling looked up, blushing. "I did see some people with dark skin."

"You saw the Blacks then." Ebb gave such a sickening smile that it made Anna Claire queasy, again using that other awful word. "Are you a Black-lover, Miss Darlin'?"

Anna Claire looked back at Tommy whose eyes were wide.

Miss Darling tried to turn her attention back to the class, but Ebb coughed and yelled loudly throughout the classroom, "Black-lover."

Miss Darling shut her eyes and pursed her lips. "I will have *no one* using that dreadful word in my classroom!"

Ebb only smiled, knowing he was much bigger and stronger than the sweet little teacher. She knew he was far too big to make stand in the corner or whip with a ferula, and she rarely ever had to use the ferula anyway. She was not sure of the next step in this altercation.

"Blacks ain't human, Miss Darlin'. For all your schoolin', you should know that by now."

Miss Darling walked over to him and pointed her finger towards the door, her hand shaking and her eyes narrowed. "Leave this school now."

Ebb only smiled more and laughed. "What will you do if I don't, Black-lover?"

Miss Darling swallowed, her hand shaking even more, and her voice trembling. "Please leave."

"*'Please leave,'*" he mocked, looking at his friends. Not even his friends laughed.

"I mean it, Ebenezer," said Miss Darling in a voice no one had heard before. "Leave my school at once. If you do not leave, I will have to expel you," Miss Darling said softly.

"I ain't goin' nowhere and you ain't expellin' me," Ebb gritted his yellow teeth, his eyes glaring.

"I will do as I please in my school," answered Miss Darling, standing up straight and looking poised.

Even though Ebenezer Drummond was the oldest and biggest student in the little schoolhouse, and Miss Lucia Darling herself was only a small, twenty-seven-year-old woman, she pursed her lips and fixated her eyes right on Ebb. "Get out."

"Make me."

Miss Darling sighed. "I do not have the physical strength to throw you out of my classroom, but I will call for help if I must."

Ebb kept his glare, standing up even straighter. "You ain't doin' nothin'."

That's when Tommy slowly started to stand up from his seat in the back. He didn't want to draw attention to himself. He slowly backed up towards the door, all the while looking over at Miss Darling. He pointed to the door and raised his eyebrows, signaling for her to let him go.

Miss Darling quickly glanced over and gave a nearly imperceptible nod to Tommy. Tommy ran out the door at that moment. He ran as fast as he could because he knew Ebb would certainly have heard him leave the schoolhouse, which would leave Miss Darling without him in the classroom to handle the mess.

He raced over to the end of Clover Street, where he ran into one of the legislators, Mr. Henry Wits. Tommy knew that Henry Wits was just the man to go to. He was strong, moral, and very frightening when angry.

"Mr. Wits, Mr. Wits!" Tommy cried, out of breath and face flushed. "Help! We need help!"

"What's goin' on, boy?"

"The school-" Tommy said between breaths. "Trouble in the school. Miss Darlin'- Ebenezer- he's threatenin' her- she said leave- he said no-"

"Slow down, son," Mr. Wits said, putting his hand on his shoulder. "I can't understand what on God's earth you're talkin' about."

"Ebenezer Drummond is threatenin' Miss Darlin'. She told him to leave because he kept sayin' this word, and he wouldn't leave. She said she was gonna expel him, but he kept sayin' the bad word, so then he said he wasn't gonna leave and she wasn't gonna be able to do anything about it. She looked awful scared, Mr. Wits!"

Mr. Wits patted him on the back. "Let's go."

He and Tommy ran through the street and up to the schoolhouse, ignoring the people asking what was wrong.

"What's goin' on in here?" Mr. Wits asked through gritted teeth.

Tommy looked over and saw poor Miss Darling against the wall, Ebenezer holding her there by the collar of her dress. The students were standing up, some on the other side of the classroom, looking afraid and not knowing what to do. Anna Claire had stayed at her desk and was yelling for Ebb to "Get off'a her!"

"Mr. Wits, come quick!" cried Anna Claire.

Miss Darling looked absolutely petrified. Her mouth was grimacing, and her eyes were widely pleading for Ebb to stop.

"Enough!" said Mr. Wits, thundering up through the classroom and pulling on the back of Ebenezer's shirt. He was a strong man and was able to easily pull him apart.

"What the hell is wrong with you, boy?" he asked, shaking him by the collar so that his head flew around him. "How many times are you gonna threaten your teacher? She's in here tryin' to give you a good education, and here you are robbin' yourself and your class of that. I'm sick of ya, Ebenezer Drummond! Right sick of ya! I know your pa don't care a lick about anything, but when I see him and tell him how I feel, trust me, boy, he will care then! I'll make him care. Now go, leave, and never come back to this school! You've lost your right to it! And if you won't listen to me, I'm sure you'll listen to the governor in court. Now go!"

Ebenezer shook his head and left without another word. Tommy felt a surge of relief. Miss Darling was going to be alright.

"I apologize for the trouble that boy caused you today, Miss Darlin'," said Mr. Wits, shaking his head and putting a hand on his hips. "That boy ain't nothin' but trouble! I'll see to it that he doesn't come back here. I'll be sure of it."

Miss Darling looked breathless. "Thank you-thank you Mr. Wits!"

"Now, you get back to teachin' what you were teachin'," he said, and then to the rest of the class,

"You appreciate your teacher, Miss Darlin'. She's givin' you good schoolin' here. You all should be grateful."

With that, Mr. Wits left, giving Tommy a pat on the back. Tommy sat down shakily, looking over at Caroline to see how she was fairing the distress. She was still in the back of the classroom, her hands clasped to her chest and her blue eyes wide.

"Return to your seats," said Miss Darling, a look of embarrassment on her face. "Elmer and Helen, please fetch the firewood. We will start by reciting the poem from yesterday."

She picked up her book and began reading the poem monotonously. Everyone went to their seats and watched her, their hands in their laps and their eyes fixated on Miss Darling politely. Even some of the more unruly boys were quiet and sheepish, looking down, faces pale.

Miss Darling continued on with her lessons, finishing Keats and moving on to arithmetic; however, no one could pay much attention to her. Everyone was nervous and shaky. Tommy himself felt queasy. He looked over at Anna Claire who quickly turned to look back at him while Miss Darling wrote on the board.

Tommy squirmed in his seat. Miss Darling was one of the nicest people in Gold Country and she had nearly gotten very hurt by one of her pupils. It was uncomfortable to say the least.

When school ended, the day being painfully long, Tommy went up to Miss Darling.

"Thank you, Tommy, for getting help," she said softly.

"Thank you for teachin' us," he answered, looking up at her with his sincere, sharp eyes. "You're a great teacher, Miss Darlin'."

Miss Darling blushed but smiled. "I am glad you think so. You yourself are growing as a student."

Tommy turned around and smiled at Anna Claire. The two of them walked out of the building and down Clover Street.

"I wonder what Mr. Wits is gonna tell his father," said Anna Claire, skipping along next to him.

"I don't know," Tommy sighed. "But I don't think he'll be comin' back to bother Miss Darlin' no more."

"He better not," Anna Claire pursed her lips. "I hate that Ebb Drummond! I hope we never see his stupid face again!"

"Me neither."

They walked on for a while before they ran to the saloon to grab some of the candy.

"I gotta go home or Mama will wonder," said Anna Claire.

"I'll come with you," said Tommy. "It'll help take my mind off it all."

The two walked out of the saloon, Kathleen Cooper waving at them from the counter, and began the walk to the Freiler's cabin.

"Did you see the Black people?" Anna Claire asked him as they walked through the tall grass.

"No," answered Tommy. "They didn't come in the saloon. Who was it?"

"I don't know, but there was a man who was with a woman and a little boy. I think they were his family."

"What happened?"

"Well, me and Berthie and Pete were walkin' to school, and we were walkin' by the general store when we heard some yellin'. The Black man was tellin' the store worker that he should be ashamed of himself, and the store worker said that the sign on the window said that no Blacks were allowed and then told him to go home. He called him that word Miss Darlin' doesn't want anyone to say."

Tommy repeated it in question.

"Yeah, that one," Anna Claire shuddered to hear the word again. "I don't like that word."

Tommy glanced over at her. "I don't really like the word now, either. I used to think it was just what Black people were called, just their name. But I don't think that's what it's supposed to mean anymore. 'Specially the way Ebenezer said it."

"Oh, I hate that boy!"

"Me, too."

The children walked on, both in deep thought. Tommy was happy he had come to the aid of Miss Darling and the class once again, but he had a nagging feeling that something still wasn't right. Something wasn't right about the situation, although he couldn't place his finger on it.

"I feel sad," said Anna Claire softly.

"I think I feel sad, too," said Tommy. "Somethin' ain't right."

"Yeah, somethin' ain't right," agreed Anna Claire. "I think 'cause no one helped those people. They weren't allowed in the store and the worker called them that word and they had to leave. I think that's why I'm sad. I'm glad Miss Darlin's alright, but I wonder what's gonna happen to *them*."

Tommy nodded, finally understanding what was bothering him. "Ain't no one gonna protect them. We can get people to help us, but they can't. Where can they go for help or when they need somethin'? What about when they need a doctor or more food or tools? Where can they go if the people in town don't let 'em?"

Anna Claire sighed as the cabin started getting nearer and nearer in view. "Why do people hate people just because they ain't White?"

Anna Claire didn't want to eat dinner that night. Instead, she sat with her head in her hands, sneaking food to Hero and looking at the table sadly.

"I know greens aren't your favorite, but you've gotta eat them," said Joseph, motioning with his head for her to finish her plate.

Anna Claire looked at the turnips and slowly twisted them around her fork.

"What's the matter?" asked Charlotta, looking around the table. "Has something happened at school? Why is no one talking tonight?"

Helen looked around the table and said what everyone was thinking. "There was a fight between Ebenezer Drummond and Miss Darling. It was awful and now none of us are hungry because it upset us."

Charlotta looked over at Joseph who was eating his corn fervently.

"What was the fight about?" he asked. "I can't imagine anyone wanting to hurt Miss Darlin', not even that awful boy."

"Well, he did!" shouted Anna Claire. "He kept sayin' a bad word because some Black people were in town today. He kept callin' them this bad name and sayin' they're not human. Miss Darlin' got real mad and told him that he couldn't say the bad word no more, but he kept sayin' it anyway."

"Yes, and then she said she would expel him if he did not stop saying it," remarked Caroline. "He kept saying the word anyway. Tommy was smart enough to run out of the schoolhouse and fetch Mr. Wits. Mr. Wits came running over with Tommy. Mr. Wits is stronger than Ebenezer and pulled him right off of Miss Darling. He said he was going to talk to Ebenezer's father and keep him away from the school."

"And then he left!" added Pete. "And all that time while Tommy was gone gettin' Mr. Wits, he kept sayin' that word!"

"Alright, enough," interjected Joseph. Clearing his throat, he looked around the room at the children who were sitting quietly, staring into their laps. "Children, that word isn't a good word to use. That's a word White people use to hate Blacks. You see, you remember the days of slavery in the South?"

All of the children nodded.

"Well, now that Lincoln freed them, they're wanderin' more up North lookin' for work and even gold," he took a sip of water and cleared his throat again. "They're not slaves anymore, and they should never have been. They are humans, too. Black people aren't like White people, though. They were enslaved for years. It's just now that they're free. But their freedom isn't much because they still can't do much with the freedom they got."

"Because the White people hate them?" asked Pete, taking a hearty bite out of the cob.

"Yes," answered Joseph. "Most White people do."

"Why?" asked Berthie.

"Some people think they're not quite as smart or as good as White folks," said Joseph. "But they don't know much better, bein' that they were just freed."

"Do you think Black people aren't as smart as White people?" asked Caroline, her voice soft.

"I don't know," said Joseph slowly. "Most people think so. They definitely are different."

Anna Claire gritted her teeth. There was so much she wanted to say and so many questions she wanted to ask.

"Some of the children at school are saying that Black people aren't human," Helen said, her brown eyes wide. "I don't understand."

"There's not a lot anyone can understand," said Joseph, taking another gulp of water. "Just be kind to them, but always look out. Some Blacks are waitin' for the right time to do somethin' to us. Whether it's to steal or hurt. Many of them are angry because they were enslaved for so long that some of them want revenge on White folk. Be careful, children."

Anna Claire rose from the table and put her dish into the little bucket of water. She didn't want to hear any more of the conversation, so when she came back to the table, she began talking about how good Tommy was for getting help when he did.

That night, when the children were getting ready for bed in the loft, Anna Claire pulled the buckskin hides to the side unexpectedly, causing Caroline to yell.

"You rat!" she cried, pulling her nightgown to her chest. "You know you're not supposed to be here! Go on your side of the loft!"

Anna Claire stuck out her tongue and said, "Fine by me! But I wanted to ask you what you would do if you saw another Black person."

"I would do as Papa said and turn away," Caroline answered.

"I might say hello but then I wouldn't say anything else," said Helen.

"I wanna listen to Papa," said Anna Claire, "but I don't think Black people are bad people."

"It's like Papa said," continued Caroline, "not all of them are bad, but some of them want to hurt us. That's why we ought to stay away from them."

Anna Claire looked both ways as if she was looking for someone, and then she said matter-of-factly, "I think Black people are just like us except they're Black."

Caroline shook her head. "You heard Papa. They aren't like us. They're different."

Anna Claire frowned and closed the buckskin curtain, walking solemnly over to the bed. Her father was wrong again, and she knew it.

Chapter 13- Unlikely Friends

"Iá daxpitchée!" yelled Anna Claire as she and Tommy reached the Native American camps, both out of breath and panting.

They had run to get there, being so excited to see their friend that they dashed off right after school.

"Anna Claire, Tommy!" said their friend, running to meet them.

Unlike the last time, this time they got more smiles than frowns from the tribe, and most of the people looked upon them warmly.

The boy ran up to his father, who was walking toward the teepees with a huge deer hanging from his back. He said something in their language before standing by their side.

"Follow," Iá daxpitchée motioned, the two children following their new friend to his teepee on the other side. "Stay."

After a moment, he came out of the teepee and held out a stunning beaded bracelet, with patterns in the shape of diamonds with white beads outlining the vibrant pinks and the blues. He held it up towards Anna Claire. As she reached up to admire it, he gently put the bracelet over her wrist.

Anna Claire could not believe her eyes. She had never seen anything so beautiful. Not even her aunt's finest jewelry back in Minnesota matched this. Not even the jewelry in town came close to this.

"Me?" she asked. "I can keep it?"

"Keep," he nodded. "For Anna Claire."

Anna Claire touched the bracelet slowly, feeling the edges and bumps of the beads. She could hardly look away from it.

"Play," said Iá daxpitchée, motioning for them to join some of the other children who were playing the game of hoops.

Tommy and Anna Claire watched Iá daxpitchée join the others and play for a while before playing themselves. They held the buckskin net and tried horribly to put the sticks through, although they had no idea what they were doing and failed miserably. This made Iá daxpitchée and the other children laugh, which only made Anna Claire and Tommy laugh harder at their own silliness.

After the game, Iá daxpitchée took them into his teepee and introduced them again to his mother, his grandfather, his grandmother, and his baby sister. They let the children sit by the fire. Anna Claire got to hold the baby's doll, which was made of buckskin and horse hair, and Tommy was able to admire a split horn headdress. Iá daxpitchée chatted with his family happily, and even though they could not understand the language, they felt the love and comfort in the teepee that day.

Anna Claire, Tommy, and Iá daxpitchée spent more time teaching each other words in their languages. They all felt like they were learning a lot. It was difficult at times, because Anna Claire wanted to tell Iá daxpitchée all about her life, her family, her home, school, and her and Tommy's gold hunt mystery, but she didn't know how to convey all of that to him.

"Bracelet," lá daxpitchée repeated. "Anna Claire. Like bracelet?"

"I love the bracelet," smiled Anna Claire. "Thank you, lá daxpitchée." She had gotten considerably better at pronouncing his name.

lá daxpitchée smiled, shivering in his robe of bison hide.

Anna Claire and Tommy were beginning to feel cold, too.

"Cold," said Anna Claire, wrapping herself up with her arms and shivering. "Cold."

Tommy and Anna Claire stood up as a gust of wind blew through harshly, causing them all to fall sideways.

"We have to go," said Tommy sadly. "Go."

lá daxpitchée nodded, his smile fading.

"We will come back," Tommy assured him. "Tommy and Anna Claire- we will come back to lá daxpitchée."

lá daxpitchée smiled brightly again and nodded. "Go. Come back. Goodbye."

"Goodbye!" Anna Claire and Tommy called as they ran.

They walked for some time until they finally reached the creek.

"What have you been sayin' to your ma and pa?" asked Tommy curiously.

"I tell them that I've been at the creek playin' with you. What else would I say?"

"Good idea," said Tommy. "We can keep goin' to lá daxpitchée's home!"

"We made a good friend," said Anna Claire, feeling her bracelet. "Oh! The bracelet! Mama and Papa can*not* see it! Helen and Caroline will surely find it somewhere. Can you keep it for me?"

"O' course I can," said Tommy, taking the bracelet from her hands. The bracelet was a trifle big for her small wrists. "It's too big for you now anyway. You gotta wait until it fits so you don't lose it. I'll keep it with me."

Anna Claire nodded as the two walked across the little log that crossed the creek. They both had impeccable balance and had used the log when getting across the other side of the creek. Then, they began running through the yellow-glazed grass, the sun setting in the orange sky.

"I gotta get in. I'll be in trouble," said Anna Claire. "I'll see ya later, Tommy!"

"Careful," he said. "See ya later, Anna Claire!"

"Just in time for supper," said Charlotta when she walked through the door. "You look flushed. Are you alright, Anna Claire?"

Anna Claire caught her breath and nodded. "Yes, Mama." But she was thinking of the bright blues and pinks of her bracelet, and of the little baby's rosy cheeks, and of her new friend's silly laugh, and the way the people offered them food and shelter. She thought to herself how nice it would be to live with a Native American tribe.

Anna Claire and Tommy were not the only ones making friends, as the other children had made some friends from school, and Charlotta had Nettie Clemmons. Joseph also had his good friends who turned out to be very fine people. However, Joseph was beginning to get anxious for the gold. He worked so hard that sometimes his hands bled from constantly holding the pick, and his back and shoulders ached from the weight of mining in the creek and bending down to search for the color. He still had high hopes that he would strike. There was news that a man had struck gold not very far down the creek, just a few miles away, and so Joseph must have been slowly but surely getting closer to what he had wanted for so long.

He toiled away day after day, becoming more and more adapt at placer mining where he separated little pieces of gold from the creek bed. This required hours upon hours of physically challenging work, as Joseph and his friends had to lift enormous amounts of gravel, pebbles, and dirt. In the hotter months, they had had to deal with the insects such as the mosquitos, but now that it was getting cold, the ground was getting harder and harder to break. By the time winter had come, panning for the gold was a miserable undertaking, as Joseph was forced to pick through ice and dig through the creek in the hopes of finding a little piece of the invaluable treasure.

Wearing bear skin and fox hide to keep warm, he worked tirelessly throughout the creek, stopping to sometimes have a flask of whiskey with the other men or talk about the difficulties of life in Montana Territory. The snow was, at times, above Joseph's knees, and the wind stung his face like knives, yet he went out nearly every day to pan for gold and go to the Assay office to weigh any minerals he found.

Once, he lucked out and found just a little silver, which was enough for him to buy his wife a lovely new dress.

There were other dangers besides the winter cold and the rough and tumble ways of town. Joseph had at one time encountered a bear on his way home from hunting. The bear had been thankfully a good distance away, but close enough that it could have chased and mauled Joseph to death if it was so inclined. However, the bear had merely glanced over at Joseph and kept on eating the leaves on the tree, completely unaffected by Joseph's presence.

Earlier in the season, there was another rattlesnake that had made its way to the Freiler's front yard and slithered its way around the house, sneakily creeping around the corners of the walls outside. It was spotted by a horrified Caroline when she looked toward the window and saw the long body of the snake slinking up and down the pane. She had immediately drawn attention by screaming and having everyone stay inside until Charlotta herself got the rifle and shot the snake dead.

There were long nights of wolves howling in the distance and coyotes running to and fro with each other, their long bodies moving rapidly through the grass. The family had bolted locks on the door, and the rifle stayed right by Joseph and Charlotta's bed in case it was suddenly needed in the middle of the night. There were strange bugs that found their way into the house, too, and plants that they could not tell whether or not they might be poisonous.

Despite the many privations, there were so many beautiful things about Gold Country. There were odd birds that none of the family had ever seen before, some in bright plumage of blues and reds, and the morphing of the mountains from green to orange and then brown was a beautiful sight as the seasons changed. The asters had kept their violet stars while the red swamp fire turned deep blood-red. The green ash trees near the rivers and streams had turned yellow as the maidenhair fern evolved into a confident gold. The smiles on the people's faces in town when they gathered to trade were jovial and made Charlotta feel safe and warm. Having the Clemmons's a quick walk away was a blessing, as they sometimes took turns having suppers at each other's homes, laughing and making merriment. Anna Claire thought that there could never be a happier place than Gold Country- except when she was stuck indoors alone or cooped up with just Caroline or Helen. Anna Claire had another experience that she didn't like so much.

It was a very cold November day when there was a knock at the door. Anna Claire had been bringing water inside the house in a bucket, which was nearly half her size, and she had noticed a man dressed in black on his way across the field. She had dropped the bucket, water splashing everywhere, and warned the others in the house. Joseph had been working that day and took Pete with him so that he could learn about panning for gold. It was just Charlotta and the girls in the house that day.

"Mama, Caroline, Helen!" cried Anna Claire, her dark-gold hair flying around her face. "There's a strange man wearin' all black and he's comin' this way and we gotta hide! Ya heard me, hide!"

Charlotta, her apron covered in flour, stretched her back to try to see through the window before appearing at the door. The look of pure joy on her face was indescribable as, with an almost girlish laugh, she clasped her hands together.

"I knew God would send someone!" she declared, tears filling her eyes as she opened the door.

Anna Claire ran behind Caroline's back to shield herself from the stranger, who was old, ominous-looking, and wore a cold expression upon his face as if he wanted to whip her right there on the spot.

"Hello, Mrs.-?"

"Freiler," Charlotta finished, her cheeks flushing with excitement. "You must be the traveling minister. I just knew the Lord would send someone to us! I knew it all along!"

The man, without so much as moving, bowed his gray head and held his Bible with both hands. Caroline moved herself away from Anna Claire to politely greet the older gentleman while Helen regretfully shook his hand, a repulsed look on her face as she shivered. It was as if the man himself was literally cold.

"My name is Minister Harris. It is a pleasure to meet you all."

It certainly didn't seem like a pleasure. His face was contorted in a serious, solemn expression and his eyes seemed to hold no light. Anna Claire shivered in his presence and stood with Berthie to avoid shaking hands with the grim man.

"Please, have a seat," said Charlotta, motioning him to a humble chair by the fire. "Can I fetch you some tea? A slice of cake?"

Minister Harris shook his head, unsmiling. "Thank you, Mrs. Freiler, but that will not be necessary."

Berthie, clearly afraid of the man, huddled closer to Anna Claire as they sat down, burying her little face in the corner of Anna Claire's arm.

The minister opened his Bible and read some of the text of Revelations before standing up and saying with a long, drawn-out, monotonous voice, "The good Lord has allowed you to come to this land in search of a Godlier life. You must remember that each of you has been sent here to set a good example for the people of this land. You must deliver the word of Christ and see to it that the holy book is followed at all times." He stood straight and tall before continuing. "Mrs. Freiler, you must always remain dutiful to your husband at all times, day and night." He gave her a strange, reproachful look. "Children, you must listen to your father, for it seems as though your father is a God-fearing man. You must never laugh too loud, run too quickly, or enjoy too much. Life is not for pleasure. You are alive to serve your God and Jesus Christ, our Savior. That is all. This means," he said, looking down at Caroline, "that you shall not be vain in the way that you dress or look. It also means," he said, moving onto Helen, "that you must always help your neighbor and never show a bad temper. Bad tempers are a sign that Satan has invaded your spirit, child."

He took a long, deep breath as Caroline and Helen squirmed uncomfortably in their chairs.

"Now you," he bent forward towards Anna Claire, his breath like a dead animal, and his pupils dilating. "You, child, must grow to be obedient. Ah! I can tell you have a disobedient soul, child. I can see it in your eyes. Very well then. You must work hard to control yourself. You must not divulge into sin, as sin is in your blood."

Charlotta was beginning to look uncomfortable herself, and her face grew pale.

"You must be careful not to disobey your mother and your father, and to always follow the holy book. This means, child, no laughing too loudly, no eating too much, and none of the wild music of the town. You must make yourself pure to enter the kingdom of heaven!" He turned from Anna Claire.

"And the little one here," he said, looking at Berthie, showing sickening green teeth. "You shall grow up to be the purest yet. I see you are untainted by the devilish spirit of your sister. You shall always be humble, never dress extravagantly, and do what your father and someday your husband says. God appointed men to care for womenfolk. You must choose wisely and marry a God-fearing man."

At this point in his speech, Charlotta stood up shakily and smiled. "Are you sure you do not want some tea or cake?"

Minister Harris, annoyed to be interrupted, put his hands up to deny the food and drink.

"I am very sorry, minister, as I have enjoyed this so much," Charlotta's smile was strained. "I'm afraid I have not been feeling very well today and I would much regret you catching ill. Also, the children and I are going to be making supper soon enough. We have much to do here, as you can see."

Minister Harris gave her a grim look. "You must make time for the Lord."

"Yes, and in fact, I wanted my children to practice reciting the ten commandments," Charlotta went on, finding him as repulsive now as the others did. "They must learn them properly. Oh, thank you, this has inspired us so much!" She moved to the door and opened it. "Be well, dear minister, and carry the message of the Bible throughout Gold Country!"

Annoyed to be asked to leave, the minister raised his hand as a goodbye, frowning, before he walked away across the field. Charlotta closed the door with great relief, although she did not want her children to see it so she added, "It is such a shame that he could not stay longer. He has very good messages, my dear ones."

"Do we really have to memorize the commandments *now*?" asked Helen, sinking into her chair and rolling her eyes.

"I cannot lie to the minister." Charlotta put her finger to her mouth in thought. "But- well, I do think we must get started on supper. I think tonight we can read the commandments together and that shall suffice."

The children smiled to each other, relieved that the minister was gone and that they could resume their sunny fall day without Minister Harris's grim expression. Every single one of them felt thankful, even Charlotta, although she would never tell her children so.

It wasn't just traveling minsters and circuit riders that came to Bannack. Sometimes, there would be barn dances when everyone would get together to laugh, sing, dance, and eat baked goods in the hall. This was the most fun for the whole family, despite Charlotta's conservative concerns that it was a bit too rowdy. Joseph calmed her by telling her that this was "the way in the new El Dorado" and that dancing was a good way to get by in Gold Country. The dances happened every now and again, and the Freiler children were able to see the other children around town and the surrounding areas.

Anna Claire had gotten quite used to Lisa Howler now and was able to play with her without fighting or throwing fruit on any of her dresses. The Clemmons children joined in as well as the Mast's and the O'Reilly's. There were dozens of families that would come to the hall to celebrate their lives in Montana Territory, and Anna Claire relished all of it. For the little girl, there was nothing quite like a crowd dancing to music, everyone talking, laughing, and celebrating. It reminded her a bit of the mining camps when the men used to take out their cornstalk fiddles and would start playing giddy music, the children gathering around in a circle and holding hands while the women and men would dance with each other and hop up and down, feeling alive with jollity and activity.

Joseph often took a break throughout the week to go with his friends to one of the saloons to play poker or Faro. Sometimes, he even had some liquor. The games could get rowdy and people could get angrier than a cat in water. He knew his wife would reprimand him if she had any inkling of what he was doing on those breaks, and he could never lie to his wife, so instead he just never told her about it.

Pete Freiler was amazed to meet real cowboys one day when his father took him to town. The men rode on horses and carried a bullwhip and lasso, wearing chaps and blue jeans. He had stared in awe at them when they rode down the street. One of the cowboys even tipped his hat and smiled at him. Pete was determined that someday he would become a cowboy and travel all over Gold Country!

Food could be tough to afford, and there were times when the Freiler's did not have much on their plate. But, when they were able to get enough and more, they were pleased to receive goods of bacon, dried peaches, and moose meat.

There was an array of people settling around Bannack and Gold Country. Many of the northerners had come from the Yankee Flats while the southerners scoffed at them, as they were loyal to the confederation. Described by some as "the backdoor to hell," the place was overrun with crime and disloyalty. Nevertheless, it had an odd way of drawing people in, and the family had grown attached to Grasshopper Diggings and their plain wood cabin in the fields. Memories were being made, laughter was echoing in the air, and dreams were conjured up more and more every day. They had a stable home, access to the town, plenty of resources, and enough food to ensure they would not starve. Also, they had each other, which made all of the difficult things worth it.

"It's gettin' too cold out," said Anna Claire to Tommy as they began crossing the log over to the other side of the creek where the saltbush lay in a cloud of white. "I had to beg Mama to let me go out. She said this may be the last time I can walk around the creek for a while, unless I'm bringin' in water."

"It's already snowin'," said Tommy, shivering. He wasn't wearing a coat and he looked dreadfully cold.

"You must be freezin', Tommy Cooper," said Anna Claire, looking at his light flannel shirt and his trousers which were too short for him now.

"I ain't," said Tommy, but his voice quivered as he spoke.

The two children were walking to their new favorite place- the camps of the Native Americans. They had been going there a few times now, and had learned lots of new words in the language Iá daxpitchée spoke. Iá daxpitchée had also been learning a lot, too, especially since Anna Claire gave him a full teaching lesson the last time they had come to visit.

"We are so lucky," said Anna Claire.

"Why?"

"Because we've gotten to know them. Nobody else does. That's why they think they're bad."

"Bad!" said Tommy. "They're good people!"

"*We* know that," said Anna Claire practically, "but that's not what Papa says. He says that they scalp people and want to kill all the White people."

Tommy laughed. "Grown-ups," he scoffed. "They always think they're right even though they're usually wrong!"

"Grown-ups," repeated Anna Claire with a shake of her head.

The children reached the little plateau in the field and saw the teepees in the distance. They began to run, Tommy purposefully pushing Anna Claire to the side and she doing it back, the two giggling as they entered the camps.

"Anna Claire, Tommy!" said Iá daxpitchée's mother warmly, motioning for them to come into her teepee.

They walked into the comfortable home, sitting down by the fire and warming their hands. Iá daxpitchée's mother handed them hot drinks made from berries. Anna Claire was allowed to hold the baby, the rosy-faced little girl laughing gleefully in her arms. Tommy was busy admiring a large drum that was sitting to the side of the teepee. The old couple watched with grins on their faces, quietly observing the children.

Iá daxpitchée soon ran into the teepee. His eyes gleamed brightly, and a big smile appeared on his face.

"Tommy! Anna Claire!"

"Iá daxpitchée!"

They stood up to greet him. He handed his mother a goose and she took it to the other side where she began to skin it.

"Hungry?" he asked.

Tommy nodded while Anna Claire kicked him.

"Eat," said Iá daxpitchée. He whispered something to his mother who came around with a parflech filled with bits of dried elk.

Tommy dug right in, eating hungrily. Tommy did not get to eat much in general, which could be seen in his boniness, and anything he could get his hands on he relished.

"This is good," said Tommy with a smile. "Good!" he said to the others, who looked a bit confused but happy.

Iá daxpitchée told them what he meant and then the old woman smiled as the old man laughed. They started talking in their language.

"They say they are happy," said Iá daxpitchée. "They are happy because it is good."

Anna Claire and Tommy nodded. They sat by the fire for some time until they heard the rustling of noises outside of the teepee.

Iá daxpitchée stood up quickly and shouted something before smiling even wider. "Come! It has begun!"

Anna Claire and Tommy were not sure what was going on, but they did what they were told and went outside. Sitting in a circle, groups of tribe members around them, a few of the men began speaking.

"They talk about sadness no more," said Iá daxpitchée. "They talk about the grass and the trees and the land. They talk about the beautiful."

The men continued to tell their tales, their garbs long, thick, and colorful, and their trimmed leggings and breechcloths protecting them from the winter chill. They soon began to sing and dance, their moccasins hitting the ground with thuds. Anna Claire and Tommy watched in hushed silence, admiring the way they moved, their beads flying around them and the men's long hair whipping the ground. They began to hum and then started singing in their own language.

Anna Claire turned to Iá daxpitchée, who whispered, "They sing about the sun. Sun made all."

Anna Claire wasn't exactly sure what he meant, but she could not wait to eventually find out. For the time being, she sat quietly, Tommy with his eyes wide by her side, and Iá daxpitchée smiling at them with pride.

One of the women who had been sitting next to them put her arm around Anna Claire and squeezed it. Another turned to smile at her, and another came from a teepee to offer the children more food. Iá daxpitchée's father was dancing with the other men, and his mother was carrying the baby in her arms, rocking her back and forth and making her laugh. The sun was just showing the beginning signs of sinking away. Anna Claire felt warm, happy, and loved, all comfortable and cozy by the fire at the Native American camp with her new friends.

She did not want to leave. She stayed much longer than she really should have, for her mother trusted her to be home well before the sun went down. The sun was down and Anna Claire stood up and began clapping, her and some of the other children running in a circle around the dancing men as they continued to sing in their language. She had forgotten about the cabin across the creek and the family that was waiting for her to do her chores. She had forgotten everything in those moments except the firelight, clapping and dancing, and the comfortable feeling of friends around her.

"You should go home," said Tommy, pulling her arm out of the circle. "You're gonna be in trouble and then you won't ever be able to come back!"

Anna Claire knew he was right. Anna Claire left the campfire and said goodbye to Iá daxpitchée's mother and the baby. Turning to Iá daxpitchée, she said, "Tell everyone I said I'm sorry, but I have to go home."

Iá daxpitchée thought for a moment and then nodded. "Goodbye, Anna Claire."

"Goodbye, Iá daxpitchée!"

She turned to Tommy, who had decided to stay. "Tell me all about it later!"

And the child was on her way towards the other side of the creek.

"Oh, look at you, you poor thing," Nettie Clemmons said one day as she stopped by the Freiler's cabin to bring over some homemade bread. "I can see you've been working all day!"

Charlotta laughed and gave Nettie an embrace. "What would I do without you, my dear Nettie?"

Nettie smiled as Charlotta motioned for her to sit down.

"Sometimes, it is so nice when the children are at school," Nettie said as Charlotta brought over two little plates and a knife.

"Sometimes?" said Charlotta. The two of them laughed. "How are Rebecca and Matthew?"

"Oh, the same," said Nettie. "They're both growing so much that I daresay I have to keep sewing and hemming all of the time. My hands hurt from it!"

"Rebecca and Matthew are lovely children," smiled Charlotta sincerely. "They always have a nice thing to say to everyone. Helen so loves when Rebecca comes to visit! The two of them really get on well."

"They absolutely do," agreed Nettie, taking a small bite of the bread. "Tell me, how is your family? How is Joseph?"

Charlotta sighed. "As you well know, I am not happy with Joseph and his hunger for gold, but there is not much I can do about it. I do not think Gold Country, or at least Bannack, is safe for us, but he is certain he will find the gold before it gets worse here."

"My husband is the same way," said Nettie, shaking her head. "I have told Paul time and time again that this gold mining was nonsense. I did not travel all the way from Virginia to be nothing but tired and poor!"

"I know how you feel," nodded Charlotta, touching her hand to Nettie's. "It is awful out here sometimes. The chores seem endless, the danger worse, and I have had these spells every day where my head hurts and I become dizzy. The town is wild and rough- my, it's the roughest place I ever did see! I do not think even my imagination could conjure up such a place! Sometimes it is as if I cannot breathe."

"It sounds like nerves," said Nettie knowingly. "I had those spells myself a while back, but got used to them. Mainly out of habit. No wonder, either, when everything here is such a shindy! You will learn to control the nerves more. You just keep remembering to trust in Jesus. Jesus knows the light and he will see us through."

Charlotta nodded. "You are right. I grow so concerned out here. Sometimes, I find myself missing my mother like a child! But with God, I know all things are possible."

"Yes, but it is still hard to withstand sometimes," sympathized Nettie, placing her fork on the plate. "Paul will not always talk to me about the mining. He comes home so tired he's almost dead. I can do nothing but cook and try to make him warm, but he has to be out there doing the hard labor. I worry that Matthew will follow his lead into the mining. He is already talking of wanting to be 'like his father' and find the gold."

"I well know it," sighed Charlotta. "Anna Claire is just like her father. She thinks the town is this exciting, wonderful place where all good things happen, but she does not understand how dangerous it really is. I am thankful that they have all started school to keep them busy, at least for a while. It makes me feel that town is safer with a school. Oh, I know that is silly, but just having a school reminds me that other mothers and fathers are around here, and that there will be people wanting to protect the children."

"My children are asking a lot of questions recently," Nettie lowered her voice. "Mainly about the 'other' people around here. They want to know what makes us all different from each other. I do not know how to answer them."

"Nettie, I am having the same problems with mine! Just the other week, there was that fight at school."

"Yes, yes, Rebecca told me all about it!"

Charlotta shook her head. "It sounded awful. It is a good thing Mr. Wits came when he did, otherwise...well, anyhow, it was a horrible thing. My children could not stop talking about it. My Berthie is far too young to understand what was happening, and Pete is almost as confused as she is, and Anna Claire-well, Anna Claire has talked nonstop about them and how curious she is about them. Helen and Caroline are listening to their father and taking caution. I must admit, I do not know how to feel about all of this."

"We must keep our children safe from them," said Nettie. "We will all have to stick together."

"We must not let anyone hurt our family," agreed Charlotta, sipping her tea.

"I have told my children to stay far away if they were ever to see one!" went on Nettie. "I won't have my children seen with the likes of them."

Charlotta nodded, but felt a bit ill.

"I think I may lie down a spell," she said, standing up. "I feel one of those nerve attacks coming on again."

"Don't let me keep you," said Nettie, standing up and putting a hand on her friend's arm. "I should get back home before Matthew and Rebecca come home, anyhow. We have supper to tend to. Don't forget what I said about the dance in January! I think we should all go together. It will be such a splendid time."

Charlotta smiled, her whole face brightening like it always did when she truly smiled. "I will talk to Joseph. I think it sounds like quite a nice idea."

Meanwhile, all the way in the town of Bannack in a little dusty saloon, Tommy Cooper was sitting in his room, thinking of Caroline Freiler, the girl he most adored. He so hoped for Caroline to finally look at him with the same love and admiration that he had for her. He wished, prayed, and pined for her, and whenever he saw her, he paid special attention to her, chattering as fast as a bird when she was present, and offering to bring her candy from the store. Caroline was very annoyed with Tommy, although she had affection for him as a member of the family, and told Tommy more than once that she wished he would stop attempting to make her love him. It was a sad chase, really, and very hard for little Tommy, who, at merely eleven, truly believed the pretty Caroline was the only one for him.

Caroline herself was wrapped up in Jacob Mast and the two of them had been courting for quite some time now. Caroline was inwardly planning what it would be like if he were to take her as his wife and if they started their household together. Caroline was only turning fifteen, but now old enough to think of marriage. She wanted to please her family, have a husband, a home, and children. In fact, it is what she lived for and what she believed her true purpose in life was. She was a natural homemaker- good with chores, with quilting, with making things smell fresh and look pretty. She was also smart, an excellent cook, and very proper. She knew she would make someone a good wife.

But the real question remained: Did Caroline truly love Jacob? She was certainly fond of him as he was Godly, kind, and interested in her. But was that love? Did she want to make a home with him? She thought that she did, but deep down inside, she wasn't sure, and she was too young to understand what she wanted.

Of course, in Tommy's mind, Jacob was not the boy Caroline should marry. If only he was older, then he could make her see!

This jealousy built within Tommy slowly until it festered inside of him like bile. He began to hate Jacob Mast and cast nasty looks towards Jacob whenever he was also at the Freiler home. Jacob was confused but did not think for a second that this little boy was so interested in Caroline.

Anna Claire was just happy that she was still a little girl and did not have to worry about courting. She decided a long time ago that she would not court ever, at any time, and no one could make her, not even her mother or father. She was not like Caroline or her mama. She did not swoon, she was not prim, and she did not care a lick about impressing a boy. It was all silly to her, and sometimes she thought she would rather *be* a boy, as they seemed to have all the fun anyway.   Later that day, after school was out and Nettie Clemmons had left, Tommy gained his courage and walked up to the Freiler's door, knocking on it with purpose. He did not even tell Anna Claire during school that he was going to be coming. This was something that Tommy had to do alone.

Helen answered and let him inside. She informed him that Caroline was outside in the back of the house doing the wash. Without another word, he went around the back of the house, where he found her and Charlotta dunking the clothes into the bucket of water. Anna Claire stood on the other side of them, looking bored as she began to hang the clothes on the wire.

"Tommy!" she exclaimed, dropping a pair of pantyhose onto the cold and muddy ground, much to the dismay of her mother and sister.

"I have something to say," said Tommy, his face serious and his back up straight.

"Tell me you brought candy!" cried Anna Claire, her face glowing in excitement. "I've been yearnin' for candy all day!"

Tommy shook his head and then turned his eyes on Caroline, whose long hair was wet at the ends from dipping the clothes into the bucket. She looked at him with a cautious smile.

"Hi, Tommy," Caroline said cheerfully. "Would you like to help us with the wash? You must learn how to wash properly."

"Caroline Freiler," said Tommy, wanting to waste no time. He looked over at Anna Claire, who was shaking her head as if to warn him not to do it. He looked over at Charlotta, whose eyebrows were narrowing and her head tilting in wonder. Then he looked over at Caroline, who was beginning to feel queasy. "I love you. I know I'm just a boy, but when I grow up, I want you to marry me. Please, say you will?"

Caroline and her mother stared, their mouths hanging slightly open. Neither knew what to say.

"Tommy, you shouldn't have told her that!" Anna Claire cried, her hands to her face. "What an awful idea!"

Caroline stood up, turned around in embarrassment, and walked around Tommy to go back into the house.

"Is she angry?" asked Tommy, a puzzled expression on his face.

"I do not think she is angry," said Charlotta, suppressing the urge to laugh. "I think she is surprised. I am surprised! I think your intentions are lovely, but you are far too young to be asking a girl for their hand in marriage." She stifled laughter with her hand and cleared her throat. "You must wait for a very long time. Give it time, Tommy dear."

Tommy, disappointed but understanding, nodded and said, "I'll give it all the time I've got! I love Caroline and I will make her my wife someday!"

Charlotta controlled herself and managed to only smile. "That is a good idea, Tommy. A very good idea."

Tommy felt angry and humiliated. He only meant to tell Caroline how much she meant to him, and it backfired.

Feeling silly, he and Anna Claire ran from the house into the bright prairie sun, Anna Claire happy to be allowed some relief from the washing.

"She don't love me," said Tommy sadly. "She thinks I'm too young. I know she does."

"Of course, you are," Anna Claire nodded practically. "I told you already, she will never love you! And I still don't understand how you can like such an annoying goat like Caroline!"

"She's not a goat!" Tommy said indignantly. "Anyway, once I get the gold, she'll want nothin' more than to marry me."

Anna Claire laughed again. "She'll never marry you! Anyway, she wants to marry Jacob Mast. What do you wanna get married for?"

"Because Caroline is the most beautiful girl in the world!" sighed Tommy dreamily as they began walking to the creek.

They now had to walk in a foot of snow, both wearing scarves and hats- Tommy's clothes old and ripping apart- and both utterly cold. They were still allowed to visit the creek that day, so long as they promised not to step on the ice. There may have been parts of the creek that were not completely frozen and they could not risk falling into the ice and drowning. They had heard that a girl had drowned the year prior in the creek after falling in and not being able to pull herself out.

"I hate this," said Anna Claire, throwing up her hands and looking around her. "I'm always so cold!"

"Me too," said Tommy, shivering and putting his hands up to his nose. "Even in my room it's always cold. I have to wear my coat to bed!"

"Sometimes when we wake up, there's snow on our blankets that got through the roof. Sometimes even on our face," said Anna Claire. "Mama checks on us sometimes just to make sure we're still breathin' 'cause she says we can get sick if we get too cold."

They were about to reach the sage bushes and little trees on the creek when Tommy stopped very suddenly and grinned.

"There's *one* good thing about wintertime," he said mischievously.

"What?" But before she even finished the word, she felt a shocking ice-cold slap on the cheek.

"You-you!" She cried, picking up snow and forming it into a ball.

"Shin out!" Tommy called gleefully, picking up more snow and pelting it at Anna Claire.

Anna Claire formed another ball of snow in her hands before she got hit in the chest, falling backwards. Laughing, Tommy helped her up before throwing another snowball in her face, making her nose red.

"You'll get it, Tommy Cooper!" Anna Claire shouted, taking an armful of snow and shoving Tommy to the ground.

"Fine! Fine!" he yelled, laughing. "You win!"

They laughed so hard that their eyes filled up with tears. When they looked at each other, they noticed it had begun snowing again.

"I gotta get back to the saloon," said Tommy. "See ya later, Anna Claire!"

"See ya later, Tommy!" And with that, Anna Claire ran into the house, her nose stinging and her hands red and raw.

"Oh, you're covered in snow!" cried Charlotta upon her arrival. "Anna Claire, what were you doing?"

"Tommy started hittin' me with the snow and so I hit him back, but then he hit me again and I fell so I hit him and he fell and then we both fell!" Anna Claire explained in one big breath, her high-pitched voice exhausted by the end of it.

"That is naughty," was all Charlotta had the energy to say as she began to warm up water in the pot. "I want you to go up to the loft and change into your nightgown immediately. Then come right back down!"

Anna Claire, out of breath, ran up the loft, shaking off the snow that had fallen on her coat. She changed into her nightgown and came downstairs like her mother told her to. Charlotta had her sit in the chair and wrapped a blanket around her shoulders, giving her a hot cup of soup.

"It is quite cold enough," said Charlotta sternly. "I do not need my children going outside and bringing more of the cold in here!"

Anna Claire nodded, still not regretting the snow ball fight.

"Mama, do you think Santa Clause will come fow Chwistmas?" asked Berthie, coming over to sit in Anna Claire's lap.

Charlotta's face paled. "I am not sure, Berthie. We will have to wait and see. Remember, we are all alive and well, and that is what matters the most!"

Berthie nodded somberly.

"I want a new hat," said Helen. "Either for Christmas or my birthday! They're both coming up."

"And my birthday is only four days after Christmas!" reminded Caroline, looking up from her sewing.

"Yes, it is certainly the time of the year when money disappears," said Charlotta with a sigh.

Berthie held the doll she had gotten recently for her own birthday, kissing it on the cheek.

"I gave hew a name," she said.

"What is the name, dear?" asked Charlotta, coming over and pretending to have interest.

"Alice," Berthie answered, "just like my fwiend at school!"

Charlotta smiled and ran her fingers through her light hair. "That is a nice name."

"Alice is a little darling, Mama," said Caroline as she set the table. "She always wears her curls in pigtails and has the cutest pinafore!"

"That is wonderful to hear."

"When will it be Christmas?" asked Pete impatiently. "I want to make the Christmas tea!"

"Next week, moron," answered Helen, slowly washing the silverware in the bucket.

"That mouth, Helen!" said Charlotta. "One more outburst from you and you are going to the loft."

Helen huffed and slowly made her way over to the bucket of water, where she dumped the rag in. She even more slowly made her way to the windows, where she began wiping them, frowning.

"I wish I could get that train set from the drug store," said Pete, moving his arm up and down while pretending to have the toy in his hand. "That's what I want from Santa Clause!"

"All I want for Christmas is for everyone to be glad," said Caroline, smiling at Charlotta.

"Oh, dry up, Caroline," said Anna Claire with a roll of her eyes. "You want Jacob Mast to kiss you!"

Pete and Berthie began to giggle, Pete making kissing noises with his lips.

"'Oh my darlin', Oh my darlin', Oh my darlin' *Caroline*!'" sang Pete, Anna Claire joining in.

"That is quite enough!" snapped Charlotta firmly, raising her voice more than she usually did.

Caroline stood up from the table, tears in her eyes. "Mama, may I please be excused?"   Charlotta nodded.

"You all just want to ruin everything!" Caroline yelled as she climbed up the ladder.

Anna Claire and Pete were still smiling when Charlotta walked over to them.

"Anna Claire, go clean the outhouse. Peter, go get some water and start scrubbing the barn."

"But we hate those things!" said Pete.

"Exactly," said Charlotta.

"Please, Mama!" begged Anna Claire. "I don't wanna!"

Charlotta shook her head. "Go. But be back here before dark!"

The children did not ask any more questions before going off to do their chores.

Charlotta sighed and turned around to look at Helen and Berthie. Helen was still washing the windows slowly, and Berthie held her "Alice" doll in her hands. Charlotta thought of admonishing them, for Helen should have been quicker and Berthie should have been offering to help, but at the moment, she decided to sit down and stare at the log wall in front of her.

"Are you alright, Mama?" asked Helen as she turned around.

Charlotta nodded, feeling the day's activities hitting her body. "Yes."

Helen looked at her as if she did not believe her, but then said, "Do you want me to make you some soup, Mama?"

"I am so tired of soup!" Charlotta said before she could stop herself. Now she herself was sounding like an impertinent child!

Helen's brown eyes went wide.

"I'm sorry, Helen," she said quietly. "I'm very tired today. No, thank you, dear."

Still with raised eyebrows and wide eyes, Helen walked away from the windows and began to pluck the chicken on the other end of the table.

Charlotta was truly tired. She just needed a

moment- just one moment- to stare into the vacant-ness and feel nothing.

Soon, somewhat begrudgingly, she stood up and helped Helen pluck the rest of the chicken before putting it into the oven. After some time, she summoned Berthie over, who was now on the floor playing with her doll, so that she could see what a properly-cooked chicken looked like.

Anna Claire and Pete came in as the evening started to settle. They both looked miserable and smelled awful.

"Wash your hands and your face," said Charlotta. "Use the soap."

Anna Claire went first to the pan of water when Pete shoved her out of the way.

"I'll give you a lickin'!" yelled Anna Claire, pushing him back with the side of her body.

"Not another word," sighed Charlotta, "or you will both be going back out there with the lamps tonight."

The children settled down. The chicken was ready and the table was set, Caroline feeling calmer and coming back down from the loft to help. Now, they waited for Joseph. They waited and waited and waited.

"I suppose this is going to be another night where he is late," mumbled Charlotta. "Let us say grace."

She bent her head down, the pieces of dark curly hair falling out of its clips and her eyes shutting gently.

"'Our Father in heaven, hallowed be thy name. Thy kingdom come, your will be done, on Earth as it is in heaven. Give us this day our daily bread, and forgive us our sins, as we also have forgiven those who sin against us. And lead us not into temptation, but deliver us from evil. Amen.'"

"Amen," the children said.

"You may eat now," Charlotta nodded, looking fervently over at the door and hoping Joseph would barge in at any minute.

He didn't barge in until much later, when the food was eaten, the plates were clean, and all of the children were in bed.

"There's my beautiful wife," Joseph said, placing his hand gently around her neck and kissing her.

"I have really missed you today," Charlotta sighed, taking his hand. "Sit down. There is most of the chicken still left."

"Thank you, my darlin'," he said, sitting at the table while taking his big black boots off and shaking the snow from them.

"I was beginning to get worried," Charlotta stated. "It is so cold and it got so dark!"

"I bring the pistol with me every day, so you don't have to worry," assured Joseph as Charlotta handed him the plate of chicken and corn.

"I know, but I can never be sure what can happen out here in this strange land."

"We will persevere," promised Joseph. "I will always come home."

Charlotta smiled. "I do fret, but I know you are safe."

"Clemmons and I walked home together after the pannin'," Joseph said in between big bites of chicken. "We had a good laugh today when we thought we spotted a bear in the dark, but it was a shanty instead!"

The two laughed merrily for a moment.

Charlotta stood up to refill his cup of water before sitting down again.

"The children were fighting again," she said. "First, Helen called names. Then they were teasing Caroline about Jacob Mast. Anna Claire and Pete continued to fight even after I made them clean the outhouse and the barn."

Joseph kept eating hungrily. "Well, it seemed like it was a hard day for everyone. I got no gold, not even dust, today."

"Oh, dear. I'm sorry."

"It was just so cold; Paul and I could hardly see anything. The creek was frozen solid. The snow covered everything. I picked and picked but hardly got anywhere. Paul didn't get nothin' either and his nose looked like it was plum frozen!"

"I hope it will be better tomorrow," said Charlotta, feeling herself wanting to fall asleep.

Joseph looked at her. "You're tired, dear. Go to sleep."

"I still need to clean the plate and the fork. I need to check on the children and get more firewood for the morning."

Joseph looked at his wife and gently pulled at her arm.

"I will do that," he said, standing up.

"Nonsense, Joseph, I-"

"Go to bed," Joseph smiled. "I will do what is needed. I am not as tired as you are. Those children are more tirin' than minin' for gold!"

They laughed and Charlotta kissed his cheek.

"Thank you," she said, walking over to the hanging buckskins and parting them. As soon as she changed into her nightgown, she felt a wave of exhaustion hit her like wind. She got herself into bed, her head hit the pillow, and soon she was asleep before she had any time to even realize it.

Chapter 14- Christmas in Gold Country

"Help me hang the stockings, dear," said Charlotta to Anna Claire, who was staring into the fireplace and imagining what it would be like to be a traveling singer. "Anna Claire, enough daydreaming. Come help me hang these stockings."

Shaking her head as if she was waking up from sleep, Anna Claire hopped from beside the fireplace and took a long stocking from her mother's hand. She smiled when she saw that it was her own tattered red one on which her mother had sewn her name when she was a baby. She felt a ping of holiday nostalgia before it was gone, and she was back to daydreaming about more important things again.

"Mama, must I stay here tonight?" asked Caroline, patting her long black curls with her small hand. "You know that Jacob has invited me to dinner at his home and-"

"We have discussed this matter quite enough," said her mother, pursing her lips. "It is Christmas Eve, and you will be spending it with your own family. You shall see Jacob once the season is over."

"Oh, Mama!" pouted Caroline, who so rarely pouted that it was an odd sight for the other children. "Mama, please! Jacob wants me to go so badly, and I never get to go anywhere anymore, and I hate it!"

Charlotta turned to look at her, her face growing ashen and her eyes glazing. Caroline knew to stop arguing then and grumbled as she helped her brother hang the stream of painted popcorn across the window.

"When will Papa be home?" asked Helen, scrubbing the floors with soapy water.

Charlotta sighed. "I am not sure I know, dear. I do hope he will be home soon. Supper will be ready in an hour and our Christmas decorations will be all prepared!"

"I'm hungry *now*," complained Pete.

"I want hot cocoa."

"Me, too!" chimed in Berthie.

"We will drink hot cocoa tomorrow," said their mother as she took the warm bread from the fireplace, hair falling out of its bun around her face. "Please, let us stop complaining. Let us thank the Lord and remember the sacrifices He has made for us. We are celebrating the birth of Jesus Christ. Let us pray to God and show gratitude for all that He has given us."

Caroline, determined to stop complaining, bent her head down in silent prayer, her black silky curls falling into her lap. Pete sat down in the chair and crossed his arms. Helen and Berthie held each other's hands and smiled. Anna Claire snuck away from them and into the kitchen, where she felt she could breathe again, away from everyone. While there, she sat on the floor and held Hero's head to her own, kissing his cheek and telling him that she loved him as he happily licked her face. She came back into the main room shortly after prayer had ended. Her mother was admonishing Helen over something, so that she did not notice Anna Claire's brief absence.

"I cannot wait until Papa sees what we have done!" exclaimed Caroline happily, admiring the little holiday napkins she had made. "Perhaps I will give Jacob one next time I see him."

"Shut up about Jacob," said Anna Claire, walking to the front of the cabin. "No one cares a lick!"

Caroline made a face. "No one cares about silly little girls, either!"

"Stop that!" said Charlotta, her hands in her hair, feeling as if she was about to burst from irritation. "Do not talk to each other that way! You are sisters."

Anna Claire hung her head and pretended shame before giving Caroline a nasty look. Caroline, returning the look, went over to the window where she dramatically watched the snow falling from the sky.

The night was dark and beautiful. There was a large blanket of glimmering snow as far as their eyes could see, and the little candles burned softly, the shadows of the flames dancing on the walls. Their cabin was decorated with red and green popcorn, the beautiful little pine tree that Joseph had cut down for the family in the corner. The few ornaments that they had taken with them in the big trunk from Minnesota hung on top, as the cozy stockings hung from the fireplace. The little manger scene which Charlotta had been given as a child was situated on the little round butter churner in the corner of the room, nearest the kitchen, and all of their fur coats hung on the nails next to the door. They could hear the wind lightly pushing and pulling the house, and there was a chill inside, despite the very warm fire.

It had been snowing for weeks at Grasshopper Diggings. Anna Claire and Tommy would often go with Pete and Berthie to sled on the little hills up near the town. Sometimes, they would even cross the frozen creek unattended, slipping and sliding and laughing joyfully on the ice together. The winter had begun quite harshly, although the Freilers were used to long, difficult winters as they were from Minnesota where winters were very cold and harsh.

"I wish we had a piano like Lucy Grimm," sighed Helen glumly, looking over towards the empty wall. "What we have is scarce," agreed Charlotta, "but we must never forget to be thankful. Some children have never even heard the sound of a piano. Some children are out in this harsh cold right now with nowhere to go."

Helen looked down, embarrassed at her own selfishness.

"I miss Jacob," sighed Caroline.

"I wish we could eat now!" exclaimed Pete. "I'm starvin'!"

Charlotta threw her hands in the air. "Why are we all so miserable tonight? It is Christmas tomorrow. We have food, we have God, and we have each other."

"You're right, Mama," said Caroline, coming over and touching her arm. "We have far too much."

Anna Claire nodded and said, "We should all say one thing we're grateful for!"

Charlotta looked stunned for a moment. "That is an excellent idea, Anna Claire. Let us!"

Anna Claire looked down in thought, surprised at her mother's proud reaction. "I'm grateful that Tommy steals candy from the saloon and brings it to school."

Her mother's face fell. "Well, the idea itself was good, at least."

"I'm grateful that I have Jacob," said Caroline dreamily, a finger wrapped through one of her dark, silky curls.

"And you, Helen?" asked their mother.

"I'm grateful that I have nice hair," she said matter-of-factly, stroking her long, lightened brown waves. "That is vain, Helen!" cried Charlotta, frowning.

"Well, I'm grateful that we are gonna get to eat a big gobbler!" said Pete, rubbing his stomach.

"What about you, Berthie?" asked Helen. "What are you grateful for?"

Berthie went to the window and sighed. "I'm gwateful that it's snowing!"

Her large brown eyes could not part with the little flurries that were falling down from the dark sky and lightly touching the stark white ground.

"That is a very nice thing to be grateful for," said Charlotta, going to the oven and taking out the little balls of dough that had flattened into molasses sugar cookies.

The children crowded around the tray of treats, all anxious to get a bite.

"Let them cool," warned Charlotta with a smile as she placed them on top of the oven.

It was only a moment later when Joseph walked through the door, holding a large turkey in a wooden box, one from Salt Lake that he had purchased at the market.

"The turkey!" exclaimed Pete, his eyes going wide.

"Papa!" the girls said, running over to embrace him.

Joseph rubbed their head with the top of his hand and laughed. "I never saw so many children so happy to see a turkey before!"

"Silly Papa!" said Caroline. "It is *you* we want to see!"

They helped him sit by the fireplace to warm up and eat cookies. His face was red from the cold, and his hands felt like ice. Anna Claire helped take off his boots and gloves before hanging his icy coat up on one of the nails by the door and coming to sit beside him.

"You're so cold, Papa!" she said, warming up his hands with hers. "Poor Papa!"

"I'm alright, Anna Claire," he said with a smile, his eyes glistening, the hair around his chin white with ice. Everyone else had gone into the little kitchen, so it was only the two of them now.

"I want to go huntin' with you next time," said Anna Claire with gusto, sitting up straighter. "I can do it, Papa, I promise! I can do anything Pete can do, too! Like hunt and sow the seeds, and fix the house. I can do it, Papa!"

Joseph laughed and tweaked her lightly freckled nose. "I know you can, my wild girl. I don't doubt it for a second."

"This means you'll take me huntin' with you?" she asked, her eyes lighting up, hair glowing in the light.

"Maybe," sighed Papa. "Maybe someday, my little Anna Claire."

Anna Claire felt disappointed. Why couldn't she hunt, fish, harvest, and cut down trees, too?

Papa noticed the disappointment and added, "Someday, we will go into the woods together and I'll teach you how to shoot."

Anna Claire perked up immediately. She leaned over, kissed his cheek, and stated, "You'll be so proud of me!"

"I already am," said Joseph, giving her a squeeze.

The rest of the family came back from the kitchen holding the tray of cookies, a large loaf of home-baked bread, a little cup of butter, and mash potatoes. It was not very much, but for the family, it was exactly what they had wanted.

They gathered at the table, said their prayer, and began to eat, everyone impressed with the molasses cookies. Anna Claire was so hungry that she didn't even sneak Hero, who had a little red ribbon tied around his throat, any food. Instead, Hero got a nice helping of the turkey on his own little plate for the night. Everyone seemed especially hungry after the long wait to eat, and they hoped to finish their plate in a hurry to get to the cookies.

Charlotta, Caroline, and Helen began to work on cleaning up while Joseph took the younger three outside to look at the moon and tell them the story of Christmases he experienced as a boy. He talked about his brothers and how he and his brother James used to play pranks on Christmas Eve. James had died when he was still just a boy. "Why do young people die, Papa?" asked Berthie innocently, her eyes round like saucers.

Joseph sighed, his breath floating into the sky. "I reckon I wish I knew."

Anna Claire huddled closer to her father, as she was beginning to shiver from the cold.

"When is Santa Clause gonna come?" asked Pete with curiosity, his teeth chattering. "Do you think I'll get the train set I saw in the store?"

Joseph smiled. "Maybe, but I'm not Saint Nikolas, so I can't say for sure!"

The children laughed and Berthie dropped down into the snow, squealing with delight.

"It's a nice night," Joseph added. "I'm sure it was just as nice of a night when Jesus Christ was born."

They lapsed into silence for a few moments. They could hear the wind swooshing in the distance and the sound of muffled laughter from inside the home. The snow fell and made crystals in their hair while their cheeks turned red. They went inside in a few moments lest they catch a cold, and soon it was time for the Freiler children to go to bed.

"I just *know* I'm gonna get the train set from Santa," said Pete excitedly as he hopped into bed. "What do you think Santa's gonna bring you?"

"I want the dolly that I saw in the window!" pronounced Berthie with her arms outstretched. "The one with the blue wibbons!"

Anna Claire watched the snow falling from the window and looked up into the sky. She hoped that Santa Clause would be able to find her even though she wasn't in Minnesota anymore. Although she had been through very harsh moments during her journey to Gold Country and while living there, she had not lost her childish hopes.

"I want books," she said. "I hope he brings me books."

"That's dumb," said Pete. "Books are boring."

"They *are* not! *You're* dumb," cried Anna Claire, lunging over at him and throwing his own pillow at his face. Pete fought back until they were both laughing too hard to speak.

"I'm gonna read every book there ever was someday," said Anna Claire, standing up and walking to the window again. "I'm gonna learn all about the cities and New York and London and Indian royalty and even the people in Africa. I'm gonna learn it all. And then when I'm all grown up, I'm gonna go everywhere."

"You can't learn *everything* and go *everywhere*," said Pete, shaking his head of bright hair. "That would be too much! No one could!"

"I can do it and I will."

"How can we make tomowow come fast?" asked Berthie, sitting up in bed and holding one of her little dolls. "I wanna eat cookies and see my gifts!"

"Me, too," agreed Anna Claire, looking up at the big and very bright moon in the sky above the home. It seemed to be smiling down at her, the craters looking like a big face. Sometimes, depending on Anna Claire's mood, the moon would look like it was crying or very sad. When Anna Claire was scared, it looked scared too. And when Anna Claire was very happy, like she was on this night, so the moon looked cheerful, jolly, and overwhelmingly glad.

"Tell me a stowy," said Berthie, snuggling down in the covers, her big eyes beginning to look tired. "I can't sleep! I'm too excited!"

Anna Claire went back over to the bed and kissed the top of her head. "You both want to hear a real scary Christmas tale?" she asked, lowering her voice in an attempt to sound menacing.

"You sound stupid," said Pete, "but tell the story."

"There was once a little boy just like you, Pete," began Anna Claire, blowing out the candle on the little dresser and smiling in the dark. "The little boy was happy because he wanted a train set for Christmas. Well, when he woke up- he did get a train set! Santa had given him what he wanted! When he went outside, he was so happy he got to play with his new train set-"

"Is this story about me?" asked Pete suspiciously from under his blanket.

"Anyhow," continued Anna Claire, "just as he was about to take the train to town, a hill, a huge snowball came down and hit him in the face and killed him! He was dead! That's the end of the tale."

"Oh, shut up!" said Pete. "At least I'll be gettin' what I want for Christmas! You'll probably just get coal."   "I suppose we'll see!"

The children fell asleep shortly after, Pete beginning to snore lightly and Anna Claire's arm around Berthie. That night, Anna Claire dreamed of tall white trees and an adventurous little boy who looked a lot like Tommy going to the jungle and swinging from the trees. She was happy to be spending Christmas in Gold Country.

The next day, once Helen had gathered water in the pan and everyone rinsed their fingers and washed their faces, the family had a breakfast of eggs before Joseph read from the family Bible that had once been Charlotta's grandfather's. They each got a small gift for each other. Pete got his train set, Berthie got her new doll, and Anna Claire received a book about the Revolutionary War, which she treasured with all of her heart. Helen received a new pair of gloves, and Caroline got a new pearly hair-comb that she decided to wear that day. Joseph and Charlotta themselves received little trinkets from the children including a new bowl from Caroline, two hand-sewn ornaments for each parent from Helen, pieces of candy from Anna Claire that were no doubt taken from Swiner's Saloon, a carved iron knife from Pete that Joseph taught him how to make, a silver necklace Joseph made for Charlotta for Berthie to give her, and a hat that Charlotta had made for Joseph for Berthie to give him. All in all, the gifts turned out to be heartfelt and generous.

Caroline, finally allowed to see Jacob, hastened to get ready and left the house in a flurry, nearly forgetting her scarf and gloves. The others sat together and sang Christmas carols. They even let Hero have a cookie.

While they were drinking hot chocolate, Anna Claire happened to look out the wintry window to see a familiar figure running through the snow, the white fluff up to his waist. Without pause, she ran over to the door, flung it open, and let the chill into the house, running through the snow in her nightgown. She was wet with cold and her legs grew numb within a moment, but she was so happy to see Tommy that it didn't matter.

"You came on Christmas Day!" she exclaimed, running into Tommy and knocking him into the snow.

"I told ya I would!" said Tommy, standing up and brushing snow off of his shirt. "It's freezin' out here; what're you doin' in the snow?"

Anna Claire smiled. "I haven't seen you all week, not since Mama's been makin' us do all the Christmas preparin'!"

The children walked back in, Charlotta opening the door and scolding Anna Claire for being careless again.

"Tommy, you made it here!" said Joseph, offering a chair by the fireplace. Tommy shivered as he undid his boot laces and took off his tattered wool coat. "We were hoping you'd come."

"We have something for you," Charlotta smiled, walking slowly to the other side of the room.

"Wait 'til you see it!" exclaimed Anna Claire.

Charlotta walked over, her eyes gleaming, and handed Tommy a coat made of ox fur. It was long, warm, and finely sewn. Tommy had never had a coat like this. He had always just worn his old tattered one since he was about eight, which he had long outgrew and which didn't cover him nearly enough in the cold.

Tommy stood up and put the coat on, his face brightening.

"Oh, gee," he said. "It feels warm. Thank you! I don't reckon I ever had a coat like this before!"

He took it off and held it in his hands, feeling the softness and admiring the breadth of it.

"The girls helped me make it, and Pete went with Joseph to find the ox," Charlotta said softly. "We are so glad you like it."

"I told you he would like it!" exclaimed Anna Claire, feeling the coat herself.

"I got you somethin' too," said Tommy, feeling embarrassed as he went over to the pocket of his old coat.

"My dear, you should not have," said Charlotta, her face softening at the boy's kindness.

"It ain't much," said Tommy, his eyes looking down at the wooden ground. He fumbled in the pocket of his old coat until he pulled out a small hand-carved wooden plaque that said, "The Freilers". "You can keep it in here or anywhere you want. It says your name, see? I made it. I thought it might be nice in the house, but you don't gotta do nothin' with it."

It was not much of a plaque. It was small, only as big as his pocket, and with no fanciness to the lettering, yet it was finely crafted. And it was from Tommy, and created from his heart.

Charlotta's eyes stung with tears, and Joseph stood up to give the boy a firm pat on his back.

"This is the finest thing that has ever been carved," said Joseph kindly.

Tommy gave them a wide smile, his blue eyes sparkling with pride. He felt warmth and happiness that he had not felt in a while bubble up inside of him as he allowed Charlotta to embrace him.

"I like it," said Helen. "It says our name. Thank you."

Anna Claire grabbed the plaque from her father's hand. "It's perfect! He did it all by himself! You did, right Tommy?"

Tommy nodded bashfully, his foot scraping the ground.

"It is delightful," agreed Charlotta, taking it from Anna Claire and examining the craftsmanship. "You have a true gift, Tommy. Use it well." Tommy, feeling quite proud of himself, wished that Caroline were there to see his woodworking.

"Where's Caroline?" asked Tommy, looking around.

"She went to see Jacob Mast," said Helen with a roll of her eyes. "Her *lovely* beau!"

Joseph smiled. "She's fifteen in four days. She's gettin' old enough to begin thinkin' of marriage."

Tommy's stomach churned a bit and he just barely kept himself silent.

The Freiler's and the one little Cooper went into the kitchen to drink hot cocoa and have their Christmas dinner. It was a true feast that night, as there was real sugar, bone marrow butter, turkey, and cranberry jelly. After they ate, Charlotta began preparing pieces of the turkey to take to the Clemmons's, and Joseph went outside with Peter to get the horse ready. They were going to take their annual Christmas ride together, this time with Tommy and without Caroline. This would be the first year that Caroline did not come on the ride. Joseph had a brief moment of sadness when he thought of Caroline not being there to go sleighing with them.

Joseph took the bells from the little stable and led the horse out with his reins. One by one, the children walked into the red wooden sled, holding hot stones to keep warm, while Charlotta went over to the Clemmons's to deliver some of the turkey and cookies. Once they were all in the big sled, Joseph then sat atop the horse and directed it to begin moving.

The snow fell lightly, and the whole world looked dark except for the candles that were brightening in the windows. The children were getting warm, the fleece blanket that was over their legs covering their waists. Joseph began the journey, the children laughing and teasing each other. He went a bit faster across the field and turned around towards the creek, making the sled slide to the side a bit. Berthie and Pete began laughing as Joseph pretended to fall off the horse, and Helen looked truly frightened for a moment.

Anna Claire felt so small in the world, which seemed so big to her. She looked up at the sky and watched the stars, bright and still. The snow seemed calm compared to the sleigh that was rolling on through it, making long tracks. It was so cold that her feet felt nearly frozen and her little nose ached, but all the discomfort was worth it for the ride in the sleigh. She thought of the Christmases in Minnesota with Cousin Katie, and for a moment, she felt sad, but in another moment, she felt happy again when she looked over at Tommy and saw that he had nearly fallen out of the seat.

"Is Christmas at your home always this fun?" asked Tommy, steadying his hands in front of him and pulling his new fur coat closer around his shoulders.

"Yes!" cried Anna Claire, laughing as her father spun the sleigh around again. "We have a sleigh ride every year! Papa always gets one of the horses to take us on the sleigh, but we had to leave the other sleigh at our old home, so he built a new one."

"It's a hog killin' time!" affirmed Tommy.

Joseph pulled the sleigh further out as the children held onto the front of it for support.   "Hold on!" he yelled as he went in a full circle, the sleigh slipping and sliding and the bells ringing loudly on the horse.

"I'm glad to be here," said Tommy. "Ma is real drunk today so she don't wanna do nothin'. Sometimes we have a tree, but Ma didn't want one this year 'cause last year one of her men came over and hit the tree down when he was real angry and the ornaments broke. She said she never wants to have another Christmas tree again."

"Oh no," said Anna Claire, feeling a prick of sympathy. "I suppose I wouldn't want to, either. Why does your ma get drunk all the dang time?" "She likes to, I guess," said Tommy. "I think it makes her happy and makes her forget about all the bad. Hey, Anna Claire, I finished *A Pirate's Tale* yesterday!"

"You did?" Anna Claire exclaimed, her eyes wide and bright.

"It was ace high!" Tommy agreed. "I like the part when the pirate was caught by the robbers, but he still got away in the end."

"I love it, too," giggled Anna Claire. "And you're reading now! How does it feel to read?"

Tommy smiled. "It ain't as bad as I thought it was gonna be."

"I told you," said Anna Claire with a smirk.

When the little ride was over, they all went back into the warm house to drink more hot cocoa and sit by the fireplace. Charlotta had arrived back, and it wasn't long before Caroline was also home, Jacob escorting her. "Come in and have some cookies," offered Charlotta, smiling as she opened the door.

"No, ma'am," said Jacob. "I must get back home. My folks are waitin' for me. Much thanks to you, ma'am."

"Thank you for bringin' my little girl home safe," said Joseph, winking at Charlotta as if the two had a secret. "Tell your parents we said hello and a merry Christmas!"

Tommy smiled to himself as Jacob left. He turned towards Caroline, whose black hair was whitened with snow, and her face was red from the cold. She shivered as she gently took off her coat and gloves, and then faced Tommy with a smile.

"I'm glad you've come!" she said.

Charlotta walked over, holding the wooden plaque Tommy had made. "Tommy made this for us."

Caroline, genuinely impressed, admired the gift and smiled again, her face brightening. "Thank you, Tommy. I'm ever so glad we have this. It is beautiful." Tommy's body felt like it had turned to jelly. To have Caroline smile at him was the best Christmas present of all.

"It ain't much," Tommy said humbly.

"Oh, but it is," said Caroline. "I mean it; you made this! It is *simply* wonderful!"

Tommy wanted so much for her to kiss him. He thought how wonderful it would be for her to walk over with her sweet face and to kneel down and touch her lips to his.

"I got my train set," Pete said to Tommy proudly, breaking his reverie. "Do you wanna see it?"

"He doesn't want to play with you!" Anna Claire broke in with frustration.

Tommy stood up from his chair and walked over to Pete. "Sure, I wanna see it."

Excitedly, Pete grabbed his train set from across the room and brought it over.

"You gotta see how fast it can go! It can go faster than fast!"

"Alright, show me then."

Pete, who looked up to Tommy very much, took him up the stairs to have more room to play with the train set while Anna Claire and Berthie played with Berthie's new doll in the kitchen. Caroline and Helen discussed the events of the day, with Caroline gushing over Jacob, and Helen telling her all about the ride in the sleigh. Charlotta and Joseph sat by the fire together, Joseph placing his hand on his wife's and looking into the fireplace. The two drank hot cocoa and talked in low voices.

"That boy is the sweetest boy to have ever come around," said Charlotta, looking up at Tommy's "The Freilers" sign. "The craftsmanship is wonderful. I must say I do not know where that boy learned how to do that."

"He is more talented and good-natured than we ever realized," agreed Joseph, taking a sip of cocoa from his clay mug. "He is a good boy, Char. I know he can be a bad influence to Anna Claire sometimes, but he's a good boy."

"He is," agreed Charlotta, "although I do wish the two of them wouldn't steal so much candy when they go to the saloon. In truth, I would rather Anna Claire not go to the saloon at all."

"I suppose so," Joseph said, "but it seems that Anna Claire is right determined to be friends with him. I can't say I blame her, Char."

Charlotta snuggled closer to her husband and put her arm around him. "I wish I had a little friend like that at her age. I only had my sisters."

"Do you think we would have been good friends if we had met then?" said Joseph with a twinkle in his eyes.

"No," laughed Charlotta, kissing him on the cheek.

Joseph thought that Charlotta looked beautiful in the firelight with her hair beginning to fall out of its tight bun and her pale face golden in the firelight. He sighed calmly, feeling thankful to have his family with him and even Tommy, who was slowly becoming like a son to him. All seemed to be well this majestic Christmas night as the snow fell softly outside of the window and the children were joyful.

"When I'm all grown up, I'm gonna marry Caroline," Tommy reminded Anna Claire as the two got into the big bed.

Tommy was to stay overnight at the Freiler's, as it had gotten late and they knew his mother would be too drunk to care for him.

"You're silly," said Anna Claire. "She'll never love you. You're too young!"

Tommy made a face while Pete and Berthie got into bed.

"Santa knew I wanted the train set!" said Pete, his smile wide and his eyes glowing. "I can't believe it!"

"He knew I wanted the dolly!" cried Berthie, giggling in her characteristically high-pitched voice. "I love the dolly. I'm gonna call hew Mawy."

"I can't wait to read my book," said Anna Claire. "It seems like it's going to be all about war!"

"I wonder if it will have a lot of blood in it," said Tommy with interest.

"'Course it will," replied Anna Claire, letting her head fall on the pillow. "Blood and rifles and lots of dead people."

"That's a book even *I* would read!" said Tommy excitedly. "I'll read it next!"

"Children, go to sleep!" called Charlotta from the bottom of the stairs.

Anna Claire snuggled down in the covers her Tommy and her siblings chuckling for being sneaky. Eventually, the room grew quiet, and Tommy and Anna Claire could hear slow-paced breaths.

Tommy lay on his side and closed his eyes. "I hope you don't kick in your sleep," he said with a grunt, moving over to the edge.

"I hope you don't snore," returned Anna Claire with equal annoyance. "Anyway, I guess we'll see. G'night."

"G'night," Tommy whispered. "Hey-" he turned to face his friend. "This might'a been the best Christmas I ever had."

It took quite a while of begging for Charlotta to allow Anna Claire to "play by the creek" the next day on December 26th. Anna Claire had done all of her chores very early in the morning- fast and haphazardly, but they were done. After reminding her mother of all of the work she had done and how good she had been behaving, she told her mother that she would only be at the creek for approximately an hour. Tommy had gone back to the saloon earlier but had promised to come by around dinner, and Anna Claire was waiting for him now.

"Please, please, please, Mama!" begged the little girl. "I did all my chores, and I did a good job, and Miss Darlin' says I'm a great student! It will only be an hour! Me and Tommy just wanna look at the ice and see the birds."

Charlotta, admitting to herself that Anna Claire had indeed been doing well, sighed and smiled. "You may go- but only for an hour! I want you back by dinnertime! You must wear your coat! Your scarf and your mittens! You must wear your hat!"

"I promise I will!" said Anna Claire happily, nearly hopping with joy. She knew she only had a precious short time to see lá daxpitchée and his friends and family, but it would be worth it. "Would it be alright if I shared some of our ginger snaps with Tommy? His ma would like them, and they don't get a lot of cookies in town."

Charlotta resisted the urge to laugh at that last part of the sentence. "Yes, of course. Why don't you go play and come back for the cookies?"

"Well... actually," went on Anna Claire, "I think that it would be better if I get them first. You know Tommy. He'll forget and I'll forget too!"

"Alright, but I hope you do not leave them by the creek!" said Charlotta, smiling and handing her the little tin can filled with iced ginger snaps.

Anna Claire grabbed them anxiously, kissing her mother on the cheek very uncharacteristically. Charlotta may have questioned this if she hadn't been so distracted tending to Berthie's sore stomach.

Anna Claire ran up the ladder to the loft where she threw on her coat, her little black-knit hat, her matching mittens, and her winter boots. She then sat by the window and watched impatiently for Tommy, who had gone home to say Merry Christmas to Mr. Dobbins, to come trudging through the snow towards the cabin. When she saw him, she clasped her hands together and walked quickly across the loft. She ran down the ladder, jumping off in glee, and shouted a goodbye to her mother and Berthie.

She ran out of the house, stumbling in the snow, and waved to Tommy, who was also clumsily running towards her as well.

"Anna Claire!" he shouted as he waved back.

"Let's go! I only got an hour!"

The two children went as fast as they could through the knee-deep snow over to the little wooded area by the creek. When they got to the creek, they approached the log where they usually walked across, only the log was caked with snow.

"How can we get across?" asked Anna Claire.

"I got an idea!" Tommy crouched down then and started picking up rocks. He began throwing handfuls of rocks at the log, so much that they began to clear off the snow.

"Good idea!" said Anna Claire, beginning to pick up rocks and pelt them at the log. And the two crossed the log.

They ran so hard through the snow that they were panting. Their cheeks and noses were icy and red, and their fingers hurt through their mittens. They knew they had to get to lá daxpitchée.

It seemed like hours, but they finally reached the camps. There were some people around a fire, but many were in their teepees due to the extreme cold. Some of the men stood up and gathered around them, smiling and greeting them in their own language. Iá daxpitchée's father came to them, his feathered headdress looking stark in the snowy background, and said, "Iá daxpitchée is in his home. You can see him."

Anna Claire and Tommy ran over to the teepee and huddled at the bottom, telling the family who they were.

"Come, come!" said Iá daxpitchée's mother.

The children walked in and were greeted by Iá daxpitchée, who stood up from the mattress and touched their arms.

"You are here!" he said. "I did not think you would come!"

"It was hard," admitted Anna Claire, "but we wanted to see all of you. And we wanted to bring you these." She held out her hands where the tin can was placed. "They're ginger snaps. My mama and my sister made them. They're delicious!"

"Delicious?"

"She means good," said Tommy. "The cookies are good."

Iá daxpitchée smiled. "Good- delicious!"

"Thank you," said Iá daxpitchée's mother, coming over and opening the tin. She took the tin from her son and went to the old woman and old man, offering them a ginger snap before taking one herself. "Very good!" she began to laugh as the crumbs spilled out of her mouth.

Iá daxpitchée's grandmother and grandfather ate the cookies and smiled, looking satisfied. They said something in their language, to which Iá daxpitchée translated, "They like."

Anna Claire and Tommy smiled.

"You want hold baby?" he asked her, picking up his little sister. "She likes you."

Anna Claire's eyes widened with delight as she took the baby from his arms. Kissing her cheek, she began to bounce her up and down, humming her own tune. The baby cooed and laughed, her rosy cheeks deepening into dimples and her big brown eyes sparkling.

"Sit," said Iá daxpitchée.

"I want to sit," said Anna Claire slowly, giving the baby back, "but we can't stay. I told my mama I'd be home soon. I just wanted to give you the cookies."

"Not stay?" asked Iá daxpitchée sadly.

"No, not stayin'," said Tommy, putting an arm around his friend. "But me and Anna Claire- we'll be back! Anna Claire's ma thinks it's too cold to be out. But we will be back soon!"

"We will try to be back soon, but if we can't, we'll come back in the spring!" said Anna Claire. "I promise, you'll see us soon!"

"See Anna Claire and Tommy soon?" asked Iá daxpitchée hopefully.

"Yes, we will see you soon, Iá daxpitchée!" Anna Claire smiled and took his hand in hers. "Soon!"

lá daxpitchée walked outside with them. Anna Claire and Tommy nodded and smiled at some of the others who were outside cooking by a fire. They said goodbye to their friend one more time, Anna Claire promising again that they would see them soon, and walked briskly away from the camps.

"He's a good friend," said Tommy as they trudged along, their legs pushing against the crisp snow. "Maybe he'll be allowed to go to the creek in the spring."

"Maybe!" said Anna Claire. "I hope we can see him and his family before the spring! That's months from now!"

"Yeah, that's forever," agreed Tommy, tripping into the snow and falling over.

Anna Claire laughed and, as she attempted to help him up, he brought her down with him, and the two began laughing, their mouths full of snow.

"I hope it ain't been an hour," said Anna Claire.

"I don't reckon so," answered Tommy, "but it'll probably be close."

They walked as fast as they could to the creek, where they crossed the log and ran through the trees. Once in the clearing, they felt safer and walked more slowly.

"If my mama ever asks, those cookies were for you," reminded Anna Claire. "Come and visit tomorrow!"

"My ma wants me to help her in the saloon tomorrow," said Tommy begrudgingly, "but maybe the day after that."

"Alright, see ya!" called Anna Claire as she struggled through the snow.

"See ya!" Tommy waved. "It'll take me all day to get home in this snow!"

"Don't get lost out there, Tommy!"

"Hey, Anna Claire?"

"What?"

"Watch out!" and with that, he quickly scooped up a ball of snow and flung it at her, hitting her square in the face.

"You're dead!" yelled Anna Claire, pelting him with more snow until he started to back away.

"G'bye, Anna Claire!"

"G'Bye, Tommy!"

Chapter 15- Winter in the West

The rest of the winter found the Freiler family in tough times. The matriarch of the family was, understandably, as stressed as ever. Keeping the family warm and fed proved very strenuous. Charlotta found herself warming stones every day to put into the children's gloves as they went off to school, knitting torn socks and scarves, making pots of tea for herself and Joseph, trying to ignore the icy chill as she completed chores outdoors, and unfroze the canned jams by placing them next to the fire until supper was ready. There was always a wintry chill in the house, regardless of how heavy everyone dressed or how long the fireplace was lit. Everything seemed to be so cold, and Charlotta could never keep her pale hands warm enough.

The children struggled, too. Walking into town when the snow was as high as they were was challenging. They often dropped their slates into the watery ice, arrived at the schoolhouse with their eyes stinging and their hands numb, and caught colds and small illnesses. Still, the days were short, and the nights were long, and the children found themselves stuck inside most of the time, tending to their chores and talking amongst themselves. Many times, they were not able to go to school because of the storms, and this often led to the children quarreling with each other because they were sad, bored, frustrated, or all three. The winter was even more difficult than the winters in the past that they were used to in Minnesota, and sometimes it became so cold that any sweat that came from hard work would immediately freeze on their bodies.

Caroline was sulky because she could rarely go out with Jacob Mast, and Peter was angry because he was not allowed to go sledding by himself on the hills. Berthie struggled with a terrible cough that lasted throughout the entire winter. Helen was annoyed with Anna Claire, and the two frequently got into disputes over every little thing, whether it was who was doing what chore, who had defied a parent, or which color egg was best. Their arguing caused a decent amount of chaos in the house, and some chores were done improperly. This led to both girls receiving punishments from Charlotta, who took away Helen's prettiest dress and Anna Claire's favorite books until they apologized to each other and promised they would try harder to be nice to each other, although the niceness only lasted so long.

The one bright spot during the winter months was that fewer men were murdered. This happened for a number of reasons. With it being harder to mine and discover gold, fewer men were targets for exploitation. With the weather being dreadful, no man or family could travel very far on the dangerous roads, and the Road Agents themselves were stuck inside most of the time. Joseph, occasionally going to a saloon with Mr. Clemmons and Mr. O'Reilly, often overheard talk of the people who got lucky in Montana Territory and struck gold, and those who gave up everything only to be penniless. This undoubtedly uneased Joseph, but he was still not deterred. Everything in him told him to stay patient and keep going with the hunt. No matter how high the risk was, the gold would be found, and his family would be safe.

Charlotta herself felt burdened with stress. Joseph had to work so hard every day just to make ends meet. Due to the intensely cold weather and all of the snow and ice, he could not pan for gold nearly as much or as well as he usually could, so the promise of finding it was at its lowest, at least until the spring. Joseph worked so hard, and Charlotta was beyond appreciative of it, but she often felt alone and unheard. Nettie could not come over as much, nor could she come over to her, as the heavy snow and ice prevented this. Charlotta was the only member of the family who knew what it was like to be the mother and the wife, and that was not always easy. Tending to the house and children were all things she had always expected to do, even when she was a child herself, but there were extra pressures of prairie life and life out west. She had to worry about the possibilities of bears coming too close to the cabin, of snakes sneaking through the door, of raising her children without a proper church, of constantly worrying if the Native Americans were going to find them and attack, and whether or not it was going to be safe to obtain supplies from town.

Life out west was difficult and truly a daily struggle. And now it was so cold- all the time so cold. Ice on the windows, the water in the buckets freezing, the snow piled up high outside of the door, and snow falling through little separations between the logs, causing them to wake up with snow on their faces and blankets. Charlotta was a resilient woman, but she knew she was not God. It was only a matter of time before she felt she would crack.

There was a bright spot soon, however, as there was to be a winter dance that January.

Dances happened quite often in Bannack, but Charlotta did not approve of them, so she and Joseph never went. However, since Nettie and Paul Clemmons were going, she figured she would take the chance and go, too. Anyhow, she was eager for company, and seeing friends would improve her mood markedly.

The men and women enjoyed company, especially during the winter months when everyone stayed inside most of the time. Everyone was anxious for fun amongst the difficulties of Western life. Most days were full of hard work, but when there was a dance, it seemed that life stopped for a brief moment so that everyone nearby could gather together in celebration of community.

Earlier in the previous month, Mr. Dobbins pronounced to Mr. O'Reilly that there would be a dance at the court hall in town, which was certainly big enough for many people. Mr. O'Reilly then relayed the news to Mr. Grimm, who then told Mr. Clemmons, who gave the news to Mr. Freiler. The word spread throughout town and the surrounding areas, and soon enough, people were excited and anticipating the dance.

Charlotta herself was even eager for the time to come. The winter was becoming so long and dreadful, and she sorely missed the company. She was fervent for connection. Anna Claire was excited because that meant that she could see Tommy again, as the children were not able to attend school for a few weeks due to the storms, and she wanted so badly to get out of the house and run around wild. Caroline was filled with joy, as she knew she would be able to dance with her Jacob finally, and spent the few days prior sewing lace around the bottom of her good dress and sleeves. Helen was neither glad nor upset about this dance, as she had no reason to be either. Pete did not want to go and would have rather stayed home, complaining that he was capable to stay alone in the cabin, to which he was not permitted to. Berthie wanted to go to the dance and was very excited to eat desserts and hear music.

"I do *so* want to dance with Jacob tonight," said Caroline as she twisted her hair into even bigger curls with her pencil, a bright smile on her face and a dreamy look in her eyes.

It was the night of the dance, and the family was in a hurry to look their best and get to the town hall. Joseph had returned from working and was outside tying the horses to the hitching post while Charlotta helped Helen put ribbons in her hair and dressed Berthie.

"I want to see Tommy!" pronounced Anna Claire cheerfully, pushing her older sister out of the mirror's way and sticking her tongue out at herself. "Tommy said he's gonna dance like he's drunk and scare everyone!"

"You are a dreadful little girl," said Caroline, lighting another candle with her small, pale fingers.

Calico slips and pants were strewn everywhere as everyone had been preparing for the night of the big dance. Bread crumbs that had fallen from supper were getting conveniently cleaned up by Hero, and the sound of children arguing and laughing permeated cheerfully throughout the home. The house was glimmering bright due to all of the many candles, and even the wintery chill could not spoil the merry mood that night.

"Stop- moving-" Charlotta said, pulling on Berthie's braids.

"Mama, it huwts!" cried Berthie with tears in her eyes, reaching up to clutch the top of her head.

"Just stay still a bit longer," Charlotta tied the final blue ribbon, and, thankfully, the little girl's hair was finished.

"I don't wanna go to this stupid ol' dance!" yelled Pete miserably from the ladder. "None of the other boys are gonna go, and I'll be the only one there! I don't wanna!"

"Quiet, Peter," said Joseph, rushing through the door and giving his wife a kiss on the cheek. She looked radiant despite her modest dress and tight bun. "There will be lots of cookies and food you can eat. Don't spoil the fun for everyone else."

Pete pouted but calmed down at the word "cookies."

"Oh, my hair, this isn't right!" cried Caroline, frantically re-curling a straying black ringlet and slamming her arm down on the table in frustration. "What shall Jacob say!?"

"Your hair is beautiful," said Charlotta with a smile. "Oh, Caroline, you are truly a wonderful sight!"

"What about *my* hair?" asked Helen, finding her hair distasteful. "I look horrid with curls!"

"You look horrid with anything!" yelled Anna Claire, wrinkling her nose.

"You see, Mama?" cried Helen angrily. "Papa, did you hear her? She is always so dreadful! Did you hear what she said?"

"I did," said Charlotta with a sigh, "but your sister is ten. You are thirteen. You cannot take such things to heart so much, my dear. I think your hair looks lovely, just like you."

Helen couldn't argue with the age difference, so she crossed her arms and glared at Anna Claire from the chair.

Anna Claire was spinning around excitedly, thinking of all the treats she would eat and the wild dances she would do. Maybe she would pretend to be an animal to scare the others, too. She would even get to dance with her papa tonight! She bent down, her short, golden braid hitting her face, and tied her shoe lace again, feeling grateful that she didn't have to have her hair curled in such a silly fashion.

Together, Caroline argued with Helen and Peter teased Berthie; they gathered themselves outside in the cold shortly before hopping into the wagon.

The fields were covered with snow, and the stars hung high and very white in the dark sky. The storm had ended, but had left Gold Country very cold and windy. The Freiler's faces reddened, and their noses and hands felt icy cold, but they laughed all the way to the town hall, talking about memories of family back in Minnesota and the new memories they were creating in Gold Country.

Anna Claire looked up at the sky and thought about all of the people around the world and what they would see when they looked up at the sky. Some places would be light as day, while others would be even darker than the sky she was looking up at. She saw a star fly across, and her eyes went big. She remembered that her aunts always told her to make a wish on a star. She wasn't sure if she was doing it properly, but she looked up into the night and said to herself silently, *I wish Papa would find gold and Mama would be happy.*

They arrived at the hall in cheerful fashion, paid the five dollars necessary for entry, and greeted the Clemmons's with excitement. Rebecca took Helen by the hand and led her over to the table where the water was, whispering in her ear about a boy they both knew. Matthew shyly followed behind, looking over his shoulder and putting his hand behind his back, unable to look at Helen. It was not much time before Caroline was dancing with Jacob, and Nettie was taking Charlotta over to the window to talk quietly about how reckless the cowboys were that had been coming into town. Joseph and Paul Clemmons were each having a drink by a table off to the side, as the liquor poured from the barrel generously, and soon approached Elmer Grimm, James O'Reilly, and Sam Chesham.

"There's been a murder over in Virginia City," said Mr. Chesham, refusing the drink offered to him and looking around to ensure nobody was listening to the conversation.

Joseph exhaled and shook his head. "When are all these rousers gonna stop? It's gettin' more and more risky."   "I don't know," said Mr. Grimm, "but my wife and I have been thinkin' of takin' Lucy and gettin' ourselves out of here."

"You serious, Elmer?" asked Mr. O'Reilly, looking at him with surprise.

Mr. Grimm sighed. "It isn't set in stone, now. But we're thinkin' about it. We're thinkin' maybe the East, where there's more people and more protection."

"I would wait," said Mr. Clemmons, tilting his head back to take a big swig of the drink.

"I don't think you should be doin' any of that," agreed Mr. O'Reilly. "Danger is everywhere, Elmer. Journeyin' to the East isn't gonna get you away from the danger."

Mr. Grimm took another drink and looked at his wife, who was talking with a group of women on the other side of the hall.

"I just wanna do what's right by her and my Lucy."

"We don't doubt that," said Mr. Clemmons. "I think you oughta be careful, especially travelin' right now. It's not safe. And it's not just because of the cold. Even if you don't have gold, it seems they're after everyone now."

"I think you'd better stay until it quiets down around here," agreed Joseph. "I thought about takin'

Charlotta and the children and leavin' Gold Country too, but it's too dangerous right now. Besides, we got a good community here. No harm will come to us. We're a big team."

He and Mr. O'Reilly hit their bottles together and pat Mr. Grimm on the back.

"Just give it some time," said Joseph. "Just a little time. We're growin' here, and that's all it'll take. We just gotta keep a trigger eye on the Agents."

"I'm not sure if all this was a good idea," admitted Mr. Grimm. "Every day, we're all out there minin' and pinin' for gold. What do we get? Meager gold dust to barely last us a week!"

"It's frustratin', that's for sure," agreed Mr. Clemmons, "but that's part of it all. It's always right when someone's about to give up that they find what they're lookin' for."

"I hope so," said Mr. Grimm, "because I'm gettin' more impatient by the day."

Joseph swallowed his whiskey. He was about to chime in that he felt the same way, but instead, he took another drink.

"I reckon I didn't think winters here would be this bad," sighed Sam Chesham, rubbing his yellow mustache. "It's downright freezin'!"

"Even Minnesota doesn't seem as bad as this," Joseph agreed. "Yesterday, I looked down and my porridge was frozen solid! I hadn't even touched it yet!"

"The minin' is startin' to hurt my fingers," complained Mr. Chesham. "I'm sick of my hands turnin' into blocks of ice every time I put them in the stream."

"It's cold," agreed Mr. Clemmons, "but the heat is even worse. We can't forget all the flies, boys!"

The men nodded somberly.

"You'd be hard-pushed to find a more interesting place than here," said Joseph.

"My daughter's takin' French lessons now," laughed Mr. Grimm. "My wife wants her to be a 'lady!' Imagine that, in a town like this?"

"Rebecca takes the singin' class," said Mr. Clemmons. "She likes it a whole lot."

"My Helen is very social," said Joseph, "but she hates singin'! She's no good at it."

"They even got opera lessons in the hall on Wednesday nights," said Mr. Grimm with a smirk. "You wanna do some opera, boys?"

The men laughed into their drinks.

"I'm surprised Charlotta lets you drink the blackstrap," said Mr. O'Reilly with a hearty laugh, elbowing Joseph in the arm.

"Only at the dances," said Joseph with a smile and a nod. "She don't know about the other times."

Everyone laughed then, the men cheering with their drinks.

"To the new 'El Dorado!'" said Mr. Grimm. "May we all get lucky and get the hell outta here!"

"To Gold Country!" they said, the drinks splashing from their cups.

The children were scattered to various parts of the large hall to find their friends, and it was not long before Anna Claire found Tommy, who had come with his mother. Ms. Kathleen Cooper was still wearing her bright red saloon dress and big makeup, immediately going over and grabbing a bottle of whiskey. The people were doing the scamper down before the double shuffle and then the western-swing, big smiles on their faces, and their feet loudly clapping the floor.

"There's so many people in here!" exclaimed Anna Claire, pulling Tommy by the hand.

"Where we goin'?"

"Upstairs!"

The children snuck up a short stairway that led to a loft in the hall. The crowd danced to a waltz below, and the conversing and laughing followed them into the loft. Anna Claire fell dramatically onto the ground with Tommy following behind her. The two of them peeked through the loft's rails, watching the ladies spin around in their big dresses and the men taking their hands with strength. The candles made the entire hall look bright and alive, and the music from the fiddle had people nearly lifted off their feet.

"Look!" giggled Anna Claire, pointing down at a woman whose gown had flown up her skirt, showing high up her legs.

Tommy laughed and took a piece of candy from his pocket, heaving it at the crowd. It landed on a young man's head, who touched his hair slightly, shrugged, and continued dancing.

"Let me try," said Anna Claire naughtily, taking a piece of blue candy and slinging it through the rails.

It hit a woman on the shoulder, who looked very much perturbed.

"Get her!" said Tommy, hitting Anna Claire with his elbow and pointing at Helen.

Laughing sneakily, Anna Claire swung the candy toward Helen, who was whispering in Rebecca Clemmons's ear. It hit Helen straight on her forehead and, shocked, she looked around to see who had thrown the candy her way, her eyebrows raised in anger and her mouth hanging open.
Anna Claire leaned back so that she would not see her as she and Tommy laughed and laughed.

"That stupid goat," declared Anna Claire. "She didn't even see me!"

"You're awful mean sometimes, Anna Claire," said Tommy with a smile, "and you're strange."

"I ain't strange!" said Anna Claire defensively.

"I meant strange as in-," Tommy paused to think, "strange as in- different! Different than other girls!" Anna Claire's face relaxed, and she nodded. "Thank you!"

"For what?"

"For sayin' I ain't like other girls! I don't like other girls. Anyway, let's get some cookies, I'm hungry."

The children returned down the stairs, watching as Helen eyed the crowd suspiciously. They watched silently at the men and women dancing and the fiddle playing until they saw Mr. Dobbins coming towards them, holding his gray brimmed hat in his hand and his face as red as it ever was.

"Mr. Dobbins!" cried Anna Claire excitedly.

She and Tommy ran and embraced him.

"My favorite youngins," he said proudly with

a big smile crossing his ruddy face. "How are ya?"

"Fine," the children said at the same time.

"Did you have some of Mrs. Grimm's cookies?" asked Mr. Dobbins, rubbing his stomach. "They're dang delicious!"

Anna Claire and Tommy shook their heads and eyed the table. Summoning Mr. Dobbins, they all walked over to where the oatmeal cookies were, which were still warm. In fact, the whole hall was so warm with all of the people's bodies and the big fireplace that they nearly forgot it was January.

"I have to tell you a secret," said Tommy, his voice getting low. "Since no one can hear us, we gotta tell you now, right, Anna Claire?"

"What secret?" asked the girl as she slowly took her hair out of her uncomfortably tight braid and let it free around her shoulders.

"Miss Darlin'!" whispered Tommy.

"What, what? I can't hear ya!" said Mr. Dobbins as he touched his ear.

"Let's go," said Tommy, leading them to the loft. When they were safely up, he said, "It's a big secret. You can't tell no one. *Not no one*."

Mr. Dobbins chuckled, his face glowing. "Alright, let's have it!"

"It's Miss Darlin'," said Anna Claire in a low voice. "Wait, I wanna tell him!" yelled Tommy in annoyance.

"You always get to say it and I never get to say nothin'!" Anna Claire cried angrily.

"We both can say it," Tommy said. "Miss Darlin' is our teacher."

"Yes- Lucia!" nodded Mr. Dobbins. "She's a real nice gal!"

"She's not just our teacher, though," said Tommy in a hushed whisper.

"What do you mean?" Mr. Dobbins asked suspiciously.

"She- she's-" began Anna Claire.

"She's Daisy's daughter," finished Tommy, ignoring Anna Claire's appalling looks.

"What?" asked Mr. Dobbins, a look of confusion on his face.

"We figured it all out," said Tommy. "Ya see, we never noticed before, but her name is Darlin' and she's come from a place far, far away and no one here even knew her before, and she doesn't have any parents 'cause she lived with her Uncle and she's back in Gold Country!"

"She's back," went on Anna Claire, "probably to see her mother's bones and say goodbye. But she don't want anyone to know she was her baby. I don't know why. Probably 'cause she's real sad about her mother bein' dead and wants to find the gold herself. Maybe she even knows there's gold in the hills 'cause that's where her grandfather put it when Daisy left. Maybe she came here to look for it, too. We're gonna tell her, but we can't tell her now 'cause she's our teacher and she'll be awful mad if she knew we found out her secret. Do you see? We found her! We found Daisy's daughter! It's Miss Darlin'! *Darlin'!*"

Mr. Dobbins frowned profoundly and closed his eyes for a moment. The children, worried, wondered what was going on.

"I don't reckon you're right," he said finally, shaking his head. "I'm sorry I got you two so caught up with all this nonsense. It ain't right. It just ain't right."

The children felt a wind of disappointment hit them in the chest. Why was Mr. Dobbins regretting all of the things he had told them and all of the stories?

"Well, why not?" asked Anna Claire. "Her name is Darlin'! How do you know she ain't her daughter?"

"For one thing, anyone could be named 'Darlin.' I don't know, youngins, I think you two have taken this too far. I thought you were done goin' missin' gettin' everyone worried and huntin' out there for treasure."

Tommy and Anna Claire looked at each other.

"We are," said Tommy. "We aren't gonna go look without a grown person. Never again. But Miss Darlin' might be able to help us find the gold. She might know what happened to her ma somehow, and how sad her grandfather was. Maybe someone who knew her mother took her and raised her far away. Maybe it was the governor!" "Why would it be her last name then?" asked Mr. Dobbins. "Last names come from fathers!"

"Because that could have been the man Daisy tried to run away with!" exclaimed Tommy. "Maybe his last name was Darlin'!"

"Her uncle *must* know," Anna Claire reasoned.

Mr. Dobbins sighed. "Just don't pull any funny stuff on them hills," he looked around the hall as if the mountains were right within his eyesight. "It's dangerous out there. I wouldn't say nothin' to Miss Darlin' until later, after you're done school, so that you don't upset her. Just think if it is true and she *doesn't* know. Think of her comin' here to be near family, and she doesn't know a thing about her real parents. Just think of that!" Anna Claire and Tommy nodded at each other.

"It would hurt," said Mr. Dobbins. "Don't tell her. Not yet. Wait a bit. Wait a few years, and she might start to discover it herself."

Anna Claire and Tommy nodded again.

"Alright," agreed Tommy.

"Good idea," said Anna Claire.

The three left the loft and joined the rest of the dance. Merriment and cheer filled the air as the people of Gold Country danced and laughed and chatted and ate, and lived. Anna Claire watched the crowd with big, glowing eyes. Caroline stared deeply into the face of Jacob Mast, who was not exactly the best dancer, and Joseph had now grabbed Charlotta by the hand and started spinning her around, her laughing in surprise. Helen and Lucy Grimm were talking and dancing with each other, and even Pete was in heaven by the dessert table, stuffing his mouth with as many pieces of sliced ginger cake as he could. Berthie watched her parents dance with a large toothy grin, her dark eyes sparkling, and her little hands clapping. It was a very good night indeed.

"When are we gonna have another dance?" asked Pete as the family left in the wagon.

"Soon, hopefully," answered Joseph, winking at his wife, who began blushing.

"So long as you children are obedient and mind what I say!" Charlotta added.

It was an icy February evening when the men stormed out of town, drunk and carrying their pistols up the snowy cold banks. Joseph Freiler had stopped for a quick drink on his way back from town to buy some medicine for Berthie, whose throat was mildly sore, and had heard part of the conversation.

"You ain't goin' up there right now this late?" said Mr. Scott Taylor, the manager of the Taylor Saloon across town.

"Better late than never," said one Mr. Adam Blarney.

"You'll be in an awful lot of trouble," Mr. Taylor shook his head, pouring a Mr. Samuel Collingsworth another drink.

Mr. Blarney laughed as he tripped over a chair. He was able to catch himself by holding onto the counter top, but not before the drink fell right out of his hand. He continued laughing idiotically, bending forward to pick up the glass.

"My, my," he slurred. "I guess I damn well near drank too much."

"Come on, Blarney, I'd say you're rightly sober to do the job!" said Mr. Collingsworth, standing up from his seat by the counter.

"You two are fools if you go this late," said Mr. Taylor, wiping some of the spilled drink from the counter. "It's already gettin' dark. They'll probably shoot you with arrows before you come anywhere near them."

"Their arrows can't match my pistol," said Mr. Blarney, holding it in the air as if to throw it.

Joseph was listening to the conversation, leaning in further after hearing the word "arrows."

"We better get a move on," said Mr. Collingsworth, throwing a dime onto the counter. "Don't say a word of this! We'll come back and tell ya how it went. Maybe we'll come back with one of their heads!"

"Oh, you should just leave them alone," said Mr. Taylor. "They ain't been doin' nothin' here recently."

"They're tryin' to keep this land that's rightly ours," broke in Mr. Collingsworth. "They've been killin' our families, Taylor. It's only right to show them that they ain't gonna be doin' that no more. We gotta show 'em. Show 'em who they're messin' with. They can go tell all their friends that we mean business."

Mr. Taylor simply shrugged and shook his head. "I think it's a lousy idea, but you fools are gonna do it anyway. Just threaten them and leave them alone!"

"Come on, Collingsworth," said Mr. Blarney, the two of them snickering as they ran out the door of the saloon.

Joseph stood up then and walked over to Mr. Taylor.

"It sounds like they're going to try to find the Crows," said Joseph. "Why?"

Now, Joseph was pitted against the Native Americans and had a deep prejudice against them, but he was not beyond some level of moral awareness that hurting them for no reason would be wrong.

"Ah, they're just joshin' around," said Mr. Taylor with a small laugh as he washed the glasses. "Those fools think they're tough; they like to play games. That Blarney is gonna go find the camps, wave his pistol like it's an American flag, and run off home before they probably even have a chance to see them. They're all talk."

"It sounded serious," said Joseph, looking at the door as if expecting them to walk back in.

"They make everything sound serious," laughed Mr. Taylor. "Those two will be goin' too late, it'll be dark soon, and then they'll probably turn back around like a couple of betsys. I'm sure they'll have a nice story tomorrow, though! Bogus, of course, but a good story nonetheless!"

Joseph smiled and shook his head. "I don't know them, but if you say they're all talk, I'm sure you're right. Do you know where the Crows are camped?"

"Some of them are far down, we think, closer to the mountains in the West," said Mr. Taylor thoughtfully, scratching his white mustache. "I don't reckon I know exactly where, but I know that folks been seein' them around. They've walked through town a couple of times, too. I'm sure someone followed them so someone might know where the camps are. I think they're over west by the mountains, like I said. I know they're close 'cause they've been to town before. One even stopped in for a drink! I gave it to him. Hey- it ain't my muss! If they can pay, they can pay! I ain't turnin' down no payin' customer. No, sir."

Joseph nodded and handed over his glass. "Well, that makes sense, sir. I guess I'd better be gettin' home to the family."

"Always a good thing to do," said Mr. Taylor with a smile.

Joseph left the saloon, sighing. He didn't like Native Americans. He never had. He would never want to help one, and he would never let his children near one if it could be helped. But to purposefully go to search them out and threaten them for a lack of reason was wrong.

"Fools. They'll probably get arrows in their chests," Joseph muttered to himself as he walked down the street, turning onto the main road.

Anna Claire woke up the next day with a sinking feeling in her stomach. She didn't know why she had the sinking feeling, but something seemed to feel wrong or out of place. She, Pete, and Berthie woke up together and went down the ladder of the loft. Anna Claire had her breakfast, did her chores, and had a typical quarrel with Helen- a perfectly normal day. But something was wrong. She just didn't know what.

Not very long after dinner, Joseph Freiler stormed into the house, his face red from the cold and his hands gritty from attempting to do some panning (although without result).

"Joseph, what ever is the matter?" asked Charlotta, dropping her rag that she was using to dry dishes onto the floor.

"I just went into town." His face was long, and he was visibly shaken. "There was an incident over at the Crow camp."

Anna Claire's stomach dropped.

"Oh my, well, what happened?" Charlotta asked, coming next to him to sit down.

Joseph and Charlotta sat at the table while Anna Claire pretended not to be interested, but was glancing over at them with furtive eyes.

"Last night I heard these two men talkin' at Taylor's," Joseph recounted. "They were sayin' they were gonna go to the Crow camp and threaten them. I didn't think much of it since Taylor told me they were always pretendin' to harm people, but that they don't really mean it. Well, they meant it this time. I just stopped into town for the butter, and I see all these men out in the street. O'Reilly found me and told me that Samuel Collingsworth was found nearly dead on the outskirts of town in the early morning, not far from here. Some miners found him. They got him to the doctor, and he's over in his office now. Collingsworth told him and some others that he and Adam Blarney had run over to the Crow camp to defend our territory. A couple of men went out to find Blarney and found him layin' dead with a bullet in his head. This is what O'Reilly told me. Collingsworth seemed almost proud of himself. He told the doctor and the men who were helpin' him up that he himself killed two Crows and Blarney had killed one. Apparently, Collingsworth killed two men, one who seemed to be the chief. But Blarney- he killed a little baby girl. They didn't find them. They had left their camp by the time they all got there. They only found the bodies of the two men, Blarney, and the arm of the baby. The Crows had packed their things as quick as possible and left right away. Nothin' was left except the bodies. The mother probably carried the body of the child with her, poor woman. They all left. God only knows where. Probably somewhere South. I wouldn't be surprised if one of them came back to Bannack. They're not gonna want to let a thing like this go. At the same time, they know they'd be in danger if they decided to come back. They might have left, thinkin' that they killed Blarney and Collingsworth. Collingsworth is still alive, who knows for how long. In the meantime, we can't take the chance of goin' into town. Not for a while. That's why I got this bag of bread from the bakery. It was expensive, but it needs to last a little while. We have to make sure these people are gone for good. They're sendin' a team to go scoutin' the area and they're gonna send a telegraph to the other towns like Virginia City and Helena to be wary. It should be safe, but we need to stay here this month, just in case. Apparently, the camp was just over down there, maybe a mile or so away from us. We got lucky not to run into them. Whoo. Boy, always somethin' goin' on around here!"

Everything went silent in Anna Claire's head. Charlotta was covering Berthie's ears as Joseph elaborated on the event while the other two girls were sitting at the table with shocked looks on their faces. Pete was standing up and staring at their father with frightened eyes. Joseph and Charlotta began talking again, but Anna Claire didn't hear what they were saying.

Before even realizing it, Anna Claire was on the ground.

"No!"

"Dear, what-" began Charlotta, rushing to her side at the bottom of the ladder.

"Noooo!" cried Anna Claire, her body leaning forward. "*No, no, no!*"

Joseph stood up and tried to pick her up, but she wriggled out of his grip. Caroline scolded her to be quiet and talk like "a human being" while Helen, Berthie, and Pete didn't know what to do but stare from a distance.

"No!" she wailed, saliva pouring onto the ground as her hair fell around her face. "No!"

"My goodness, what is the matter?" Charlotta yelled over her.

Anna Claire could only wail and scream "No!"

Charlotta tried to touch her arm, but she broke away from her grasp. Caroline then came to sit down and lift her head, but Anna Claire pushed her aside. She could not stop crying. She felt that her throat would explode from the screaming and that her eyes would fall out with all of her tears. Everything was blurry around her. She could feel her wet hair on her face and the pain on her kneecaps where she had fallen. She stopped hearing her family. She felt like she was floating in air above everything.

"Anna Claire, Anna Claire!" Charlotta was crying. "We should get the doctor!"

"I don't need the doctor!" she wailed from the ground. "I don't need the doctor! I don't need the doctor! I don't need the doctor!"

"My girl, please talk, what is it?" begged her father who was now holding her in his arms. "Did what I say scare you? I'm sorry! I'm sorry, I shouldn't have said it in front of you. I only worry. I'm sorry I scared you. We will be safe here. I've got our rifle and Hero, and I will be on guard for weeks. They won't come near us. They want Collingsworth or the men from town. Don't cry, darlin', we're safe."

Anna Claire choked on her tears, nearly vomiting. She felt dizzy and forgot where she was for a moment.

"You were wrong!" she yelled, collapsing again. "You were wrong!"

"Wrong about what, darlin'?" asked Joseph, feeling confused and helpless.

"Them!'" cried Anna Claire, speaking of the Native Americans. "They aren't bad! I know them!"

Charlotta sighed. "I know you have seen them in town, but-"

"No!" cried Anna Claire, her nose running. "I went to the camps! They're across the creek! I *know* them! I met a boy and I know his whole family! You were wrong!"

"You went to those camps?" asked her father, anger in his voice. "I always told you-"

Screaming and crying, Anna Claire fell limp into her father's arms and fell suddenly silent. She had cried so hard that she passed out. Charlotta herself was holding back tears as she helped her husband hold Anna Claire up and bring her to the room up the loft.

"You're awake," said Joseph gently, a few minutes later, putting his hand on her forehead.

Anna Claire wiped the tears from her cheeks and sat up slowly.

"You must tell me what you know," said her father, still angry but calmer.

Anna Claire began to cry again as she said, "I know I wasn't supposed to, but me and Tommy went across the creek- we didn't mean to find them; we were just walkin'. Then we saw the camp. Then we met a man who asked why we were there. He was the boy's father. We met the boy's mother 'cause she was with the man. Then they gave us bread and were nice to us. They were so kind, Papa! And then we met Iá daxpitchée. His name means 'Little Bear'. He's a little boy. Iá daxpitchée showed us all around the camps and in different homes. We taught him words in English and he taught us words in his language. We played with him. Sometimes we'd go to the camps. We met everyone there. They were all so nice. They let us dance and sing with them around the fire. They gave us food, and Iá daxpitchée gave me a bracelet and Tommy a necklace. They all wore beads with all the colors in the whole world! You should've seen it, Papa! They were kind. Sometimes his mother would let me hold the baby. The baby was such a pretty thing! She was always laughin' at us and smilin'. She loved me! Iá daxpitchée was kind to us and so was everyone else. All they wanted was to stay and be left alone. All they wanted was to live! You're wrong, Papa. They aren't all bad. They're not bad!"

Joseph sighed and closed his eyes for a moment, attempting to calm himself before yelling, knowing it would do no good at the moment. "I reckon there are some of them that are good, but most-"

"Most are *good*!" interrupted Anna Claire. "They were kind to us. They gave us food and let us sit with them, and they tried to talk to us sometimes. Papa, they're just like us. Some are bad, but just like us! Some White people are bad, too, but most are good. It's like that with other people. Most of them are good. They just wanted to be home!" She began wailing again before saying, "Papa- the baby- she was the youngest one there. She- she must have been the baby they killed. They killed her! A baby! She's just a baby!"

"Anna Claire," Joseph reached over to hold her close to him. "Maybe I was wrong about them. I'm glad these ones were kind to you. There's a lot of bad ones out there and we just want you to be safe. I'm sorry I told you. I figured you children would hear about it anyway. Maybe the baby you knew wasn't the same baby."

"No," said Anna Claire sitting up. "She was the only baby about a year old. All the others were older. She was the baby they killed- she was the baby that lost her arm!"

"My little girl," said Joseph, holding her close. "You're so disobedient! How on Earth have you been goin' to the camps this whole time? Imagine if you had been there last night! I will ride close to the camps and see if I can find them. They can't be too far. When I find them, I'll bring some food and clothing for the winter."

"They'll think you're the bad man and kill you!" cried Anna Claire.

"You are too wise for your age, despite your faults. You're right. It may be too dangerous for me to go find them. Your friend- Ia..."

"Iá daxpitchée," finished Anna Claire.

"He got away," Joseph said, wiping a wisp of hair out of his daughter's eye. "They did not kill any more children. He got away, Anna Claire."

Anna Claire took a deep breath. "I hope they don't find them!"

"They know how to be safe," said Joseph. "Collingsworth is on his death bed and the other one is dead. They won't go after them no more."

"Someone else will," Anna Claire choked. "They're hated. Everyone hates them, but everyone is wrong to hate them!"

"I will pray for their safety, and you will, too," said Joseph. "I'm sorry, Anna Claire, that I talked badly about these people- I reckon you're right. There's good and bad in every kind of people. Your friends may be goin' away, but they survived."

"I hope the men they killed wasn't his father," said Anna Claire softly, wiping her tears from her cheeks.

Joseph shook his head. "I hope so, too."

That was when there was a knock at the door. Joseph went down the ladder as Charlotta answered the door.

"Tommy, I think it's best if you go home," said Charlotta softly. "Anna Claire is not feeling well."

"It's alright, Char," Joseph said as he reached the ground. "She's feelin' better now. I think she will want to see Tommy."

Anna Claire was already out of bed when Tommy went up to the loft.

"Anna... Claire," he said, out of breath. "Everyone in town's... talkin'. Some men went to... the camp and... killed some of the people!"

"I know," sobbed Anna Claire. "My papa just told us. He knows."

"He knows about us goin' there?" Tommy asked, surprised.

"I told him," she answered. "I had to. I was cryin'. Oh, Tommy, they killed the baby!"

Tommy walked closer to her and put his hand on her arm. Without saying another word, Anna Claire fell forward into him and began sobbing into his coat.

"This is too terrible! The baby, our poor baby. And lá daxpitchée! What if his father was killed? And what will become of his poor mother? Tommy, tell me this isn't true!"

Tommy sighed, also beginning to tear up and wiping the tears away determinedly. "I wish I could. I really wish I could, Anna Claire."

Both sat in silence with each other for some time until Charlotta came into the loft.

"Dears," she said, coming over to them and embracing both children. "I know. I know how horrible this is. I am sorry. I am so very sorry! But the two of you should not have wandered so far from the creek."

"Oh, Mama!" cried Anna Claire. "The baby! The baby is dead! The baby is dead!"

"I know," Charlotta's voice cracked. "Those men did a cruel thing and they will be punished by God! Most of your friends are safe and are gone now. Please take comfort in that, my children. Most of them are safe."

"They ain't never gonna be safe," said Tommy, "when everyone's after them!"

Charlotta could not protest that. Instead, she held both of them closer to her and tried to soothe them the best that she could. She never expected to have to discuss with them a thing such as that.

Chapter 16- The Road Agents

Anna Claire and Tommy did not want to be bothered much by anyone except each other, as they were the only two who truly understood what it was like to get to know the Native American tribe. The weather was still too bad to go to school, and they wouldn't have been able to concentrate anyway. The thought of their friends running for their lives with everything they owned made them cry, and the thought of the little baby suffering and being killed made them sick to their stomachs. Neither wanted to eat, sleep, or even be near family. Tommy especially did not want to be anywhere near his mother, who continued to drink excessively and bring strange men upstairs with her during absurd hours of the night.

"Why do they have to keep comin'?" asked Tommy one day to his mother before the saloon officially opened. He was sitting at the counter while Kathleen Cooper was opening the safe box. "I don't like that they always come."

"Listen, kid," said Kathleen, "I need to make money, alright? I can only make money if they come here. The room and board is not enough. We need food and clothes, and Lord knows we need help. The men pay me well."

"But what for?" asked Tommy, feeling frustrated. "Why do they pay you only in the mornin'? And what do they do all night in your room?"

Kathleen gave him a dark stare. "I told you to stop talkin' like that! I told you they come for my company. You don't need to know anything more about it."

"But Ma, I don't like them!" repeated Tommy, his eyes beginning to fill up with tears.

"You're a lucky, spoiled boy," Kathleen hissed, leaning over towards a mirror and applying more red paint on her lips. "You're lucky I let you go to school. I could'a said no. But you're goin' to school and learnin' all those fancy words. I never went to school at your age 'cause I didn't have no school! Spoiled is what you are."

Tommy looked down and wiped his eyes. "But Ma, it gets so noisy at night, and I can hear the men yellin' all the time, and I can hear them hurtin' you! I don't want them to come around no more!"

"One more word of this," Kathleen spat, "and you will get a good beatin'. Do you understand?"

Tommy said nothing. He didn't even nod. Instead, he got up, walked to the side of the saloon, and climbed the stairs. When he got to his room, he burst into tears. All balled up on his cot, and with no clear future ahead of him, he sobbed into his arms.

After a few moments, he stood up, ripped one of the pictures of the women he had on his wall, and tore it to pieces before throwing a shoe across the room. All he had was this little room with his little posters. He just wanted it all to stop, all of it. The fighting between his mother and the strange men, the men coming and going whenever they wanted to, the drunken stupors and long, loud nights- he wanted it to be over. But he realized it may never be.

Still crying, he looked in front of him and saw the book Anna Claire had given him for Christmas. He had learned how to read quite quickly and could now understand most of the words, even some of the big ones.

Sighing, he stood up and went to look at the book. He paged through it and held it to his chest. He had more than just that little room in the saloon and more than just lonely memories. He had a best friend, too. Someone he could count on, even if she was only a little girl.

He took a deep breath and opened the book. He wanted to finish it and tell Anna Claire all about it. He clenched his jaw, determined not to cry again, and reminded himself that as long as he had the Freilers, everything would be alright.

"I don't doubt there's more gold," said Mr. Chesham during one of the days in Bail's Saloon. "They think there's more gold here than in California! Now that's somethin'! If that's true, we'll all get rich once we hit that spot."

Joseph nodded. "That's why I'm here. I believe in this."

Mr. Clemmons laughed and gave his friends a toast. "To friendship in Gold Country!"

Everyone clinked their cups together and drank down a big gulp of whiskey.

The saloon was crowded that March day as the cold and stormy weather had finally subsided a bit and the sun was beginning to peek out again. Joseph had spent a long day pining for gold and decided, after accidentally cutting his hand with his pick earlier in the day, that he was going to enjoy the rest of the afternoon at Bail's Saloon until it was time to go home for supper.

He was pleased to find his two friends there and joined them at their table. The table itself was being serenaded by a painted lady with a large bosom and white lacy frills underneath her dress, which were very clearly visible above her thighs.

"You know, I heard that the Agents got another one down on the west road," said O'Reilly with a brief look of fear across his face.

"This seems to be happenin' more and more recently," acknowledged Joseph.

"We all gotta be careful," Paul Clemmons stated, lowering his voice. "Besides each other, we can't trust anyone. Any man in here could have a pistol by his side for all we know, just waitin' for someone to call 'Gold!'"

"A man will do anything to be rich," agreed James O'Reilly.

Joseph sighed in agreement. "I only want to make sure my family's safe. You see, boys, if it was just me out here, I would be pannin' everywhere for miles and doin' everything I can to find some. With the family, I have to be as careful as possible. They need me to provide. I have to make sure I have the time to hunt, to make the tools, to give my children and my wife a kiss at night. They need all my wages. I shouldn't be usin' it for a drink, but my hand is in pain!

One can't hurt too much. I just have to make sure the family is safe and protected."

"Thanks to us Vigilantes, they are," said Mr. O'Reilly.

They cheered again for the Vigilantes and Joseph took another gulp of whiskey. It tasted very bitter and oily, but it was something, at least. "Imagine if they hadn't moved those people," Mr. O'Reilly said, in reference to the Native Americans. "They would be rulin' over the territory and sittin' their teepees all over the gold."

"They never did anything to us," broke in Joseph, trying to look unaffected. "Now think if someone came to your door, told you to get you and your youngsters and your wife out of there because it was now their house and their land? I know I would rage."

Mr. O'Reilly laughed and Mr. Clemmons took another drink, an awkward silence following.

"It's a shame that the Sheriff was in on everything," said Mr. Clemmons, cutting into the quietness. "You know they only hung him a couple of years ago."

"Yes, sir," said Mr. O'Reilly. "Me and the wife and children got here the year before after the Pikes boys struck. Plummer was made Sheriff to help the Vigilantes, and instead he was a Road Agent all along, tellin' them who had gold and when they were leavin' town. At least they got him for it."

Joseph sighed. "I'm glad we came later than that."

"Well, things are gettin' bad here again," said Mr. O'Reilly, putting his arm down on the table so hard that one of the cups spilled a bit of the whiskey.

"You know they just killed two boys the other night who were on their way to Fort Benton? Bludgeoned them to death. Then I heard they cut them up into pieces before burnin' their bodies. All for the sake of gold. Isn't a man's life worth more?"

"Men become animals at the sight of money," remarked Joseph, closing his tired eyes and taking another sip of whiskey.

"Money and women," laughed Mr. O'Reilly, who was eyeing the painted saloon lady with lust.

Suddenly, there was a huge crash and the sound of shouting as a drunken man fell over onto their table and spilled their drinks along with his own, crashing recklessly onto the floor. He rose up slowly and the others began laughing and leading him back to his own table.

"Watch it next time!" yelled Mr. O'Reilly, wiping some of the drink from his pants.

"You're payin' for my drink as soon as you sober up!" yelled Sam Chesham angrily, kicking a chair that was directly in front of him.

Joseph had drunk up the last of the whiskey and resisted the temptation to use his money to buy another one.

"What will you do if you strike it rich?" asked Mr. O'Reilly, the men coming back to sit at their table.

"You mean *when*," Joseph corrected, smiling and clearing his throat. "I'll buy my wife any beautiful dress and jewels she wants. I'll save some and give Caroline a beautiful wedding when the time comes. All that girl talks about is wantin' to get married, and seein' she's with the Mast boy, it might actually happen soon. I'll let Helen go to New York City to see the theater, like she's always wanted. Anna Claire will have a whole library all to herself filled with adventure books, and I'll buy Pete as many cowboy figures as he likes. My Berthie- well, she can have just about anything she wants. Clothes, dolls, glass figures."

"What about for yourself?" asked Mr. Clemmons. "Of course, I'll get my family everything they want. But for me, I'd buy lots of land and hire people to do the farmin'."

"I'd go to Europe and see the Sistine Chapel," said Mr. O'Reilly. "Maybe even see some family back in Ireland."

Joseph sighed and frowned. "I think I'd go to Wisconsin and visit my family there. I haven't seen them in so long."

The men nodded in understanding, for they had all left their homes at different times in their lives and it was never easy regardless of how many times they left.

"Listen boys, I got to get goin'," said Joseph, standing up from the table and patting his friends on the back. "It's gettin' later and I got to be home for supper or Charlotta will have my head!"

"I wouldn't want to make Mrs. Freiler angry," laughed Mr. O'Reilly.

The men shook hands, and Joseph walked out the door into the sunny day, the first sunny day he had seen in a long time.

Joseph found himself getting to know most of the people in town. He was determined to stay on good footing with as many people as he could so that he would have less to worry about when it came to the safety of his family. He often met people in the stores or even in the saloons whenever there was a town speech or simply a big game of poker.

Joseph began to love the town of Bannack just as much as he had any other home. He enjoyed talking with the men from the Bannack Ditch and Mining Company and walking over to Rudderfield Mill to chat with them as well. During the calm daylight hours, he took Pete to the little bowling alley and taught him how to throw a hard ball. He even let his son get a job. Pete was given a dollar every week for spending a couple of hours cleaning Bail's Saloon, in which he did on Wednesdays after school. Joseph was able to persuade his wife to go to one of the "balls" at the billiard hall, which attempted to be fancier than a regular barn dance and cost $5 in gold, no drinking allowed. They had enjoyed every minute of the dance, despite it getting rowdy, and he and Charlotta danced all throughout the night.

Joseph had gotten to know the secretary of Bannack, along with the butcher who had a bad habit of letting his hogs run amuck on Main Street. He got acquainted with the tailor as well as the dentist who had to pull out one of his back teeth once when it began to sting painfully in his gums. He became on good terms with Mr. Stuart, who was a very prominent figure in the town, as he owned the butcher shop with his brother and was part of the legislature. He became close with another legislature and cattleman who had, on one occasion, bought him a glass of whiskey upon seeing Joseph outside of a saloon. He was even known to share a drink or two with the fiddler, "Buzz."

He knew most everyone, including the engineer and surveyor and the banker. Among his friends were the blacksmith and the carpenter, who worked in the brewery and liked to tell mysterious jokes. There were others, too, that he became acquainted with, such as the Chief Justice, the Associate General, the deputy, the US Marshalls, and even the collector of Internal Revenue of Montana Territory. He played his cards carefully, always being sure to say a kind remark, a hello, and- when possible- to buy a drink for the men. He never knew when he would need someone on his side, and, as the place was dangerous enough, he could not have been more careful. No matter how many people he had come to know, there were none as dear to him as his closest friends Paul Clemmons, Sam Chesham, James O'Reilly, and Elmer Grimm. The five of them made a nice group and always had each other's backs during good and tough times.

Joseph made his living as he toiled away on his claim along Grasshopper Creek. He worked hard to find a gully where he could pick into sandstone, hoping for a speck of gold. He would dip his pan into the gravel in the water, checking the bottom for gold flakes. The power of gravity eased the find and, along with his tools, he was able to obtain some gold. There were times when his friends wanted to work on claims with each other, and that is when one of them would do the shoveling and the other would work the rocker, the big bucket that swung back and forth where the gold would bundle in the cleats on the bottom.

Joseph dressed the part of a true pioneer and bought leather breeches, made moccasins and a fur hat, and got himself a belt. Now that it was getting warm out again, he had his gauze on to keep his face from getting attacked by the flies and mosquitoes, and his cabbage hat to help keep his face from getting too sunburnt. Not only did he mine throughout the day and the evening, but in the early mornings, he tended to his little farm in the clearing which grew corn and wheat, and he looked after the animals he had accumulated through the year. On as many nights as he could, he would hunt the wild game which could be anything from chicken to moose meat. He worked very hard to make life in Montana Territory work, and, because of it, he occasionally spent some time at a hurdy gurdy in town now and then to have a drink with his friends. After all, he was doing back-bending work.

The town itself was ridden with dirty floors in its buildings, muddy roads, tobacco spit, and horse manure running up, down, and across all of the streets. Bannack was loud, overcrowded, and filled with outlaws, drifters from the Civil War, business-men, and prospectors just like Joseph who came with their families in the hopes of gaining wealth.

One April day, Jacob Mast had come over to have tea with Caroline, who annoyingly took all morning to curl her hair even more than it was naturally, and she forbade Anna Claire to come anywhere near her lest she spill something on her creamy afternoon dress. Caroline had the intention to marry young and she was determined that nothing would come between this lifelong desire.

"Anna Claire, you wretched girl," Caroline said as she looked at herself again in the mirror. At fifteen, she had grown taller over the winter months, and her once straight figure was curvy. "Do not come anywhere near me today! When Jacob is here, leave us. He does not want to see you. He is coming here for me, and I will not have you spoiling our day! I haven't seen him in ever so long."

Anna Claire rolled her eyes. "I don't care about you and your stupid Jacob Mast!" She stomped her foot on the ground and put her hands on her hips. "Besides, me and Tommy are gonna go play in the creek. It's not that icy anymore. So don't come botherin' us, neither!" she stuck out her tongue defiantly when Charlotta had walked in.

"Anna Claire, stop," she scolded. "You must stop doing that! It is uncivil!"

Anna Claire turned her back and did it to the wall instead.

"She's just jealous because she's still a little girl," scoffed Caroline.

"I ain't jealous! I ain't!"

"Do not say 'ain't'. Have you not learned a thing in school?" said Charlotta, putting a hand to her forehead.

Suddenly, there was a knock on the door. It was Tommy. Anna Claire opened it happily.

"Oh- hi Caroline!" he said in surprise when he saw the older girl.

"Hello," Caroline responded, not in any mood to talk to young children that day.

"Hello, Tommy!" said Charlotta warmly. "Would you like a good cup of tea?"

"Oh, no, Mrs. Freiler," Tommy answered sheepishly. "Thank you, but I'd rather be outside."

Charlotta nodded and smiled at his frankness, pouring some more tea for herself and Caroline.

"Let's go!" shouted Anna Claire, pulling his hand and dragging him out of the cabin.

The two children ran to the creek, kicked off their shoes, and jumped into the water, not minding the cold or getting their clothes soaked.

Splashing each other and screaming with laughter, they ducked in and out of the water before letting themselves float on their backs. Anna Claire looked up admiringly at the big blue sky above her head and the fluffy clouds that seemed to sit still.

"Are you angry that we never found gold?" Anna Claire asked her friend, who was pointing at a turtle before catching it and touching its shell gently.

"Yeah," said Tommy. "I'm mighty angry! But that ain't the end! We'll find it! There might not be treasure buried in the mountains, but everyone is here for gold. That means there must be gold around! We'll find it, Anna Claire."

Anna Claire sighed and made a circle in the water with her arms, spinning while humming loudly. "Papa says there's gold here, and he says he's gonna probably find it. When he does, I promise I'll give you some!"

Tommy splashed her again. "I just-" he faltered, shuddering. "That skeleton."

Anna Claire swam over to him, her dress dragging behind her. "That was real scary. I wish we hadn't seen that. But now we know who he was. We helped find him when no one else could!"

Tommy shook his head. "I know. It's sad though, ain't it? I mean, I wonder if he fell or jumped? Guess we'll never know for sure."

Anna Claire nodded and sat herself upon the ground, her fingers twisting a twig. "Yeah, awful sad. And you know what else is sad? Daisy Hatfield. How she just ran away."

"Because he was keepin' her there," answered Tommy, "without lettin' her go nowhere."

Anna Claire fell silent as she watched the lake, Tommy chatting about candy he had taken from the saloon. She felt a wave of sadness when she thought of Daisy Hatfield killing herself. It had shocked her and still did whenever she thought about it. What had happened? Why did Daisy do it when she had a baby? There had to be more to the story than that.

Then Anna Claire, despite trying so hard not to, thought about Iá daxpitchée and his friends and family.

"I wonder where Iá daxpitchée is now," said Anna Claire, feeling the coldness of the water finally hit her.

Tommy stopped swimming, and his whole face fell. "I've been tryin' not to think about it."

"Me too," said Anna Claire.

They were quiet for a moment before Tommy said, "Iá daxpitchée is strong. I think he'll be alright."

"His sister." Anna Claire pursed her lips to keep from crying.

"Those bastards!" yelled Tommy. "Killin' a baby! If they weren't dead already, I'd kill 'em!"

"Me too!" yelled Anna Claire. Then she added softly, "We'll never see Iá daxpitchée again."

Tommy shook his head. "We probably won't. I bet they're on the other side of the territory by now! Probably somewhere safe, somewhere better for 'em."

"I hope so," sighed Anna Claire. "I'll miss Iá daxpitchée."

"I'll miss everyone," agreed Tommy. "At least we got that necklace and bracelet to remember him by!"

The two stood up and reached the shore, where they stumbled out of the creek. Shivering, as it was still a bit cold, they slowly and sadly began walking through the little wooded area into the clearing where they could see the cabin. Before entering, they decided to sit in the grass to watch the clouds for a few moments.

The children sat together for a while, talking about horses and cowboys and what they wanted to be when they grew up. Tommy wanted to find gold and compete in rodeo shows. Anna Claire wanted to write about other countries and travel, especially to Egypt, where there were big, tall pyramids, ancient relics, Pharaoh tombs, and beautiful people.

"Mama says I'll never be able to go to Egypt," said Anna Claire dejectedly. "She says sailin' is dangerous and it's too far away to travel on a wagon or even a train, even if I did get on a big boat. But I told Mama that I don't care about sailin' and takin' a hundred trains! I'm goin' to Egypt."

"Why Egypt?" asked Tommy curiously. "If I were goin' anywhere, I'd go to India and eat Indian food and climb trees."

Anna Claire laughed. "That's all you'd want to do? Eat and climb trees?"

Tommy shot her a nasty look.

"I don't care where I go, but I ain't stayin' here!" cried Anna Claire. "I like Montana Territory and Gold Country, but I want to see the world! In a book I read once, this man got to go to Spain, Africa, France, and China in just three years! Can you imagine? I wonder how he did that?"

"I'm stayin' right here in America," said Tommy decidedly. "Maybe I'd go to India, but that's it."

The children sat in raptured silence for a while, listening to the sound of the creek drift over the little rocks and mounds, and the birds sitting above their heads in the trees. Both had dreams as big as the prairie sky and as deep as the sea. They were two children with big hearts, big ambitions, and big hopes.

"I can't wait until we can tell Miss Darlin' what we know," said Anna Claire, breaking the silence.

"Me neither," Tommy agreed, sitting up. "But we can't say it now. We gotta keep quiet, like Mr.

Dobbins said. Besides, she won't even believe a couple of kids!" He spit next to him and shook his head.

Anna Claire nodded. "Someday we'll tell her, but it ain't gonna be for a while. I don't wanna wait, but we have to."

"Yeah," Tommy sighed. "For forever.

The Freilers had lived in Gold Country, Montana, for well over a year now when the Felton brothers died on one of the roads going from Bannack. This was a big deal, for the Felton brothers were young, tough, and a big part of the community. They had helped construct the buildings of Bannack and were instrumental in organizing the Vigilantes along with the governor's nephew. It was clear why they were murdered- they were men who never gave up on finding and tracking down the Road Agents, and they were a big threat to those who wanted to rob and kill for gold.

The murder was obvious, as it was clear that they were dragged from their shanty, taken down the road in a wagon, and stabbed multiple times in the chest, the blood making tracks in the dirt. One of them had been found with their heart outside of their chest and the other one was lying face down in the dirt with the bones of his spine showing. Their faces had looks of sheer terror and there were long cuts right down their foreheads. "Papa, what was Mr. Clemmons saying?" asked Pete at dinner one night. "I heard him say that someone was killed!"

Joseph looked up at Charlotta, who had her hand on her cheek and looked horrified.

"Don't you worry about that," Joseph said with a bit of anger in his voice. "It is not your responsibility to worry. We are all safe here."

"Who was murdered?" asked Helen, taking her bowl and gulping down the soup in a very unladylike manner.

"No one," broke in Charlotta, looking at Helen. "Now put that bowl down and eat like a human and not a wild animal."

Anna Claire's interest peaked at the topic. "I wanna know! I wanna know, please tell us! Tell us!"

"Tell us!" cried Pete, smiling and banging his fist on the table while him and Anna Claire yelled repeatedly, "Tell us! Tell us!"

"Enough!" yelled Joseph with a force he normally did not exert.

The children stopped in their tracks and fell silent.

"No more talk of this! I mean it! Any more questions, and I'll give you a good lick! We are safe. That is what matters. This family is safe!"

Everyone stopped talking and looked down at their soup bowls, but no one felt very hungry anymore.

"I wonder what the weather will be like tomorrow," broke in Caroline, who was trying fruitlessly to lighten the mood at the table. "I do hope it is sunny!"

"I hope so too," said Charlotta, thanking her daughter for changing the topic with her eyes. "I was becoming so tired of the cold. We had such an icy winter this year. It is so nice that the sun is out once again! Would you not agree, Joseph?"

Joseph, a look of frustration still on his face, nodded slowly. He sighed and scratched his short golden beard with his hand.

After supper, Joseph and Charlotta sat in their room, Charlotta brushing her long dark hair by the window and Joseph changing out of his clothes which had been stained with mud from panning all day.

"Joseph, I'm frightened," said Charlotta, nervously beginning to pace on the floor. "It seems as though someone is getting murdered every day here! I read in that paper from Bozeman City that there was a group of men murdered right at Fort Benton."

"It is only on the roads, Char," answered Joseph with a sigh. "The world is dangerous anywhere. The killings are happening on the roads far away from Bannack. They aren't happening here."

"Not yet." Charlotta shivered in her nightgown, the feeling of anxiety rising like a lump from her chest to her throat. "I even read in the Rocky Mountain Gazette that there was another skirmish near Virginia City where they had revolvers and Hawkins rifles, and held up the telegraph lines," she said. "We live quite a distance from town. It would be so easy for someone to ride here and slaughter us all!"

Joseph sighed again. "I will not let that happen. Char, the Clemmons's are close by and no one has any reason to want us dead. None. I stay friendly with all the men and I never talk about gold. I haven't even found any gold worth stealin' anyway!" At this exclamation of frustration, Joseph got into bed, looking older and more tired than he ever had before.

Charlotta came to sit next to him. Leaning her head on his shoulder, her sweet face calming, she said, "I know you are doing the best you can. And you are wonderful. You work all day and still put food on the table and kiss the children goodnight. No matter how busy you are, you always find the time to talk to them and be with them. And me, too."

"I wish I could do more," Joseph said as he wrapped his arm around his wife, feeling a bit helpless. "Caroline seems so lonely sometimes. Helen is becoming selfish. And Peter can't hunt well enough yet, and Berthie still talks to her dolls. And Anna Claire-" here he paused and shook his head. "Well, Anna Claire is as wild as they come. She has no manners and heeds no warnings."

"Yes, but ever since she began school, I think she has been quite better," said Charlotta gently, caressing her husband's chest. "She has not tried to run away from home, and she has stopped incessantly talking about odd things like blood and going to Bora Bora and such likes. She has been better, Joseph. Even her teacher has seen the changes."

Joseph nodded and looked ahead out of the window. "I want to be with them more," Joseph laid down on the bed and brought Charlotta down next to him. "I want them to know I love them. I love this family. That's why we moved here. I need to find gold, get us wealthy, and give us everything we want."

"But Joseph, we already have everything we want," Charlotta smiled. "Our family."

Joseph smiled and kissed her, pulling her closer. "And this is why you are perfect." And then they blew out the candle and continued to kiss.

***

There was a nice period of happiness in Gold Country during the spring. Families began visiting each other again, barn raisings started resuscitating, and people began to hopefully plant and prepare their crops for the season. It was a time of abundance and peace.

Coffee, sugar, and bacon were only a dollar a pound, and Charlotta was thrilled to have those little luxuries. This was the season of blooming flowers and apples, of currents, prunes, and raisins, the time of year when Joseph had little trouble catching game from elk or deer. Charlotta often wrote to her family back in Minnesota of her experiences and gave her letters to Joseph. Joseph would then take them to the town post-master, who would then travel to Fort Benton to send and retrieve mail.

Charlotta planted little flowers along the side of the house, which made it more inviting and pretty. She was happy that Caroline was growing up so well and was proud of her manners. She felt that Anna Claire had thoroughly learned an important lesson after visiting the Native American camp and she had not had to worry about her as much as she had the year prior. She spent her days with little Berthie by her side, as she taught Berthie how to plant the flowers and how to cook and bake. There was no longer that awful cold in the house that had been there for so long, and the ice was finally melting across Gold Country, albeit slowly. Even Joseph had been in higher spirits, as he had a feeling that he was going to find gold that summer, now that the weather was warm and he got a new pick.

Montana Territory was so odd during this time of year, as one could find different seasons among the sloping hills and mountains. There could be brightly-colored wildflowers on the hillsides right under mountains covered with snow less than a mile apart from each other. The cattle sat atop the little hills as the horses and antelopes dug into the snow with their hooves to find hidden food. It was a gorgeous sight and one that not many people in the world got the pleasure of witnessing.

Anna Claire was happy it was spring. She didn't have to stay indoors all day counting the floorboards or spend it arguing with Helen. Even better than that was the fact that she could go to school and be with her friends and lovely Miss Darling. After showing some improvement in her behaviors, her parents were becoming a bit more relaxed. She made it a point not to mention anything bloody or gory, nothing about hating dresses and dolls (although she still did), and absolutely no word of going to see the gold in the mountains. She did her chores (most of the time), completed her figures, and attended school. She was hoping she would be allowed to go to town again with Tommy if she proved that she had learned her lesson and would never run away again.

And she did learn her lesson. She had no desire to be dragged back home from the wilderness or have to bear anymore punishments by being kept at home. She would be good, she wouldn't run away, and she would be allowed to go into town again. She and Tommy had planned for her to be able to go to town with him during the summer months. She waited a long time before asking her parents if she could go into town for fear that they would not allow her to. By the time it was May, her family had nearly put the old incident of the treasure-hunting behind them. One day, when Anna Claire knew her mother was in a cheerful disposition, she asked if it was alright if she walk into town with Tommy.

"Sure," Charlotta said with a smile. "I know you are quite finished with all of the childish running away nonsense, right, dear?"

"Yes, Mama; I'll never do that again!" exclaimed Anna Claire truthfully. She really had learned a big lesson, and seeing the remains of a man at the top of the mountain had certainly solidified that for her.

Charlotta smiled and twirled a piece of Anna Claire's hair around her ear. "Alright. You can go. Do not go into any of the saloons except for Swiner's- and only if Mr. Dobbins is there- and stay on the main road. Come right home before the sun goes down."

The family had been quite careful since the Felton brothers had been killed on the roads, but they also knew their home was as safe as possible, as they were close to town but not in town, and close to neighbors but far away from any of the back roads.

Anna Claire ran outside and greeted Tommy, and the two of them ran off through the fields into town. They spent the afternoon walking up and down the main road, looking at the chocolate in the drug store, and admiring the tall men on their big horses. Anna Claire was so thrilled to be in the town, and could not remember the last time she had felt so free and alive. Both were tempted to go into Swiner's Saloon, but Anna Claire remembered her mother's warning. Instead, they both settled by sitting on the stoop of the building, their head in their hands and their boots scuffing the stairs underneath them.

"I heard Mama tellin' Papa that some men were murdered," said Anna Claire, lifting her head up to look at Tommy. "Why?"

Tommy paused and sighed. He was worried that Anna Claire was going to ask questions. Tommy was a little boy who had grown up exposed to all kinds of adult things. He knew that Anna Claire was more sensitive than she claimed she was. Oddly, he wanted to protect her.

"I don't know," he answered shortly, looking at the ground. "I don't think little girls should be hearin' nothin' about it."

Anna Claire stood up and gave him a good shove so that he fell over to the side.

"I am *not* a little girl!" she cried resentfully. "And I can hear anything!"

Tommy sat up. "Ow," he said, rubbing his shoulder. "Well fine, but don't go tellin' me I didn't warn ya!"

Anna Claire grinned and sat closer to hear him, in awe of the danger that was around her. "It was the Felton brothers," said Tommy sadly. He himself had known them as they often came into the saloon. They had been kind to him and used to pretend to make a coin disappear behind their backs. Now they were gone.

"Who are they?"

"Two nice men who used to be really nice to me. They helped start the Vigilantes, and the Road Agents didn't like it, so they murdered them. Cold blood, too!"

Anna Claire took a deep breath, her eyes widening. "Where are the bodies?"

Tommy shrugged. "That's a strange question. They took them to the coroner, and they already had the burial. They're at the cemetery."

Anna Claire sighed. "Did they get the men who murdered them?"

"They think so," said Tommy, his blue eyes gazing up at the sky. "They just hung a couple. I saw yesterday. They saw them with blood all over them comin' back to town that night so they knew they got the right men. The hangin' was awful. The one man was screamin' that he didn't do nothin' wrong and was innocent, and the other was smilin' until they pushed him. Then his mouth drooped open and his eyes got real big and they looked like they was gonna come right out of his skull!"

Anna Claire suddenly felt queasy. She no longer thought the danger was thrilling or exciting. Instead, a permeating fear replaced her curiosity. People were *really* dying out there- real people, people that Tommy knew, maybe people she and her family knew. It was frightening. And who would be next?

"Are you scared they'll kill children?" asked Anna Claire with a shudder. "You don't think they'd kill children?"

Tommy looked at his friend, his expression calm. "I think they would. I don't think they have yet, but they probably would if they had to. Look what happened to Iá daxpitchée's sister."

Anna Claire stood up from the steps, suddenly feeling very sad.

"I told ya you wouldn't like it," said Tommy matter-of-factly. "I told ya!"

Anna Claire shook her head, not bothering to deny the fact that she was bothered by these horrible tragedies.

"I think I should go home now," she said, although it was still far from sundown.

"Anna Claire, why? Why?" Tommy stood up and put an arm around her shoulder.

Anna Claire was taken aback, as Tommy rarely showed emotion.

"What if Papa gets killed?" she cried frantically, her voice changing. "What if they kill him like they did to those other men? What if he's in danger?"

Tommy took her hands. "We're all in danger, Anna Claire. But your papa is smart. He knows what to say to people, and everyone likes him real well! If he finds gold, all you gotta do is warn him not to tell anyone."

"Papa knows," said Anna Claire, surprising herself with her own intense reaction. "He told Mama that he can't never tell no one except the Clemmons's if he finds gold 'cause word can't travel 'round here. That's when the Road Agents start lookin' for people 'cause Papa says they want gold."

"If they came after your pa, your pa would give them the gold," said Tommy. "He wouldn't fight it. He's smart. He'll let 'em have it all. They won't kill him."

Anna Claire nodded, feeling the nausea pass.

"I'll walk you back," said Tommy, taking her by the wrist.

The two walked on more somberly than they ever had before. Their world was changing and, although they couldn't see it, they could feel it happening.

And the children were right. It was slowly becoming a more unnerving time in Gold Country. With the nice weather also came the violent men. Everyone was very aware of the Road Agents and the demolition they were causing wherever they went. It was not only the Road Agents, either, as there seemed to be violence at every corner. Joseph had learned of the tragic Memphis Riots in Washington, where twenty-four Black people were killed, eight of them discharged soldiers from the Civil War. More closer deaths on the road from Bannack occurred and with every death she read about in the Rocky Mountain Gazette, Charlotta pleaded with Joseph to leave Gold

Country. However, stubborn and determined, he convinced her that staying was the right thing to do.

It wasn't merely violence on those who struck gold that occurred. There were many attacks on people based on race and ethnicity. Those who were of Chinese descent were often chased away or had no choice but to settle on worked-out claims where there had been little chance of discovering gold. There were signs on many of the stores, such as "No Chinese" and "No Blacks Permitted," and- of course- there were many attacks on Native Americans in Gold Country. Most of the attacks were unprovoked and unwarranted.

Meanwhile, amidst all of the drama, Anna Claire and Tommy were very interested in their pretty and kind schoolteacher, whom they were convinced was the lost baby of the Hatfield's, and only the two of them knew this supposed secret. Anna Claire, as much of a spitfire as ever, had gotten into another big fight with a boy in school and was punished by staying home while her class was able to attend a girl's birthday party outside in the beautiful weather. That was a true punishment for Anna Claire: the inability to go outside. If there was any way to properly punish Anna Claire, it was to make her sit inside her home doing nothing. It was during this time that she watched her oldest sister have a breakdown.

Caroline had returned from town on her feet one beautiful spring day, despite the fact that Jacob had picked her up in his wagon and transported her to town. Her hair was uncurled and drooping over her shoulders from the heat, and there was a long expression on her face. Charlotta had the children doing their chores and noticed the look on Caroline's face when she walked through the door. After greeting her and seeing to it that she was alright, Caroline began to weep into her arms profoundly, sobbing so loudly it woke Berthie from her nap.

Anna Claire listened from the kitchen as Caroline explained that she and Jacob had quarreled over his wish to avoid spending as much time with her and how she felt hurt by it. Jacob had ended the courtship and told her he wanted to court a "more Christian girl," which hurt Caroline deeply, as she considered herself to be the epitome of young Christian girls.

"Oh, darling," Charlotta consoled, taking her head into her chest. "Jacob knows not what he is talking about. I went through the same thing at your age. I was courting someone who liked another girl better than me. It is awful! Oh, it is unbearable! But it will get better. I am so sorry, dear."

Caroline continued to sob into her mother's chest as Anna Claire and Helen, who came out of the kitchen, looked at each other with wide eyes. Helen raised her eyebrows to ask Anna Claire what had happened, and Anna Claire gritted her teeth and held her finger across her neck to tell her that Caroline no longer had a beau. For a brief moment, she and Helen shared a sentiment of concern.

Helen approached Caroline with Anna Claire by her side.

"Oh, just go away!" cried Caroline dramatically, her nose running and her eyes red. "Go away! Oh, Mama, make them leave me!"

Charlotta gave her children a look and shooed them away with her hand.

The two girls went up the ladder to their loft, but were listening. Caroline wept about how much she would miss Jacob and how she thought that they would get married. Charlotta comforted her the best that she could and reminded her of how beautiful, sincere, and Christian she was.

It was around this time that Tommy Cooper showed up at the door, interrupting the sadness with his sparkling blue eyes and awkward half-smile. Anna Claire saw him from the window and leapt downstairs faster than a jack rabbit. When she answered the door, Caroline cried harder.

Tommy saw the look on his dear Caroline's face and rushed to her aid. Charlotta shook her head at him to leave her alone, but he did not catch this reference and instead put his hand on her shoulders.

"Jacob ended it with her," said Anna Claire practically. "That's why she's crying."

Tommy's eyes went wide. "Gee, Caroline!"

Caroline, not wanting to be bothered with a little pest, brushed his hand away from her shoulder. "Go away, you little- oh, just go away!"

"I'm sorry," muttered Tommy, but he then looked her way and said, "Jacob's a fool."

Caroline perked up just the slightest bit and managed to smile at him. "I am sorry for my rudeness. Please forgive me."

"I could never be cross with you," said Tommy, his eyes shining. "You know, maybe you and I could go to town sometime and-"

Caroline began weeping again even harder, and Charlotta flicked her wrist for the two children to get out of their sight.

Tommy and Anna Claire ran out of the door and through the bushes and trees to Gold Creek. "She's such a baby," said Anna Claire, shaking her head. "Stupid baby! Crying over some stupid boy!"

But Tommy's face was glowing. "She was smiling at me! She smiled at me!"

Anna Claire shoved him with her elbow, and the two took off their clothes to jump into the creek as they normally did, the sun beating down upon them and the leaves falling green from above them.

"Let's explore," said Anna Claire as she dipped her head into the water, making her golden hair look darker.

They opened their eyes underwater and made funny faces at each other. Then the children, feeling free and happy, got back into their clothes and ran through the sagebrush, laughing and hollering all the way. Anna Claire informed her mother that she was going into town then. She and Tommy ran through the fields with energy, hollering through the grass and shouting at the sky.

"Wanna see somethin'?" Tommy asked with a mischievous grin when they reached town.

"Yes!" answered Anna Claire with all of her enthusiasm. What sort of thrilling adventure was Tommy about to take her on now?

"Follow me."

Anna Claire happily followed him as he walked down towards the town and then away from the town, pausing as he reached the other side of Main Street. Anna Claire squinted her eyes to see little white things that were standing on the ground. When she got closer, she saw that they were stones and crosses.

"It's the cemetery," said Tommy in a hush.

"I didn't know the cemetery was so close!"

"Well, where d'ya think we bury all the dead people?"

Anna Claire shrugged and walked fearlessly over to where the graves lay. They were odd, as most of the gravestones were kept inside small wooden fences that wrapped around them, and some of them only had letters on them, not even names or dates. Some of them were so small they could hardly be seen, while others were a bit taller and grander.

"This is strange," said Anna Claire, touching a stone softly with her hand. "I do like strange things!"

"Don't touch!" yelled Tommy, pulling her back. "Mr. Dobbins says it's not polite to touch the graves. Maybe it angers their ghosts."

"Oh," answered Anna Claire, impressed by this knowledge.

The two walked through silently, Anna Claire trying to imagine what the people may have looked and been like when they were alive.

"Someday, we'll be as dead as they are," said Tommy somewhat sadly.

Anna Claire shuddered.

As they were walking around the graves, tak-ing in the solemn atmosphere of the little cemetery, they both stopped in their tracks.

"Tommy, look!" cried Anna Claire, tugging on his arm, which was tanned from the sun.

"I see it." He said this in such a serious way that it frightened Anna Claire a bit.

There, a small, humble grave without a wooden fence, was a stone that read "HATFIELD."

"This can't be Daisy's," said Tommy. "They buried her on the other side of town. Mr. Dobbins told me she wasn't buried in the cemetery."

"Then it must be Old Man Hatfield!" Anna Claire announced, taking a step back from the grave. Tommy turned to her. "I never noticed before. I usu-ally never really read the names. I used to come here to sit sometimes when I was sad or when Ma was an-gry with me, but I never read the names."

Anna Claire sighed. "It's him, Tommy, it's gotta be!"

"It probably is," said Tommy. "I think Minnie was buried on the land, so this ain't hers. This has gotta be Old Man Hatfield's grave."

"I wonder why we found it just today," Anna Claire thought. "Maybe his ghost is tryin' to tell us where the gold is!"

"Maybe," said Tommy. "That was smart, Anna Claire. Maybe it's true, and maybe he wants us to find the gold, and this is his way of tellin' us."

The two fell silent again, and this time the si-lence seemed very, very loud. They stared for a while at the little white stone that read "HATFIELD" before they remembered that they were hungry and went off to steal candy from the saloon.

The sky had darkened when it was time for supper at the Freiler's. This time, Tommy was invited. The two ate the sweet-tasting calf's foot jelly as if nothing was happening, but as everyone spoke, Tommy and Anna Claire snuck sneaky glances at each other. They were both dreaming of gold and thinking of what David Hatfield might have been like when he was younger. Only *they* knew the truth about the secret, and only *they* would be able to put all of the pieces together.

Chapter 17- Unbelievable Sights

It was something neither Tommy nor Anna Claire would ever forget. It haunted their daydreams long after it happened and presented itself in nightmares that they dealt with on and off throughout their lives. It officially tainted the way the children saw the world and made them grow up just a little bit more than they were before. They could never go back and unsee what they saw. They could never fix what happened. All they could do was watch-watch and then remember.

"This is awful," said Charlotta in the doorway one night, Joseph coming in from tending to the animals. It was very late, and the children were all in bed.

Joseph walked through the doorway soundlessly, almost too quietly. He didn't know what to say or how to reason with his wife, for she was right-things were getting very dangerous. That he could not deny. And this, he knew, would only make Charlotta more anxious than ever to leave Gold Country, even if doing so would prove to be more dangerous than ever.

"Well, what do you have to say?" she poked, following him into the small kitchen, a dripping spoon at her side.

"Not now, Char," he said in a low and gruff voice, a voice that was very much unlike him. "I'm exhausted. I went to that dang creek for the thousandth time and once again found nothin'. I haven't even found silver in months. I'm goin' mad tryin' to see gold out of every rock every day! I know you think I'm a failure and what I'm doin' here is foolish. I know you do."

"I never said that!"

"You didn't have to." He walked slowly over to where his wife stood and sighed. "We cannot leave Gold Country. Everything we have built is here. We have been here well over a year now. We have a family in these parts, Char. People that love us and care for us. We cannot just load the wagon and leave. The children are settled now. They go to school, they have friends, *we* have friends. You must understand that."

Charlotta put her hand to her cheek in the way she so often did when she had questions. "How did it come to this? Yes, Joseph, we have built a life here, a good one even. We are accustomed to it here now. You know how dear Nettie is to me, and even little Tommy Cooper. I love your friends and their wives. I know we have friends here, Joseph. You don't have to remind me of this. But another man is dead because of these Road Agents- another man! Another reason to be worried for our children's safety."

Joseph turned around sharply and glared at his wife. "Yes, someone has died. Someone is always dyin', Charlotta! We cannot build our entire lives upon that fact!"

"Why not?" cried Charlotta, her voice cracking.

"Stop flyin' off the handle over everything!" Joseph paused and took a deep breath. "I know it has not been safe around the roads. But here, we are safe. I know there's been some fightin' in town as of late which is why we must be more careful when lettin' the children go into town. But we *are* safe here. We have so many friends, and I know most of the men. They won't hurt us. I know my way around this land now, Char. I know the people. The Road Agents do their dirty work in secret, at night, away from everyone on the roads, far off from here. We will never go on those roads at night- not ever! We will be safe."

Charlotta's resolve not to cry broke and she began sobbing into her husband's chest. "May the good Lord protect us. May He give us strength and keep us in His arms."

"We will pray," said Joseph, more softly than he had been speaking before. "We will pray and all will be well. We will stay here as long as we can. If any more blood will be shed, I will think of leaving."

"Do you promise?" asked Charlotta, her hair strewn carelessly out of her loose bun. "Do you promise if it grows very dangerous, we will leave?"

"If it becomes very dangerous close by and not just on the roads, then we will leave. We will go somewhere else, although I must say that I don't know anywhere much safer than here."

"Minnesota was safe," muttered Charlotta, still weeping.

"Nowhere is safe anymore," said Joseph, turning around. "It is far better to make a place safe than it is to try and run away from a dangerous one. Running has never gotten anyone anything he desires." He looked down at his leg and thought bitterly of the war in which he so bravely tried to fight but couldn't.

"I know you think of the war," said Charlotta. "Stop blaming yourself! You got hurt, you were injured. You wanted to defend the Union and you did your duty. You did not run."

"I don't wish to talk of this," Joseph snapped, feeling the pain of humiliation sting him again.

"You don't want to talk about this, but you will talk about how it is a good choice to keep our family here to be in peril?" Charlotta's voice rose with every word, and she felt her face getting hot.

"Peril!" scoffed Joseph. "You are being insensible. Insensible!"

"What else would you call it?" Charlotta spat. "A place of comfort?"

"Yes, I would, because we are very fortunate to live here in Gold Country, where we know people who care about us and where the children can have a school now. Do you not understand the importance of minin' for the gold, Charlotta? Do you not understa-"

"Oh, I understand!" Charlotta threw her hands in the air as her eyes narrowed. "I understand that you want gold so badly you would put your own family in danger!"

Now, Joseph's face turned bright red, his eyes twitching. "Don't you ever say that again! I have done everything in my power to make sure this family has what it needs! You have no idea what I have sacrificed!"

"What *you* have sacrificed?" Charlotta's voice cracked, her lips trembling. "What about what *I* have sacrificed? My mother, my sisters, my friends, my nieces and nephews, my church! I have sacrificed it all! For what? For you to go on a wild goose chase!"

"Listen, you must stop talking as if I have done evil! I did this for our family!"

"Of course," laughed Charlotta sarcastically. "I suppose we will all be rich and dead then!"

"I can't even believe-"

"Mama? Papa?" said a little voice, breaking their conversation.

They turned around to see small Berthie, standing there with her blonde hair over her eyes and a tired frown on her face.

"Dear, it is much too late," said Charlotta, wiping the remaining tears from her eyes. "Why are you awake?"

Berthie came over to them slowly as Joseph reached down to pick her up.

"What is the matter, my darlin'?" asked Joseph, giving her a kiss on the cheek.

"I can't sleep!" she proclaimed, wiping her eyes.   Charlotta held her closer. "Let me warm up some tea. I am sure it will help you to sleep."

Berthie nodded while Charlotta got the kettle prepared. Joseph gave his little one a kiss on top of her head, placed her back on the ground, and left the kitchen, scowling at his wife as he walked away.

Charlotta was beginning to believe her husband was foolish for thinking all would be well when it was frightening in Gold Country. All she could do, being a woman and a wife, was hope that her husband was right and that she was, as he thought her to be, completely wrong.

The next day, Anna Claire had woken up early, done her chores haphazardly, and ran to town before anyone had even risen. Tommy had told her the day before that there was to be a big event in town where they were going to hang a man for murder and treason- a man who had pretended he was a Vigilante but was actually a Road Agent.

Anna Claire had never seen a man get hung before! She couldn't wait to see the man fall, the neck twisting and the eyes bulging out like Tommy said they would. Maybe his whole neck would be ripped off, and the head would fall to the ground, oozing of blood and pus. The mere thought of this justice excited Anna Claire so much that she could not sleep, and so the morning came slowly.

Anna Claire ran to Swiner's Saloon just after the morning chores, which she completed as early and as quickly as possible. When she found the saloon to be locked, she waited on the steps patiently as the sun slowly rose, first orange and then gold before she could no longer watch it any more.

"Anna Claire?" said Kathleen Cooper, her lips bright red and her bosom busting at the seams.

"Tommy's Ma!" greeted Anna Claire cheerfully. "Where's Tommy?"

"He's still asleep, child," answered Kathleen Cooper, leaning against the railing and twirling a piece of her red hair in her finger. "You can come in for now and wait for him. It may be a while. He don't like gettin' up early, now."

Anna Claire smiled and followed the woman into the saloon, thinking to herself how exciting it was going to be to see someone die.

Kathleen began serving drinks early on, eyeing Anna Claire carefully as the little girl impatiently knocked her shoes on the chair next to her and stared around the saloon anxiously.

It certainly seemed to take a while before Tommy emerged and walked downstairs with a yawn, fully dressed, but his chocolate-brown hair messy.

"Anna Claire!" he cried, rushing to the table as she jumped up.

"When is it!? When's the hangin'? We didn't miss it, right?" she asked, her eyes full of wonder.

"Soon!" said Tommy. "They said in the mornin'. Dang, I hope we didn't miss it. Let's go!"

The two of them ran out of the saloon, Tommy not bothering to bid his mother goodbye, and towards the opposite side of the street. Here, they walked up over the little hill behind the drug store where the gallows stood menacingly. People were beginning to crowd around already, and they soon saw the prisoner being dragged by a couple of big men with long faces.

"That's him!" cried Tommy, pointing a finger at the criminal. "That's the man who killed the Dennis man! It's him! He did it!"

Anna Claire struggled to see in between all the people, as she was so small.

"Help me see!" she yelled. "I wanna see him die!"

Tommy rolled his eyes and bent down so that she could step on his back. Anna Claire saw the culprit along with the men and watched as they began talking about the crimes the man committed.

"I wanna see, get down!" yelled Tommy, standing up so that Anna Claire had no choice but to trip. "Here, look around this man."

Anna Claire took Tommy's advice and squinted between a man's arm. She watched as they continued talking. The man who was to be hung, referred to as "Hammond", looked angry but very distraught at once. He was a slightly older man with a long face, thick whiskers, and cold, sad eyes. Anna Claire felt a chill hit her bones when she looked at him, even though it was a perfectly sunny May day.

The talking felt like forever. Anna Claire and Tommy began to grow antsy and couldn't stand still. It was beginning to drizzle slightly, and the two of them were bored and anxious while waiting for the event to begin.

Eventually, everything grew silent. Everyone stopped talking, even the crowd. It was going to happen at any moment!

Anna Claire looked over at Tommy with an excited glance. Standing on her tip toes, she peered between the shape a man made with his arm and elbow. The man at the gallows was now looking nervous and the anger on his face had washed off. He was looking at the sky as if to curse it or pray, one or the other, maybe both. The men pushed him towards the gallows and a reverend began to say a prayer for the soul of the man.

Anna Claire felt nervous herself for the man. She couldn't imagine being the one up there having to die. She squirmed as the man began trembling. He made a guttural frightened sound that she would never forget, his aged face beginning to shake. It all moved so fast from this moment.

The man looked at the ground as the men held him up, helping him stand on a little wooden whiskey box that had been propped up on the gallows. One of them pushed him toward the hanging rope, pulling it down and over a bit. He then swiftly put the criminal's head into the loophole and, with a very short pause, another guard kicked the whiskey box forward. The man, with one more open-mouthed look at the sky, made a retching sound as he fell, the noose tightening around his neck.

He wriggled and writhed for a moment, his legs moving as if trying to run. His eyes bulged and his tongue protruded from his lips. The crowd cheered heartily. Anna Claire knew she should be happy the man was dead- and she was, for he had committed terrible, unspeakable crimes. He deserved to go down in a worse way than those he had murdered. Yet, for a moment, Anna Claire felt a pang of pity before the sick feeling came over her. She had just witnessed a killing.

Tommy, knowing what to expect, still felt his nerves rising and his body trembling. He looked over at his friend, who had stopped grinning and was biting her lip anxiously. When they looked back at the man, they noticed he had stopped moving and was hanging lifeless, his last memories reduced to the rope.

Tommy pulled Anna Claire's hand out of the crowd. They moved passed the happy and cheering people, including some of the other children who were being warned about the fate of criminals, and walked silently down the dusty road of town. The road had now turned to mud that went past their ankles, and the smell of horse manure was especially strong. They walked stiffly for a while as they passed Bail's saloon, the meat market, and the butcher's shop. They took a turn outside of the town and walked for some time up a big hill before stopping and sitting down breathlessly.

Tommy looked over at Anna Claire, regretting his decision to let her come to town to see the spectacle. Anna Claire looked so small and fragile sitting there in her already dirty, pink gingham dress and hands around her bony knees. Tommy felt his heart drop for a moment and an instinct to protect his little friend from the sight she had just witnessed- all because he wanted her to see it with him.

"I'm sorry," he whispered, his throat feeling dry.

"What are you sorry for? I wanted to come." Anna Claire's face had grown paler, and her eyes were still wide and frightened.

"I didn't- I didn't know it'd be so scary," said Tommy, feeling guilty as he placed a hand around her back. "That was the worse killin' I ever saw! You're too little to see somethin' like that." "We're almost the same age, you fool," Anna Claire snapped, but with less gusto as her usual insults.

"I shouldn't have let you see that," continued Tommy, shaking his head of messy brown hair, his oval face downcast. "I didn't know it'd be like that. I didn't know it'd be so scary like that."

Anna Claire felt a calmness rush over her- an eerie calmness that took the place of her nerves but also made her feel numb.

"I'm glad he's dead," she said finally, picking up a rock and throwing it. "He should be." Tommy nodded, afraid to look at her.

The two stood up shakily, Anna Claire with a determinedly stiff look on her face.

"It wasn't *that* scary," she said, although she could feel her hands sweating.

"It was though," Tommy echoed her thoughts, his piercing eyes shining. "I never saw nothin' like that before. This was different than the other times."

Anna Claire nodded and began to walk forward, Tommy following hesitantly.

"I wish I didn't see it," she said suddenly, watching the crickets hop in the grass as she walked through.

"Me too," confessed Tommy, looking over his shoulder as if someone was going to come up behind them.

"I couldn't imagine being hanged," said Anna Claire. "Imagine standing there on a box knowing you're about to die. Just think of it. I wonder what it felt like when he was strangled by the rope. I thought it would be fun. But now I'm thinking of how much that probably hurt. Now he's dead."

Tommy walked a little faster to catch up with

his friend. "He was a hard-case, Anna Claire. He had to die."

"I know," Anna Claire sighed. "But I don't wanna see nothin' like that ever again!"

"Me neither," agreed Tommy, shuddering from the rain as it began to pelt down in thick drops. "Never again."

When Anna Claire arrived home, she kicked off her boots and sat at the table. Charlotta had never seen such a look on her daughter's face before.

"What is the matter, Anna Claire?" she asked gently, coming over and placing her hand on her arm.

Anna Claire shrugged. "Me and Tommy saw someone die. The murderer got hanged."

Charlotta gasped, feeling faint.

"How- why- *why* did you go to see such a horrible thing?" and as she spoke those words, she knew there was no way that she would ever be able to protect her young daughter from seeing a sight like that and, frankly, it was too late to restore the innocence she had before she witnessed this disturbing event.

Anna Claire shrugged again. "I wanted to see him die. He killed people. He deserved it! He's dead now. Good riddance!"

Charlotta resisted the urge to cry. "Well, are you alright?"

"Sure," said the girl. "He needed to die. It was strange to see him die. He looked all scared, and his eyes were bulgin'. Do people always have that look on their face when they die?" Charlotta sighed and played with Anna Claire's hair. "No, my dear. This man was hung. He had a strange look because his neck was in the rope. Please, dear, don't think of this anymore. I know it was frightening- it must have been.

"It wasn't," lied the little girl, turning up her nose. "I wasn't scared at all!"

Charlotta wished this were true but knew that it wasn't.

"I wish you had not seen such a thing," she said sternly. "I do not want you to ever go and see something like that again. I think it is time that I forbade you to go to town once and for all."

"But Mama, Tommy said-"

"I don't care what Tommy said." Charlotta pursed her lips. "It is dangerous around Gold Country now. You are not to go anywhere without telling me first, especially not town or any of the roads leading to it. Tommy is always welcome here, you know that. Your papa will take you into town if you so wish. But no more town alone or with Tommy, not for now."

Anna Claire felt her face grow hot. "Fine, but I ain't gonna be happy about it!"

Charlotta couldn't resist a small smile. "I know, but you will thank me someday."

"No, I won't." Anna Claire kicked the chair and sulked.

Charlotta stood up and thought to herself how in the world she would ever explain to her ten-year-old child what she had witnessed.

Tommy and Anna Claire had nightmares for many nights after the hanging. They went to sleep thinking of standing at the gallows, closed their eyes thinking of a box kicked underneath their feet, and woke up in a sweat as they saw themselves with the noose around their necks. It was a horrible time for both of them, and they wished with everything that they hadn't seen what they had seen. Although both were tough little souls, they were only eleven and ten years old. The children inside of them weren't quite as brave as they so often seemed.

Joseph was livid when he found out that the children had seen the hanging, but knew, like his wife, that there was no way he could make them unsee what they had already seen. Joseph himself concentrated all of his efforts on his mining and finding the coveted gold he so wanted. Day in and day out, sometimes panning with his friends and sometimes panning alone, he sifted through the mud and dirt to find anything, even silver. Day in and day out, he had no luck, despite truly believing in his soul that he was going to strike it rich. His wife had long been doubtful, and now she was even more aware of how far away Joseph's dreams were and how silly she thought he was being.

Gold Country was known now as a dangerous place to travel and Bannack was associated with blood around Montana Territory. The children even stopped going to school for a while when there was a shoot-out in the saloon nearby, and they finished their studies at home. No one had died, but it was dangerous all the same. Tommy and Anna Claire were particularly upset for not being able to see Miss Darling now, at least not for a few weeks, and Anna Claire was angry that she would be home for some of the biggest chores the family had to do.

Charlotta was beside herself with keeping house and caring for her children. Caroline was still distraught about Jacob, and Helen was always irritated and angry with something. Anna Claire was as wild as ever, and Pete continued to play pranks. Berthie kept coming down with colds and was bedridden for many days at a time. And, worst of all, Joseph was taking so many risks being out late at night panning for something that he would most likely never find. Charlotta was beginning to grow angrier and more frustrated with Joseph than she had ever been before. Her patience was wearing thin.

It was a beautiful day in May when Tommy came to the Freiler house with Mr. Dobbins.

"Would I be able to take the little lady into town?" Mr. Dobbins asked Charlotta with a grin, looking at Anna Claire as she held the broom, her mouth open in a wide smile.

Charlotta nodded. She knew Mr. Dobbins would never let any harm come to the children.

"Mind what Mr. Dobbins says," Charlotta said to her. "Listen to him and don't go traipsing off anywhere!"

"I won't, Mama!" yelled Anna Claire enthusiastically as she dropped the broom. She couldn't have been happier to get away.

The three of them began walking across the field, the sun in their faces and the air soft and clear.

"Mr. Dobbins," said Anna Claire happily as she skipped next to him, "I haven't been to town in so long! Not since the hangin'."

Mr. Dobbins shook his head. "Tommy told me. I wish you youngins hadn't seen that."

"It was scary," admitted Tommy, his body already browned from the sun. "Especially his eyes! They were bulgin'!"

"Alright, youngins," Mr. Dobbins said as he frowned, "no more sad talk about hangin's and killin's."

"But we wanna talk about it," said Anna Claire.

"Yeah, that's right!" agreed Tommy, moving in front of them.

"What do you wanna know?" asked Mr. Dobbins patiently. "I can't tell ya everything, but I can tell ya some things. Only the things that are important to know. I reckon you gotta tell youngins the truth sometimes. They grow up to know it anyway."

The children smiled at each other.

"Why are so many people gettin' murdered?" asked Tommy. "I know it's 'cause of the gold, but why do they do it if they just go to jail or get hung?"

Mr. Dobbins laughed. "Jail's a joke for some of 'em. They all think they'll either not get caught or- if they do- be able to escape the noose. And they do. Most of the time. We got lucky to find some of 'em and hang 'em. Ever since we found out that Plummer, the Sheriff, was a part of the gang back a couple years ago, it seems more and more men think they can get away with the same foolery. Which don't make no sense since Plummer himself was hung! Men are daft, I tell ya."

"Why is there gold here?" asked Tommy as they walked through the fields.

"Well now," said Mr. Dobbins, "we don't quite know. What I do know, though, is that they found gold in Grasshopper Creek and then a bunch of people staked their claims. Before the gold rush, this place was as quiet as they come. There was no big town, only a few cabins in the hills. Then all these people started comin' here and all those fancy business folks followed with all their fancy stores and fancy shops. You know they even spelled the dang town's name wrong?"

"They did?" asked Anna Claire with wide eyes.

"Sure. The town was 'Bannock' with an 'O' because of the native folks who lived in these parts. But then they got rid of them and forced them off their own dang land and misspelled the name of the town 'Bannack' with an 'A.' If I ever heard anything more stupid! Then you got all those folks from California who either found gold and wanted more, or ain't find nothin' and came here a'lookin'. Don't get me wrong, some of the folks are good people, like your family, Anna Claire. I like your father a whole lot and we're good friends. But some of the others came with their guns a'blazin' and their knives in their pockets to frighten the whole damn place. Now there's so many murders in these parts that you'd think the roads were paved with blood. It's common doin's now. This is why greed don't do nobody no good. Everyone might as well go on to Virginia City since they got more deposits there now."

"Why are there all those posters?" asked Anna Claire, referring to the posters with the mystic numbers "3-7-77."

"Well, a grave is three feet wide, seven feet long, and seventy-seven inches deep," replied Mr. Dobbins. "The Vigilantes put those up to scare the robbers. I don't reckon it's workin' much, but without the Vigilantes this place would be bloodier than ever. Before all this, we traded fur. Now everyone wants the gold. All those men comin' on steamboats up the Missouri River to Fort Benton. Some of them went to other towns. That's what they reckon anyway."

When the three of them arrived in town, Mr. Dobbins took them to the drug store and bought them ice cream. It had been such a long time since Anna Claire had ice cream, and she loved ice cream the most, next to pie. She and Tommy both chose chocolate, and Mr. Dobbins treated himself to a vanilla. They sat for a while on a bench under the sun, watching the people go by- the children in their overalls, the little girls in their pigtails, the women in their dresses much too hot for the season, and the men riding the horses.

"I don't care if it's dangerous. I love it here," said Anna Claire as she licked some of the ice cream from the side of her hand. "I wanna live in Gold Country forever!"

Mr. Dobbins sighed, taking his hat off. "I hope ya'll stay here. I hope it gets safe and quiet again. Anyhow, I'm glad you folks came. You're some of the good ones."

Anna Claire smiled, finishing her ice cream.

"I hope I never get hanged," mused Anna Claire as she and Tommy strolled back from town, the tall grass hitting their knees.

Tommy laughed. "What would you do to get hung? You ain't a murderer or a robber!"

"Well, I'm only ten. What if I become one? I could picture me killin' someone if they ever hurt my family!"

"I hope you don't get hung," said Tommy sadly. "Listen to that!" Anna Claire put her hand out in front of Tommy to stop him. "Do you hear that?"

They stopped and listened to the bird flying over their heads, swimming in the big Montana sky. They laughed when the bird ducked lower, seemingly coming after them.

"Dang!" cried Tommy.

"Did you see that!?" cried Anna Claire.

They laughed some more, Anna Claire beginning to skip through the grass, humming a tune.

"I wonder when there's gonna be another murder," said Tommy, running ahead of her.

Anna Claire shrugged. "Not sure, I reckon."

"I really hope no more. Everyone's gonna leave, and then I'll be lonely all by myself again."

"We're never gonna leave," said Anna Claire confidently. "Papa said so!"

They walked and talked some more until they entered the clearing before the Freiler's cabin.

"I gotta go home," said Tommy.

"I gotta go eat supper," said Anna Claire, and the two parted ways.

When Anna Claire skipped into the house, there was a loud noise and the sight of Helen running towards her. Before anyone could stop her, Helen jumped upon Anna Claire, hitting her on her head and her arms.

Anna Claire screamed. "Stop! Stop! What are you doin'? Stop!"

"Helen, no!" cried Caroline, her hand over her mouth.

"Stop this!" shouted Charlotta, rushing to their side.

Joseph ran to the aid, grabbing Helen and keeping her from clawing Anna Claire's face.

"You brat!" Helen screamed.

"What is happening?" Charlotta looked over at Joseph. "Helen, if you want to see tomorrow, you had better calm down now!"

Still flailing, Helen let out one last scream before going limp in Joseph's arms.

Anna Claire was too surprised to move. She backed away, her eyes wide.

"That little brat," Helen spat, pointing at Anna Claire, "took my favorite book and ripped all the pages out!"

Anna Claire's eyes went even wider.

"Why do you think it was Anna Claire?" asked Charlotta.

"Because I know it is! It's always her!"

Anna Claire put her hands up. "I did no such thing, you stupid fool! I did no such thing, Helen Marie!"

Charlotta went over to Anna Claire and calmly looked down at her. "Did you rip apart Helen's book?"

"No!" said Anna Claire honestly. "I don't want your stupid book, you idiot!"

"Little brat!" cried Helen, her body getting tense again, and Joseph holding her tightly.

"Alright," said Joseph, still holding onto Helen. "Who ripped Helen's book apart? I want honesty!"

"She did!" spat Helen, pointing an accusatory finger at her sister.

"Did not!" yelled Anna Claire, walking over to her and slapping her in the face, causing Helen to jump up. Joseph placed his hand around her waist while Charlotta grabbed Anna Claire's arm. "You stop this right now!" she said to them, her face flushed.

"I want someone to tell me what happened to that book!" yelled Joseph, his voice growing louder.

Everyone looked around the room. Pete stood in the corner laughing.

"Pete?" Joseph asked, turning to look at him.

"It's just a stupid book!" he cried. "I was gonna give it back!"

Charlotta walked over and spanked him once very mildly.

"Stop, Mama!"

"Now, I'm at sea. Why would you do that, Peter?" asked Joseph, letting go of Helen who was watching with big eyes.

"I don't know!" cried Pete. He had stopped laughing and now had tears coming down his red face. "I wanted them out of the book! I wanted to make Helen mad. I was gonna give them back! I promise!"

"You little worm!" yelled Helen, stomping her feet. "If you were older, I'd spank you too, and hard!"

"Stop this! Stop this now!" said Charlotta, holding the shoulder of Berthie who had come to stand next to her, sucking on her thumb.

Still crying, Pete ran up to the loft and back down the ladder, giving Helen the torn-out pages. Some were completely curled at the top and ripped on the sides, making it impossible to read alone unless stuck back into the book on the correct pages.

Helen took the pages and sobbed. "My favorite book! When shall I be able to get another? I hate you, Peter!"

Caroline shook her head and walked over to Berthie to comfort the frightened child.

Joseph took a look at the cover without its pages, which made it look limp and empty.

"I'll find it somewhere," he said gruffly. "It'll take me a while, but I'll find it somewhere." Helen crossed her arms and glared at Pete, who was wiping his snot from his nose.

"What do you say to Anna Claire?" asked Charlotta, hands on her hips.

Helen took a deep breath and nervously glanced Anna Claire's way. "Sorry, Anna Claire."

Anna Claire made a face before walking past her. "I hate you, Helen!"

"Both of you, upstairs! Now!" yelled Charlotta. "But I didn't do anything!" cried Anna Claire angrily.

"You hit your sister! Now go!"

Both girls stalked up the ladder angrily, Anna Claire sticking out her tongue and Helen elbowing her. When Anna Claire entered her side of the loft, she threw one of her pillows on the ground. There was not much else she could throw at that moment.

"Are you alwight?" asked a tiny voice, entering the loft.

Anna Claire immediately calmed. "Yes, Berthie. I'm alright. Helen is just stupid. But I'm alright."

"Can you tell me a stowy tonight?"

"Sure. So long as you eat!"

The rest of the night was spent with Anna Claire and Helen glaring at each other while they were eating, and Pete looking down at the table, his eyes red and swollen.

"Children," Caroline muttered, rolling her eyes and touching her curls.

Chapter 18- Springtime in the West

Life in the winter was the hardest, but spring came with its own burdens.

School was easier to get to now, and classes luckily resumed with Miss Darling once the news of the saloon shoot-out had calmed down. Anna Claire did well in her classes, especially when it came to matters of reading and writing, and she made her parents proud with her frequent high marks. All of the Freiler children were doing well in school- even Helen who was the laziest of them all. They were all good at different things, and where one was deficient in, the other was proficient. However well they did in school, it was not comparable to the little boy who sat in the back, the one that had only just learned to read and who had nearly no upbringing whatsoever.

Tommy Cooper just seemed to get it all. He picked up reading quickly and everything else seemed to come to him with as much ease as breathing air. He caught on to arithmetic extremely well, as numbers had always made sense to him, and excelled in the subject of science, as he was curious and detailed. Although he had some work to do in matters of creativity, such as writing poetry, he nevertheless understood the works well, and his presentations in front of the class were nearly theatrical. It was evident that Tommy was not only smart but *extremely* bright, and the only aspect holding him back was his sporadic attendance.

"You are doing very well," Miss Darling said one day, keeping him after school while Anna Claire anxiously awaited outside the schoolhouse. "I thought you were not going to be able to finish the Third Reader. But, Tommy, there is a good chance that you will. Your marks have been outstanding. The one thing that is holding you back is your lack of attendance."

Tommy looked down at the ground, but Miss Darling lifted his chin up gently.

"I know it is so difficult when you are the only one pushing yourself to go to school," she said softly, looking at him with empathic eyes. "I can see clearly that you rather like school here. You have your friends, and you are interested in learning. Why do you not come every day this spring? The weather is no longer an excuse."

Tommy shuffled his feet. "I dunno."

"Give me a real answer, Tommy Cooper," Miss Darling said sternly but kindly.

Tommy sighed. "Most of the time I like it, but my ma doesn't like schoolin' so much. She says it's makin' me spoiled."

Miss Darling sighed and looked ahead of her. "I see. Tommy, you are not spoiled for being able to go to school. School is a privilege, yes, but one that everyone should have. You are a child of Bannack. There is a school in Bannack. You are entitled to go to that school, no matter what your mother says. This does not make you spoiled. This makes you appreciative of what you have. Some children never get to go to school and you *can*, Tommy. It would be a shame if you wasted this opportunity. Especially since you are one of the brightest students I have ever had."

Tommy looked up at her with an expression of careful hope.

"I'll try to come more," he said, meaning it. "I really will try, Miss Darlin'!"

Miss Darling smiled and tapped his shoulder. "I hope so. Now go to Anna Claire. I know she's waiting for you!"

Tommy smiled and began running to the back of the classroom.

"Oh, Tommy!" yelled Miss Darling before he walked out.

"Yes, Miss Darlin'?"

"You *are* bright. Do not let anyone else tell you otherwise."

Tommy smiled again and nodded, running out to talk to Anna Claire.

"Are you in trouble?" she asked anxiously, grabbing his arms. "What'd she say?"

Tommy shook his head. "I ain't in no trouble. She said I'm bright, is all."

"Really?" asked Anna Claire as they walked down Clover Street past the general store.

"She said she wants me to come to school more."

"That's a good thing, Tommy!" said Anna Claire happily. "You *should* come more. The school gets awful quiet and boring without you."

Tommy nodded. "I like goin' to school but my ma doesn't like when I go. She wants me to stay home. But I usually don't listen to her and go anyway, and then she forgets by the time I come home."

They kept walking fast, eager to get to the Freiler's cabin so that they could play in the creek.

"I wish Miss Darlin' would make me stay late to tell me I'm smart," said Anna Claire. "I love Miss Darlin'! She's the nicest teacher I ever had!"

Tommy nodded, the two turning onto Main Street and walking past all of the horses and wagons.

"You always get good marks," said Tommy. "At least in writin' and readin'."

"That's 'cause I like it," Anna Claire replied. "I don't like arithmetic so I can't pay attention to it. But you can do anything!"

Tommy smiled. "I never thought I was smart. I always thought I was dumb 'cause I couldn't read."

"Like my mama says, sometimes people are smart, but they don't show it because they never had the chance. My papa says everyone is smart but in different ways. I think they're both right."

"Me too," agreed Tommy as they turned down an alleyway and made their way toward the little hill.

"I wonder if we're all gonna go to the dance next week," said Anna Claire. "Mama still hasn't decided. I think she doesn't wanna go, but I know Papa does 'cause he has been trying to tell her good things about it. He says there's gonna be cake and apple pie. I love apple pie! He said that nearly all of the people we know will be there, like the Clemmons' and the Howlers! You'll go if we go, right?"

Tommy nodded. "Sure, I will. Why not? Maybe I'll ask Caroline to dance!"

Anna Claire scoffed. "I think she'll throw pie in your face. She doesn't want to be courted by a little boy!"

"I ain't little!" Tommy puffed out his chest to seem bigger and walked ahead of Anna Claire. "I'm gettin' taller. Mr. Dobbins said so!"

"Maybe, but you're still eleven."

Tommy wrinkled his nose.

"I wonder where lá daxpitchée is now," remarked Anna Claire sadly, walking backwards and nearly tripping over her boots.

"Somewhere far away from here," Tommy answered. "Hey, why are you walkin' backwards like that?"

Anna Claire laughed. "Because I can!"

They walked on for a while, admiring the bright blue sky above them.

"lá daxpitchée was a good friend," said Tommy. "I hope wherever he is, he's safe. And his family, too."

Anna Claire frowned. She tugged on Tommy's arm to stop him from walking.

"What's the matter?"

"Promise me you'll be my friend forever?" she asked, looking at him with wistfulness.

"O' course," Tommy said. "What's the matter with you?"

Anna Claire sighed. "If we ever get mad at each other or somethin' I don't wanna stop bein' friends. Sometimes people get mad at each other and never talk again. You're the best friend I ever had."

Tommy took her hand. "We'll always be friends, Anna Claire! I mean it! I won't never get so mad at you that you won't be my friend."

"Say you promise!" demanded Anna Claire, shaking her hand from his and putting it on her hip.

"But I just told you-"

"Promise me!"

"I promise, I promise," Tommy said, turning around to continue walking. "Gee, you get odder every day."

Anna Claire ignored that last comment as she turned to happily begin walking again. She knew he meant what he said and that they would always be friends, come rain or shine. Even if something happened and she had to leave Gold Country.

"I don't reckon I understand this," said Joseph that night during supper, looking at Helen with confusion. "You're tellin' me that you want me to buy you an outrageously expensive dress you saw in the store window just because your friend Lucy has one just like it? I just wanted to make sure I got it right."

Helen nodded. "Please, Papa! Lucy's is pink and this one is blue, but it's such a dark, pretty blue! It even has the ruffles on the sleeves!"

"You are thirteen-years-old," said Charlotta, shaking her head and giving Joseph an incredulous look. "You are far too young for such a fancy dress."

"But you said Caroline can start thinking of marriage and she was only fourteen then!" cried Helen. "I'll be fourteen next year!"

Charlotta sighed. "I know dear, so maybe when you are fourteen, we can get you the dress."

Helen crossed her arms and began to pout.

"You're even uglier when you're sore," laughed Anna Claire.

"I hate you!" Helen spat, stomping the ground with her foot.

"Stop it," said Charlotta. "Both of you. Otherwise, the two of you will not go to the dance next week."

Both Helen and Anna Claire perked up at this.

"That's right, children," said Joseph. "We're all gonna go to the dance at the hall, as long as everyone behaves. If not, no one is goin'."

Caroline cleared her throat and said sweetly, "That means we must all be good as gold. That means all of you had better not ruin this for me!"

"Caroline," said Joseph.

"You think everything is about you!" quipped Helen.

"Enough," said Joseph again. "If you can get through a whole day without fightin' with each other, we'll think of goin' to the dance. But if any of you misbehave-" he gave them all a playful but menacing look, "no one is goin' to this dance."

"I wanna go! I wanna go!" shouted Berthie, patting Hero on the head as he jumped up to steal her food.

"Me too," said Pete. "I know there's gonna be apple pie!"

"I love apple pie; we *have* to be good!" agreed Anna Claire.

"Sorry I said I hate you," Helen grumbled from across the table.

"Sorry I said you're ugly," muttered Anna Claire.

Charlotta smiled. "See? It is possible! Can you believe it, Joseph?"

Joseph smiled too, his soft brown eyes gleaming. "A true miracle in the Freiler home."

"I wanna dance with you, Papa," said Berthie, standing up to hug her father.

Joseph picked her up and held her in his lap. "You will be my first dancin' partner!"

Berthie laughed as he tickled her stomach while Charlotta stood up and began carrying the plates away from the table.

"I'm tired," said Anna Claire suddenly, yawning and slinking down into the chair.

"You are never tired this early," Charlotta remarked, putting a plate down. "Do you feel ill?"

Anna Claire shook her head. "No, I'm just real tired, Mama."

Charlotta walked over to make sure she didn't have a fever.

"You feel fine," Charlotta breathed a sigh of relief.

"I couldn't sleep last night," said Anna Claire. "I kept thinking about Iá daxpitchée and his family. Where could they be now?"

Charlotta and Joseph looked at each other.

"Dear, you must understand that Iá daxpitchée is gone and you will not see him again," said Charlotta gently. "He is with his family and his family is taking care of him. They know safer places than here for them to be."

Anna Claire frowned. "I miss them."

Joseph stood up and walked around the table to put his hand on her shoulder.

"I know you do, Anna Claire," he said. "You have a good, kind heart like your mother. Your friends will be alright, even if they are far away."

"But his sister wasn't alright," Anna Claire choked, thinking of the round baby with the rosy cheeks, trying not to cry.

"I know," said Joseph. It was the only thing he could say. "Stand up."

Anna Claire did what he said. He then put his arms around her, enveloping her in his great, big embrace. For a few moments, Anna Claire felt safe again.

"Now go off to bed," he said. "It's late and you didn't sleep last night. The other girls will help your mama clean up tonight."

Helen and Caroline glanced over at each other, both pursing their lips in frustration but knowing they had to behave.

"Alright, Papa," Anna Claire answered, embracing her mother before walking up the ladder to the loft.

When she changed into her nightgown, she looked up at the sky. The moon looked big and full, and reminded her of an enormous stone.

Soon, Berthie came up to join her and the two stood by their little window for a while.

"Tell me about Old Man Hatfield," demanded Berthie, tugging on her sister's arm.

"Not again," sighed Anna Claire. "I always tell you that story. Let me tell you a different one to-night."

"Alwight," Berthie answered with disappointment as the two climbed into the little bed.

"Well, there once was a big dragon that lived in a forest," began Anna Claire, "and the dragon didn't like people very much. He liked to pick them up and eat them 'cause he was big and hungry."

Berthie shuddered and laughed, hiding herself under the covers.

"Well, one day there was a man who tried to come near the big dragon without gettin' eaten 'cause he wanted to tell everyone in town that he could do it. He said hello to the dragon and the dragon said nothin'. Then the man said that he wanted to be friends with the dragon, but the dragon picked him up and opened its mouth."

"Oh!" cried Berthie from under the covers. "Does he eat the man?"

"I'm gettin' to that part!" said Anna Claire in frustration. "Anyway, the man said that if the dragon didn't eat him, he would give him lots and lots of gold. More gold than the dragon had even heard of! Well, then the dragon put him back down and told him to get him the gold. The dragon knew where he lived 'cause it was right down the lane. When the man came back, he had lots and lots of gold for him. The dragon was happy until he realized he had no use for gold. So, he opened his mouth to eat the man, but the man said that if he didn't eat him, he'd give him lots and lots of fish! So, the dragon put him down. The man came back the next day with fish. But when the dragon finished the fish in just one bite, he opened his mouth to eat the man. The man said that if he didn't eat him, he could have his beautiful daughter all to himself! The dragon was very interested and dropped the man. Well, then the next day the man brought his beautiful daughter and presented her to the dragon. The dragon was happy and let the man go free, but kept his daughter imprisoned. Well, the daughter was smart. She slowly began making the dragon his suppers until he trusted her to make his supper all by herself. One day, the daughter used poisonous mushrooms for the supper and the dragon ate all of them 'cause they were so delicious. And then the dragon fell down and died because he ate the mushrooms. The daughter didn't even need another man to come and rescue her. She did it all herself 'cause she was smart and smarter than even her own father. She lived to tell everyone about the big dragon who got fooled by mushrooms."

"She didn't die?" Berthie asked, peeking her head from the covers.

"No," said Anna Claire with a smile as she bent down to kiss her sister's head. "She saved herself."

Berthie sighed with relief. "That stowy was scawy, but I still liked it."

"Just remember you can always count on yourself," reminded Anna Claire as she snuggled down into the covers. "And me, too."

***

The days came when there seemed to be more and more to do as spring was quickly turning

533

into summer. The purple bitterroot sprang up in lovely layers and the prickly pear bloomed in ruby red bulbs despite its thorns. Anna Claire enjoyed the sound of the singing meadowlarks and staring at the clouds while swimming in the creek. Charlotta was able to boil the broadleaf cattail for dinners and add linseed for flavoring, making the most out of the family meals. To add to the summer beauty, prairie snowballs emerged confidently from the sandy soil and the western wild winger opened up like a hundred gingery hearts. Sweet-scented bluebells colored the land with their bulbous, violet flowers while western spring beauty reached toward the sun in colors of white and pink.

Charlotta and Caroline spent much time mending and sewing aprons and skirts, and hemming shirttails as well as tending to their little garden and sugaring the strawberries and raspberries. They spent a good amount of time separating the cream from the milk and then churning butter, which was simply done by someone stepping on the little paddle throughout the day as they went in and out of the room. Sometimes, on the very rare occasions when Joseph was home at night, Charlotta would go into town with Nettie Clemmons and join the town's literary society. Charlotta's love of books never failed her, even when she was exhausted to the bone. This was a nice opportunity to meet some of the pioneer women, at least the ones she considered moral and suitable for her to associate with.

Everyone was very busy preparing for summer. Weaving and spinning occupied much of Charlotta's days as she turned wool into yarn, and then weaved the yarn with the loom to create fabric. Joseph was able to cleverly make a little extra money here and there by burning lumber and selling the ash to make potash. The children gathered the tomatoes in abundance, used with salt to eat stewed or stuffed.

Joseph got the family together for games of chess, the pieces made from the bottoms of corn cobs, for this had been a favorite game of his when he was a boy. Pete and Berthie could be spotted outside the house playing "graces" with their hoop. Charlotta sometimes read parts of books to everyone when she wasn't reading the Bible aloud. Helen liked to bake, and enjoyed making breads and pies in the oven while Anna Claire dried the vegetables and placed them above the fireplace. Shirts and other items of clothing were boiled before being taken out to dry on the line outside, and the floors had to constantly be washed and scrubbed. Not to mention the little outhouse outside that needed to be covered with dirt after it filled up and the structure placed elsewhere. Unfortunately, Anna Claire was responsible for seeing to it that there was some lye in the outhouse and enough corn leaves to last the week. Everyone pulled together and did what was needed to be done.

"I am very proud of you, children," said Charlotta as she put her beautiful long hair up in pins. "I cannot believe it, but you have proven yourselves worthy of going to the dance. You have behaved all week. I am very pleased."

Helen put up her nose and said smugly, "Well, I knew *I* would behave just fine. It was the little ones that I thought were gonna mess everything up."

Anna Claire finished lacing up her boots and ran over to the door.

"Let's go!" she cried anxiously. "I want to see Tommy!"

"I want to see Rebecca!" said Helen.

"I just want the apple pie," shrugged Pete as he emerged from the ladder, one boot on his foot and the other hanging from its laces in his hand.

The Freilers walked out of the cabin and out into the warm June air. Caroline stepped very daintily into the wagon while the others hopped in with chaotic loudness.

"Stop!" begged Caroline. "You're hurting my ears!"

The other children were laughing, even Helen, and talking about the excitement of the dance.

Dances were not infrequent in Bannack, but the Freilers were usually too busy to worry much about them. Besides, Charlotta often worried about the safety of the dances. But tonight, she knew some of their friends would be there and many of the good men that they knew, so she felt confident to bring her family.

"I can't wait to eat pie!" said Pete, standing up in the wagon.

"Sit down!" yelled Caroline. "You'll get yourself killed!"

"Why do you only think of pie?" asked Helen. "I want to see my friends!"

"I want to see my friends, too!" cried Anna Claire. "Tommy promised he'd be there. He better be there or I'm gonna kick him real hard when I see him!"

The wagon rolled along, the children excited and the adults possibly even more so, as it seemed to have been a long time since the last dance they had been to.

When they tied the horses and wagon to the hitching post in the back of the billiard hall, they all walked in with smiles on their faces.

Rebecca approached Helen and the two girls immediately ran to another smaller crowd of girls who were standing in the corner, looking at boys and giggling. Berthie followed Pete who ran right to the food table. Anna Claire stopped to watch the sight. And what a sight it was!

Anna Claire never forgot the feeling of all of the people, the women's colored dresses swaying against the floor and the men's boots hitting the ground with loud thuds. Her father had taken her mother into the room to dance with her, and she was staring up at him lovingly. The fiddles were playing merrily and the candles were burning brightly around the windows.

"What's the matter with you?"

"Tommy!" shouted Anna Claire, turning around sharply. "I thought I might be awful bored when I didn't see you here!"

"Well, I'm here," Tommy said flatly. "Anyway, let's dance!"

"I ain't dancin', Tommy Cooper," Anna Claire wrinkled her nose.

Tommy began laughing and grabbed her arm. "We're at a dance! Mr. Dobbins says you have to dance at a dance. And Caroline won't dance with me. I already asked her and she said no. Come on, let's dance!"

He tugged her arm and began spinning her around. Anna Claire laughed as the two ran through the crowd and started dancing ridiculously, Tommy making chicken wings out of his arms and Anna Claire spinning around him until she was nearly dizzy.

"You two are silly!" yelled one of the men good-naturedly as he danced with his wife.

Anna Claire and Tommy smiled to each other and continued to dance- or rather run around wildly- until they were both nearly sick from spinning.

"Let's go get water," said Tommy, grabbing Anna Claire's arm and running her through the crowd. As they wobbled through all of the people, they caught the eye of some of the adults. Some were amused while others were clearly annoyed with the children's behavior.

Anna Claire could not stop laughing. Her eyes filled with tears and her face was flaming red.

"I love dancin'!" she cried as Tommy poured a glass of water from the pitcher into one of the glasses.

"I can't hear you!" yelled Tommy.

"Just forget it!" said Anna Claire into his ear.

They took their water and went over to the side of the billiard hall, watching the dancing people. Charlotta was now dancing with Mr. Clemmons and Joseph was dancing with Mrs. Clemmons.

"I think we gotta tell Miss Darlin' soon," said Tommy.

"But Mr. Dobbins said we shouldn't tell her 'cause if she don't know it might hurt her, and if she does know she's not gonna want anyone else to!" said Anna Claire. "I thought we were gonna wait 'til we were older and could go back to the mountain without gettin' in trouble."

"I was thinkin' that," said Tommy, "but your ma and pa won't let you go in a hundred years. And I don't wanna go without you."

Anna Claire half-smiled at the last comment.

"I can't do it without you," Tommy went on. "But it'll be years and years and years. It'll take forever. We need to tell her now. And if she don't know the secret, then it's up to us to tell her the truth! How would you feel if someone knew a big secret about you and never told you?"

Anna Claire considered. "You're right. We gotta tell her!"

"We'll think of the right time," said Tommy. "Hey, let's go back and dance!"

The two began to laugh as they spun each other in circles again and again until they both became nauseas.

"Stop behaving like this!" yelled Caroline as she walked over and put her arm out to stop the spinning. "You're embarrassing the whole family!"

Tommy stopped immediately and put his hand through the top of his hair. "You're right. You heard her, Anna Claire."

Anna Claire rolled her eyes and pulled Tommy away from her older sister.

"Go away, Caroline!"

Caroline did, in fact, go away, and the two younger ones walked over to the side, Tommy looking around him as if someone was going to pop up right behind him.

"Now look," he said, "we might be riskin' a lot by sayin' somethin'. But this can't stay a secret. We're too young to find the gold and Miss Darlin' has a right to know who she is!"

"Maybe we should tell," Anna Claire agreed. "I guess we can tell. But can we wait for a while? I want to be prepared. Look- she's over there dancin' with that man! I don't wanna tell her now. I think maybe when we go back to school in the fall."

Tommy nodded. "Alright, we'll wait. We'll do it your way. But I ain't waitin' forever!"

The rest of the night went well. There was more dancing, fiddling, and eating treats. It was nice for everyone to get away from household chores, mining, and the daily toils of life for a while. Caroline was found dancing with another boy from school, and even Helen was asked to dance by one of the boys. Berthie stuck by Pete and the two mainly stayed by the food. Anna Claire and Tommy spun each other around in more circles until they couldn't stop laughing.

"Do you think we'll ever find Old Man Hatfield's treasure?" asked Anna Claire dreamily.

Tommy nodded. "No. I *know* we'll find it."

It was a rare moment when Charlotta had a day to herself. There was much to be done, but Caroline insisted that she wanted to keep house for the day to let Charlotta take a break. Charlotta had to admit that she had been feeling more worn down than usual and was anxiously awaiting a time when she could enjoy the beautiful Montana air without worrying about washing clothes or picking the weeds. Besides, Caroline was old enough now to be left alone to tend to the chores without being looked after.

Charlotta walked through the lovely plum milkvetch, taking in deep breaths of clear Montana Territory air and letting herself relax. She admired the caribou grazing from the distance and the heath aster with their dainty white flowers. Beautiful, mountainous scenery surrounded her and, letting herself sit on top of a blanket with an apple in her hand, some may have thought she resembled Anna Claire for a moment- sitting with her legs crossed and biting into an apple carelessly. She even felt somewhat freer than she normally did being in the open blue sky and gazing forward at the snow-capped mountains. Smiling, she thought of fond memories of girlhood with her sisters and all of the fun they had running around their yard.

She was transfixed in the moment- under the sky and the mountains- which is why she was completely startled at the sound of an unfamiliar voice.

"Are you alright?"

Charlotta looked up and her eyes went wide.

"I didn't mean to startle you," said the man, taking off his wide-brimmed hat.

He was tall, in his forties, and Black. He had a big smile and some wrinkles around his dark eyes.

"Oh, oh," fumbled Charlotta, not knowing what to say. "I didn't know anyone was out here!"

"My name's George Watson," said the man, holding out his hand, his smile bright and wide.

Charlotta was stunned. At first, she just stared up at the man. But she hastily became a proper lady again and took his hand gently. She had started standing up when he began to protest.

"Don't stand up on account of me," he said. "Do you mind if I sit a while? I'll sit over here. I haven't anyone to talk to in a long time 'cept my wife. She's a great girl, but I don't always like to worry her."

Charlotta couldn't decide if she should run or stay still. She had never actually interacted with a Black person before and she had heard terrible tales about Black men hurting and assaulting White women.

"I won't hurt you," he said, practically reading her mind.

Charlotta smiled slightly, feeling uncomfortable, but better now that he had sat a good bit away from her.

"It's a fine day," he said, looking over at the mountains. "Where are you and your family from originally?"

Charlotta swallowed and put her hands around her arms. "We- we've come from Minnesota."

"Minnesota! That's far!" said the man. "My folks and I traveled from Kentucky. Once we were freed after the war, we could go wherever we wanted to."

Charlotta felt herself growing very awkward.

"I took my family and we came out here," the man went on. "I'm glad we did. They had a lot of problems with Black folk down in Kentucky! They still have problems with Black folk here, too, but I haven't had as many death threats as down in Kentucky."

Charlotta looked at his face and studied it for the first time.

"You received death threats very often?" she asked.

The man nodded and sighed. "White folks in Kentucky don't think we should've been freed. They liked to see us pickin' their fields and servin' their suppers. I think it takes time for people to get used to ideas when they're new. Freed Blacks are new so it'll take White folks some time to get used to it."

Charlotta felt herself feeling guilty suddenly.

"I'm sorry you received death threats," she said sincerely.

"It just takes some time for people to get used to new ideas," repeated the man, still grinning in his friendly manner. "Anyway, it's much better up here. People out here in the Northwest are used to gettin' used to new- their whole lives are new! We're settlers, so nothin' is familiar. Everything is different."

Charlotta nodded. "That is surely true. Sometimes I feel as though things are *too* different here."

"I know it hasn't been easy on you womenfolk either," said the man. "My wife is havin' such a time with her garden, and not a lot of folks in town will let us come into the stores for seeds and groceries. It can be real hard to eat. But luckily, I've got a skill for huntin'." He playfully patted his rifle by his side.

Charlotta frowned. "Do they not let you in the stores?"

"Not usually," sighed the man. "But sometimes I can go into the grocery store on the other end of town past Maple Road. Usually there's two owners there and the one don't like me much, but the other one always lets me in to choose food."

Charlotta glanced over at him sympathetically. "Food can be so scarce as it is. I cannot imagine not being allowed to go to the stores. I- I'm very sorry."

"Don't be sorry," he smiled. "It ain't so bad for me! I feel worse for my wife and my daughter. I can handle bein' turned away, but I can't handle seein' them turned away. My little girl don't know anything else but bein' treated bad by White folk. I always tell her that people need to get used to the idea of us bein' free to make our own way in this country. She's only ten so she don't understand what makes the people hate her so much."

Charlotta tilted her head sympathetically. "Oh, that is awful. I am sorry for your little girl, and for your wife. I have a ten-year-old girl myself- she is one of five, and the fieriest of all of them!"

The man turned to look at her and laughed. "My name's George Watson," he repeated. "It's a pleasure to meet you."

"Yes," said Charlotta, blushing. "It is a pleasure to meet you as well. My name is Charlotta Freiler."

"Do you live far?"

"Not very, just a bit through the fields across there," Charlotta pointed to the left side. "And yourself?"

"I live on the other side of the fields close to town," George answered. "I've been huntin' in the woods over there all day, but have had no luck. I'm hopin' not to come home empty-handed tonight, but I needed a rest. I'm glad to find someone else is out here too and it's not just me!"

Charlotta laughed. "I needed a rest, too. My oldest girl is keeping house for me today. She insisted I take a few hours to rest. I thought it would be better here than at home, for the younger ones wouldn't leave me alone for a second!"

"I know that's right!" laughed George.

"It's been difficult here," sighed Charlotta. "I've missed home so much. Well, what used to be my home. My husband always wants to be a part of a great adventure, and when he heard about the rush, he just needed to try it. So here we are!"

George smiled warmly. "I've been hopin' that gettin' a little gold would give us somethin' in the world, but no luck so far."

"Neither us," answered Charlotta.

The two fell into a silence for a moment. They could hear the faint sound of a hunting dog in the distance and some birds flying above.

"Was your journey very hard?" asked Charlotta, not being able to imagine being Black in America in general let alone having to travel throughout different territories and states.

George nodded. "It was. Our little girl became sick at one point and we were worried it was somethin' serious. But she recovered faster than a horse! But it was terrible gettin' the wagons and the horses and donkeys to cross those rivers and streams. They nearly drowned! It was even harder findin' food sometimes because in certain places we didn't have much luck. But my wife is big on prayin', and she said prayers through the whole journey that we were gon' make it safe and sound. I have to say, I think God heard her prayers! We're here and that's a dream."

Charlotta smiled softly. "I am happy you and your family have made it safely."

"It wasn't easy, as you know, but well worth the trip," George turned around to look at the mountains. "See?"

"Yes..." Charlotta was a bit confused.

"Those mountains, they represent everything that America is all about," George sighed happily. "They represent climbin' your way up 'til you make it to the top. Findin' your footin' even if the climb is steep and the rocks are rugged. Knowin' that no matter who you are or what your place is in this world, that there's some hope you'll get to the top. That's the way America is now, and that's the way it's gotta be for us."

Charlotta's heart stirred. She smiled warmly and gazed up at the mountains.

"I know you have said that you have been having hard luck today. How about you and your wife and daughter come to eat with us tonight?"

George glanced over cautiously, as if she had asked him something outlandish.

"I'm not sure how your husband would feel about a few Black folk comin' to eat with his family," said George, this time not smiling.

Charlotta sighed, feeling that guilt bubble up inside of her again. "My husband will be just fine. My children will be happy to get to know you all. I would be glad, too."

George smiled his big bright smile again and nodded. "Your offer is kind, ma'am, but I couldn't ask that of you or your family."

"Please," insisted Charlotta. "We haven't had good company over in so long. My ten-year-old would probably get along well with your ten-year-old. Let me make you some dinner, at least just tonight."

George nodded. "You've talked me into it!"

Charlotta and George stood up from the ground and began walking back to the Freiler home.

"Our home is down there, I'll show you," said Charlotta. "It is very easy to find once you get to town. We aren't far away at all- scarcely a mile!"

"That shouldn't be hard," said George. "Tell you what. I'll let the wife and daughter clean up a bit and then we'll come around. Would 'round six o'clock be alright with you, ma'am?"

Charlotta nodded and smiled, her blue eyes sparkling.

"I'll do our best to get us out here in time!" said George.

"Do not fret," answered Charlotta. "We will have plenty of food. This has been a good week for us. Please do not worry if you are late."

"I'll try my best not to be," nodded George. "Thank you for your kindness. You sure looked frightened when you saw me!"

Charlotta blushed furiously, angry with herself. "I- oh, I'm sorry. I'm just not used to- well, seeing..."

"A Negro," finished George. "It's alright ma'am, you can say it."

Still blushing, Charlotta pulled her bonnet closer around her face as they reached the part of the clearing where the cabin was visible.

"That is our home," said Charlotta. "If you keep walking down and towards your left, you'll reach town quite quickly."

"If it's any trouble," said George, "do not feel bad if you must tell us to leave. I don't want your husband gettin' angry with you."

"He will be just fine," assured Charlotta with a laugh. "I am glad you're coming."

Joseph came home looking tired after the long day. It was around five o'clock, and Charlotta was running around the house cooking up a storm and seeing to it that the table was set early and perfectly.

"What do we have here?" asked Joseph as he hung his hat on the wall.

Charlotta smiled. "Joseph, I met a man today when I was taking a walk."

"Oh, don't tell me you're leavin' me for some stranger you met on a walk!" teased Joseph with a grin.

Charlotta rolled her eyes. "Joseph, he is a very nice man. He was out hunting today, but he didn't have much luck at all. We were talking about our families. He has a wife and a little girl! They came here all the way from Kentucky."

Joseph was impressed. "That sure is a long way!"

"I hope you don't mind, dear, but I invited him and his family for supper."

Joseph sighed. "I am tired and not much in the mood for company, but it sounds like the family could use one of your good home-cooked meals. I'm happy to meet them."

"Well, you'll like them very much… but…"

Joseph paused and came over to hold her head in his hands and kiss her face.

"Yes?"

"They're Black, Joseph. Not that it makes a bit of difference, but they're Black."

Joseph inhaled sharply and took a step back. Caroline and Helen were watching this conversation unfold from across the room where they were sewing.

"Why would you invite Black folks to the house?"

"Joseph, you said it yourself that it is important to be neighborly!"

"But with Blacks?" Joseph shook his head. "Charlotta, this has gone too far. You know they don't like White folks. You know they try to hurt us."

"Not George," said Charlotta firmly.

"I don't want Black folk eatin' in front of my children in my house!" shouted Joseph harshly.

"Please," pleaded Charlotta. "Just meet them. If you do not like him or his wife and little girl, we can let them go."

Joseph sighed. "I don't like this at all, Char."

"It is the neighborly thing to do," Charlotta looked over at Caroline and Helen who both had incredulous looks on their faces. "Right, girls?"

They looked from her over to their father, not knowing whose side they should be on, and nodded slowly.

Joseph sighed and kicked off his boots.

"Black people are comin' to the house?" cried Pete, running down the loft ladder and jumping down as hard as he could. "I can't wait!"

"Yes, Peter," said Charlotta as she placed down the lace napkins around the table. "And they will be our special guests. I realize I have not done my duty as a mother to teach you children right from wrong in *every* way, including the color of a person's skin. We are all children of God, and I am sorry if I led you to think any differently."

Helen closed her mouth and looked over at Caroline who looked just as confused.

"It is right to be kind and treat others as Christ would want us to," said Charlotta with a quick nod of her head. "I am sore at myself for not having more conversations about these matters. Anyhow, you will get to know George and his family tonight."

"You are right, Mama," said Caroline, standing up and walking over to her. "You are good to remind us."

"What time are they comin'?" asked Anna Claire who was climbing down the ladder. "Are there any children?"

"They have a little girl just your age!" said Charlotta with a smile. "They will be here in about an hour so we must all make sure we look nice and clean!"

Joseph said nothing, but instead glared at his wife.

The children hastily ran to the creek to fetch water while Charlotta took the liberties of making sure the outhouse smelled as good as it possibly could, all considering.

Anna Claire was happier than ever. She couldn't wait to possibly make a new friend!

It was not long after that when the Watsons arrived on foot. George wore the same shirt and trousers as he was wearing before, and his wife and daughter wore gingham dresses, although very old and tattered-looking.

Joseph walked outside cautiously, his rifle hitched to his trousers.

"Thank you for havin' us over, sir," said George, coming closer and reaching out his hand.

Joseph took his hand and shook it firmly. Suddenly he looked calmer. "Glad you're here. Hello," he said to his wife and the little girl.

His wife did not smile but looked afraid. The little girl was slightly hidden behind her mother's dress, also looking trepidatious.

"Please, do come in," said Charlotta cheerfully, motioning them with her arm at the door.

They all walked in, George smiling brightly and his wife and daughter looking around them nervously.

"Don't be afraid!" said Anna Claire loudly, causing George's wife to be startled. "There ain't nothin' to be afraid of here. Except maybe Pete because he smells bad."

"Shut up!" said the sore Pete.

Charlotta was mortified. "I am so very sorry. Anna Claire and Peter, stop this instant or you will be going to the loft!"

George laughed heartily. His wife looked around the cabin suspiciously, holding her daughter close by her side.

"Please, sit and be comfortable," said Charlotta as everyone sat down at the table, one of the little benches on the side being used to seat Berthie and Pete to make room for the guests.

"A dog!" said the little girl suddenly, smiling as Hero went up to her and began licking her face.

"He's a good dog," said Anna Claire with a smile. "Aren't you, Hero?"

"I like dogs," said the little girl, finally looking calm.

"Let me introduce myself," said Joseph, also looking calmer. "My name is Joseph. That is my wife Charlotta and these are my children, Caroline, Helen, Anna Claire, Pete, and Berthie."

"Hello," said George, nodding his head each time he looked at a child. "I am George and this is my wife, Abigail. Our daughter's name is Hope."

"It is a pleasure to meet you both," said Joseph with a friendly smile.

"Yes, we are so glad to have you," added Charlotta as she spooned the mashed potatoes onto the plate.

"Tell me about Kentucky," said Joseph. "My wife tells me that's where y'all are from?"

"Kentucky," sighed George. "Oh, bad times there. Very bad times. But we are happy to be up here in the North now! There are so many new opportunities for Hope."

Anna Claire caught Hope's eyes and smiled.

"It must have been difficult," said Joseph, clearly not knowing where to begin.

"The travels weren't easy," said George. "I was tellin' your wife today that the rivers were the worst part since they were so deep. We thought the horses would drown! But they got through it, even a part where their heads were under water."

"That's scary!" said Pete, his eyes wide. "And they didn't drown?"

"No," answered George in his friendly way. "They kept goin' right through! Frightened us and the horses."

"We had to cross a big river, too," said Pete.

"It was weal scawy," added Berthie with a nod.

"I don't doubt it," said George, taking a spoonful of applesauce. "The journeys are sometimes long and fierce, but we can't doubt in the Lord's goodness."

His wife smiled then for the first time. "That is true, George. We mustn't never take the Good Lord and all He's done for us for granted."

"Amen!" said Joseph, looking fully relaxed now.

Seeing his contented expression, Charlotta smiled to herself.

"Joseph, they have been having a much more difficult time than we," she said, looking over at George who nodded silently. "They have not been able to go to the grocery stores to get food, and they have received death threats already."

Joseph looked concerned. "I'm sorry to hear that."

"It's not so much myself I'm worried about," said George, glancing over at his wife and daughter. "It's my womenfolk here I'm frettin' over."

"Why do people want to kill you?" asked Pete, his mouth full.

Charlotta narrowed her eyes. "Peter."

"It's no trouble at all," said George. "You see, sometimes people don't like other people 'cause they might be different than they are. Myself and my family look different than other people because we're Black folk. Most people don't like that much."

"Why?" asked Berthie, her head tilted in such an innocent way.

George sighed. "Sometimes I don't know. But then I remember that it takes people some time to get used to new ideas. Black folk are no longer slaves in this country, and some people don't like it too much. But, you see, once people get used to new ideas, they tend to change their minds. Especially when they meet those people."

Charlotta glanced over at Joseph and pat her mouth with her napkin to hide her look of satisfaction.

"I think it's a real shame that people don't like you," said Helen practically.

George smiled. "We do, too." He patted his daughter's small hand.

Caroline, who had been staring at the family intently, finally broke her silence.

"Why do people think Black people are bad?"

Everything went silent for a horribly long moment. Charlotta looked sharply over at Caroline, as did everyone else. Before anything could be said, George broke out with his smile.

"Well," he said, "that's a really good question. People sometimes don't like what they don't know, because they don't know what they don't understand. Because we're different, White folks sometimes think badly of Black people, whether they got a reason to or not. Some Black folks do bad things which makes people hate them more. Other folks do bad things, too, but Black folks are already hated so it's easier to think of us all as bad."

Caroline's face went red and she stared down at her hands. "I am very sorry."

George shrugged. "It's not your fault, sweet girl! Like I said, people have to get used to things. I'm hopin' someday people will get to know more Black folk so they know that they aren't all bad. That might change things in this country."

Pete lifted his head up from his plate. "I like Blacks!"

Charlotta could not have turned redder. "Peter Freiler!"

George burst out in affectionate laughter. Soon, even his wife and daughter were laughing.

"What?" asked Pete in confusion.

Joseph shook his head.

"It sounds stupid when you say it like that," said Anna Claire bluntly.

Charlotta cleared her throat. "Anyhow, we are so glad you are here. You are always welcome."

"That's right," said Joseph confidently. "You must come here to eat again!"

The rest of the night went pleasantly well with lots of talking and laughing. His wife had become more comfortable and shyly engaged in the conversation as well. Anna Claire and Hope kept looking over at each other. When the dinner was over and everyone was talking, Anna Claire asked if she could show Hope the loft.

"Alright, but not for long," said Charlotta. "It is getting late and I'm sure our guests are getting tired. Although you are welcome to stay as long as you like!"

"That is very kind of you," said George. "Hope, go see the loft and then come back in a few minutes."

Anna Claire took her new friend by the hand excitedly and began walking up the ladder. Hope looked happy to have someone her age to talk to.

Hope was a very beautiful little girl with brown eyes that sparkled and dimples in her plump cheeks. She had her father's big, broad smile and her hair was voluptuous, two ribbons tying it from each side. She was just a bit taller than Anna Claire and a bit plumper than Anna Claire.

"This is the loft," said Anna Claire. "It isn't much, but you can see the moon from the window!"

Hope smiled and looked outside. "I can see it already!"

Anna Claire giggled. "I always wonder if some-day people will ever get to touch the moon. My sister Helen says I'm stupid for thinkin' that 'cause people can't fly."

"Well," said Hope, "people can't fly, but that don't mean somethin' else can't!"

Anna Claire's eyes went wide. "You're right! I never thought of that!"

Hope smiled as Anna Claire showed her some of Berthie's dolls.

"I hate dolls," said Anna Claire. "My sister Berthie loves them."

"I don't like dolls neither," said Hope, scrunching her face. "I don't understand the purpose for them."

Anna Claire's heart soared in her chest.

"I don't either!"

The two girls got to talking about the silliness of dolls until Charlotta called from the bottom of the ladder for them to come downstairs.

They obeyed reluctantly.

"Did you have a nice time?" asked Hope's mother.

Hope nodded and smiled back at Anna Claire. "Mama, I made a friend."

Charlotta looked over at Joseph, and George looked over at Abigail with small smiles.

"I'm awful glad to meet you!" shouted Anna Claire, giving her new friend a quick embrace.

Hope smiled and the family members said their goodbyes, Joseph telling them to come again and Charlotta stuffing their hands with corn muffins.

"It was a pleasure to meet you," said Joseph, shaking George's hand heartily.

"You as well, you as well!"

"Please come again," said Charlotta. "Anytime."

"You must come to our home as well," said Abigail with a shy smile. "We will have you over soon!"

When the families parted ways, the children waving from the door, Charlotta couldn't help but smile.

"I was right," she whispered to her husband.

Joseph grabbed her waist. "You always are."

Chapter 19- Gold Fever

It was not long before there was to be another dance in town; this time, a dance in which there was to be no children allowed. Joseph had convinced Charlotta to go with him, and Caroline was to watch the other Freiler children while they were at the dance, a chore in which Caroline was very unhappy, as she wanted so earnestly to be considered an adult.

Charlotta stood in front of the mirror getting ready. She put on her necklace and earrings, the only jewelry she had brought with her from Minnesota, and placed her hair high up above her head. She was actually happy about going to the dance. She was so tired of everything being the same routine and was anxious to get away from the isolated cabin in the field. Also, Nettie would be there with Paul, so she knew it would be a good time.

"Are you ready, dear?" asked Joseph, opening the buckskin curtain and coming to put his hand around her shoulders.

"I am," Charlotta answered, turning around to smile at her husband, who came forward to kiss her.

"Always so beautiful," he said before opening the buckskin curtain again.

"Oh, Mama, you look pretty!" said Helen, coming over to admire her mother's necklace, which she so seldom wore.

"Mama, so pwetty!" agreed Berthie.

Anna Claire knew her mother was beautiful, but she always thought she never needed jewelry to look nice.

"We are off to the dance," said Joseph, rubbing his growing beard. "I don't want to hear a bad report from Caroline about any kind of funny behavior. Do you understand?"

"Yes, Papa," the younger children said at once.

"I promise I will watch them exceedingly carefully," said Caroline, glancing over at Anna Claire and narrowing her dark eyebrows.

"I will miss you," said Charlotta to the children before Joseph grabbed her by the arm and opened the door into the warm air.

"G'bye!" yelled Pete, running after them to give Charlotta a quick kiss on the cheek.

"G'bye!" Berthie cried, waving and running to stand by the window.

Anna Claire was dreading this. Caroline would not stand for any type of imperfect behavior, and she knew she would not be able to get away with anything that night.

"Now, first, we shall read from scripture," said Caroline, walking briskly over to the little table by their parents' bed to collect the Bible.

The rest of the children walked begrudgingly over to the table. They knew that if they disobeyed Caroline, she would tell their parents and they would get into immense trouble.

"This is horrid," Helen whispered to Anna Claire, who nodded in response. For a mere second, they shared a moment, that which was shattered by Caroline's insistence that each child take turns reading from the scripture.

Caroline, black hair in her usual curls hanging down and that all-too-familiar serious look in her eyes, read first from the scripture and then passed it around. Anna Claire did not like reading the Bible- she thought most of the stories could not be fully taken literally, and everyone was so strict about it. She read her part and hated it, but she knew she had to if she did not want to get punished by her mother and father.

"Now, Mama expects us to do some of the chores, which we should do whilst she is gone," said Caroline, pursing her lips. "Helen, you get some buckets of water and begin heating them up. Peter, go tend to the animals and make sure they have plenty to eat. Anna Claire, begin cooking the chicken. Remember to pluck out the feathers first. Berthie, you will be with me. We will do some sewing."

Anna Claire rolled her eyes and went over to the bucket by the fireplace where the chicken was kept. She took it and put it on the pan on the table, beginning to pluck the feathers one by one. This seemed like such a tedious task and it took a long time for Anna Claire to clear even a side of the chicken off.

"You are entirely too slow," Caroline scoffed as she walked over to her. "Pluck faster. Then put the pan in the oven. Remember to turn it!"

"Fine," grumbled Anna Claire, plucking a bit faster but still daydreaming.

"That took you long enough," said Caroline a few minutes later with her hands on her hips as Helen brought in the second bucket of water.

"It was heavy!" yelled Helen, giving her older sister a scowl.

"Get Pete," Caroline ordered her. "He cannot possibly still be tending to those animals. They were already washed earlier today."

Helen sighed loudly and walked out of the door.

"Keep practicing that stitch!" Caroline shouted over to Berthie, who was sitting on the stool and looking dreamily out of the window. "Careful not to prick yourself!"

Anna Claire took a chair and sat by the fireplace, turning the chicken over arbitrarily with the metal spatula. She wished that Tommy would come over and save her from the boredom.

"What are you looking at?" asked Caroline, coming over to Anna Claire. "Look at the chicken! Oh, you are a hopeless case!"

"I don't care a lick!" Anna Claire couldn't help herself. She stood up and put both of her hands on her hips. "Tell Mama and Papa how bad I've been! I don't care a lick! I'm tired of you bossin' me around, Caroline Charlotta Freiler!"

Caroline's bright blue eyes widened in surprise.

"Well, I suppose you are more of a hopeless case than I had even thought you were," she said with her nose up in the air. "How can you go through life being *you*, Anna Claire?"

"It's better than bein' a jackass!" Anna Claire narrowed her eyes and pursed her lips. She looked a bit menacing, and even Caroline was put off.

"I will tell Mama and Papa what you called me!" cried Caroline dramatically as she threw the rag she was holding onto the ground. "Oh, you are a wretched, evil little girl!"

Anna Claire suppressed a smile. She knew that she had succeeded in scaring her sister.

Charlotta found herself happy at the dance. It was such a relief to be away from the isolated cabin, the work, and-yes- maybe the children just a bit. Being a mother was exhausting, but being a pioneer mother felt almost impossible.

She had the first dance with Joseph before dancing with Mr. Clemmons, Mr. O'Reilly, Mr. Grimm, and Mr. Chesham. She hadn't felt so wonderfully alive in a long time. The drinks were flowing through all the men's glasses, and the skirts of the women were swirling around and around. The man played the fiddle loudly and danced while he did it, causing it to be more spirited than it already was. However, there was a part of her that felt like something was missing.

It was the Watsons. She felt that they should be there, enjoying the liveliness and the dancing. The only reason they weren't there was that their skin was dark.

"What's the matter, Char?" Joseph asked, putting his hand around her waist.

She sighed. "Mr. and Mrs. Watson would love to go to a dance like this. They would get to know so many people! It is a wretched shame that they cannot be here."

Joseph nodded. "I agree with you, my dear, but there is nothing we can do about it."

Charlotta shook her head. "This is precisely the problem."

Before she knew it, Mr. O'Reilly grabbed her by the hand and led her to the middle of the hall. They danced for some time before Charlotta retreated to where her husband was talking with Paul and Nettie Clemmons.

The hall was lit by lamplights and the fiddles sang to the sound of dancing feet. Smiles were on most of the faces, and merriment was felt throughout the whole building. Charlotta couldn't stop thinking about the Watsons and how much fun they could be having if they were there. She considered telling Nettie, her dearest and truest friend, but even Nettie would judge her if she knew she had befriended a Black family and had let them into her house. So, she kept quiet.

"It's bleeding!" shouted Berthie from the stool. She had cut her little finger with the needle.

"I told you to be careful, Bertha," said Caroline, getting another rag from the cupboard and lightly covering Berthie's finger in it.

"He's here," said Helen, opening the door, letting Pete into the house.

"Whad'ya want me to do now?" asked Pete with a grumble.

Caroline walked over to him and licked her finger, wiping a smudge of dirt off of his face. "You should be the first to bathe after I do! Helen, bring the water buckets over here. We'll put them above the fire. Anna Claire, turn over the chicken and move it to the side. We need to make room for the buckets."

Helen watched as the water heated up into the buckets and Anna Claire finally took the pan out of the oven.

Caroline retrieved the lavender soap and proceeded to wash herself and then her siblings with rags and the heated water.

"I don't need you to wash me," said Helen. "I'm thirteen-years-old!"

"Very well," Caroline sniffed. "I do hope you know what you're doing and wash yourself correctly."

When it was Anna Claire's turn, she cringed and winced as Caroline scrubbed her body hard with the rag, practically scratching her with it. Caroline used the rag so roughly that parts of Anna Claire's body were red. Then, at the end, Caroline dunked her head in the other bucket of water and soaped her hair until she practically choked from the foaming water.

Anna Claire then ran up the ladder into the loft where she put on her nightgown. She had wanted to rest and read for a while, but Caroline called from down the stairs, "Anna Claire! Come!"

"No!" cried Anna Claire, picking up her book and hiding her face with it.

"Come here at once! You must help me set up the plates for Mama and Papa! They will surely be hungry when they get back from the dance."

Grumbling, Anna Claire threw herself out of the bed and ran down the ladder to throw the plates on the table unevenly, the spoons and forks crookedly situated around them. Almost as quickly as she came down, Anna Claire went back up to the loft and opened her book again.

"Anna Claire!" called Caroline from the bottom of the ladder. "Come down! We are going to do our teeth and I am going to brush your hair. You never get the knots out!"

Anna Claire sighed angrily and took her time coming down the ladder.

Caroline was helping Pete brush his teeth. "You must ask me before going up to the loft."

Anna Claire bit her lip. She knew she was already going to get into big trouble for calling her sister a jackass, so instead she decided to be quiet.

"Helen, let me do your hair properly!" said Caroline.

"I'm too old now!" complained Helen angrily, grabbing the brush from Caroline's hand. "I can do my own hair."

Caroline nodded as if it was her idea. "I suppose you are right. You are almost a young lady now."

Helen scowled and rolled her eyes, beginning to brush out her long, golden-brown hair around her thin, tan shoulders.

"Come," said Caroline to Anna Claire. She helped her brush her teeth, Anna Claire spitting into the bucket.

When Helen gave Caroline back the brush, she took it and began brushing through Anna Claire's knotty gold hair, brushing so hard that Anna Claire had tears in her eyes from the pain. Then, she brushed Berthie's long white-blonde hair, which was always perfect and knot-free, and kissed her on the cheek.

"The only one who has not complained is our Berthie, and she is only six," sighed Caroline reproachfully. "I am disappointed in all of you tonight! I am sure Mama and Papa will be, too, when I tell them!"

"Why?" cried Helen, coming and standing face-to-face with her sister, as she was finally as tall as she was. "I was perfectly fine! I did everything you said *and* the chores!"

"You were spoiled about it."

"That is not true, Caroline!" yelled Helen, taking the brush out of Caroline's hand again and throwing it onto the ground. "I'm going to tell Mama and Papa how you treated us tonight and see how you like that!"

"You brat!" said Caroline. "I am the oldest! I decide who does what!"

"The oldest yet the most horrid," Helen muttered, walking up the ladder.

"I heard you!"

"I don't care!" Helen shot down at her from the loft.

"I'm tiewd," said Berthie, yawning. "I want to go to sleep."

Caroline sighed. "I did want to read a few Bible verses before bed. Also, everyone must focus on their recitation and parse sentences from school. But, oh fine, everyone just go to bed. Most of you do not listen anyway."

Pete, happy to hear this, dashed up to the loft. Anna Claire was next, grabbing Pete's foot when he was trying to climb, causing him to slip.

"Anna Claire, stop!" yelled Pete, pushing her shoulder.

Anna Claire laughed as the two entered the loft, finding Helen sitting on her bed with her arms crossed.

"She is so awful!"

"I know," answered Anna Claire. "We can tell Mama and Papa the way she talked to us and made us do everything for her."

Helen nodded. "She'll be sorry!"

"Children!" yelled Caroline from downstairs. "I am going to get ready for bed! I am going behind the curtains so no one can see me!"

"We don't care!" shouted Pete as he climbed into bed.

"Stop wigglin' in your sleep," Anna Claire whispered to him. "I can't sleep when you do that."

Pete stuck out his tongue and kicked her purposefully. Anna Claire took her pillow and threw it into Pete's face, causing Pete to jump out of bed and take his own pillow and hit her across the head with it.

"You little toad!"

"Enough!" yelled Caroline. "Mama and Papa will be here at any moment. Would you like them to hear you like this?"

Anna Claire gave Pete a last push on his shoulder as they crawled back into bed. Berthie was next, holding tightly to her doll.

Not long after they were in bed and Caroline was washed, Charlotta and Joseph walked through the door with smiles on their faces.

"Did you have a lovely time?" asked Caroline, coming to take off her father's boots.

"We did," smiled Charlotta. "It was so nice to see the Clemmons's, and I talked with Mrs. O'Reilly quite a bit."

"They were bad, Mama," began Caroline, shaking her head and sighing. "Sit down and I'll tell you all about it."

"Mama, why can't Hope go to school with us?" asked Anna Claire one day.

It was the end of June and school would soon be out for the season.

Charlotta was hanging the clothes on the line outside. "It isn't safe for her to go to school with you. She would not be accepted at your school, my dear."

"Miss Darlin' would love Hope!"

"I know she would," answered Charlotta, "but it's not Miss Darling that would have the problem. It would be the board and the parents. They would not like it if a Black girl went to school with White children."

"Why?" Anna Claire was so confused. "She's smart!"

"I'm sure she's very smart," answered Charlotta, "but unfortunately many people do not care. They do not want their children to be near Black people. It is sad, but it is the way people think."

"But why, Mama?"

Charlotta said. "Remember what George said? People don't like what they don't understand. People don't understand Hope and her family yet."

"Just like Iá daxpitchée," said Anna Claire sadly.

"Yes," sighed Charlotta. "Maybe there will be a time when children like Hope and Iá- I'll say, I can't pronounce his name- can go to school with White children. It will take a long time for people to get used to the idea."

"It's not fair," said Anna Claire as she walked away.

"What's the matter?" asked Caroline, coming to her side and putting her hand on her shoulder.

"Get away from me!" yelled Anna Claire, squirming away and beginning to walk through the fields.

When Anna Claire got to school, she sat with her head in her hands and a pout on her lips. It wasn't fair that all the other children went to school and her friend wasn't allowed just because she was different than they were. She looked over at the window sadly and thought how much fun they could all have together if only Hope was there.

Miss Darling soon entered the classroom and began cheerfully lecturing. Tommy slumped in his seat just as she was getting started. Since he had spoken with her, he had not missed a single day of school, although had been late a few times.

Anna Claire looked around the classroom. She knew she may get into trouble for asking, but she had to try.

"Yes, Anna Claire?" questioned Miss Darling.

Anna Claire cleared her throat and took a deep breath. "I have a friend. Her name is Hope. She's

Black. Can't she come to school? My mama says she can't 'cause people won't like it, but you wouldn't mind, right, Miss Darlin'?"

Lucia Darling stopped short as the rest of the class began muttering to each other.

"Well," she began, her eyes soft, "to answer your question, I would not mind. I would not mind at all. Black children deserve as much of an education as anyone else!"

The class was silent. Some of the older boys began laughing quietly while some of the girls' faces were shocked. No one said anything for some time.

"Well, maybe Hope can come and meet everyone and then she can go to school!" said Anna Claire happily. "My mama says the board won't like it or the townsfolk. But you wouldn't mind! I know you wouldn't, Miss Darlin'!"

Miss Darling sighed, looking at a loss for words. "Of course, I wouldn't. But it isn't all up to me. It can be dangerous for a Black person to go against what the townspeople want. I would welcome her in school with open arms, but that could be dangerous for your friend."

Miss Darling looked a bit angry for a moment, as if she also was sick and tired of the townspeople.

Anna Claire sighed, feeling disappointed.

"Why did you say that?" whispered Helen, tapping her shoulder from behind her. "You could've gotten us into a lot of trouble! No one should know we talk to Black people."

Anna Claire shrugged and frowned. "I was only sayin' the truth. And you heard Miss Darlin'! She would if she could."

"Girls," warned Miss Darling with narrowed eyes.

They stopped speaking at once and looked into their books. Anna Claire looked back at Tommy, who was sounding out the words in the book.

"Who's Hope?" asked Tommy outside during their break as everyone ate their dinners.

"My new friend," said Anna Claire proudly.

"How d'ya meet her?"

"My mama met her father when she was takin' a walk and they started talkin' so she invited his family over. I met him, his wife, and Hope. Hope's my age. She's ten, too."

"Is she nice?"

"Nice! Is she ever! She's the nicest girl I ever met! And she's smart and hates dolls, too!"

Tommy laughed. "Well, you don't like her better than me though, right?"

Anna Claire smiled. "I don't think I could like anyone as much as I like you, Tommy Cooper. But for a girl, Hope is pie!"

Tommy looked over at Caroline, who was eating her sandwich daintily on the stairs with her feet crossed.

"Stop lookin' at my sister!" Anna Claire forced his face to the side with her hands.

"Gee, I can't help it," said Tommy dreamily. "She's the prettiest girl in the whole wide world!"

"Oh, you would say that, wouldn't you? Hope is real pretty, too. I wish she could go to school with us. She would love it. She's smart and likes to learn. Hope might come again in a couple of weeks to eat with us, and then we might even go to her house to eat with her family. Papa wasn't sure he was gonna like them 'cause he said that Black people are usually bad, but he does like them! Mama was right. She knew we'd all like them once we got to know them."

"I'd like to meet her!" Tommy exclaimed.

"I'll tell you when she's comin' over and then you can come to eat with us," said Anna Claire with resolve. She couldn't wait for her two good friends to meet each other. "Just don't call her that word! The one Ebb Drummond said!"

Tommy shuddered. "That's not a nice word. I'll never say that again."

Anna Claire smiled, glancing up at the clouds. "Maybe Hope will wanna go to the creek with us. We'll have to show her, Tommy. Hope will love it!"

Tommy nodded. "Fine. But we ain't tellin' her about Old Man Hatfield!"

Anna Claire frowned. "Well, why not?"

"It's a secret, remember?" asked Tommy, clearly agitated. "I'm sure Hope is nice, but the treasure is between us and Mr. Dobbins. We can't risk anyone else knowin' or anyone else tellin' Miss Darlin'."

Anna Claire sighed. "You're right. Just in case. But maybe when the treasure is found, we can tell her!"

"Not until the treasure is found," Tommy reiterated.

Charlotta had been over the Watson's some number of times to drop off baked goods. She felt sorry when she saw their little shanty and barely any food on their table, and she made it her mission to feed them when she could.

Nettie Clemmons was growing suspicious, as Charlotta didn't come to tea as often as she had before, but Charlotta did not want Nettie to know she was seeing the Watsons. She knew Nettie would not approve and may, in fact, judge her for it, as kind of a woman as she was.

It was a very hot day when the Watsons came over for supper again. The children had done their chores early in the morning, as they were excited to see the Watsons. They didn't have company often, and the Watsons were nice people.

Anna Claire had told Tommy to come over that night, and, although unexpected, Charlotta allowed him to stay for supper.

"I wish you would have told me," she said as she began preparing the fish. "I love when Tommy comes, but we almost didn't have enough food with the Watsons coming! It is a good thing we are able to provide enough."

"Yes, Mama," answered Anna Claire. "I'll tell you next time, I swear!"

"Do not swear!" reprimanded Charlotta. "You may promise, but do not swear."

Anna Claire nodded.

"Anna Claire, you look dirty," snapped Caroline as she went up to her face with a rag. "Let me wash your face."

"No!" said Anna Claire, squirming away.

"Let her help," said Charlotta sternly.

Anna Claire sighed unhappily and allowed Caroline to scrub her face with the rag.

"Can we go to the creek?" asked Anna Claire. "Not for long! I just want Hope to see!"

Charlotta shook her head. "It is up to her parents."

Tommy and Pete burst through the door, Pete laughing loudly at something Tommy said.

"You think I can do it, Tommy?"

"' Course, Pete. I'd bet money that you'd win a horse race!"

Pete's face shone. He loved it when Tommy paid special attention to him and thought Tommy was the bravest older boy in the world.

"When Hope's here, we can go to the creek!" yelled Anna Claire enthusiastically.

"*After* supper," Charlotta reminded her.

It was only a couple of hours later when the Watsons arrived on foot to the Freiler cabin.

"Hey!" called George, coming to shake Joseph's hand.

"Nice to see you!" said Joseph sincerely, also shaking hands with Abigail.

"Hope!" yelled Anna Claire, running out of the house to hug her new friend.

Hope smiled shyly and glanced over at Tommy with wide eyes.

"This is Tommy," said Anna Claire. "He's my best friend. This is Hope!"

Tommy held out his hand and Hope took it hesitantly.

"Well, now you finally met each other," Anna Claire said as the families went into the cabin. "We can all be good friends now!"

Hope's dark hair was in two big braids and she wore an old cotton dress, a shaded blue. She had a deep, sad look in her eyes, but when she smiled, her whole face lit up.

"I do hope you like fish," said Charlotta, a worried look crossing her face.

"I love fish," George answered as everyone sat down.

Charlotta placed the fish on the plates while Caroline brought out the fluffy, hot bread.

"Let us say grace," said Charlotta when they had come to sit down.

During the prayer, Anna Claire snuck looks at Hope and they smiled at each other.

"I'm awful hungry!" yelled Pete, picking the fish up with his hands.

"Can I give it to Hewo?" asked Berthie, looking hopefully at the dog.

Charlotta pursed her lips. "You will not give your food to Hero. You will eat your supper tonight."

Berthie stuck out her bottom lip and sulked.

"This is delicious," said George, nodding in pleasure at how good the food was. "Joseph, your wife can really cook!"

"I know it!" said Joseph with a laugh. "I married her for some reason!"

"Joseph!" Charlotta shook her head.

"Mama is the best cook," said Berthie, slowly taking a bite of the fish. "I don't like to eat, but I'll eat it if Mama makes it."

"I don't blame you, child," George said with a smile. "Abigail is a wonderful cook, too. Next time, you will all have to come to our house! Granted, the house ain't big, but we'll make room for all of you!"

Charlotta looked up and smiled. "That would be lovely. Thank you, Mr. Watson."

"No more 'Mr. Watson,'" said George. "Call me 'George.'"

"As long as you start calling me 'Charlotta!'"

George nodded and everyone ate. Caroline was staring at the Watsons, clearly curious about their differences, and Helen was looking at her hands.

After supper, the adults sat at the table to chat.

"Mama, Mr. Watson, Mrs. Watson," said Anna Claire, "can I show Hope the creek? It's real close! It's right down there! She'll love it. It's real nice."

George glanced at his wife who nodded.

"Stay close, Hope," he said sternly. "Come back soon."

"Those children love that creek!" said Joseph as the children headed out the door.

The three of them skipped along, laughing and chatting, all the way to the creek.

"It's nice!" agreed Hope, looking around her at the tall, thin trees and the magpies fluttering over their heads.

"It's too cold to swim today," said Tommy, "but maybe next time! You'll have to come swimmin' with us soon."

"I'd like that," said Hope with a smile.

"Where ya from?" asked Tommy as they sat down, not caring about the dirt underneath them.

"Kentucky," Hope said slowly.

"Gee, that's real far!" said Tommy.

Hope looked at the ground before saying, "It was a really long trip, but we had to leave. Our owners wanted to make us stay, but they treated us badly so Papa said we had to get far away from Kentucky. We left in the middle of the night when the owners were sleepin'. Papa said they don't own us anymore, but they still were tryin' to keep us. We weren't sure if they were gonna find us. Either way, it was a risk, Papa said. 'Cause if we got caught and the owners found us, we would get a bad beating. One time they beat me so bad I almost lost my eye! Mama mended it, though. If we stayed there, we would still get beat and possibly die. Papa said the best thing to do was to escape."

Anna Claire was stunned. She looked over at Tommy, whose blue eyes were wide and his jaw open.

"We had to run on foot for a while until Papa was able to get a wagon with horses. It took a long time though because no one wanted to help us. Papa had to use every penny he had gotten from the own-ers for food, and it wasn't much. We had to be real careful and never speak of the owners. We would tell people that we were freed and let go. It was a lie but we had to lie, otherwise they'd send us back and we wouldn't be able to leave again. Papa said it was our only chance at a life. We were awful sore and hungry, but Mama was good at cookin' vegetables and leaves. It's all we had. When we finally got the wagon, we were able to travel, but no one was very nice. One of the men tried to hurt Papa when he saw him on the wagon and started throwing rocks at him. Another time, a mean man with a black beard came up with his wagon and tried to crash into it to make it fall. Oh, Papa was so mad! But we kept goin'. We didn't have a lot to eat 'cause we didn't have no money for food so we always had to stay where there was water nearby. Papa was good at catching fish. Once, the native people helped us. They saw we were hungry and cold so they gave us fur coats and buffalo meat. It was good! We were nice and warm for a while, until someone stole the coats from our wagon a few days later. Papa said that some of the Yankees didn't want to fight for us to be free, but only so they can take advantage. Even in the North, it's dangerous. We still can't get a lot of food 'cause no one wants to let us in the stores. Sometimes they do, dependin' on who's workin' there. Mama said that if it wasn't for Papa, we'd starve to death. Papa's real good at huntin'. I don't understand why we're not allowed in the stores. We didn't do nothin' wrong and we never stole nothin', not even from the owners. Papa always says people don't like change and don't want Black folk to be free. I don't understand why not, but Mama says it's because we were free labor. But I always wondered why it was only us and not the Whites, too?"

Anna Claire and Tommy were stunned. They didn't know what to say. Finally, Anna Claire rested her hand on Hope's.

"That sounds scary," she said, "but now you have friends! We can help with food. Papa knows everyone and they all like him. And Tommy steals candy from the saloon all the time!"

Hope's eyes went wide. "And you never got caught stealin'?"

Tommy laughed. "I live there! Ma sees me steal sometimes, but she usually don't care. She don't care about nothin'."

"I can't believe how many people tried to hurt you," whispered Anna Claire sadly.

"That wasn't half of it!" exclaimed Hope, looking at the ground and playing with a stick. "When we were with the owners, Papa got sick and couldn't work one week and every day they whipped him. Once, their daughter offered me food and I ate it, but the owners didn't like that so they gave me a beatin' I never forgot! That's back when I was eight. One time, the owners got awful mad at us 'cause they thought we weren't workin' hard enough and made us watch a hangin'. One of our friends stole somethin' from the owners- I think it was bread- and they hung him. I didn't like seein' him get hung 'cause he was real nice."

Anna Claire and Tommy both shuddered.

"We saw a hangin', too," said Tommy.

"It was scary," said Anna Claire. "But it must have been so much worse for you since he was your friend! We didn't know the man who got hung."

Hope nodded sadly, holding herself with her arms.

"When do you think people will start seein' us as just like them?" she asked, looking out at the water. "I know we're Black folk, but we're still human. Just like everyone else."

Tommy and Anna Claire looked at her and then at each other, at a loss for what to say.

"I don't know," jumped in Tommy, "but once people get to know ya, they'll like ya! We just gotta get people to know ya."

"No one wants to know us," said Hope, making a little hole with the stick. "We can't go nowhere. They don't want us to go in stores or the billiard hall or the saloons."

"Come to my saloon," Tommy said. "My ma works there. I'll tell her to talk to Mr. Swiner. He owns the place. If she asks him, he might say yes."

Hope nodded. "Maybe he will."

"When do you think we'll see you again, since you can't go to school?" asked Anna Claire.

"Will your mama and papa let me come over to play?" she asked, her eyes hopeful.

"I'm sure they will!" replied Anna Claire. "Let's go tell them."

The three children ran through the trees and back to the cabin.

"Well, there you are!" said George with his big smile.

"Mama, Papa, can Hope come back over to play?" asked Anna Claire, out of breath.

The adults smiled at each other and nodded.

"Hope is welcome anytime," said Joseph sincerely.

The children grinned at each other.

"Can Hope come by tomorrow?" asked Anna Claire.

Abigail Watson smiled. "Tomorrow, Hope is going to help me with the garden. Maybe the day after, if that is alright with Mr. and Mrs. Freiler?"

Charlotta and Joseph nodded at each other.

"I think that's a splendid idea!" agreed Charlotta, taking Hope's hands. "I am glad Anna Claire has a friend like you."

Hope smiled happily and took her mother's hand as they went out the door. George grabbed his hat from the nail on the wall and bowed his head to Joseph. Everyone waved as they walked across the field, Anna Claire waving the hardest.

"She's nice," said Caroline, as if surprised.

"She's a lovely girl," Charlotta agreed. "It is a shame she cannot go to school with you all."

Anna Claire frowned and turned to her father.

"Do you think Hope will ever be able to go to school?"

Joseph sighed. "No, my girl. No, I don't."

Chapter 20- Ghosts and Gamblers

Life that summer appeared to be eventful that year, and the family seemed to have grown even closer. Montana Territory was as beautiful as ever, as the clear water sparkled around them and the little animals slowly emerged again. People in town were jollier, and there was an overall feeling of festivity in the air, not unlike a holiday.

Anna Claire and Tommy were enjoying playing games in the fields and swimming in the creek again. There was a lot of laughter at the Freiler's home, and Charlotta and Joseph seemed to be in peaceful states. Summer had begun in a happy fashion, as the Freilers had produced a small but successful truck-patch where they grew pumpkins, squashes, and potatoes. Charlotta brought the girls to quilting bees, and the younger children had fun sliding down the haystacks in the barn.

Montana Territory bloomed with mushrooms, wildflowers, elderberries, and white yarrow. The sloping hills burst with plants and wildlife, animals and produce, and intervals of earth enriched by spilling water. The meadows were dewy again and covered with soft grass and river bottoms. Animals came out of their respective caves and homes, emerging to join the beauty of nature. Even the sagebrush along Grasshopper Creek seemed to come alive with the touch of summer. All was well for a while in Gold Country.

"Let's go to the loft!" said Anna Claire one day to Tommy after playing in the creek.

The two had come back to the house and were the only ones there. Charlotta had taken Berthie to town to go shopping, Helen was spending time with Rebecca at the Clemmons's house, Pete was out hunting with Joseph, and Caroline had gone on a walk. Anna Claire was excited to be by herself and happy that no one would be asking her to do chores or bothering her.

"I like the loft," said Tommy, coming to the left of the ladder and walking around the buckskin hides that separated Anna Claire's side from Caroline and Helen's. "It's even bigger than my room!"

"Not by much," said Anna Claire, climbing on the bed and jumping on it. "Come on, it's fun!"

"Won't we ruin it?" asked Tommy cautiously.

Anna Claire shrugged. "I don't care. We can always get more hay. Jump with me!"

Tommy did as she asked, and the two hooted and hollered for quite a long time until Anna Claire lost her balance and fell to the side of the bed.

"Are you alright, Anna Claire?" asked Tommy, coming to her side and crouching down.

Anna Claire nodded and began to laugh. "My backside hurts, but it was awful funny!"

The two laughed and began to jump on the bed again until they heard the ominous voice of Caroline shouting from the ladder. She had returned from her walk.

"Stop that foolishness now!" she called. "I could hear you before I even came into the house!"

Anna Claire put her hands over her mouth to keep from laughing out loud. Then she and Tommy slowly crept down from the bed. Anna Claire went over to her dresser and picked up a book called *Peter and the Elf*.

"You should read this next," said Anna Claire. "Pete thinks this book is about him, but the Peter in this book is much smarter than Pete. You'll love it 'cause there's this one part of the story where the boy Peter almost gets eaten by a wolf!"

"Really?" Tommy gently took the book from her hand and skimmed over the red cover with his hands, his fingers tracing the engraved lettering.

"What are you children doing up there?" yelled Caroline from down the loft. "You had better not be touching my things! I don't want to come up there after you!"

"I don't care a lick about your things!" yelled Anna Claire saucily. "Leave us alone!"

"I shall not, not if you will speak to me in that manner!"

"Let's go say hello," said Tommy eagerly, practically skipping across the floor.

As usual, his face dropped and his eyes grew bigger when he saw Caroline, who was sitting in the chair already knitting.

"Hi there," he said, feeling dizzy. She looked so pretty in her bonnet!

"Hello," sighed Caroline politely but with irritation.

Anna Claire thudded down the ladder loudly and ran to the table, pushing Caroline with her hands so that the chair nearly tipped over.

"Anna Claire!" she shouted, putting her hands out in front of her. "Stop it! Oh, stop it, you wretched little girl! Wait until I tell Mama on you."

"Go ahead," Anna Claire shrugged. "I don't care!"

Caroline shook her head and fixed her curls back around the bonnet.

"You look real pretty, Caroline," said Tommy, dizzy with affection.

Caroline rolled her eyes. "Can you children please let me knit?"

Anna Claire grabbed Tommy's hand and flew out of the door.

"She still don't like me," sighed Tommy when they were safely outside.

"She don't like anyone!" said Anna Claire. "Do you have the book? Good. Let's go into town and find Mr. Dobbins."

The two walked off across the field, the sun beating pleasantly down on their little faces as a warm breeze rolled through. They talked about silly little things children often talk about, things that don't mean all that much unless one is a child, such as what type of candy was their favorite and which child in school brought the best dinners. By the time they had reached the town, they had talked so much that they were worn out.

"Mr. Dobbins!" said Tommy happily, pointing to the plump, gray-haired man on the other side of the street.

"Mr. Dobbins! Mr. Dobbins!" shouted Anna Claire as loudly as she could.

Mr. Dobbins, newspaper in hand, turned around to smile and wave at the children, who ran to him eagerly.

"Mr. Dobbins!" yelled Anna Claire, out-of-breath. "We've been meanin' to have a word with you!"

Mr. Dobbins's eyes twinkled in amusement. "A word, huh? What could that be about?"

They strolled along the street, Anna Claire pulling at Mr. Dobbins's sleeve. "Do you believe in ghosts?"

Mr. Dobbins laughed now, his wide-brimmed hat nearly falling off of his head. "Ghosts, huh? Well, sure, I do."

Tommy's eyes went wide and Anna Claire's mouth dropped open.

"Have you seen one?" Tommy asked.

Mr. Dobbins nodded. "I swear I did. When I was a young boy, not much older than you, I went out to feed the cows late at night. My pa had died real young so I had to do all the man's work in the house. When I went to the barn, I heard a weird creakin' sorta noise. I looked to where the sound was comin' from but I didn't see nothin'. I went about my business and did the feedin' and then when I turned around, I seen it. It was a figure, all dark but outlined in the brightest blue light you'd ever seen. He was just standin' there lookin' at me. Didn't say a word. Scared me so much I nearly threw the lantern on the ground! I sure as day saw that man. I even remember his eyes bein' real sad and a pipe stuck in his mouth. I yelled and yelled and couldn't move for a while and then he was just gone. He plum disappeared. My brother went to check on me 'cause I was screamin' so loud. He thought I was dumb 'cause he didn't see nothin', but I know what I saw, youngins. No one believed me. But not even a week later, I saw that man again. This time I was upstairs and he was near the tree next to the window. He kept on starin' into space, smokin' that pipe of his. But I blinked and he was gone then, too. I didn't see that man no more and never saw him again."

"That's scary!" said Anna Claire.

"Well, you wanna know the scariest part?"

Anna Claire and Tommy both nodded eagerly as they turned the corner towards Swiner's Saloon.

"I found out about a year later by someone my pa used to know who still came over to check up on my ma that some man had died not even a mile away from us, before I was even born. He used to smoke a pipe and died when he lit a bunch a' hay by accident. Burnt down his whole farm, he did. He went up in flames and smoke right with it. I know that was that there man I used to see."

Anna Claire shivered with delightful fright. "What else did you see, Mr. Dobbins?"

"Well," he said with a pause. "I confess that's just about the only ghost I reckon I ever saw- at least that I know of- but I do believe they are as real as you and me. My ma's seen 'em, my brother and sister seen 'em, and I have a lot of friends who seen 'em, too. Now I know that your mama and papa wouldn't be too happy with me tellin' you that story, little miss," he nodded at Anna Claire, "but you asked me and I wasn't gonna lie."

"I'm glad you didn't lie," said Anna Claire. "I want to see a ghost! Do you think Old Man Hatfield is a ghost?"

"Oh, here we go again with that," laughed Mr. Dobbins.

"If he's a ghost, maybe we can talk to him!" reasoned Tommy.

"You don't really talk to ghosts," answered Mr. Dobbins pensively. "You can look at them and sometimes they'll look at you if they notice you, but they usually don't speak. At least from what I heard everyone say."

Anna Claire and Tommy looked at each other as they entered the saloon, Kathleen Cooper there with her big red smile and her big red hair.

"You children want some bread? Just made it!"

Anna Claire nodded, and Tommy shook his head.

"You don't look so good," said Anna Claire to Tommy. "You just stopped talkin'!"

Tommy shook his head again, not wanting to explain why the sight of his mother was becoming more and more difficult to bear. "I'm fine."

Mr. Dobbins noticed this change also, but had more of an idea what was really going on. He then pat Tommy on the back. "You look like you're gettin' taller to me!"

This cheered Tommy up. "I think I am!"

Anna Claire giggled. "You always think you're gettin' taller!"

"Well, Mr. Dobbins sees it, right, Mr. Dobbins?"

The older gentleman smiled and nodded as Kathleen came back with the plate of bread and a knife along with a smaller plate of butter.

"Bread with butter!" said Anna Claire. "We haven't had butter in a long time!"

"Well, eat up," said Kathleen with a wink, putting an arm on Mr. Dobbins's shoulder. To Tommy, she added, "Stay out of my way tonight. I got me some company. Stay in your room."

Tommy didn't look up from the plate of bread. He merely nodded in embarrassment.

"Why don't she like it when you're around company?" asked Anna Claire.

Tommy shrugged. "I don't know. She thinks I'm a pest and don't want me botherin' no one."

Anna Claire caught the expression on Mr. Dobbins's face as he pursed his lips and his eyes went soft.

"You don't bother no one," he said, patting his hand on Tommy's back. "You know your ma. She's one helluva interesting lady! She don't mean no harm. You know your ma."

Tommy nodded, but still did not smile.

Anna Claire caught the sadness in his eyes and realized that there was more sorrow in Tommy than she had ever noticed before.

"I wish you didn't have to stay here," she whispered to him. "I wish you could come home with me and sleep there like on Christmas."

"My ma said I can't do that no more," said Tommy sadly. "She said it makes her look bad if I don't sleep at home. But she also don't want me knockin' on her door or botherin' her neither."

Anna Claire reached out and touched his shoulder. "I'm awful sorry, Tommy. She sounds like she can be real mean to you."

"Well," shrugged Tommy, "she could be worse."

Anna Claire figured that was true but she still felt badly for her friend.

The three pals ate the bread and butter before Mr. Dobbins was off to do some fishing.

"Can you come for supper?" asked Anna Claire, looking at Tommy before heading out the door. "I'm sure Mama won't mind. She loves you, ya know!"

Tommy looked back at his mother, who was watching him closely with her hand on her hip.

"Can't," he said, looking at the ground. "Ma probably wants me to help her today 'cause we're gettin' big company."

Anna Claire was disappointed. "Alright. Well, I guess I'll see ya!"

"Guess so," answered Tommy flatly, turning around without saying another word.

Anna Claire walked home feeling confused and down-trodden. She knew Tommy got sad sometimes, but she never saw him look quite the way he did that day in the saloon- like his whole heart was breaking.

Joseph became more and more disappointed with every day. He had days where he found enough gold dust to get the family through a week or even more. Sometimes, he could even buy little treats like butter and coffee. Yet, most of the time, he worked for hand-to-mouth living. Sometimes, regretfully, he stopped into a saloon to gamble on one or more occasions, making a little more gold dust and sometimes losing more than he made. This was a bad habit for which he was trying to compensate by gambling more to make more, although this rarely worked. He soon realized he needed to stop or he would inevitably destroy himself and his family.

He was grateful to have the days when he could work with his friends, and was even more grateful that he was able to find anything at all, but his dreams of striking it rich were becoming less and less real to him. He dreamed of buying his wife the fanciest dress in town and of buying his children anything they asked for, but he was beginning to realize that this lofty hope might never actually come true.

Day in and day out, Joseph mined. July was prime mining weather and he spent most of the days outside in the sun, sluicing and panning and hoping to see more than just shreds of gold. Many days later on, he would go hunting instead and it would never be certain whether he would retrieve game or not. Most of the time he did- he was an excellent shot- but other times he could not find the animals.

Charlotta was overwhelmed with chores day in and day out. She looked forward to those very brief moments where she would have some time to read in bed or even to walk to Nettie Clemmons's house for tea. Now that it was summer, she could more easily travel across the field. However, Berthie had been getting stomach aches for weeks and she did not want to leave her alone. The Watsons came again and they also had the Freilers over another time as well. These times were nice for everyone, but both families were very busy, and their houses were not close by each other.

Besides, there was always so much for Charlotta to do. There was planting and tending to the little garden, helping to feed and care for the animals, churning the butter, making soap, fetching water from the creek, scrubbing the windows, canning fruit, cooking vegetables, hemming clothes, and washing boots. Just as one chore ended, another one would be waiting for her. She was used to chores- she had grown up with them- but life in Montana Territory seemed packed with endless chores, chores that she could never fully catch up with.

The children were invaluable on the little farm. They helped to cook, clean, and tend to the animals, and rarely did they complain. Even Helen, who always complained, was beginning to mature and complete the work without much of a fuss. Caroline, prim and dainty, did not care for the hard labor that was a huge part of the work, but she learned to do it the best she could dutifully. Pete was learning much from his father and was already catching game and bringing home big fish. Berthie stayed close to her mother and learned from her, but she was often getting sick or wounded. Every fall she took, she bruised up her arms and legs or cut herself easily on a thorn or the edge of a chair. Her stomach hurt much of the time, especially after eating, and many times she would be very tired or her throat would hurt. Berthie had always been a sensitive child and Joseph had bought every medicine he possibly could from town to keep in the house for those tougher days.

The children all did well on their oral exam at the end of the year, although Anna Claire nearly did not pass her arithmetic portion. Anna Claire strangely missed school, as it was over for the year now, but was happy to play with Tommy and Hope. The three of them had a strong connection, and Anna Claire and Tommy debated if they should tell Hope their big secret.

"I don't know, Anna Claire," Tommy hesitated. "We don't want anyone knowin'!"

"Well, who is she gonna tell?" reasoned Anna Claire. "She can't even go to school!"

Tommy considered. "That's true. Oh, well, we might as well tell her so long as she don't tell her parents. They might not let her play with us anymore."

So that is what the children did.

"We gotta tell you a secret," Tommy said at the creek one day, Anna Claire and Hope taking off their boots to get into the water.

"A secret?" asked Hope, her eyes wide. "What kind of secret?"

Anna Claire and Tommy glanced at each other and nodded.

"Tell her the story, Tommy," said Anna Claire, urging him with a nod of her head. "Go on, tell her!"

"Alright, alright, I'm gettin' there! Alright, Hope, you just gotta listen real carefully. It's a long story so you gotta be ready for it. It'll really surprise you, now."

Tommy told the story of Old Man Hatfield from beginning to end, and then both he and Anna Claire told her how they had tried to climb up the mountain for gold, but only found a man's dead body instead.

"You climbed all the way up a mountain?" Hope asked in awe, truly impressed.

"We sure did," Anna Claire answered. "It wasn't like what we thought it'd be and we didn't bring enough food or water. And it was too hot. And we didn't really know where we were goin'."

"We were younger than," said Tommy with a shake of his head. "That was last year!"

Hope nodded, her eyes big.

"When do you think you're gonna tell your teacher that she's Daisy's baby?" she asked.

Anna Claire sighed and took off her dress, dipping her body into the creek.

"I don't know," she answered. "We were thinkin' of tellin' her soon, but what do you think?"

Hope shrugged. "I guess you should. I would wanna know if I was her."

"That's exactly what I told Anna Claire!" shouted Tommy. "If I was a child of the woman who ran away from her father and killed herself on account of his death, I'd wanna know."

Anna Claire nodded. "We're thinkin' of tryin' to tell her this year. I reckon now we really should."

Hope nodded. "That story; it's real interesting. Do you think it's true?"

Anna Claire and Tommy stared at her. They never actually sat down to really think this all the way through.

"'Course it's true," said Tommy. "Everyone is always talkin' about it. Anyhow, Mr. Dobbins was here long before any of us and he would know!"

Hope nodded again, wading in the water and looking at the top of the trees.

"Y'all think maybe 'Darlin'' wasn't the baby's name, but just somethin' Daisy called her?"

Tommy grinned. "Nah, Darlin' was her name! Mr. Dobbins said so."

Hope shrugged.

"It *is* an odd name to be a first name," said Anna Claire. "I always thought Darlin' was the last name."

"It has to be," nodded Tommy. "That's why it's gotta be Miss Darlin'!"

"Can I help you find the gold someday when y'all go back to the mountain?" asked Hope as she stopped swimming and came over to sit on the grass.

Tommy and Anna Claire glanced over at each other, neither of them knowing how to respond to the question.

"We won't be able to go for years probably," said Anna Claire. "When we're older and we won't get in trouble for goin' again. But, hey, if you're still in Gold Country- well, maybe you could come, too. Right, Tommy?"

Tommy sighed and twisted his mouth in thought. Then he raised up his chin and smiled. "Yeah! Then we'll find it faster and we can all split it up!"

"What would you do with the gold?" Anna Claire asked their new friend.

Hope grinned. "I would buy all the stores and the school so that the White people couldn't keep us from goin' inside them anymore."

"That's a perfect idea," said Anna Claire.

Tommy jumped into the creek, splashing them in their faces and making them laugh.

"Either way, I'll tell ya one thing," said Tommy, lifting his head out of the water, his brown hair sleeked back. "I'm never gonna stop 'til I find that gold."

Chapter 21- Fourth of July

"I am ever so excited!" cried Caroline on the Fourth of July, fixing her big black curls around her face.

"You just want to meet another boy," hissed Helen, using the pencil to curl her brown hair.

"Helen," scolded Charlotta, shaking her head. "We will have a grand time, indeed! Oh, where is Peter?"

"Right here!" called the little boy, running down the ladder with his good pair of overalls on.

"Very good," smiled Charlotta, placing her boots on her feet.

"I got a feelin' there's gonna be food!" said Joseph as he came around the table and tickled Berthie.

Berthie laughed and held out her arms to be picked up.

"Anna Claire!" cried Charlotta, glancing over to see the middle child lying on the ground, her feet in the air, watching the ceiling as if transfixed by it.

"Oh, my goodness, Anna Claire! Get up!" yelled Caroline, her dress swishing around her as she walked over.

Anna Claire plopped her feet down loudly on the floor and yawned.

"You're going to get your dress all dirty!" yelled Charlotta, coming over and helping her up.

In fact, getting the dress dirty was the entire point of why Anna Claire was sitting on the floor.

"I don't want to wear this!" she said. "Why can't I wear overalls like Pete?"

"Because you're a girl!" said Helen matter-of-factly. Over the summer, Helen had grown considerably and was now an entire foot above Anna Claire. She was even taller than both her mother and Caroline.

"Precisely," agreed Caroline as she applied rouge to her cheeks. "Girls don't wear overalls."

"Well, why not?" asked Anna Claire, a question for which no one had a direct answer.

Anna Claire tugged at her knee-length maroon calico, hating the itchy feeling around her neck.

Joseph got the horses ready as Charlotta and the children went outside in the hot summer sun. Charlotta, in a good mood, sat down in the wagon and kissed the side of her husband's head.

"Are we all ready?" she asked happily, her blue eyes sparkling.

"Yes!" said Peter and Berthie at the same time.

"Sure," Helen rolled her eyes and crossed her arms.

"It shall be lovely!" said Caroline, taking out her little mirror and admiring her reflection.

"I got it!" yelled Anna Claire, grabbing the mirror from her hands and pretending to throw it onto the ground.

"Mama, she's trying to throw my mirror out of the wagon!" yelled Caroline in a high-pitched shriek, falling over Anna Claire to grab it. "Give it back immediately!"

Anna Claire laughed before throwing the mirror into Caroline's lap.

"You are a horrible little girl!" yelled the oldest Freiler child, turning her head away from her.

Anna Claire smiled to herself, satisfied that she was able to get a rise out of her sister.

The wagon rolled on for a short while until they reached the outskirts of town. Joseph tied the horses behind the billiard and everyone jumped down.

"Happy Fourth of July!" exclaimed Paul Clemmons, shaking hands with Joseph and nodding at Charlotta.

"And to you!" said Joseph with a big smile, his arm around Anna Claire.

"I think there's goin' to be a pie eatin' contest later," Paul said, eyeing Pete. "You should try it!"

"I love pie!" declared Pete, licking his lips.

"Hey, it's Tommy!" cried Anna Claire, turning her head and waving at her friend, who was running through all of the happy people in the street. "Please, please, can I go?"

Charlotta smiled. "Don't get your dress dirty, Anna Claire."

Anna Claire waved goodbye to her and her father before running towards Tommy, right through the middle of the parade, nearly getting hit by a horse.

Tommy's mouth was already stained with chocolate, and his chestnut-brown hair was ruffled around his face.

"Tommy!" cried Anna Claire, jumping toward him, her sweet tooth getting the better of her. "Where dy'a get the chocolate?"

"Mr. Blake is givin' it out!" cried Tommy, grabbing Anna Claire's arm and pulling her to the grocery store, where little chocolate morsels were being handed to the children.

As the two of them ate their chocolate, they sat on the steps for a few moments, watching the crowds of people. There were so many people that it was hard to see. Men, women, and children were walking through the street, wearing their best attire. All of the stores had their doors open, people bustling in and out of them hastily, and everyone was giddy.

"You wanna look up ladies' dresses with me?" asked Tommy mischievously.

Anna Claire pouted. "Nah. Not today."

"What's wrong with you?" Tommy plopped another piece of chocolate in his mouth.

"I hate Helen and Caroline," she answered. "They're awful! They are stupid and awful and terrible!"   "Well, ignore 'em," said Tommy plainly, eating the last piece of his chocolate.

"Easy for you to say," Anna Claire said. "You don't have to live with them!"

Tommy sighed. "Well, let's have fun. We don't gotta be with them now."

The two stood up and ran around the town, laughing as they bumped into people.

"Tommy!" cried Anna Claire, laughing so hard she was coughing. "Wait for me!"

Tommy shouted as he bumped into a man and watched his hat fall to the ground, the man grumbling angrily.

The two children laughed as they reached the end of the road.

"Look, there's where they're havin' the pie contest," said Tommy. "Wanna watch people get sick?" "Yes!" agreed Anna Claire heartily.

The two sat on the side in the dirt, Anna Claire's dress getting covered with mud and hay.

"I want apple pie," mused Tommy. "Maybe I can steal some."

"Let's," agreed Anna Claire. "I haven't had apple pie in so long! Mama hasn't made it in a while. Pie is my favorite thing in the whole world!"

"My ma makes real good apple pie," Tommy said. "She don't make it much, but it's real good."

"Why does your ma have so many friends who are men?" Anna Claire asked in confusion.

Tommy shrugged. "I don't know. I know they give her money to be their friend, though."

"I wish people would pay me to be their friend! Would you pay me to be your friend, Tommy?"

"I don't gotta," said Tommy. "You'd be my friend either way!"

Anna Claire nodded. "I suppose so."

"This town has gotten so big since the gold rush," said Tommy. "There's so many people here now! It used to be quiet 'round here. There wasn't no town here when I was real small."

"I liked it at the mining camps better than our house," said Anna Claire. "It was so excitin'! There were all these men, and they all told ghost stories, and all the children were naughty like me, and we played games all day long!"

"Sounds like a good time."

"It was," agreed Anna Claire. "It was the greatest! Mama and Caroline didn't like it, but me and Pete liked it."

"Pete's funny," said Tommy. "You gotta bug on your face!" He placed his finger and flicked the little beetle off of her forehead.

"Thanks!" she said, before sighing and glancing over. "I wish we could go find the treasure now."

"I told ya, when we're a little older and we're allowed to go to the mountain. If we get caught like last time, I'll never see you because you'll be stuck in your house forever!"

Anna Claire nodded. "I know. I want to find this treasure. We *are* gonna find it though someday, right?"

"'Course we are."

"I can't wait 'til we tell Miss Darlin'," Anna Claire's eyes lit up. "She'll be so surprised! And then she'll love us even more when we give her some of the treasure!"

"She might be sad, too," reflected Tommy. "The fact that her mother killed herself and she was taken to a city far away! She might be awful sore about it."

Anna Claire played with the string on her boot. "I can't wait 'til we tell everyone. They'll know we're heroes! We solved the mystery!"

"Now we wait," said Tommy.

They sat in silence for a moment, when Anna Claire stated, "I wish Hope could come to town."

"She would love it," mused Tommy, frowning. "All of the cookies and candy and pie! And all of the people!"

They both sighed and thought of their friend, who was alone with her parents down through the other side of the fields.

"I can't believe I've lived here for over a year and I'm gonna be eleven next month!" said Anna Claire cheerfully. "Then we'll be the same age!"

"Only for a couple months," scoffed Tommy. "Hey look, it's Mr. Dobbins!"

The two children shot up from the stairs and ran through the street to greet their friend, who bent down to hug them.

"Happy Fourth of July, youngins!" he said, clapping their backs with his hand.

"They gave out chocolate, Mr. Dobbins!" yelled Tommy.

"I can see that on your face," he laughed. "And look at you, little miss. You look nice!"

Anna Claire shuddered. "I hate dresses. Mama made me wear it."

"Anna Claire hates dresses," Tommy said very seriously.

"Well, now I guess I can understand that," said Mr. Dobbins with a smile. "Have you two been gettin' yourselves in any trouble today?"

Anna Claire and Tommy looked at each other, smiling.

"No. We just bumped into people on purpose," said Anna Claire.

"Oh golly," Mr. Dobbins shook his head. "Well, I suppose it's better than other things."

"Do you know where we can find apple pie?" asked Tommy, standing on his toes and looking around him.

"Follow me." Mr. Dobbins led the children over to the bakery. He went up to the front, bought two small pieces of apple pie, and handed them to the children.

"Oh, thank you, Mr. Dobbins!" Anna Claire exclaimed.

"Well, now, where's my money? You gotta pay me, 'course!"

Tommy and Anna Claire looked at each other.

"But we don't have any money, Mr. Dobbins!" said Anna Claire, her face falling.

Mr. Dobbins laughed and scuffed their hair. "I'm jokin', youngins. What you *could* do is tell me who won the pie contest?"

"We don't know," said Tommy. "We left before it ended. It wasn't as fun as we thought."

"It was boring," seconded Anna Claire.

"I guess it *is* boring to watch other people eat pie if you can't eat it yourself," said Mr. Dobbins with a smile.   The three of them wandered around the streets for a while, watching auctions and seeing the reenactment of the Declaration of Independence in which some of the townsmen played the roles of the founding fathers, including Mr. Grimm. Anna Claire found her mother at the store buying a new China teacup and saw her father talking with a big group of men, his laughter loud and booming. Anna Claire smiled. She loved it when her father laughed- it made her feel safe.

The three of them entered Swiner's Saloon, where they greeted Kathleen.

"Want me to sneak you some whiskey?" asked Tommy to Anna Claire.

Anna Claire shook her head. "That was disgusting!"

"No whiskey," said Mr. Dobbins firmly. "Not for either of ya! I'm gonna go to the counter and have a drink now. You youngins be good!"

Tommy and Anna Claire escaped the crowd by running upstairs and into Tommy's room.

"Are you ever gonna take these stupid pictures down?" asked Anna Claire, looking at the posters of the scantily-clad painted ladies.

"Why would I? They're beautiful!"

Anna Claire scrunched her face and sat on the ground. Tommy sat in front of her, and the two crossed their legs.

"I wish we had more pie," said Tommy, "but it was nice of Mr. Dobbins to buy it for us."

Anna Claire nodded. "And we got chocolate!"

Tommy smiled. "Yeah!"

"I can't wait until Hope can come," sighed Anna Claire. "Maybe next year!"

"I told her that they could come to the saloon, but I ain't seen them yet," frowned Tommy. "I don't know why."

"I think it might still be dangerous for them," said Anna Claire. "Even goin' into town is dangerous, let alone goin' in a saloon."

"Yeah," sighed Tommy.

The two were quiet for a moment when they heard a loud noise coming from under the window. They stood up to look outside, where a crowd of people were laughing at a frightening-looking clown.

"I'm tired," said Anna Claire, yawning. "I need to find Mama and Papa soon or they'll never let me come back."

"See ya," said Tommy. "I gotta go help my ma."

"See ya," answered Anna Claire as she left the room and hopped down the stairs.

She glanced over at Kathleen, whose red lips were even more red than usual and whose red hair was out of a bun and spilling over her large chest.

When the Freiler family all found each other, they went through a few stores, Joseph purchasing some coffee and butter, until it was time for the fireworks.

"Maybe Tommy'll let me watch them from his window," said Anna Claire. "I'll be able to see 'em better."

"We don't care, just go!" yelled Helen.

"You may go if you care to," said Charlotta. "Not for very long. Come back after the fireworks."

Before Charlotta could finish her sentence, Anna Claire ran down the street and around the corner to the next street, where Swiner's Saloon was. She was disappointed when Kathleen informed her that Tommy was going to be busy behind the bar helping her serve drinks. Anna Claire saw him momentarily and waved at him, but Tommy didn't see her because of the crowd.

The fireworks had begun, but instead of sitting with her family, Anna Claire sat in front of the saloon, her head in her hands. When it was over, the Freilers left town happily and jumped into the wagon, each telling each other fun stories of the day. Anna Claire felt glum. She suddenly missed Tommy. Why couldn't she live with him in the saloon and eat candy all day?

"What's the matter, dear?" asked Charlotta when she noticed Anna Claire still sitting in the wagon when everyone had gotten up.

Anna Claire shrugged. She didn't know what was wrong. She just wished she was in town with her best friend Tommy, laughing at people and talking about gold. She suddenly felt very lonely.

Charlotta took her hand and walked into the house before bending down and kissing her cheek. "I love you, my girl."

"I love you, too, Mama," answered Anna Claire.

She walked into the house forlornly, scuffing her boots through the door. Hero greeted her as she walked in, her bending down and Hero licking her face.

"What's the matter with you?" asked Pete, coming from behind her. "Didn't you have fun?"

Anna Claire shrugged and walked over to the window.

"I wonder where Iá daxpitchée is now," she said softly.

Caroline and Charlotta looked over at her and Charlotta came by her side sympathetically.

"I am sure he is safe with his family," she said, squeezing Anna Claire's shoulders. "You mustn't think about it much anymore, dear. It will only cause you pain! Trust in the Lord that your friend is where he is meant to be right now, for whatever reason that is."

Anna Claire sighed and continued staring out of the window. She watched as her father and Pete went outside to go hunting, her father wearing his chaps and his gumboots and Pete with his trousers.

"I wish I was a boy so I could go huntin'," said Anna Claire out loud. "It ain't fair that I can't just 'cause I'm a girl! It don't make no sense, does it, Mama?"

Charlotta sighed and gave Anna Claire an amused but firm look. "It does make sense, Anna Claire."

"How come?"

"God made man and woman for different reasons," said Charlotta. "God made men to work hard and provide food for the family. God made women to help men and serve them in the household."

"What if I don't wanna help no man?" said Anna Claire as she sat down at the table.

Charlotta sighed again and shook her head at the ceiling. "Anna Claire, you must not say things like that. That is very naughty."

Anna Claire closed her mouth, but she had so many more questions. What was so different about girls than boys? Why were boys considered stronger and smarter? Why couldn't she, too, learn the tricks and trade of the men? Why was it her brother that got to go outside and fish and hunt and learn about animals while she was stuck indoors learning how to sew? It just seemed so unfair.

She went into the kitchen with her sisters to help prepare the food for that night's supper. Charlotta was happy to have calf's foot jelly, as this was a rare treat, as well as carrots and beans. Anna Claire had a hard time concentrating. She wanted to finish making dinner so that she could run to the creek.

"You're so dirty, Anna Claire!" yelled Helen, scrunching her face. "Mama, Anna Claire stinks! Can't she bathe tonight?"

Charlotta paused. "That may not be a terrible idea. It is almost time for our baths anyway. We should all bathe tonight after supper. Helen, begin getting the water from the well."

Helen sighed, not realizing the consequence of her request, and reached down to obtain one of the little wooden buckets.

The girls prepared supper and then set the table, waiting for their father and Pete to return. When they came home with a moose on the back of the horse, they sat down and ate before Charlotta got to work skinning the moose.

Joseph stood up suddenly and grabbed Anna Claire's hand.

"What is it, Papa?"

Joseph smiled. "Come with me."

Anna Claire, happy to oblige, followed him out into the warm night air.

When Anna Claire looked over at him, she noticed he brought out his rifle.

"I think I oughta teach you a thing or two about this rifle and shootin'," he said with a twinkle in his eyes, bringing the rifle closer to Anna Claire and putting it in her hands. "Now, see here," he said, bending down to her height and moving her arms and hands where they needed to be. "That's right. You gotta always make sure it's in there. When you see your target, you always want to check just to make sure you're right and you're not shootin' anyone who doesn't need to be shot. Now, focus and aim. Take this and push this here. Then lift your shoulder up. Yes, like that. Good. Now don't get too stiff! Loosen your body. There. There! Perfect! I couldn't pose better myself. Now you'd pull and aim. That's it. Just like that. Dang, I reckon you could shoot as well as Pete."

Anna Claire's face brightened and she smiled widely.

"Thank you for teachin' me, Papa," she said. "Can I go huntin' with you and Pete?"

Joseph sighed but smiled. "Maybe. Sure, once can't hurt."

Anna Claire was elated.

"Oh, thank you, Papa!" she leapt into his arms and buried her face in his chest. "I won't disappoint you, Papa!"

"I know you won't," he said, affectionately, ruffling her hair with his hand. "Now go inside and help your mama!"

Anna Claire nodded, still smiling, and skipped inside happily. Her father had taught her how to use the rifle and- better yet- he was going to let her go hunting with him! This day had been a good day after all.

After she helped Charlotta skin the moose and wash the dishes, they all had their baths. When the baths had ended, she ran up the ladder naked to get into her nightgown.

"Shameful, Anna Claire!" cried Caroline from the keg.

"Anna Claire!" yelled Charlotta in surprise.

"I forgot to bring my nightgown down!" Anna Claire answered, going to the end of her bed and throwing it on. She was still floating in the clouds about the possibility of going hunting.

"Let us read the Bible," said Charlotta when Anna Claire had come down, everyone in their nightgowns.

Anna Claire didn't mind that night. She sat at the table and held Hero in her lap, the dog grunting and kissing her cheek. She looked around her at the sight of her family- her beautiful mother holding the Bible upright and proper while reading, her father sitting with his foot on his other knee, staring at Charlotta as if she was a fairy from another land. She looked over at Caroline, whose pale face was illuminated by the candles and her usual stern look soft with awe. She watched Helen, originally looking bored and unhappy, now look serene, her long brown hair in two braids down her back. Looking beside her, she saw Pete who- not able to pay much attention to the Bible- was now letting the dog lick his face and laughing quietly to himself, his golden hair shining and his whole face lighting up. She looked across from her at Berthie, who had come over to sit in their mother's lap. Berthie was sitting still, a solemn expression on her face and a soft look in her big brown eyes. She looked like a small angel sitting there all bright and attentive.

Anna Claire was so happy! She knew her papa didn't treat her like the others did. Her father understood her and knew what she could do. Her siblings were there and, although as annoying as they were, Anna Claire still thought they all looked so nice on that night, the candlelight flickering on their faces and their eyes calm and glad. This feeling bubbled up inside of her, and she went to bed that night very proud and very happy.

"You know what, Berthie?" Anna Claire said as they climbed into bed.

"What?" she yawned, her voice tired.

"I just love you so much," she whispered, her heart feeling full.

Giving her a kiss on her cheek, Anna Claire tucked her little sister in first before getting into bed herself.

"I love you, Anna Claiwe!" said Berthie before falling asleep into dream world.

Chapter 22- El Dorado

On a beautiful August day, Joseph let Anna Claire come along to watch him pan for gold. This was thrilling for Anna Claire, as she wanted nothing more than to be a part of the excitement. She was allowed to pan a bit herself and was absolutely delighted. She had always enjoyed watching Joseph do anything, but panning for gold- it was beyond her wildest hopes.

And so they went, Joseph with his leather breeches and his belt from which held a hunting knife, and Anna Claire carrying the shot pouch.

"See here?" her father said, bending down and pointing into the sluice box. "All that dust there is gold!"

Anna Claire's eyes sparkled, and she hopped into the air.

"You found us some gold dust!" said Joseph happily, grabbing his daughter closer to him and kissing her on the top of her forehead. "Looks like you found enough dust to last us at least a week!"

Anna Claire gushed with pride. She bent lower to see the gold dust as her father scraped it into his buckskin poke.

"How do we know when we're rich?" she asked, taking the pick and digging into the pebbly bedrock.

Joseph smiled. "That is a good question. Well now, it depends. To really be rich, we'd need just about a few pounds of gold nuggets. I reckon about that. That would give us some money to last a long time. What we usually do out here is try to separate the loose gold from the dirt and all this gravel here."

Anna Claire wet her hands in the water and kept placer mining. She had a lot of youthful energy, and Joseph was actually glad to have her there working hard by his side, even if she was small and light.

They worked for quite a while until Joseph said, "Well, now, that might be all the gold we're gonna get today."

Anna Claire frowned. "But I wanted to find more!"

"I know," sighed Joseph. "Me, too. But it's almost suppertime now. And didn't I promise you that I'd let you go huntin' with me one day?"

Anna Claire's heart soared. "Today!? You wanna take me today!?"

"Only if you're ready," said Joseph with that familiar twinkle in his eye.

"I am, Papa!" she declared, hopping up into the air again.

Joseph smiled, ruffled her hair, and they walked two miles home.

When they got there, Anna Claire and Joseph drank some water before Anna Claire changed into a different dress, an older dress where it did not matter if it got dirtier. She then allowed her mother to put her hair into two short pigtail braids before she was ready to go hunting in the great outdoors.

Charlotta herself was not very fond of the idea, and she begged Joseph to be extra wary for her. As the two of them headed out of the door into the sunshine, she called out, "Don't let Anna Claire shoot by herself!"

"I'll be right by her side!" yelled Joseph with a laugh.

The two of them rode through the fields for a very long time while Joseph told Anna Claire all about hunting with his six brothers and how much fun they used to have camping out at night.

"Can we stay out in the timber tonight?" asked Anna Claire eagerly.

"No, darlin'," said Joseph, patting her back. "That wouldn't be safe tonight. Plus, we didn't bring nothin' with us to do all that! But maybe we can someday."

Anna Claire was a bit disappointed that they could not spend the night camping amongst the wild animals, but cheered up when her father bent down and said, "Look!"

Anna Claire looked through the trees. There, in all its glory, was an elk.

"Do as I told you," said Joseph quickly, the two jumping off of the horse, putting the rifle in her hand. "Remember to bend! Yes, like that. Up more. Alright, now!"

The first shot did not go so well and it only scared the elk away.

"Don't be sore," said Joseph. "This was only your first try. Do you know how long it took me to kill?"

"No, Papa!"

"It took me four separate times goin' huntin'!" exclaimed Joseph.

Anna Claire's eyes went wide. "Really?"

Joseph nodded. "That's right! I wasn't much younger than you, either. It's tough. We'll try again."

The two kept on walking through the woods, slowly and as quietly as they could. It took a while but after some time, they spotted a deer grazing on some of the leaves.

"I can do it, Papa," Anna Claire whispered, taking the rifle from her hand. Bending down and stretching out her leg, she aimed the rifle right at the deer, took a deep breath, and shot.

"Anna Claire!" shouted Joseph in surprise. "You did it!"

The deer had gone down immediately. Anna Claire felt a bit sad for the deer. But she grew happy when she realized she had hunted all on her own, not even needing her father to aim for her.

"I did it, Papa!" she cried, jumping up and down in circles. "I did it! I got 'em!"

Joseph was as surprised as she was. "You- you certainly did, my girl. Let's get this one home! We're havin' veal tonight!"

They were both elated and Anna Claire had never been so proud of herself.

Joseph went to the deer, pat its head as if to apologize, and said a prayer silently in his head. "All God's life is precious, Anna Claire. God made animals for us to eat, but we still must respect them."

Anna Claire nodded somberly, her eyes wide. Then, she helped her father get the deer onto the horse. Anna Claire was allowed to ride the horse with the deer on the back while her father walked beside her.

"Mama will be so proud!" she gleamed, her eyes shining in the bright sun as she moved up and down on the horse. "I did it, Papa!"

Joseph looked at his middle child with fondness. He couldn't believe that his little daughter, who was nearly as small and light as a feather, had successfully aimed, shot, and killed their supper for the week. "You did it. You really did it."

It was approximately a week after Anna Claire went with Joseph to watch him pan for gold and go hunting when the unthinkable occurred.

One day, when Joseph came home with the happiest grin on his face and a look of pride unlike any other, Charlotta's heart dropped and she ran to embrace him. The children, perplexed, watched them questioningly until Caroline dropped her handkerchief and went to hug Joseph, too. That is when she explained that Joseph had managed to strike extremely nearly impossibly lucky- he had found a pretty good chunk of gold while panning down the creek. That was the day he and Paul Clemmons decided to go panning together, and they had both found great sources of the rich mineral.

Things went quickly after that. Joseph got his gold weighed at the Assay office and turned it into money. Although it was not as much as some panners were rumored to have made, it was more money than the Freilers ever dreamed they would have. It was enough to significantly change their lives if they spent it wisely. The whole family was very proud of Joseph and Joseph, and despite his shame for being unable to fight for the Union, he was extremely proud of himself. Anna Claire thought her father was a true hero and, upon finding out the news, wanted to race to town to tell Tommy, but her parents made her wait. Word was not supposed to get out, for finding gold could be very dangerous business.

The summer ended with a huge victory. Joseph had done the very thing he said he would. He had struck gold, and plenty of it! The final amount came to over $5,000 for both the Freilers and the Clemmons' each. The Freilers wouldn't have enough to buy a steamboat, but they certainly had enough to get themselves out of the poor house and save for their children's education. They then had high hopes that perhaps Peter would go to college, for he was a bright young boy and the only male child.

The family didn't tell anyone about the gold except for the Clemmons's, who had been there with them. Then only Mr. Grimm, Mr. Chesham, and Mr. O'Reilly knew about their success, and were even given money themselves to get by with Joseph's insistence that they take something because they had helped him so much in Gold Country. The families celebrated at the Clemmons's barn, and all of their children had new clothing, which Charlotta managed to buy quietly.

The cellar and kitchen were full of food and goodies now. Charlotta had plenty of French onion seed for flavoring the chicken and turkey, syrup, dried fruit such as apples, raisins, and peaches, and sacks of flour to make breads and pies. Joseph even spoiled himself with Natural Leaf Tobacco, a treat he only caved in to on rare occasions, and Charlotta was able to receive paints for the chairs, turpentine for soap, table linens, and some lovely perfume.

Caroline finally got a string of pearls around her neck that she had always wanted. Helen was able to get a beautiful new cap for the winter, and Pete got a painted puppet. Berthie had a new porcelain China doll, and Anna Claire was allowed to have a new book. Joseph had bought Charlotta the fancy boots she had been eyeing in the store, and bought himself a big coat to take with him on those dark nights when he was hunting and it was cold. Those were the treats allotted to each family member. Now that they had a little fun, the rest of the money would be saved and put in a savings fund until the Freiler parents figured out what they were going to do with all of that money. They knew the danger of this spreading word all over town and they knew they had to keep this a secret until things in and around Gold Country became safer.

***

Anna Claire turned eleven in August, and she was allowed to pick out ingredients to make a very big and tasty cake for her birthday. Later in the week, Tommy was even given a new pair of boots, and Hope and her family were provided with food, medicine, and materials for clothing. They didn't know about the gold, for Joseph was careful not to discuss that with anyone besides his family and some of his friends, but thought that Joseph just got lucky with a little extra. Joseph thought about possibly building a nicer and larger house, but that would signal to everyone that they had gold, which could put the family in danger. They did not know what to do because if they bought nice things, the people would know that they had money, so Charlotta bought fabrics secretly by going into different stores and wearing two different bonnets each time. Joseph quietly bought food from the town and himself a new rifle to hunt with.

Unfortunately for Anna Claire, her mother made her a beautiful yellow dress with a ribbon around the waist and ribbons around the sleeves. Along with the insultingly yellow dress, she bought her a matching bow. Anna Claire thought it was the most horrid thing she had ever laid her eyes on, but Charlotta insisted she wear it for special occasions.

Anna Claire was dying to tell Tommy about their amazing streak of luck. One day, a couple of weeks after Joseph had made his discovery, she promised that if she could go into town, she would not tell Tommy. Anna Claire promised sincerely that she would not tell Tommy anything about finding gold, right before running off to town to tell Tommy the astonishing news.

Tommy was sweeping the floors when Anna Claire burst through the swinging doors, her eyes wide and her mouth open in a smile.

"Where have you been? Tommy, I need to tell you somethin'!"

"Go away," he said, pushing her away with his hand.

Anna Claire's face dropped. "What's wrong with you?"

Tommy sighed and slowly walked over. He leaned down and whispered in her ear. "I ain't allowed to go outside no more. Ma told me she wants me to help her here now."

Anna Claire looked around at the saloon, which only held a couple of men.

"That's no fun, Tommy," she said with a frown. "Why's your ma makin' you do all that stuff?"Tommy shrugged. "I don't know. But that's why I haven't been comin' over. I've been busy here." He continued sweeping the floor as Kathleen walked through the doors in the back of the saloon. Upon seeing Anna Claire, her face brightened.

"Tommy, why don't you take a break?" she said. "Go play with your little Anny-Claire friend."

Tommy dropped his broom and smiled. Anna Claire grabbed his hand and the two ran out of the saloon, walking along the dirt street.

"I need to yell you somethin'"", said Anna Claire, motioning him to walk up the hill and down one of the little roads out of town, the one that led to the graves.

"Well, what is it then?" asked Tommy, his face browned from the sun.

Anna Claire made him sit down at the top of the little hill overlooking the cemetery before talking.

"You're sure actin' funny," said Tommy suspiciously.

Anna Claire's smile widened.

"But you gotta tell nobody!"

Tommy rolled his eyes. "Alright, alright, just tell me!"

Anna Claire lowered her head and looked around her before whispering in his ear, "My papa struck gold." "Gold!" yelled Tommy loudly, nearly falling backward.

Anna Claire motioned for him to stop.

"Shut up, shut up! No one can know! Remember? The Road Agents?"

Tommy quickly looked around him to make sure no one could overhear their conversation.

"Yes," he said, shaking his head. "I won't tell nobody. Anna Claire, you know what this means?"

"I'm rich?" she answered innocently.

"More than that," said Tommy. "We could take some of the money and get new shovels to go to the mountain and get the gold!"

Anna Claire laughed. "We can't do that. Shovels ain't gonna do that and you know it."

Tommy nodded. He really just wanted to have another adventure with Anna Claire, but he decided not to tell her that.

"I knew Papa would do it!" Anna Claire went on. "Mama wasn't sure, but I knew he would do it!"

"What are you gonna do with all that money when you can't use it?"

Anna Claire thought about it. "I don't know, but we're gonna save it now. My mama and papa want to help Pete go to college, but I think he's too dumb to go. I wish I was a boy so they could save up for me to go to college!"

"Or we can buy all the chocolate in town!" mused Tommy.

"Mama and Papa won't let me do that!" said

Anna Claire. "But I promise I'll try to buy you some chocolate."

"Gee, thanks!"

The two talked for a while before Anna Claire had to head back home.

"Now, remember what Mr. Dobbins talked about," said Tommy, lowering his voice.

"Don't tell nobody about the gold," finished Anna Claire.

"That's right," Tommy smiled. "Gee, I'm awful happy he struck it rich. It's hard to believe, but you're rich now, Anna Claire!"

Anna Claire smiled, but then cringed. She wasn't sure how much she liked the sound of that now that she thought about it. She remembered seeing the fancy family in town that one day and shuddered. She never wanted money or gold to change her into someone who was pretentious or stuck-up.

"I won't tell," she said. "By the way, that don't change nothin' about me, Tommy Cooper! I can still fish and swim and run better than you! This don't change nothin'."

Tommy shook his head. "No, but it does mean you're a rich girl now."

Anna Claire wanted to protest, but realized he was right. She *was* a rich girl now. What would that mean for her? What would that mean for her friendship with Tommy?

"I'm not gonna change," she reiterated, looking straight into his eyes.

Tommy shrugged. "Well, I'm happy for ya. I am!"

Anna Claire waved goodbye, made Tommy swear not to tell anyone about the gold again, and ran off back to the cabin. She realized that she was no longer a "poor" pioneer girl. She was one of the lucky ones, one of the little girls whose father struck it remarkably rich and would benefit greatly from this providence.

"I ain't any different," she told herself as she walked home.

That night, she couldn't fall asleep. She was thinking of all the wonderful books she'd be able to read soon, now that the family had money. Sneaking by the ladder to listen to Charlotta and Joseph talk, she leaned over and closed her eyes. "Charlotta,   I know," Joseph was saying. "I just think leavin' here is a mistake."

"A mistake! Joseph, you promised."

"I promised we'd leave if it got more dangerous, and it hasn't! Look at the Fourth of July! Not one thing happened and everybody was in town!"

"I know, Joseph, but what are we going do with all that money just sitting there and no bank to put it in? What if the house burns down and we lose it? We won't be able to do anything! We'll have to live poor for the rest of our lives since it's too dangerous to have money here!"

Joseph sighed. "I think this place is gonna be safer. The Vigilantes are gettin' stronger. I think we got a nice home and a nice town that the children can grow up in. We have friends here, Charlotta!"

Anna Claire could tell by her voice that her mother was crying.

"Alright," she said softly. "We will stay. On one condition! If it gets more dangerous, you won't fight me on it. We shall go."

Joseph sighed and began pacing. "Alright, Char." Anna Claire quickly leaned back and ran to the bed and under her covers. The thought of leaving Gold Country was terrible and made her feel sick to her stomach. They couldn't leave! Not ever. This was her home.

Joseph was exhausted as he left town one night. The drug store had just closed, and he had picked up some White Pine Compound for Berthie, who had come down with another cold. It was a warm September night and there was just beginning to feel a chill in the air in Gold Country. Joseph could not wait to get home, have supper with his family, and get into his warm bed.

He began walking up the trail from the town, the town lights shining down. He was thinking about what he would buy Charlotta as a surprise gift when he suddenly felt a large pressure on his back and a painful weight on the back of his head. In a mere second, he had fallen to the ground in one big swoop. Before he knew what he was doing, he was calling out and flailing his arms in the air. He could hardly see among the chests of his attackers, but he saw them- two big, strong men pounding him from above his head, yelling and grunting.

Joseph grabbed whatever he could in front of him, which was the collar of one of the attackers, until he felt a pair of hands around his neck and a punch to the nose. His body fought back as blood poured from his face. He began feeling dizzy and falling unconscious. The attackers beat him full force and just as Joseph felt as though his pain would make him faint, he felt the relief of the attackers rise from around him and the sound of yelling and shouting out. Joseph could vaguely make out the voice of Mr. Clemmons and Mr. Chesham angrily swearing as they began punching the attackers, screaming that they would kill them. He heard the sound of thuds and knocks until he was aware that his friends were by his side, lifting his head and wiping blood from his nose.

"Get him up!" said the voice of Mr. Chesham, grabbing his legs as Mr. Clemmons grabbed his shoulders.

Joseph's face hurt too much to open his eyes, but he was aware of the yelling and the pain as he was being carried down the road. He did not know what was going on, but he knew his friends were by his side and they had scared away his attackers. Everything suddenly became black as he passed out and fell limp.

Joseph was taken to Mr. Chesham's cabin due to its closeness to town. While there, Joseph could hear the sound of Mrs. Chesham crying out and tending to him with water and a soft rag. He was aware that he had started to groan in pain and everything hurt, from his head down to his knees. He had been injured- and badly, at that.

"You're gonna be alright, Joseph," said the voice of Mr. Clemmons. "We took them down. They're gone now- they got away. I don't know where they went, but they got the hell on out of there."

Joseph found it hard to breathe. He tasted

blood in his mouth, and his eye stung when he tried to open it. Mrs. Chesham continued to treat him with water before putting something smooth over his wounds, making them feel raw. It felt like mere minutes but it was over an hour later when his wife came to the Chesham's cabin.

He could hear Charlotta crying beside him, her hand holding his.

"You're alright now," she said gently over and over again. "You're alright."

He tried to open his eyes, but all he could see was the top of the cabin, dim with candlelight, before everything went dark and he fell asleep.

It had been nine days since the attack. Anna Claire did not want to leave the house, although school was now in session and her parents were urging her to go. Joseph had been recovering quite quickly, all things considered. His nose was a bit more crooked in the middle and he had bruises all over his body, but most of the swelling had gone down.

Anna Claire was horrified and frightened. She didn't want to leave her father's side, where she had stayed for those nine days, helping her mother and sisters tend to him. Pete and Berthie helped by bringing water and doing some of his chores that he couldn't do. Pete also started hunting more and was bringing in the game- as much as he could, which was not a whole lot yet, except for small animals, but enough to keep some food on the table.

Tommy had come to the door once and Anna Claire explained that her papa was sick and she needed to help him. She was told not to get into too many details with anyone just yet, so she didn't explain the whole horrible event to her friend yet. She was eventually forced to go to school in October. It was the last thing she wanted to do, but she had to do it.

She was glum the first couple of weeks, even though Tommy did his best to make his friend laugh, including getting himself in trouble by standing on his desk- but it was no use. Anna Claire felt awful for her father and her family.

Miss Darling understood, as Charlotta had brought her a basket of wildflowers and cornbread while explaining to her what was happening at the Freiler home, and one day, when she saw Anna Claire crying during lunch, she let her leave school early.

Tommy knew something was very wrong with his friend. Anna Claire didn't cry often at all. She just didn't. It wasn't something she did unless she was extremely distraught. Grabbing some candy from the saloon one day, ignoring his mother when she told him to "get back here and help me clean these durn dishes," he ran to the Freiler's house, on a mission to visit his favorite family.

"Come in," Charlotta said when he appeared at the door with his candy.

Tommy walked in and was surprised to see how bad Mr. Freiler looked. The skin around his eyes was gray and his body was covered in bruises and sores.

Walking over to his side, Tommy offered him a piece of candy, to which he laughed heartily and denied. "Thank you, son," he said, "but Mrs. Freiler has been spoilin' me with her sweet bread. Share some with the children."

Tommy heard the sound of footsteps jumping down the ladder and turned around to see Anna Claire flying at him.

"Oh, and you brought us candy!" she said. She looked much more like herself than she had earlier.

Tommy grinned and held some candy out for her and Berthie, who was standing next to her shyly. Both of the girls took the candy, eagerly plopping them in their mouths. Helen came inside from the barn at that moment and helped herself to some of it as well. Tommy's eyes widened when he saw Caroline, her sitting in the chair at the table and sewing. He offered her some candy, to which she politely but regretfully declined. "Why don't you children go and have some fun," said Joseph. "Anna Claire, be back by supper!"

Anna Claire hesitated.

"He has us," Charlotta reminded her, touching her husband's hand with her own.

Anna Claire kissed her father's cheek gently before letting Tommy grab her hand and lead her outside into the fresh but crisp air.

"Let's go to the creek," he said, his mouth filled of licorice.

Anna Claire abided, and the two walked quickly through the little wooded cluster of trees and down by Grasshopper Creek. They sat some minutes quietly, Anna Claire looking for fish in the water and Tommy enjoying his candy.

"Your pa looks awful bad," said Tommy after a while.

Anna Claire bent her head down. "I know. We still don't know who those attackers were. No one can figure it out. It was so dark that Mr. Chesham and Mr. Clemmons couldn't see much of their faces. They said they didn't recognize their voices, though, so they might be from out of the town somewhere else. Why my papa?" She frowned as she picked up a stick and started making a circle in the dirt in front of her. "Why'd they gotta hurt my papa? He don't do nothin' wrong to nobody!"

"I'm sorry," said Tommy, his face downcast. "That's plum awful. I know we can find 'em! Those cowards- they couldn't even stay to confess what they did! Cowards, both of them!"

Anna Claire continued to frown and stare at the ground.

"Don't be sad," said Tommy. "I know I'll find them. No one hurts your pa!"

"You won't be able to find them," Anna Claire snapped.

"Well, I can try," Tommy said softly.

"I don't know where they went. Papa said it was two of them just attacking him. We all think they know he has gold and they were trying to get it from him." "Probably," said Tommy. "But Mr. Chesham and Mr. Clemmons got 'em and they won't be comin' back no more!"

"What if it happens again?" asked Anna Claire with her wide green eyes.

Tommy sighed and handed her another piece of candy. "He can't go to town at night no more. Bad things happen around town at night."

"Tommy- somethin' real bad might happen again."

"Don't worry, your pa is a strong man."

"No, Tommy. Somethin' else."

"What?"

Anna Claire paused and bit her lip. "Mama said that if it got more dangerous here, we'd have to leave." Tommy's heart dropped. "Leave? You mean- Gold Creek? Grasshopper Diggin's? Bannack?"

Anna Claire's voice trembled. "Gold Country."

For the first time in a very long time, Tommy felt like he was going to cry.

"I don't wanna leave. I can't leave. This is my home!" said Anna Claire sadly. "I can't imagine livin' anywhere but here! Where there's the mountains and the lakes and town!"

"You don't gotta leave," said Tommy. "They can't make you! You'll have to run away. You can hide in the cellar at the saloon. My ma won't tell no one."

"Oh," sighed Anna Claire, "I don't think so, Tommy. If they make me go, I won't have a choice. I'll have to leave Gold Creek, Bannack, Miss Darlin', Mr. Dobbins, Mr. Clemmons and the others, Hope, you..."

Tommy stood up. Her words felt like knives. Anna Claire was his only best friend in the world. Her family was his family. She wasn't even going to fight to stay? She would let them take her away without another thought?

"I have to go," said Tommy abruptly, standing up and turning around.

"Well, why?" Anna Claire was confused.

Tommy turned around sharply. "You won't even try to stay! You don't want to stay! You don't care a lick about me, Anna Claire Freiler!" And with that, he ran out of the wooded grove and through the fields, leaving Anna Claire alone by the creek.

Anna Claire began to cry then. It began as little tears, but soon turned into sobs. She didn't want to leave Gold Country, and she *did* care about Tommy. He was her truest friend and best friend she'd ever had. She just *couldn't* leave.

Anna Claire stood up, brushed the dirt off her dress, and ran out of the woods where she stayed crying by herself for a long time. Would Tommy ever want to be her friend again?

The whole family was deeply affected by Joseph Freiler's attack and each responded in a different way. Charlotta's heart jumped in her throat at the slightest sound of anything amiss. Caroline concentrated all her efforts on studying, so much so that she would skip supper or not eat at all. Helen brushed her hair constantly until it started falling out in bundles, and she refused to do her school assignments. Pete stopped talking and went nearly mute, which was absolutely cause for concern. Berthie had nightmares and kicked and tossed in her sleep. Anna Claire was angry and took it out at school, where she got into repeated fights with the other children. None of the fights were pleasant, but there was one in particular that caused huge trouble.

It was a Tuesday, a beautiful but cold day at the end of October, when Anna Claire got into the worst fight of her life so far.

"Hey, the strange girl!" said Jimmy Bales, one of the older children, laughing with his friends as he sat at his desk at school. He threw a piece of chalk at Anna Claire's head to get her attention. Miss Darling had to take a quick trip to the outhouse, and so the children were left inside to do their arithmetic assignments.

Anna Claire was good at many things, but she was not good at ignoring people- especially when they were being rude. She slowly turned around and shook her head at him, causing Jimmy and his friends to laugh more.

"Look at the little girl sittin' there with her little slate and her little ribbon," said Hans Elkmann, throwing another piece of chalk her way.

"Ain't you gonna turn around, little girl?" asked Parsley Kent, sitting back into his chair, his freckled face turning red from laughter.

"She's too afraid," scoffed Jimmy. "Poor li'l Anna Claire Freiler. Angry because her pa got the livin' devil beat out of him!"

That was all that was needed to be said for Anna Claire to forget about getting into trouble. Turning her head, she slowly stood up from her chair.

"What did you say?" she asked, her eyes narrowing in the way they often did when uncontrollably angry.

"Look!" cried Hans. "She stood up!"

The boys collapsed into more laughter. Anna

Claire stomped her foot, took her chalk, and threw it hard at Hans's head before going over and kicking Jimmy in the shin.

"You li'l rat!" cried Jimmy, standing up and grabbing Anna Claire by the elbow and causing her to fall.   This was Tommy's turn to interject. Standing up, he went over and pulled Jimmy around the neck as Parsley began hitting him. Hans had grabbed Anna Claire by her other arm and clenched his fists, swearing at her. Tommy threw Jimmy's head on the desk before rescuing Anna Claire by standing in front of her.

Compared to Hans, Tommy was little. Hans laughed, and Tommy stood up straighter than ever, determined that nothing would happen to his dear friend.

"Hurt me," he said bravely, pushing Anna Claire back and causing Hans to drop her arms. "Don't touch her!"

"Aw, look, the little girl has a li'l sweetheart!" laughed Jimmy.

"Ooh, you want to save your li'l sweetheart, don't you, Tommy?" mocked Parsley.

"Let her go!" Tommy demanded, puffing his chest.

"What on Earth!" cried Miss Darling as she entered the schoolhouse, her hands to her face.

Hans let go of Tommy, and he, Parsley, and Jimmy sat back down in their seats. Tommy gulped and took his seat down the next row. Anna Claire was still fuming, glaring at the other three boys with a look of absolute hatred.

"Anna Claire?" Miss Darling waited.

"I hate you all!" she screamed, her voice cracking, as she leapt toward Parsley and put her hands around his throat before slapping him, quickly turning to kick Jimmy in the stomach. Hans grabbed her by the back of her hair, and Anna Claire punched the back of his head, causing Hans to twist her arm before throwing her onto the ground.

All of the children had stood up by this point. Some were screaming for a fight while others were carefully waiting by the doors in case things got worse.

"Don't fight him, Anna Claire!" Helen was saying by the door. "Stop fighting him! Don't fight him, Anna Claire! Stop fighting!"

"No!" Berthie wailed, her eyes full of tears.

"Don't you hurt her!" screamed Tommy, standing up again and jumping onto Hans, who couldn't see with Tommy's hands over his eyes.

"Stop, stop!" Miss Darling was crying, her face frazzled and her hands up to her cheeks. "Please, stop!"

Miraculously, the boys calmed down fairly quickly. Tommy ran to Anna Claire's side and helped her stand up.

"I hate you all!" she repeated, her face as red as a tomato. Even the little freckles that crossed her nose were red.

Miss Darling gently held her waist and led her out of the building.

"Anna Claire! How could you be so reckless?" she said with tears in her eyes, bending down to look at the little girl.

Anna Claire was beginning to cry, too. "They kept throwin' chalk at me and callin' me little, and they said I was angry 'cause my papa got beat up! They made fun of my papa! No one makes fun of my papa!"

Miss Darling's face softened. "I agree with you; those boys were very wrong. They will be punished. But you cannot go around losing your temper like this, Anna Claire! You will someday get yourself into a lot of trouble doing what you just did!"

Anna Claire was still shaking from the incident.

Tommy had come out, but Miss Darling shooed him back into the schoolhouse.

"Anna Claire, go home," she said. "I know your sisters and your brother will tell your mama and papa, so I won't have to find them. You shall indeed be in much trouble. Are you alright?"

Anna Claire nodded, wiping her nose and clutching her elbow, which was hurting from the fall.

"Go home," Miss Darling repeated. "I will take care of the others in there. Go home and feel better. Come back tomorrow with better resolve. Next time, let me handle them. You must stay out of trouble."

Anna Claire nodded and turned around. She walked slowly throughout the town, looking into the windows of the stores, until she decided to go home.

"Why are you home so early?" asked her mother, although she believed she already knew the answer.

Anna Claire frowned. "Miss Darlin' said I could leave. She's not even angry with me! Jimmy and Parsley and Hans attacked me and talked about Papa and said he got beat up, and called me little. They threw chalk at me and grabbed my arms, and I hit them back and they *deserved* it!"

Charlotta sighed, feeling a small amount of pity for her child. "We shall talk about it later. For now, just go to your chores."

Anna Claire was happy to oblige. She did not want to talk about anything at that moment.

Life continued on in this way for some time. Joseph was not able to gather with the Vigilantes due to his injuries. He was healing quickly, but was still recommended by the town doctor to stay in bed. He hated not being able to pan more gold, and being bedridden was not something Joseph was used to, but Charlotta forced him to. The family struggled to do their daily work, and they were in over their heads with autumn chores. Most concerning of all, Joseph was back at the mine before he was even fully healed. But, as he had told Charlotta, the gold wasn't going to wait for anyone.

Chapter 23- Sharing Secrets

It was not lost on Charlotta that life in Gold Country was getting even more dangerous than it was previously. Along with tending to her injured husband, she also heard more of the news from town, which detailed murders on the roads to the other gold rush towns. Mrs. Clemmons, worried about the safety of her family, often came to the Freiler home to discuss the increasingly dangerous atmosphere. It was not just Joseph who was getting attacked. There were now multiple people getting attacked about a mile or two away in the other direction of town. Word spread very quickly in Gold Country. People knew people who knew other people. With the Vigilantes, it was easy to get word on what was happening.

Charlotta was overall exhausted with caring for her husband, taking care of the house, and raising all of the children. It was a blessing that she had Caroline, who at fifteen could do most of the chores herself. With this, though, she also wanted Caroline to have a chance to grow and have experiences, which is why she would allow her to take walks into town or go to one of the dances. As long as she was accompanied by someone- usually one of the boys from town who was smitten with her- she could go occasionally.

Helen was able to do most of the chores herself, but there were still some things that she couldn't do, such as sew on a button properly or cook a good turkey. Charlotta also wanted her to experience more than just daily chores and wanted her to be immersed in nature, to make friendships, and to go to some of the (less rowdy) town gatherings. This is why she be-gan taking Helen to the literary club in town on Wednesdays. It was a mere couple of hours, but a couple of hours they both relished, as Helen got to at-tend with Lucy Grimm and Rebecca Clemmons, and Charlotta got to enjoy the presence of Nettie.

The three younger ones were more challeng-ing. Anna Claire was always getting herself into scrapes while Pete laughed everything off as a joke. Pete had begun to talk again after being mute for nearly an entire month, and that was a relief. Yet, he was not completely himself and seemed to be fearful of the littlest of things. Berthie was constantly sick with various illnesses- colds, flues, sore feet, eye in-fections, ear infections- anything that needed to be treated. The town doctor had come to the Freiler home on more than a couple of occasions to treat the small girl, and the family was worried about her health. She also had been suffering from stomach-aches more recently which had been very trying on Charlotta.

Charlotta did the best that she could under all of the circumstances and stress she was under. It was difficult to be a wife and mother, especially one in a developing new land. Her husband still talked about staying in Gold Country even though it was more dan-gerous than ever, and she had not gone very far with convincing him that it was time to leave. She hated the feeling that danger may be on the doorstep. How-ever, she had made dear friends and that was some-thing very important to her, and this was the one as-pect of staying in Gold Country that Charlotta agreed with. Without her friends, she didn't know how she would have survived all of those months of changes and disaster. So, inwardly, she prayed that there would be more law enforcement or a stable government coming to Bannack soon.

"Well, hello, little Anny-Claire!" said Kathleen Cooper as Anna Claire entered the saloon.

It was several days after Tommy had abruptly left Anna Claire at Gold Creek and Anna Claire wanted to make amends.

"Hi, Tommy's ma!" she answered, skipping up the stairs to where Tommy was. She knew he would be in his room because that was where he always was on Sundays. He never went anywhere on Sundays and his mother didn't make him either.

"Hey, Tommy!" she said with a knock on his door. He didn't answer at first. She knocked four times, threatening to break the door down, until Tommy finally opened it up.

Anna Claire gasped.

"What happened to your eye?" she asked, walking towards him and putting her hand on his cheek. "That looks awful!"

"Stop it," grumbled Tommy, stepping back away from her and squinting his right eye, a black and blue ring circling it.

Anna Claire was worried now.

"What happened, Tommy? You got hurt!"

"Yeah, well, oh well," he grumbled.

"How did that happen?" Anna Claire closed the door behind her.

Tommy turned around to face the cot. "I fell down the stairs."

Anna Claire laughed. "That is just like you, Tommy Cooper!"

"It's not funny!" yelled Tommy harshly, sitting on the cot frowning.

"Alright, alright," said Anna Claire. "It's not funny then! How did you fall down the stairs?"

"I just did, alright?"

Anna Claire tried to make eye contact, but he wouldn't look at her. Instead, he had his head towards the ground, staring at his bare feet.

"I'm sorry I laughed," she whispered sincerely.

Tommy didn't answer. He turned away from her again to face the wall.

"I wanted to thank you for helpin' me at school last week," Anna Claire said. "Those boys are just awful!" There was a long pause. "Well, don't you wanna go to the cemetery? We can see the Hatfield stone again!"

"No."

"Alright, well maybe we can find Mr. Dobbins somewhere! He'll be glad to see us!"

"No, Anna Claire," Tommy said, still refusing to look at her.

"What's wrong with you?" she asked, hand on her hip.

Tommy shrugged. "I'm just tired. Go home, Anna Claire. Just go home."

"But"- she started, her face falling. "But I wanted to have fun!"

"Go home!" he stood up then and began push-ing her out, his hands shoving her shoulders back.

"Fine!" cried Anna Claire. "Fine! I'll leave! And maybe I won't come back!" She began to walk out of the door when Tommy relented.

"Alright, wait!" he said.

"Why?" She was thoroughly insulted.

Tommy sighed, calming down. "I changed my mind. Maybe we can go lookin' in the stores for Mr. Dobbins."

Suspiciously, Anna Claire re-entered the room. "How did you fall down the stairs and hit your eye like that?"

Tommy stopped. "Fine, I didn't fall down the stairs."

"You got hit!" declared Anna Claire. "I knew it! Who hit you? Was it that stupid Jimmy from school?"

Tommy looked down at the ground and shook his head.

"Well, who then?"

Tommy sighed deeply and looked over at his friend. "My ma's friend. I've gotten hit before by her friends, but never this bad."

"What do you mean?"

"Sometimes Ma's friends strike me," he ex-plained softly. "My ma has a lot of men friends, and they come to stay the night here a lot. Remember I told you that people pay my ma to be their friend?"

Anna Claire nodded, her eyes getting bigger.

"Sometimes if they get angry or they're real drunk, they'll hit me if I say somethin' wrong."

Tommy looked back down at the ground, his cheeks flushing.

"Why do they hit you?" Anna Claire sat down next to her friend.

"Like I said, when I say somethin' wrong," explained Tommy, his eye twitching in pain. "Sometimes I don't even say nothin' either and they hit me anyway. Usually when they're drunk and angry at Ma. They hit her sometimes, too, but Ma says that it's alright 'cause they give us money, so they're allowed to hit us."

Anna Claire's heart sunk. She felt her whole body tense up in anger.

"No one hits you!" she yelled, standing up and pointing her finger at his face. "No one should hit you!"

Tommy shrugged. "Calm down. They pay my ma real good so it's alright. Even Mr. Swiner says so!"

"No, it's not alright!" said Anna Claire, her voice shrill. "I'll kill 'em, I'll kill 'em!" Her eyes began to sting and her hands were clenched in fists. She could not remember the last time she was so angry. "It's not alright for anyone to hit you! It's not alright!"

Tommy, a bit touched by his friend's vengeful attitude said, "We can't do nothin' about it, though. If I were healed, they'd be under grass! But I'll tell you somethin', someday I'm gonna get big and tall and they won't be able to touch me!" He nodded his head as if confirming it for himself. "Someday I'll take them to the ground! They won't be walkin' or talkin' for weeks!"

"We'll get them," agreed Anna Claire, her face scrunched up and determined. "We'll get them someday. When you get big and tall, no one can ever hurt you again!"

"Never," he agreed. He broke out into a smile. "I'm only twelve, but I won't be twelve forever! Someday I'll be bigger than they are and I'll get them good!"

"If I ever see them they'll be sorry!" said Anna Claire, her face red. "I might be little, but I can kill them!"

Tommy chuckled. "That's awful nice of you to say, but you'll end up in the hoosegow. Anyhow, you don't gotta worry about me. Soon I'll be so strong all I'll have to do is look at them before they go runnin'!"

"No one touches you, Tommy," reiterated Anna Claire, her voice softer than it was before.

The children talked for a while before playing with the marbles in Tommy's room.

"I don't wanna leave Gold Country," said Anna Claire suddenly, playing with the marble in her hand.

Tommy frowned again. "You can't leave. You just can't! You gotta stay. We gotta think of a way for you to stay here!"

"But if Mama and Papa move, I gotta go with them."

"No! You can stay here. I can hide you in the cellar, remember? They'll never find you!"

Anna Claire considered. "Maybe."

"It's the perfect plan!" Tommy went on. "If they say you have to move, we'll make the plan. My ma won't even notice you're there and Mr. Swiner won't be bothered by it. Before then though, we won't worry about it. I don't wanna think about it."

"I don't either," agreed Anna Claire. "But if they say I gotta go, then we gotta plan it, Tommy."

"Deal." The two spit in their hands and shook them.

It was only a few days later that Anna Claire, after doing all of her chores and begging and persuading, took Berthie to town. The littlest Freiler had been talking about town nonstop and wanted to see the dolls in the windows, smell the baked goods from the open doors, and watch all of the different people. They were permitted to go as long as they wore their woolly clothing, which was uncomfortable and itchy although very warm. "You must be careful with her," said Charlotta, one hand on her hip. "Do not lose sight of her! And Berthie, you be a good girl now, and stay with Anna Claire and Tommy! Oh, I suppose it is alright for you to go into town in the daylight, seeing how many friends we have there. Just be careful and do not wander outside of town. I mean that, Anna Claire. If I find out you left town- oh, you will be sorry!"

"I know, Mama," said Anna Claire as she grabbed Berthie's hand and began pulling her out of the door.

"I get to go to town!" cried Berthie enthusiastically, her round, brown eyes full of wonder. "Where's Tommy?"

Berthie, attending school diligently and being surrounded by Charlotta, had finally lost the adorable mispronunciation she had for so long.

"He's waitin' for us at Swiner's Saloon," Anna Claire answered. "I told him I'd come today when I saw him yesterday."

The two children skipped across the field, the wind blowing their hair and making their dresses lift slightly off of the grass. Anna Claire couldn't wait to show Berthie how much fun she and Tommy had whenever she went into Bannack. The only time Berthie ever went into town was when the whole family would go together, like on the Fourth of July, but this time she would get to see the real fun.

"Me and Tommy have lots of good times in town," said Anna Claire, taking her sister's hand and twirling her around. "We can take you to the cemetery. It's real creepy there. We can steal you some candy, too, but you can't tell Mama or Papa! Like I said, I'll let you come and have fun, but *only* if you promise not to tell. If you tell, we'll both get in trouble and I won't take you to town again!"

"I promise I won't tell," said Berthie softly, a smile on her face and her usually pallid cheeks rosy pink.

When they got to town, Anna Claire let Berthie stare into a few of the stores before walking into Swiner's. Berthie peered at some of the dolls in the window. Joseph had been able to buy her some new dolls recently, but still did not want to buy too many for fear people would know how much gold they actually had.

"Little Ber!" cried Tommy, using his pet name for her, when he saw them.

"Tommy!" Berthie ran over and hugged him.

"Let's get Berthie some candy," said Tommy, smiling as he ran to the back of the saloon. In a few minutes, he popped out with some licorice and caramels.

"Ooh," said Berthie happily, placing one in her mouth.

Anna Claire took some of the candy from Tommy's hand and began putting them into her mouth all at once.

"Let's go to my room and plan the day," Tommy said as they ran up the stairs.

When they entered Tommy's little room, Berthie pointed to all of the pictures of the painted ladies.

"Why are their dresses so short?" she asked innocently.

"Never you mind, Berthie," snapped Anna Claire. "Those are just Tommy's stupid pictures."

"They're not stupid!" Tommy went over to the window and looked outside.

"I told Berthie we could go to the cemetery," said Anna Claire, "and then maybe we can play."

"We can go into all the stores, too," said Tommy, smiling kindly at Berthie.

"Anna Claire told me that there's ghosts in the cemetery," said Berthie, noticeably shuddering.

"But they're not around in the daylight," Anna Claire added quickly.

The three children ran out of Swiner's Saloon and to the cemetery, where they read all of the engravings and thought of what it was like to be dead.

"Look, he was eleven like me," said Anna Claire sadly, pointing to the grave of a boy who had recently died.

"I knew this lady," said Tommy, looking at the grave in front of him that read, "MRS. NELLIE GABLES-1801-1863." "She was a real nice lady. She always called me her 'little man.'"

"Ain't dyin' sad?" mused Anna Claire, bending over to look at the very small grave of a man.

"Mama said death isn't sad," said Berthie, "because then you go to heaven and meet Jesus!"

"Maybe," shrugged Anna Claire.

After inspecting all of the graves, they began to go into each of the stores, aweing at everything that was in them. They walked through the bakery, the masonry, the blacksmith's, the grocery stores, and the meat market. They ran into many people in town, such as Mr. Chesham, and even their teacher Miss Darling, who greeted them cheerfully with open arms.

"I never knew how much fun town is!" cried Berthie, her mouth in a wide grin.

"It's the funnest!" shouted Anna Claire. "Tommy, remember how I told you that I told Berthie about Old Man Hatfield?"

"Yeah," said Tommy, taking a cigar from under his bed and lighting it.

"Well, maybe Berthie can help us find the treasure when we go back- when we're older," said Anna Claire.

"Yeah! Berthie, do you want to go into the mountains and treasure hunt with us?" said Tommy, offering Anna Claire the cigar as she scrunched up her nose and brushed it away with her hand.

"Yeah!" said Berthie, jumping up excitedly. "I can do it!"

"Well, we might have to wait a while," said Tommy, "when we're all a little older. That's 'cause Anna Claire can't get caught again runnin' away. We gotta be old enough to be allowed to go, just the three of us with Hope."

"Why can't Papa take all of us?" asked Berthie, frowning.

"Papa doesn't believe," said Anna Claire, "and we've already asked Mr. Dobbins, but he said he's too old and he doesn't think it's safe. So that leaves us four."

"Us four," repeated Tommy, nodding seriously.

"I can't wait to find the gold!" Berthie said with a little jump in the air, her straight, flaxen hair flying behind her. "Don't forget to bring me with you!"

"No one can know, just like I told you," reiterated Anna Claire. "But we gotta wait probably a couple years at least. We need to tell Miss Darlin'-"

"Shh, not yet, Anna Claire!" yelled Tommy, a finger to his lips.

"Tell Miss Darling?" asked Berthie with curiosity.

"Oh, yes..." said Anna Claire, grimacing. "I meant that we have to tell Miss Darlin' about our adventure someday when we're older!"

"Oh," said Berthie, believing the lie.

Tommy and Anna Claire looked at each other and took a deep breath. They almost told Berthie a little too much about their big plans.

"We better go," said Anna Claire, grabbing Berthie by the hand. "Mama said only for a while and not too long."

"Alright," said Tommy disappointedly. "Little Ber, you gotta come back!"

"I'll come back!" she agreed happily.

"See ya later, Tommy," said Anna Claire.

"See ya," called Tommy.

The two girls ran quickly out of the saloon, mouths full of candy, and down through the streets. Anna Claire was proud of herself for being able to keep an eye on her sister and for not being tempted to go anywhere where she may not have been allowed to. Best of all, Berthie had fun, and Berthie so deserved to have fun. She was always very dependent on their mother, and did not like much to do other things, so getting her into town with just the three of them was wonderful.

The thought of possibly leaving Gold Country made Anna Claire's lips tremble. No, she would not think of it. She didn't have to think of it. Not yet, at least.

Tommy Cooper could not bear to lose the Freilers. Charlotta and Joseph had been practically like an aunt and uncle to Tommy. He still had some hope that someday he would court the beautiful Caroline. He liked joking around with Helen and Pete and being like a big brother for Berthie. But he especially loved being Anna Claire's best friend.

He had to find out who had attacked Mr. Freiler and find the criminals. He would find them and then tell Mr. Dobbins, who would tell the others. They would be hung for their crimes, and Bannack would be a safe place again. That way, the Freilers would never have to leave him!

Tommy crept up behind one of the graves one November night. He had decided that enough was enough. He wasn't going to let these evil men get away with their cruelty any longer! He was going to accost them and show them that someone knew who they were and would not let them get away with it. He was going to scare them, see them, and tell the people of the town.

He squatted next to the gravestones, anxiously awaiting the possibility of seeing a Road Agent. He knew it may not happen, as one could never tell where a Road Agent may be and when they were coming, but Tommy had a feeling it would be on the road out of town by the cemetery.

He sat there and waited for what felt like a very long time. He looked around him to make sure no one had followed him and was watching him. After a while, he thought about getting up and leaving, but instead, he heard the noise of a wagon. It was very dark, but he could see from a distance a family, the one who was leaving their settlement after they had made their lucky strike. He watched carefully as they rode in their wagon, a little lantern lit in the back.

Tommy shivered in the cold as little flurries began to fall from the sky. He was thankful he had the ox fur coat given to him by the Freiler's for Christmas that year before, as he would have frozen otherwise. He breathed warm air into his hands and waited for a while. That's when he saw it.

Almost right as they ascended the little hill not far from the cemetery where Tommy was hiding, a few men rode up to the wagon. It appeared to be calm for a moment, but then quickly turned sour when he heard one of the men yell, "Get out!" and the family hastily leaving the wagon.

Tommy watched with wide eyes as they took a big, long sack out of the wagon. Tommy couldn't- *wouldn't*- let them get away with it!

He found himself running in that direction before he even knew what he was doing.

"No!" he cried, as he ran as fast as he could towards the wagon. The man and woman both looked frightened and shocked as he ran over to the men, gripping the sac on the other side and fighting them.

"I'll kill ya! Leave!" Tommy shouted, pulling the sac with all of his might. "Leave! Get outta here!"

"No, son, please!" begged the man from the wagon. "Don't get hurt, son! Let them take it!"

"Give it back to them!" continued Tommy, kicking and flailing his arms around the men.

One of the men laughed, and Tommy felt something hard hit him on the top of his head. That is when everything went black for a moment-or, at least, what felt like a moment.

When he opened his eyes, the men were gone, and so was the wagon with the family.

He sat up slowly, his eyes feeling heavy and his head hurting. He had tried to stop the Road Agents, but that didn't work out too well. He was still too small, and no one was afraid of the little Cooper boy from town. He sighed when he thought of how silly he was. How could he possibly think he, as a little boy, would be able to fight off the powerful Road Agents? He thought of just how many Road Agents there could be and realized that there would be no way to know for sure which ones had attacked Mr. Freiler. They could be anyone, anywhere. There was no telling. All Tommy could do now was wait and make another plan, hopefully a better one than before. If he could just see some of them, Bannack and Gold Country would be one step closer to being safe.

Chapter 24- The Vigilantes

Joseph had become a part of the Vigilantes and had, along with the other men, gone to town and threatened those who were thought to be Road Agents. They told them that they would slit their necks or shoot them down if they kept robbing people of their gold and tracing them down the roads from Bannack. Joseph wore a bandana to cover his face and was able to avoid confrontation for the most part, as there were men who got there quicker, but he still had moments of pinning men against the wall with a knife at their throat and pointing a pistol at more than one Road Agent.

Charlotta wasn't aware of exactly what the Vigilantes did, as Joseph was discreet. She knew that they protected the townspeople, but she thought they were simply walking around and warning others of danger. If she had known the amount of aggression and peril involved with being a Vigilante, she would have never forgiven her husband for sacrificing himself like that.

To keep themselves safe, they could not tell anyone about their success. It was wonderful to have money; however, the Freilers were frugal. They kept the money safe under the floorboards of Joseph and Charlotta's bed. Charlotta worried often if anyone would find the money, but Joseph was determined that it was safe, as he kept his rifle close. There was also the slight problem of not being able to benefit much from the money. They were able to get food in plentiful and little treats here and there, but they had to be very careful not to draw too much attention to themselves.

The children were going through their own trials and tribulations. Caroline began courting one of the boys at school while Tommy sadly pined away for her. Helen decided to sneak out of the cabin one night to go into the town with Rebecca Clemmons, and the two were caught by Mr. Grimm, getting into an enormous amount of trouble. Other times, she was late for supper and refused to study, which made Charlotta worry. Peter was overcome with the fact that his family had money and incessantly bragged about money at school, causing Joseph to remind him to keep this to himself lest he anger the other parents and cast an undesired light on the family.

Anna Claire was always Anna Claire. She still got into fights at school, but usually they would end before it became physical- *usually*. Tommy remained arduous to defend her honor and never let so much as a negative word slip out of someone's mouths without ripping them apart. Anna Claire was plotting her way to save Tommy from his mother's suitors, and seriously considered hiding in the saloon and stabbing the men in the chest with a knife when they were least expecting it.

"I want to sneak out and then I can hide," said Anna Claire to Tommy one day after school. "I'll stay in the cellar until I hear him comin'. Then, I'll climb up the stairs and wait until he leaves. If he tries to go into your room, that's when I'll jump out with the knife. I'll have to stab him real hard 'cause he'll be way bigger than I am, but I'll get him good! Then you'll come to my house, and Mama and Papa will take good care of you. You could be like my brother! Wouldn't that be somethin'?"

"That won't work," said Tommy. "You'll go to jail- or worse, they'll hang ya! Thanks anyway."

"No one can hit you," Anna Claire repeated, pacing around the schoolyard. "Maybe I can wear a bandana around my face like the Vigilantes and no one will know it's me!"

"It's too risky," said Tommy. "They'll catch you, and you could be killed. I'm not gonna let you get killed."

"Well, then what are we gonna do to make it stop?"

"It doesn't happen often," said Tommy, wiping his nose on his sleeve. "I never know when one of them is gonna hit. But I promise next time, I'll be ready. I'll have the knife myself under the bed if they try anything! You don't gotta worry about me. I don't need a girl worried about me."

Anna Claire sighed. "I'm not just any ol' girl."

"Look, I can take care of myself," said Tommy.

Anna Claire was worried, but knew she should stop talking.

"Let's go on the other side of town, across that field," she suggested. "I told Mama I'd be stayin' over to study with you."

"But I've never been over to that part of the land," said Tommy. "Only a little bit. Why you wanna go over there?"

"Maybe there's somethin' we haven't seen before," Anna Claire took his hand. "Remember, that's how we found Iá daxpitchée! Just for a little bit."

"Not far," reiterated Tommy. "You know Gold Country's not safe."

"Just down a bit," Anna Claire promised.

The two walked the opposite direction than they usually did and left the town. After walking up some small hills, they reached a plateau of flat land that they walked through for several minutes.

"There ain't nothin'," said Tommy. "I told you!"

"I wonder what we could find if we had the horses. I bet we'd find so many things out there!" Anna Claire stared ahead of her, the golden fields rippling in the wind.

"Probably skeletons and old cabins and rusty flasks!" Tommy now looked intrigued.

"Anyway, are you still readin' like I told you?" asked Anna Claire, narrowing her eyes at him.

"Sometimes I do," said Tommy. "Honest, I do! I didn't this week, but I've been readin' a lot and I know a lot of new words now."

"Good," said Anna Claire, "because if you can read, you can go anywhere in the world and do just about anything!"

"It's alright," admitted Tommy reluctantly.

"I'm gonna write someday," said Anna Claire. "I don't care what I'll write about so long as I write! Maybe I'll write about the Crow people and how they had to leave their homes when all the White people came along. Or maybe I'll write about the English Kings and Queens and royalty. I could write adventure stories with lots of blood and bones, and mystery ones, too."

"My ma likes love stories," Tommy rolled his eyes. "Disgusting."

Anna Claire scrunched her face in agreement. "I'll never write a love story! That's 'cause I wouldn't know how and I wouldn't want to. That's boring."

"And disgusting," added Tommy again.

The two lay into the grass and watched the clouds in the sky.

"It's gonna get dark soon, so I'd better go," said Anna Claire. "Mama and Papa will be awful mad if I'm not there!"

"Alright," said Tommy.

"Well, aren't you gonna walk with me?"

"Not today," said Tommy with a sigh. "I'm feelin' real relaxed. I just wanna look at the clouds for just a little bit and then I'll go back."

Anna Claire shrugged. "Fine. See ya later!"

"Bye!" called Tommy.

Tommy stayed where he was for hours. He did not want to go home. He did not want to see his mother getting drunk or meet whichever man would be accompanying her for the night. He did not want to wake up with bruises and cuts all over his body. So instead, he stayed right there in that field, imagining all of the things he would do when he eventually found the treasure.

It was hours later when Tommy finally woke up. He sat up on his elbows and looked around him at the dark field and sky. He stood up shakily and glanced over towards the town, where he could see the lights. He began to walk away from his spot back towards Bannack.

Suddenly, he heard the voice of a man yelling in his ear, the feeling of him being tripped to the ground, and a strong blunt to his cheek. Before he knew it, he had a sack over his head and was being dragged down the field.

Terrified and screaming, he kicked and flailed his arms and legs until he was told to "shut up, boy." He had never been so frightened. He felt a terrible pain on the top of his head as the man grabbed his hair. He stopped then and struggled to breathe as he was taken what seemed to be a very far distance away. Finally, he felt the sack being lifted from his face as he was kicked and tossed to the side.

It was four tall, big men wearing bandanas over their mouths. One of them wore a hat and had a long beard. Another one had red hair.

"We know what you've been doin'," said the long-bearded one, taking a rock from the ground and throwing it at Tommy's head. "Tryin' to gum us, are ya?"

Tommy groaned and covered his face with his hands.

"You gotta stop tryin' to figure us out, boy. If you keep doin' that, you're dead." This was the red-headed man, coming over and spitting tobacco right on his chest.

"You fired into the wrong flock. We're gonna let it go this time, 'cause you're a kid- but if you were a li'l older, you'd be cold as a wagon wheel by now!"

The long-bearded man also spit on Tommy before cackling menacingly.

Tommy shut his eyes and trembled, silently begging for the men to leave.

"Stop tryin' to protect this town," said the red-haired one. "You can't be any older than twelve. You ain't gon' be able to do nothin'. But if we see you creepin' 'round here and there talkin' about gettin' the Road Agents and savin' the people of the town, we'll have no choice but to put ya under grass. Do ya understand, boy?"

When Tommy didn't speak, one of them kicked him in the chin.

"Now consider this your warnin'," said Long-Beard. "I don't give warnin's out very much. I don't think they serve much of a purpose. But 'cause you're just a kid, we're gonna let this little scrape go for now. But don't you ever, and I mean *ever*, try huntin' us down or gettin' in our way again. Next time we ain't gonna be so kind."

"Yes, sir," Tommy choked, holding his stomach and trying as hard as he could not to vomit.

"Good. I trust your little friend will help you here." And with that, the men got on their horses and rode away down the other end of the field. When Tommy looked up, he didn't know where he was at for a moment. He was sore and beaten, and more tired than he could remember being.

He got his bearings and was able to direct himself back to town. When he crept into the saloon, the blood that was running from his nose landed on the ground and then some on the door handle. All was very quiet, and there was only one light next to the counter. It must have been in the early hours of the morning already for there to be no people.

Tommy, his entire body sore and hurting, walked up the creaky stairs and climbed into bed, groaning in pain. He could hear the sound of laughter coming from his mother's room. Unable to hold it back, he rushed to the bucket and vomited, his stomach painfully throbbing.

Life in Bannack seemed to be getting more and more chaotic every day. What was going to happen now?

Tommy had not been to school for four days and his mother had said he was sick each and every time Anna Claire tried to check in on him. Miss Darling and the Freiler children were beginning to become concerned for the little Cooper boy, for Tommy's attendance at school had been markedly improving before this.

"He can't *still* be sick," said Helen to his mother, as she had come with Anna Claire to Swiner's. "Please, let us talk to him."

Kathleen Cooper sighed. "He won't be happy that you did, but go on." She motioned with her arm for the children to walk up the stairs, to which they did hastily.

"Tommy!" Anna Claire knocked loudly. "Tommy, open, open!"

"Go away!" he yelled.

"We're comin' in!" cried Anna Claire, opening the door to see Tommy peaking under his covers.

"Go away, I said!"

"Tommy!" exclaimed Helen, gasping. "Tommy, what happened to you?"

Tommy sighed and slowly sat up, revealing his bruised cheeks and a large cut across his face.

"Tommy!" cried Anna Claire, her eyes welling up with tears. "No, Tommy." She ran to his side and sat down next to him. "Who did this to you? I'll kill them! And your ma too!"

Tommy shook his head. "It wasn't any of them."

"Then who?" questioned Anna Claire.

"Who did it, Tommy?" demanded Helen, hand on her hip.

"I don't know," said Tommy honestly. "It was a few days ago, the day we went on the other side of the town and walked. I fell asleep, and then someone dragged me with a sack over my head and beat me. They didn't tell me who they were. They just told me to stop lookin' for Road Agents and protectin' the town. They wanted me to stop tryin' to find them. They let me go and told me they'd kill me if I kept on tryin' to find out who they were."

"The Road Agents," said Helen, frowning.

"Oh, Tommy," Anna Claire reached forward and touched his hand, which was scratched up as well. "Tommy, you look awful."

She couldn't explain the sadness and anger that were in her heart at that moment. She couldn't believe someone had attacked her best friend and left him like that- grown men, at that.

"You shouldn't try to find them anymore," said Helen, sympathetically brushing her hand over his ear. "You can't ever do that again. You gotta protect yourself and stay away and stop gossiping!"

Tommy nodded, his head still aching slightly.

"I can't believe they did that to you!" cried Anna Claire in rage, the redness coming back to her face. "Oh, I wanna kill them! Murder them in cold blood! I'd do it too, if I knew who they were and I wasn't so little."

"Be quiet, Anna Claire," said Helen, rolling her eyes.

"Maybe you can come home with us!" said Anna Claire to Tommy. "That way you'll be with us, and Papa will kill anyone who'll hurt you!"

Tommy shook his head. "Nah. It'll be alright. Ma needs me here. I help her a lot. I just gotta stop talkin' about the Road Agents. And we all gotta realize that these men- they knew what I was doin'. They know us. They could be anyone. Even our friends."

Helen and Anna Claire looked at each other and shuddered.

"Well, I think you're safer not talking about it at all," said Helen. "Don't worry about the Road Agents. There's nothing you can do, even if you knew who they were! You have to stop talking about it and telling everyone you're gonna catch them. It looks real suspicious, Tommy."

Tommy nodded regretfully. "I know that now."

"It seems like someone's been listenin' to our conversations," said Anna Claire pensively. "How else would they know you talk about the Road Agents?"

Helen rolled her eyes. "He always talks about them! Right, Tommy? You talk about them in school during lessons, while everyone is eating dinner outside, when you're in the stores, and even in the saloon. You're always talking about the Road Agents! It's not a secret that you wanna stop them."

Tommy sighed. "Well, look what good it did me."

Anna Claire walked over to him and placed her hand on his shoulder.

"I know you're tryin' to be brave and all," she said, "but sometimes it's alright to be scared. Sometimes bein' scared is what protects us."

Tommy looked up at his friend and smiled slightly. "I suppose I gotta stop talkin' about the Road Agents out loud, but that don't mean I have to stop thinkin' about them! I'll find out sooner or later who they are."

"Well, keep your mouth shut for now!" said practical Helen, pulling on Anna Claire's sleeve. "Let's go. Mama will be upset if we're not back soon."

Anna Claire nodded and turned to Tommy. "Remember what I said. Sometimes it's alright to be scared. It's alright not to be brave all the time."

Tommy nodded as they closed the door. Then he laid back down and pulled the covers over his head, feeling considerably more cheered up but also very fatigued. Anna Claire was right. Sometimes it was good to be frightened- sometimes being frightened helped people get away from bad situations. Still, Tommy felt that there was more he could do despite being a child. He felt the responsibility of an adult upon him, as he had practically raised himself anyway, and had a more mature understanding of the way the world actually worked. He felt it was at least partly his responsibility to help his friends and the people of the town, even if he was still just a little boy.

Tommy was not as frightened as the men may have thought he was, in fact. Tommy was also not very good at taking orders from people, either, so having the bravado of a grown man in a child's body, he decided to leave the saloon one night and carefully track the Road Agents again. This time, he made sure to be quiet about them and did not tell a single soul of his desire to protect the town. He knew this plan may work, as it was different than his last one of merely going up and yelling at them. Tommy, although young and foolish, was also bright and carefully hid next to the billiard hall until far after midnight when the town was quiet.

When he heard nothing for some time, he went into the outskirts of the town past the cemetery and waited. Again, it felt like he had been waiting a very long time. It was cold and his hands shook and his feet were numb in the snow. It was about an hour when he saw the figures of five men come from the other direction. Before he even knew what was happening, the men had approached a sixth man who was riding his horse in the other direction.

Tommy watched them with an open mouth and wide eyes as the group of men crowded their own horses around the man's and stopped him. He gasped as he watched them pull the man off of his horse and stab him, the man's body contorting grotesquely and letting out one last moan of pain before falling to his side. It looked to Tommy that the man was stabbed in the heart. The other men quietly untied a packsaddle from the back of the man's horse. Upon opening it, they were thrilled when it revealed hunks of the glittering substance so obsessively craved.

Tommy knew it was foolish, but he had his plan. He forgot about being cold and now was shaking from nerves, but he still had his plan. He knew he had to do something about all of this, at least in some way.

Tommy ran over to the men then. A couple of them glanced backward to see him, and two of them tackled him to the ground, punching him in the face.

"So, you wouldn't listen," the one man said.

"I'm sorry!" cried Tommy, desperately trying to get a look at the man's eyes. It was dark and he really could not get a good look at them. "I'm sorry! I just want some of the gold for myself!"

The men laughed at him.

"You want some gold?" said one, taking a piece of gold from the murdered man's sack, putting it in his mouth, and spitting it out at Tommy's face. "Well, that's too bad! Only we get the gold!"

"You're right," cried Tommy desperately. He knew if he died, he would never see Anna Claire or the Freilers again. "You're right. I just wanted to be a Road Agent like you! That's why I wanted to figure you out! I wanted to show you that I can do it, too! See, I'm real fast and no one would suspect me!"

Tommy's face was red and determined, his eyes shining with false confidence and his body tense from his lie.

The men looked at each other and nodded.

"Fine, we can respect that, son," said one. "And maybe we can use you someday. But you're too young now. You won't be no use to us now. We'll give you a piece of gold if you don't say nothin' of us. Of course, if you do, we'll have to kill you and your fine ma. Believe me, we all know your ma." They laughed. "But since you admire us Road Agents so much, then you'll have no trouble takin' the gold and keepin' the secret? Maybe if you prove you can keep a secret, we'll let you in the gang a little sooner."

Tommy, breathless, could only nod.

"Just give him a piece," said another one with irritation.

Tommy felt the press of what felt like a small rock in his hand and the tug on his hair as one of the men pulled him down and hit him on the shoulder so that Tommy fell face-forward in the muddy grass.

"Tell no one and your ma will live to see another day!" said one of the Road Agents, letting out a sickening laugh. "Like I said, don't say nothin' to no one and maybe we'll think about lettin' you in our gang and gettin' rich! Now mosey on outta here!"

Tommy was too surprised to move. He hugged the gold in his palm as he walked home, exhausted and his face swelling. He hadn't been able to get a good look at anyone. He realized with a heavy heart that he may never be able to find and identify the Road Agents, no matter how much he wanted to or how much he fervently tried to reveal their identities. And even though Tommy decided to be more careful

in his search, and even though he reported what happened to Mr. Dobbins and Mr. Freiler the next day,
innocent people still ended up dead.

Chapter 25- Blood and Chaos

It was well into December, and it was very cold in Montana Territory. Even their long johns and petticoats couldn't quite cover the blasts of wind that hit them repeatedly. The cabin was frozen to the touch, and the grass became brown and hardened. There were little bits of frost around the windows of the houses, and the fireplace became essential for surviving the winter in Gold Country.

The children were usually responsible for hitting the flintstones with steel until there was a flame. Then, they would take a piece of flax and light the wood of the fireplace. During the colder months, it was crucial to keep the fire going. Helen had this responsibility. Before retreating to bed, she covered the fireplace with ash, allowing it to safely burn throughout the night. Upon waking up, she removed the ashes to put the wood down. Then, she would use the bellows kept next to the fireplace to light it. On some of the autumn and winter nights, the children would place coal under the mattress to make it more bearable to sleep, as they often woke up with frost on their faces. On particularly cold days, Charlotta would prop up the tin foot warmer and fill it with hot coal for when the feet needed particular attention.

Caroline had the responsibility of ironing the clothes, and she did it dutifully, as she loved making imperfections smooth. She enjoyed pressing and seeing to the petticoats, and even insisted that the long johns be ironed as well. In the mornings, she was also responsible for heating the potatoes in the oven so that they would take them to school. The children would then carry the potatoes to keep their hands warm as they walked to school and, most of the time, it served as a suitable dinner.

Charlotta always made sure that everything was long since canned by this time. She had harvested her corn, cabbages, carrots, radishes, and apples, and placed them in the root cellar where everything was boarded up and held other pickled food next to the herbs. She and Caroline were responsible for most of the food preparation.

"I wish we didn't have to go to school all the time," said Peter as the five Freiler children walked to the little schoolhouse.

"We didn't go to school much last winter," Caroline reminded her siblings, walking a bit ahead of the others so as to not be embarrassed by their presence should anyone her own age see her. "If only I could wear the nice dresses so that I could hold my head up high at school!"

"I'd much rather go to school than stay home all day with the chores," Helen said, her nose in the air.

"I like to go to school because I can see my friends!" said Berthie, skipping along happily.

"I like to go to school because we get to see Miss Darlin'," said Anna Claire. "I like Miss Darlin'. She is the best teacher in the whole world!"

"She is a good teacher," admitted Caroline. "I do like the way she teaches arithmetic. She makes it seem so simple!"

"I like her because she's nice," Helen said, "and smart!"

They walked on for some time until they reached town, crossed over Main Street, and onto the other side of Clover Street. Anna Claire saw Tommy and immediately ran to him.

"Anna Claire!" he said, book and slate in hand. "Do you wanna come to the saloon after school and eat candy?"

"Yes, but only for a little while!" said Anna Claire. "My mama wants me to help her with the canning today."

The two walked into the school building and sat at their desks. Tommy and Anna Claire snuck a glance over at each other. This was going to be a particularly good day at school. They had both decided that for the story assignment, Anna Claire would tell the story about Old Man Hatfield. They knew that Miss Darling probably didn't even know her own history and that she was the baby left behind, but if she did know, her facial expression would give her away. If she didn't know, she might connect the name with herself. It was a risky plan, for if Miss Darling became upset or angry, they would no doubt get into enormous trouble.

The overall assignment was for the children to stand in front of the classroom and tell a fictional story that they have heard before, preferably from a book they read, and tell the class the main points of the story. This was not a book Anna Claire was going to speak about, but it was something much better.

"Class," said Miss Darling gently as she walked over to the chalkboard, "remember that your presentation needs to be at least five minutes long. Who would like to go first?"

Anna Claire raised her hand, but Lisa Howler was called on. A few children were called on before Anna Claire was finally able to go to the front of the class.

"For my story," she began, winking at Tommy who was looking uneasy. "I chose to talk about the legend of Old Man Hatfield and Daisy."

Other than Anna Claire's siblings, most of the children looked puzzled. Miss Darling herself cleared her throat and took a deep breath. Anna Claire's subject matter, although not from a book, was in line with the instructions to talk about (what she thought was) a fictional tale.

And so went the story of Old Man Hatfield, the wife who died and left him with the daughter Daisy, and Daisy whom left him for the world only to find that he had passed away once she came back home. With that, Anna Claire explained, she committed suicide (Miss Darling nearly lost her breath at this part). Her child was still out there somewhere and no one knew where- but they knew that the baby's name was *Darling*. And Darling would be all grown-up by now.

Anna Claire and Tommy both looked at Miss Darling anxiously to see the expression on her face. Miss Darling's eyes were wide and her mouth was slightly open. She certainly looked shocked.

It seemed obvious to Tommy and Anna Claire that Miss Darling was affected by the story, especially the part where her name was mentioned. Tommy and Anna Claire looked over at each other again and smiled in knowingness.

"That was-" began Miss Darling, still stunned, "a lovely presentation. A bit morbid, I'm afraid, but you presented it well. Thank you, Anna Claire."

Anna Claire sat back down in her seat confidently as she and Tommy smiled at each other again. They knew the truth. Miss Darling just *had* to be the baby left so many years ago.

Tommy was up next and he did a surprisingly good presentation on Oliver Twist, a book which he had gotten from the Freilers and one he was quite fond of. Everyone liked it because he spoke with force and intrigue, and Miss Darling was obviously impressed. He had already been doing much better at school now that his attendance was back up, and this presentation would surely raise his marks significantly.

After school that day, Tommy followed the Freilers back to their home.

"Tommy's comin'!" said Pete happily as he stood next to him.

"Are you gonna play with me?" asked Berthie hopefully.

"Sure," said Tommy, glancing hopefully at Caroline. "Why don't y'all come to the creek with us?"

"It's December!" pronounced Caroline, her hands around her arms. "It's too cold."

"I have reading to do," scoffed Helen.

"I'll go! I'll go!" yelled Pete.

"Me too, me too!" shouted Berthie.

Tommy was secretly (or not so secretly) disappointed that Caroline would not be joining them at the creek. He frowned and began walking slower, looking at the ground.

"Tommy?" asked Anna Claire, playfully lifting his chin. "Come on, you namby-pamby. It'll still be fun, just the four of us. Who needs stupid Caroline."

"Who said I care?" Tommy kicked the dirt under his feet and then walked ahead of her.

When they arrived at the Freiler house, Charlotta had made pumpkin pie for them. They ate it together at the table, talking and laughing amongst each other, before Tommy, Anna Claire, Pete, and Berthie went to the creek, bringing Hero with them.

"Tommy, look at this!" said Pete, jumping up to touch a tree branch while Hero jumped, too.

"You're gettin' taller!" lied Tommy, understanding the importance of feeling big when one is merely eight-years-old.

"He ain't gettin' taller," spat Anna Claire, throwing a rock across the creek.

"I am, too!"

"Look!" laughed Berthie, pointing to a grasshopper. "Look how fast it jumps!"

Anna Claire stood next to her and crouched down so that she was her height. "Yeah, it sure does! You know that's why they named it Grasshopper Creek when they started settlin' here?"

"Oh!" laughed Berthie as she ran to try to catch the grasshopper. Just as she was going to catch it in her hands, it jumped away from her. "Oh no, he got away!"

"It's alright, Berthie," soothed Anna Claire. "You'll catch one someday!"

"Gee, I wish it was warm so we could go swimmin'," said Tommy, picking up a stone and flinging it into the creek's waters.

"Me too," said Pete, trying unsuccessfully to reach a higher branch.

"Do you know we're rich?" asked Berthie, happily sitting on the muddy ground.

Tommy put his finger to his mouth. "Shh! You should never say that, Little Ber! It isn't safe! When people find out other people are rich, they try to steal from them."

"Little Ber" put her arms around her knees and lifted them up to her chin. Hero wiggled up next to her and began licking her face, causing her to burst into little giggles.

"Yes, Berthie, we can never tell anyone that we're rich except Tommy!" reminded Anna Claire, plopping down next to her in the mud. "We could get killed."

"I don't wanna get killed!" said Berthie sadly.

"Alright, then don't tell no one we're rich!" stated Anna Claire. Putting her arm around her younger sister, she squeezed her shoulders and said, "When people are allowed to know we're rich, Papa will buy you any doll you want."

"Any?"

"Any."

Tommy began to cross the log that was stretched over the creek and crossed it back, his arms helping him balance. He then helped Pete do the same, but Pete nearly lost his footing and had to hold onto Tommy.

"Imagine if there were sharks in here!" Pete said.

"Sharks don't swim in creeks, stupid," said Anna Claire haughtily.

"I know that, dim wit," answered Pete. "I was just sayin'!"

Tommy and Pete came over to sit with the girls.

"What's it like bein' twelve, Tommy?" asked Pete.

"Twelve sounds so big!" said Anna Claire, beginning to dust some of the mud off of her hands.

"It ain't much," admitted Tommy. "It's still not old enough to do much. Maybe next year when I'm thirteen, people will start takin' me seriously."

"I wanna be twelve!" said Pete, looking over at Tommy in awe.

"Me too," said Berthie, although she was completely distracted by a golden leaf that had landed in her hair.

The children sat for a while by the creek. The skies began to turn a brighter but deeper blue which seemed to fall over Gold Country like a blanket, making everything a bit darker.

"I don't like when it gets dark so early," said Pete. "We can't stay out and play!"

"The dark is scary," Berthie shuddered. "I don't like it at all!"

"The dark ain't so bad," said Tommy, looking up at the sky. "I think it's peaceful."

"Well, I don't like it," sighed Anna Claire. "Now we all have to go home."

Sullenly, they stood up from the mud, all of their clothes quite dirty, and began to walk out of the little woods and into the clearing. When they reached the cabin, Anna Claire turned to Tommy.

"Go in," she said to the others. "I'll be right there!" She then whispered to Tommy, "Can you believe Miss Darlin's face? It *has* to be her!"

"I think so," agreed Tommy. "She looked like someone could've knocked her over with a feather. She must be the baby!"

"When should we ask her?"

"Not now," said Tommy slowly and carefully, his watery-blue eyes gazing upward. "We should wait until school ends."

"But why?"

"If she gets angry, we'll be in an awful lotta trouble and my marks are finally good," Tommy sighed. "It's gotta be soon, but not *too* soon. She might know, but if she doesn't know, she's gonna be in a shock. We'll have to be real gentle with her. She might not know she was the baby of Daisy Hatfield."

"She might not know," Anna Claire repeated. "If she does know, she might know where the rest of the gold is. Then we could *all* be rich for the rest of our lives!"

"Well, we can't say nothin' yet. At least not for a couple months."

"But that's forever away."

"Yeah, but we can't, Anna Claire."

Anna Claire nodded. "Alright. I gotta go inside now before Mama gets cross."

Tommy waved his hand and began to run the other way. "Remember, don't say anything to anyone what we know about Miss Darlin'!"

"I won't!"

Anna Claire hurried into the cabin smiling.

"What are you so happy about?" said Helen, making a face as she wrote on her slate.

Anna Claire stopped smiling abruptly. "Oh, I was just thinkin' of how good my presentation was today. It was better than yours!"

Helen scrunched her nose and Anna Claire stuck her tongue out.

"I hope Papa is home soon," said Caroline wistfully. "Maybe we can read the Bible together."

"That would be lovely," said Charlotta as she floated down the ladder from the loft, basket in hand.

Caroline sighed, her long black locks hitting the chair. "With all of the work I have done today, I would love to hear about God."

Anna Claire resisted rolling her eyes. God had always felt like a foreign concept to her, especially when described in the Bible.

"I'm hungry," said Berthie at the table.

"Your father said he will try to be home early tonight," Charlotta smiled, looking more peaceful than she had in a long time. "Let us wait for him before we eat."

"But I'm hungry!"

"Berthie," snapped Charlotta, narrowing her eyes.

Berthie was quiet then. She ran to the window to stand next to Anna Claire. "Can you tell me a story tonight?"

"Sure," sighed Anna Claire, anxiously awaiting her father's return from the cold darkness outside.

"Tommy did good on his presentation, Mama," said Helen from her chair, still working on her slate.

"I am happy to hear that," Charlotta smiled. "Tommy is very smart. Look how quickly he learned how to read! He is far smarter than everyone realizes. I know he is an odd boy, that is for sure, but he is the nicest little boy you could ever meet."

"Is Papa almost home?" asked Pete impatiently. "I wanna eat!"

"We shall eat when your father gets home, Peter," said Charlotta. "I don't know when he is coming home." She swallowed and clutched her stomach, feeling that tight knot of anxiety again. Since her husband had gotten attacked, every time Joseph was so much as five minutes later than anticipated, she panicked.

The Freiler matriarch and children waited for some time before Joseph Freiler walked through the door, shivering in his fur coat. When he entered, the children stood up to embrace him.

"I'm a lucky man!" he said, his eyes sparkling as he placed his hat on the wall.

"We can eat now!" exclaimed Berthie. Everyone laughed.

"I'll tell ya," said Joseph, coming to sit down as Charlotta began bringing the duck out. "Today was tough. No one even found gold dust. Not a speck of it!"

"Well, we must have found the last of it," said Charlotta, pursing her lips at her husband.

Joseph ignored that comment and turned to Anna Claire. "You look happy tonight!"

"I am," she smiled. "I did a great presentation."

"She told that stupid Old Man Hatfield story again," piped Helen with a roll of her brown eyes. "It's the silliest, most boring story in the whole world!"

"Well, *I* reckon it's a good story!" said Joseph, patting the top of Anna Claire's head affectionately.

"Tommy's presentation was the best one," Helen said, using the poking iron to spark up the fire. "You felt like you were in the book, the way he talked about it!"

"I'm glad to hear he's doin' better in school." Joseph smiled, cutting into the duck.

When it was time for bed, Anna Claire tucked Berthie in, and the two huddled together under the covers.

"Can you tell me the Old Man Hatfield story?" she asked, her big eyes wide. "That's my favorite!"

Anna Claire sighed. "I just told that story in school today!"

"Please?" Her voice was quiet but hopeful.

Anna Claire smiled. "Fine, just tonight! This is the last time for a long time!"

"Alright, Anna Claire."

"Well, there once was a real nice man named David Hatfield..." Anna Claire told the story again, herself even beginning to be a bit sick of telling it, before giving her sleeping sister a kiss on the forehead and closing her eyes.

It was two days later when Charlotta walked across the fields and over to the little cabin on the other side past town the next day. It was a good three mile walk, and her feet were sore as she knocked on the Watson's door. She couldn't take the chance of taking the mules or horses with her to the Watson's.

"Oh, Charlotta!" said George merrily. "Come on in!"

"Thank you," Charlotta said, nodding her head. "Hello, Abigail!"

Abigail Watson smiled cheerfully and motioned for her to sit down at the little table.

"Where's Hope?" asked Charlotta, looking around her.

"I let her go for a walk," said Abigail. "Only around here. She is not allowed far without us."

Charlotta nodded and thought about the possible circumstances if Hope were to run into Whites.

"I do confess," began Charlotta, "I wish Hope was able to go to the school with all of the other children. Anna Claire says it all of the time! We all want Hope to be able to go to school. The teacher, Miss Lucia Darling, is wonderful."

"I wish so, too," said Abigail sadly.

"But that ain't gonna happen," added George, a touch of anger in his voice. "No one wants my little girl in their classroom on account of that she's Black. She wouldn't be able to go to school without them kickin' her out."

Abigail nodded and looked over at Charlotta helplessly.

"I know," she sighed. "But I did have an idea. I am not a school teacher, but I almost was one and I must say I know quite a bit, having read many books in my youth and even now. I would be honored to come once a week and tutor Hope. I'm afraid I have far too much work to come daily, but I believe I could make the trip once a week."

Abigail looked over at her husband in shock.

George paused, thinking it over. "That is kind of you, ma'am. It really is. We couldn't take so much from you."

Charlotta smiled gently. "It's not too much. I would be happy to. Hope is a smart girl and if she cannot go to school, she should at least know what the other children do."

"Hello!" said Hope as she walked through the door, her hair out of place and her eyes sparkling.

"Hope!" said Charlotta. She looked over at George and Abigail.

George nodded knowingly and tapped Hope on her arm.

"Hope," he said, "how would you feel about Mrs. Freiler comin' over and givin' you some schoolin'?"

Hope's eyes went big and she smiled brightly. "Me? School?"

"Well, it wouldn't be a real school," said Charlotta, "but I could teach you what the children know and are learning. You are smart and you will be able to catch up with them easily! I would come here once a week. Will Thursday afternoons be suitable?"

"Suitable?" asked George, standing up. "It'll be more than suitable! We can't thank you enough, ma'am!"

"Yes! Please come!" Hope clasped her hands together in excitement. "Hear, Mama? Papa? I'm gonna learn, just like all the other children!"

The parents smiled at her.

"I know you must be eating soon," said Charlotta, "so I will be back next week. But for now-" she reached in the little tin pail and pulled out a book, "this will teach you some things about reading and letters. Also, please take this. It is a calligraphy plate. It will help you to learn the alphabet."

"She knows a bit from us but not a lot," said George. "This is perfect."

Abigail's eyes filled with tears. "Bless you, bless you!"

Charlotta smiled warmly and stood up, giving Hope a little squeeze.

"I will see you next week!" she said. "How about you all come for supper tomorrow night?"

George and Abigail looked at each other, then at Hope who was pleading with her eyes.

"I say that's a good idea!" nodded George. "Thank you, ma'am."

"Remember, call me Charlotta," she reminded him gently, opening the door. "I will see you all tomorrow then!"

And that is how Charlotta began to teach little Hope arithmetic, literature, and history. Charlotta provided some of her books, and Anna Claire let her borrow a dime novel of her own. Throughout the winter, Hope learned many lessons and, although far behind the children her age, she was tough and a fast learner. She studied often and practiced all week long. Charlotta was impressed by how quickly she was learning and how much time she dedicated to her studies. Charlotta had become much closer to the Watsons now. When they could, they would make the trip to eat supper at each other's houses. It was something that had to be kept a secret, for if anyone knew, they could potentially harm the Watsons and even the Freilers for their camaraderie.

Bannack was not getting less dangerous in general. There were more mentions of murders and robberies than ever before, and Charlotta had just about enough of it all. It wasn't bad enough that pioneer life was so hard, but now she had to live near one of the most treacherous places in the entire country! She was becoming more and more furious with Joseph, as he was convinced that he would be able to find even more of the gold. There were times when Charlotta cried, nearly begging him to leave, and although he would try to soothe her, he would not budge despite his earlier promise that if it were to get more dangerous, they would leave.

The house was frozen over throughout the entire winter. There were not quite as many brawls at the saloons or even murders, as the winter frost held a layer of protection, but they knew that come spring, there would be more.

"Another Christmas in Gold Country," said Anna Claire happily, hanging up her stocking.

That Christmas Eve night, Joseph and Charlotta had gone to visit the Watsons and the Clemmons's and to bring them food, leaving the children at the cabin alone.

"This time, we're gonna get real good presents," said Pete sneakily. "We don't even need Santa Clause this year!"

"That's right, because we have money now!" said Anna Claire.

Caroline was curling her hair with a pencil. "It does not matter if we have money or not. Anna Claire; stop acting so spoiled!"

"I was only sayin'!"

Helen came barreling down the loft with a smile on her face.

"What are you so happy about?" asked Caroline, wincing as the pencil came a bit too close to her face.

"I'll be fourteen and Mama says I can have a beau when I'm fourteen," she giggled and sat on the ground, curling up next to the fireplace. "It's cold!"

"Beaus are not everything you think," said Caroline. "You are hardly ready for one! You are as stubborn as a mule and as clumsy as a clown."

Helen made a face and looked over at Anna Claire.

"Why do you look so miserable?" asked Helen.

Anna Claire sighed as she finished placing the ornaments on the tree.

"I wish Hope was here," she said sadly. "It isn't fair that they can't go wherever they want!"

"It is sad," agreed Helen.

"I wish they could be here, too," admitted Caroline.

There was a moment of silence before it was broken by Berthie's singing of Christmas carols.

"Doesn't anyone want to sing with me?" she asked in her lilting voice.

"No," snarled Pete. "I hate Christmas carols! Christmas carols can die!"

Caroline shook her head. "Don't talk about death tonight, Peter. It is so morbid, and it's Christmas!"

"Christmas is tomorrow," reminded Pete with a smirk, his eyes twinkling and his cheeks red from the firelight.

Suddenly, the children stopped what they were doing when they heard several loud knocks in a row.

"That doesn't sound like Papa or Mama," said Caroline.

"It must be!" said Helen.

"Who else could it be?" asked Anna Claire, her heart beginning to race.

The children stood up and stayed still, not knowing what to do.

The knocks came again, this time louder and for longer than before. It was certainly not their parents.

"I'm scared," said Helen, her fingertips to her teeth.

"I'm not going near that door!" Caroline agreed, moving towards the back of the cabin.

"Y'all are scaredy cats!" said Anna Claire haughtily. "I'll answer it."

"No, it could be anyone!" cried Caroline. "Look out of the window!"

Anna Claire hesitated and then did what she was told. Upon wiping the foggy window with her hand, she saw someone she was not sure she'd ever see again.

Without bothering to explain herself, she opened the door despite the protests from her siblings.

"It's Jim! Jim Turner!" she exclaimed proudly, a smile on her face.

And Jim Turner it was, looking very happy but very blue from the cold.

"Jim! Come, sit!" cried Caroline, rushing over with a blanket and helping him to a chair by the fireplace.

"I'm sorry to intrude on ye folks like this," he said, "but I was on my way from my niece's and thought I'd say hello. I'm thankful ye remember me at all!"

"Hello!" shouted Pete from across the room.

"Hello, Peter!" Jim called cheerfully, waving his hand in the air. "You've grown since the last time I saw you!"

Pete brimmed with pride.

"Who's that?" asked Berthie, nervously holding onto Caroline's hand.

Caroline smiled and bent down. "Don't be afraid, Berthie. You know him. You just don't remember because that was a long time ago now and you were too little."

"Oh, little Berthie!" he cried, resisting the urge to give her a hug. "Look at how ye've grown!"

Berthie didn't smile but instead glanced up at Caroline with a concerned expression on her face.

"Jim! I can't believe you're here!" said Anna Claire, enveloping him in a big hug. "You're so cold!"

Jim smiled and stretched his arms out to get a better look at her. "How old are ye now? Ye were nine last I saw you!"

"Eleven!" she said proudly. "Haven't I grown?"

"Ye certainly have!" said Jim. "Look at yer hair! It's longer now! Ah, it is so nice to see you again. Tell me, how are ye all doin'?"

Anna Claire smiled. "We're alright! How are you, Jim? I've missed you!"

"Where are my manners?" said Caroline suddenly. "I'm going to bring you a cup of hot chocolate!"

"Much obliged," answered Jim. "I'm alright, too, youngin. Just travelin' around as usual. Ran into a couple a' outlaws, but nothin' unusual. It's nice to see all of ye. Where are yer ma and pa?"

"They went to bring some food to our friends," said Helen. "Stay! They'll be back soon, I suppose!"

Jim smiled, his eyes twinkling just as they had before.

"And how is the other one- your friend, Tommy?" he asked.

Anna Claire grabbed the cup of hot chocolate from Caroline's hands and gave it to Mr. Turner. "Oh, Tommy's fine!"

And sure enough, almost as if the universe had decided fate to be, there was a quick knock on the door and Tommy appeared, falling through the door and bringing a bunch of snow with him.

"Tommy!" Anna Claire jumped at him and grabbed his hand. "Look! Look who's here! It's Mr. Jim Turner!"

"Mr. Jim Turner?" asked Tommy incredulously. "It really *is* you!"

Mr. Turner smiled and shook hands with the boy.

"Now ye've gotten taller yourself."

"It's good to see you, Mr. Turner!" said Tommy, his mouth still agape in disbelief.

"Here you are," said Caroline, coming back into the room with a tray of oatmeal cookies and hot cocoa. "Please, have as many as you desire."

"Thank ye, dear," he said, taking a cookie and throwing it into his mouth. "Ye'r prettier than ever, Caroline!"

Caroline blushed. "Thank you, Mr. Turner."

"Tommy is gonna marry Caroline," Anna Claire whispered in his ear, "but she doesn't know it yet."

Mr. Turner laughed and pretended to put his finger to his mouth in silence.

"Mr. Turner, did you see Santa Clause?" asked Pete sincerely.

Mr. Turner looked at the ground. "I can't say that I have. Although I did think I seen a reindeer on the mountaintop, but that could've been my bad eyes."

Pete's face brightened. "I bet that was Santa Clause!"

"I wanna see him, too!" shouted Berthie, becoming more comfortable with the man who looked frightening from the outside, but was tender-hearted within.

"He usually only comes when all youngins are sleepin'," said Mr. Turner. "He might come later, I expect."

"I wish you could stay here always," said Anna Claire, looking at him with admiration.

"You could come stay at the Goodrich Hotel!" said Tommy, pleading with his eyes. "Lots of people stay there!"

"Maybe someday, but tonight I have to get goin'."

"You can't leave yet; you just got here!" exclaimed Anna Claire in disappointment.

"It's far too cold," pressed Caroline. "You will have to stay here for the night."

"Nah," said Mr. Turner. "I got to meet a friend in Virginia City in just a few days. I gotta get there fast, ye see."

"Well, wait until Mama and Papa come home," said Helen. "They would love to see you again."

And that they did. Upon opening the door and seeing the giant man in their cabin, Joseph immediately lifted his rifle as Charlotta screamed and ran toward Berthie.

"Mama, Papa!" said Anna Claire impatiently. "It's only Mr. Turner!"

Their expressions were confused and Joseph gripped the rifle tighter.

"It's Jim Turner!" she said again. "You remember. He saved me and Tommy when I got lost down the creek!"

Charlotta's face began to relax as she leaned forward to inspect the man. Joseph began to carefully put the rifle down by his side.

"My God!" Joseph cried, his eyes going wide. "Jim Turner! How could we forget? You saved our daughter!"

Now recognizing him, Charlotta leapt over and embraced him, tears in her eyes.

"I promised I'd come back someday, didn't I?" Mr. Turner said with a grin.

And that was Christmas Eve. They stayed up late, eating cookies and drinking hot chocolate and listening to Jim tell more stories of his travels. Anna Claire and Tommy rattled on about school and

Bannack while the others were raptured up in his tales. Joseph and Charlotta were happy to see him, but he had to leave almost as quickly as he came.

"I'll be back in these parts again someday," he said as he walked out of the door, giving Tommy and Anna Claire a wink. "Now be good this year! Remember to listen to your ma and pa!"

"Don't leave, Mr. Turner," begged Anna Claire sadly.

"You are welcome to stay the night!" Charlotta said again.

Mr. Turner smiled and pat Tommy on the back. "I wish I could, but I gotta get to Virginia City. It was awful nice seein' ye folks. I knew I'd come back to the area someday! And I'll come back again, God willin'."

The children and parents gave Mr. Turner a hug and Joseph helped him to his wagon, giving him lots of cookies and filling his canteen with hot chocolate. Then, the Freilers and the one Cooper went back inside to warm up and finish the hot chocolate.

"Mr. Freiler, Mrs. Freiler," Tommy began, not knowing how to ask. "Is it- could I-"

"Stay here for the night?" Charlotta finished with a gentle smile. "Of course. We wouldn't have it otherwise."

Tommy smiled, relieved.

It was not much later when everyone went to bed, Tommy sharing the bed with Anna Claire, Pete, and Berthie as he did last year. When they awoke the next morning, the sun shining across the snow outside, they were finally able to see their presents.

Charlotta had made Joseph a new hat and gloves. Joseph had bought his wife a fine ruby necklace from the jeweler in town. Berthie not only got a new doll but she got two new outfits for her dolls. Pete got a cowboy figurine and a pair of silk mittens. Helen received new stockings and brown leather boots. Caroline was given a beautiful pink muslin dress to wear for special occasions like the dances. Anna Claire got not only one book but three books, all classic adventure books that she couldn't wait to read. Tommy, sitting by the fireplace and looking a bit out of place, was then given his very own pocket watch.

"You're gonna need it, son," Joseph said, patting the top of his head with his hand. "I bought this from the watchmaker. I hope you like it."

Tommy was thrilled. He never had a watch before, and now he could be like all of the men he saw at the saloon and the merchants in town.

"*Yeah*, I like it!" he declared, turning the watch over and over in his hands. "A real watch! I can't wait to show Mr. Dobbins!"

Joseph and Charlotta looked at each other and smiled, happy to have pleased the little boy.

Tommy's face fell. "I forgot to bring your gift. I forgot it at the saloon."

Charlotta stood up and gave him a hug. "Don't think another second about it!"

"Don't worry about it, son," said Joseph.

"Can I tell you about it?" asked Tommy eagerly.

The parents were surprised he had actually gotten them something and they nodded.

"Well," began Tommy, "wait 'til you see it! I made you another sign but this time it's a real big one and it says 'Family.' You gotta see it!"

The Freilers smiled warmly.

"That is thoughtful," said Charlotta.

"Thank you, son," said Joseph.

The others said their own thank yous before Tommy grabbed Anna Claire by the hand.

"We're gonna have a snowball fight!" he called. "Who wants to come?"

"I do!" shouted Berthie, running after them.

"Me too!" yelled Pete, tripping over his boots.

"Maybe I would, too," said Helen, trying to look bored but looking excited instead.

"Children, keep your mittens on!" called Charlotta. "Do not take anything off! Do not get snow in your clothes!"

"We won't, Mama!" called Anna Claire as they ran out into the crisp air, snowballs in hand.

And then they played. They ran, chasing each other, snow in their boots and faces. They felt alive as they hit each other and fell. Even Helen was laughing and throwing snowballs. It was a wonderful time.

In fact, it was one of the last wonderful times the Freiler children would have all together.

"They'll like the sign an awful lot," said Anna Claire as she sat on Tommy's cot in the saloon.

"Do you really think so?" Tommy asked, proudly showing off his very well-crafted "Family" gift.

"Yeah," said Anna Claire. "You know what?"

"What?"

"I think Mama and Papa wish you were their son, too," she said. "You *and* Pete."

Tommy looked up, stunned. "Why would you think that?"

Anna Claire shrugged. "They like you an awful lot. They talk about you like you're a son. They care about you."

Tommy smiled. "Do you think Caroline is startin' to notice me, too?"

Anna Claire nodded, causing Tommy's face to brighten excitedly.

"Only as a little brother," she added, watching as Tommy's face fell. "What do you expect, you're only twelve!"

"I won't be twelve forever," said Tommy, frowning. "She'll love me someday, you'll see, Anna Claire!"

Anna Claire laughed at the thought. "I bet you a hundred dollars she won't!"

"I bet you a hundred dollars she will!"

"How about this- in five years, if she still doesn't like you, I win!" declared Anna Claire.

Tommy grinned. "Fine! Five years- I'll be seventeen. I'll be all grown up. She'll want no one more than me!"

Anna Claire spat in her hand and shook his hand. "The bet has been settled! Now all we gotta do is wait five years."

"That sounds like an awful long time," said Tommy grimly. "Oh, well, it'll be worth it! I'll prove you wrong, Anna Claire! In five years' time, Caroline and I will be talkin' about marriage! You'll probably be alone."

"Fine with me!" shouted Anna Claire. "I told you, I'm never gonna court. I don't wanna and I ain't gonna. No one can make me! I'm gonna write and travel the world! I'm gonna see everything! Just you wait and see."

"I hope we remember in five years," mused Tommy. "What if we forget about the deal?"

Anna Claire considered. "Well, we can't. I'll write it down, and so we'll have to remember."

Tommy smiled. "Don't you forget!"

Anna Claire rolled her eyes. "I never forget anything, Tommy Cooper! In five years, I'll be gettin' ready to travel the world and you'll be no closer to courtin' Caroline than you are right now!"

"We'll see about that."

And Anna Claire, rushing to get home, took the quill and wrote on a small piece of paper, "January 1867- THE BET. Tommy Cooper bets that he and Caroline Freiler will be courting by January 1872. Anna Claire bets that he will not be courting Caroline by January 1872. Anna Claire will be getting ready to travel the world."

Satisfied, she stuck the piece of paper in her little trunk of clothing, where she would open it again years later.

Chapter 26- The Sickness

It was a cold February morning, not long after Joseph took the family on a short trip to town, when Berthie suddenly arose from the bed beginning to cry in pain.

Anna Claire turned over, still half-asleep, and slowly opened her eyes. "Berthie, what's wrong?"

"My stomach!" she cried, beginning to wake the others up. "It hurts!"

"Berthie, what ever is the matter?" cried Caroline, running to their side of the loft and holding her sister.

"I have to go to the outhouse," Berthie gasped, running down the ladder and right out of the door.

"Where is she goin'?" asked Joseph as he threw his pants on.

"The outhouse," said Anna Claire. "She said her stomach hurts."

"It must have been all that candy you let her have," snapped Charlotta, coming over and shaking her head at her husband. "You know how sensitive her stomach has been of late! I knew all that sugar was a terrible idea, but you never listen!"

Joseph pursed his lips. "Char, stop this. She was allowed to have a little treat. She needs to stop being babied so much! It's not good for her constitution."

Charlotta shook her head again and they waited. They waited a while before Helen offered to go check on the little girl. Then, the others waited some more.

"I'm going to see what is going on," said Charlotta, putting on her boots before running out of the door.

Some time later, they all walked into the house, Helen and Charlotta helping Berthie walk.

Berthie was still crying, her face white as ash and her lips the same color.

"What's wrong with her?" asked Pete, backing against the wall.

Joseph rushed over to help and picked Berthie up, sitting by the table.

"Did I give you too much candy?" he lamented. "I'm sorry, my girl!"

Berthie cried and cried, sounding so defeated and frightened. She was clutching her stomach, her white-blonde hair falling over her face, and her eyes were becoming red from rubbing them.

"How can I help, Berthie?" asked Anna Claire gently. "What can we do?"

"I am going to make some soup," said Charlotta, rushing into the little kitchen. "Joseph, go and find the doctor. Caroline, go with him and get some laudanum from the general store. Peter, please go to the loft and make up the bed. Helen, go grab some water. Anna Claire, stay with me."

Everyone did what they were told and went their separate ways. The other chores of the day would have to wait. Berthie was sick.

After countless of trips to the outhouse, a chamber pot was put up in the loft. This made it easier so that Berthie didn't have to keep running to the out-house. When changing and cleaning out the pot, Charlotta gasped at what she saw. When looking into the chamber pot, she saw red- it was blood.

"Bloody Flux," confirmed the doctor, feeling Berthie's feverish head, before requesting to speak to Joseph and Charlotta privately in the little kitchen.

"No, it can't be," said Charlotta. "We take every measure to keep her clean!"

"She must have contracted it from touching someone," said the doctor, "or perhaps from some-one in town. You went to town the other day, didn't you?"

Joseph nodded, tears in his eyes. "How do we stop it, doctor?"

The doctor's face had gone from red to pale.

"We will treat the symptoms with laudanum, but I am afraid there is not much we can do except watch her and pray to God he spares her. But I must warn you both that I have seen this before. There is little we can do except help her to eat and use the laudanum. There is a chance she will recover, but the chance is very small."

"No!" Charlotta fell to the side, leaning on her husband for balance. "No, that cannot be!"

"She will recover," said Joseph determinedly. "We will have her drink and eat, and we will treat her with the laudanum. She doesn't seem so bad, yet, doctor. Please, is there anything else we can do?"

The doctor, looking utterly defeated, shook his head. "The bloody flux is particularly difficult to treat. We don't know exactly what it is or how to stop it, but we know it usually drains the patient completely until they succumb to it. Berthie is very young and very fragile, and is already sensitive to this earth. I will not lie to you, as my duty is to be truthful. The chances of recovery are very small. You must tend to her the best you can, but prepare for the worst. Her face has gotten paler and her lips are whiter than they were even a few minutes ago."

"What can we do?" begged Charlotta, wanting an answer. "I will not lose my Berthie!"

"We're not losin' her!" shouted Joseph, so loudly that all of the children jumped up, startled. "Berthie is just fine. Doctor, she is young and fragile, but she is also determined. She will fight this, you'll see. We're not throwin' up the sponge. You'll see, doctor!"

The doctor frowned. "I have examined the child. I am afraid that the chances are small."

"Is there nothing else that can help her?" cried Charlotta, wiping the tears from her cheeks methodically.

"Make sure she drinks plenty of water and try to see if she can keep food down," answered the doctor, his eyes concerned and his tone soft. "That will help her feel more comfortable. I advise she stay in bed until- she should stay in bed now."

"How long until she's cured?" asked Joseph in a loud, booming voice.

The doctor paused and stared at him with an expression of acute sadness.

"How long!?"

The doctor turned his head. "Berthie may have about four or five days left. The chances of her getting well are very minimal; so minimal, in fact, that they are barely there."

Charlotta was hyperventilating as she hit the ground with her knees. She couldn't speak or even make a sound. The tears were coming down and her mouth was open but there was no sound coming out.

"I will be back tomorrow to check on her," said the doctor sadly, turning to walk out of the kitchen. "Here, take this sheep sorrel. It will help with the symptoms a bit."

"You'll see, she'll be feelin' better by tomorrow!" yelled Joseph confidently, even though there were tears in his eyes, too. "You'll see, doctor!"

The doctor did not reply but instead he walked out of the cabin, his eyes heavy and his body slow.

"What's happening?" asked Caroline from above the loft.

"What did the doctor say?" asked Helen.

Joseph stopped, turned around for a moment, and then turned back around again to face his children.

"The doctor said she is very sick." His throat felt dry. "She is very, very, very sick."

The children looked over at Charlotta who had stood up but was now looking at the ceiling with her hands clasped together, clearly praying.

"Mama, Papa, what precisely did the doctor say?" Caroline held her stomach, breathless.

"She has an illness which is causing her to bleed," Joseph answered. "When she goes to the out-house, she bleeds. The doctor does not think she will get better, but we will prove him wrong, won't we, children?"

They were stunned. They looked at each other and did not speak for a moment.

"Of course, he's wrong, Papa!" said Anna Claire with a laugh. "It's just a little blood! I get blood-ied up all the time. I'll tell her stories and read to her so that she won't be bored while she's gettin' better."

Caroline walked over to her father and touched his arm. "I will make sure the other chores get done. I will prepare the dinner and supper, and I'll make sure Berthie has clean blankets."

Helen, who looked more startled than she ever had, ran to give her mother a hug, stifling tears. "I'll make sure she's eating and drinking. I'll keep get-ting the water and giving her the laudanum."

"What can I do?" asked Pete in a mature way he had never asked before.

Joseph rubbed his forehead with the palm of his hand. "Peter, stay by me. We're goin' to the Clem-mons's. Perhaps Paul and Nettie have gone through this before with one of theirs."

Charlotta took a seat and lifted her head, look-ing hopeful for a moment.

"Yes, Nettie and Paul, they will know what to do! Yes, that is a splendid idea. Ask them if they have any medicine that helped with their children. I am sure Rebecca or Matthew have had this before!"

Anna Claire put her fingers in her mouth. This was the first time she had done this in years.

"Please," choked Charlotta, beginning to cry, "go to the Clemmons's. We need to know what to do to save her."

"We will, Mama," said Helen, tears in her own eyes, coming over to embrace her mother again.

Joseph said nothing as he left the house, rifle in hand. Caroline's eyes were wide, and her face had grown very white. Helen was crying with Charlotta and Pete had backed himself up against the wall, staring at Helen and Charlotta with wide eyes. Anna Claire had already begun walking up the ladder.

"Anna Claire, wait!" called Caroline, looking at Charlotta. "Mama, is this contagious?"

"I don't know," Charlotta answered, her voice shaking. "My mother had it before and lived through it. We must trust God to protect our girl. In the meantime, do not touch Berthie. Only stand away from her."

Anna Claire walked somberly up into the loft. Her sister was paler than she ever had been and her lips looked sore and gray. Her eyes were closed, and one hand was over her stomach. Tears were still on her cheeks and she was breathing in little choked sobs that made her chest tremble. Berthie had always been frail and accident-prone, always the first one to get sick, and now it was catching up to her in the worst way.

"Berthie," whispered Anna Claire, stretching her arm out to touch her small hand despite being told not to touch her. "I'm here, Berthie. I'm right here. Can't you look at me?"

Berthie opened her eyes and then shut them again, tears still trailing down the side of her face.

"You're gonna be just fine," said Anna Claire. "It's just a little blood. Remember the time I fell down the stairs in Minnesota? I got so much blood on me! You'll be fine, but you gotta eat! I know you don't like to eat, but you gotta this time."

Berthie weakly looked up and nodded.

"Good," said Anna Claire. "We're gonna help you get all better! But first, I'm gonna tell you the Old Man Hatfield story. I'll tell you the story all day long if you want."

Berthie gazed up and put on a small smile.

Meanwhile, Charlotta was making soup and using the last of the flour to make bread. Caroline took to washing all of the clothes, Helen fetched water back and forth in the buckets, and Peter had run with Joseph to the Clemmons's house.

When Joseph came back, he had Nettie by his side. Charlotta burst into tears and ran to hug her friend. The two hugged and cried for a moment until they both went to check on Berthie and help feed her soup. Paul was not at home, as he was out mining at the creek.

"I am so sorry, Charlotta," wept Nettie. "Rebecca and Matthew never did get the Bloody Flux. I know it is dangerous. We must make sure she keeps drinking!"

It was difficult, but Berthie did as she was told and drank water and ate the bread and soup. Nettie helped Charlotta bring up the bowls and clean the chamber pot, which continued to be full of blood. The children completed the necessary chores for the day and then completely immersed themselves in helping Berthie to get well. Joseph had decided to go to town and ask the townsmen if anyone knew anything about the Bloody Flux and if there was anything else he could do besides give Berthie the laudanum.

When Joseph came back home, he looked utterly heart-broken and defeated. Nettie made him and Charlotta cups of tea before she went back home to her family.

"Oh, Joseph!" Charlotta said, crying into her hands.

"It's not over," Joseph insisted in his booming voice. "It's not over. Not yet. Berthie is eatin' and drinkin'- is that not a good sign?"

Charlotta nodded weakly, looking up towards the loft.

"We just have to wait it out," Joseph reminded her, standing up to put his arm around her back. "I'm sure in a day or two, she'll be just her old self!"

The children stayed away from Berthie. Charlotta decided to stay with Berthie in the left side of the loft while all of the other children slept on the other side of the loft. She agreed not to go anywhere near the children until Berthie was well and it was sure that she was also well. She went outside to clean the chamber pot, but that is all she did out of the loft. She couldn't take the chance of giving this disease to the other children.

That night, Berthie was up vomiting into the chamber pot. All of the children woke up to the sound of the choking as well as her crying. Charlotta was crying, too, and yelling, "Joseph! More blood! Joseph! More blood!"

Joseph stumbled up to the loft, but Charlotta put her hand out to prevent him from coming any further.

"We have to look out for the other children," she said in a voice that didn't seem like her own.

Joseph put his hand to his head. "She must stop bleedin'!"

"She is vomiting blood," cried Charlotta, her voice shaky. "Joseph, what should we do?"

Joseph was at a loss for words. "I'm goin' to get more water."

When he came back up to the loft, Berthie was still leaning over on the bed, vomiting into the chamber pot, blood dripping from her lips.

"Joseph, help!" cried Charlotta frantically as she rubbed her daughter's back. "Get the doctor!"

Joseph ran to fetch the doctor. He had never run so fast in his life, not even when he was fighting for the Union. When he came back, Berthie had stopped vomiting blood but had used the chamber pot again, also producing blood.

The doctor looked sadder and more concerned than he even had before.

"The best we can do is to keep her comfortable." He gave Joseph a small bottle of medicine. "Have the sweet child take this. It's morphine. It will comfort her."

"She'll be alright?" asked Joseph as he took the bottle.

"No, she will not," the doctor answered seriously. "There is no hope; you must be prepared. Berthie is dying. She may have a day or so left, but she is dying very quickly. You must begin to prepare yourselves."

With that, Charlotta began shrieking, falling to the floor, and banging her hands on the wood.

"Oh my God," Joseph said, also falling to the ground and leaning over. "No, not my Berthie! Not Berthie!"

"I am very sorry," said the doctor softly. "There is nothing more we can do. Give her a spoonful of morphine tonight and tomorrow morning. If she is alive tomorrow night, give her another. I will come back tomorrow to check on all of you."

Charlotta and Joseph could barely hear him over their screaming.

Caroline herself fell onto the ground on the other side of the room and wailed. Helen had both her hands around her body as she sobbed, her face turning red and saliva dripping from her mouth. Pete stood next to Anna Claire with his eyes wide, and Anna Claire was staring at the doctor.

"Make her better!" Anna Claire yelled, storming over and grabbing the doctor by his coattails. "Make her better! She can get better. Make her better *now*!"

The doctor unclasped her hands from him and shook his head sadly, tears in his eyes.

"I am sorry, dear child. For all of you, I am so sorry. There is nothing that can be done when it progresses to this level. Give her the morphine at night and in the morning. I will come by tomorrow."

The doctor left the house, wiping tired eyes, as Anna Claire ran up to the loft.

"Don't touch her, Anna Claire!" yelled Charlotta through her tears.

Anna Claire, not heeding her warning, walked over to Berthie's bed and grabbed her hands.

"Berthie, Berthie, you can't sleep yet!" she said, tears beginning to graze down her cheeks slowly. "You have to wake up! We have to get you better. That dumb ol' doctor will see when he comes tomorrow that you're better. You need to eat and drink. I'll tell you the Old Man Hatfield story all night long and all day long. Don't go to sleep yet!"

Berthie opened her eyes weakly and smiled softly, her big brown eyes piercing, as if she had gained years of wisdom in only moments. It was as if she was looking into Anna Claire's soul.

"Anna Claire," said Caroline, coming into the loft and pulling her away. "We must stay on the other side of the loft. We cannot get sick, too. We have to care for Berthie."

Trembling, Anna Claire nodded as Caroline turned her around and embraced her, letting Anna Claire cry into her dress.

"Caroline," she wailed, holding onto her back. "We gotta save her!"

"Shh, dear," Caroline cooed, gently rubbing her back. "Help me cook supper and then we will tend to Berthie."

Anna Claire wiped her eyes with the back of her hand and allowed herself to be led down the loft.

Charlotta had curled herself up on the floor as she held onto the leg of one of the chairs while Helen fell beside her, her head in her lap. Joseph knelt down to put his arm around them while Pete was holding his hand, standing up by his side.

"We have to be strong for Berthie," said Caroline, her chin up as she wiped the remaining tears from her eyes. "Anna Claire and I will be cooking. Helen and Peter, go fetch more water. Mama and Papa- go lay down for some moments."

"No," said Charlotta, standing up slowly on shaky legs, grabbing onto the table for support. "I will stay upstairs with Berthie."

"And I will wash our blankets so that Berthie can have clean ones," said Joseph, standing up slowly and pursing his lips. "Berthie deserves the best we can give her."

And the best they did.

Chapter 27- Death Be Not Proud

Hero stayed loyally by Berthie's bed the whole time. It was even hard to get him outside. It was as though he knew instinctively that the little girl was very sick and wanted to comfort her. Caroline and Anna Claire made the supper, cooking the moose meat and throwing a little cherry pie together, as Berthie loved pie. Charlotta stayed upstairs with Berthie, holding her hand and telling her stories of when she was a little girl. Joseph had run to help Helen get the water, and the two of them washed blankets and one of Berthie's other dresses along with her tights. The house was cold, and Pete kept it warm by bringing in the firewood and seeing to it that the fire did not die.

Berthie was able to have a couple of bites of pie, which gave Charlotta some hope, although Joseph was beginning to understand that his youngest would not get better. The family stayed upstairs in the loft, Caroline reading Psalms while Charlotta kissed the top of Berthie's head as she held her hands. Berthie had to use the chamber pot often, and they all helped her, carrying it down the ladder and washing it, blood swishing around the bottom.

Berthie had stopped vomiting, at least, and was finally able to go to sleep. She woke up consistently throughout the night to use the chamber pot but she was no longer crying.

The others took turns. Charlotta was up most of the night, not daring to take her eyes off her little one. Joseph got some sleep, as he knew it would likely be the only sleep he would get for a long time, and Pete eventually fell asleep, too. Helen and Anna Claire sat up in bed for a long time, silent with their knees up to their heads, looking at each other every so often in disbelief. They both fell asleep too, Helen nodding out first before Anna Claire, who had fallen asleep without giving permission.

The light peered through the room. Anna Claire's heart dropped the second she opened her eyes. She got out of Caroline and Helen's bed, climbing over Pete, and ran to Berthie's side. Charlotta was feeding her soup, Berthie was opening her mouth, and Anna Claire sighed in relief.

"She's better, isn't she, Mama?" sighed Anna Claire. "Right, Mama?"

Charlotta looked grave.

"She is eating, which is a good sign," she answered. "Right now, we have to wait for the doctor."

"That doctor doesn't know what he's doin'!" yelled Anna Claire, waking the other children up. "He said Berthie wouldn't get better, but look- she's gettin' better! We don't need that doctor!"

Charlotta looked at her with watery blue eyes.

"Anna Claire!" yelled Joseph from downstairs. "Come and help me tend to the animals."   Relieved to be out of the house, Anna Claire did what she was told as the other children slowly started to wake.

Caroline immediately took to making more soup and bread as well as keeping the fire going. Helen washed the other blankets and put an extra quilt on Berthie, as it seemed to be even colder than the day before. Pete walked to and from the well, the snow almost up to his chest, and dragged the water bucket in and out of the house. Charlotta stayed by Berthie's side, cleaning out the chamber pot and keeping Berthie as warm as she could be. Joseph and Anna Claire had been working with the animals, and then came back inside to help Berthie take her morphine. Berthie herself looked very calm, despite the fact that she had heard the cries and shouts from the day before.

The doctor came in the late part of afternoon. He was surprised to see that Berthie was still alive, but when he went to check on her, he frowned deeply.

"There's a lot more blood," he said, coming down the ladder.

All the rest of them were down on the first floor. Charlotta was holding onto Joseph while the children stayed close to them.

"How can we make the bleeding stop?" asked Charlotta, refusing to give up.

The doctor sighed again. "It won't. You see, the Bloody Flux causes the bowels to bleed until too much blood exits from the body."

"We can use the blankets to stop the blood," said Charlotta fiercely.

"That won't do," said the doctor, his face paler than ever. "That will only start an infection and it would be very painful for the child."

"Well, damn it, what do we do?" yelled Joseph, nodding his head and pounding his fist into the wall next to him. "I'm not lettin' her die!"

The doctor looked utterly defeated.

"God will look after her. What is God's will, will be. Berthie may only have today. Spend it wisely. I suggest you read the Bible and give her your prayers. Then, say goodbye. She is dying, and there is no way to save her."

"No!" cried Charlotta, falling to the floor again as her husband leaned down to pick her up.

"I'm dying?" said the smallest voice in the house.

Berthie had hobbled to the edge of the loft and was looking down at everyone.

The doctor was shocked. He looked over at Joseph and then at Charlotta.

"No, dear," Charlotta said. "Nonsense. Get back into bed. I will be there soon."

Berthie looked around with her big brown eyes and got back into bed.

"You can give her morphine every few hours," said the doctor. "I will be back tomorrow. If there is some miracle and she lives the night, keep feeding her soup and bread in the morning. And give her the laudanum."

Joseph angrily walked to the door and waved at it, signaling for the doctor to leave. The doctor sadly walked out, and the door slammed in his face.

"Useless," scoffed Joseph bitterly.

Charlotta was already going up the ladder, Anna Claire trailing behind her.

"Am I dying?" Berthie asked again with her tiny little voice, putting the head of one of her dollies onto her pale cheek. Her lips were gray and her face was white, and her eyes were big and wide, her pupils hardly visible, like she was looking through their souls and was somewhere else entirely.

Charlotta shook her head but could not force herself to say it.

"It's alright, Mama," said the child. "I don't think I mind dying. I'll get to go back home."

Charlotta began sobbing and holding her hands, while Anna Claire stared at her sister in disbelief.

"You always said God does miracles!" said Anna Claire frantically, pulling on her mother's hand. "You said God can do whatever He wants! Maybe a miracle will happen!"

Charlotta bit her lip and closed her eyes. "Maybe, Anna Claire. Maybe."

"Mama," she choked, feeling her whole body shake, "can I have a few minutes with Berthie? Just to tell her the Old Man Hatfield story?"

Charlotta looked at her, then at Berthie, and stood up.

"Oh, Anna Claire," Charlotta ran to her, picking her up and kissing the top of her head. "Oh, my girl."

Anna Claire kissed her mother on the cheek and then sat beside her little sister. When she looked at her, Berthie looked different. Very, very pale, and her eyes deeply sunken into her face. She had grown so thin in just a couple of days and her white-blonde hair hung in strings down her little shoulders. She was clutching onto Hero, who was slowly licking her arm in a very gentle way, as if he knew it was nearing the end.

"Hi, Berthie," Anna Claire said as cheerfully as she could, although her voice was breaking along with her heart. "Do you wanna hear the Old Man Hatfield story?"

Berthie smiled gently and gave a small nod.

"Alright," said Anna Claire. "Once there was a nice man. His name was Davie." Anna Claire had started to cry. "He was real nice to everyone he met and everyone liked him. He got married-" she stopped here and began to sob quietly before continuing. "He got married to Minnie. Minnie was a nice girl he met. Minnie was a good wife and they had a baby and named her Daisy."

Anna Claire watched her sister gently close her eyes as she softly rubbed her little hand.

"Well, Minnie got thrown off the horse and died. So, he had to raise the baby all by himself." Berthie took a deep breath, still slightly smiling. "So, then he was strict with Daisy and didn't let her go nowhere or do nothin'. Daisy was angry." Anna Claire began to weep profusely despite trying to be brave, wiping her nose with the sleeve of her dress. "Daisy was angry. So, she left when she grew up. She went out to find the world. David Hatfield was real bitter and angry that she didn't stay with him so he ran after her and chased her. She didn't come back for a long time." Anna Claire felt Berthie's hand relax. "Well, David Hatfield was so sad and angry that he got mean. Real mean! No one liked him anymore. Daisy had found a man, and the two ran off together, but the man left her alone with their baby. They named the baby Darlin'. When Daisy came back to see her father, she found out he died from a heart attack. She was so sad that she killed herself. I know it's sad, Berthie, but you remember the good part? Old Man Hatfield buried a treasure up in the mountains. Daisy probably knew where it was. Maybe she told whoever took her baby, Darlin'. Darlin's alive out there somewhere. We think it's Miss Darlin', our teacher! Berthie, you gotta get better! You're comin' with us, remember? In a few years, we're all gonna climb the mountain again and we're all gonna find the treasure! But you gotta get better so you can come! I ain't goin' without you." Anna Claire began sobbing again, unable to speak for a long while. She tucked the blankets tighter around her sister and kissed her on the forehead. "You must be hungry. Do you want some soup?"

Berthie didn't answer. Anna Claire looked down and gently tapped her on her shoulder. Berthie's body felt limp to the touch and her eyes were slightly open but looking at nothing. Hero had stood up on the bed and was putting his paw on Berthie's little arm.

"Berthie, wake up, you gotta eat," said Anna Claire, her heart dropping into her stomach. "Wake up, Berthie!" She pushed her shoulder again, but Berthie did not move. "Berthie! Berthie! Wake up! You gotta eat!" Charlotta came up the ladder at that moment, Caroline following.

"She's not movin', Mama!" cried Anna Claire frantically. "She's not movin'! Make her move!"

Charlotta felt her head and crumbled onto the bed, sobbing into the quilt. "Oh, my baby. My baby!"

Caroline fell next to her mother and wrapped her arm around her. Helen and Pete, hearing the commotion, ran up the ladder then.

"She's dead?" asked Pete, tilting his head and looking at his sister's face.

Caroline looked back and nodded sadly.

"No," Helen began to weep, her hands up to her eyes. "No, no, no!"

Soon, everyone was crying, even Pete, who was next to Berthie's head, staring at her as if she would wake up. Joseph came in from getting the firewood and panicked when he didn't see anyone.

"Char!" he called from the main room. Instead, he was only met with sobbing.

He ran up the ladder and put his hand to his forehead when he saw his daughter lying there, lifeless and white.

"Oh God," he said, his whole face distorting in grief. "Oh God."

Helen ran to hug her father while Caroline held her mother. Charlotta had her head on the bed on Berthie's chest while Joseph came over to embrace Pete.

"Anna Claire," Joseph said, his voice cracking, but his arms open.

But Anna Claire didn't want to be held. She didn't want anyone to try and comfort her. She couldn't be comforted, and she knew that.

Turning on her heels, she ran through the loft and down the ladder. When she reached the ground, she sprinted ahead and out the door, running as fast as she could despite all of the snow. She ran and ran until she fell into the snow, her face red and tears freezing on her cheeks.

"Berthie, no!" she wailed, her nose running and saliva dripping slowly from her mouth. "No, not Berthie! Not Berthie! Not my sister!"

The pain was unlike anything she had ever experienced before. It felt like someone had stabbed her heart with a knife and yanked it out. She couldn't understand how Berthie had just been there and now was suddenly gone in the blink of an eye. She was fine and laughing just three days ago!

Anna Claire threw her head into the snow, not caring about how cold it was. She didn't want to exist in that moment. She wished she were far away from there. She wished she could be wherever Berthie was, whatever heaven lie above the sky.

She did not come home until Helen ran out to find her and bring her back. Helen herself had a wet face as she dragged Anna Claire up from the earth.

"Come on, Anna Claire," said Helen. "Stop it! Get up!"

Anna Claire glared at her. "Why did it have to be Berthie? Why couldn't it have been *you*?"

Helen was stunned and said nothing as the two walked back to the house. Anna Claire knew she had said something bad to her sister that she could never take back, but at that moment, she was too sad to care. She just wanted her Berthie back.

The next couple of days were surreal. Joseph went to town that very day and purchased a beautiful white coffin with flower engravings on the side, made by the prominent coffin-maker, Mr. Ferguson. It was clearly the most expensive one there. Charlotta would not leave her daughter's body for hours, her hand holding her lifeless one, and her head on her chest. Joseph ran into Mr. Dobbins while he was in town and told him the tragic news. He stated that they would have the viewing the next afternoon, and anyone that loved Berthie was welcome to come and pay their condolences. He was able to make the trip to the Watson's home and told George and Abigail, who told Hope. Hope had taken to Berthie and was quite sad to hear of her passing. They would not be able to attend the wake for obvious reasons, and they gave Joseph a handful of food to take home with him. Even Hero was distraught and sat by Berthie's coffin throughout the next day, hardly leaving her side. His heart was broken, too.

Joseph and Charlotta laid the little girl out nicely in the main room once they had gently washed her body and dressed her in her best dress. They had moved the table to the back of the room and placed the coffin on top. Berthie looked peaceful and calm, as if she was just sleeping. Charlotta had taken three of her dolls and placed two of them around her little girl, keeping one doll for the family. That night, no one left the room. They sat on the bench and the chairs, staring at the little girl in the coffin with the white face and the white hair.

Anna Claire wanted to shake her on the shoulders to wake her up, but she knew it would not be possible. Berthie was gone, and she wasn't going to come back, no matter how hard her family willed it to be. Instead, Anna Claire sat there and studied her face like the others. Berthie looked so beautiful. She was lovely in death, just as she was in life, only now she no longer had to suffer with painful ailments and chance injuries. Now, she could finally be at peace.

Tommy had found out the horrible news from Mr. Dobbins that day, who could barely talk. Tommy had been helping his mother at the saloon and the snow had kept him indoors, so he had not even heard that Berthie was sick. He was stunned. He was told by Mr. Dobbins not to bother the family that day, and that he could come the next day to say goodbye at the Freiler home.

The next day was a hard one- one of the most difficult days the Freilers had ever known. No one had gotten much sleep the night before and Anna Claire refused to leave her sister's body, sleeping on the floor next to the table.

In the morning, Caroline had ensured that the family ate some oatmeal. No one wanted to, but they knew they needed some energy to get through the day. Joseph had, the day before, talked to Mr. O'Reilly who got in touch with a man who used to be a pastor. That day, the man came to the Freiler house and stood by the coffin. In what seemed like a very short time, the house became packed with solemn people wearing black and weeping into handkerchiefs. None of the Freilers had anything black to wear, so they stuck to the darkest colors they could find. Anna Claire didn't want them to take her sister away, so she kept a close eye on Berthie's body.

Caroline stood next to Charlotta, giving her friends from school small hugs when they walked past her. Helen, somber and serious, shook hands with people and couldn't even smile when Rebecca came up to hug her. Pete was half-hiding shyly behind Charlotta as Joseph stood on the other side, greeting the mourners with a shake of the hand and a small, albeit tight, smile, thanking them for coming to see their little Berthie be put to rest.

"Anna Claire!" Tommy proclaimed as soon as he ran inside the house.

Mr. Dobbins hushed him, and Tommy remained quiet until it was his turn to walk by the family.

Joseph's eyes filled with tears as he saw Tommy, giving him a hard shake of the hand and a very heart-breaking smile.

"I'm sorry, Mr. Freiler," peeped Tommy. It was all that he could say.

He hugged the family and, for the first time, did not care about how beautiful Caroline looked. This time, he only cared that she was hurting and had lost her sister.

"Anna Claire," he said when he came up to her.

Anna Claire knew he was in front of her, but her eyes hurt from rubbing them so much and the lack of sleep that she could hardly see him.

"Anna Claire," he repeated, putting his arms around her. "I'm sorry, Anna Claire. I'm awful sorry."

Anna Claire's body was tight. She didn't hug him back but instead looked away. Tommy wanted to stay, but Mr. Dobbins moved him along.

When it was time, Joseph and Paul Clemmons lifted the coffin and walked outside into the cold air, the snow finally easing up and beginning to melt. They gently placed the coffin on the wagon and hitched the horses to it. They, along with everyone else, rode and walked over towards the creek. The weather was crisp and cold, but the sun was shining.

Joseph and Mr. Clemmons began digging through the snow and then into the ground. Most of the women were crying, especially Nettie who was holding onto Charlotta and helping her stand. The children stood together, staring at the coffin. There was not a dry eye among the group and even the men were teary. Mr. Dobbins ensured that Tommy did not bother the family and kept him away from Anna Claire, which was a hard thing to do as all Tommy wanted was to give her a big hug and tell her how bad he felt.

Anna Claire's heart broke all over again upon seeing the little stone with the engraving, *"Bertha Freiler: 18th of November 1859- February 6th, 1867."* She began to sob loudly, falling next to the grave and screaming Berthie's name over and over again until Joseph picked her up and held her. This was unbearable for Tommy, as he knew his friend needed him, but he could do nothing to ease her pain.

The old pastor said some soothing words and read some quotes from the Bible. Nothing made sense to Anna Claire. It was all just words. Meaningless, useless words. It all seemed to go fast for Anna Claire- so fast that it seemed as though everyone was gone just as quickly as they had come.

The Freiler house was piled with food- pies, cakes, fruits, even meat. In any other circumstance, this would be too good to be true. In this one, nobody cared about the food or wanted to eat. The food sat there for a while until Charlotta reminded everyone that it was wasteful to let food spoil.

Over the next few days, Joseph kept busy. He kept mining, tended to the animals, and began building more chairs, even though more chairs were not needed. Charlotta kept herself going by packing food, but she mainly stayed in bed. Caroline was the one who had to step up during this time and clean the house, tend to the meals, bring in the water, wash her siblings, wash the clothes and blankets, and make sure the other children were kept clean.

No one talked much. No one wanted to talk much. Pete had stopped with his joking and pranking, and Helen did her chores without one single complaint. No one felt like doing anything for that matter, and, besides chores, they sat around miserably.

Charlotta never stopped crying, and the minute she experienced a reprieve, she started crying all over again. Joseph barely cried at all. He couldn't stop and think. He had to make the chairs before starting to make another table, and then more chairs for the Clemmons's. He then began building a little shed to store some more of the farm materials, which were more useful than chairs, but still unnecessary at this time. He often worked on this instead of sleeping. He couldn't sleep- not after knowing she was gone.

Caroline had toughened up to take care of her siblings and parents, and this was the first time Anna

Claire ever truly respected her. Caroline waited until she was alone at night to do her grieving and, as soon as the sun rose up, she was on her feet again, doing the household chores and feeding the family. Helen helped without whining at all, which was a very bad sign, and Pete became irritable and angry, not wanting to talk or listen to anyone. Anna Claire felt like she was in a dream. She hated sleeping in the bed that her little sister died in. She hated seeing the empty seat at the table, and the feeling that there was one less person saying grace. She hated that the house was so quiet during cooking and that there was no little girl anxiously awaiting to hear her stories. Anna Claire felt helpless. She just wanted her little sister back, but there was nothing she could do and no place she could go to see her or hear her little voice.

Joseph found comfort in a very old poem published in 1633 by Dr. John Donne called "Death Be Not Proud." He read it aloud to his family along with the Bible every single night for weeks:

"Death, be not proud, though some have called thee
Mighty and dreadful, for thou art not so;
For those whom thou think'st thou dost overthrow
Die not, poor Death, nor yet canst thou kill me.
From rest and sleep, which but thy pictures be,
Much pleasure; then from thee much more must
 flow,
And soonest our best men with thee do go,
Rest of their bones, and soul's delivery.
Thou art slave to fate, chance, kings, and desperate
 men,

And dost with poison, war, and sickness dwell,
And poppy or charms can make us sleep as well
And better than thy stroke; why swell'st thou then?
One short sleep past, we wake eternally
And death shall be no more; Death, thou shalt die."

Chapter 28- New Journeys

Nothing was the same without Berthie.

There was no sweet laughter filling the house, no "dollies" all over the floor, no high-pitched voice asking questions, and no little arms stretching out for hugs. The sweetest and kindest of the Freilers had passed away, and now it was up to the rest of them to make some new kind of meaning out of their lives.

March was so awful for everyone that it went by terribly and painfully slow, as if a year had gone by. Tommy had come to the door a few times to pay his respects and check in on the family, but no one wanted company, not even Anna Claire. Finally, Joseph explained to Tommy that the family was in grief, and when one is grieving, company can take an emotional toll on a person. He asked that he wait some time before coming back, to give everyone some space while they processed the loss.

Tommy himself was destroyed. He loved his "Little Ber," and had no time to adjust to her death, as he had not even known she was sick. She went so quickly. He had no time to say goodbye to his little friend. He stayed in his room by himself most of the time. If he couldn't see the Freiler's, he didn't want to see anyone.

Grief came like a cloud over them and settled there. But grief was not the only calamity going on in Gold Country. The roads to Virginia City were still unsafe, men were still being murdered in cold blood, and the Road Agents continued to terrify everyone in and around Bannack. It did not help that strange men, some who very possibly could have been Road Agents, were staying overnight with Tommy's mother. Tommy was beginning to understand that something else was going on besides drinking and talking. He wasn't sure exactly what, but he knew it was more than that.

It was a miserable time for most people. Bannack seemed to be getting more dangerous, the people had lost a precious little soul, gold was getting harder and harder to come by, and Tommy missed his best friend.

Dear Mor,

I cannot bear to have lost my child. I am sorry that you did not get the chance to say goodbye. Berthie loved you so much. I know you loved her, too. I confess my heart may never heal from this pain. Every day seems harder than the last. Berthie spent most of her time by my side. Never there was a sweeter and more loving child than our Berthie.

The days are long and wretched. Caroline has been a blessing and has been doing what I cannot do now. Joseph is beside himself. The children do not want to do anything. Anna Claire has even stayed at home and refuses to leave the loft except for chores. Anna Claire had a special bond with Berthie, as she used to tell her stories before bedtime. There were so many nights when I caught the two of them talking late at night! I scolded them, but now I would give anything to hear that again.

The others are devastated beyond recognition as well. Helen cries and cries and Caroline refuses to cry. Pete looks sad and tired all the time, and always looks at Berthie's empty spot at the table. This is too much for my heart to bear. I do not want to do anything but leave this terrible place. It was once becoming my home, but now all I think about is that Berthie died here. I have lost all of the connection I had with this place.

Joseph and I will be moving; it is just a matter of time. Where will be go, I'm not sure. I hope somewhere far away from Bannack and Gold Country. I do not want these constant reminders that Berthie's soul is no longer here with us. Please continue to pray for us, Mor. I will write to you when we have found a house.

Yours sincerely,
Charlotta

"I think it is time," said Charlotta softly one April day as the rain pelted on the roof of the house.

The children were busy with their chores, and Charlotta and Joseph had a few moments to speak.

Joseph nodded solemnly. He no longer cared about finding more gold- in fact, he didn't care about the gold at all anymore. He had lost what was more valuable than any amount of gold, and money didn't matter anymore except for the purpose of taking care of the rest of the family.

"Yes," he agreed, taking a long breath in. "I believe Ponderosa Valley will be suitable. It's North from here and much safer. It's a bigger town with a lot of people, and they don't have the kinds of problems we have here. I was talkin' to Mr. Grimm, who knows an investor who has some money. The man is sellin' his house. What do you say about Ponderosa Valley?"

Charlotta's eyes brimmed with tears. "I'd rather go back to Minnesota."

"I know, Char," said Joseph, "but makin' that journey now would be too risky. We barely made it here last time! Ponderosa will only take a couple of days on the road. We would leave very early so we can be far away from here by the time the night falls."

Charlotta, crying softly now, nodded. "I have heard of Ponderosa Valley being safe and very nice."

Joseph managed a small smile. "The house is beautiful. It has two floors, real panelin', and even some plumbin'. It'll be a nice life, Charlotta. We have the money now."

"I don't care about the money."

"I don't either," admitted Joseph, "but it will be important for the children. We want Pete to go to college, Char. Imagine the life he could have! Caroline would be more eligible for a wealthier suitor, and so would Helen. Ponderosa Valley will be a good place to start again."

Charlotta nodded flatly, staring into space. "I don't care what we leave and what we take anymore. I just want to get far away from here as soon as we can."

"Then it's settled," Joseph nodded. "I will talk to Mr. Grimm today. It is a great thing that his friend is selling that house. We have more than enough money to buy it without any loans. That house sounds real nice, Char! Can you picture us livin' in a house with plumbin' and four bedrooms and a parlor? You're gonna be real happy there, Char. You'll see."

Charlotta nodded again, looking as if she did not care if the roof collapsed right on top of her.

"It won't be the same without Berthie," she said, her voice cracking.

Joseph's face fell. He looked at Charlotta, but didn't know what to say so he walked out of the door instead.

When he got to the little barn, he collapsed on the ground with the hay and sobbed bitterly. No matter how strong he tried to be or how much he worked, he would never be able to repair his broken heart. He would never hear the sound of his child's voice, tell her stories of his boyhood, watch her grow up, or wrap his arms around her again. She would always be seven years old, and he would always remember her that way.

He stood up shakily, brushing the hay from his pants, and began washing the animals. Everything was gray, and nothing seemed to matter to him anymore.

It was late April now, and over two months since the disease had taken the youngest Freiler child. Tommy could not wait any longer. He had not been to the Freiler's cabin in over a month. He had heeded Mr. Freiler's wishes, but he needed to see how his friends were doing after their horrible tragedy. One Saturday, he jumped out of bed, put on his boots, and ran through the town over the hill and into the fields on the way to the Freiler's home.

"Oh, Tommy!" said Caroline when she answered the door, surprised.

"Hello, Caroline," Tommy said. "I'm awful sorry about Berthie. Can I come in?"

Caroline looked around. "Please wait here."

When she came back, she smiled. "You can come in. I asked Mama and she said it was alright. She's sleeping, so you must be quiet. Anna Claire is in the loft reading."

Tommy nodded and walked in sheepishly. He looked up at the loft and saw Anna Claire staring down at him.

"Anna Claire!" he said, walking up the ladder stairs.

"Tommy," she said before bursting into tears.

Tommy walked over to his dear friend and put his arms around her, letting her cry into his shirt.

"It's been so awful," she said, wiping her nose with her sleeve. "We miss Berthie so much. Mama just sleeps, and Papa works all day and night. He keeps makin' chairs that we don't need. We don't do nothin' but sit around. It's so awful, Tommy. None of us have wanted to do anything. We pray for Berthie's soul a lot. Mama says she knows she's in heaven 'cause she was an 'angel on earth.' She was, wasn't she, Tommy?"

Tommy nodded, feeling a lump in his throat. He wiped his eyes before Anna Claire could see that he was struggling not to cry.

"Do you wanna go into town?" asked Tommy. "That oughta cheer you up! Come on, we can have candy!"

Anna Claire shook her head. "Mama and Papa say it's gotten worse, and I can't go to town anymore, not even with you, unless they come with us. Mama sleeps a lot and she don't like it when we disturb her. Papa ain't comin' back probably 'til it gets dark outside. We can go to the creek, though! I haven't been there since-" she paused.

"That sounds like a good idea!" said Tommy quickly.

"I have to ask Caroline," she said with a whisper.

The two children walked quietly down the loft, careful not to wake Helen as she was also sleeping.

"Caroline," said Anna Claire, walking up to her as she cleaned the windows. "Can me and Tommy go to the creek? We won't be too long!"

Caroline looked as if she was about to protest, but instead sighed. "Yes, you may go. Don't be too long; I need your help with the animals."

Anna Claire nodded and grabbed Tommy by the hand.

The two children walked into the fresh air, the birds chirping around them and the grass finally green. They didn't say anything for a while. They found that, for the first time, they had nothing to say to each other.

They sat on the bank, Anna Claire twisting a piece of grass with her fingers and Tommy tapping his boot. They didn't speak, but they watched the water together, comfortable with the silence. Tommy, sensing his friend's sadness and feeling helpless to do anything, placed his arm around her. She began to cry softly, leaning into him and burying her head in his shoulder. They continued to say nothing but the silence said everything.

After some time, they stood up and brushed the dirt off of themselves. They walked away from the creek and back into the clearing.

"I'm awful sorry, Anna Claire," he said finally, looking at her with dread and sympathy. "I'll never forget Berthie. I miss her lots."

Anna Claire nodded. "Promise you'll never forget her? Not ever?"

Tommy shook his head rigorously. "I swear on Old Man Hatfield's grave that I will never forget Berthie!"

Swearing on Old Man Hatfield's grave was very serious, so Anna Claire felt satisfied.

"I gotta go, Caroline wants me to help with the animals," said Anna Claire. "Come back, Tommy—don't forget!"

"I won't forget!" he promised as he began to walk away. "I'll come back soon!"

When Tommy went to sleep that night, he felt an overwhelming sadness fill him up. He had never seen Anna Claire look so hopeless before. It wasn't like her. She never let anything get to her. The death of her sister had finally taken a piece of her that could never be replaced. Tommy knew deep down that she was forever changed in some way.

Tommy had trouble falling asleep that night. He tossed and turned, turned and tossed, and finally sat up in his bed with a huff. It was eerily quiet in the saloon, which Tommy was not used to, but that only lasted a brief moment, for in a minute he heard the sound of men banging down the door and yelling cuss words.

"Open up, harlot!" screamed one of the men as the door finally gave and the men entered, their boots loud and booming on the wooden floorboards.

"Where is that woman?" asked another, the sound of his feet walking around the floor.

"In her bedroom, of course," said another one with a sickening laugh.

Tommy recognized the voices. He had heard them before. In fact, he had heard them the time he was beat up in the fields and left for dead.

He braced himself as he heard them walking up the stairs. It sounded like about five men walking up. Tommy felt a gust of fear and considered jumping out of his window, but that would have been a bad fall.

One of the men barged into Tommy's room. Breathless, Tommy reached under his bed and grabbed his knife.

The man, wearing a black bandana and a black coat, laughed. "Now I'm all balled up. Why you got a knife in your hand? Don't worry, boy. It's not you we want. It's your whore of a mother. She's been tellin' tall tales about us. Tellin' people we're killin' people on the road. Tryin' to get us all hung. She's gonna have to pay."

"No!" cried Tommy, leaping at the man with his knife. The man pushed him against the wall, grabbed the knife from his hands and put it to his throat.

"Shut your damn bazoo! Move one muscle and you're done," the man said, letting Tommy fall to the ground.

"Don't you hurt my mother!" cried Tommy, his whole body shaking with fear, surprise, and anger.

"That's it," said the man as another man came into the room behind him. "Tie 'im up!"

The other man took a long yellow rope and pushed Tommy towards his bed, tying him up against the post and putting a handkerchief in his mouth so that he couldn't talk.

Tommy struggled to spit the thing out and yelled through the cloth, but his voice was barely audible.

He could hear the sound of the men opening the door to his mother's room across the way. He could hear the sound of his mother waking up and screaming. Then he heard the sound of beating while his mother continued to yell and sob. Then he heard one of the men make a loud noise and a sound that resembled slicing. Then, he heard laughter as the men ran down the stairs. One of the men, the man that had pinned him against the wall, looked into his room and spat, "Good luck, son."

Tommy, crying and unable to talk, screamed through the handkerchief as loudly as he could. He couldn't move because of the rope, and the men had taken his knife. All he could do was wait.

It was awful for the next couple of hours, and Tommy's breathing was ragged because his nose was clogged. He felt hope when he heard the sound of people rushing into the saloon and gasping. He could hear them talking and becoming upset at what had occurred. It wasn't long before someone had run upstairs and found him on the floor, tied up to the bedpost, a handkerchief filling his mouth.

"My God!" said the man, pulling on the rope and taking a knife from his pocket to cut it. He removed the handkerchief simultaneously.

"My ma!" Tommy choked, finally being unleashed. "My ma! They hurt my ma! You've gotta help her!"

The man looked at him with wide eyes and turned around to walk into his mother's room. A few men had come up and were yelling and hollering.

"What in the-"

"My God!"

"What in the devil's name happened here?"

"Who done it?"

"Evil sons of bitches!"

"That poor woman. Who's gettin' the deputy?"

"I'll do it."

Tommy squeezed through the men, anxiously attempting to get to his mother. When he saw her lying on the floor, a large pool of blood next to her head, he screamed.

"No, Ma!" he fell onto the floor and began to yell. "My ma!"

Mr. O'Reilly was one of the men there that morning, and he picked the little boy up and held him.

"I'm sorry, kid," he said. "It looks like the Road Agents did their evil work here."

"But my ma!" he continued to sob. "Why did they kill her?"

"I reckon I don't know…" said Mr. O'Reilly, his voice trailing off.

"This damn cussedness has to stop!" chimed in Mr. Wits.

"The Road Agents kill anyone who tries to interfere," said an older man with a wide-brimmed hat. "Your ma must have done somethin' to set 'em off."

"I'm sorry, Tommy," said Mr. O'Reilly sympathetically, patting his back and looking straight into his eyes.

Tommy couldn't speak. He felt the world moving around him. He fell into Mr. O'Reilly's arms then and everything went gray. He had passed out.

When he woke up, it was nearly an hour later, and he was lying in Mr. Dobbins's bed out of town with a cold cloth on his head.

Mr. Dobbins had tears in his eyes. He put his hand on Tommy's forehead and peered at him with his sharp grey eyes.

"You awake?"

Tommy nodded, taking the cloth off of his head. "My ma is dead!"

Mr. Dobbins sighed. "I know, youngin'. I know."

"They came this mornin' and killed her!" Tommy sat up in bed and jumped up on the ground, ignoring Mr. Dobbins's pleas to sit back down. "Why would they do it? Why did they have to kill my ma? What she done to anybody?"

Tommy's face was red and his eyes sunken in his cheeks. He looked as if he hadn't slept in weeks.

"That's what I gotta explain," said Mr. Dobbins, helping Tommy drink a glass of water. "I warned your ma about this."

"About what?"

"About talkin' too much about the Road Agents," he said sadly. "Your ma has been talkin' 'bout them for months and how she's gonna run off and tell the deputy. All this hearsay. Your ma didn't always have the best company, you know that. Some of them were probably Road Agents themselves and heard her talkin' about catchin' 'em. They probably killed her so she wouldn't be able to talk no more."

Tommy felt breathless. "Why did they have to kill her? Why couldn't they just stop seein' her?"

Mr. Dobbins closed his eyes, trying to find the right words. "It seems like your ma may have already suspected a Road Agent. We're still lookin' into it and we got a lot of investigatin' to do. But what we do know is that your ma is dead and those damn Road Agents killed her."

Tommy's head hurt and he was shaking.

"I'm sorry, Tommy, but we gotta get out'a here," Mr. Dobbins paused and brushed Tommy's hair out of his face affectionately. "Bannack ain't nothin' but trouble. I was hopin' it was gonna get better, but it's gettin' worse out here."

"Where will be go, Mr. Dobbins?"

Mr. Dobbins shook his head. "I reckon I don't know. Nowhere near here, though. Now, we just gotta prepare for the wake. Mr. O'Reilly and Mr.

Grimm are seein' to the body. She'll be laid out at Swiner's tomorrow and then we'll bury her in the cemetery."

Tommy couldn't quite believe what he was hearing. Although she often disappointed him, Tommy loved his mother and this news was hard to bear.

"You gotta eat somethin'," said Mr. Dobbins. "You haven't eaten all day long."

"I don't wanna eat," cried Tommy. "Ma's dead!"

"I know," Mr. Dobbins sighed, letting him cry into his shoulder. "I know, my Tommy boy."

Ms. Kathleen Cooper's murder was investigated by the governor who sent some of the Vigilantes in a group to track down the Road Agents, as Tommy was able to give them enough information for some of the suspects. One of them had already been held in suspicion for another murder and was easily caught. The Road Agents were able to track down another one by a bandana that had fallen in the saloon, belonging to one particular Road Agent. There was some justice involved in the woman's gory death, which gave Tommy and Mr. Dobbins some kind of comfort, however only two of them had been caught so far. They were both put in the little Bannack jail on the outskirts of town where they awaited their official execution date.

Ms. Cooper was laid to rest at the cemetery the day after her untimely death. Tommy helped the men carry her body in the coffin, which was a big honor for a twelve-year-old boy. The reverend said

some kind words and read from a Bible. Tommy began to feel numb and did not cry when they put her
in the ground.

The Freiler's, despite going through their own
grief, attended the funeral. Anna Claire was kept by
her parents' side, much like Tommy by Mr. Dobbins's
during Berthie's funeral. Not many people attended
the funeral. Kathleen, although so popular around the
town, was not respected and few people wanted to
go see "the harlot" put to rest. It was a bitter end to a
life so plagued by financial burdens and the enormous
weight of caring for a child. It didn't seem fair that she
was so easily accessed in life, but no one seemed to
care about her once she was dead and could not en-
tertain anymore.

Upon walking back from the cemetery, Anna
Claire broke away from her family and ran to
Tommy's side.

"I'm awfully sorry, Tommy," she said. "I wish
she didn't die."

Tommy frowned and nodded, but didn't look
at his friend. Instead, he kept walking straight, his chin
firm and his head held up high.

Anna Claire knew not to push him. She walked
by his side and said nothing, until she was pulled away
and he and Mr. Dobbins walked together.

"We need to talk," said Mr. Dobbins as they
arrived back at his shanty.

Tommy sat down numbly, feeling nothing.

"I didn't want to do this so soon," he continued, "but it's best you know this now. There ain't a
more proper time for you to know."

Tommy couldn't imagine what this news could be and, frankly, couldn't care less. Whatever it was, it could not be more important than the death of his mother.

"Now, you're gonna be awful sore at me," said Mr. Dobbins, pacing around the shanty nervously. "Please, just listen to me. Don't talk at first, just listen."

"What is it, Mr. Dobbins?" asked Tommy, beginning to feel sick.

Mr. Dobbins sighed and pulled up a chair to sit beside him.

"It's about Old Man Hatfield."

Tommy's interest peaked for a moment, and he began to listen intently.

"Tommy-" Mr. Dobbins looked stricken. For a moment he couldn't speak. Then, shakily, he said, "There's somethin' I've kept from you this whole time and I'm cruel angry at myself for it, too. Now that your mother's gone, well, it's best you know now."

Tommy felt a lump in his throat. He clutched his stomach nervously.

"Tell me, Mr. Dobbins!" he cried, standing up and sitting back down.

"The story is true," said Mr. Dobbins, "but we don't know nothin' about gold. There was a rumor he hid his gold in the mountains, but it was just a rumor. I don't think he did hide gold in those mountains, Tommy. He wasn't a rich man. My mother told me he did, but my mother told a lot of tall tales."

Tommy breathed in slowly.

"Why didn't you tell me that?" he asked, his face falling. "I was lookin' all over for that gold! Even Anna Claire was lookin'!"

Mr. Dobbins sighed. "I reckon I thought you kids would get a kick out of it. I wanted it to be somethin' fun. I went too far and I'm sorry, Tommy boy."

Tommy felt like crying again, but instead swallowed his tears. This was all too much disappointment for one day.

"There's some more," said Mr. Dobbins, looking around the shanty as if someone would appear at any moment.

"What?" Tommy's bright blue eyes went wide and studied Mr. Dobbins's face closely.

"The rest of it is true," he went on, sighing and putting his head in his hand. "All of it. His wife passing away, Miss Daisy Hatfield, Darlin'- all of it."

"Oh, alright," said Tommy, a bit confused.

"But I've been keepin' somethin' from ya, boy. Somethin' important."

Tommy bit his lip as his knees moved up and down in his chair.

"Tell me! Tell me, Mr. Dobbins!"

Mr. Dobbins looked away, his eyes brimming with tears. "I'm so sorry, but there's a reason I didn't tell you! I knew Miss Daisy Hatfield."

"I know," Tommy nodded. "You told us."

"I loved Miss Daisy," Mr. Dobbins went on, his eyes seemingly looking at something far away. "Fell in love with her. I wanted her to love me, but she fell in love with that other fella. That scum who left her with a baby. You see, Mr. Hatfield did love his daughter, and when she left, he was heartbroken. When she had the baby and came back, and she found out he died from a heart attack, it killed her inside, it did. So, she finished herself off. She drank poison, Tommy. She passed away in her father's house, and no one found her for days. It was only until someone went to deliver mail that they found her on the ground."

"She used poison?" Tommy was surprised.

Mr. Dobbins sighed. "Tommy, it's not the only thing. Please understand, I love ya an awful lot. I couldn't tell you 'cause your mother wouldn't have liked it."

"What wouldn't she have liked?" Tommy's eyes were growing bigger.

"Tommy, your mother knew Miss Daisy. They were good friends."

Tommy was surprised. "Really? How come she never said nothin'?"

"She couldn't," said Mr. Dobbins. "Kathleen really did love ya. I know she had a hard time showin' it, but she loved ya."

Tommy's head was spinning with confusion. "How could she keep that secret from me?"

"Because," Mr. Dobbins continued, "she was told not to tell. You see, Miss Daisy had a baby she called Darlin'. A handsome baby, too, with big blue eyes and light brown hair. She called that baby Darlin' all of the time, so much so that everyone started thinkin' that was the baby's actual name. But it wasn't." He stopped and looked up at the ceiling, taking a deep breath. "You see, the baby's real name was Thomas. Thomas Wister."

"The baby was a boy?" Tommy asked uncertainly.

"The baby," breathed Mr. Dobbins, "was *you*."

Tommy felt the whole world spin around him. He leaned over in his seat and clasped his hands together, his whole body shaking.

"I was Darlin'?" He couldn't believe what Mr. Dobbins was saying. He suddenly felt very faint again. "I'm Miss Daisy's lost baby?"

Mr. Dobbins nodded. "You are, Tommy boy, but you're not lost no more. I'm sorry I didn't tell ya. Your mother- the mother that gave you life- was real good friends with the mother that raised you. Before she killed herself, she gave you to Kathleen Cooper to raise you as her own and never tell you the truth. Kathleen was devoted to her friend. God knows Kathleen has her faults, but her friendship is like no other. The two of them were inseparable. There was never one without the other. Like I said, Kathleen had her faults, alright, but she's loyal as hell! She raised you and never told you a single thing."

Tommy stood up, his eyes brimming with tears. "That can't be true! She's my mother! My father stopped seein' us!"

"He did," sighed Mr. Dobbins, "but Ames Cooper was not your birth father. Jeb Wister was."

Tommy felt dizzy and sat down again.

"I couldn't tell ya, Tommy. Your mother didn't want you to know that she killed herself. She didn't want you to think she left you. She loved ya. Both your mothers did. Daisy wasn't right in the head. She didn't kill herself 'cause of you. She killed herself *for* you. She didn't think she had it in her to be your mother."

Tommy's mouth was dry and he felt like he was swallowing bricks.

"So, she gave me to my ma, so that I wouldn't know about it?"

Mr. Dobbins nodded. "That she did."

Tommy didn't know what to say or what to think. All of this information was too much for him and he fell mute.

"I know this is a hell of a lot," said Mr. Dobbins, wiping sweat from his forehead, "and I know you must be awful mad at me for keepin' this secret. I was just tryin' to do what your mothers would have wanted. I was tryin' to respect Daisy's wishes. I loved her. It killed me when she went off with that Jeb fella that broke her heart and left you both."

"David Hatfield is my grandfather," said Tommy slowly, "and I never even knew it."

"I know, son, I know," Mr. Dobbins himself was at a loss for words. "I was plum devastated when Daisy...ended it all. I knew that I would always try to protect her little boy."

"So that's why you've always been around," said Tommy, looking at the ground. "Because you had to."

"No, son," Mr. Dobbins sighed. "In the beginning, I did promise to make sure you was safe. But time went on and- Tommy, you're like the son I never had! I love ya. I wasn't gonna tell you all this until you were older, but with your ma dead now- well, it's time you knew."

"Who else knows? Everyone?"

"No," said Mr. Dobbins. "Kathleen raised you like you was hers. No one knew except the three of us- and, well, Kathleen's daft husband."

Tommy stood up again, trying to process this information.

"I can't- I don't believe you!" he cried. "Stop lyin' to me!"

"Tommy boy, I ain't-"

"Stop lyin' to me!" And with that, Tommy ran out of the shanty and through the fields.   Tears blurring his vision, he ran and ran and ran. He ran into town and ran through the streets, ignoring some of the men who tried to catch his attention to talk with him. He kept running and running as fast as he could, until he was out of breath and his feet hurt. Without even trying to, he landed on the doorstep of the Freiler's cabin.

"Tommy!" said Charlotta when she opened the door. "You look a fright! Poor boy. Come in."

"Anna- Claire," he said between breaths.

Charlotta nodded as Anna Claire came running in from the kitchen, her little apron still on.

"What's a matter, Tommy?" she asked, her dress covered in flour. "You look like you've just seen a ghost!"

Tommy took a deep breath.

"Can we go to the creek, Mrs. Freiler?" he asked, wiping a tear from the corner of his eye.

Sensing he needed to talk, she nodded.

"I'll be back soon, Mama!" said Anna Claire.

"Take your time," Charlotta replied gently.

Tommy grabbed Anna Claire's hand and pulled her towards the creek. They walked through the grass, past Berthie's little gravestone, and through the trees. Anna Claire had never seen Tommy actually cry before. She had seen tears in his eyes, yes, but he never truly cried in front of her.

When they got to the creek, they both plopped down, took off their boots, and put their feet into the water.

"You're cryin'!" said Anna Claire. "Oh, your ma! I'm awfully sorry, Tommy. I am. I'm sorrier than you could ever know!"

Tommy nodded and then looked at her fiercely.

"I gotta tell you somethin'," he said, throwing a stone in the creek.

When Anna Claire arrived back home, she couldn't think. She had just gone back to school, but she couldn't do her arithmetic. She could hardly finish her chores, and accidentally spilled the bowl of flour all over the kitchen floor.

"What is the matter with you?" asked Charlotta.

"He's Darlin'!" she cried uncontrollably.

"What ever are you talking about?"

"Tommy!" she exclaimed, just as her father walked through the door with a deer over his shoulder.

"What about Tommy?" asked Joseph, placing the deer on the hide by the fire place.

Caroline and Helen had walked into the room upon hearing the commotion while Pete had walked down the ladder.

"Mr. Dobbins had a talk with Tommy today," continued Anna Claire breathlessly. "Mr. Dobbins said he was in love with Daisy Hatfield!"

"Oh, not this again," Joseph sighed.

"Papa, just listen!" Anna Claire stomped her foot on the ground. "Daisy Hatfield gave her baby up before she killed herself 'cause she didn't know if she could raise the baby. She gave the baby to her closest friend. They both knew Mr. Dobbins and Mr. Dobbins promised he'd watch out for the baby. Her friend was Miss Cooper. Baby Darlin' is *Tommy*!"

Charlotta and Joseph looked surprised despite themselves.

"You're telling me that this whole time, Tommy didn't know he was Daisy's son?" asked Charlotta, her eyebrows raised.

Anna Claire nodded. "Mr. Dobbins just told him. All this time, we thought our teacher might be the baby. But Mr. Dobbins said that Tommy was the baby. She left him with her friend who's Tommy's mama. She raised him with Mr. Dobbins helpin'."

"Oh my!" exclaimed Charlotta, looking at Joseph.

"And there might not even be gold in the mountains!" said Anna Claire with sadness.

"I could have told you that," snapped Joseph. "Anna Claire, I knew that was part of a tall tale."

Anna Claire nodded. "You were right. But the story was true. That means that Tommy is Old Man Hatfield's grandson! He never knew it."

Joseph and Charlotta were surprised, but they didn't want to cave in to Anna Claire's fancies too much.

"That is surprising," Charlotta nodded. "How strange!"

"It is," Joseph admitted. "Is he sure?"

"Yes," said Anna Claire. "Mr. Dobbins told him today. And he told him he was gonna tell him when he was older, but 'cause his ma just died, he thought Tommy should know. His real name was Thomas Wister!"

"Poor Tommy," said Caroline, coming to stand next to Anna Claire.

"We never knew it! But now we know some of the mystery. The baby was never really lost- he was right here the whole time!"

Charlotta and Joseph looked at each other and sighed.

"May I go to town to see him?" Caroline asked, much to the shock of everyone.

Charlotta's mouth dropped, and her eyes grew bigger. "Why...why, yes, Caroline. Of course."

They were all staring at Caroline. No one could quite believe that she had requested on her own to go visit little Tommy Cooper.

"Give him a kiss," Anna Claire said with a chuckle. "That'll cheer him up!"

"Oh, stop it," Caroline said. "I am going to bring some muffins over to him. He is still staying with Mr. Dobbins?"

Anna Claire nodded.

"How do you know where Mr. Dobbins lives?" asked Joseph suspiciously.

Caroline swallowed and looked at her feet. "Arnold and I went there once. He wanted to say hello, so we went."

"See, she's *not* perfect," Anna Claire gloated.

Charlotta pursed her lips. "Well, in that case, go right along! Take the muffins."

Caroline nodded, going into the little kitchen to put the muffins in the tin pail. She walked out of the house and right across the field. Her heart hurt in so many ways, and now it hurt for Tommy, who had lost two of his mothers all in one day.

"Caroline!" said Mr. Dobbins as he walked out of his lop-sided shanty.

"Take the muffins," she said hastily. "I want you both to have them. Anna Claire told us what has happened. I know Tommy is much disturbed by the news."

Mr. Dobbins frowned and sighed. "I feel downright wretched about the whole thing."

Caroline, not sure if she should be angry with Mr. Dobbins or not, smiled quickly and then frowned.

"Caroline?" asked Tommy slowly, coming from around the back, no shoes on his feet.

Caroline smiled and walked over to him.

"I brought you and Mr. Dobbins some muffins," she said. "I hope you find them suitable. I made them myself."

For a second, Caroline looked like a little girl again. Her eyes sparkled, her cheeks flushed, and she looked at her muffins with pride.

Tommy tried to smile, but he couldn't. Once upon a time he would have been thrilled to receive a muffin from Caroline. But now, he could barely bring himself to lift his head.

"Gee, thanks," he mumbled.

Caroline saw the look of deep sadness on his face and felt truly sorry for her young friend. She carefully walked closer to him, bent down so that Tommy could feel her breath on his ear, and gave him a small kiss on the cheek.

"I hope you feel better," she said as she walked away, her ringlets bouncing.

Tommy couldn't believe it. He put his hand up to his cheek and found himself smiling. For a moment- just one moment- he almost felt happy again.

"She's a pretty one, ain't she?" Mr. Dobbins said with a wink.

Tommy nodded. "The most beautiful girl on Earth!"

Anna Claire was listening next to the loft late that night, trying to hear what her parents were saying. They were talking low so it was quite difficult, but she strained her ears to listen anyway.

"If it wasn't for you and your stupid gold!" Charlotta cried, her voice cracking. "That *damn* gold!"

Anna Claire was stunned. Never once in her entire life had she heard her mother swear- in fact, she had always said swearing was one of the worst sins.

"Char, you know I was tryin' to do what was right for our family!" Joseph spat, his voice rising and then lowering.

"Look at how that turned out," cried Charlotta as she sniffled. "Our little girl is gone! She is dead, Joseph! If we had stayed in Minnesota, this never would have happened! Everything and anything for your Almighty Dollar!"

Joseph paused for a long time.

"You're right," he said finally, sounding completely defeated.

Charlotta sighed.

"You're right," Joseph went on, his voice shaking. "We shouldn't have come out here. I shouldn't have brought you all up here with me. I should've come here by myself and came right back. I should've never let the children come out here. This place was unsafe and I knew it. This happened 'cause of me."

Charlotta sighed again. "Joseph," she said much more softly. "I'm sorry. This is not your fault. You could have never known this would happen. I still don't understand how this happened or why God would do this to our little girl."

Anna Claire could hear the sound of Joseph walking towards Charlotta and Charlotta's stifled cries as she leaned into him.

"We're leavin'," said Joseph firmly.

"When?" Charlotta asked softly.

"As soon as possible," Joseph sighed. "I don't wanna be here anymore than you do. We gotta get goin' soon while the weather's still good. It shouldn't be a long trip. Grimm said it'll take about three days, give or take."

Charlotta sighed. "We will pack and move this week, then. Have you spoken to Mr. Grimm's friend?"

"I did, Char. The house is ready. He leaves in a day and will meet us when we get there to give us the key. Mr. Grimm will let him know when we leave so that he can be there when we come."

"A key?" asked Charlotta, a small bit of excitement in her voice. "It will be nice to have a house with a key."

"Our lives are gonna start off brand new," said Joseph. "Soon, we'll have everything we've dreamed of!"

"Almost," added Charlotta sadly.

"I know it's been the worst of times," Joseph went on, "but this is a chance for our family to start over. This is what we have to do."

"Well, then, we shall tell the children tomorrow and say our goodbyes."

Anna Claire put her hands to her mouth to stop herself from saying anything. She realized then that everything was about to change.

"Tommy!" Anna Claire yelled as she walked up to Mr. Dobbins's shanty that very next day.

"Anna Claire!" Mr. Dobbins called. "Tommy just left! He's lookin' for you! You must have missed each other!"

Without saying another word, Anna Claire turned on her heels and sped away through the fields. She found Tommy not too far away from town.

"Tommy!" she called, running to him as he turned around.

"You're here!" he said, surprised.

"Of course, I'm here," she said haughtily. "Listen, Tommy. We might have to do the plan."

"What plan?"

"The one where I hide with you," she was breathless, leaning over and wiping her hair from her face. "Mama and Papa wanna leave. And they wanna leave fast! I think the house makes them sad 'cause Berthie ain't here anymore and they think Gold Country is gettin' more dangerous. They wanna leave next week, Tommy!"

Her eyes stung with tears, her little freckled nose turning red and her green eyes worried and watering.

"No, you can't leave!" yelled Tommy. "You're my best friend!"

"You gotta tell Mr. Dobbins! I'm sure he'll hide me!"

"He won't," said Tommy in a panic. "I don't think he will! He likes you, but he ain't gonna lie to your pa!"

Anna Claire paced around in a circle. "What are we gonna do? We can't be separated!"

Tommy hid his face in his hands, crying again.

"Why is everything goin' wrong?" he asked, more to himself than her.

"I don't wanna leave you, Tommy," Anna Claire began to cry, too. "You're the best part of Gold Country! You're better than all the gold anyone ever found here!"

Tommy suddenly pulled her toward him and embraced her.

"Mr. Dobbins says he wants to leave here, too," he said. "He thinks it's gettin' worse and don't want nothin' bad to happen to me."

"We'll be apart!" shouted Anna Claire, her nose running and her little face stained with tears. "You might be a hundred miles away from me! We might never see each other again!"

"We can't let that happen!" said Tommy helplessly. "Stop cryin'. We're gonna find a way. I'm gonna come up with a plan."

"Maybe we can run away to the mountains again?" asked Anna Claire frantically, still pacing back and forth.

"That's too dangerous," said Tommy. "I ain't lettin' you get hurt! I'll think of somethin'. Don't worry. Nothin's gonna separate us!"

"We're best friends!" nodded Anna Claire, drying her eyes and pursing her lips. "They're not gonna separate us! They can't!"

"They ain't gonna!" spat Tommy. "We'll show 'em! Give me some time. I'm gonna come back tomorrow. Try to be home."

"Mama wants me home now anyway," replied Anna Claire. "She don't like me goin' anywhere around here anymore."

"Good," Tommy took a deep breath. "Then I'll come tomorrow. You better be there, Anna Claire!"

"I already said I would, now shut up about it!"

The children went their separate ways then, both of them trying to formulate some kind of plan to stay in Gold Country- or, at least, not be separated from each other.

Later that night, Joseph broke the news to the family that they would be leaving in exactly four days. This wasn't much time for Anna Claire to come up with a brilliant plan. In two days, they were having people over for a goodbye gathering. What could Anna Claire do?

"What did they say?" Tommy asked her at the creek that next day.

"Four days," she said sadly. "We're leavin' in four days."

"Mr. Dobbins wants to leave soon, too. We don't know where though. Where do they wanna take you?"

Anna Claire sighed, her lips trembling. "To Ponderosa Valley! That's not even near here! Papa said it's days away!"

Tommy stood up, feeling like someone set him on fire.

"This can't be!" he wailed. "I don't know what to do! I can't think of anything! If we run, they'll catch us anyway. We're still too little."

Anna Claire started crying and reached up to touch his finger. "Remember when we became blood brothers? No matter what, even if I never see you again, we'll always be connected. Nothin' can really separate us."

Tommy wiped a tear from his face. "I'm sorry I couldn't think of anything! I'm so sorry!"

The two, both of them crying now, sat back down in the mossy mud.

"What if this is the last time we're here?" reflected Anna Claire. "Mama and Papa are gonna want me helpin' with the chores and packin'. This might be the last time we sit here."

"I wish Mr. Dobbins knew where he was goin'," Tommy shook his head, his brown hair falling over his forehead.

Anna Claire glanced up at him, her eyes growing wider. "Tommy, that's it!"

"What?" he snapped.

"Mr. Dobbins!" she stood back up and leapt in the air. "Mr. Dobbins is leavin', but he doesn't know where you're gonna go!"

"So?"

"Are you stupid, Tommy Cooper? *So* that means we gotta tell Mr. Dobbins that he needs to move to Ponderosa Valley!"

Tommy's eyes widened. "Yeah, we can tell him Ponderosa Valley is the perfect place!"

"It is, it is!" exclaimed Anna Claire excitedly. "Papa says it's more like a city than a town, and a lot safer, and there's more people but not too many people. It's perfect!"

"But where will we live?" asked Tommy, his face growing excited, too.

"I don't know," said Anna Claire. "Maybe Papa and Mama will let you stay with us! Or maybe he can build a cabin there!"

"We gotta make it work," said Tommy with a nod of his head. "I'm gonna tell him. I'm gonna tell him we gotta move to Ponderosa Valley!"

"I gotta go back and help Caroline," she said, before giving him a quick hug. "I'll see you in two days when we say goodbye to everyone."

And the two children made another plan, their last plan at Gold Country. But would it work?

"I really don't know," Mr. Dobbins sighed. "I'm an old man! I don't know if I can travel that far!"

"I'll help you, Mr. Dobbins!" begged Tommy. "It's safer than stayin' around here! You said it yourself!"

Mr. Dobbins sighed. "Maybe we can go."

"Yes!" Tommy jumped in the air and hollered.

"But I gotta consider everything. I gotta consider where we're gonna live, where I'm gonna be able to build somethin' new, where you're gonna go to school."

"Anna Claire talked to her papa and her papa said they have a school there, and that there's lots of people but not too many people, and that it's the safest place in Montana Territory!"

Mr. Dobbins couldn't help smiling. "You're really attached to Anna Claire, ain't ya?"

Tommy shrugged. "She's my best friend. And I think once Caroline gets to know me, she'll want me to court her! She already gave me a kiss on the cheek. You saw that, Mr. Dobbins!"

Mr. Dobbins began laughing heartily. "The Freilers are my friends. I trust them. They've been good to us. I know how much you love them, and they love you. I say, where they go, we'll follow!"

Tommy jumped up and cheered again. He ran over and wrapped his new guardian in a tight hug.

"Alright. Oh, alright," Mr. Dobbins said sheepishly, not used to all of the affection.

"I can't wait to tell Anna Claire!" exclaimed Tommy.

"You can tell her tomorrow at the goodbye gathering," said Mr. Dobbins. "In the meantime, let's go into town and get some supper!"

"Supper?" Tommy was confused. "We don't got the money to eat at the restaurant!"

"Well, I've been savin' some money for a special occasion- and what's more special than this? I got my boy, we're leavin' this dark town, and we're goin' with the Freilers!"

Tommy's smile could not have been wider. "Let's go, Mr. Dobbins!"

And with that, the two young men (at heart) walked into town to the restaurant, laughing and talking all the way.

The goodbye gathering was a sad one, and was made even sadder by the lack of the Watsons' presence. The beginning was filled with dancing, food, and laughter, and some small trinkets for the Freiler family to take with them to their new town. But as the hours went on, it was more evident that they were really leaving forever, and that would mean leaving some very dear friends.

"I'm gonna miss you all," Joseph said to his friends. "It's been a pleasure workin' with you, but more of a pleasure bein' your friend."

Mr. O'Reilly held out his hand for him to shake it and then Mr. Chesham did likewise. Mr. Clemmons simply patted him on the back, as did Mr. Grimm.

Charlotta was beside herself with losing Nettie.

"If you ever decide to leave," Charlotta told her, "please consider Ponderosa Valley. It truly does sound like a nice place."

"We will probably move back East," said Nettie, touching her arm. "But if we ever come back to Montana Territory, Ponderosa Valley will be the first place we shall go!"

Charlotta gave Nettie a small hug. Trying not to cry, she put her arm around her.

"Thank you for all you have done for me and my family," she said. "I wouldn't have gotten through everything without you. I would have never gotten through Berthie-"

"Don't," said Nettie gently. "You don't have to say a single thing. I understand everything! Oh, Charlotta, I am going to miss you horribly."

"I will surely miss you more," Charlotta said, letting out a sob and burying her head in her friend's shoulder.

Some of the children came to say goodbye, too. Helen was tearful when she was saying goodbye to Rebecca and Lucy, and Caroline was tearful when saying goodbye to Jacob Mast, even if he had broken her heart.

"We love you all and will miss all of you!" yelled Joseph to the little crowd. "Thank you for bein' part of our lives. We will pray for each and every one of you. May God be with you all and keep you safe!"

"Bless you!" added Charlotta.

When people began leaving, Mr. Dobbins pulled Joseph to the side. Anna Claire and Tommy watched with sneaky looks on their faces.

"What do you think he'll say?" asked Tommy.

"I don't know," Anna Claire shrugged.

After a few minutes, Joseph's face broke into a big smile.

"Charlotta, children!" he called. "Come!"

Everyone gathered in front of the cabin, wondering what was making Joseph so happy at that moment.

"Mr. Dobbins has decided to leave as well," said Joseph, unable to hide his own excitement. "He wants to go to Ponderosa! He'll be travelin' with us!"

Charlotta brought her face to her hands as her eyes lit up. For a moment, she looked as young as an adolescent.

"This is wonderful news," said Charlotta. "We love you, Mr. Dobbins, and we are so happy you will be joining us."

"I got my own wagon," continued Mr. Dobbins, "but we'll be together. Right, Tommy boy?"

"Right!" Tommy said, looking at Anna Claire happily.

"Oh, Tommy," Charlotta began to cry again as she came over and enveloped him in her arms. "Our

Tommy! You will be coming with us. We won't have to lose you, too."

Tommy smiled, embracing her before everyone started to hug and laugh.

Tommy gave quick hugs to Helen and Pete before standing nervously in front of Caroline.

"You look awful pretty," he said with a sheepish grin.

Instead of scolding, Caroline gave him a big squeeze with her arms. "I am glad you'll be coming with us, Tommy."

Joseph cleared his throat and paused, a broad smile on his face. "I also have some more good news. I spoke to the Watsons and they need to leave here, too. They decided it would be best to go where they already know people. They're comin' to Ponderosa, too!"

Anna Claire was shocked. She looked over at Tommy whose mouth dropped.

"That's ace high!" Tommy said, jumping in the air.

"Now Hope will be our friend forever!" yelled Anna Claire, running to her father and giving him a hug, letting him pick her up.

"We'll all meet here in two days' time, early mornin'," said Joseph, looking happier than he had in months.

"I am so happy, Papa!" cried Anna Claire. "We don't have to lose everyone!"

Then she became sad again when she thought of Berthie not coming with them to Ponderosa Valley and leaving her behind.

As if reading her mind, Joseph said, "Berthie is comin', too. In our hearts. That is where she will always be."

Anna Claire sat by the creek, her thoughts swirling around in her mind. She could not believe that this would be one of the last times she would be sitting by Gold Creek. It had become home to her for the last two years and she didn't know how she would get on without it.

She moved her finger in the water so that it made little currents while she splashed with her feet. Her father had done it- he had struck gold and the family was rich! They were one of the very few fortunate ones whom this had happened to, as it was much rarer than not, and the family had survived through it- all but one little slip of a girl with long white-blonde hair and big brown eyes.

Anna Claire thought of the times she had with Berthie. The times they would play at the creek together and go swimming, the times they tricked their siblings together, the nights where they stayed up late and told stories. Things would never be the same again.

Anna Claire herself was not the same. She had done a lot of growing up in the past couple of years and had to learn many of her lessons the hard way, yet she stayed strong and determined, just as she always had.

She was going to leave Bannack and Gold Country for a long time. It filled her heart with sadness to think of leaving so many friends behind and the exciting place she grew to love. She didn't want to leave but, at the same time, it was too difficult to stay now that Berthie was gone. The family needed a fresh start.

"I'll miss you, my beloved creek," she said out loud, standing up and brushing the dirt off of her dress before putting her boots on.

She looked out over the water before slowly walking through the trees. She was surprised when she reached the clearing and found her father there, looking at Berthie's little gravestone.

"Papa!"

"Anna Claire!" he said with a small smile. "I thought you'd be here."

"I miss Berthie, Papa," she said with a long sigh, coming to stand next to him.

Joseph reached his arm around her and pulled her in close. "I do, too. I miss her, too."

Suddenly, they both found themselves crying, wiping their noses, and looking down at the grave-stone.

"Remember what I said?" asked Joseph, turning to look at her with his soft brown eyes.

"Berthie will always be in our hearts," Anna Claire finished. "But Papa, it's not the same."

"I know, Anna Claire," he sighed. "I know. Things won't be the same from now on. We will always love and miss our Berthie, and she knows. She's safe and sound now, my girl. She's watchin' us, and I can guarantee she's laughin' at you for gettin' mud all over your dress."

"Oh, Papa!" Anna Claire laughed, swishing her dress around her to see the globs of mud stuck to them.

"Not everything changes," Joseph teased with a twinkle in his eyes. "You know, Anna Claire, you taught me a lot."

"Me? *I* taught *you*?" asked Anna Claire with wide eyes. "How?"

Joseph smiled and looked behind him at the little cabin in the clearing.

"You did," he went on. "Oh, boy, you sure have pluck, my girl! You don't let anything stop you! You taught me what it was like to love people- all people. What it was like to see a person for who they are, not just for the color of their skin or anything else. You taught me to be humble and grateful for all we have. My girl, you taught me a new way of seein' the world. You taught me grace."

Anna Claire smiled, her little face shining.

"I'm so glad!" she said, taking her father by his hand. "Now, we will go to Ponderosa Valley and Berthie will come with us wherever we are!"

"That is right," nodded Joseph. "Let us go and help your mother with supper."

Anna Claire nodded and the two walked back to the cabin hand in hand. They had been having some very bad days since Berthie's untimely death, but in that moment, all seemed promising again.

That night, after taking their baths, Caroline came up to the loft where Anna Claire was standing by the window, looking up at the moon again. Everyone else was downstairs finishing up some last-minute chores.

"What are you doing up here?" she asked, walking closer.

Anna Claire sighed, bracing herself for Caroline's scolding. "I did my chores already!"

Instead of scolding, Caroline put her arm around her shoulders. Anna Claire stiffened up and took a step to the side.

"I'm sorry if I've been harsh with you," Caroline said gently, a look of true sincerity in her eyes. "Maybe I've been too bossy. I just want to see you grow up to be a proper young lady, so that you'll have many opportunities for happiness."

Anna Claire slowly looked over at her, surprised. "I'm happy not bein' a proper lady."

Caroline smiled. "For now, yes. But manners are important. You know what is even more important than manners?"

Anna Claire shrugged.

"Sisters," Caroline said, looking down at Anna Claire in such a mature way that Anna Claire had never seen before. It was evident that losing Berthie and taking care of the household had significantly changed her. "I am sorry for always being angry with you. I hope you can forgive me. After Berthie- oh, nothing is more important than loving your family!"

Anna Claire bit her lip, too surprised to know what to say at that moment.

Caroline bent down a bit to embrace her. Shocked at her own reaction, Anna Claire hugged her back, willing tears to go away unsuccessfully.

"I could never bear to lose you," sobbed Caroline, holding Anna Claire as if she would never let go.

"I don't want to lose you either," said Anna Claire truthfully. "I'm sorry for bein' so naughty all the time."

Caroline stepped back and smiled. "You aren't so naughty *all* of the time. You have a kind heart, which is the most important thing. Even more important than being proper."

Anna Claire smiled, and the two girls embraced again.

"How about you come down and I'll make you some tea?" asked Caroline gently, one strand of curly black hair hanging down from her loose bun.

Anna Claire nodded. "Alright. Hey, Caroline?"
"Yes?"

"Do you ever think people will be able to go to the moon someday and touch it?"

Caroline laughed. "Oh, Anna Claire, the thoughts you have! I don't think so. But I suppose one can never know! God does work miracles."

Laughing, the two walked across the loft and slowly down the ladder, Anna Claire's heart feeling full as if someone had slowly begun stitching the broken pieces together.

Two days later, it was time for them to move. It was sad and heart-breaking. They were leaving a place they had come to know and appreciate for over two years, a place where they had fought so hard to make work, a place where they would have to leave the body of a beloved little girl. A place that had been home.

Joseph got the wagon hitched and everything they could take packed up, the horses ready to go. The other things that were too much to take with them, they gave to their friends. It was strange to see the cabin all empty, and it gave Anna Claire a very depressed feeling. She thought of Bannack and everything she would miss. The beautiful sloping hills and rich, meadowy intervals, Grasshopper Creek and the cottonwood trees, the liveliness of town, and the people who became her friend. She was sad to leave- very sad, in fact- but her joy of moving with Mr. Dobbins, Tommy, and the Watsons overcame some of this gloominess.

Mr. Dobbins had gotten to the Freiler home early and had Tommy all ready to go. The Watson's, a bit later than anticipated, arrived after that.

"Well, I guess we're ready," said Joseph with a smile. "To Ponderosa Valley we go!"

"To our new adventure!" joined in Mr. Dobbins, raising his fist in the air.

"Mama?" asked Anna Claire, pulling on her dress.

Charlotta managed a small smile. "Yes, darling?"

"Do you think we'll be happy in the new place? Will we like it?"

Charlotta sighed and pulled her close. "I hope so, Anna Claire. I do hope so."

Getting the maps ready and making sure the canteens were sealed tightly, they began to step into their wagons, Hero happily jumping in and licking Anna Claire's face, his paw holding her shoulder.

"We're always gonna be friends now!" said Tommy to Hope, who was waving from the wagon, too. It was settled that the Watsons, as well as Mr. Dobbins and Tommy, would stay with the Freiler's in Ponderosa Valley for some time before building a home of their own.

"I'm hungry," said Pete, rubbing his stomach. "Tommy, you bring any candy?"

"' Course, I did!" Tommy answered, throwing some over to Pete and giving the rest to Hope and Anna Claire.

"Don't eat too much now!" said Charlotta, a smile on her rosy face. "Save some for later."

"I suppose I'll have to be in this wagon with *you* for days," snapped Helen to Anna Claire, crossing her arms and moving to the other side of the wagon.

Anna Claire stuck out her tongue before Caroline gave her a firm but soft look.

The wagons were ready to go, and everyone had their belongings packed- or, as much as they were able to bring with them. Mr. Dobbins, his face plump and jolly, waved from his horse and Joseph tipped his hat, waving back. They had hidden the money in Charlotta's dress in case they were to come upon any unfortunate circumstance. With the rifles and everyone traveling together, the journey would be much safer.

"Wait!" Tommy called to Anna Claire. She looked behind her and stepped outside of the wagon, tripping over her laces. "Here."

Anna Claire held out her hand and saw the beautiful, beaded bracelet, given to her by their dear friend, Iá daxpitchée.

Anna Claire smiled and put the bracelet on her wrist. It was still much too big for her.

"See ya at home!" she called to Tommy as he jumped into Mr. Dobbins's wagon, everyone beginning the long journey to Ponderosa Valley, Montana Territory.

"See ya at home!" he answered, hope brimming in his eyes and a smile wide on his face.

Acknowledgments:

www.legendsofamerica.com

www.grunge.com

www.goldrushnuggets.com

historynet.com

iamcountryside.com

freepages.rootsweb.com

beaverheadsouthwes.wixsite.com

chalkboardchampions.org

Chrisenss.com

Library of Congress

www.brucegourley.com

www.heritageall.org

ereferenecedesk.com

gardenia.net

Fieldguide.mt.gov

Beaverheadwatershed.com

Lifeonspringcreek.com

Bannack State Park- fwp.mt.gov

DiscoveringMontana.com

BannackMontana.com

LegendsofAmerica.com

Montanahistory.com

About the Author

Kirsten Miles is an award-winning author in the heart of New Jersey. Kirsten has published a novel titled "The Hummingbird Lullaby," which debuted on August 1, 2024. This is an LGBTQ+ romance that delves into love, sacrifice, and identity. The novel has been given

a 2025 certificate of exemplary literature from Book-Fest. This novel has also been voted #1 Featured Book of the Month, trending across diverse genres in Literature at BooksBrew, and was ranked 5/5 for books among the featured booklist at BooksBrew Fest. This novel was also a finalist for the American Legacy Book Awards and was rated 5 stars by Reader's Favorite. Kirsten has a new book coming out this summer of 2025 called "Heroes of Gold Country," a western, which has won the "Highly Recommended" award of excellence by The Historical Fiction Company. Kirsten has also self-published a novel titled "Senior Year" under the pseudonym of Lily Caverton, which details mental health issues. This novel won the 2024 International Impact Book Award for Teen Mental Health Fiction. She has published a short story in the Lothlorien Poetry Journal. Kirsten has also published several poems, including "If Love Was a Color" in the 2019 edition of "New Jersey's Best Emerging Poets." She lives with her wife and their two dogs, with whom she has many adventures!

www.ingramcontent.com/pod-product-compliance
Lightning Source LLC
Chambersburg PA
CBHW062057290726
48975CB00001B/8